THE EAGLE *and* THE RAVEN

the EAGLE
and the
RAVEN

PAULINE GEDGE

CHICAGO
REVIEW
PRESS

Cover design: Sarah Olson
Cover illustration: Leo and Diane Dillon

This unabridged edition is reprinted by arrangement with the author
© 1978 by Pauline Gedge
Foreword © 2007 by Donna Gillespie
All rights reserved
This edition published in 2007 by
Chicago Review Press, Incorporated
814 North Franklin Street
Chicago, Illinois 60610
ISBN-13: 978-1-55652-708-1
ISBN-10: 1-55652-708-X
Printed in the United States of America
5 4 3 2 1

This book is for Sylvie, who turned
a little patch of garden into an estate,
and cut the flowers beautifully.

FOREWORD

*T*HE FIRST CENTURY A.D. was a tumultuous time for barbarian tribes in the path of the expanding Roman Empire. As Rome muscled its way into territories occupied by others—humbling, occupying, displacing—worlds came to an end. History gives us the testimony of those who could write, leaving those with oral traditions cloaked in mystery, so we can only imagine the grand and noble stories that remain untold. This is what Pauline Gedge has accomplished masterfully in *The Eagle and the Raven*, a sprawling epic that dramatizes the full story of the British resistance to the coming of Rome, taking us through the reigns of Caligula, Claudius, and Nero. Lifting a veil as obscuring as an Albion mist, she shows us the people of Britannia in those catastrophic moments that must have been, as ordinary men and women made the desperate decision to capitulate or fight. It would have been bitter for the proudest among them to see how numerous were the pragmatists poised to collaborate, to discover that foreign gods were stronger than your own. When the legions came, the Britons couldn't have known the future; it must have been as though the sun were no longer to rise. In Gedge's novel we feel intimately their terror as disciplined, better-armed soldiers landed on their beaches. And their humiliation as ancient tribal centers were torn down to be replaced with Roman towns, and free people became tenant farmers harried with harsh taxes and the brutal means of collecting them. "All we wanted was to be left alone," are the words spoken by Gedge's protagonist Caradoc (history's Caratacus), the British chief who leads the resistance. "Such a little word, freedom, such a small request, and yet the asking of it has consumed the soul of a nation."

In 1978, when *The Eagle and the Raven* was first published, historical novels set in Roman times were not so common as they are today; even more uncommon was the Roman novel that revealed empire building from the perspective of the conquered tribes who left no record. In this pioneering book, Albion's struggle is told through the story of Caradoc, the war leader who for a decade managed a brilliant guerrilla campaign against the new overlords—and then ultimately through the better-known Boudicca, the warrior queen who leads the resistance into its titanic final act. In the novel, these two embody the passion for freedom. Their homegrown antagonist, personifying those who believed the imperial occupation would bring a better way of life, is realized in the character of Aricia (history's Queen Cartimandua) who sets in motion a ruthless plot to make certain her own vision for the island is carried out. Of these three figures the ancient historians give us maddeningly little—Boudicca is of "terrifying" appearance; we are told that "a great mass of tawniest hair fell to her hips." Of Caratacus and Cartimandua we are given even less. From tantalizing scraps Gedge evokes living individuals; she shows us the darker workings of their minds, probes their psyches with a thoroughness that brings out their common humanity. She illustrates well how ambiguous the day's choices would have appeared to a first-century Briton. For the benefits Rome brought must have been apparent to some: Improved farming techniques. Fabulous trade goods from afar. Paved roads linking towns. Relative peace among the tribes. Literacy (at a rate not to be equaled until the nineteenth century). Britannia's transformation from misty redoubt to cosmopolitan island. Almost immediately, occupiers became neighbors, then relatives, as Briton intermarried with retired veteran soldier. But then, this was a warrior culture. Personal honor and tribal pride, meticulously maintained for the next generation, was the most treasured possession. In the person of Queen Boudicca the empire builders collided with a pride too implacable for them to understand, and it nearly cost them their new province.

It's intriguing to note that on the British side, two of the three most powerful principals in the political drama are women. The Roman historian Tacitus, describing Boudicca's revolt in *The Agricola,* states, "The whole of the island rose under the leadership of Boudicca, a lady of royal descent—for the Britons make no distinction of sex when they choose their leaders." To the Romans this must have seemed a striking cultural trait. In the *Annals* Tacitus states that when Caratacus was finally brought before the emperor Claudius, the famous British freedom fighter gave to the empress Agrippina "the same homage and gratitude as he had given the emperor." That Tacitus would mention this at all reveals his surprise. But Caratacus was only acting in accordance with the ways of his tribe. Gedge illustrates this rare equality well; her women are forces to be reckoned with. This too sets *The Eagle and the Raven* apart—at first publication it was one of very few novels set in classical times that featured women as unfettered political agents. Robert Graves had depicted a politically potent Livia in *I Claudius,* but she was an anomaly; supreme power could never have been hers by right. In fact, Romans tended to count "legitimatized" female power—equal inheritance, matrilineal descent—as a sign of barbarism. Gedge shows us that contemporary with imperial Rome was a nearby island where women assumed every role in society—they might be warriors, healers, druids, poets, tribal leaders—and this *was* legitimatized by custom. It is difficult for us to imagine, but Gedge does so with startling veracity. She presents us with adolescent girls training with the sword, women debating in war councils, a hereditary queen receiving the unquestioned obeisance of her subjects—and skillfully makes these interludes appear as natural as all others in this complex story.

Despite her tale's solid grounding in history, Gedge never forgets that a novel is foremost a work of art. With her lyrical descriptions of place, she splashes colors onto the page that rouse the senses, bring the moist forest close, allow us to feel the lonely spaces between settlements, in the characters' hearts. The action surges across a broad canvas with an attention to composition that for me recalls a nineteenth-century classical painting, for the story has a powerful symmetry, a strong frame. In tales spun from history's scattered remains, a novelist must know what to select if she's to craft a story that feels like a living whole. *The Eagle and the Raven* ends where it begins—in the soul of Caradoc, who birthed the resistance.

It is difficult to believe this landmark book was ever out of print. I'd like to think that the muse of history watched over it, shepherding it into the hands of a new generation of readers. It's a tome to retreat with for a week, to immerse yourself in, a novel that no one infatuated with Roman history—or with grand stories passionately told—should miss.

Donna Gillespie

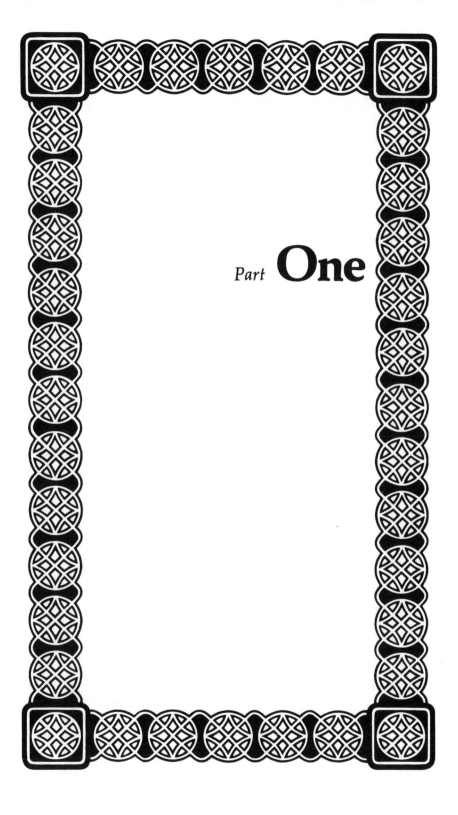

Part **One**

Autumn, A.D. 32

CHAPTER ONE

CARADOC PUSHED HIS WAY through the dense thicket of briars and found himself out in the open at last, free of the forest's somber shadows. With a sense of weak relief, he sheathed his sword, hugged his cloak more firmly about him, and squatted for a moment on the gentle slope of the bank, watching the sullen flow of the river as he recovered his breath and his bearings. For a while he had believed himself lost and had thrashed about in the pathless halls, knowing full well the panic that seized him. For this was Samain, and even his father's best warriors, men who feared nothing and no one, were afraid on this day and were not ashamed. The sky had been gray all day, and now a bitter, driving wind had sprung up. It would bring rain, but he lingered, unwilling to rise from the damp grass, yet anxious from the swift coming of night and from the trees at his back which spoke of dark secrets he could not understand. He shivered, but not from the cold, and, morose, he huddled deeper into his cloak, thinking of all the Samains he had seen come and go.

His earliest memories were full of the same fear that had gripped him in the forest, of his father, Cunobelin, sitting like a great bulk of shadow, gazing into the fire, of Togodumnus his brother, and Gladys his sister, silent and uncomprehending, clinging together at his father's feet, while his mother lay on the bed and held him close, her arms stiff. The eerie autumn wind would whisper round the doorskins, and the fingers of night would rustle above in the thatching. They would sit thus through the dark, slow-moving hours, the children dozing and waking again to see the fire burned low and Cunobelin leaning over to lay more wood upon it, and only when the pale, reluctant dawn crept shamefacedly into the room would any of them dare to speak. Later, after porridge and bread and a piece of honeycomb, they would gather in the Great Hall, anxiously counting the chiefs and freemen as they straggled in, afraid to ask if any had been taken, afraid to ask who had been spared. Then, in the late cold morning, the cattle slaughter would begin, and for days the reek of blood would hang over the town. Samain. How he hated it. Another night of terror, another day of killing, another year almost over.

A sudden splash of color caught his eye and he turned. His brother had emerged from the trees where the path wound down to the riverbank. Togodumnus was not alone. Aricia walked beside him, her black hair streaming out behind her and the long folds of her tunic pressed tightly to her lithe body, her blue cloak and Tog's crimson flapping against each other. They seemed to be arguing, and they stopped and faced one another, their voices rising vehemently, but they were still too far away for Caradoc to catch any words. All at once they burst out laughing, and Aricia's hands, her long white fingers, fluttered in the fading light. The pale butterflies of spring. For a moment Caradoc was dazzled by their flight, but soon he rose, and, at the movement, Togodumnus saw him, waved, and began to run down the path. Aricia caught at her cloak and vainly tried to wrap it around her as Caradoc slowly went to meet them.

"We lost you!" Togodumnus shouted, coming up panting. "Did you make a kill?"

"No. He bolted into a thicket, but by the time the dogs had found a way in, he had vanished. Where is my horse?"

"Aricia tethered him and then we looked for you. She was angry because the gate will be closed soon, and it looks as though the night will be stormy. She wanted to leave you to your fate." He grinned. "She didn't want to spend Samain Eve in the woods."

"You were the one who cast fearful glances over your shoulder, Tog, and I was the one who had to lead Caradoc's horse," Aricia protested hotly. "I am afraid of nothing," she said, smiling at Caradoc in mute complicity.

It was late afternoon and the light was failing rapidly. In the north, the clouds billowed ominously, piled one on top of the other by the

4

force of the wind, and the three hunters hurried toward the horses and mounted quickly. Togodumnus led the way, cantering easily beside the water; Aricia swung into a gallop beside him, and Caradoc brought up the rear. Once the first gate was past, they would still have to go six miles, through straggling clusters of huts, beside farmsteads, skirting meadows. In an hour they would be drinking warm wine beside their own fires, their feet to the friendly flames.

Caradoc suddenly thundered past Aricia and motioned Togodumnus to rein in. "The dogs!" He shouted, waving his arms furiously. "We forgot the dogs!"

"You fool!" Togodumnus swore at him. "Where did they go after they lost the boar?"

"They went charging off into the underbrush on some other scent. I whistled them and they came and then I started back for the path. Why call me a fool? You two are the greater idiots for not following when they were hot for a kill!"

"You are both fools and idiots," Aricia broke in, her voice betraying a verge of panic. "Cunobelin forbade you to take out the dogs because they are bound for Rome the day after tomorrow. But what did that mean to you? Just another admonition to be ignored." She gathered up the reins and kneed her horse. "Well, you can go back into the woods and hunt for them, if you dare. I am cold and tired. I'm going." She trotted past them and then picked up speed. In a moment the dusk swallowed her and the young men were alone. They eyed one another, aware of the growing dimness and the unnameable things that waited in the trees beyond.

"What shall we do?" Togodumnus said. "That vixen—— It was her idea to hunt today and well she knows it. Some night I shall catch her and tie her to a tree, let the Raven of Nightmares have her."

"Hush," Caradoc hissed. "She'll hear you and She'll come. We must get home. Tomorrow we can tell father and take our punishment."

Togodumnus shook his head, but Caradoc had already started for the gate, and Togodumnus followed. The wind had risen to a shriek, clawing at their hair and their heels, and the horses snorted and stretched into a wild gallop. When they reached the first gate, they fell off their horses and ran across the dyke, dragging the reins in their sweaty hands. As they tumbled headlong toward the gate the gate-guard came running out, his torch held high.

"I was not going to wait for you another moment, Lords," he grumbled as he slammed the big wooden gates closed behind their horses. "Such foolishness, to keep me sitting by a naked gate on this night of all nights!"

The man's sword was in his other hand. But what could a sword do against the demons of Samain? Caradoc wondered. "Has Aricia been through?" he asked. The man nodded. "And dogs? Have any dogs been through?"

"Yes, indeed. A pack of them an hour ago, lathered up and worn out."

Togodumnus clapped his brother on the back. "There! The hounds have more sense than we! Thanks to you, freeman. Go back to your hearth." The man sheathed his sword and turned away.

"Now for bed," Caradoc sighed as they mounted. "And not even a rabbit to show for a wasted day. Father will surely notice Brutus's ripped ear."

"Of course he'll notice, and he'll take a heifer from each of us for the price of the hound. What ill luck!"

"How could Samain Eve bring anything but bad luck? And just when my honor-price has been going up."

"It's a good thing that your honor-price depends on more than your cattle. What surety did Sholto offer you for the loan of your two bulls?"

"He has pledged himself and his kin to me. He is a good man to retain. I told him that if he oathed to me instead of to you I would give him one of the bulls and buy his wife a Roman drinking cup, of silver."

"Caradoc! No freeman's loyalty is worth a whole bull! Besides, I offered him a bull and a heifer."

"Then why did he decide to oath to me?"

"Because you never make your freemen do anything but count your precious cows! Oh, a curse, it's beginning to rain. Perhaps it will turn to snow."

"Too early in the year," Caradoc answered shortly, and they finished the ride in silence, their shoulders hunched into their cloaks, water dripping from their elbows and heels and driving cold into their faces.

The way was dark as they followed the rough, winding path across the little fields. The peasants would be huddling together in their hovels, the chiefs and freemen in their wooden huts, and they passed no one. Occasionally they heard the restless lowing of cattle, brought in from summer pastures and herded together within the wooden palisades, but even the wild animals had gone to ground and it seemed to the two youths that they were the only living things left on earth. Caradoc and Togodumnus plodded on, their horses' hoofs falling quietly on the sodden, leaf-strewn path. Beside them, they could see Aricia's track in the wet grass, the horse's prints already filling with black water, but soon the night was fully dark and they could

6

see nothing but the thin ribbon of road that wound slowly and hypnotically beneath them. Togodumnus began to sing quietly under his breath but Caradoc hushed him once more, ashamed of the fear that welled up inside him. Already seventeen, he had killed his man and raided for cattle; he had hunted deer and boar and wild wolf. These things he could face and understand, but the nebulous, drifting spirits of Samain, the demons who waited this night to drag their victims to the woods, these he could not turn to best with a slash of his sword. He felt them now, standing just within the cover of the gaunt, leafless branches meeting over his head, watching him with hatred, wanting to do harm. He gripped the wet reins ever tighter and spoke quietly to his horse. Togodumnus began to hum but this time Caradoc left him alone. One more bend, and they would be home.

They finally dismounted inside the second gate, their thighs wet and chafed and their hands blue with cold. The stable servant ran out to meet them; he took the reins from their stiff fingers and led the tired horses away without a word.

Togodumnus took off his cloak and watched the water trickle between his fingers as he wrung it out. "Will you sleep tonight?" he asked his brother.

Caradoc shook his head. "I don't think so. Hot wine and dry clothes for me, and then perhaps a song or two from Caelte to keep the vengeful ones from my door." His voice echoed against the darkened huts. "Tomorrow we can breathe again, but in the meantime you can go to the kennels and check the dogs. It was your idea to take them out."

"No, it was not! Aricia and I got into a fight. She said I was too much of a coward to disobey Cunobelin, she said I had no guts! Besides, you lost them, not me."

"Oh Tog, why do you listen to her? You know she will get you into trouble."

Togodumnus's eyes glistened. "Not as much trouble as she will make for you, my brother, if Cunobelin ever hears what you and she are about all the time."

"What do you know about that?" Caradoc asked him sharply, grinning.

"Nothing. Only rumors. Well, a good night to you Caradoc, and good hunting."

"Tog! Come back!" Caradoc shouted, but Togodumnus was already striding between the silent homes on the steep hill to his own little hut. Caradoc resignedly moved west into the deeper shadows of the tall earthwall, his footfalls sounding fatally loud in his ears. He soon

7

came to his father's stables, where a gush of warm, sweet-smelling air engulfed him for the moment, but then he turned, passing the blacksmith's forge and the harness maker's shop, and so came to the kennels.

He counted the cages carefully and stopped at last, squatting, calling softly. The hounds ran to the fence and quietly pushed their cold noses into his hand. He quickly ran his eye over them once, twice. There was one missing. Caradoc groaned to himself as he started to count again, not certain which one was gone. Brutus, half his ear hanging over his nose, watched him reproachfully. Finally Caradoc cursed out loud. It was Caesar. The one dog prized above all others of this litter, the one that had been especially trained for Tiberius himself. It would be that one, Caradoc swore, remembering why Cunobelin, with his sly humor, had given the beast such a name. It was not for Tiberius's sake that the dog was so blessed, but for that of Julius Caesar, who had come to Albion twice and gone away twice, never to return. Cunobelin had remarked to his sons that Julius had not, after all, been a very good hunter.

Caradoc stood irresolutely, his hair sticking to his forehead and his cloak, heavy with water, hanging from his shoulders. He did not doubt that Caesar had led the dogs back home. Putting himself in Caesar's place, he suddenly realized where the dog would be——somewhere warm. Caradoc turned to begin his search, starting with the blacksmith's, then the harness maker's, the stinking tanneries, the stables. Determined he left the fourth circle and walked slowly up to where the freemen commoners lived, an area of squalor and confusion. He knocked on walls and pushed aside doorskins, frightening the tribesmen who at first saw in this dark, sopping figure a cunningly disguised spirit. Minute after minute passed, and at last he had to admit defeat.

He swung abruptly into the climb to his own house, but when he came out above the buildings perched on the slope, the wind caught him and he staggered and almost fell. All at once the skies opened further, releasing a black wall of ice-tipped, stinging rain. He began to run, and, as if at the awkward movements of his body, his pent-up panic was unleashed and pushed him on.

What am I doing out here on this night when time stands still and the earth is poised on the brink of a terrible nothingness? he thought, horrified. Some fey spirit has entered into Caesar so that I will search for him, and when I find him he will take me in his mighty jaws and drag me back to the forest.

He struggled on into the teeth of the gale, blinded, vaguely aware that he was passing the Great Hall, instinctively and mindlessly veer-

8

ing away from the shrine of Camulos until at last his numbed fingers felt the heavy skins of his own door. He thrust them aside and tumbled within, standing, panting, his eyes closed, while water ran from his body and pooled under his feet. He was stunned for a moment by the sudden cessation of noise, the storm now only a steady shushing on the thatching of his roof, the wind an impatient prowler, throwing itself against his walls, to no avail.

Soon he relaxed and opened his eyes. A solitary oil lamp burned on a little table opposite the door. Soft hangings covered the walls, and, at one end, curtains were drawn back, revealing a low bed with a blue and red cloak trailing across it. But this was not his hut. Beside the bed was another table, a mirror lying on it, and with it a gold head circlet, a pile of bronze arm bands, and a brightly enameled girdle that snaked to the floor. With a whine of welcome Caesar rose from his place before the smoking fire and padded across the room toward him.

Aricia spun round in shock. "Caradoc! You gave me a fright! What do you want?"

He hesitated, torn between an embarrassed confusion and overwhelming relief that he had found the dog. There was no demon here, only a dog, and a girl. She was standing barefooted on the skins that covered the hard clay floor, and her white sleeping tunic fell around her like drifting snow. She held a large comb in one hand, and her black hair fell straight and thick to her knees, spreading over her pale arms and gleaming in the firelight as she stepped toward him. He mumbled an apology and turned to go, an irrational anger rising in him, but she spoke again and he paused.

"How wet you are! Have you been looking for the dogs all this time? Take off your cloak or you will catch cold."

"Not tonight, Aricia," he said firmly. "I am soaked and tired, and angry with you for keeping Caesar here. And I am angry with Tog for leaving me to seek on my own. I am going to find my own hearth."

She laughed. "What a sight you are, with that black scowl on your face and your hair hanging down your back in strings! I didn't find Caesar and keep him here. He ran to me not half an hour ago. I was about to call for someone to take him to the kennels when you fell in. As for Tog, you know you have to take him by the scruff of his neck and shake him if you want anything done. Why are you so annoyed?" She went to him swiftly, tugged the cloak from his shoulders, and, gingerly holding it out, walked to the fire and laid it down. "Warm wine from the land of the sun," she said gently, picking up a jug that sat in the embers. "Have a cup before you brave the night again, Caradoc. And talk to me. It is Samain, and I am lonely."

9

He sensed Caesar's brown eyes upon him. Go now, he told himself. Go before once again your honor lies around you like pieces of smashed pottery. But she had poured the wine and as she held it under his nose, the spicy fumes steamed in his nostrils. He took the cup and warmed his hands around it, feeling his fingers tingle with new life. Then, he stepped further into the room and turned at the fire to let the heat penetrate his stiff legs.

"I thought you did not fear Samain," he remarked.

She looked at him swiftly and went to sit on the edge of her bed. "I said that I was lonely, not that I was afraid. But you are afraid," she mocked.

"I have good cause to be," he retorted, swallowing a great gulp of wine, feeling it burn its way into his stomach and spread its glow throughout his chest. "I am a chieftain. The demons delight in attacking royalty on this night."

"So am I of royal blood," she said tartly, sitting straighter. "Have you forgotten? Have I been at Camulodunon so long that I seem just one more of Cunobelin's spawn? I have not forgotten," she finished softly, looking down at her hands, entwined softly in her white lap.

He emptied his cup and reached down to pour himself another. "I'm sorry, Aricia," he said. "Sometimes I do forget. You have been here for so long and we have all grown up together—you, me, Tog, Eurgain, Gladys, Adminius. How many years has it been since father began to call us the Royal War Band?"

She closed her eyes as if some memory pained her, and he watched her covertly over the rim of his cup. She is so beautiful, he thought in growing resignation, looking at the pale complexion that never tanned with the summer sun, the delicate chin, the long black lashes lying on such high cheekbones. He wondered just when he had ceased to think of her as a hunting companion and begun to see a stranger. When she opened her eyes he recognized the enticing mysteries hidden there, intriguing confusions that he was too young to recognize as insecurities. For a while they scanned each other, he too tired to look away, mesmerized by her black eyes, she not seeing him, feeling back into the past.

Suddenly she giggled. "Caradoc, you are steaming."

"What?"

"Your breeches are drying out and the steam is rising in clouds! You look like some river god, emerging on a winter morning. Do take off your clothes or go away and stop making my little nest all damp."

"I suppose I had better take Caesar to the kennel," he said reluctantly, feeling the wine swell his tongue and turn his limbs to lead.

10

Shaking her head, Aricia stood up quickly. "Do not tempt your luck! We have already had more than we deserve tonight. Leave him here with me, or take him to your own hearth." She glided to him, her tunic rustling, bringing with her a whiff of Roman perfume. "I am truly sorry for the trouble I've caused today. Tog only insisted on hunting because of a dare I made. If Cunobelin is very angry I will help you both pay Brutus's price. I don't suppose the traders will want him."

"No, I don't suppose so." He felt his legs trembling loosely with fatigue and he saw her mistily, through a haze of wine fumes. Seeing his hesitation she began to smile. Ah, not now, not tonight, he thought to himself unsteadily. But it was too late. Already his hand was reaching out, lifting a lock of her hair, running it through his fingers to feel its thick, smooth texture. He raised it to his face, breathing in its perfume and its warmth, and she did not move until he had finished.

"Stay with me, Caradoc," she said slowly, looking at him enquiringly. "You want to stay, don't you? I am a Samain demon tonight. Do you feel the spell that I am placing on you?"

She spoke half in jest but he felt the bewitchment stealing over him like a sweet, familiar song. He knew that he should rush to the door with a protecting spell on his lips, but, as always, he only looked at her with hot stupefaction. He and Tog had often joked about this black witch of whom they were so dangerously fond, and they teased her unmercifully about the paleness of her northern skin in the same way that they teased Eurgain about her long silences, or Adminius about his precious collection of boars' teeth, but they did it without malice and without forethought, the unthinking words of friends of long standing. If she irritated him lately he put it down to the coming of winter, the time when men looked to the months ahead with tight belts and empty bellies, a time of year when he merely existed. And, if he sometimes wanted to slap her for her superior airs and her fiery will in an argument, well, she was, after all, just a girl, only a fourteen-year-old girl struggling to become a woman.

As she brought a handful of her own hair to her face, and closed her eyes, he felt a rush of heat from his loins. "You have no choice, spoiled Caradoc," she said quietly. "My bed is far more comfortable than the damp forest floor."

Outside, the rain drummed down. The wind had dropped to a low, persistent moan and inside the room the untended fire was dying, hissing now and then as stray raindrops found it. She reached up to his neck, removed the golden torc, and laid it carefully on the floor. She reached up to unbuckle his heavy belt, and as she did so the sword slid onto the skins. Still he made no move.

11

A weakening struggle went on within him and his eyes followed her every motion, but when the thin fingers touched his face he surrendered, grabbing her by her arms and pulling her sharply against him.

After all, he told himself, it is Samain. Raven of Panic, you will not find me here, he called silently.

A moment later she pulled away from his grasp. "You are making me wet," she said evenly. "Take off your tunic, and your breeches. No, I will do it for you. You are standing there as if I have put a holding spell upon you."

"You always do. Aricia . . ."

She put a finger to his lips. "No, Caradoc. Don't speak, please." Her voice shook. Stooping, she drew the short tunic over his head, and as she did so, he saw a flare of mockery in her eyes.

How strange, he thought. I never noticed before that her eyes are flecked with gold. He grasped her again, kissing her roughly, clumsily, feeling her hands warm on his naked back, losing himself in the softness of her mouth. Her magnificent hair fell tangling over his arms, and as he felt her press against him he caught her up and threw her on the bed, twitching the curtains closed behind them and cutting off the light of the lamp. He looked at her in the dimness as she lay waiting, arms outstretched, her hair spread wide upon the pillow, her thin-lipped smile both enraging him and inviting him to pain.

"Tog knows," he whispered.

Her smile widened. "I don't care. Do you?"

"No," he said softly.

"Then stop talking."

In his wine-befuddled eagerness he tugged at her sleeping tunic and heard it tear, and then her breasts were under his fumbling fingers, his greedy mouth. She drew in her breath sharply and hissed, and the rain continued to fall, monotonously and dreamily.

He could not restrain himself and it was over very quickly, but tonight she did not complain. It was always like this, an uncontrollable surge, the desperate, compulsive hunt for her, then the sharp, painful satiation. He rolled onto his back, his head on one arm, and gazed at the dim roof above him, wondering how and why as the little needles of shame began to prick. I have done it again, he thought despairingly. It was one thing to tumble a slave in the fields, or even the willing daughter of a freeman commoner, but this was Aricia his friend, Aricia who had shared in every escapade he and Tog had devised, Aricia, daughter of a ricon whose lineage stretched back much farther than his own. He wanted the earth to swallow him. He

12

wanted the demons of Samain to come and take him to their caves. He wanted to die.

She turned on her side, propped herself on one elbow and, not bothering to cover herself, pushed her hair back impatiently. Incredulous, he felt desire stir in him again.

"Caradoc?"

"Yes?"

"Marry me."

He thought for a moment that he had not heard her right, but then realizing, he sat bolt upright.

She wrapped her arms about her knees. "Yes, you heard me. I want you to marry me. I beg you, I implore you, Caradoc. Marry me!"

"What are you asking of me?" he said sharply, his mind temporarily freed from its drugged preoccupation with her.

She put a hot hand on his arm. "Are we not old friends?" she whispered. "Would it not be so easy, so very easy, to take the next step and become pledged to one another?" Her grip tightened on his arm. "It's not such a great thing that I ask. After all, you can take other wives."

He laughed then, clearheaded. "You mean Eurgain, I suppose. Oh, no, Aricia. We have had great pleasure together, but I do not think we should speak of marriage. Now I must go." He hurriedly swung his feet onto the cold floor but she restrained him with a force he had not known she possessed.

"Why not? Don't you think that I have a claim on you, Caradoc?"

"What claim? Do you mean this?" He bent to kiss her but she squirmed away from him and flung open the curtains. The dim lamplight showed him a face shadowed with emotion, lips barely controlled, eyes brimming with tears.

"I will play no more games with you, Caradoc. Where are the words of love you whisper to me in the darkness?"

"Love has nothing to do with you and me, Aricia, and you know it." He left the bed and dressed quickly, stepping into breeches that were still damp, pulling his wet tunic over his head. "I have made no promises to you."

She reached out and clung to the curtain as if her muscles had melted with her hope. "Caradoc, I am desperate. Do you know how old I am?"

He buckled on his sword belt. "Of course I know. You are fourteen."

"The age of betrothal."

His busy fingers paused and he glanced at her, sensing the truth.

"Very soon an embassy will come from my father, to take me home." The tears overflowed and splashed onto her hands and she shook them off angrily. "Home! I can scarcely remember the barren moorlands and poverty-stricken huts of my birthplace. Oh, Caradoc, I do not want to go. I do not want to leave you and Tog and Eurgain, and Cunobelin who is like a father to me. I do not want to go away to a place I fear, among fierce, uncouth men!" Her voice faltered, and, sobbing, she slipped to the floor. "I, too, hate Samain and the rains of winter, the loneliness that will come. Must this night go by with no demon come to claim me and no man to wed me?"

He went to her then and knelt beside her, and took her awkwardly into his arms, feeling sympathy rise within him for the first time. "Aricia, I didn't think, I didn't know. Have you spoken to Cunobelin?"

She shook her head violently, her face hidden in his neck. "He cannot keep me. My father will want me in Brigantia, for there are no other children to rule after him and the chiefs will certainly elect me." She looked up then, her eyelids swollen, her skin whiter than he had ever seen it. "If you care for me at all, do not allow this thing to happen to me. I will bring you the greatest dowry the Catuvellauni have ever seen. All of Brigantia! All of it, to share with me. You and I, ruling there together."

"But what of my own tuath? What of my own kin, and the freemen who depend on me? I don't want to go to Brigantia any more than you. Can't you refuse to go, Aricia?" He disengaged himself firmly and stood up. "Forgive me, but I cannot interfere in a matter between foreign kin. I . . ."

"You what? You are content to use me, and now you pity me? Keep your pity! I want no man's anxious looks." She brushed the tears from her cheeks and faced him. "I could make trouble for you, Caradoc, for dishonoring me and yourself, but I will not. I know my father will send for me soon, I have begun to dream about it, but when I go you will be sorry. There will be a hole in your life that will not be filled. I will remember. I swear by Brigantia the High One, goddess of my tribe."

He looked at the defiant face, the widely gesticulating hands. "We have used each other," he reminded her quickly. "How has this thing happened, Aricia? How have we ceased to be what we were?"

"Because we have been growing, and you have been too stupid to see it!" she shouted. "You must have known that I love you, you must have seen it, but you stand there with your jaw hanging down like an ignorant Trinovantian peasant! Leave me alone!" She flung herself onto her bed and did not move. For a few seconds he looked at her

14

miserably, wondering whether he was seeing the real Aricia or another one of the masks she slipped on so easily, but he could not linger and he snatched up his cloak and pushed past the doorskins, out once more into the darkness and the rain.

A few steps took him to his own door, and once inside he dropped the still-sodden cloak onto the ground. Fearachar must have come to stoke the fire, for it was blazing brightly and the room was comfortably warm. He quickly stripped and wrapped himself in a blanket, then sat with his legs stretched out to the red flames, his head in a whirl, wishing for the first time in his life that he could live Samain Eve over again.

He had touched more than Aricia's body tonight. Somehow he had flayed a raw nerve, a part of her that lay exposed, not yet covered by the droll, whimsical, often hard veneer she showed to the rest of them all too often, and he did not like what he had seen. He had not believed her capable of either tears or pleadings, and he wondered if she was lying in the dimness, caught in surprise at herself.

But marriage! His feet were too hot and he sat up, drawing them in under his chair and reaching for the wine placed ready for him. He had no wish to even consider the prospect with her. She was not the kind of woman to bear the sons of a Catuvellaunian chieftain, and his immediate refusal had come from a deep part of him, a part that he, too, did not know existed. He did not deny the spell she exerted on him. They knew each other too well. At least he had thought that they did. He remembered the day she had come to Camulodunon, all big frightened eyes and pathetic, childish haughtiness. Even then, though he himself had been but a child, his heart had gone out to her. For ten years they had all hunted, feasted, and fought together, terrorized the peasants, infuriated the freemen, lied and cheated for each other, and suddenly, between one dawn and the next, it was all over.

It had always been understood that he would marry Eurgain. She was a noble, the daughter of his father's chief tribesman, and even before she and he and the others had formed Cunobelin's War Band they had held a great affection for one another. She was tall, also, but more slender than Aricia, a fragile girl, silent, not beautiful but with an aura of peace and assurance that had begun to lure many to her. She had the deep, honey-colored hair and cornflower blue eyes of the best of his people, and she seemed to know his thoughts even before he spoke them.

Eurgain.

A vision of Aricia immediately arose in his mind, naked, black-eyed, shameless, hair falling to her hips and beyond, and he squirmed in his

15

chair. If she loved him as she said she did, how cleverly she had concealed it! Did she, then, hate Eurgain? She had given no sign of that either. Or was she putting on a last, desperate pose, faced with the prospect of the long, lonely ride back to her birthplace? How could it be that he had lived beside her day after day and did not really know her at all? He put a hand over his eyes, overcome with the desire to take those few steps back to her room, to walk in, to say . . . what? I lust after you, I am eaten away with desire for you, but I do not love you? What am I, of what price my honor if my father and my friends were to see me now!

He left the fire and went and lay on his bed, his eyes closed, still ashamed of himself, still wondering what would have happened if he had behaved as a freeman ought to behave. If he had walked out the door before she wound those soft arms about his neck. But it was weeks, months too late, and already his will had been weakened. He was vaguely aware that the rain had stopped, though the wind still muttered fitfully beyond the thin walls. He fell asleep, but even in his dreams she snared him like a rutting, netted boar.

He slept late the next morning, waking sluggishly to the sound of his servant whistling as he raked over the ashes of the dead fire and began to set a new one. A shaft of pale sunlight flowed under the doorskins, bringing with it cold, crisp air that blew the last of the night from Caradoc's head. As he sat up, Fearachar glanced toward him.

"A good morning to you, Lord. How pleased I am to see that you have been preserved and no demons saw fit to disturb your slumbers."

"And a good morning to you, Fearachar," Caradoc responded automatically. "I'm hungry." Feeling clearheaded, he stood, pulled on his breeches and a clean tunic, strapped on his sword, but suddenly the night came back to him. His torc did not lie on the table by his bed. With a shiver he realized he had left it on the floor of Aricia's hut. Fearachar glanced up to see the dismay on his master's face, but then rose, dusted off his hands, and produced something from the folds of his short red cloak.

"The Lady Aricia asked me to give you this and to tell you that though it is the badge of a freeman, to her it sometimes seems more like a yoke of slavery." Caradoc snatched at the torc and slipped it about his neck. "The Lady also said that she has taken Caesar to his kennel. It was foolish of you, Lord, to borrow the dogs. Your father will be angry."

"Perhaps. But what is that to you?" Caradoc said rudely. Yoke of slavery! How dare she!

16

"I am a freeman," the servant said, hurt. "I may have lost my honor-price but not my honor. I may speak my mind."

"Fearachar, when you have found your mind you may indeed speak it, but please find it first." Caradoc slung his red-and-yellow striped cloak around his shoulders and fastened it with a silver brooch. He put on plain bronze arm bands, and slipped his feet into leather sandals, then combed his hair, flung down the comb, and strode out into the morning.

He paused outside his house to sniff the clean air. The storm had moved on to trouble the north, and the valley lay before him, beyond the motley cluster of huts where smoke spiraled from the roofs and children romped in the thin, pale sun of winter. From where he stood he thought he could just make out a haze that was the river, and farther toward the horizon the dark blur of the forest, its plumes smoking with mist. The sky was washed blue, dressed in shreds of white cloud. More clouds, gray, hung in the north. It would be fine until the evening.

He strode down the winding path, calling for Cinnamus and Caelte as he went, not waiting for them as they ran, but the three of them reached the entrance of the Great Hall together and went inside, on their way greeting the chiefs who hung about, waiting for Cunobelin.

A smell of hot broth and pork fat met them as they entered the darkness and they went immediately to the great black cauldron that hung from iron chains over the massive fire at the center of the Hall. They ladled the steaming broth into wooden bowls, took cold pork and bread from the slave who sat behind platters heaped high with both, then found a corner and sat, drinking their broth with the utmost concentration, their eyes still unaccustomed to the gloom.

The Great Hall had been built five years before Caradoc's birth, when his father had swept upon the Trinovantes and taken their tribal territory for his own, setting up his new capital and his mint here, at Camulodunon. Caradoc's grandfather, Tasciovanus, had also conquered the territory but had not held it for long, withdrawing tactfully back to Verulamium when Caesar Augustus had come hurrying to Gaul. But Cunobelin had bided his time, waiting to strike at the Trinovantes once more, when Rome was smarting and demoralized by the loss of three legions in Germania. This time Rome had shrugged her imperial shoulders and Cunobelin had settled down to rule one of the greatest gatherings of tribes in the country. He called himself ricon now, a king, and though he was old his ambitions still consumed him. Caradoc well remembered his father and his uncle going off to war when he was ten, and now his uncle, Eppaticus, ruled the northern Atrebates, and Verica, their true chieftain, was left with nothing but a strip of coastline. He had protested to Rome on numerous occasions, but Rome had better things to do than send good men to die in Albion for one insignificant chief. And besides, Cunobelin controlled the southern trade with Rome. He kept that city supplied with dogs, hides, slaves, cattle, grain, and, once in a while, raw metals—gold and silver—from the inland territories of the tribes who traded respectfully with him. In return, Rome sent wine, and silver tableware and drinking cups, bronze-plated furniture, pottery, ivory, but most of all, jewelry for the chiefs, their horses, and their women. The river was always busy. Ships plied up and down, traders swarmed all over Catuvellaunian territory, news went back and forth, and Cunobelin watched it all, silent and unblinking like an old, wily spider, weaving webs of deceit and successfully holding Rome in one hand and his dark policies of expansion in the other.

He trod a narrow, dangerous path and he knew it. To make war was to invite Roman intervention, for Rome would allow nothing to interfere with her precious trade. But to rely too heavily on the good-will of Tiberius was as foolish a move as to trust one's life to the shifting sands of the marshy estuary of his river, and, besides, a great deal of his power depended on his keeping the chieftains happy. He let them raid sometimes, to give them something to do, and though there had often been formal protests from Caesar, it was a tribute to Cunobelin's statecraft that no more concrete objections ever materialized. He was content, for the time being, to hold the land that he had, but his glance ever strayed—northeast, to the rich Icenian lands, and west, to the hills of the Dobunni. He left the Durotriges of the southwest alone. They were a warlike, fierce people, thoroughly intractable. He could only conquer them with a full-scale assault, which would mean irreparable damage to his trading connections. They kept to themselves, following the ways of their deep ancestors, and he knew he would have to wait for a more favorable time to lead his war band against them.

Now Dubnovellaunus, chieftain of the Trinovantes, nursed his wounded pride in Rome and his people farmed for the Catuvellauni. Cunobelin had built the Great Hall in the first flush of his new conquest. It was of wood, spacious and airy, its roof vaulting high above, its wooden pillars carved tortuously by the native Trinovantian craftsmen into curling, sinuous leaves, plant tendrils that wrapped dreamily around one another, and half-hidden faces of men and beasts that peered out, sleepy and mysterious. Cunobelin and his family did not particularly like the native art. They preferred the honest, open faces and designs of the Roman potters and silversmiths, for sometimes, of

18

a lonely winter evening, the complex, secretive work of the native artists seemed to come alive and move softly, speaking of a time when the Catuvellauni had been nothing but a dim prescient warning carried on the night breezes.

The roof was vented so that the smoke from the fire could escape, and all around the walls hung shields and iron swords, javelins and thrusting spears. Hanging on the central pillar was the wizened, wrinkled head of one of Tasciovanus's fallen foes, held there by a knife through his hair. No one could remember who he was, but he was carried into every battle, and hung in Cunobelin's tent whenever the ricon was away from Camulodunon. Caradoc and the others had ceased to notice him years ago, and now he swung above the company, his sunken eyes watching the comings and goings, his gray locks stirring in the constant draft.

"No hunting today," Caradoc said to his friends. "I suppose you both want to go and watch the slaughtering."

Cinnamus wiped his generous mouth on his sleeve and put down his bowl. "I had better watch," he said. "My freemen tell me some of my herd is missing, and I have a feeling Togodumnus will be rubbing his hands this day. If he has touched my breeding stock he had better look to his weapons."

Caelte leaned his back against the wall. "We have guests," he said softly, "and here is Cunobelin."

The Hall was almost empty, for the morning was advancing and already the autumn slaughtering had begun on the flat land by the river. Caradoc turned his head to watch his father come striding into the dimness, surrounded by his chiefs. With him came a short, fat man whose braided hair hung over his cloaked shoulders, and a little girl. They went immediately to the cauldron, and Cunobelin himself served the guests broth and bread, then looked about for a place to sit. The chiefs served themselves noisily, already quarreling over the pieces of meat that floated so appetizingly in the brown soup, and Cunobelin steered his guests toward the three young men. They stood up, as Cunobelin approached, and Caradoc tried to divine his father's mood. He wondered if Cunobelin already knew about Brutus.

"Ah, Caradoc," Cunobelin boomed. "This is the Lord Subidasto, chieftain of the Iceni, and this is his daughter, Boudicca." Caradoc nodded to the man and smiled briefly at the girl, then he presented Cinnamus and Caelte.

"Lord, this is Cinnamus, my shield-bearer and charioteer, and this Caelte, my bard. You are welcome in our Hall."

They all clasped wrists and then sat down, Caelte immediately talking to little Boudicca. Cinnamus excused himself and went out,

19

and Caradoc turned to Subidasto, feeling his father's calculating gaze upon him.

"You have come far, Lord," he said. "I hope your stay with us will be one of rest and peace." They were the words of formal greeting, but Subidasto laughed harshly. How rude he is, Caradoc thought. I am only trying to repeat the words of formal greeting as I'm sure father has done.

"That depends on your father and our talks together," he said. "We have much to discuss."

Caradoc looked at him closely. He had been wrong about the fat. Subidasto was enormous, yes, but his girth was not loose or flabby. His arms were full of tight muscle, his mouth firm and unyielding, and he had the pale blue, piercing eyes of a man who spends all his time out-of-doors, looking into far distances. Is there trouble here? Caradoc wondered. Is that why Subidasto has claimed the immunity of Samain? What is my father plotting this time? He glanced at Cunobelin but read only merriment in the close-set eyes, in the heavily wrinkled face.

"Peace, Lord!" Cunobelin said. "First there must be good eating and drinking tonight, and plenty of music, and of course the rites of Samain. Then we will talk." He scrambled to his feet. "But if you've eaten for the morning, let me show you Camulodunon."

Subidasto's mouth set in a hard line of disapproval but he rose also, nodding reluctantly.

Caradoc suddenly found Boudicca's round eyes staring at his face, and it made him uncomfortable. "Father," he said. "Will you excuse me? I must go and see to my herd today."

Cunobelin dismissed him, but said quietly, "There is also the matter of my dogs, Caradoc. Brutus has a ripped ear and cannot now be sold. How did that happen, I ask myself, when the guards at the kennel have had orders not to let those dogs out of their sight? There must be a settling here."

"You know everything, father," Caradoc said, grinning. "Have you spoken to Tog?"

"Yes, and to Aricia. The three of you owe me two heifers. Breeding stock." Cunobelin was smiling back.

"Now father!" Caradoc protested. "Take a carcass. I cannot afford a live heifer."

"I'll fight you for it if you like," Cunobelin said indifferently.

"No, father, no." Caradoc shouted with laughter. "I have no wish for more scars, but a breeder gone will be a sore loss."

"Then take Cinnamus and Fearachar and go raiding," Cunobelin said. "How do you think I got rich, Caradoc?"

Caradoc saluted him ruefully and turned on his heel, but he felt a small hand steal into his own and hold him back. He looked down to see those brown eyes still fixed solemnly on him.

"Can I come with you?" she whispered.

His heart sank, but before he could refuse, Cunobelin said, "Take the child down to the slaughtering, Caradoc, and amuse her for a while. Do you object, Subidasto?"

Subidasto hesitated. He was evidently torn from moment to moment by the wish on the one hand to be as objectionable as possible and on the other not to offend these most powerful people, but finally he shook his head, and so Caradoc left the Hall with Boudicca trailing behind him. They walked into the sun and took the path that led straight down to the gate. It stood wide, and beyond it Fearachar waited, sitting on the ground, a sour look on his face, the reins of Caradoc's horse held loosely in his hands.

"I have been waiting for you for a long time, Lord," Fearachar said reproachfully as he handed the horse over to Caradoc. "I am cold and hungry."

"Then go and get warm and have something to eat—but I don't think we have left you much," Caradoc retorted. "Boudicca, can you ride?"

The chin came up. "Of course!" she said. "But not . . . not horses like him, only chariot ponies. There are not many horses as big as that in our country," she finished, blushing.

Caradoc lifted her and set her on his mount's back, jumping up behind her and gathering up the reins. "Shall we go fast?" he asked her, and she nodded vigorously, winding her fingers into the horse's mane as he dug in his heels and swept down the gentle slope into the meadows beyond.

In an hour they came to the river flat, and even before they rounded the bend that would reveal the water and the marshes and the tall, leafless willows, they could smell the slaughtering—the sickly sweet, wet smell of freshly spilled blood—and they could hear the high, panic-stricken bellowing of a thousand cattle who were about to die. As they cantered around the bend, all the ground from forest to water became a thick mass of pushing, jostling people and closely herded beasts. The din was tremendous. A little way up the bank Caradoc picked out Togodumnus, and with a shock of remembered shame and excitement spotted Aricia next to him. They were sitting close together on cloaks on the grass, their steaming breath mingling as they talked. As he drew rein and got down, and Boudicca slid off the horse's back to stand beside him, Adminius came striding up the slope.

21

"Caradoc, where have you been? I've had my people running all over the place, looking for you!" He came to a halt, panting, his handsome face flushed. "There's trouble down there. The freemen are fighting. Sholto says you offered him a bull and a heifer from your breeding stock, but Alan says no, you offered only one bull, and that for slaughter for his family's meat. And Cinnamus is down among his cattle, screaming and swearing, for it seems that he is short twelve beasts."

Aricia chuckled, Tog nodded in mock solemnity, and Caradoc cursed. "Well, Adminius, why come to me? You are senior next to father. Go and sort it all out."

"Because I've got cattle missing too!" he roared. "Tog, I'm sick and tired of creeping into your compounds in the dead of night to steal back my own cattle! Where is your sense of honor? And you with the highest honor-price of the lot of us. I'm going to complain to father!"

"Oh sit down, Adminius," Togodumnus said lazily. "How could there be anything but trouble when the freemen rush to drive their cattle first to the slaughter? No wonder the traders stand back and laugh at us. If Cinnamus spent more time caring for his beasts and less crossing swords with you, Caradoc, he'd know that he lost cattle this summer through disease. And as for you, Adminius, I think I'll bring a case against you for trying to steal my cattle. You've just admitted it, you know."

The color mounted in Adminius's face and he rushed at his brother, pouncing on him, and soon they were rolling on the ground, fighting and kicking.

Aricia sighed. "You had better go and see what has happened, Caradoc," she said.

When he met her eyes he was conscious of a tightness in his loins, but she spoke evenly and her eyes told him nothing. It was as if the night had never been. Well, perhaps it hadn't. Perhaps it was not Caesar who was the demon, or Aricia, but he himself who had spent the whole night of Samain in a fit of delusion. She looked away, sighing in a great gust of steamy breath, and the very hopelessness of the set of her shoulders told him he had not dreamed the night. She was too quiet, too calm.

"Leave the little one with me," Aricia said. "Who is she, anyway?"

"Boudicca, daughter of Subidasto, chieftain of the Iceni," he said carefully, pulling his cloak around him. A yell of rage came from the two wrestlers and he repressed an irritated urge to kick them both in the rump.

"Come and sit here, beside me," Aricia said to the girl. "What do you think of the Catuvellauni?"

22

"You have fine horses, and much cattle," Boudicca answered promptly, "but my father says that you all suffer from a disease."

Caradoc turned, amused. "Indeed?" he said. "And what disease do we have?"

"It is called the Roman disease," she replied, lifing her limpid brown eyes to meet his own. "What is it, do you know? And will I catch it? I do not want to be sick."

Aricia and Caradoc looked at each other for one astounded moment, then Aricia burst out laughing. "I do not think, little Boudicca," she gasped, "that either you or your father are in any danger of being struck down by this, this terrible disease. It seems to afflict only the Catuvellauni."

"Oh. Then I do not wish to sit here. I wish to ride Caradoc's horse again."

The child is quick, Caradoc thought. She knows that we are laughing at her father. He nodded to Aricia and strode away, torn between laughter and anger at old Subidasto's temerity. Roman disease! How little he knew Cunobelin, to imagine that the Catuvellauni were only pawns in the ironclad fingers of Rome. We are first, and only, freemen, masters of ourselves. In that is our pride.

He plunged into the crush of excited, shouting people and they made way for him, muttering as he passed. They were mostly peasants, small and dark-haired, but there were also many native Trinovantian freemen and former chiefs, from whose stock his mother had come. Here and there a Catuvellaunian chieftain bowed to him, and by the time he had forced his way to the bank of the river he had four nobles at his back.

Here the stench was overpowering. Blood pooled on the grass and trickled in rivulets down to the water, and great piles of carcasses waited for the tanners to come and skin them and the butchers to haul them away and dismember them. The air was clouded with flies even though the first frosts had come and gone. Alan stood next to Cinnamus, the sleeves of his tunic rolled up, his arms bloody to the elbows. Sholto was berating them both, shaking his fists and stamping on the ground while the crowd watched, waiting for the blows that must come. Caradoc stepped forward.

"Alan, a good morning to you. And to you, Sholto. Shall I pick you up and throw you into the river? Why do you argue with my freeman?"

Sholto glared at him. "I am your freeman too, Lord, or have you forgotten our bargain? I oath to you for a bull and a heifer, breeders, but Alan here calls me a liar!"

Caradoc looked at him speculatively for a moment, watching the shifty eyes slide away from his. He did not like Sholto and was already regretting his offer to take the man on as his chief, but the honor-price was a sore point between himself and Tog, and Sholto had a large kin and many cattle. He was a whining, lying miser, but he could fight, and so could his freemen and his women.

"I do not call you a liar, Sholto, but I call your ears hard of hearing. Alan is right. I promised you only a bull for your winter store, and a silver cup for your wife. But if you prefer, you may take a breeding heifer. I do not care. Or you may want to consider Togodumnus's offer, but make haste. My cattle wait for the knife."

Alan smiled slowly, folding his red arms, and Sholto chewed his lip and thought furiously. Togodumnus was young but he had many freemen in his train. Too many, and they squabbled all the time. But Caradoc could keep order among his men with a word or a joke. He had a way with people and, moreover, he was honest in his dealings. Such a lord could not be manipulated or rapidly impoverished. Sholto spoke sullenly.

"I will take the breeding heifer, Lord."

"A sound decision. Well, Alan, you can get on with it. Cinnamus, why are you foaming at the mouth?"

"That brother of yours has gone too far this time!" Cinnamus came close to him and spoke in a low, forceful undertone. "Twelve of my fattest slaughter stock are among his cattle. I know them. My head freeman knows them. I am going to present a case to your father tonight, Caradoc, and I am going to be recompensed for Togodumnus's light fingers."

"How can you prove your loss?"

"All my people will take the oath for me!"

"So will Tog's. There has to be more."

"There is." Cinnamus smiled grimly. "All my cattle were marked this spring, nicked in the ear. We shall see how Togodumnus can worm his way out of that!"

The crowd was drifting away now, disappointed because there had been no fight, and already the tanners and butchers with their knives and hooks were moving among the piles of dead beasts. Caradoc looked to the forest bank, but Aricia, Tog, and Adminius had gone. So had Boudicca with his horse.

"Cin, why don't you go to Tog and tell him what you've told me. Then demand from him twelve of his cattle as well as your own back. That will hurt him far more than my father's justice, and I would hate to see you and him shed each other's blood over a few cows."

"A few cows!" Cinnamus swore and spat on the ground. "Fine for you, Lord, with your vast herd, but I must count every beast twice. A drop of Togodumnus's blood would go a long way to assuage my heart, and a lot of others, too. Even his own chiefs are wary of his theiving ways."

Caradoc knew it was true. Tog was sixteen and he had great charm, a gift that rescued him from scrape after scrape and caused his chieftain freemen to cluster around him like fawning dogs, but he was dangerously close to losing his father's patience and the admiration of his kin. Cinnamus could easily kill him, Caradoc knew. The young man who stood before him, frowning angrily, had been trained from birth as a warrior, a cold fighter whose reflexes were lightning swift and who could destroy without mercy. That was why Caradoc had chosen him as shield-bearer and charioteer. But he had also been chosen because he was generous and quick to laugh, and he and Caradoc loved one another.

"Do what you think best, Cin," he said at length. "It is your feud. But think of the consequences to your family if Tog decides to make it a blood feud."

"He never would. Not him. If you speak to him, Lord, I may be content. Tell him I want my cattle, and the others too, and tell him also . . ." He paused, his green eyes smiling into Caradoc's own with an edge of pure ice to the humor. "Tell him also that if he enters my compound again I will order my freemen to kill him." He nodded and walked away, striding loose-limbed and tall by the river, the sun glinting on his golden hair, and Caradoc turned, making his way slowly back along the path to the gate.

Halfway there he met Togodumnus, one hand on his horse's flank and the other around the little figure perched atop like a tiny sparrow in a big tree. Boudicca waved to him and then clambered down, her eyes sparkling with success.

"I rode him all by myself! I did! I even made him trot!" She stroked the smooth neck of the animal, sniffing at his warm smell, and her red hair, loosed from its braids, floated in a great aureole about her face. Caradoc watched the square, blunt little fingers moving over the brown coat while the horse stood patiently, his soft muzzle quivering.

"Good," Caradoc said absently, and they moved slowly on. "Listen Tog, I've just been talking with Cinnamus. He's very angry with you over those cattle."

Togodumnus sighed with exaggeration. "What cattle? I stole no cattle. They must have strayed."

Caradoc stopped in the path and took his brother by the shoulders. "You are a fool, Tog. Cinnamus is deep and dangerous. He thinks. And he knows your habits." Togodumnus shrugged.

25

"Do you know what he has done?" Caradoc asked. Boudicca was watching and listening with interest, and Tog shook his head, smiling. "He marked his cattle last spring. All of them."

Togodumnus whistled. "Then I am in trouble. I suppose he wants them back."

"He wants your blood, but he will take the cattle back, along with twelve of your own and a promise to leave his goods be. Otherwise, he will kill you."

They resumed the walk in silence, but as the gate neared, Togodumnus stopped. "I will do that," he said. "I like Cinnamus."

"Then why do you steal from him, and from everyone else?"

"I do not steal from you!"

"A chieftain does not steal from any member of his tuath," Caradoc said pointedly. "Even if he is starving."

Togodumnus laughed. "Then he is a fool."

CHAPTER TWO

THAT NIGHT THE GREAT HALL was crowded, and the huge logs on the fire spat and crackled as the fat from the roasting pigs dripped onto them. Samain was over. The cattle were slaughtered and would soon be salted, and men knew that the winter would be without want. The breeding stock was safely in the byres, the grain filled the big urns and storehouses, and the weather could do its worst. Mead, beer, and red Roman wine flowed freely, conversation rose loud and excited, and Caradoc, Cinnamus, and Caelte battled through the throng to their appointed places. Cunobelin sat on the floor on skins, wrapped in his yellow cloak, his thick gold torc flashing in the firelight and his gray hair lank upon his breast. Beside him were the guests, Subidasto and little Boudicca, who was chattering to her father. To Cunobelin's left knelt Adminius, his eyes on the pigs, his mouth watering, and Caradoc and his followers went to squat beside him. Togodumnus had the next place but he had not yet arrived, and Aricia sat beside Subidasto, for, though she had been at Cunobelin's court for many years, she was still regarded as a guest and had a special and permanent place at all feasts.

Caradoc looked for Eurgain and spotted her at last, far down the

Hall with her father. Gladys, his sister, was with her too. Eurgain felt his gaze and turned to smile at him. She had on a new tunic this night, tightly patterned in green and red, and she wore silver anklets and a thin gold band on her brow. Her father was rich, almost as rich as Cunobelin, his master, and Eurgain possessed trinkets from all over the world.

Gladys saw him but gave no sign. She was wearing a black coat, and her dark brown hair, braided in one long plait, hung down her back and coiled on the floor. She was a strange one, Caradoc thought. Nineteen years old and not married from choice, she wandered in the woods, with no fear of the gods who watched her jealously, collecting plants and small animals, and gathering queerly shaped driftwood from the beach she often went to with the traders. Yet for all her abrupt, unwelcoming air she was Cunobelin's chosen confidante and often his advisor since the death of their mother. Perhaps father took comfort in her calm wisdom. She had ceased to be part of the Royal War Band after that time Tog and the others raided from the Coritani and three people had been killed, one of them a child. Gladys had been incensed with Tog and from then on had refused to meet any of them outside Camulodunon, and Caradoc was sorry. There was something intriguing and commanding about his sister, but he could not penetrate her cold exterior.

The slave turning the spit signaled to Cunobelin and there was a hush as all eyes turned to the meat. Cunobelin rose with effort, his knife in hand, and after carving off a haunch with flourish, laid it on a silver plate and presented it to Subidasto.

"The choice cut, for our guests," he rumbled, and Subidasto took it with thanks. A low table was brought to him, and then Cunobelin carved the rest of the pigs and each man or woman received a piece commensurate with his or her station in the tuath. Far in the back by the open doors a fight had already broken out over who had been cheated of his correct joint this night, but no one but the protagonist took any notice of the brawl. Fearachar brought Caradoc his meat and bread, and Cinnamus and Caelte waited for their servants to do the same, and the Hall quieted as bellies were swiftly filled.

Suddenly Caradoc stopped eating. He had caught a flash of white close to Subidasto. He craned forward as Togodumnus slipped down beside him and whispered, "Do you see him? Is he not awesome?" Caradoc felt cold and his appetite left him. He pushed the dish away and took a mouthful of wine, his eyes never leaving the spare, white-clad man with the gray beard and sharp eyes who was sitting motionless, neither eating nor drinking, though his gaze wandered over the company.

27

Druithin! What was the old bird of doom doing here? Caradoc wondered, alarmed. The Druithin hated the Romans with steadfast fanaticism, and it had been a long time since one had been seen anywhere within the sphere of Cunobelin's influence. This one must have come with Subidasto. How awkward. No Druid could be killed anywhere, and a traveler needed only to be in the company of such a one to be safe. Caradoc sensed his father's unease as well. Cunobelin was speaking in quick, dying spurts, his eyes, too, on the old man, and the smattering of Roman traders who always managed to insinuate themselves into every feast were whispering excitedly. But the regal figure was calmly ignoring them all, his hands folded loosely in his lap, a little smile on his lips. He should have been served first, of course, before Subidasto, Caradoc thought. How ill-bred he will think us! Caradoc drew his plate to him again and began to pick at his food, feeling the presence of Druithin magic like a secret smoke. The person of the Druithin was sacred, even to the Catuvellauni.

Presently Cunobelin wiped his greasy mouth on his cloak and clapped his hands. Silence fell. The fire could be heard crackling cheerily, and outside, where it was full dark, a swift squall of rain pattered on the roof and gusted on the rising wind. Servants ran to close the doors and the people settled themselves more comfortably on the floor while Cathbad, Cunobelin's bard, rose with harp in hand.

"What will you hear tonight, Lord?" he asked, and Cunobelin, with one squinting eye on Subidasto's shadowed face, called for the song of the defeat of Dubnovellaunus and his own triumphant entry into Camulodunon.

Cathbad smiled. The song had been sung many times, but Cunobelin never tired of hearing of his own prowess, or that of his ancestor, Cassivellaunus, either, who had fought the great Julius Caesar and driven him back to sea not once, but twice. It was so well-known that many people joined in, and soon the Hall was full of the deep-throated music, and the people linked arms and swayed to and fro, caught in the thrall of heroic deeds and brave deaths.

But the Druid sat still, his head lowered, looking down at his white-clad knees. Caradoc wondered if the sacrifices had escaped his notice, but then thought that probably they had not. The Romans did not encourage human sacrifice, and this afternoon's rites to the Dagda and to Camulos had included only the slaying of three white bulls. Not for ten years had a human victim been fed to the sacred arrows, and it seemed the Dagda had not minded.

The song ended and the wine jugs passed quickly from hand to hand. What more does a man need? Caradoc thought contentedly. A song to hear, a jug of wine to drink, an honorable enemy to fight, and, of course, a woman to love. He glanced at Aricia but she too was watching the Druid, her mouth parted and her eyes half-closed.

Togodumnus leaped to his feet and shouted, "Now let us hear of our first cattle raid, Caradoc's and mine! Twenty beasts we took. What a day that was!" But Caradoc pulled him down.

"No!" he called. "I want to hear 'The Ship.'"

"No, no," several voices objected. "Sing us a happy song!" But Cathbad had already begun the doleful tune. Aricia's head shot round and he deliberately met her eye, allowing the plaintive, sweet lay to slow his heartbeat. For a moment she looked at him, but in the gloom he could not read her expression, and when he looked away he felt Eurgain's eyes upon him, questing and puzzled. Cathbad reached the last high note and left it to flutter in the darkness of the vaulted ceiling but Caradoc was the only applauder, and Cathbad bowed in his direction. Aricia got up abruptly and went quickly out the door.

"Now," said the bard, his fingers idly plucking the strings. "Shall I sing a new song? One that I have just composed?" Cunobelin nodded. "It is called the 'Lay of Togodumnus the Many-Handed, and the Twelve Lost Cattle.'"

Togodumnus rose with a roar of anger while laughter exploded around him. "Cathbad, I forbid you to sing such a song! You have been talking to Cinnamus!" Cunobelin waved him down and then summoned Cathbad. They whispered together and then Cathbad straightened.

"I cannot sing the song," he said sorrowfully. "My royal master always breaks out in a rash of apprehension when I eulogize Togodumnus together with cattle." He launched into a raucous drinking song to drown Togodumnus's spluttered expletives, and they all screamed it with him while the rain pelted down. When it was over Cunobelin rose and Cathbad retired to his spot by the wall.

"The time for Council is here," he said. "Chieftains and all freemen take heed. All others leave." No one moved but the few slaves and traders, who slipped out into the night. It was only the chiefs who ever had anything to say, but all freemen were allowed to hear how the affairs of the tuath were being settled, and they drew closer to the fire. Caradoc saw the Druid rise. He came closer, sat down by Subidasto and whispered to him, and Subidasto nodded. Boudicca was asleep, curled up in her father's cloak.

"Our guest may now state his business," Cunobelin said, and went to sit beside Caradoc. "There will be trouble here," he said in a low voice, "and harsh things said. This Subidasto does not like us."

"Does the Druid not speak first?" Togodumnus leaned over and whispered.

Cunobelin shook his head. "He will not speak."

Subidasto was on his feet now, his legs astride and one hand resting on his sword hilt. He slowly surveyed the company, cleared his throat carefully, and began. "Does any man here deny me my immunity?" No one spoke. "Does any man here deny the Druid his immunity?" Again there was silence. "Good." Subidasto nodded. "I see that you have a semblance of tribal dignity left." He hurried on, ignoring the muttering. "I am here to protest against the repeated and unnecessary raiding carried out by the Catuvellauni into Icenian territory. My people have lost their flocks and herds, their servants, and even their lives." He thrust out an arm as thick as a young tree trunk. "Why? Because, as usual, your ricon chooses to ignore the bounds of his tuath. He rides roughshod over the territorial rights of others as well as those of myself. Where is Dubnovellaunus? Where is Verica? Cunobelin's sons are rapacious and cruel, and his own greed is uncontained even by his age. He looks ever beyond his own people, seeking new conquests, and I know," he shook a fist at Cunobelin, "I know, that it is only his true master in Rome who prevents him from making full war upon me and mine." Cunobelin stiffened but did not respond. His turn would come. "I demand to be left alone," Subidasto shouted. "I demand an agreement, I demand hostages to back that agreement, and I want a full and proper restitution of all that my people have lost to you, you wolves of Gaul!" He stood for a moment longer, thinking, then with a twisted smile gestured to Cunobelin and sat down.

Cunobelin paced to the fire, turned, and folded his arms. He appeared to ponder, head down. Now speak, you silver-tongued old fox, Caradoc thought. Put the Icenian firmly in his place. Cunobelin lifted his head and suveyed the Council with a question in his eyes, then raised his arms appealingly.

"Who am I?" he asked, and his chiefs answered, "Cunobelin, Ricon!"

"Am I a Roman?"

"No!"

"Am I a wolf of Gaul?"

"No!"

"Yes!" Togodumnus whispered in Caradoc's ear, and the Druid glanced sharply in their direction as if he had heard. Cunobelin spoke to them all, but his words were for Subidasto.

"You come from far, Icenian chieftain, with wild rumors in your ears and lies to tell. Of course we raid. Who does not? Do your chieftains spend their time raising children? We raid the Coritani, and the Coritani raid us. We raid the Dobunni, and the Dobunni raid us. We all lose animals and men, but that is the luck of the game. We are warriors. We do not work on the land. We fight. Will you stand and swear to us that you and your chieftains have not taken Catuvellaunian lives and cattle? I did not hear you protest when I rode into Camulodunon with my chariots and my men, crushing the Trinovantes and sending Dubnovellaunus running for the coast. And I have heard rumors of my own, Subidasto. Are the Iceni not pushing west and discomfiting the Coritani themselves? No?" Subidasto muttered something. "We will have an agreement, if you like." Subidasto's head jerked up in shock but Caradoc smiled to himself. He knew what his father would say and he knew Subidasto's outraged answer. "I will cease to raid you and you will cease to raid me, and to seal the bargain we will exchange hostages. I will give you one of my sons. Who will you offer?" A slow, anticipatory smile spread over his face. Subidasto swallowed noisily and his hand went out to rest on Boudicca's fiery hair.

"I have only my daughter," he said quietly, "and well you know it, Cunobelin!"

Cunobelin clucked sympathetically. "But my friend, something that hurts must be sacrificed to seal such a solemn bargain. Little Boudicca would be quite safe here. She would learn every gentle art of living. She would imbibe the culture of a rich and various tribe."

The inference was obvious, and Subidasto flushed hotly. "I am as rich as you, wolf of Gaul, and as for culture, I prefer the Icenian way of life to this . . . this cheap Roman muddle!" Cunobelin did not reply. He merely stood there smiling, his eyes almost hidden by the seamed flesh of his face. He could have pointed out that fully six generations had gone by since his ancestors brought the fire and the sword from Gaul to Albion. He could have raved that he was no man's servant, let alone Tiberius's in Rome, but he did not.

He bowed to the company. "Is the Council over?" he called, and they all shouted back, "It is!"

"Then to bed. I trust, Subidasto, that our poor Roman hovels are comfortable and to your liking?"

Oh father, easy, Caradoc thought. Do not tempt the man to a show of arms, for you will have to kill him. But Togodumnus craned forward eagerly and was disappointed when Subidasto rose without a word, gathering the warm bundle of child into his arms and walking regally out of the Hall. No one else stirred, and Caradoc saw that the Druid had gone. He rose and stretched, yawning.

"Tog, you can supervise the loading of the dogs tomorrow," he said. "That at least you can do for your folly."

"But I have much to do!" Togodumnus protested. "Aricia and Adminius and I . . ."

"You can do it," Caradoc said firmly over his shoulder as he left the Hall. He stood for a moment on the threshold and gulped great drafts of the heavy, wet air that beat upon him. He drew it down into his lungs with relief, closing his eyes and turning his face upward so that the rain washed his face with its cold, clean fingers. Cinnamus passed him, bidding him a polite goodnight, and Caelte paused beside him. "Do you want my music tonight, Lord?" he asked, but Caradoc declined. He was tired but pleased with the day. Perhaps he should go and talk to Aricia, to find out what she thought of the mysterious member of the Druithin. All at once he opened his eyes in shock, setting his lips firmly against his thoughts and his feet upon the path to his door. Not tonight, Aricia. By the Dagda, not tonight!

The light from his fire and his lamps shone out under the doorskins, and Fearachar stood without, huddling dejectedly into his short cloak while the rain dripped off his long nose.

"I have been waiting . . ." he began in an injured tone, and Caradoc cut him short.

"I know!" he snapped, not amused tonight by the servant's whining. "For a long time. Go away, Fearachar. I have no patience with you tonight."

"Lord, I have been waiting here to tell you that you have a visitor," Fearachar concluded in a morose but satisfied tone. "Seeing that you wish no commerce with me tonight I will forbear to tell you who it is." He sniffed once and sneezed twice. "I am getting a cold." He bowed perfunctorily and walked away quickly, his back hunched.

Caradoc just stood there, his heart beating wildly. Aricia! He pushed past the skins and ran into his room, but it was not Aricia.

The Druid sat in the bronze-plated Roman chair, his long legs stretched out before him and his hands, as before, still in his lap. The firelight haloed him, throwing his bony profile onto the wall, magnifying it and giving it life, and to Caradoc it seemed as if the man had grown, become grotesque. He stopped in fear and confusion, but the man did not turn his head.

"Come in, Caradoc ap Cunobelin," the Druid said, his voice young and strong.

Caradoc took three steps and looked openly at the face. He was not old, this priest-philosopher. He was perhaps not more than half Caradoc's own age again, and the beard that earlier had seemed gray was in fact pale gold. What do I say? he thought in a panic. What do I do? Has he come to put a spell upon me?

The man laughed softly. "Why are you afraid, Catuvellaunian warrior? Come and sit."

Caradoc recovered his wits and walked to the other side of the fire,

32

then lowered himself onto his stool and leaned forward to gaze into the orange depths of the flames. He felt curiously shy and could not look full into the thin face. The Druid slowly sat up straight, pushing his hands into the folds of his deep sleeves.

"Forgive me for intruding, and for startling you, Caradoc," the Druid said at last, after a long and speculative scrutiny of the youth before him. He nodded to himself, for what he saw seemed to satisfy him. The boy's face was broad and cleanly boned, the nose broad, too, but not ill-formed. The chin was square and cleft, like the father's and the two other brothers', a sign of pride and great stubborness. But whereas the eyes of the young Togodumnus were never still, never fixed for long in thought or observation, these brown eyes even now lifting to meet his own were steady and acutely perceptive, full of a wisdom that the boy was perhaps unaware he possessed. The hair fell dark and softly waving from a high, wide forehead, and the hands . . . The Druid stirred. Hands told him everything the eyes could not. These hands were large-palmed but not fleshy, the fingers long but blunt at the tips, the hands of a man who could combine foresight with impetuous action. So. Here was another tiny fruit of possibility, as yet tart and unripe, but to be watched carefully. He leaned toward Caradoc, and stretched out his arm. "I am Bran," he said.

Somehow, unwillingly, Caradoc found himself grasping the wrist of the man in friendship, and finding it well-sinewed and very warm, his fear seemed to flow from himself into the other and to be dissipated somewhere in the depths of the white woolen gown.

Bran sat back once more with a smile.

"What do you wish of me?" Caradoc asked.

"I wanted to meet you," Bran said, raising one shoulder, "and I think that if I had sat down beside you in the Hall tonight you would have gotten up and run away. Am I right?"

Caradoc flushed angrily. "The House Catuvellaun runs from nothing and no one," he said hotly. "But I will confess to a certain unease when I saw you there."

"Why?"

"Because the Druithin are no longer seen in these parts. The traders . . ." He broke off.

"The traders, being good and loyal sons of Rome, drove us away. Yes, I know." The pleasant voice held no hint of bitterness. "And so the sons of Cunobelin forget that the Druithin do not exist to cast spells and make magic." He was amused now, his eyes twinkling, and Caradoc felt like a clumsy peasant. "But we are still useful, Caradoc. What would your father have done if Subidasto and his daughter had not come under my immunity?"

"Father would have kept Boudicca and perhaps slain her father, and then he would have made war on the Iceni."

"And called it self-defence, as he did when Tiberius sent to ask of him why he marched against Dubnovellaunus. Oh, his hospitality is unimpeachable. He would have feasted Subidasto, and enquired as to the health of all his tuath, but Subidasto would have met with an accident on the long ride home, and Boudicca would have settled here and been happy."

Caradoc's glance slipped to the fire again and he did not reply. Any chieftain would have done the same. Why, then, did this Bran make him feel so dirty?

"Perhaps you are not aware, Caradoc, how much your father is hated and feared outside his own territory. I travel all the time, I carry news and messages, and I know what other chieftains say."

Caradoc looked up sharply. "He does not care, and neither do I. Why should we? Is there any ricon who is greater than Cunobelin?"

"There is Tiberius," Bran reminded him gently.

"I do not understand," Caradoc replied curtly, and Bran shook his hands free of his robe and put them together, rubbing one small palm against the other. Caradoc's eyes were drawn to them, those hands, cruel and capable, like the talons of a falcon.

"I think you should begin to care," Bran said softly. "You members of the House Catuvellaun are ringed with enemies, but you cannot see beyond your meager dreams of conquest and aggrandizement. Do you really think that Julius Caesar was beaten back by Cassivellaunus? I tell you that the weather defeated him, the weather and the tides of the sea. And Rome does not forget. You and your father are living in a fool's dream world."

Caradoc began to tremble. He could not help himself. It was not Bran's words but the tone of his voice that played on old and long-forgotten scars, older than the lad himself. "Sir, are you a seer?" he cried out.

Bran threw back his head and laughed. "No, Caradoc, no, not I. I am of a different order. I read the stars, but not to tell the future, only to discover the hidden secrets of the universe. I sniff the wind of men's words, and so divine the trends of the tribes and the slow washing of the tides of history. Do not fear me. Yet, Caradoc, I am wiser than you and your crafty old father. Count your days of gay ignorance. They are not to last."

Caradoc rose. "Now I know you for what you are!" he said unsteadily. "Of course! It is just as the traders say. You and your fellows wander abroad, inciting hatred in the people against Rome because you suffered under Roman hands, and you always find a willing ear and stir up men's fears of slavery." He walked to the doorskins, holding them back with one white-knuckled hand. "Please leave. Tomorrow men will begin to wonder what the magic-maker was doing in the hut of Cunobelin's son. This I do not want, nor to hear any more of your insane talking!"

Bran stood and walked to him silently. He was smiling faintly, not at all insulted, and as he left he placed a light hand on Caradoc's shoulder. "Remember me and my seditious words," he said. "When the hour of your greatest need comes, I and my brethren will be waiting. We may meet again, whether you will it or no."

He passed out swiftly and Caradoc let the skins fall, drawing in his shaking breath. He was cold. He went to the fire and squatted, letting the heat beat upon his face, then ran back to the door and bellowed for Fearachar. After a time the man came, bleary-eyed and half-asleep, and Caradoc ordered him to fetch Caelte. There would be music, and laughter. Was the man a seer after all? He shrugged, but the movement of his broad shoulders did not lift the dark load of doubt and unease that had settled around him. He felt as if all his warm flesh had been stripped away and his bones left to rattle in a cold, foreign wind. Caelte played and sang for him, told him jokes, and in the end berated him soundly, but Caradoc turned his face to the wall and would not reply.

In the morning, he and Cinnamus went together to the harness maker's shop, where Caradoc's chariot was being repaired. They passed the kennels, hearing Togodumnus shouting and the kennel guards swearing. A few traders hung around the door, slates in hand, waiting impatiently for order to be restored before the dogs were taken down to the barges and thence to the river estuary where they would board the ships bound for Gesioracum and Rome. Caradoc did not stop. Let Tog sort it all out himself and perhaps learn a lesson, he thought.

The harness maker was sitting outside his shop, surrounded by his awls and knives and strips of leather, and in a bowl at his feet lay a pile of dark red coral studs mounted in bronze, waiting to be fitted to the harness of some chief. "A good morning, Lord," he said, remaining seated as Caradoc approached. "You've come for the chariot, I suppose." He indicated his door. "Go in and take a look. It will cost you a silver coin."

"Pay him," Caradoc said to Cinnamus, and ducking his head, he entered the dim interior. His chariot lay on its side, and where the hidden tree stump had ripped the wickerwork to shreds with its jagged teeth, the harness maker had woven a new side. He grasped it firmly and heaved it upright. It came easily, and he examined the work closely, prodding and pulling until he was satisfied, then went back outside. "The work is good," Caradoc said. "Who are the coral studs for?"

"The Lady Gladys. She has ordered a new harness for her horse, and new leather boots, also studded, and a new belt picked out in silver, for her sword."

"Oh. How beautiful they are!" He squatted and ran his hands through the pile, feeling the cold smoothness of them, then he rose. "Cinnamus, I'll take the chariot out today. Get the horses yoked, will you, and I'll meet you outside the gate."

He retraced his steps, noting that the kennels were quiet and the dogs and Togodumnus gone. On the way to his hut he met Gladys, swathed in green, her black eyes veiled by the gray morning and her hair hidden in the hood of her cloak. "Where are you going?" he said, stopping to speak with her.

She waved toward the river. "I'm going to the sea, with the traders. I am wasting away for want of seeing the rocks and the sand and the salty breakers."

"I saw your new leathers, and the coral. They're very pretty. Where did you get them?"

"They were a gift. I was also given a handful of pearls." She changed the subject abruptly and he guessed that some infrequent suitor was trying his luck again. "I hear you had a visitor last night, Caradoc."

Was she smiling? "I suppose all the town now knows that the Druid came to me," he said angrily. "But Gladys, there was nothing I could do. He was there when I arrived."

"What did he tell you?"

"Why should he have told me anything? He talked a lot of nonsense and I grew impatient and sent him away. That is all."

She moved past him. "Take care, brother of mine," she said smoothly. "The Druithin are poison."

Before he could reply she was gone. He strode to his hut, strapped on the heavy iron sword in its finely wrought bronze scabbard, barked at Fearachar, and strode out again, down to the gate. The day was damp and clammy. Fog hung about the lower slopes of Camulodunon and the sky was unrelievedly heavy with gray cloud, but he did not feel cold within his long, bright woolen cloak, and only his ears and the tips of his fingers tingled as he ran to meet Cinnamus.

The chariot was harnessed to a pair of ponies, shaggy and sturdy, not particularly fast, but steady, the horses that the people of Albion bred many years ago, before his ancestors brought the big riding horses with them in their flight from Gaul. The children learned to ride on them, for they were docile and good-natured. Now the two stood quietly, muzzles together and ears twitching at the sound of his coming.

Cinnamus handed him the reins. "Shall I come, Lord?" he asked, but Caradoc shook his head, stepping up between the two big, iron-rimmed wheels and placing his feet apart. Already he felt content and untroubled. Cinnamus turned away and Caradoc shook the reins, trotting along the wide path, his cloak floating out behind him, his hair streaming with it on the freshening wind.

As he approached the steep slope he dismounted and led the ponies down, and then across the dyke, then mounted again and called to them, rolling ever faster toward the river, veering east under the trees. The mist enfolded him, beading on his arms, his hair, hanging shimmering in the folds of his scarlet tunic. Around the next bend, he knew, was a smooth, straight stretch of track, mossy and even, halled over by the massive oaks, and he slowly came to a state of nerve-tautening concentration, wrapping the reins about the frontal bar of the little chariot and balancing with arms outstretched. The ponies' gait never varied. Whistling and chucking to them all the time, he placed one foot up and onto the yoke, seeing the stretch open out before him. With infinite care he tested his foothold, raised himself, feeling his unused muscles protest. Then he was up, standing lightly on the yoke, and still the ponies thundered on. He stepped out, ran to the ponies' wide backs, ran back, ran up again, glorying in the perfection of his body, in its instinctive, humbling skill. Then he jumped down onto the wicker floor and took the reins again. The track narrowed now, began to twist, and branches whipped at his face. He crouched, reined in, and turned about, preparing to repeat the performance, but suddenly he heard hoofbeats on the turf and he stood waiting while the ponies steamed and wheezed.

It was a woman on a horse. It was Aricia, her hair braided in three plaits, the short tunic of a man covering her and her legs clad in men's breeches. Her cloak hung almost to the ground. The mist parted to let her through, and when she saw him she kneed her horse and trotted up to him, sheathing the knife she had drawn.

"Caradoc! So your chariot is running again." Against the vivid blue of her cloak her skin was pale ivory, but under her eyes there were dark smudges. "That's good. I've been down to the pier with Tog. Your father refuses to take more wine for the dogs. He wants money instead, and the Romans are busy haggling with him. I think the presence of the Druid last night upset them and today they are viewing Cunobelin with some suspicion."

She was talking too fast, avoiding his eye, and her embarrassment was communicated to her horse. It shuffled and sidled nervously, and its ears were flattened to its dark head.

"What are you doing out here?" he asked her.

She showed him the pouch slung across her shoulder. "Looking for hazelnuts, and perhaps the last of the brambles."

"That's servants' work."

"I know. But I value every moment I spend from now on in your woods and meadows, Catuvellaunian wolf!"

They smiled at each other and Caradoc got down, taking her reins and his own and winding them around the nearest branch. "Shall I help you?"

"If you like. There is none to see the mighty Caradoc picking nuts, and I have changed my mind about wanting to be alone." She shivered slightly. "I did not realize how thick the mists were. At least the wind cannot find us in here."

They left the track and struck out into the trees, and their breeches were soon soaked with the droplets of dew showered on them from the lacy maidenhair ferns and their footfalls muffled by the damp carpet of russet leaves and bilious, wet green moss. Not far from the path they found a hazel thicket, thin twigs standing stiff and brittle, and their feet crunched on the nuts that had already fallen to the ground. They picked busily for a while, content with the deep silence of the wood and the company of each other. Every movement they made seemed to echo a hundredfold in the weighty stillness. Caradoc cracked open the nuts between his strong young teeth, chewing the tangy meat, and Aricia's fingers flew in and out of the thicket.

"Where is Boudicca this morning?" Caradoc asked her.

"She and Subidasto left sometime in the night," she said without turning, her arms raised to reach the highest clusters. "Very rude of them, I thought, to go without the cup of farewell."

"Did . . . did the Druid go with them?"

She lowered her arms and grinned at him slyly. "Of course. How transparently anxious you are! Everyone is talking about your midnight visitor."

He groaned. "Not you too, Aricia. No words, please. I do not know why he selected me for his silly maunderings and I do not care. Now shall we walk on, and find some blackberries?"

He lifted the pouch now bulging with nuts and they sauntered on with no fear of being lost. He had grown up in these woods—they belonged to his family—and in the daylight hours he had explored every inch of them, and he knew the burrows and sets of every mole and badger, every fox and rabbit. They passed the big oak that was so

38

good for climbing, and the little clearing with the ring of mushrooms that had always been "safe" ground to the pursued when he and Tog had hunted each other. They pushed their way into the dense thickets of trailing bramble bushes whose arching stems with the cruel thorns tore at their clothes and their hands.

"There is no room in the pouch for berries," Aricia said. "Let's just eat them. There are so few left now. Most of them have rotted."

They lifted the fuzzed purple berries gently, and crushed them in their mouths, savoring the sweetness, and their fingers and mouths were soon stained with the dark juice. The mist was very thick in here, white and wet, and the cobwebs festooning the gaunt tree trunks were weighed down with thousands of shimmering, pear-shaped crystals. But it was not cold. Only still and secret and private, a hushed world within a world.

Presently Caradoc raised his head. "Listen!" he whispered, and she paused, berry halfway to her mouth. In the silence the steady trickle of water could be heard. "A new spring has opened somewhere close by," he said. "Come!" They followed the sound, and after a while found a clearing, not open to the sky but clear on the ground. Long, wet grass stood there, and pine needles lay dark around the feet of the surrounding trees. In the center, a well of water bubbled up and trickled away through the grass in two little channels already grooved in the spongy turf.

Aricia knelt and fumbled at her girdle. "A new goddess has come to live here," she said with awe. "Quick, Caradoc, have you any money?"

"No, but I have my ring." He drew it reluctantly from his thumb, and together they approached the spring, laying Aricia's bronze coin and his own gold ring in the ice-cold, pure water, and for a moment they stayed there, hypnotized by the quiet tinkle of the gushing water.

Soon Aricia sat back on her heels with a sigh. "Such a beautiful, hallowed place," she said. "But I think we should go. Someone may steal our horses."

He put a hand under her elbow and helped her to her feet, then found that he could not let her go. She was a bright-clad and living thing here among this quiet, mute-colored wetness. Her breath was a warm cloud, her skin perfumed, and there was no one to see them and no one to know. Only they themselves would see his shame well up again. He took her other arm and turned her roughly to face him, then lowered his head and found her lips, cold, resistant, tasting of berry juice. For one moment she relaxed against him, then stiffened and wrenched her head away. He dropped his arms, feeling foolish.

"Son of a dog," she said viciously. "Will you marry me?"

"No."

"Do you not love me?"

"Aricia."

"It would not matter," she whispered, her breath hissing into his face. "What you feel for me is something stronger, isn't it, Caradoc? You will never be rid of me. Don't think you can brush me aside, for I am buried deep inside you." She touched his loins and he started as if he had been scalded. "There, in a place where your mind has no power. If you do not marry me you will have no peace, not ever."

"You are wrong," he flared, his reckless pride stung. "Already I have had enough of you, Aricia. You have nothing more to give me and I am sorry we began this. You are no longer a pleasant diversion."

"Liar!" She slapped him across the face with the flat and then the back of her hand, once, twice, and turned on her heel, pushing blindly through the undergrowth. He ran and caught her up, heedless of the branches and thorns that caught at his hair and whipped across his forehead, bringing blood.

"Aricia, listen to me! Tell your father that you will not go! Tell him. . . ."

But she shouted over her shoulder, "Perhaps I should go! Perhaps I have been here too long and Subidasto is right! Where is your honor, wolfling? What wasting disease invades the mighty Catuvellauni?"

When she reached her horse she leaped upon it, tore the reins from the tree and whipped the animal madly, and it careened down the path in a startled gallop, mud flying from the hoofs. Caradoc followed slowly in a mood of exasperated despondency. The pouch had been left behind, and so had a certain vision of himself, shattered among the tall grasses where the goddess combed her wet hair and played with his golden ring.

When he arrived back the stables were in pandemonium. A crowd of freemen pressed about the open circle where the horses were walked in the early morning, and Caradoc heard enraged shouts even before he handed the reins to the stable slave and tried to push his way through. There stood Cinnamus, a grim smile on his face and his drawn sword in his hand. Togodumnus was shedding his cloak and tying back his hair.

"What is it? What has happened?" Caradoc called to Cinnamus as Togodumnus tugged his sword from its scabbard.

"Your brother has accused me of freeing all his breeding stock in the night, Lord, and driving them far afield." Cinnamus turned to reply, a look of pure, venomous delight in his calm green eyes. "He has rounded up some fifty of them, but apparently thirty are still wandering in the woods. How he comes to blame me I do not know." The eyes dared Caradoc to interfere but showed no guilt. Cinnamus had merely thought again about the agreement and decided upon his own revenge. He had nothing to reproach himself for. "Come then, Lordling whelp," he said, bringing his sword whistling down in a great arc. "Teach me the lesson you promised me, for I have need of such learning."

Togodumnus stepped toward him, teeth bared, and Caradoc stepped back. He could do nothing. It had gone too far for words. But do not kill him, Cinnamus old friend, he prayed, or I will then be forced to kill you to prevent a blood feud. Cinnamus knew this, but his anger had burned slow and long, and all watching read Togodumnus's death in his eyes. Caradoc turned and sent a servant running for Cunobelin, then sat down cross-legged on the wet ground. The crowd did the same and the two young men circled one another, testing their defences. With a cry Togodumnus hurled himself upon Cinnamus, aiming a slashing blow at the legs, but Cinnamus sprang up and the blade cut only air. Before Togodumnus had time to regain his balance, Cinnamus moved in with a great swing that curved straight for Togodumnus's neck, but the lad slipped on the slick earth and the blade did nothing more than rip his tunic from his shoulder. Cinnamus waited for Togodumnus to rise, saying nothing, not taunting, and Togodumnus raised his sword, grasping the hilt in both hands. Cinnamus stood still, watching, waiting, knowing where the next blow would fall. His shoulder tingled in anticipation, and then it came with the full force of Togodumnus's weight behind it. Cinnamus moved like lightning, and there was a jarring, crunching sound as the blades slid together. All at once Togodumnus was on his back, his sword just out of reach, and Cinnamus moved in for the kill.

Caradoc sprang up, drawing his own sword and shouting bitterly, but his father thrust him aside. "Enough, Cinnamus," Cunobelin said quietly. "Let the lad get up." Cinnamus did not stir. He and Togodumnus regarded each other without expression, panting a little, still locked in combat with their eyes. "Cinnamus," Cunobelin said, "if you kill him you will die. You know this well. If you must feud with him, wait until he is older, but let him up now. I do not want to lose a son, or one of my finest young warriors, in this foolishness."

Cinnamus blinked and lowered his sword arm, then contemptuously kicked Togodumnus's sword within his reach and walked away, loosening his hair as he went. Caradoc found that his own sword arm was sore from the effort of Cinnamus's capitulation.

Tog began to grin. "A narrow escape, that one!" he said, leaping up.

41

"My thanks, father. Now call Cinnamus back and have him restore to me all my cattle."

Caradoc groaned. Cunobelin took two strides, and with one blow of his big fist knocked his son to the ground once more. "Be quick, Togodumnus," he shouted, "and grow up, before your honor-price is worth no more than the price of your sword!" He flexed his fingers, grunted, and walked away. Caradoc knew what that blow had cost his father, for no one could speak against Tog and not feel Cunobelin's anger. A buzz of approving conversation broke out, and Togodumnus's chiefs went to him and helped him to get up, restoring his sword to him and soothing him with soft words. But Togodumnus shook them off and stalked away, the tatters of his torn tunic making him look a little ridiculous.

Someone tugged softly at Caradoc's arm and he looked around. It was Eurgain, dressed in yellow and blue, her dark blonde hair parted in the center and falling down her back.

"What a terrible thing," she said, a crease of worry between her long, feathered eyebrows. "Cin would have killed him if Cunobelin had not come."

"Of course he would. And a happy circumstance, many would have said."

"Caradoc!"

"Well, it's true. Tog is loved and also hated by everyone, and there are many who are tired of loving and forgiving a liar and a cheat no matter how much charm he has." Caradoc looked around him and then lowered his voice. "Eurgain, I must talk to you. Where can we go?"

She hesitated, scanning his face swiftly, aware of some almost indefinable change in him, a new soberness, a sense of stress. "Come to my hut. We can break our fast on cold pigeon if you like."

They walked side by side and in silence up the hill, following the path that took them behind the Great Hall to the very edge of the massive earthmound, where Eurgain had a house with a window. The window made her room very cold in the winter, covered as it was by skins which let in the wind no matter how firmly they were tacked down, but she did not mind. She liked to sit with her arms folded on the sill for hours on end, looking out west above the forest to the gently rising hills and the hazed horizon beyond. She and Gladys were very close, indeed the Royal War Band had gradually been breaking up into smaller groups as its members matured—Aricia spreading dissent among all, but spending most of her time with Caradoc or Togodumnus, Gladys and Eurgain growing more companionable, and Adminius, the eldest, withdrawing from them all. The woman and the young girl shared a love of wild, lonely places, an

42

affinity for solitude and oases of quiet. Gladys loved the sea. She went often, and would not come home for days, taking food and a sword and her warmest cloak, and sleeping alone in some dark cave on the beach. She would hold a mystical commerce with the ocean that was far from easy or safe, and what she learned she never divulged. Eurgain's longings went to the hills, the open, bare spaces of her country where the wind tore at her and rippled the long gray grasses, and the curlews and plovers swooped overhead. She would lie on the hilltops, her arms outstretched and her eyes closed, feeling the slow pulse of the earth beneath her, feeling the swing and rhythme, majestic and eternal, of the silent rock. If it rained, so much the better. Rain enclosed her, wrapped her in her dreams, and, like Gladys, none knew her thoughts.

She and Caradoc passed within her doorskins. The fire burned, and the light was very dim. Caradoc lit a lamp and she went to the window and dropped the skins with an apology.

"I thought that it might snow today and I had Annis take out the tacks so that I could wake and see the world," she said. "But all we get is gray sky, and I do believe it is warming to rain again." She spoke quietly, her mind feeling for his.

Caradoc glanced about him. Nothing ever changed in here. Stepping into Eurgain's room was like stepping into a place where one might wait in perfect tranquillity for a glimpse of eternity. Her Palmyran hangings were soft, muted, very rich. Her jewels always lay in the same place, piled on a table beside her bed. There was only one chair, a Roman couch used for dining. She had many lamps, all intricately and beautifully cast and polished. Some were by her bed, some hung on slender chains from her thatched ceiling, some stood on the big table where she kept her crystals and her precious star maps and paper. For Eurgain could read Latin. Not well and not fluently but certainly better than Caradoc himself, and though she did not tell him so, she had spent an hour with the Druid, poring over the star maps, sorry that he had left so soon. It was a dangerous thing to do, she knew, yet with her father's wealth came a certain haughty disregard for public opinion, and as it turned out, no one had seen Bran come and go but Tallia, her servant.

"Light the other lamps," she said, going to sit on the edge of her bed, still puzzled at his air of abstraction.

The afternoon was advancing and the light was already fading away, but as Caradoc moved about the room the friendly, quiet glow increased and he felt his muscles and his mind relax.

"Now," she said when he had finished. "Sit on my couch and tell me what you want."

He did as he was bidden. What do I want? he thought, and such was the stillness and peace of the room that all his confusions fell into niches and he could view his troubles clearly. I want to be finished with Aricia. I want you to make me feel clean again, Eurgain. I want a new position in the tuath. I want roots among my kin, new anchors against my restlessness, but most of all, oh most of all, dear Eurgain, I want to be rid of Aricia!

He cleared his throat. "Eurgain, we have been promised to each other for a long time now, and it is time I was wed. Do you agree?"

She did not move. She did not color, or blink, or sigh. She merely sat there looking at him, the lamplight flickering on her hair and making shadows in her tunic. But slowly a deep sadness, a hurt, passed over her face and he saw it.

"Caradoc," she said calmly. "Something is wrong, I know it. Why do you come to me now, at this strange time, and blurt out your proposal as though a demon were at your back? Have our fathers not pledged us to each other? There was no need for this."

"I want a betrothal now, Eurgain. We are both of age and I tire of an aimless life."

"Aimless? How can you say that, you a warrior with an enviable honor-price, in full health and leading a hundred chiefs?" He was lying, she knew, and a knife turned in her heart. "It's Aricia, isn't it? The rumor is all over the tuath."

He started, then rose and began to pace in agitation. "I should have known better than to think I could keep my foolishness from you. You are right. It is Aricia."

"Are you in love with her? Do you want her for your wife?"

"No!" The word exploded into the room, and she heard all that there was to hear in the force of its passing. "She is troubled because she knows her father will send for her before long and then she will have to leave us. She is trying to press a claim on me, Eurgain."

"Say no more!" Anger lit her words. "I, too, have a claim on you, Caradoc, but I would not dream of presuming on a childhood agreement!"

He stood still and pushed a bemused hand through his hair. "I know, I know. Will you still forgive me, Eurgain?" he said with difficulty. "I'm a weak-kneed peasant, I admit it. Will you still accept me?" He felt suddenly as though the course of his whole life hung on her answer, doom or pardon, slavery or freedom, and he watched the wide blue eyes, the small nose, the large, pensive mouth, in an agony of waiting. Finally she sighed.

"I will accept you, Caradoc," she said, but her voice was flat and

44

tired. "I have waited long enough. You think you know me, but you do not." She rose and drew close to him and he took her cold hands in his own. "I am a sword-woman and the daughter of a sword-woman. Never insult me, dear one, by underestimating me."

He enfolded her mutely. He could not find the words to tell her that he loved her because from their earliest years their lives had been intertwined and had formed a bond that would not be easily broken. No matter what he said at this moment she would not believe him. Aricia, he thought, but the pain was already subdued. Aricia. He cradled Eurgain gently in his arms.

She drew away slowly, her hair netted in the rough embroidery of his tunic. "Will you eat now?" she asked him, as though she had not just been torn apart, as though the sweet fantasies of all her fifteen years had not been turned to dust and blown stinging into her face. She had never controlled herself with such iron determination before and her chest ached with pain and her eyes smarted. A sword-woman does not break down, she told herself. She does not show fear.

"I think I should go and talk to father," he said, knowing he could not eat. "And then I should go see Sholto."

"Watch that man, Caradoc," Eurgain said. "Father says that he has a large honor-price but no honor."

"Yes, I know," he replied. "But he swells my ranks." He bent and kissed her cheek, and left her.

Cunobelin was in the Great Hall, talking to his chiefs as Caradoc and Fearachar plunged into the gloom and went to join them. The big fire was out and ashes lay scattered about the floor. Lamps burned high on the pillars but their brave circles of wan light only served to darken the shadows around them. Caradoc heard the chiefs burst into raucous laughter and watched them disperse before going to Cunobelin, who turned to him, smiling.

"Well, Caradoc, this has been an unlucky day for me. First those greasy traders refuse to give me money instead of wine because of that cursed Druid, and then my son nearly gets himself killed by my favorite chief. Now what ill news do you bring me?"

"*My* chief, father. Cinnamus is in my train," Caradoc reminded him, and they sank cross-legged to the ground together. "Bring wine, my friend," he said to Fearachar, who was hovering in the background. "And then get about your business." Fearachar went to the end of the Hall, drew wine from one of the newly landed jars standing there, and then brought it back and served them.

"From today's shipment," he said. "Probably a bad vintage. Those

45

Romans will cheat you as soon as look at you," Fearachar said and then left.

"To the eternal night of the tuath," Cunobelin said, raising his cup, and they drank together, pouring their dregs onto the floor for the Dagda and for Camulos and for the goddess of the tribe, aging now, even as Cunobelin himself aged. Cunobelin licked his lips and folded his arms and leaned back against the wall. Caradoc heard the slaves behind him begin to lay another fire, chattering as they padded among the ashes.

"Now," said Cunobelin. "What is on your mind?"

"I want to get married, father. I want a betrothal to Eurgain as soon as possible."

Cunobelin looked at him carefully, his small pig eyes sharp. "That is quite reasonable. And what does Eurgain say? Is she ready?"

"She agrees."

"Hmmm. And what of Aricia?"

Caradoc kept his eyes on the floor between his knees. How astute his father was. "I am not sure what you mean," he said.

"Of course you are! You are not the first man to be caught between two fires. Do you love Eurgain?"

"Yes."

"Caradoc, if you want to marry Aricia I will be content. Eurgain's father and I can work something out. You may have to pay her some cattle, and a bauble or two, but she would understand."

"I know she would, but I do not want to marry Aricia!"

Cunobelin looked at him curiously. "Why not? I would, if I were younger."

"Because I don't want to go off to Brigantia."

"That's not the real reason, and you know it very well, but I suppose it will do. The chiefs of Brigantia are fierce men, Caradoc, and rough. They can fight. They would certainly not welcome a foreign ruler. But think . . ." he went on slyly. "Think what it would mean for us. Brigantia ruled by a Catuvellaunian warrior." They met each other's eye and burst out laughing. "You know, Caradoc," Cunobelin went on quietly, leaning close to Caradoc's face, "I once considered making war on Aricia's father, taking his head. Brigantia is very large: all our people, and the Trinovantes too, could fit within it twice over. Did you know that? Aricia is heir to a vast, unkempt, poverty-stricken kingdom, which nevertheless has some of the best warriors anywhere. But I decided that it wasn't worth the trouble. The Coritani lie between us and Brigantia, and they would have had to have been trodden down first, and somehow I did not think that Augustus, or

46

Tiberius, would like that." The flames of the new fire danced across his seamed face. "No," he said, leaning back again. "Aricia has been an admirable hostage. Brigantia has minded its own business as I knew it would, and so have I. Do not be too hard in your judgment of her, my son. It will not be easy for her to leave her pleasant life here and go home to try to control a horde of tough wildmen."

Aricia's sojourn among the Catuvellauni had had two aims. Her father had sent her to absorb a way of life proper to the daughter of a chieftain. Many young nobility had passed in and out of Camu-lodunon, where power and luxury were greatest. It was the custom, but Cunobelin had begun to wonder lately whether perhaps in Aricia's case it had been a mistake. The spirit of childish willfulness that had won his approval had grown with her, and as she matured it was becoming an obstinate selfishness. She was too easily lured by the blandishments of luxury around her, and of course, by spoiling her outrageously he had contributed to her blithe presumption that every pleasure, good or bad, was due her. She had also been sent as a hostage, in the days when Cunobelin and her father were treating with each other. One of Cunobelin's sons had gone to Brigantia in exchange, but the distance between the two tribes and the ever present threat of Roman intervention had caused Cunobelin to discard one of his many tortuous ambitions. His son had died in Brigantia and Aricia had become his pet.

"Caradoc," he said, "marry them both, and keep Aricia here. Then her father will make war on us, Tiberius will champion me as the undoubtedly innocent party, and there—we have a foothold in Brigantia!"

Caradoc smiled wryly. "What about the Coritani?"

Cunobelin yawned prodigiously, scratched his head, then smiled slowly into Caradoc's brown eyes. "I have been considering them lately. Yes, I have. Do you know what they own, Caradoc? Salt! Plenty of lovely salt. I think a few raids into their southern flank would not go amiss, and then perhaps a little war, if Tiberius does not send an objection to the raids. He may even approve. Salt for trade!"

Caradoc cut in. "Father," he said delicately, feeling the quicksand under his words, "just how closely are you tied to Tiberius?" He could not ask what he wanted to—is Tiberius Ricon of the Catuvellauni?

Cunobelin stared past him for a long time, breathing lightly, and the clanking of pots and the echoing of the slaves' voices as they began to prepare the evening meal wafted toward them. The Hall was more crowded now. People hung about the fire to exchange the news of the day, and the rain had begun, drumming on the wooden walls in monotonous rhythm.

At last Cunobelin stirred. "All my life I have walked a narrow bridge," he said quietly. "On the one side is the dyke of my dreams, full of battle and conquest, a kingdom for the Catuvellauni stretching in uniform length from the wild lands of the north to the uncouth mines of the western peninsula. All men using my coins, Caradoc, all freemen raising their cattle and crops for me and my tuath. Think of it! I think of it constantly, but now my days are coming to an end. The goddess and I grow wrinkled and feeble together, and the chiefs whisper of my ritual death and of the goddess becoming young and strong again. But not for me the drowning cauldron of Bel, the fire of Taran!" His eyes burned and his lips drew back from yellowed teeth. "Not yet!" He slumped a little. "On the other side of the bridge is the gaping throat of Rome, her imperial tentacles reaching for me like the cold bodies of a thousand snakes, but I walk free and alone, between the two, for I am Cunobelin, Ricon, and neither Rome nor my fading dreams shall take me. What would you do, my son?" he said gently.

Rome had tried to force a foothold in Albion, and Rome had failed. The traders flooded the lowlands because the Catuvellauni allowed them to do so, and Caradoc thought privately that his father was indeed growing old, and soft, and full of groundless fears. "I would move against the Iceni, father, and then the Coritani, and then Verica, huddling by the ocean, and the Durotiges and the Dobunni, what is left of them, and I would not stop until my name was feared from one end of the earth to the other."

Cunobelin watched the handsome face, the glowing eyes, and a warm pool of paternal pride spread within him. "Would you indeed! So would Tog. But Adminius . . . ah, there's a deep one, my oldest child. Adminius would go to Rome and see the city of his dreams. He would talk with the emperor, and come back with a thousand togas and a thousand thousand new ideas. Well, Caradoc, the chiefs will have to make the final decision. It will be far from easy for them. Three sons!" He began to laugh, struggling to his feet while about them curled the aroma of boiling pig and roasting steer. Caradoc stood, too, and his father slapped him on the back. "I will announce your betrothal to the Council," he said. "There will be no objections—at least, not among the chiefs. Poor Aricia."

Caradoc was flicked on the raw. "If you feel so sorry for her, marry her yourself!" he snapped, tugging his cloak around him with irate pettishness, and left the Hall.

CHAPTER THREE

*I*N THE SPRING, when the frail white snowdrops and shiny yellow celandines carpeted the meadows, and the woods were a riot of fresh green leaves and drunken bird song, an embassy arrived from Brigantia, to take Aricia away. The winter had been mild, with days of wind and rain, gray skies and brooding, clinging mists, but few frosts, and spring had come early. Caradoc's betrothal to Eurgain had been announced to the Council and no voice had been raised in objection. Indeed, everyone had got drunk and sung the night away, and Aricia had withdrawn proudly into herself. Caradoc had hoped that with his new relationship to Eurgain the old, heat-seared helplessness of his lust for Aricia would be mitigated, but he found to his shame and dismay that if anything it had intensified. Aricia avoided him, and he saw no more of her than her cloaked shadow fleeing around a corner in the mist, or her shrouded, tall figure gliding from the Great Hall. His days were full of the tension created by her deliberate absence, and he found his daydreams wrapping all too easily around her. He knew very well that she was not the woman for him, and he, bewildered, did his best to struggle free, but the mindless rivers of desire flowed on within him, in a place where he could not reach, even as she had said, and Eurgain watched his pitiful attempts to extricate himself with a great, omnipresent pain. She loved him, she had always loved him, and she was prepared to lay aside her pride enough to marry him, although in the evenings, when he was full of wine, her name came hard to his lips. Aricia would go, and Eurgain waited with grim patience.

Togodumnus had spent the winter months licking his wounds. The fight with Cinnamus had not shaken him, but his father's reaction to it had, and his chiefs had told him politely but firmly that though they were his to command they were not his peasants and they could change alliegance if they chose. He coldly reviewed his honor-price and came to the conclusion that it was high enough. He stole no more cattle from the members of the tuath, but he, Caradoc, and Adminius went raiding in Coritani territory twice before the sticky brown buds on the trees burst forth, and the Coritani, with outraged affront, began to throw up huge earthworks just within their border. Cunobelin was satisfied. "It is a beginning," he said. "We must move slowly." And then the calving began, and the sowing, and men's spirits rose and spread wide like the carpeting of bluebells that were flung down with a prodigal hand by the god of the woods.

On a soft day, when the river ran warm and green and the sun dimpled upon its breast, six men drew rein outside the far gate. Their tunics were soiled and wrinkled. Brooches and bracelets of curious, tormented design adorned them, and their bronze torcs were almost hidden under matted beards that gave their dark faces a wild, graceless look. The cloaks that lay slung across their horses' backs were scarlet, fringed in blue tassels, and each man had a bronze shield across his shoulder. Their eyes burned under high, tanned foreheads, flicking sharply over the river, the trees beyond, the gate, and the cool shadow of the outer earthwall, restlessly seeking. The tallest man strode forward to greet the gateguard, who had come hurrying, his sword drawn.

"Good morning to you, Catuvellaunian," the man said, his voice deep but ragged with weariness. "Put up your sword, we come in peace. Send to your master. Tell him that Venutius chieftain of Brigantia is here, and then bring us food and beer, for we are tired and thirsty."

The gateguard gave them all a quick, disapproving glance and beckoned them into the dimness of his little gatehouse. They followed slowly, chafed and stiff from long days of riding, and uneasily they sank cross-legged to the dirt floor while the gateguard set meat and bread before them, and dark brown, strong mead. He left them reluctantly to send a servant riding the six miles to Camulodunon and then to see to their horses himself. He approached the beasts warily, wild animals these, skittish and jumpy, decked out in more of the flamboyant, foreign bronze whose contorted faces of unknown gods leered at him. He cursed softly as the horses backed away from him, their harnesses trailing and their ears flat to their heads, but one of the men called a word of command from the shadow of the gatehouse and they stood still immediately. The gateguard led them to the stable, calling his servant for help, while the men within drained their mead silently, their eyes still probing cautiously. They began eating when the gateguard returned, wolfing the food without apology, then settled their backs to the wall, their legs stretched out before them and their hands on their sword hilts. They still did not speak. After a while they seemed to doze, but when the gateguard rose to go outside he found himself transfixed by six pairs of unblinking eyes trained on him in unbroken hostility and he sat down again, trying to decide how long it would be before a message would come and he could be rid of his unwelcome guests.

At last, after two silent hours, the sound of hoofs was heard, and then the jingle of harness and men's voices. Venutius and his Brigantians came fully alert and rose quietly. They left the stuffy gloom of the gatehouse and went blinking into the sun, and the gateguard

50

reached for his beer with vast relief. Caradoc and Cinnamus had dismounted, but their chieftain escort remained seated on the broad backs of their horses, their hands surreptitiously sliding to the hilts of the swords they had hidden under the folds of their cloaks. Caradoc and Cinnamus advanced and saluted.

"Welcome to Camulodunon, chieftains of Brigantia," Caradoc said, looking at them with candid interest. "May your stay here be one of rest and peace." Although Caradoc was tall, Venutius was a full head above him, and Caradoc found his wrist taken in a viselike grip. He resisted slightly, out of pride, and Venutius smiled slowly at him, his white teeth appearing amidst the tangle of red beard.

"I thank you for your greeting," he said, and they dropped their hands. "I am Venutius, my lord's right-hand man, and these are my kinsmen."

Caradoc greeted them all with affability, conscious of their latent power, a raw, almost wild undercurrent of brute strength and clean animal cunning. He knew that Cinnamus was eyeing the weird, repellent designs on the shields and brooches with the same fascinated stare.

"And I am Caradoc ap Cunobelin," he said finally, turning to see the Brigantians' horses being led from the door of the stable. "My father waits for you with eagerness, and even now a calf is being slaughtered in your honor." The niceties of greeting were thus dispensed with and the mounted Catuvellaunian chiefs relaxed, their sword hands sliding to their harnesses once more. Caradoc, Cinnamus, Venutius, and his men swung onto their horses and the cavalcade set off up the winding track in the direction of the town. After a while Camulodunon appeared as a smudge of black smoke and a vague gray hump on the horizon, but it was still quite a ways off.

Caradoc and Cinnamus talked a little as they rode, to put these strange men at their ease, but their efforts went unrewarded. The Brigantians said nothing, watching with hard eyes the slow unfurling of this peaceful, green countryside, and Caradoc knew that when the embassy returned home the Brigantian ricon would receive a full report on the Roman-loving Catuvellauni—the numbers of their cattle, how many fields were tilled, how many traders had been passed and greeted on the road, how great the forests were. Caradoc did not mind. The chieftains would also see the rings of massive earthwalls encircling the town, the might of the huge gate, the depth and danger of the dyke. Let them look, and be amazed. Yet they did not seem amazed. Venutius pointed out a peasant and his wife, who were sowing in bare feet, their tunics tucked in their leather belts, and he made some comment in an undertone to his kinsmen that produced a series of dry chuckles. But other than that the ride was an uncomfortably silent one. Caradoc and Cinnamus caught each other's eye and smiled sympathetically, thinking of Cunobelin's reaction, but Caradoc thought also of Aricia, and the smile left his face. So she was to go. He had dreaded and longed for this day, but now that it was here he could think only of Aricia's own fear, and the miles between Camulodunon and Brigantia that she would have to ride with these unpredictable freemen-chiefs for company.

They dismounted again at last, and the gateguards saluted and waved them through. The afternoon had begun and the sun, now shining full and filtering through drifting wisps of lazy cloud, made them sweat as they waited for the stable servants to lead their beasts away. Then Caradoc gestured to Venutius and they walked up the slope together, past the stables and kennels, past the craftsmen's shops, up past the disorderly, dirty sprawl of freemen-commoners' huts where women sat on their skins and gossiped, to the wooden huts and neat paths of the nobles' and chieftains' circle. The shrine of Camulos was open, and as he passed Venutius cast a swift glance inside. The three-faced god squatted in the close darkness, ugly and menacing, and Venutius barely restrained himself from spitting as he strode by. Roman-lovers! he thought. Even their gods were enclosed in dark shrines, like the gods of Rome. He wanted nothing more than to take the lady and be gone.

Caradoc halted before the doors of the Great Hall, where Cunobelin stood with his chiefs ranked beside him, his arms folded and glittering with bronze bracelets, his gray hair plaited on his breast, his eyes half-closed against the sunlight. Venutius stepped to him and saluted, and Cunobelin smiled, offering his arm for the other's clasp, noting Caradoc's tense face. So the sheepherders of Brigantia had discomfited him! So much the better. Let him watch and learn. He snapped his fingers, and his chiefs parted.

"Welcome to Camulodunon, son of Brigantia."

"Your hospitality is boundless, Cunobelin, Ricon," Venutius replied, his voice a deep, rolling rumble that made Cunobelin's own sound high and thin. "We are tired. We have ridden with haste, for our lord is dying, and wants his daughter home." A murmur sighed through the crowd.

"I have had word of your coming," Cunolebin said smoothly. Caradoc looked at him with astonishment. It was possible, of course, for his father kept a keen eye on the borderlands, but if it were true he had not said a word to anyone. Cunobelin turned. "Enter now and give me your news. You can bathe and rest, and we will feast. Afterwards you can repeat your business to the Council."

"Ricon, much as we would like to while away the hours in pleasantries, we have great haste," Venutius replied quietly, but coolly. "Send for the lady, I ask you, and have her traveling wain prepared. Her father's strength fails and we dare not linger."

Cunobelin turned back, astounded, and some of the chiefs whispered angrily. To refuse hospitality was the height of rudeness, but what else could they expect from such wild northmen? "But you will surely eat the calf that has been slain for you, and change your clothing? Besides, it will not be easy for Aricia to pack her belongings. She has been here very long and has many precious possessions." None missed the hint of reproof that bordered on a cool statement of Catuvellaunian superiority, but though Venutius's jaw tightened, he answered Cunobelin with the same indifferent calm.

"Cunobelin, we must indeed wash and change and eat," he said slowly. "However, may the feasting be swift and the Council dumb, for whether we will it or no, we must be gone before tomorrow's dawn."

Iron lay under the words, and Cunobelin's men gathered into a belligerent knot, scowling openly at the strangers, but Cunobelin finally smiled again in perfect understanding. None of them, not Venutius and his chiefs nor Cunobelin and his band, cared when death came to Aricia's father. They were speaking not with their words but with their wills, and the game was as old as the tribes themselves. Cunobelin loved it. He played it with consummate skill and knew how to reduce an opponent to a faltering child without saying one harsh word. But these Brigantians did not enter into his machinations, not yet, and today he did not want to play, so instead of opening the next move, he shrugged, bowed, and led the way inside, leaving his back to the foreign swords. Venutius followed, his back exposed to the Catuvellaunian chiefs, and Caradoc watched the little ritual and wanted to laugh. The older his father became, the more these little games amused him. Caradoc put a hand on Cinnamus's shoulder.

"Go and find Aricia, and tell her that the time is here," he said. His voice shook and the green eyes rested on him in understanding before Cinnamus turned away. Caradoc fought a desire to run to his house and seal the door, but he walked slowly after the Brigantian chiefs and into the smell of stale pork drippings and woodsmoke.

Cinnamus found Aricia outside the gate, a few paces in under the trees, picking bluebells. He stood quietly for a moment, watching her bend and straighten, her arms full of the rich blue flowers. He felt no pity for her. She was a foreigner, beautiful, yes, with a veneer of Catuvellaunian culture, yes, but ultimately she did not belong to his tuath. Besides, she was nothing but trouble and she knew it. Caradoc was moody and sharp-tongued because of her, and even Togodumnus had been looking after her lately, an odd, reflective light in his eyes. Such a one could bring dissent and even murder to a ruling house, could weaken the unity and strength of the tribe. He saw more in her than either Caradoc or Togodumnus. He saw a plotting, cold mind behind the lustrous eyes, a dangerous lack of human affection, and he did not like her. He was glad that she was going.

He took a step and she stiffened and whirled, her fingers seeking the knife that was always at her belt, the blooms fall in a damp shower over her feet.

"Cinnamus! You startled me. What do you want?" She did not care for the blond, green-eyed young man. He was so quietly sure of himself though his clothes were threadbare and his ornaments few, and she was annoyed she could never meet his eyes. She bent and began to gather up the flowers.

"Forgive me for frightening you, Lady, but Cunobelin has sent for you and you must go at once. Your kinsmen are here."

Puzzlement clouded her eyes, but as he continued to stand there politely, looking past her to the cool depths of the wood, she straightened and pink flushed her cheeks and receded, leaving her deathly pale.

"My kinsmen, Ironhand?"

He saw the tremor shudder through the long, delicate fingers, and one by one the blooms began to fall again, already wilting. She leaned suddenly against a tree trunk, feeling weak, breathing in shallow spurts, trying to regain some control of herself, then with a savage movement, flung the remaining flowers behind her and walked to him, the skin of her face stretched tight over the fine bones, her eyes hollows of dark misery. "Lead on, then," she said, her voice high, and he turned and threaded his way back to the path and the open gate beyond.

She paced behind him, saying nothing, and together they wound their way up through the town to the Hall. Smoke spiraled from the roof, and already they could smell the roasting calf. They went in to find the Hall full of chiefs and idle, curious freemen, come to catch a glimpse of the northmen, and the conversation rose and fell around them as the wine cups were filled and emptied. Cinnamus turned aside, going to Sholto and Caelte who stood just inside the door, heads together, while others of Caradoc's chiefs clustered nearby. Aricia walked on alone to where Cunobelin and Caradoc waited.

"They have come at last," Cunobelin said gently as she came up and stood before them, her face a mask of stiff, emotionless control. "I sent them to the guest huts so that they could wash and change their

54

clothes. We exchanged such news as we were able. Will you hear it?"

Her lips trembled and for the briefest moment her gaze rested on Caradoc, then wandered from his tanned face to roam the Hall, seeking an escape, seeking a reprieve. Togodumnus came over and thrust wine into her cold hands. She drank slowly and then nodded. Cunobelin put a heavy arm across her shoulders and urged her down onto the skins, and his sons followed, squatting easily before them. Behind, in the shadows, the groups of men broke up and came and ringed them, squatting or sitting cross-legged to hear what went on. It was their right, but Aricia hated them for it. She clasped her hands in her red lap and sat straight-backed. She saw Eurgain and Gladys come in, take wine, and stand together hesitantly by the door, and she looked away. But wherever she looked she saw only eagerness for news, a callous greed for something to hear, and her eyes found no rest. Cunobelin spoke again, but softly, so that only his sons and his chiefs caught the words.

"Your father is dying, Aricia, and you must go to him swiftly. Your Council awaits you in Brigantia, and your kingdom. You must go to your house and have your servants pack a wain." The word was passed quickly to those in the rear, and whispering rose and then died away. Aricia answered him without moving.

"You are my father, old wolf, and this is my tuath. I will not go."

"No daughter of mine would speak thus," Cunobelin said sternly. "You have a duty to your people. You have no brothers, and Brigantia awaits your rule. Will you say that I have failed in my responsibility to you, that I return to your father a weak-kneed, spoiled brat?" Her eyes burned with unshed tears and she gulped the wine, knowing that he spoke harshly to help her bear what must come, but she felt a pang of resentment nonetheless. She shook back her hair and faced him.

"I know my duty, Cunobelin, but it is a hard one. Can I not be forgiven for wishing to lay it aside? I came here as a hostage but you brought me up as a daughter. Shall the parting of such kin be without pain? Do you feel nothing?"

He embraced her. "I know my loss," he replied, "but I also know Brigantia's gain and the gain of this tuath. Will there not be commerce between us, and Samain meetings, and good relations, now that my daughter goes to rule another kingdom?"

She laughed then, a sound without mirth. "Or shall I become what my kin want me to be, a wild hill-queen, loving no one and suspicious of all?" She rose. "I will go to pack, and meet these, my . . . my kinsmen." She said the word with contempt and swept past them. Eurgain moved to speak to her but was brushed off deftly, and excited talk began again while the sun poured through the vents, mingling with the smoke and making pale puddles of light on the ash-strewn floor.

That evening, every chief and freeman in Camulodunon attended the feast, and the din and laughter were full of the heady undercurrents of diversion. The members of the royal family sat together with their bards and shield-bearers and Aricia sat with them, dressed deliberately in her best tunic, the one striped in red and yellow and embroidered with gold thread. The thin circlet on her forehead was of gold, as were her bracelets and anklets. She sat on her cloak, her tunic folding softly around her, and she felt the eyes of her strange kinsmen regarding her in speculation. She sensed suspicion in them, a vague, uneasy dislike. Well, let them hate her, she said to herself. She did not care. They would have to obey her, and they knew it.

She ate little and drank much, and her kinsmen, who disdained the Roman wine, quaffed their cheap local beer and watched her from their place beside Cunobelin and his chiefs. Cunobelin's bard played and sang, but his words were drowned by the noise. Caradoc talked easily with Sholto and Cinnamus, conscious of a spreading contentment and a guilty relief. Togodumnus and Adminius quarreled and finally came to blows, but at Cunobelin's word, retired sheepishly with black eyes and bloody noses, to drink some more and flirt with the women. Gladys and Eurgain sat together, both glittering in the dark light of the smoking torches, their attendants twittering beside them. Outside the wind blew, soft and wet, and now and then a gentle, warm rain fell. At length Cunobelin sent the slaves out and called for Council, and Venutius rose and told them all gruffly and quickly why he had come.

Aricia watched him carefully. He was handsome in an overpowering way. A physical strength emanated from the long, thick, breech-clad legs, the booming voice, the matted red hair, and his men hung on his words as though he were the most silver-tongued of bards, singing to them of victories to come. Yet he was young, scarcely older than Caradoc. She sipped her wine, relishing it with fatalism, knowing that she would drink no more of it for many a year to come, unless somehow she could turn her beer-drinking savages into Catuvellaunian freemen. When Venutius sat down, his sharp animal's glance reaching her, she looked at him and then away to where Caradoc was fingering his tightly braided brown hair and listening intently to Tog's whispers. Venutius was a challenge she would have to meet if she was to do with Brigantia what she would, but perhaps he would prove easier to tame than the sophisticated sons of Cunobelin. One of the chiefs was speaking now but not in dissent, and she knew that the smile on Cinnamus's face had nothing to do with the effects of the

56

wine. They are glad that I am going, she thought bitterly. All of them. Well then, I will also go gladly. She smiled at Venutius and he smiled back slowly, warily, and looked away. Perhaps she was not as Roman as she looked, his new queen.

In the predawn mist, when the dew lay heavy on the ground and the trees reared like ghostly warriors beyond the gate, Cunobelin, Caradoc, Togodumnus, and the others gathered to share the cup of parting with Aricia and her chieftains. Two wains stood ready, moisture beading on the manes and flanks of the ponies yoked and waiting to draw them, the rich tunics and cloaks, the fine jewels and drinking cups, the beaded curtains covered with hessian to protect them from the morning's dampness. Aricia stood by her horse, her hood thrown back, her eyes shadowed with stress and weariness, and Venutius stood by her, already possessive.

Cunobelin's shield-bearer brought her the cup, bowing slightly, and she took it and sipped, then handed it back, and he passed it to the others, who were huddling in their long cloaks. When all had finished he took it away and Cunobelin stepped forward and held her to him. For the last time she rested within the circle of his strong arms and looked into his wrinkled, sly face. "Go in safety, walk in peace," he said. Then Caradoc stepped to her and kissed her cold cheek. "Forgive me," he whispered into her wet hair, but she did not respond. Adminius came to hug her next and she still stood like a stone sentinel, but Tog sought her mouth and muttered something in her ear and it brought a fleeting smile to her stiff lips. Eurgain enveloped her in warm arms and perfume, and suddenly Aricia found herself melting. The two girls clung together, and Aricia whispered, "Take care of him, Eurgain. He needs you more than me." Gladys strode up and kissed her, pressing something warm and smooth into her palm. "A talisman," she said, and Aricia opened her hand and looked down. It was a tiny piece of driftwood that seemed to writhe on her skin, four snakes intertwining. The wood had been oiled and polished and a pin set in it so that it could be worn on a tunic or used to fasten a cloak. As Aricia stood gazing at it, Gladys's strange comfort brought tears to her eyes at last and she mounted quickly, and, after settling her cloak around her, drew up her hood and nodded to Venutius.

No one called farewell or waved, and she disappeared quickly into the mist. The wains rumbled after her, and Cunobelin turned abruptly to the gate, Gladys and Eurgain going with him.

Togodumnus turned to Caradoc and smiled. "What will be her fate, I wonder?" he said lightly. "Shall we make war on her in years to come, do you think?"

A hole that will not be filled . . . Caradoc thought with a pang of deep regret, and then her face was before him, the gold-flecked eyes wide and the arms rising to encircle him. He blinked and smiled back at his brother. "Who knows?" he answered carefully, but he felt the thread that bound him to her lengthening, stretching, growing taut around him with no sign of a break. He did not think that he had seen the last of her.

A week after Aricia's departure, on a breezy, sunny morning, full of the delicate odor of yellow gorse flowers, Caradoc and Eurgain shared the cup of marriage. The wedding was on the grassy lawn that swept from the earthwall of Camulodunon to become grazing meadow and the short spears of young crops. Eurgain wore a silver circlet on her brow, and her dark golden hair fell loose about the blue folds of her tasseled tunic. Caradoc was arrayed in scarlet. He stood tall and proud while the wine in the cup sparkled red and the gathered chiefs and freemen waited to cheer and sing when the words that would bind the two of them together were pronounced.

He had chosen his wedding gifts with great care. A necklace of blue glass beads from Egypt, a bolt of silk from the island of Cos that shimmered rainbow colors when Eurgain took it up wonderingly and ran it through her fingers, a pair of hunting dogs, and two drinking cups of the purest silver, shipped especially, straight from Rome.

Her dowry had been the greatest ever brought to a warrior of the tuath—two hundred cattle—and as Caradoc took her hand and kissed her soft lips and the uproar broke out around them, he felt Togodumnus's grinning, wry face by his elbow. Now Caradoc had the highest honor-price of any of his kin. He chose gifts for his chiefs also, careful to offend none of them, but for Cinnamus he had fifty breeding cattle and a new cloak. Cinnamus had protested hotly, talking of the shame of patronage, but Caradoc pointed out to him that he was merely buying future loyalty, and Cinnamus, after weighing the words in cool silence, finally nodded and accepted the magnificent gift, knowing that he would eventually earn it in Caradoc's train.

Cunobelin had presented the couple with the largest house in the town. It had two rooms, two hearths, and twice the work to keep clean, as Fearachar had pointed out under his breath. Eurgain had spent a happy day hanging her lamps and arranging her belongings, and she had persuaded Fearachar to open a window for her, low down. The view was not as sweeping as the one from her own house, but she knew she would have little time for star-gazing. She was sorry, but her house soon acquired the brooding, peaceful aura she carried with her everywhere, and her inarticulate longing for the silence of the far-off hills was turning now to Caradoc, her love. The Feast of Beltine was coming, fertility burst forth wherever she looked, and the sun was warm on her face as she turned and smiled at him shyly, putting out a hesitant hand to touch the waving dark hair that framed his brown face. He was hers. Aricia was gone. He would come to love her in time, but if not, it did not matter. He would need her, and with that she would be content.

CHAPTER FOUR

V ENUTIUS STRUCK OUT WEST when they had left behind the bulk of Camulodunon and the knot of silent, shrouded people. He set a brisk pace, and Aricia rode beside him, her throat tight with pain and her hand still curled around the magic serpents. With no more sound than the soft footfalls of their beasts and the occasional jingle of bronze harnesses, they passed like wraiths under the fog-hung trees. They followed the same path that had often echoed to the shouts of the Royal War Band as it merrily hunted the wild boar, and Aricia resolutely shut her ears to those beckoning memories of days far off and gone forever. The straight stretch where the warriors practiced their chariot skill glided under her hanging feet, the ground began to rise slowly, and the trees thinned out. In a little over an hour the second gate was behind them, and Aricia turned once, seeing the shallow, slow-moving flow of the river, the forest, the gateguard motionless in the early morning light, the massive defences soaring behind him. She looked ahead to where the track wound up to the crest of a rolling, grassy hill and disappeared over the top, and to where the way was lined with spreading oaks and the thin, willowy ashes whose little leaves tossed in the new wind.

"We must not take much time in reaching the border," Venutius said. "A Druid waits for us there to see us safe through the land of the Coritani, but he has business elsewhere and will not stay overlong if we are delayed." She said nothing, leaving his words unacknowledged, and, with a low call to the horses, they started up the path, the wains trundling in their wake.

They stopped once on a wind-raked hill that gave them breathtaking views of the land lying under them like a blanket, patched here and there with dark forest, dyed with the bright green of young barley, oats, and wheat, embroidered with slow silver trace of rivers far away, and the blue haze of spring tinging the horizon under the midday sun. They ate quickly, sitting on the grass, and the men talked and laughed, their tongues loosed now that the all-insinuating reach of Cunobelin was a thing for tales and song. But Aricia was quiet, eating slowly, and her eyes traveled the wide sweep of the sky. She tried not to look ahead, telling herself that this was merely a trip, a short, pleasant spring jaunt to worship a goddess in the woods perhaps, and soon she would say goodbye to these unwanted companions and go home. It was a dangerous game to play, but it was the only way she knew to keep at bay the tides of homesickness and grief. Venutius sat beside her, passing her meat and cheese, and giving her strong beer from his goatskin bag. He watched her out of the corners of his brown eyes, but they eventually mounted and rode on, and she still did not grace him with the smile that had warmed his blood in Cunobelin's Hall.

At twilight of the third night, when dusk crept upon them from secret places among the trees, they crossed into the lands of the Coritani, riding beside deep pits in the earth, pools of darkness, and raw gashes in the ground where the people had taken soil for the new earthwalls that hemmed the riders in. But Aricia, tired, dirty, and cold, took no interest in the defences that had been thrown up against the Catuvellauni. A little way ahead a solitary light burned and Venutius called a halt, going forward quietly on foot to see what it was. The others sat motionless, Aricia drooping on her horse's back, her eyes heavy and her hands curled stiffly about the reins. They listened to the stir and scuffle of the wild animals in the undergrowth and watched the blurred stars wink out.

Before too long Venutius came back, his approach as silent and stealthy as a slinking stoat. "It is the Druid," he said, "and some of the chiefs of this people. The lady can rest here for the night, and there will be hot water for her in which to wash." As if, thought Aricia dully, all I want, soft southerner that I am, is a bowl of hot water. Venutius, you are a fool. Her horse plodded dejectedly the last few paces and she slid wearily to the ground, throwing the reins to the servant who had come running. She walked into the hut, ducking her head and blinking in the brightness of the fire. A Druid sat there, warming his hands, and for a moment she thought it was Bran, but then he turned his head and greeted her amiably, and she saw that this man was much older, a swarthy, bearded man with twinkling eyes and bronze rings tied into his hair.

The Coritani chiefs rose and greeted her with the words of hospitality and she answered them automatically while her men stood behind

60

her like dark shadows. These chiefs could barely hide their churlish disdain of her, the Catuvellaunian cub, and soon they bowed and went away and she sank onto the skins by the fire, letting her cloak slide from her shoulders.

"Set a watch over my wains," she called to Venutius. "The Coritani are a thieving people."

The white-clad figure on the other side of the fire chuckled. "They are no more rapacious than your foster tribe, Lady of Brigantia," he said. "They are my own people, so watch your words. I am a noble of this tribe, and if you insult them I will vanish in the night and they will come and cut off your pretty head." He was joking with her, but she was in no mood for jest and she stared into the heart of the fire. Well, let them come, then, and take her head, it would not matter to her.

The Druid rose and stretched, then cracked his knuckles until she winced. "I can see, Lady, that my jokes are out of season," he remarked. "So I will go to my rest. A servant will come before long, with hot water, for which you will, of course, pay him—in Cunobelin's coin, if you do not mind. Although the Coritani spit upon his name, they eagerly seek his money. A good night to you." He went out, the doorskins swishing to behind him, and after a moment she tiptoed to the door and peered out.

"Do you need anything, Lady?" a voice spoke in her ear, and she withdrew hastily muttering, "no, no." She went back to the fire, and sleep filled her head, driving out the hunger. At least she was well guarded. The servant appeared as she was dozing, propped against the wall, and she asked him for hot meat and warm wine, to be brought in half an hour. "That will cost you two bronze coins, Lady," he answered promptly.

"I will pay you when you have delivered the things to me!" she snapped at him, and he smirked and went out. She shed the short male tunic and the loose breeches gratefully, tossing them on the floor and then washing herself thoroughly in the scalding water. Then, refreshed, she dressed in the clean clothes she had brought in a leather pouch, and loosened her hair, unbraiding it and combing it in long, slow strokes. The servant came, carrying a tray with hot beef, bread, last year's apples, wrinkled and tiny, and a jug of cold, frothing mead. He put down the tray and bent to throw more wood on the fire.

"I asked for hot wine," she said sharply. "Do not tell me that the Coritani drink no wine for I know that they do, and in abundance. Bring me wine!"

He straightened and looked at her insolently. "I have been told that the Brigantians drink only strong mead and barley beer," he said. "Your pardon if I took you for one of them." Before she could shriek at him he was gone, returning in a while with a drinking cup full of wine. He went to the fire, picked up the red-hot poker, and thrust it into the cup, and the wine sizzled and began to steam, its rich aroma filling the hut. She almost snatched it from him.

"Now go away. The hospitality of this tuath leaves much to be desired," she said, flinging two coins at him. He caught them adroitly, bit them, and left grinning, and she sipped the hot wine thankfully, sinking to her cloak beside the crackling fire.

Early the next morning they were on the move again, riding northeast to find the coast. The Druid rode beside Venutius, talking gaily, and Aricia, her spirits renewed, rode behind then, listening and smiling at the give and take. The morning was overcast, and far away, flashes of lightning played about the gloomy marshes of the Iceni territory, but the air, although close and sticky, was not warm, and all the company wore their cloaks. At the end of the day Aricia could detect a new scent all around them—raw, bracing, the tangy smell of the ocean—and when they camped near a circle of rough stones that leaned together as if tired of the hundreds of years they had stood, she fancied she could hear it, the dull booming that made her think of silent, black-clad Gladys and the tall-masted ships of Rome. She took out the serpent brooch and lay holding it in the dark, and whether the talisman did indeed have some soothing power of its own, or whether she was becoming used to the ways of her new chiefs and felt less alone, she slept deeply and awoke with hope, to bird song and another gray morning.

They reached the ocean that day, and left all trees behind them. The country that opened out was barren, a place of rolling, grassy slopes, each folding into the other, on and on without end, a place where the wind never ceased to whisper of loneliness and quietude and of hawks and eagles, hanging, wings outspread, in the cloudy, wind-tormented sky. They drew rein on a cliff, and Aricia got down and walked to the edge, keeping her balance with difficulty as the gale sent her hair whipping behind her and her cloak wrapped itself tight around her knees. Below her, where black and gray rocks lay like the rotting teeth of the land itself, and the sand, wet and cold, hissed malevolently under the ocean's torturing hands, lay the heaving water, swelling and receding sullenly while the gulls bobbed on the waves and flapped screaming over the beach. Black seaweed lay strewn here and there, shiny and thick, and, through her keen, flared nostrils, she could smell it, too, the scent of life itself. After several deep breaths she turned again, fighting her hair and her cloak, and mounted, and they picked their way back to the track that would run beside the sea until it veered inland, where the river of Brigantia spent itself.

Five days later, in the evening, they came to where the river spread out and mingled with the sea, to a place of marsh and long-legged, long-beaked birds who stepped delicately in the mud and probed for grubs with their sharp bills. The sun had almost gone, and pink shafts of light lay over the surrounding country like the drifting gossamer of spiders' webs. The men were excited. Aricia could tell by the way they laughed more freely, their voices carrying far in the still, sweet air.

The Druid turned to her and reined in, bringing his horse to walk beside her. "Well, Lady," he said, "tomorrow you will see your home."

Already she had seen country she never knew existed, and a curious thrill went through her. She smiled at the man. "Long has it been since I left these parts," she replied. "I was not yet six when my father took me to Cunobelin."

"Have you any memories?"

She frowned, tunneling past the bright visions of yesterday to an older time. "I am not sure," she said slowly. "Sometimes I think I can remember the odor of sheep, and a huge stone house as big as the Great Hall itself, but perhaps these are only dreams."

"Perhaps." He watched her closely but saw only cheeks colored by the evening breeze and eyes clearer than the stars. "Tell me, Lady, did the seer of the Catuvellauni tell the omens for you before you left Camulodunon?"

She glanced at him swiftly, shock in her face. "Why, no. The seer at Camulodunon has not been consulted for many a year."

He sighed. "A pity. I should like to have known what he said about you, but of course the Romans do not encourage such practices." He spoke without a sneer in his voice and she did not know how to answer him. The hustle and obscenities of the Roman traders seemed so far away here.

"I suppose you will be leaving us soon," she said, and he nodded.

"We part at the border. I am traveling west, through Cornovii country and on to visit the Ordovices for a while."

"Oh? Who are they?"

He gave her a look of pure amusement, and his eyes sparkled. "They are a very fierce and uncivilized tribe who inhabit a country of snowy mountains," he said solemnly. "They have no chariots or horses, and they live in stone huts. I do not think you would like them very much."

Just then Venutius called a halt by a little stream that emerged from the eaves of the wood, and they dismounted and began to make camp. Aricia sat by the river, watching the pink glow turn to gray and then to dusk, excitement reaching her too, carried on the brisk, happy voices of her chiefs and the wind that brought to her the hint of a vast high country waiting for her on the morrow. Soon that smell mingled with the odor of woodsmoke from their cooking fire and she went to join the circle of men who ringed it. One of the chiefs had caught a hare and they ate well, washing down their meat and bean gruel with icy river water. Then they reclined on their cloaks, telling stories, singing snatches of old fighting songs, and listening to the night noises beyond the friendly circle of the fire's orange light. Aricia fell asleep contentedly on the ground, rolled in her cloak, her head pillowed on Venutius's horse blanket.

Noon of the next day brought them to the border. A light drizzle was falling, not enough to soak them, but enough to make them fasten their cloaks tightly around their necks and draw up their hoods. Although Aricia could see no sign that Brigantia lay before her, the men drew their swords and flung them into the air, catching them by the hilts and swinging them around their heads. "Brigantia! Brigantia!" they shouted, and when Aricia looked about for the Druid she found that he had left them, had melted away somewhere into the trees.

It was said that the Druithin had no fear of wooded places, but Aricia shuddered, imagining him riding alone and unprotected under the hostile eyes of all the spirits there who had no love for humans and who lived only for Samain, when they could carry a person off, never to be seen by mortal eye again. Something else took her, too, a sudden fear and foreboding. She felt somehow that if she crossed the border of her land she would immediately change and become something alien even to herself. And though men would see and speak to Aricia, Queen, yet she would no longer be Aricia but some dark, evil thing that lived in Aricia's body, which no one would ever know, not even herself. She shivered again, but the men had started to move and her horse followed them, crossing over some strange invisible line that marked the marches of Brigantia.

The rain thickened as the afternoon wore on, but the men still sang, and at last, when they could no longer see where they were going, they stopped at a peasant's hovel, pegging their horses and squeezing inside. The hut stank, and a cold wind whistled through the neglected wattle walls. Venutius coaxed the fire into new life, and the lengthening flames revealed an old man and a young woman, sitting with big, dark eyes fixed on them all, their bare feet tucked under rude sacking and their faces all but hidden by tangled masses of black hair. Aricia went to them and tried to talk, but they stared at her in dumb fear and at length she left them and took off her cloak and held it to the fire. It began to steam, and a picture of Caradoc stole unbidden into her mind. He was standing before her fire in the cozy room at Camulodunon, his eyes black and glazed over with desire, his hair stuck to his forehead and his shoulders, and his breeches steaming. She wrenched her mind away after one agonized flash of longing and turned to hold a pot steady while one of her chiefs poured the water that was to be heated for soup. Rain trickled through the moss-choked thatch above them and it soon made cold pools under their feet. They ate uncomfortably, sharing what they had with the pair, who suddenly sprang to life, snatching the bowls held out to them and eating like famished wolves.

"Are all your peasants this poverty-stricken?" Aricia whispered to Venutius.

He was galled at the way the word "your" slid off her tongue. "No, Lady. Only here, close to the border, where the Coritani often raid and the people are parted from their sheep and their goats. They suffer grievously but will not leave their land to move farther in."

The night was spent in damp, cold misery and they were astir early, in a fever to pack up and be gone. They left a bag of dried beans, a ham, and two cheap knives with the peasants, who did not thank them but stood staring into the drab dawn as they rode quickly way.

The river began to narrow and soon they left it, striking out into the knee-high grass. The land was dotted here and there with small copses, but for the most part it was bare, and in the slanting rain Aricia thought that she had never seen a more desolate place. She shivered and sneezed throughout the rest of the journey, never dry, never warm, dreaming more and more of the huge warm stone house of her childhood, praying that it existed.

At sunset on the third day since they had crossed the border, Venutius grunted, reined in, and pointed. "The heart of Brigantia," he said, and she looked, her heart sinking. No gates, no defences, no neat, tree-lined paths, no people visible, only a collection of poor, miserable wattle huts, smoke curling slowly and sullenly from their thatched roofs, and a few half-starved curs that slunk amid the old bones and offal of feasts long past. Shock swelled her tongue, and she could not even cry out. Venutius rode forward and she followed him blindly, every nerve in her shouting negation, and they dismounted for the last time. He put his hands to his mouth and called out. Slowly, silently, as if they were wraiths of the mist taking concrete form in answer to Venutius's voice, the doorskins of the huts parted and men began to flow toward them, tall men, spare, with beards that hung upon their thick tunics and eyes that seemed to gather together and fly to her, holding her in a vise. They came soundlessly, but she stood her ground, knowing instinctively that if she stepped back she would lose a kingdom. Behind them the women glided, tall also, dark-haired and pale-skinned, dressed in wild-patterned tunics that covered their leather-shod feet. Their eyes, too, held the latent ferocity of the barren hills, and they looked at her without respect and without fear. They all came to a halt and there was a deep, pregnant silence, broken only by the pattering of the rain.

Aricia flung back her cloak so that they could see the sword at her belt. "What ails you, all of you, that you stand gazing at me as if I were the Raven of Panic in human form? Do you not know a Brigantian flaith when you see one?" she said haughtily, though she was shaking with fever and her head swam. Suddenly smiles broke out and the people surrounded her, touching her cloak, her hair, bidding her welcome, speaking the words of hospitality one by one until Venutius turned and addressed them.

"Prepare fire and food, and go about your business. The lady must see her father, and then she must rest." The crowd scattered, but Aricia was not too sick to notice their instant response to his bidding. She wondered whether Venutius had brought her all this way only to challenge her right to rule. She and Venutius walked on through the huts, the chiefs behind them, leading the horses, she swaying a little, sweat breaking out on her forehead. Venutius stopped by a house built, she saw with unutterable relief, of stone. It stood in the center of the village, surrounded by a palisade of tall wooden stakes, and six chiefs lounged at the entrance, leaning on their shields and talking, impervious to the rain. They straightened and saluted Aricia, and Venutius gestured with one brawny arm. "Lady, your father awaits you within. He is very weak and may not even know you, but I think the expectation of your coming has kept him alive, and now he will not linger long. I will see that you get dry clothes and food in a little while." She smiled wanly up at him and he saw the sweat on the white forehead, the fever-glazed eyes, the trembling hands. A pang of concern went through him but he did not show it, and turned on his heel to go inside.

It was warm and dry within. A fire burned at the central hearth, and sheepskins covered the dirt floor. As she bent her head and entered, a woman rose from a stool at the bedside, but Aricia saw her only through a fog of sickness. She heard her own voice greet the woman but it seemed to come from someone else far away, and the woman's polite reply reached her tired brain as mere gibberish. She shed her heavy cloak and the woman took it, putting it over one arm and going out. Aricia turned to the low bed with a growing sense of unreality, her heart beating faintly and rapidly.

She lowered herself onto the stool and leaned forward, but it was not Cunobelin who lay there sinking into his last sleep. It was a wizened, gnomelike little man with a thin, drooping mouth and wispy gray hair like a baby's. He was scarcely breathing, and she thought for a moment that he was already dead, but then the blue-veined hands lying inert on the blanket quivered and she leaned closer, feeling the fever begin to gnaw at her back. "Father?" she said loudly, feeling the terrible, ridiculous nonsense in the word, and he opened his eyes with effort and turned his head. They were brown eyes, rheumy and vague, and they searched the room for her. She stood and bent closer. "Father, it is I, Aricia. I have come." He saw her then and his eyes wandered over her face. The hands lifted, fell back, and she reached out and clasped them with her own. It was the hardest, most distasteful thing she had ever done in her life, but she took the brittle fingers, feeling the coldness of death in them, and he smiled very faintly.

"Aricia," he whispered. "Home at last. You have not changed at all, little one."

She felt a tremor pass from his hands to hers and he closed his eyes for a moment, marshaling his strength. "The chiefs are like children," he went on slowly. "Swift to anger, loyal to death. Treat them as children. Leave the Carvetii alone. We have a treaty with them, and with the Parisii. Ride against the Coritani and teach them a lesson. Listen to the Druithin. Observe the sacrifices."

"Hush, old man!" she whispered back fiercely. "Be at peace. Am I not of your flesh? Will I not rule the Council well?" Her head ached, and black spots flickered and burst before her eyes.

His hands went limp and she sat back with relief, but before he closed his eyes he said, "Venutius. Great honor-price. Much power, but loyal to House Brigantia. Give him . . . give him . . ." He sighed and slept, and after a moment she rose from the stool and staggered to the fire, sitting beside it, exhausted, and laying her head on her knees. Give him what? Her thoughts echoed in the battleground of her fevered mind. Give him myself?

She fell into a deep, troubled sleep and the woman found her there, moaning and ill, and sent for Venutius. He came and picked her up as though she were a wisp of straw and carried her to the guest hut, laying her gently on the bed and stoking the fire until it roared halfway to the ceiling. He put a hand on her burning brow and then looked down on her as she tossed and muttered, this pampered child, this royal woman. I could kill her now, he thought. I could pick up the pillow and smother her and the chiefs would never know that she did not die of the fever. But instead he smoothed the wet black hair from the tiny face and spoke sharply to the woman who stood waiting. "Undress her and dry her thoroughly. Pile the skins on her and keep the fire high, and send for me when she awakes." He went out quickly, mud spattering from his boots, and the rain drummed on the thatch like a mad lullaby.

For four days she lay sick, and in that time the rain stopped and a strong summer sun shone out. Her father died on the third day, passing peacefully in his sleep, and his chiefs carried him to his resting place on a bier, arrayed in all his finery, his sword and his spear beside him. They were not sorry to see him go. If he had recovered they would have killed him, for Brigantia the High One was an ugly, incompetent hag, who wandered screaming and cackling over the bare hills, reproaching them for their timidity in not dispatching him a long time ago so that she could grow young again. One of the chiefs had seen her, standing high above the village, her black robe streaming out behind her and her gnarled hands clenched, and Aricia's father had known that, naturally or unnaturally, his time had come. He wanted only to see his daughter, and having seen her he let go his hold on life and slipped away contented. The funeral would not take place until Aricia could attend, so his body lay deep in the barrow, in a dark, quiet place surrounded by his bronze and silver ornaments, his chariot, his drinking cups, his beer, and his meat. As soon as the stone house was empty, the servants unpacked her wains, exclaiming over the richness of her tunics with their thin, fine texture and their silver and gold embroidery, the softness and length of her gay cloaks. But they thought her brooches and anklets and thin metal headbands crudely decorated, and they handled them with contempt under Venutius's watchful eye.

On the fifth day Aricia sat up and called for water and fresh fish. The servant went to her and saw the clear eyes of returning health, and Aricia ate and drank and slept again to the sound of the sheep calling on the long sloping hillside beyond the village and the dry smell of a sun that had come to stay. On the sixth day she got up and sat wrapped in blankets before her door. She leaned against the wall and closed her eyes, her sun-starved body basking in the gentle warmth, listening to the people coming and going. Sometimes the footsteps stopped and there were whispers, but she did not open her eyes, drowsing between reality and fantasy, and healing in the strong yellow light while the busy life of the village went on around her, bringing to her a certain pleasant stability. Her dreams had been dark and frightening, the dreams of fever, full of blood and darkness and the tortured faces of those she knew, but now she rested in the real world, and it made her inexpressibly glad.

On the seventh day she moved into the stone house, and that night she went, unsteadily but purposefully, to the great fire that had been lit outside the village just under the dimpled feet of the first long slope that stretched to a summit five miles away. It was twilight, warm and full of the scent of grass and wildflowers, and she sniffed the little breeze with pure delight as Venutius came to greet her, smiling, and her chiefs rose, crashing their swords on their shields and shouting her name. She sank cross-legged onto her cloak, and the sparks roared and leaped into the black, velvety sky now hung with winking stars. The whole village was there, along with chiefs and their wives and families from miles into Brigantia, and the laughter and chatter grew louder as the meat, smoking and dripping, was apportioned and the beer passed from hand to hand. Venutius squatted beside her and she talked to him quietly, stirred by the strength of him, glancing now and then at his rugged face, and he smiled slowly back at her, his eyes boldly meeting her own, feeling the urges within her yet warned by what he read in her eyes. It was the same way that Caradoc had been warned. There was calculation there, and cold reasoning, the flaws of insecurity and self-hate, but above all there was lust, for him or for power or just for a full life, he did not know. He was a warrior, a seasoned fighting man already scarred from many raids, and she was just a child. Or was she? He drank his beer reflectively, and she was silent. At last he stood and bellowed, and the company drew closer to him. The fire was dying, but still the night was soft and warm and no cloud hid the white crescent moon.

"It is time for Council," he shouted. "All slaves depart. All freemen draw near." No one stirred. The Brigantians kept few slaves, and even the servants were proud people, bereft of honor-price but not of freedom. Venutius took off his sword and laid it in the grass, and the chiefs swiftly followed suit. "Let the Druid speak first," he declared and sat down. Aricia stiffened and peered into the crowd. A man had risen and was moving forward, his white robe slashed with red in the light of the fire. He carried his cloak over one arm and he came and bowed perfunctorily to her, but his eyes stayed on the dark bulk of the hill behind her. Then he turned and an expectant hush fell. For a moment he did not speak. He looked up at the stars, and among the eager faces turned to him, and then began to walk quietly up and down before them, his hands behind his back.

"Freemen and women," he said, his voice friendly. "You gather tonight to elect a new ruler, someone to replace the one who has guided you for many years, and you gather also to welcome his daughter, returning after long years far from you, her people. To some of you, what I have to say will make you angry, to some it will come as words torn from your own doubting hearts, but I beg you all to consider them. You know me well, Brigantians. I come and go. I wander at will among the tribes, I bring to you the wisdom of my travels, and I also bring truths that it is good for you to hear. I am asking you not to elect Aricia, chieftain's daughter." Strangely, no whispering broke out, and Aricia felt the mood of the crowd concentrated utterly on the Druid in breathless anticipation. Beside her Venutius stirred but did not look at her. The Druid stopped his slow pacing and stood facing them all. He was so close to Aricia that his robe brushed her feet, and she drew them in under her. "My reasons are few, but damning. Day after day the refugees among our people from the stricken countryside of Gaul pour into Albion, fleeing from the slow march of Roman aggression, bringing with them tales of such horror and degradation that the tribes who give them shelter sometimes do not believe them. Where do these people go? They seek succor from you, from the men of the west, from the Cornovii. They make the long journey to the sanctuary of the holy island, but to the mighty Catuvellauni they do not go. Why?" He paused, and the crowd leaned toward him, their eyes shining in the flickering light. This man, Aicia knew, was no potboy when it came to the slow swaying of simple people. When he spoke again his voice was pitched lower, deeper. "Because the Catuvellauni have grown fat and arrogant on the wine of Rome. Because a freeman who does not love to eat from Roman dishes and barter in the Roman tongue is not safe, even among his own brothers! And this child of yours, this chieftain's daughter, has lived among them since her earliest days, drinking in the milk of Roman thought, lying on Roman cushions, enjoying every foreign luxury, while her sisters saw their children impaled on Roman spikes and their fathers chained to work in Roman mines. When you look at her, freemen, what do you see? I see a strange, unnatural being, half Catuvellauni and half Roman, but I do not see a free Brigantian!" He strode away abruptly, melting into the press of seated people, leaving dark hints to insinuate themselves into the minds of his audience.

They looked at her with the natural curiosity of her return overlaid with a dawning hostility. They looked at their chief tribesman, Venutius, with longing. They whispered and stirred, but no one rose to speak. At last they looked at her and waited and she knew she must get up and defend herself. She had never spoken in Council before and she was afraid, but she stood slowly, feeling the last vestiges of sickness weaken her knees and bring sweat to her neck. She looked far back, to where the ungainly huts blotted the field. What are they to me, these simple fools? she thought. Let them send me away and go back to their mutton and their filthy huts! But a mettle rose in her, and she spoke.

"People of Brigantia," she said, her voice low but carrying clearly. "I have heard myself described as half Catuvellauni and half Roman, and I stand amazed. Have the Druithin lost their famous powers of memory? Do they not remember that royal children leave their homes and go to other tribes, so that when they return to their own they may serve them better? And the sons of the chiefs often go to Mona, to the home of the Druithin, to learn all the wisdom of the ancients. Is this a new thing? Not to my father, who sent me to Cunobelin to learn." She did not mention that she had also gone under great pressure from Cunobelin, as a hostage, but Venutius knew and he raised his head and shot her a keen, cool glance. She went on, a strange thrill taking her, a slow rising excitement within her. "But sons and daughters return. My father went to the Coritani in his youth. Are the Coritani your friends, then? Do you not hate each other still, even as you hate the Catuvellauni? Then why do you suspect me? I have merely done as my father did, and his father before him. Look at me, freemen!" She pulled angrily at her hair, showed them her arms and her face. "Am I not raven-haired, and am I not fair-skinned as you are? I am Brigantian and you know it. And you also know the Druid's unspoken fears. I am a woman. Will I long for the little fields and gentle woods of the Catuvellauni? Will I miss my friends and seek to bind them to me, and in the end betray you, my true kinsmen, in my weakness?" Well, will you? Her own thought mocked her, and she lowered her arms and breathed deeply. "You have been ruled by a woman before, and she was a great warrior. I am the last of my line, a line that stretches back beyond the confines of Albion to the northern reaches of the places where the sun is always hot and strong. I am my father's daughter and thus your daughter, too, and I have an undisputed right to your loyalty. The Druid has played shamelessly on your fears, but I have no fine words with which to win your love. Perhaps you wish to consider the claim of Venutius, for he is well known to you." She had struck a chord. Some of the faces went blank and there was a general scuffling. "Then consider it. But remember that only I can prove royal blood, and if you cast me out you dishonor yourselves." She sat down abruptly, not knowing what she had said, her heart pounding, and Venutius immediately rose and began to speak.

His words were few for he had already come to a decision and he knew the people would do as he wished. Before his ride to Camulodunon he had been consumed with bitterness at the thought that he, with his vast honor-price and the adoration of all the tuath, should have to bow to a girl who spoke with the accent of the southlands and whose eyes would be full of disdain at the sight of the rough land he loved, and traveling with her had flung him further into turmoil. Her speech was heavily accented, yes. Her clothes were soft and rich, her eyes held mute rebellion and a cold repudiation of him and his kind, yet there were mysteries within her, layers to be peeled back, and a stubborn disregard for the hard discomforts of the journey that spoke of hidden strengths. He had been told by Cunobelin that she could fight and hunt, and hold her own among free people. He had not believed, yet now, remembering her silent doggedness as they rode hour by hour through mud and rain, he was not so sure. He wanted time to get to know her better and besides, he had vowed an oath to her father to serve her faithfully at the risk of his dishonor, and he valued his honor above all things. That, and his freedom. He had considered the loss of his honor when he had almost succumbed to the urge to murder her, but he had not considered the loss of his freedom.

"I do not care what you do, all of you," he said to the Council, "but I vowed my lord my sword and my life, and here is the daughter of my lord. Her claim is unanswerable and you know it. I do not care where she spent her childhood. I care only that she is home again, among the people of her tuath, and the goddess can once more run across the hills with the fleet lightness of her earliest days." He bent and swept up his sword, and flung it down before her. Then he went to regain his place at her side and she turned and smiled at him faintly. There was a pause in which she could sense indecision, then one by one the other chiefs, muttering and grumbling, did the same. She watched the pile grow, but her thoughts were on Venutius. What do you want of me, hillman? she thought. Why didn't you take your sword and knock off my head? She knew why, thought she knew, and the hollow places within her began to fill with another warmth.

At last she rose. "I accept your oaths," she said. "Take back your swords. Tomorrow we will sing for my father, and then we will begin our life together."

She and Venutius left the bright circle of the fire and walked slowly to her house. The moon was full risen now, caught in a wisp of bluish cloud, but the rest of the sky was clear, and she was tired, needing another healing sleep and another day of inactivity. They reached her door, and suddenly he reached inside his tunic, bringing out a small purse. He extracted a coin and held it up before her face. They both stood in the deep shadow of the gray stone wall and all she could see of him was the glint of moonlight on his fierce eyes and the pale movement of his fingers.

"Lady, do you see this?" he said softly. "This is a Brigantian coin, not well made, maybe, not silver, but clean, Lady. No Roman hand has ever touched it, nor Roman craftsman put his crude design upon it." He bit it automatically and stowed it away again. "Tell me, is it true that Cunobelin employs Roman artists and silversmiths in his shops and forges?"

"Yes, it's true."

He exclaimed in disgust, muttering something to himself in an undertone. "Do not take your people lightly, Lady," he said aloud. "The Catuvellaunian river hums day and night with the sounds of barter, but we also trade from the bays of our coast, for things we value above the fripperies Caesar sends Cunobelin. We trade for bright swords and helms of bronze, for pots and dishes made by those who follow the ways of our fathers. In return we give them sheep hides—and this." He delved into his tunic again and pressed something hard and cold into her hand. She stepped into the moonlight and looked. It was a thick bronze thumb ring, set with a pear-shaped stone of unusual weight, and its facets glittered balefully at her as she moved it to and fro. It was black. It had no instant appeal, it did not bring forth cries of admiration and envy, but as she looked at it, it drew her gaze ever deeper into itself, exerting an unwilling fascination and a desire to own, to stare forever. She handed it back.

"What is it?"

"It is jet, Lady, jet, as black as night. Not beautiful as the amethyst, or the bright corals the Catuvellauni love, but it is the stone of your country and reflects it with truth. It is a country of loneliness and secrets, hard and rough, yet it can compel if you will let it." He took a step and she raised her head, her breath stilling in her throat. A whiff of desire came to her from him and he put his large hands on her head, stroking her hair, and they came to rest on her slim shoulders. "It can also destroy," he whispered, "if you are weak, and bring to it fear and loathing."

On an impulse she stood on tiptoe and brushed the bearded cheek with her lips, but even as she felt a rush of gratitude toward him she also felt contempt, a recoiling from him and his wild people and this dirty place. Fumble all you will, you fool, she thought with an inward smile. Before long I will be able to do what I like with you, all of you, and your bays will be full of traders bringing me wine, and this place will rise high upon the earthwalls I will construct, and I will bring cattle to mingle with these stupid sheep. She moved gently from his grasp but not from his eyes. She had seen eyes like that before, watching her intently from the thick underbrush as she rode along the forest paths with Caradoc and Togodumnus, the eyes of an animal that did not reason its danger but sensed it.

Venutius smiled through thoughts gone suddenly dim and confused, and she smiled back, reaching for her doorskins. "You do not need to harangue me, my friend. I do not deny that I came here as a stranger, but I am young, and I prefer to face change and adventure rather than turn and run." With another thought she let the skins fall and turned to him again. "Tell me, Venutius, are the Druithin seen often in this land?"

"Of course. There are always one or two of them staying in the guest hut."

"I see. Well, a good night to you."

"Sleep in safety, Lady."

She went in, letting the skins fall into place with a soft sound behind her. Her servant had gone to her own bed but the fire danced on, and the shadows on the walls danced with it. She walked to her bed and sat down slowly, the night silence lapping her in peace for a moment. Then she lay back, picking up the talisman Gladys had given her and fingering it gently. The Druithin will have to go, she thought. Somehow I must see that the people turn against them, but it will not be easy and I will have to take much time and planning to accomplish it. The fire suddenly spat and a log rolled slightly. A deep grief seized her, a wave of homesickness. For two weeks she had not laughed, nor seen a single person with whom she could share the last fifteen years of her life. She was among strangers, and they would all, always be strangers. She was alone. She turned on her side and wept at last as the thing she had sensed while she hesitated at the border to her land, the dark, unknown thing, came closer.

In the morning, under a hot sun, the chiefs gathered outside her father's barrow. A fire had been lit, pale and powerless, dwarfed by the light that poured over and around it. All the freemen stood about it, Aricia with them, dressed in yellow and blue, and with gold circlet on her unbound hair and her sword strapped to her waist. Venutius stood next to her, his red hair cascading down his back and his tousled beard combed. He carried his shield slung over one arm and his helm was on his head, for they had come to salute a warrior, not an old, worn-out dotard. Her father's shield-bearer and his bard stood apart, the latter with his little harp in his arms, and at last the Druid came, his white robe shining in the sun. The sacrifices had been made while she lay tossing in her fever and his presence was not needed, but he was there out of respect, and some perverse show of almost impudent immunity caused him to come and stand beside her, smiling a greeting.

When the assembly was ready the bard walked to stand under the shade of the small earthmound and, after tuning his harp, began to sing. He sang of feasts long gone, of her father and his wife striding young about the hills in the pearly dawns, of herself as a baby. He told them of how her father had met the goddess by the sea and kissed her, and of how his rule thenceforth had been just and fruitful. When he had finished, her father's chiefs began to sing, softly at first, beating time on their shields with supple brown hands, their hair stirring in the wind. The sun glinted on their myriad bronzes— brooches, bracelets, thick torcs, all twisted and tortured into the nightmare patterns and suffocating tight-tangled curlicues of the northern artisans. They reminded Aricia of the strange shapes carved about the Great Hall at home, in Camulodunon, but here, where they belonged, they had a power and a life far beyond the dark, unheeded, smoke-dulled pillars where Cunobelin wove his lies. The song strengthened, took wings, soared into the clean air as others joined in, but the Druid was silent, and Aricia, tears trickling down her cheeks, did not know the words. The rhythmic majesty of the music and the sight of these great, bearded men leaning on their swords and singing moved her, and in a blinding moment of self-realization she knew she was not worthy of them, these innocent people of the unsullied hills. The music changed, became mournful, and died away, and the bard took it up again, singing of her father's slow aging around the fires of his middle age, his loneliness, his longing for the wife now lying peacefully in her long sleep under the heaped earth. The chiefs sang again, their chorus and the bard's high voice blending, and Aricia, already living on nerves stretched to their limit by the events of the past days, broke down, laid her head on Venutius's chest, and cried. He went on singing but his arm held her tightly to him, and she closed her eyes while the tears continued to well from beneath the white lids. When the singing was done the men stepped forward one by one, eulogizing their dead lord in brief poignant speeches. Then it was Aricia's turn. She went to the hole in the earthmound and turned to face them, feeling frantically for words that would not come. What can I say? she thought in a panic. Lies, only lies. Can I say that I loved him, that I missed him? Can I say that I spared him one thought when Cunobelin and I gambled the evenings away together? She swallowed more tears and began to speak, and once again that odd thrill of approaching power overtook her, so that words began to flow glibly from her red mouth, and deep silence fell. Lies! her mind screamed at her. All dirty, dishonoring lies! Then her voice gained strength, intoxicated with itself, and the tears ceased to fall as she began to realize that she was holding the people as the Druithin could do. Power expanded like a slow-rising sun within her, pouring a thrall over the wrapt gathering, and when she had spoken the last word and went back to her place, taking Venutius's hand, she did not know that Aricia had gone away and the embryo of someone new pressed Venutius's hand and smiled into his eyes with a promise and the invisible threads of a holding spell.

Winter, A.D. 40

CHAPTER FIVE

FEARACHAR SLIPPED OFF THE LEASHES and the dogs catapulted into the underbrush, their deep excited baying a deafening cacophony of confused sound.

"They have the scent!" Cinnamus shouted. "After them!"

"Don't lose them, Fearachar!" Sholto yelled. "Keep them in check!"

But the dogs did not respond to Fearachar's frantic whistling and the group plunged on their trail. It was another winter morning, still and cold. There had been a frost in the night, which had melted quickly in the sun, but here, under the trees, patches of white still lay, and the men's feet crunched the brittle grass, their breath rising as steam to hang in the branches above them and their faces red and pinched with cold. Togodumnus leaped a small bush and disappeared along the path, passing Fearachar and running out of sight, and Caradoc, his son, Llyn, and Cinnamus pounded after him. Caelte paused to fasten his cloak more tightly around his shoulders, then he picked up his spear and ran too, crashing through the trees. There was no need for silence now. The dogs had the scent and the boar would be very close, clumsily feinting this way and that, angrily darting to find a stream, or the densest bush in which to wriggle. Fearachar whistled again, but the dogs took no notice. He could hear the echo of their tumult somewhere off to his right and he plunged on, seeing the flick of scarlet as Togodumnus forged ahead. Caradoc,

Llyn, and Cinnamus soon caught up with him and together they stumbled on, Caelte panting behind them. Suddenly the trees thinned and they heard Togodumnus give a great shout.

"There he is! What a big one! Where are the nets?"

Caradoc pointed beyond the boar that stood still for a moment, wheezing and befuddled. "Vocorio and Mocuxsoma have them. They should be there, a little to the left. Where are those confounded dogs?" Fearachar whistled again in a rage, and at last the dogs came loping, red tongues hanging out. At the sight of them the boar charged again, away from the men and on into the brush and the dogs forged after him, fanning out in response to another whistle. "Tog, stay where you are!" Caradoc called. "Cin, Fearachar, take the right hand. Caelte, you and I will move ahead. If the nets are set where they ought to be we shall have him neatly trapped."

"My kill, my kill!" Llyn begged, his brown eyes fixed in pleading on his father, but Caradoc shook his head briefly.

"Not yet, Llyn. Your mother would never forgive me if you were hurt. You're not old enough." The eyes lost their spark, but Llyn shrugged philosophically and Caradoc smiled down at the tousled head. "Carry my spear," he offered, "and if I make the kill you can have a tusk."

"What is a tusk, father, compared to my knife in his throat?" Llyn said, but he hefted the long shaft proudly, and Caradoc ran on. Suddenly a wild, animal shriek went up, a call of pure rage, and a great squealing began. Togodumnus was tugging madly at his spear, entangled in a vine that snaked behind him, and Vocorio and Mocuxsoma struggled to hold the net while the boar thrashed, tossing his head sharply, his tusks and one foot wrapped in the tough leather. The dogs barked and ran up and down in a frenzy of excitement, and the little red eyes of the boar blazed at them even as he wrenched himself free.

"Look out!" Cinnamus screamed. "Vocorio, throw the net!" The man ran forward as the boar shook his head and charged straight at the nearest dog, his short legs drumming over the ground. The net fell over him and he rolled onto his back, threshing and squealing in a high-pitched agony of fear. Llyn shoved the spear at his father and ran forward, tugging at his knife, but Caradoc pulled him back firmly. "No, Llyn. Behave yourself."

"It is my kill," Togodumnus said, and he heaved his spear free of the vine and strode forward, but Caelte barred his way.

"No, Lord, it is mine," he said, and the boar was suddenly quiet, lying under the net as if dead.

"You killed three days ago," Togodumnus protested.

"And you yesterday," Caelte persisted, but Togodumnus refused to concede.

"That was only a deer," he said in an injured tone.

"Nevertheless, this boar is mine. Do you want to fight?" Caelte looked calmly into the sullen face but Togodumnus dropped his spear and turned his back like a spoiled child, shaking his head.

"Really," Llyn said loudly, "the boar is mine but father will not let me kill it."

Togodumnus turned back. "Of course not!" He came forward. "Watch this, Llyn, and you will know how wise your father is." He walked slowly to the boar, and Caelte watched anxiously in case he suddenly drew a knife and robbed him of his kill, but Togodumnus made no move to his belt. The boar still lay inert but its tiny eyes followed his every step. Tog came to a halt, raised a hand as though he held a knife, bent over, and the boar suddenly sprang to life with a grunt. It lunged at Togodumnus, its leather-held tusks scooping viciously to rend, and three of the strong leather thongs parted. Togodumnus skipped quickly away and the boar struggled furiously, one tusk stuck into the ground where Tog had stood a moment before.

"You see?" said Tog, grinning. "If you had gone to slit his throat he would have had you, Llyn, and even now you would be lying on the ground with your leg ripped to the bone."

Llyn smiled back. He loved his uncle very much, drawn to the sunny glow of well-being and radiant charm. He loved his father, too, but at the age of six he still feared and respected him too much to feel entirely easy in his presence. As for his grandfather . . . Llyn wrinkled up his nose and sheathed his knife. Cunobelin was like a fat, smelly old spider, crouching in his Hall all day, and Llyn avoided him as often as he could.

"Well, Caelte, get on with it," Togodumnus said, and Caelte took out his knife and circled the boar, waiting for the moment when the red eyes were distracted. Then he ran in, grasping a tusk and drawing the knife cleanly through the gray, bristled throat. Blood steamed on the white grass, rapidly melting a tiny pool of frost and showing the green blades beneath.

"A neat kill," Caradoc approved. Vocorio and Mocuxsoma waited for the twitching of the dying beast to subside, wary still, then began to tie its legs to the pole they had brought, and Caradoc turned to Fearachar. "The dogs are unruly," he said. "They will have to be worked a lot harder if they are to be ready to be shipped in a month.

78

That black one with the gray muzzle should be trained on his own. He hangs back until the others have done all the work. Then he hops in and shares the glory."

"Like someone else I could name," Fearachar grumbled, one eye on Togodumnus as he talked to Llyn. "Well, I had better have a word with the trainers." He stretched. "A good morning's hunting. Now for wine and hot broth." Vocorio and Mocuxsoma swung the pole onto their shoulders and started back to the track where the horses were tethered and a wain waited for the kill. Cinnamus, Llyn, Caradoc, and Togodumnus followed together, and Sholto and Caelte swung along behind them. Fearachar was left to catch the dogs and leash them, and the sound of his whistles and blows slowly faded.

"Was it really your kill, Caelte?" Llyn asked, and Sholto cuffed him playfully on the ear.

"Be patient, little cub. You have at least another year before you, and even then your father may not allow it."

"Then I shall have to go off on my own and do my killing in secret."

Caradoc laughed but there was a warning note to the sound. He put his arm across the sturdy shoulders, feeling a rush of pride, glad that the boy was showing signs of taking after him and not Eurgain, though he loved her. Llyn had his own dark brown hair, but there were red lights in it when the sun smote his head. The square chin, still molded with the soft bones of youth, was undeniably cleft, a true sign of the members of House Catuvellaun, and the body was well made, already muscled. Llyn walked with his father's regular, dogged stride that ate up the ground confidently, but he had Togodumnus's full-throated, infectious laugh that spread merriment. Sometimes, when Llyn was sunk in thought, Caradoc imagined that he saw Cunobelin in the veiled eyes and the secret smile, but Llyn was not often still enough to be plunged into introspection. He ran about Camulodunon and the surrounding country with three or four of his own friends and spent much time hanging around the stables, waiting for permission to ride the big horses. He had given up the chariot ponies a year ago, but sometimes he would grudgingly ride one to keep his sisters company.

Little Eurgain was five, blonde and headstrong, already chafing to ride something more spirited, and Gladys was four, dark like her aunt, a quiet child who never cried. She was disturbingly like the young Aricia, looking at the strange world of the Catuvellauni with haughty, wary eyes, and more than once, creeping to his knee, she had flung open the gate of Caradoc's memories. For a moment the tearing, aching need would be there in all its impossible sweetness, immobilizing him with the strength of its remembered odors and colors. Even now, seven years after Aricia had ridden away into the mist with tears in her eyes and her mouth set tight against the pain of parting, she could reduce him to almost physical impotence, and in the time it took to lift his daughter onto his lap he would have relived every frenzied encounter, every whispered word, every act of violent repudiation, and be once more obliged to chase the lingering memories away by an act of the will. He was more than happy with Eurgain and knew that he had made the right decision. He would rather lose his honor-price than her. Their seventh year together was almost over and he had teased her, asking her whether now she would take her herds and the children and return to her father, having had enough of married life. In the seventh year by custom she could have done it, but she only laughed. "I have had my eye on Cinnamus for a time," she had said, trying to keep a straight face. "He greatly interests me, but I think I prefer being first wife to you than second to Cinnamus."

"Cinnamus likes his women to be fierce and quarrelsome," Caradoc had flashed back, a tiny whip of jealousy flicking him. "He would not know what to do with you."

She had come close to him, her blue eyes still dancing. "But Caradoc," she had said smoothly. "He told me the other day that all men need some variety. Perhaps he tires of Vida's teeth and claws and wishes for a change." She had kissed him then before he could explode, her mouth still quivering with mirth, knowing that he and she were bound together forever.

Caradoc looked down at his son as they neared the edge of the wood. "Never hunt alone, Llyn. If you lay injured in the forest, who could bring you aid? There may not seem to you to be much difference between bravery and recklessness, but no man respects another who is reckless."

Llyn did not reply. They broke through the trees to find the horses waiting patiently and the stable servant sitting on the bank. He rose to greet them and they mounted, Llyn jumping off a humped root to fling his leg across his horse before it trotted away without him, and set off for home. The sun was bright but held only a frail, watery warmth, and the men were more than ready for a fire and hot wine. The wain creaked after them, laden with the boar and all their hunting gear, and Vocorio and Mocuxsoma perched on the back, singing, their legs dangling, as Llyn cantered up and down the path, shouting and hooting.

They led their horses under the cold shade of the gate and Vocorio and Mocuxsoma jumped down from the wain, leaving it standing beside the wall. The freemen would come and skin the beast, saving the tusks for Caelte, and the gear would be taken to the armorer for cleaning and mending. All of them walked past the stables, the kennels, up through the freemen's circle, and so to the flat ground before the Great Hall where a chill wind pulled at their cloaks and heightened the color in Llyn's already pink cheeks. A crowd was gathered there, standing in loose groups talking or squatting on the ground. Beyond them they heard the clash of weapons and they went forward to see. Llyn tugged excitedly at Caradoc's sleeve. "It's mother and Aunt Gladys!" he said. The chiefs and freemen made way for them and they found a place and sat. Llyn was pulled down beside Sholto and warned to be quiet. Any sudden cry or movement could end in tragedy on the practice ground where no killing was intended. Llyn knew this well and he sat very still, his eyes shining and his mouth open.

His mother and his aunt circled each other, swords high. Both women wore breeches and short tunics, and their hair was plaited and strapped tight to their waists. Their left arms were empty. Caradoc preferred Eurgain to work with a shield but she seldom did and neither did Gladys, though they knew that they ought to become used to the extra weight. Gladys had just shrugged when Cinnamus took her to task over it. "I am not likely to go to war," she had said, "and I have vowed never to raid again, so why should I be encumbered?" Cinnamus disapproved, everyone disapproved, but the women took no notice. Gladys's trainer called something and the two of them closed. Then, as swift as a gust of wind, Eurgain slipped under Gladys's upward swing and brought her sword in a neat horizontal slash that would have sliced her sister-in-law in half if Gladys had not seen it coming, continued her backswing, and spun away. Both were tired, and sweat ran down their faces and their breath came in little gasps. Gladys was the more powerful of the two, with a clean, forceful style, but Eurgain was lighter and quicker. They were well matched. Eurgain pressed her advantage, pursuing Gladys with a series of short slashes back, forth, back, forth, and the crowd tumbled to get out of the way. Then Gladys turned and stabbed. It was not a common ploy. The swords were meant for great slashing sweeps, not for close stabs, the points blunt though the blades were honed to a sharpness that would slice through a wisp of grass floating in the air. Nevertheless, the point of Gladys's sword grazed Eurgain's neck and dark blood welled and began to course down the front of her sweat-stained tunic. She ignored it, whirling low for another blow, arm singing down, but the trainer called "Enough!" and the women immediately dropped their swords, staggered to each other, and laid their heads on each other's shoulders, panting. Caradoc rose and went to them, Cinnamus joining him.

"Eurgain should train with me," Cinnamus said as they crossed the scuffed bare patch of earth before the doors of the Hall. "Her stroke is good but she throws herself off balance by pulling up and back too far."

"I don't think she cares enough about her skill to pit it against you and perhaps lose her head," Caradoc replied as they came up to Gladys and Eurgain, now sitting on the ground. They squatted, and Llyn flung his arms about Eurgain's neck. She winced.

"You were very good, mother," he said seriously, "but you keep your feet too close together for proper balance. One day Aunt Gladys will kill you by accident because you slipped."

Gladys smiled, wiping her face on her dirty tunic. "Aunt Gladys would not be so careless," she said. "I am always prepared for accident, Llyn, and your mother and I have been pitting swords against each other since before you were born. We know what to expect of each other. Did I hurt you, Eurgain?"

Caradoc eased back the neck of the tunic but the wound was not deep and she shook her head. "Not much. Well, Cinnamus, what did you think?"

"Llyn is right," he said promptly. "Part your feet and do not swing so high."

Gladys sighed. "I am tired and thirsty. And very dirty." She rose abruptly and walked away slowly and Eurgain rose also, a hand to her neck, the blood still seeping between her fingers.

"Llyn," she said, "run to the house and tell Tallia to prepare hot water. Caradoc, did you have a good hunt?"

"Not bad, but the dogs are very undisciplined. Caelte made the kill."

"I thought it was Sholto's turn."

"Actually," Llyn broke in, "it was my turn, but father . . ."

Caradoc slapped him on the rump. "Get about your mother's business!" he said, and Llyn ran for the house. "He wants so much to make a kill," Caradoc told her, "but even if I allowed it I don't think he has the strength yet to kill cleanly."

"He wants to fight with iron instead of wood, too," Cinnamus said. "He is a persistent child."

"Keep him at the wood!" Eurgain said sharply. "Don't give in to him, Cin."

"I have no intention of letting him kill himself," Cinnamus said, and Caradoc kissed Eurgain on one hot cheek and turned away.

82

"We need drink and food," he said, "and you need water and clean clothes." He and Cinnamus went into the Hall and Eurgain walked slowly up the hill to her house, hearing Tallia playfully scolding little Eurgain while the child laughed delightedly. Llyn came out but did not run to her. He waved and vanished in the direction of the kennels and she climbed the last few yards wearily, her body glowing but tired.

Cunobelin sat alone on blankets wedged into a corner of the Hall, his stiff, swollen hands around a drinking cup and his legs folded under him. None of his men were with him and Caradoc wondered angrily where they were. No chietain was supposed to walk, sit, hunt, or fight without at least two of his chiefs beside him, and it was suddenly brought home to Caradoc how old his father had become, how dull in wits and immovable in body. Cunobelin gazed in front of him, his face expressionless, and when Caradoc had eaten and talked for a moment more with Cinnamus, Caelte, and Sholto, he drew wine, picked out a handful of dried peas from the sack behind the door and went over to his father. Cunobelin's head turned slightly but he gave no other sign, and Caradoc sank cross-legged beside him. He saw Togodumnus and three of his chiefs come in but they settled themselves at the farther end of the long, dark room. Caradoc knew that they were discussing the hunt while Tog relived it with the gestures and words hallowed through a thousand years of storytelling. He wondered whether Adminius would return from his raid before this evening. Cunobelin had kept up a steady pressure on the Coritani in the last five years, and Adminius and sometimes Caradoc, himself, had spent much time lying cold and wet in the woods, waiting for night, in order to slip over the border to kill and to steal. The Coritani could do little. Cunobelin insulted them and drove them to a fury simply by creeping around their vaulted hill forts and striking deeper and deeper toward their capital.

They had no king, the Coritani. They were ruled by a Council and two judges who could never agree on whether it would be better to declare war on the Catuvellauni or keep protesting to Rome, and while they dithered, Adminius, Caradoc, and Togodumnus struck again and again. The Coritani hoped for great things when they sent angry emissaries to Rome. Tiberius had died after forty-five years of rule. He had been a just and clever man, farsighted, using the army and the law to create the Pax Romana, but he had had definite views on the place of Albion, and that place was outside the Pax. Albion was good for trade, but too expensive for conquest, and Tiberius declared his western border to be the coast of Gaul. Beyond that was the ocean, and the ends of the earth. But Tiberius was dead and

Caius Caesar strutted in Rome, a pimply seventeen-year-old, burning to show what he could do. At present he was uncomfortably close, nosing out conspiracy in Germania and massing his unruly, undisciplined legions for a push across the Rhenus, but Cunobelin and his sons dismissed him as they had dismissed Tiberius. Rome had tried Albion, and Albion had slammed the lid on Rome's fingers. There was no more to be said, and Caius could spend his time harassing his long-suffering generals and embarrassing the senate all he wanted. The Coritani hoped for a change of imperial policy toward the predatory Catuvellauni, but so far they could only hope, while Caius dithered in Germania and his troops rampaged through the countryside.

Caradoc sipped his wine and crunched on the peas, and Cunobelin seemed to ignore him. Caradoc could hear his labored breathing, the air wheezing in his lungs, and his glance strayed to the blue-tinged, arthritic fingers, bare of rings, for Cunobelin could no longer slip them over his swollen knuckles. At last Caradoc spoke gently. "Are you well today, father? Where are your chiefs?"

Cunobelin slowly swung his head. The tiny pig eyes that had always gleamed in mischief or wrath were sunken and filmed over, and the heavy flesh of his face now hung pendulous and white. The gray hair was undressed, hanging in greasy strings, and Cunobelin's neck was so enlarged and puffy that the ring of his golden torc bit deep, half-buried in the folding, pale skin. He took a long time to smile at his son, if it could be called a smile. It was more of a grimace, and a waft of sour breath assailed Caradoc's nostrils, wine fumes and a stomach in turmoil. "When am I ever well these days, Caradoc?" the old man said hoarsely, with great effort, and Caradoc realized that Cunobelin was deeply, soddenly drunk. "As for my chiefs, if you can find them, ask them yourself what they are doing. They will not hesitate to tell you. They plot against me, and thus they are ashamed to look me in the face." He raised his cup with both hands and took a long swallow, and wine dribbled from the corner of his mouth and trickled down his neck. Then he put his head against the wall and closed his eyes, breathing stertorously.

Caradoc did not answer immediately. He knew the chiefs of the tuath, all of them, and he knew that if they had grievances they would shout them out at Council and not go slinking about behind their lord's back. It was far more likely that his condition alarmed them and they did not know what to do. For a year Cunobelin had not left the Hall. He ate and slept there on a pile of old blankets. He made Cathbad sing to him by the hour the songs of his life, his loves and conquests, his dreams, his hundreds of raids, but not of his failures, not of the skeins of ambition collected to weave into a picture that still lay, its colors fading, in the dimness of his mind. His chiefs could see that the end was coming, everyone could see it, but Cunobelin was as strong as he was complex and he lived on, weakening but still fighting back death, the last enemy. Eventually the interest of the tuath had declined and they had gone about their business. The chiefs did not want to kill him, Caradoc knew that. They would rather he died by his own will, if not by his own hand, but things were bad. It was obvious that the goddess tottered unsteadily, her powers of protection waning. The summer had been wet and many of the crops had rotted in the ground and could not be harvested. There had been a late frost in the spring, and many calves had died. Something would have to be done, but they stayed their hand out of love for the man who had raised them all to unimagined wealth and power and given them a kingdom. All this Caradoc pondered as he listened to the conversations going on around him, well away from the invisible circle of isolation that Cunobelin had drawn. Then he took the cup firmly from the cold hands and threw it across the Hall.

"You have drunk enough," he said. "If you are to die, then at least do it as our fathers have done, with clear eyes set steadily to the next life and a laugh on your lips! What ails you? Are you afraid?" That word went deep as Caradoc knew it would, pricking somewhere under the thick layer of intoxication and despair, and Cunobelin grunted and heaved himself upright, steadying himself with hands beside his knees, on the floor.

"No, I am not afraid," he rasped venomously, his words slurred and broken. "I have seen death too many times to be afraid. I sit and remember all the things I have not done and an anger curdles within me. My body will not obey me anymore, but my spirit leaps and dances, mocking me, so I drink and I wait. Perhaps they will have the guts to dispatch me after all." He attempted a chuckle, gasping and shaking, and Caradoc looked away, sickened. He had seen Cunobelin roaring drunk, fighting drunk, but never like this, twisted and bitter, huddling in his corner like some foul insect and brooding.

"Perhaps it is time they did," he said, his grief and disappointment strangling him. "And if they do not, perhaps I will. A sacred knife, father, flung in the sunlight, an honorable death for the good of the tuath. You care only for yourself, sucking on your dead dreams of conquests that can never be, while the Dagda hates the goddess for her ugliness, and the power of the tuath is shaken. Kill yourself, die with pride! What has happened that you squat here in the dark and destroy us all?" He got up clumsily, throwing his empty cup after his father's and tossing the peas on the floor. He went out, mad to breathe fresh, untainted air, to see men walking and laughing. Togodumnus's sharp eyes had seen what had passed and he followed Caradoc, running to catch him up as he strode down the hill.

"What did he say to you to make you so angry?" he asked curiously.

Caradoc stopped and Togodumnus saw his face. "He will not die," Caradoc said, a pain beyond tears making his voice break. "He sits there consuming himself day after day, but today he was worse than I have ever seen him and I fear for us all. If he lingers another season the Catuvellauni could once more be nothing but a few scattered kin wandering in the forests. And he is strong. He could wake and ride again if he chose!"

"He doesn't choose," Togodumnus replied. "He has run out of time and he knows it, and it galls him beyond bearing. The chiefs want to kill him but they don't dare."

"How do you know?" Caradoc asked sharply, and Togodumnus showed a crooked smile.

"Gladys told me. They came to her because she knows him better than any of us, but she sent them away and told them to make up their own minds. I think she is disappointed in him too." Caradoc did not trust himself to speak again, but left his brother without looking at him, and went on toward the gate.

Adminius returned that evening with his chiefs, driving thirty head of Coritani breeding stock before him. The night's feasting had begun and the Hall was full. He went straight to Cunobelin, who was drinking again in his corner, and gave him a full account of the raid, but Caradoc, watching them, noted that his father gave no sign of having heard a word, or even of being aware that his eldest son squatted beside him. After a moment Adminius rose and went and sat among his own chiefs and Cunobelin continued to drink. "It was a successful raid, apparently," Cinnamus whispered in Caradoc's ear, "but I think Cunobelin is wrong to push so hard and so fast. Any day now we may find ourselves facing a maddened Coritani war band, and we with no lord to lead us in battle."

Sholto had heard. He leaned over Caradoc to where Cinnamus was mopping up his gravy with a piece of bread. "I disagree," he said. "We have three lords to lead us, Adminius, Caradoc, and Togodumnus. Let the Coritani come. I, for one, would welcome a clean fray for a change." Sholto then retired to finish his meat.

Caradoc stared into the fire, his chin cushioned in his hand. We have no lord, he thought, for surely the man who was once my father, the fat hulk in the corner, is no longer lord, and the Council sits in silence night after night, powerless without a ricon. But Adminius is the eldest. It is his place to act. Why should Tog and I take the responsibility? He knew that Adminius would shrink in horror from patricide, steeped in Roman mores as he was, and his thoughts went round and round, getting narrower and narrower as the night progressed. His little girls left Eurgain and came to him, snuggling onto his knee, and he held them and kissed them, but still his mind would not be still. Servants flung more logs on the fire and the sparks showered around him. Cunobelin did not call for music and Cathbad sat with Gladys, his harp across his folded legs, but Gladys's eyes, like Caradoc's, strayed often to the dark corner from which emanated an almost visible odor and the shadow of the power that had once been.

He saw Tallia hovering by the door and he sent the girls to bed. He was tired too, and his head ached. At last he rose, Cinnamus with him, but just then a sudden, frozen silence fell. All eyes swiveled to the corner behind him and he whirled round, the quality of the silence causing him to reach for his sword. The shadow in the corner was moving. It stirred, grew tall, and Cunobelin stepped unsteadily into the firelight. In the startled hush he staggered forward and came to a halt, swaying, in front of Caradoc. Cinnamus moved, drawing closer to his lord, and Caradoc felt Togodumnus come up quietly behind him, for the glaring red eyes, the bared teeth, belonged not to the father he had known but to some renegade old boar. Cunobelin was struggling, marshaling all his forces to speak, but Caradoc's hand remained on his sword hilt and the men with him were poised for whatever might come, for all knew how the wild boar could feint defeat and yet rise at the last and maim and tear in a paroxysm of malevolent and reckless hate.

Cunobelin spoke, his voice a cracked, almost incoherent rumble, his breath a cloud of foul odor. "Kill yourself, die with pride you say to me, my son, with the callous ease of youth, you who have killed but not faced an enemy who will not be turned aside. I can wrench no hostage from the darkness that waits for me, and he comes for me without pity, the Chieftain of the Night." His head dropped toward his massive chest but he lifted it again with a monumental effort, and the company hung breathless, watching the final disintegration of a once mighty man.

"One of you," he shouted, searching the dimness for the faces of his sons, "one of you will pick up my cloak, and wear the torc of ricon, and then beware! For death will stalk you too, even if you live in pride and with contempt for him as I have done. Greedy and pitiless brutes that you are, come then, and slay me!" He fumbled at his belt, trying to draw his sword, but no one moved.

Caradoc stood rooted in a terrible paralysis that gummed his tongue to the roof of his mouth and turned his limbs to stone. He felt a hand steal into his own. It was Eurgain, white and shocked. "Do something, Caradoc," she whispered. "Don't let his memory be sullied by this awful madness," but still he could do nothing and Cunobelin began to cry soundlessly, his hand falling from his waist. All at once he lunged at them and Cinnamus drew his sword with a ringing clatter, but the old man rushed past them, staggering out the door. Gladys hurried after him, calling his name, and Cathbad ran also. Cinnamus sheathed his sword, Togodumnus made for the door, and then suddenly the whole company surged into the night. Still no one broke the silence. Caradoc, with Cinnamus, Sholto, Vocorio, and Caelte, pushed his way to the front and pelted after Gladys, heedless of the cold wind, the clear, star-dusted sky. They could hear Cunobelin shouting somewhere beyond the last circle, and Gladys was still calling, a note of pleading and fear in her voice. They ran, their feet falling lightly on the frost-hard ground, and they found Gladys leaning against the wall of the stable.

"He's gone," she managed. "Taken Brutus and his horse." Caradoc made as if to plunge into the stable, but Togodumnus pulled him back. "Let him go, Caradoc," he said urgently. "You heard how he spoke to us. It's you and me, now, and Adminius. Let the old fool go!" With an oath and an unthinking savagery, Caradoc wrenched himself free and sent his brother spinning.

"This is not the way!" he shouted. "To your horse, Tog!" The stable servant, under Gladys's shouted command, was already leading out two horses and Caradoc tore the reins from his grip and leaped up. "Move, Tog, move!" he hissed, his eyes already on the gate standing open, and Togodumnus reluctantly swung himself onto the beast's back, aware suddenly of the people who clustered around them. Eurgain stood beside Gladys. She was cloakless and shivering, but she seemed not to notice, and Adminius stood there also, his arms folded across his broad chest. He had not gone for a horse, and Caradoc, already thundering toward the gate, knew that his older brother would presently walk back up the hill to his own comfortable hut, drink some more, and calmly await any news. He jumped to the ground, led his horse quickly down the steep path and across the dyke, mounted again, conscious of Togodumnus behind him, and together they whipped at their beasts and galloped toward the black smudge of the wood.

For two hours they hunted, impeded in their tracking by the night. While Togodumnus whistled for Brutus, Caradoc often got down and knelt on the crisp grass, searching for the hoofmarks of Cunobelin's mount, but the frost was hard and the ground frozen. There were tracks but they were old, made when the mud was thick and soft, and then iced into iron-hard pits. He learned nothing but he and Tog did not turn back, riding ever deeper into the forest that closed about them in the cold solitude of early winter. At last they drew rein and sat looking at each other, baffled.

"Perhaps he did not come this way," Togodumnus offered. "He may have gone east to the river, and from there down to the sea."

But Caradoc shook his head briefly, thinking. He was sure that Cunobelin had made for the woods in the mindless flight of a dying beast, seeking without reason a dark hole in which to crawl and suffer alone. If they gave up now his father might never be found, and if they went back to Camulodunon and waited for Cunobelin's horse to come home in daylight the task would be impossible. "We'll just have to stay here and listen for the horse," he said reluctantly. "Are you cold, Tog? We could light . . ." But just then Togodumnus flung back his head, making an impatient gesture with his hand and Caradoc fell silent. They sat uneasily, craning their ears, and far away they heard it, the whining.

"This way!" Togodumnus said, and they set off with no path to follow, dismounting and leading their horses, moving quietly through the thick tangle of dead briars and trailing vines that hung motionless in their way. The low, bewildered whining grew louder. Brutus heard them coming and ran to meet them, his tail between his legs and his half-severed ear flopping. They quickly tethered the horses and drew their swords as if by unspoken, tacit agreement, why they did not know. There was a growing atmosphere of danger, a strange new coldness reaching to wrap them in its spell, and they kept together while Brutus went and sat by the horses and would not come when Togodumnus called him softly.

Then they saw him. Caradoc caught a pale glimmer on the ground, and with an exclamation he ran forward and Togodumnus followed, the sword held tight in his grasp. Cunobelin lay huddled against the trunk of an oak, his head bent below one shoulder and his legs flung out before him. As his sons bent over him, the faintest whisper ran through the naked branches high above, a half-mocking, half-sorrowful sigh of wind, and in the strengthening moonlight the black bars of shadow passed over his face, swaying back and forth, but the eyes did not move. They only stared up at the pair, empty and poignantly defenceless, bereft of all the intricately woven cloaks of deceit, of plot and counterplot, that had long veiled them, and the gray hair had settled into the long grasses. "His neck is broken," Togodumnus said. "Look at the trail he left behind him."

Caradoc peered into the gloom ahead, seeing the branches snapped and hanging drunkenly onto the forest floor, the clumps of bramble violently cloven through, and he looked down on the loose, still form, marveling. "What a ride! His horse must have stumbled, or thrown him, and he must have died instantly. We had better get him home, Tog. We'll put him on my horse and I'll ride behind you." They hesitated for a moment, not yet willing to lay hands on him, not willing, in the very helplessness of his heavy body, to admit an ending. But they were tired and cold and they knew that the rest of the kin would be congregated in the Great Hall, hanging about the fire, waiting for news. Finally Caradoc bent and took Cunobelin gently under the shoulders, and Togodumnus wrapped his strong arms about the thighs that weighed like two chunks of stone. Together they staggered to the horses with their burden, their sinews cracking and their breath puffing into white clouds around their heads. Somehow they raised him, laying him across the horse's broad, warm back. His head had not moved, so sudden and complete had been the neck's shattering. Then Caradoc wearily eased himself up behind his brother and they set off slowly, and Brutus padded dejectedly by his master's dangling heel.

They walked the horses right to the door of the Hall and then dismounted, and Gladys came running out, white and distressed. When she saw their burden she stopped, shock taking all expression from her thin face, but Caradoc went to her and spoke quietly.

"No, Gladys, we did not find him in the woods and slay him as he wandered, though we would have done so if necessary, you know that. He had a fall and broke his neck. It was not the most honorable end for him, but better than many." She seemed to relax then, and she sighed, going to the body and putting a hand gently on the bloodied head. Behind her the members of the tuath drifted, and Caradoc sensed relief, not sorrow. Cunobelin had outlived his tribal value, and though they would remember him with respect and even awe, and listen time and again to the songs and poems of his reign, they were glad that new blood would lead them and a new era was beginning. Togodumnus walked straight into the Hall, his thoughts already on fire and wine, but Gladys, Caradoc, and Eurgain paced beside the horse as it carried Cunobelin to the guest hut, and three of Cunobelin's chiefs went with them to see to the body. It would be washed and dressed in gold-embroidered tunic and breeches. The hair would be combed and his helm set upon his head, and his sword placed in his hand. Gladys left them, and Eurgain and Caradoc wended their way slowly to their little house. Llyn hovered at the door, his shining head haloed in the glow of the light behind him, and when he saw his father he ran down the hill to meet him.

"Father, what has happened!? Is Cunobelin found?"

Caradoc, obeying some instinct that bent him with a need to hold his son, went down and kissed and enfolded him, feeling the heat of the strong young body, the thick hot blood, the beating of the healthy heart. "He's dead, Llyn. He galloped into the forest, and the goddess took him. It was a right and proper death."

"Oh." Llyn shrugged his father off and turned back to the door. "He would rather have died in battle, I think, but he didn't have the strength. He waited too long. Well, I will go to bed." He yawned until his jaw cracked, pushed back the doorskins, and slid into his bed. Caradoc and Eurgain followed. The room was warm and dimly lit, full of the soft sounds of sleeping children. Llyn murmured a good night to them, already set to plunge into his dreams of hunting and rabbit snaring, and the little girls stirred, their faces flushed and loose. Caradoc put wood on their fire, then he and Eurgain slipped into the adjoining room where the curtain was drawn back from their big bed and the flames of their own fire flickered restlessly, nudged by the draft from Eurgain's window, now tacked tightly shut. Caradoc sank onto a chair and leaned back, closing his eyes, and Eurgain quietly removed his cloak, took the torc carefully from his neck, and slipped the boots from his damp feet. She reached for his bracelets but he caught her wrist, pulling her down onto his knee, and for a while they sat without moving, arms about each other, his chin on the top of her dark gold, warm-smelling head. The night was silent. Far away they heard an owl hoot twice and Eurgain fancied that she caught the echo of a wolf howl, so distant that it might have come from another world where Cunobelin walked, young and free once more.

She stirred but did not leave her husband's encircling arms. "What happens now?" she asked. "What will the Council do, Caradoc? Will they elect Adminius?" She was uneasy, and she sensed that her question had also awakened a disquiet in Caradoc. He tightened his hold on her and she felt him shake his head.

"I don't know. Adminius is very sure of the vote, and for a long time he has been strutting about like a ricon already, but if I were a chief I would think twice before laying my sword at his feet."

"Why?"

"He's too much of a thinker, Eurgain, and not enough of a fighter. Besides, he spends too much time with the traders."

She sat up and he released her. "What do you fear? That Adminius will do more for Rome than send hides and slaves and dogs?"

"Perhaps. And the chiefs want war. They are restless and quarrelsome. They will vote for Tog."

"No!" She got off his knee and stood looking down on him, a rush of love and protective jealousy filling her. The square face framed in dark hair, the warm, smiling mouth, the brown, steady eyes, she knew him so well, better, she thought, than he knew himself, and she found it hard to believe that none of the hints and whispers rife in the tuath had reached his ears. She began to undress slowly, dropping her anklets and circlet on the floor by the bed, pulling her blue tunic over her head, and loosening her hair. He watched her with satisfaction, waiting for her to speak again. She always took her time, his Eurgain. She was never in a hurry, and her words were always worth waiting for. She sat on her stool, holding out the comb, and he got up and took it from her, and drew it through the heavy tresses with long, slow strokes, and she closed her eyes and smiled. "How pig-headed you are, Caradoc," she said. "What do you think of all the time?" She opened her eyes and took up the bronze mirror, holding it so that she could see his face as he worked. "The whole tuath is divided into factions. Some favor Tog, and a few Adminius, but most of the chiefs are declaring that they will vote for you." His hands were stilled and his eyes met hers in the mirror, then he resumed his slow combing. The hair under his fingers was gleaming in the firelight and he lifted it free and sifted it thoughtfully.

"If I am elected Tog will fight me," he said, "and no matter what, I will refuse to kill him. Adminius will not fight. He will immediately begin to plot and make trouble. What of Gladys? Her claim is just as strong as mine." He went on combing though the hair fell straight and tangle-free, feeling her calm strength flow toward him, and presently she tugged her head away and put down the mirror, swiveling to face him, placing her hands in his. The comb slid to the skins.

"They will not elect Gladys while there are men in the kin to take the ricon's torc," she said, "you know that, Caradoc. I think you ought to prepare for a stormy Council meeting." He began to undress and she went to the bed and got under the covers, lying on her side with her head pillowed on one arm. Then he came to her swiftly and she held back the blankets for him. In the other room Llyn began to snore, and little Gladys cried out in her sleep. Caradoc lay on his back with an arm around her and she snuggled into his shoulder. He turned and kissed her forehead, but they lay with eyes open, their thoughts seeking the other's, meeting, meshing. At last she whispered, "Caradoc, there is a way of compromise."

"I know," he said shortly, and long after she had relaxed against him, her slow breaths warming his chest, he gazed into the darkness of the curtains and pondered.

The next day passed slowly. Caradoc took some of his chiefs and visited his breeding stock to discuss the coming season with Alan. Cinnamus, Vocorio, and Mocuxsoma went to the river to gossip with the traders and Llyn went with them, streaking up and down the bank, climbing on and off the barges while the men sat and talked desultorily, exchanging the news and watching the water glide by. Eurgain and Tallia took the little girls and went riding, for though the rain clouds had come in the night to hang black and thick over the town, the rain held off and the day had warmed. Togodumnus and Adminius spent the time in Adminius's hut counting boars' teeth, laughing over old raids, drinking beer, and watching each other. Their minds were far from hunting or stealing, and their eyes tried to ask the questions that would uncover a new hostility in each other as if they were afraid of plain speech. Only Gladys sat outside the hut where Cunobelin's body lay guarded by his hoary chiefs. Her knees were drawn up under her black cloak, her chin was on her knees, and her eyes remained blank while her mind seethed with questions and propositions, exploring one avenue the future might take after another. She found herself longing for a seer and a Druid, the one to tell the omens and set her fears at rest, and the other to take charge of the Council. But she knew that the Great Hall would be full of inquisitive Romans, traders and her father's own craftsmen, all wanting to hear what their future would be, and no Druid dared cross the country of the Catuvellauni unless he was acting as guide for some chief. Down on the flat land before the gate, beside the line of barrows where his ancestors rested, Cunobelin's funeral pyre grew, and the day wore on.

The evening's feast was brief. Only the children and a few freemen felt lighthearted enough to laugh. The rest of the people, chiefs and freemen and women, ate quickly and went away. Adminius did not come to the Hall at all, and neither did Gladys. Togodumnus called for music, but both Cathbad and his own bard refused to sing, and Caelte refused also, keeping his temper with difficulty. Caradoc dismissed him, fearing a scene, and Togodumnus came and squatted beside him, smiling gleefully. Cinnamus glowered at him, obviously wanting very much to be dismissed also, but Caradoc only signed to him to take his place and hold himself ready for action, his hands speaking in the language all his chiefs knew. Togodumnus smiled all the wider. He seemed very happy about something, and his light brown eyes sparkled at them and his darting hands played soundless music. The Hall was almost empty now, and the fire dying, the shadows lying long across the floor. The wrinkled head hung quietly on his pillar, the weird leaf tendrils and deadly curling vines writhing about him. Togodumnus hitched himself closer to Caradoc, sat and crossed his legs, and looked at Cinnamus out of the corner of his eye, but Cinnamus carefully kept his gaze fixed down on his feet.

"It's you and I, Caradoc, just as I said," Togodumnus declared. "Adminius will not be elected. Cunobelin's chieftains told me so." He leaned closer and Cinnamus stiffened, but Caradoc, looking deep into the bright, feverish eyes of his brother, saw something there that he had never seen before, a burning, naked flame of ambition whose light could not be concealed. "What I want to know is this," Tog pressed on. "If I am elected, will you fight me?"

Caradoc continued to look into those baleful eyes, searching for the gaiety and good-humor and finding only a driving force of reckless self-love. Was this a momentary fit, the kind of mood he was subject to from time to time, or had his brittle, unstable character changed under the pressure of his nearness to power? Caradoc glanced away.

"If you are elected in the proper manner, of course I will not fight you," he said. "Why should I? In any case, such a thing is forbidden once the vote is cast."

"I know, but it's happened before." He blinked, hooding his eyes, and the fire seemed to go out, but Caradoc could see the embers glowing still when he looked back.

"And what if I am elected?" he countered. "Will you accept the decision quietly, Tog, or will I have to kill you?" He knew that he would not kill Tog, and the compromise which had occupied his mind all day would work, he thought, providing Tog had a shred of dignity left.

Togodumnus laughed shortly, bunching a fist and bringing it to Caradoc's chin. "What makes you think you'll be chosen?" he asked. "But if you are, I'll fight. I want the Catuvellauni, Caradoc, for my very own."

Cinnamus broke in. He had listened to the conversation in an ever mounting anger and now he could not contain himself. "Nobody owns us!" he hissed. "We belong to ourselves, Togodumnus ap Cunobelin, but we allow our royalty to direct us, that's all. If you fight and kill my lord then you must fight and kill me, and then Vocorio, and Mocuxsoma, and all the other chiefs who will not be slaves to you or any. Only with men like Sholto will you have success, for he is less than a man." The inference brought an immediate flush to Togodumnus's face and he tried to spring to his feet, his hand on his hilt, but Caradoc grasped him and forced him back to the skins.

"Sholto?" he questioned sharply. "What have you been up to, Tog?"

Togodumnus pulled his arm free and shook down his sleeve, scowling at Cinnamus. "Nothing!" he snarled. "Ask the Ironhand, whose long nose is ever poked into everyone else's business. But you ask too late. I will be ricon, Caradoc, and don't try to stop me." He rose in

94

one lithe motion and strode away, his sword rattling in its scabbard.

Caradoc turned to Cinnamus. "You forget yourself," he said coldly. "You should know better than to interfere between two lords, and besides, I will not allow you to deliberately goad Tog into another fight."

Cinnamus looked at him calmly, and a tiny smile came and went on his mouth. "Lord," he said quietly, "if I goad him long enough I will have the pleasure of killing him. He is souring, and the pranks of his youth are no longer sufficient for him to vent his energies. He is becoming a rogue boar, your brother, the black moods coming more frequently and staying longer. Beware him, Lord."

Caradoc said nothing, aware that Cinnamus spoke not only from observation but also from a deep personal dislike, and perhaps his words were tinged with exaggeration. Tog had always been a creature of moods, flying from elation to glumness and back to elation, a fey, dancing spirit living from impulse to impulse. But was he really changing? "What of Sholto?" Caradoc demanded, and Cinnamus narrowed his green eyes in amusement.

"Sholto is very pleased with himself and cannot curb that spiteful, gossiping tongue of his. Togodumnus tried to bribe him. He has been going about among the chiefs, offering them cattle and money—not openly, Lord, but in the manner of hints, telling them that wealth can be theirs if they vote for him. He began this long before Cunobelin ailed to his death, and I am surprised you knew nothing of it. Most of the chiefs turn a deaf ear, but Sholto is most definitely interested."

Caradoc did not know whether to laugh or to rush after Tog and slice off his head, but laughter prevailed and he chuckled dryly. "How childish he is! He would denude himself of his honor-price in exchange for a few noncommittal words. As for Sholto, get rid of him, Cin. I made a mistake when I took his oath. Tog is welcome to him." They sat in reflective silence for a while. The Hall was empty, but in Cunobelin's corner the blackness still harbored a pale, lingering presence and the shrouded vestiges of a now impotent power. Caradoc wondered whether his father had foreseen the faltering indecision of the Council and the inevitable division of the family. Probably. Cunobelin would have laughed at it, though, and dared fate to gamble as it would. He got up slowly, Cinnamus rising with him, and they left the Hall, their footfalls echoing drearily to the vaulted roof. Tomorrow they would burn Cunobelin and then . . . Then another tomorrow, bringing with it a wind of change that would blow away the past and bring the future down among them like a howling gale. He said goodnight to Cinnamus and went down to the gate, but instead of passing through it he turned aside and climbed the earthwall, sitting high above the river valley in the darkness, shrouded in his cloak, his hair ruffled by the night wind. He thought long and deeply, knowing that his life and the good of the tuath hung upon a slender thread, and that thread was his brother's ability to accept the only alternative that was open. Then slowly, peacefully, a sense of destiny took him and stilled his thoughts as he struggled to anticipate the Council's decision, and whichever way he turned the eye of his mind he saw only himself alone. Of Togodumnus there was no trace.

CHAPTER SIX

T HE TUATH GATHERED by Cunobelin's funeral pyre in a cold, late dawn of light that silvered only the edges of the heavy clouds and then faded again. All were arrayed in their best, and the otherwise sullen morning was gay with scarlet and blue, red, yellow, and white. The chiefs wore their bronze helms and carried their coral-studded, pale pink and blue enameled shields, laying their arms along the massive crests, their spears a thicket of iron-tipped formidability. Caradoc stood with Togodumnus and Adminius, each of them surrounded by his chiefs.

Caradoc wore a cloak striped with blue and scarlet. Gold bracelets glinted dully on his arms, and his brooch was of amethyst set in gold. He wore the sword given to him by his father when he had reached his manhood and had made his first raid. It was an iron sword, plain-hilted, but its scabbard was bronze, worked in a pattern of sea-waves, the curl of each wave set with a pearl. His torc was also of gold, the torc of royalty, a twist of bright metal ending at each tip in the open mouth of a hound. He rested proudly on his shield and waited quietly, the freemen and freewomen of his train spreading out behind him to the bulk of the earthwall and the wooden gate.

Eurgain waited also, holding little Eurgain and little Gladys by the hand. She was wearing a tunic of russet embroidered with silver flowers, and her cloak was of russet, also, slashed in green. A thin circlet of plain silver adorned her head, and this day she and Gladys had left their swords propped up inside the door of the Hall.

No wind blew. It was perfectly still, as if the Dagda and the goddess held the breezes tight in their hands out of respect for the man who came now, borne on a great bier by four of his chiefs. Caradoc turned, watching the slow, ponderous sway of the thing, feeling no grief but a deep pride that this was his father, a man who had lived to the full and died well, a man whose place it would be impossible to fill. Togodumnus watched also, pride lighting his eyes, and Caradoc had no doubt that Tog believed himself the one who would not only emulate but surpass Cunobelin in word and deed. Behind the bier Cathbad and Cunobelin's shield-bearer walked, the latter carrying the heavy shield high over his head, the last office he would perform for his master. Gladys came next, her rough black cloak thrown back to reveal a plain white tunic. Her only ornament was a cluster of pearls worn high on her shoulder. It was obvious to all that she was suffering, yet her head was held high and the tears slid unbidden down her face. The chiefs halted for a moment beside the pile of brushwood and logs, shifting their grip. Then at a cry they lifted Cunobelin, setting him high above the silent hordes of people, and Adminius, Togodumnus, and Caradoc moved forward to take the flaring torches from the servants' hands. Immediately a great clamor arose as the chiefs drew their swords and beat upon their shields, crying out, "Ricon! Ricon! A safe journey, a peaceful journey!" and Caradoc saw Llyn grimace and cover his ears as he bent and thrust the flame into the wood. It burst into crackling red fire, the little twigs curling and already ash gray, and the shield-bearer ran and placed the shield gently on Cunobelin's bosom. Then Cathbad plucked a string of his harp and the note vibrated sweetly, carrying far, mingling with the roar of the greedy flames.

"I will sing to you of Cunobelin," he said, "and the getting of his honor-price." Then all the people stood still and Cathbad took them back in time, and they found themselves remembering incidents they had forgotten years ago, the feasts, and famines, the times of laughter and the times of sorrow. Such was the bard's consummate skill that Cunobelin seemed to stand before them as he had so many times before, his burly arms folded, his gray hair whipping about his wrinkled face, those tiny eyes surveying them all with more than a hint of amusement and malice. Gladys had sunk to the ground and covered her head with her cloak. Caradoc watched the greedy, indecent haste of the flames, eating slowly upward while his father waited, hands folded calmly under the protection of his shield, his sword beside him. Now Cathbad sang of the times of tension, the preparations for war with the Brigantians, the embassies and emissaries, Cunobelin's sealing of a pact with the Coritani that allowed his war band an unscathed passage to the borders of Brigantia, and at last the coming of a small, black-haired girl.

Caradoc felt Eurgain's eyes sweep over him and he kept his face tight while the memories, unbidden and unwanted, floated like mist in his mind. Seven years. His throat tightened with the old, sweet longing and he bowed his head, closing his eyes against the present. . . . There will be a hole . . . ah, you witch, he thought. They say you are married now, to that tall, fierce son of the hills whose beard fell to his waist and whose hand was never far from his sword. I suffered when they told me. But I have Eurgain, my beloved, and what do you have? A House torn with bitter quarrels and a tuath weakened by your ambitions and your greed. Poor Venutius. Does he long for you, even in the midst of his rage, watching you mesmerize the people like a black snake? Caradoc opened his eyes and turned his head, a movement of pain, a stern dismissal, and his gaze met Eurgain's. She smiled tremulously, seeing the naked bitterness, and he smiled back in relief and shame.

Cathbad fell silent, bowed to them, and retired, and Adminius began the funeral songs. They all joined in, a thousand voices swelling, a tide of victorious music that reduced the fire to a low spitting background, stamping their feet, shaking their shields, and Gladys wept on. Far in the east the clouds were breaking, and shafts of brilliant sunlight sliced like great golden swords to touch some meadow miles away, but here the morning was still dull, and the smoke from the pyre rose in a straight black plume to spread out and hang over the huts and halls of the town. For an hour they sang, song melding into song, a tapestry of shining memories. Then the eulogies began. Cunobelin's sons fronted the fire one by one, their words carrying far in the heavy air, giving those yesterdays a fleeting, poignant resurrection, and the chiefs stood also, acting out the raids and feasts with glittering, excited eyes and wide, uninhibited gestures. Only Gladys would not speak. She stayed motionless on the ground, just out of reach of the blossoming heat, and her grief spoke of Cunobelin's power and presence far more eloquently than any word of hers could have done. Finally the host gathered closer together, linking arms, turning their faces to where the sun poured forth a glory far away, and sang the last song of farewell and blessing, swords, shields and spears cast in a heap before them. Then they scattered quietly, while behind them the flames tongued up, curled, and licked at the white tunic, the knotted, defenceless hands, with a clean, mindless hunger.

Caradoc and Eurgain went to their house, the subdued, awed children straggling behind them, and Togodumnus and Adminius retired to the Great Hall with their chiefs to sit around the fire and watch each other with speculative, veiled suspicion. Gladys sat on, her face uncloaked now that she was alone, gazing into the holocaust. Her brief, violent spasm of sorrow had spent itself and left her empty, and the memories filled her mind without rancor and without regret, spilling into her consciousness from some deeply buried well and bringing back to her days of coarse laughter and long night talk, hot arguments and rough, fatherly embraces. Her eyes traveled the shriveling, smoking corpse without recognition. This bubbling, stinking flesh was not Cunobelin, and she wiped away the tears that still lay on her cheeks and she smiled.

All that day and far into the night the flames fed steadily, and the town was quiet. At dusk Caradoc stood in his doorway, watching the pillar of sparks shoot red into the night sky, his mind resting at last. He and Eurgain had spent the day discussing the coming Council meeting, and they had decided that Caradoc should propose his compromise if the chiefs voted solely for him. There was no other way to avoid bloodshed with a Togodumnus who seemed to have flung all caution onto the fire with his father, and every nerve in Caradoc shrank from the necessity of killing his brother and beginning his rule under the shadow of violence and resentment. He knew he could kill Tog. He was a dogged, stubborn fighter whereas Tog leaped in, arms and legs flying in a wild, undisciplined attack that often succeeded, but it if did not, he rapidly tired, resorting to tricks and feints. He had decided to speak also if the vote went to Togodumnus, for he and Eurgain were convinced that the Catuvellauni in Tog's hands would rapidly become a quarreling, disorderly tuath, bullied by Tog and his young, headstrong chiefs.

Caradoc leaned against the lintel while behind him the girls shrieked and fought as Tallia tried to coax them into bed. Llyn had gone off with Cinnamus, fishing probably, and had not yet returned. Perhaps Tog would kill him anyway, before the Council or in some secret place, but something in Caradoc spoke denial. Tog could be selfish and cruel, but his moods and impulses were always strewn throughout the town for all to see. And what of Adminius? Caradoc slid to the ground and squatted on his doorstep, frowning. He did not know Adminus well, no one did. He came and went as he chose with an understated, smooth confidence, and he did not apologize to anyone for the fact that he disliked fighting and preferred hunting, or that the company of the traders pleased him more than the company of his own kin around the feasting fire. He assumed without question that the title of ricon would fall to him, and he watched Tog's frenetic scurries from chief to chief with a superior smile. Tog was the baby.

Tog would always be the spoiled, unmanageable child, never taken seriously by anyone. What would Adminius do? Caradoc knew but did not bring the thought forward for conscious rumination. He hoped he would be wrong.

By morning the fire had eaten its fill, and Cunobelin's chiefs gathered up his hot ashes and put them in a tall, curved gray urn. Later the urn would be buried, together with meat and bread, weapons and dogs, and the old man's jewels and enormous tunics, but now they set a guard over it and left it, eager to attend the Council. The morning had begun to clear. The solid cloud cover was breaking into long, ragged gray streamers, stretched across the sky like the bellies of the traders' cats, while the wind stroked them into longer and longer shapes. It was cold, but the oppression of the day before had lifted, and the town was alive again with noise and laughter.

Adminius and Togodumnus had been first to take their places in the Great Hall soon after sunrise, their chiefs jostling each other out of the way as they fought for the best positions, and Caradoc and Gladys went in together, Eurgain following with Llyn, all of them surrounded by Caradoc's chiefs. Cinnamus saw Sholto seated defiantly among Togodumnus's men, his sour face marked by resentment, and Sholto deliberately tried to turn his back as Caradoc's entourage swept by. Behind them the freepeople pushed, chattering excitedly, and when the Hall was so full that everyone was squashed knee-to-knee, and those closest to the fire kept edging nearer, nudged by those behind them, the traders came, slipping in one by one to stand at the back in the shadows. Caradoc had ordered Vocorio and Mocuxsoma to stand at the doors and make sure that they did not enter armed, but even so, the sight of them all massed far back, unrecognizable as individuals in the dimness, made him uneasy. He was not sure how he feared them. They were adventurers for the most part, the mongrels of the empire, here in Albion to make fortunes and live more dangerously than they would at home, but they were not uncivilized hillmen like Aricia's Brigantians. They got drunk sometimes, and made a lot of noise, and then fights would break out between them and the freemen, but on the whole they were simple rough men with no guile in them. Apart from the spies, of course. Caradoc shut his mind to that avenue, an avenue that seemed always to lead him to Adminius.

"I wish we had a Druid," Gladys said to him anxiously. "Then there would be no fear of the tuath disgracing itself. I'm afraid, Caradoc."

"You?" He smiled into the clouded eyes. "Have you been hatching your own plots, Gladys? Are you going to try to sway the vote?" But she would not laugh. She sat straighter, her black braid wound in her lap, and he noticed that her scabbard was empty. "Where's your sword?" he asked sharply, and for an answer she quietly lifted the skirts of her tunic, not looking at him. The naked blade lay under her knees.

"Today the kin of the House Catuvellaun will be sundered," she said. "It could not be any other way, and so I am resolved not to speak. My heart is full of sorrow, Caradoc, for the days when we all loved one another, and yet the good of the tuath is more important than the love of its ruling kin. My only fear is that the new rule will begin in blood, under bad omens. How I wish we had a seer, also!"

"Will you shed blood?" he persisted urgently. "Gladys, why do you sit on your sword?"

She turned to him savagely. "Because I will not lay it at the feet of Adminius if he is chosen, nor at the feet of Togodumnus! And not at your feet, brother of mine. I will not be trapped into an allegiance that will fetter me if my mind should change!"

"Who did Cunobelin favor?" he asked. "Why did he never speak?"

"Because he wanted to keep your loyalty, all of you, and because he wished to end his days in peace. But he had his choice, as you well know." She would have said more, but a hush fell, and Adminius stepped into the open space left for the speakers and turned to face his kin.

Togodumnus tensed into high-strung concentration, Caradoc felt Eurgain's hand steal under his elbow, for restraint or comfort he did not know, and the chiefs rested their big hands on their fringed knees and watched, their predatory hawks' eyes alive. Adminius began to speak but immediately the crowd was shouting, "Your sword, your sword," and after a moment he shrugged ungraciously and wrenched it from its sheath, dropping it to the floor. He began again and the muttering subsided, but as he spoke he kept glancing down at it and across at his brothers, and Togodumnus grinned insolently up at him.

"Catuvellauni!" he said. "Freemen of the tuath! My words will be brief and I ask you to consider them well. I speak first because my claim is greatest, that you all know. I am the eldest, Cunobelin's firstborn, rightful heir to the title of ricon. I will not bring you new conquests. Cunobelin did that. I will not bring you famine and death. Togodumnus, if you are foolish enough to elect him, will do that. I will bring you more wealth—bronze and silver for your wives and your horses, fine dishes, bigger and warmer huts, more grain and cattle. Why should I offer you war? Why should we expand any more? We are already greater than any other tribe and our coins are coveted from Brigantia to the mines of the Dumnonii. How have we become so mighty? I will tell you." He paused but no sound filled the small silence. He sensed hostility but he plunged on. "I will be honest with you, chieftains. I will not lie to gain your vote. We have grown in strength and riches because it is Caesar's pleasure to have it so." He had expected a great outburst of rage, a wave of furious denials and name-calling, but the silence only deepened and he was bewildered. For a moment he forgot the thread of his words, and he stood looking down at his sword and hitched back his cloak, and all the while the fire could be heard roaring steadily. He searched the far reaches of the Hall, trying to divine the sympathy of the traders, but between them was a solid ocean of emotionless, upturned faces. He continued less confidently, an awful awareness growing within him. He was a man of comfortable assurances, blind to all save his own superiority, and the thought that the chiefs did not trust and admire him had never before entered his head. In his arrogance he had not considered failure. A tussle with Togodumnus perhaps, soon quashed by his own level-headed maturity, but defeat, never. Now he felt as though he were crawling from beneath warm skins to stand naked in the pitiless frosts of deep winter, and for the first time in his life he faced a reality that was not of his own making, and the props of his claim and his blood began to teeter. "Caesar's pleasure," he repeated slowly. "Our ties with Rome have been growing. For a hundred years we have been allies in all but name, my friends. If Rome withdrew her imperial support from Albion we would be reduced to poverty and impotence in less than a year." Is that true? he asked himself, doubting for the first time. But why should he doubt when his Roman friends insisted day after day that it was true? He squared his shoulders. "I must be elected so that our prosperity is assured. I will make our relationship with Rome official. I will sign agreements, and thus protect our trade and our tuath forever." The people before him had turned into wooden images, a forest of frozen statues forever sitting under the holding spell of his words. Even their eyes did not move. He felt that there was more to say but his thoughts were confused. He stood awkwardly for a moment, the only breathing being in that warm, red-shadowed place, then he bent abruptly, picked up his sword, and sat down.

For ten long heartbeats no one moved. Caradoc was stunned, though he had expected Adminius to say the things he had said. Somehow it was more shocking to hear it with the ear than to imagine it, and he had hoped, oh how he had hoped, that at the last his brother might change his mind. But no. Adminius was Rome's tool. He glanced behind him at the traders, sensing rather than seeing the quiet satisfaction ripple through their ranks, and at the movement of his head the crowd loosened, sighed, then shook off the spell and came to life.

Togodumnus flung his sword into the center and stepped after it, tossing back his cloak and planting his feet wide, his face a mask of grimness but his eyes blazing with success. Adminius was more than a fool. Adminius was dead. He and Caradoc exchanged a swift glance, then Togodumnus shouted at them all. "I will not follow the custom of the Council. I will not boast of my exploits, I will not strut before you, I will not smear honey on my words. I will say only this. My brother is a traitor, and any who vote for him are traitors too. What will Caius Caesar put in the agreement Adminius tells us will do us good? Will he kindly give us all and take nothing? You know! Adminius would sell us all to Rome for a few more paltry toys, and Rome would send us a governor to rule the Council, and soldiers to rape our women and consume our grain. This is what Adminius wants. Before our very eyes his tribal soul has been dying. He is no longer one of us. I say that our ties with Rome are becoming a hanging rope, and unless we cut the knot, and soon, the noose will draw tight. Drive out the traders! Burn the ships! Then let us turn to the Iceni, and the Dobunni, to make war, and do as my father wished. He did not have the courage. He feared Rome in his old age, but I do not. Do you?" He taunted them, and Caradoc, alarmed, watched the chiefs scuffle and murmur angrily. Tog was pushing hard and Caradoc felt his muscles ache with the urge to action, any action, anything to end this futile, stupid game. But he waited, knowing that Tog had the right to speak his piece and that afterward he would be calmer, more amenable. Either that, Caradoc thought, or one of us will die. Togodumnus whirled and began to pace before them, his tall, graceful body arched, his light brown hair swinging with him and his eyes darting over them.

"Elect me, chiefs and warriors, and we will return to the ways of our fathers. We will make war and once more the Catuvellauni will be full of honor, hard and mighty. I will give you Subidasto on the end of my spear. The head of Boduocus will swing before my hut. Verica will be drowned in the sea, and all will be ours! What do you say?" He raised his arms and suddenly the chiefs surged into life.

For years Cunobelin had held them firmly in check, offering them raids and cattle like tidbits thrown to a starving dog, but now Togodumnus offered them a hunk of meat as high as a mountain and they pounced upon it with ferocious hunger. They bawled his name, screaming Ricon! Ricon! They rose to their feet, madness in their eyes, and in the rear Caradoc saw the traders stampede toward the door. He rose, Cinnamus and Caelte with him, trying to draw his sword, but the press was too great. He could hear Gladys shouting, and he saw Vocorio run to the doors, the little girls held high on his shoul-

103

ders. Where was Llyn? Then he was swept against a wall. He pulled his knife from within his tunic and prepared to force his way to where Gladys had jumped on a table, brandishing her sword. "Caradoc has not spoken!" she was yelling. "Caradoc must speak!" Cinnamus and Caelte were belaboring the men closest to them with fists and knees, and the crowd swayed and gave.

Then Caradoc saw Togodumnus. He was bent almost double, creeping through the outer shadows, knife in hand, to where Adminius was locked tight in the crush, looking about him with bewilderment. In another moment the knife would be buried deep in Adminius's back and Tog would have severed the last ties of reason. Caradoc launched himself forward, kicking his chiefs out of the way. He heard Gladys scream, "Adminius! Look out!" Caradoc lunged for his brother and he and Tog went down. Adminius swung round, the babble began to die, and after a fierce spasm of resistance Tog released the knife and lay limp. Caradoc sprawled on top of him, feeling his hot, quick breath on his neck, his muscles jerking, then he scrambled up, taking Togodumnus by the arm and hauling him to his feet. Tog's face was flushed. Sholto bent and swept up the knife, handing it to Togodumnus, but Caradoc smoothly interposed and took it himself. Adminius leaped forward, taking Togodumnus by the neck, shaking him as a dog shakes a rat, then he flung him backward, but he did not go for his sword.

"You cowardly fool!" he shouted. "Is this how you will rule the tuath? A knife in the back for all those who will not do your bidding? Chiefs and freemen, take warning. How do you like your new ricon now?" He turned and left them and the people parted, so great was the rage and bitterness on his face. He did not call for blood. He knew a challenge would be useless, and though he might be the victor, still the chiefs did not want him for ricon. Gladys jumped down and ran behind him, her hand on his arm, but he swept out the door and into the fitful sunlight, Gladys following, caught in the eddy of his swift passing.

"Now, Tog," Caradoc said quietly, handing him his knife. "It is my turn to speak, and you will listen. Be ashamed, chiefs and freemen," he called to them angrily. "To what ignominious end have we come that the Council should be held so lightly? Sit down. Sit down!" In silence they folded away from him and onto the floor, but Togodumnus walked to him and laid a hand on his shoulder.

"I will be ricon," he whispered. "The chiefs will listen to you because they have been shamed, but you saw how they rose to me. They will not be leashed again, Caradoc." The lean hand tightened, quivering with excitement, but Caradoc gently disentangled it from his

104

cloak. To his right, where Mocuxsoma stood with sword at the ready, Eurgain and Llyn waited. Eurgain had removed her cloak and her fingers stroked the hilt of her sword, and Llyn's eyes were fixed meditatively on his uncle.

"Oh sit down, Tog," Caradoc said lightly though his heart raced and his knees shook. "You are not Cunobelin and never will be." He took a step that brought him into the full glare of the firelight, turning his back on Togodumnus, and Cinnamus and Caelte closed in behind him. "People of my kin," he said quietly. "Lords of the tuath. Today you see a terrible thing. Brother against brother, greed and ambition where once there was harmony and friendship. You have rejected the claim of Adminius and I think you are wise to do so, but you have not yet voted for Togodumnus. Tell me, are you children, wild and thoughtless? Will you follow Togodumnus to war and strife?"

"Aye, we will have him," someone muttered, and the mutinous whispers ran through the company and gained strength. "Togodumnus for ricon. A clean tuath, an honorable war." But there were also angry voices. "Caradoc for ricon!" Caradoc raised his voice again before the sighs could become another eruption of violence. "Even among yourselves you are divided," he said loudly, bitterly. "Some favor Togodumnus because they tire of too few raids and too many feasts, and some of you look to me for guidance, knowing my temperance in all things. We could sit here all day and all night and come to no decision." He glanced at Eurgain and she nodded imperceptibly, her face white and her mouth drawn. "To you, chiefs, and to you, Tog, I propose a compromise." The restless bickering died away and all eyes swiveled to him. "The tuath will divide." He paused, and in the breathless hush he looked to his father's corner, fancying that he heard a low, dry chuckle. "I will stay here in Camulodunon, with all those who choose to stay with me, and you, Tog, can go back to Verulamium, from whence we Catuvellauni first came, and rule in the west. We will strike coins together, and have treaties between ourselves never to make war on each other, and share the trade, but you and I will both bear the title of ricon." He stood quite still. Now, he thought, will Tog accede or will he fling himself upon me? He felt his whole body become stiff. He did not turn his head but he felt his brother leave the shadows of the wall and stalk forward on noiseless feet, and he poised himself, watching the eys of those who sat before him for a signal.

Suddenly Togodumnus began to laugh. He leaped before Caradoc, his gay face contorted with mirth, flinging wide his arms and laughing. Then he embraced Caradoc, and roared at the startled company. "A compromise! Of course! What else should I expect from the wily

Caradoc, true son of his father?" He burst into loud peals of laughter again but Caradoc, watching his eyes, saw that they were quite cold. Finally Togodumnus became calm. He lowered himself to the floor and Caradoc sat unwillingly beside him, while the chiefs began to rise, unsheathing their swords and moving forward. "I agree!" Togodumnus shouted. "Now all who wish to ride with me to Verulamium come now, and pledge me your swords. How many do you think will pledge to you?" he said softly to Caradoc, but Caradoc only smiled, his relief still too great for words. He knew that this might be just the beginning of his troubles. Tog and he would spend many hours thrashing out agreements and safeguards, and even then Tog might someday disregard them all and come sweeping over Camulodunon with his war band. But for the present, all was well and he watched the swords come clattering before his folded knees in a haze of weariness and deep, wrenching sadness. Eurgain laid her sword across his lap and knelt and kissed him, and Llyn flung his arms about him, but he was aware only of Tog beside him, chaffering the men and gleefully counting the swords as they fell. Then Caradoc rose and dismissed them all. They came and recovered their weapons, leaving the Hall in a satisfied silence, and Tog let out a sigh and leaned back, his chiefs settling beside him. Cinnamus and Caelte squatted easily beside Caradoc, and Eurgain sat far back, a glimmer of light in the dimness.

"Well!" said Togodumnus, stretching and smiling into his brother's face. "You managed that very adroitly, I must say. I would never have killed you, Caradoc, not really. You know that, don't you?"

"No, I don't," Caradoc snapped. "And neither do you. I wish you would learn to control your impulses, Tog. None of us is safe around you. Are you pleased with my plan?"

Tog grimaced. "Well, not exactly pleased, but I see your wisdom. Even if we had not fought, and whomever had been elected, there would still have been strife among the chiefs. This way is better. I'm surprised I didn't think of it myself."

"You were too busy sizing up Adminius."

Tog sighed, and a queer light came into his eyes. "Ah yes, Adminius. We will have to kill him, Caradoc. Otherwise he will go on skulking about behind our backs, making trouble between us and stirring up the traders."

"I know," Caradoc said reluctantly. "But it must be done properly and openly, and with the chiefs' consent. Your way was utter madness."

"It would have saved us a lot of trouble."

They sat for a moment without speaking, Caradoc's heart heavy with thoughts of his elder brother, and he felt Eurgain's sympathy reaching him, a warm, invisible cloud of peace from the shadows. His chiefs squatted quietly, looking at the ground. The anticlimax was somehow paining and unsatisfactory, as if something had gone wrong, as if threads were left untied and unseen problems were not settled, and Caradoc felt his own formless anxiety battle with Eurgain's hovering calm. He stirred.

"Your chiefs will want immediate action," he said. "What will you do?"

Tog gave him a wide smile of pure contentment. "I will war with the Coritani and finally subdue them. Then I will overrun the Dobunni. That should not take long. Boduocus sleeps all day. Then," he rubbed his hands together. "Then for Brigantia! You know, Caradoc, I think that when I have beaten Aricia in war I will marry her." Caradoc raised his head sharply, and in Togodumnus's eyes he saw his own obsession mirrored. "Yes, brother of mine," Tog said quietly, "I too am sick, and I have no Eurgain to apply soothing salves." He straightened and laughed and the moment was gone. "What will you do? What of our plans for Verica?"

"Verica will have to go," Caradoc replied. "We need his mines. He won't sell us his iron, he sulks, so we will have to take it for ourselves."

"And then?"

Caradoc shrugged. "The perhaps the Iceni, and the Cantiaci. Who knows?"

Togodumnus struggled to his feet. "Who indeed?" he remarked lightly. "Will you continue to shake hands with Rome?"

Caradoc rose, too, and stood thinking. If he assented he might be feeding the fires of conquest in Tog, fires that often leaped in him also. If he denied, Tog would wonder then whether all the fuss of the Council was simply in order to put Caradoc in Cunobelin's place. He lifted his eyebrows, smiled, embraced his brother. "I do not know," he said. "Let us deal with Adminius first," and they linked arms and went into the damp, sun-drenched day, their chiefs pacing behind them.

Adminius strode on down the hill with Gladys running after him. He passed the harness maker's shop, and the blacksmith's, and the kennels where the trainer called a cheeery greeting, and at last he turned in at the stable. Gladys panted after him, stumbling as the sunlight was cut off and the steamy, pungent air enveloped her, then she followed the sound of harness clinking. To right and left the horses stood, tails swishing idly, munching on their hay, and normally she would have stopped by each one to stroke and speak quietly, but she moved on. Adminius was harnessing his mount, his fingers fumbling angrily with bit and leather, and she squeezed between his horse's broad flank and the farther wall and watched him. He ignored her, his face a stiff scowl, the mouth pulled tight and the eyes black holes of burning misery. He rammed the bit into the horse's mouth and flung the reins over its neck.

"Where are you going, Adminius?" she said softly.

He did not answer, bending beneath his horse's head and pushing her roughly out of the way. Suddenly he stopped and laid his forehead for a moment against the rippling brown hide. "I am going to Caesar," he said harshly.

She stepped forward abruptly. "No! No, Adminius, how can you consider such a thing? Will you be like Dubnovellaunus then, hanging about Rome, bowing and scraping to the senate, suffering every indignity? And for what? Stay here."

"They will kill me," he said, eyes narrowed. "Caradoc and Tog. In a moment they will remember that I am free and they will come for me. They cannot let me live, Gladys, and you know it. But I will be revenged. Caesar will listen to me. He's mad, everyone knows it, and the right words can control him. I will ask for justice, and Caius will give it to me because I will tell him . . . " He swung away from her and mounted and she stepped out of reach of the sidling hoofs. "I will tell him that the Council elected me, and my brothers drove me out. The traders will back me up. I will tell him that if he does not help me all his trading connections in Albion will be broken."

"You dare not!" she flashed at him. "What of your honor-price, your freedom? Adminius, if you leave then the Council will pronounce you unfree, a slave, and all your riches will be forfeit. Is that what you want?" He sat looking down on her, teeth bared, hands clenching and unclenching on the reins.

"What is the goodwill of the tuath to me?" he ground out. "Henceforth I am a Roman." He wrenched the torc from his neck and flung it at her. It struck her on the cheek, grazing her, and then fell with a tinkle to the floor. "What are the Catuvellauni but a mud-caked rabble of quarrelsome, ignorant peasants?" he screamed. "When I return it will be to see you all ground under the boots of Caius's legions!" He kicked his horse viciously in the ribs and the animal snorted and made for the door, Adminius bent low on his back. Then man and horse were gone and Gladys stood shaking, dabbing at her bloody cheek with her sleeve. The horses had stopped chewing and their heads had turned, the liquid brown eyes rolled toward her in enquiry. She calmed them automatically, with silly, soft words pouring from her lips, and she picked up the torc and walked unsteadily to the entrance, passing out under the sun. Already the men were running toward her, Caradoc and Togodumnus in the lead, and she waited for them, a hand on her cheek, her eyes squinting in the bright light. The shreds of cloud had thinned to nothing and the blue sky held only a white, warm radiance.

"Where is he?" Togodumnus panted, coming up. "Where has he gone?" But she turned to Caradoc, meeting the dark eyes calmly.

"He has gone to Caligula," she said. "He has gone for vengeance." She turned away then to hide tears, while Togodumnus burst into derisive laughter. Caradoc came and put an arm about her.

"Are you hurt?" he asked gently, and she shook her head, mutely holding the torc out to him. He took it in wonderment. "Does he knew what he has done?" he said, and she nodded, Adminius's own words falling from her lips like poisoned berries.

"Shall we go after him?" Sholto asked eagerly, but Togodumnus spoke.

"Let him go, the arrogant fool," he said scornfully. "Caius cares no more for us than Tiberius did. He will not make war for the sake of one more disgruntled chieftain." He spread his arms expansively and raised his face to the benison of the winter sun. "Now we can proceed! Let the war band come to arms! Oh, Caradoc, an empire as great as Rome's for you and me!" Cinnamus met Caradoc's wry smile with a whimsical, quick grin, and Gladys stifled her tears and moved away.

"Where are you going?" Caradoc called to her as she passed under the black shade of the stable's entrance, and she paused and said contemptuously, "To the sea."

CHAPTER SEVEN

CARADOC, TOGODUMNUS, AND ALL THE TUATH prepared for war on a great tide of excitement. Not for thirty years had the war band gathered, but now Camulodunon hummed to the sound of impending battle. The blacksmith's forge glowed day and night. The Great Hall was full of people who hung about to gossip at all hours and watch the freemen run in and out on their errands, and the big fire was always hung with boar or steer. The chiefs spent much time by the river, dashing up and down in their chariots, and their freemen sharpened and polished the bright swords and massive shields. The women were restless also, caught up in the constant, feverish flux, and fights often broke out among the wives of the freemen's circle, as the bragging and strutting men drew their women into their own heated arguments over who deserved the title of champion.

Caradoc and Togodumnus had decided to divide their force and strike simultaneously at the Coritani under Tog, and at the Atrebates under Caradoc. The spies crept back to Verica and the Coritani, and those tribes made their own preparations, cursing Caius Caesar for his lack of interest in their plight, and cursing the Catuvellauni for their rapaciousness. Llyn spent all his time begging Caradoc to let him fight too, and the little girls chased each other around their house with wooden sticks. The women were not going to fight—Caradoc had decided that they were not needed—but they would, of course, follow the warriors with the children in wains, and watch the excitement from the nearest high point. Caradoc and Tog were blithely convinced that no tribe would be able to stand against their own. They spent hours in Tog's hut, drinking wine, talking of how the enemy chiefs would fall before the chariots like wheat before the shining blades of the reaping scythes, and any misgivings Caradoc may have had were swamped in Tog's enthusiasms.

Eurgain said little to him of how she felt. Vida stormed and cursed at Cinnamus because she was not to draw blade, Gladys spent more and more time in her cave, watching the breakers roll in and weaving her own strange enchantments, but Eurgain went about her duties quietly and dumbly. Caradoc tried to tease her out, but she seemed to be withdrawing, drifting back to the time before he had married her. She once more sat by her window in the early afternoons, chin in hand, her blonde hair stirring in the cold winds, and her eyes fixed broodingly on the distant, tree-covered hills. She still played with the children, and rode and hunted, and attended the Council meetings. She still went into his arms with the same warm willingness, wrapping her sweet freshness around him. But she and Gladys no longer sparred though the other women battled on the practice ground, and Caradoc was too busy to unravel the tangled obscurities of her mind. He and Togodumnus had decided to strike in the spring, when the tribes would be busy with sowing and birthing. The Catuvellaunian peasants who wanted to fight were to be armed, at the chiefs' expense, but many of them were to stay on the land to see to the cropping and the stock.

The time went by. Samain came and went, a momentary lull in an otherwise keyed-up and preoccupied Camulodunon. In a month the chiefs were ready and once more they gambled and quarreled around the great fire. In six weeks Togodumnus and Caradoc prepared to say goodbye, for Togodumnus and his men were to spend some time at Verulamium, seeing to the fortifications in the unlikely and laughable event that the Dobunni or the Coritani should chase the Catuvellauni home.

Then one afternoon, when Caradoc and Togodumnus were standing outside the stables watching their chariots being harnessed before they set out to race each other along the path that ran under the leafless trees of the wood, Cinnamus came pounding up from the gate, his horse lathered, his tunic streaked with sweat, his face an urgent message of fear. He clattered to a halt before them and tumbled off his mount, leaning against the beast for a moment to still his heaving chest, then motioned to the stable servant to lead the horse away. He turned to Caradoc. "The traders!" he gasped, and Caradoc left his glittering harness and went to him, sending Fearachar for water from the trough. Cinnamus wiped his gray-spotted face on the corner of his cloak and then bent, hands on knees and head hanging, struggling to get his breath. He had ridden from the river at full gallop and his heart still pounded out the rhythme of his horse's flying hoofs. Fearachar ran up with water in a wooden bowl and Cinnamus straightened, plunging his face into its coldness. Then he took it and drank deeply, handing it back and grinning crookedly at the men who were watching him in puzzlement. "Lord, the traders are leaving," he said. "Already five boats have gone with the tide and another ten wait. They will not talk. All they do is sit on the bank, their belongings around them, but the wine merchant was more amenable."

"Wait a moment, Cin," Caradoc said. "Get your breath," but Cinnamus was already recovering. He squatted on the hard earth, and Caradoc and the chiefs squatted with him.

"Caius Caesar is moving," he said. "He is within a day's march of Gesioracum, and three legions, perhaps four, march with him. The merchant says he is going to cross the water."

No one spoke. Cinnamus's words hung in the frosty air, and Caradoc looked at the ground while behind him his ponies shuffled restlessly and the wheels of his chariot rolled back and forth. Then Togodumnus swore, a loud, rude expletive that startled them all, and jumped to the earth.

"We know who is with him, too!" he shouted. "That thrice damned Adminius! We should have pursued him and taken his head, Caradoc. Now look what he has done!" Caradoc looked enquiringly at Cinnamus, and Cinnamus nodded once.

"It is true. Such is the madness of Caligula that he imagines Adminius to be offering Rome the whole of Albion, and he is coming to claim it. The traders want no trouble. They will sail to Gaul and scatter, waiting until the legions have come and conquered, and trade begins once more."

"What of Caius's generals?" Caradoc asked. "Surely they are sane enough to see that Adminius is only a fugitive, not a ricon. In any case, a ricon from Albion who voluntarily sold his tribe into slavery would obviously be mad."

"Of course they know," Cinnamus answered him. "But how can they persuade Caesar and keep their heads? Pity them, Caradoc. And hope that one of them can somehow convince the emperor that Adminius is a criminal fool."

Togodumnus spat into the dirt and scowled. "Let them come!" he said. "What did the wits of Rome say when Julius Casesar slunk home, his tail between his legs because the mighty Cassivellaunus sunk his teeth into the august rump? 'I came, I saw, but failed to stay.' Rome met its match in the Catuvellauni a hundred years ago."

"It was not Cassivellaunus who defeated Caesar, it was the weather and the tides of the sea," Caradoc said automatically, then he frowned in shock. Who had told him that? Togodumnus stuck out his tongue in the direction of the river and then laughed.

"Rubbish! Is that what Julius said? I suppose he had to say something." The chiefs laughed, their momentary anxiety dissipating as swiftly as a summer mist, and they all rose and passed their interest to other things. They walked away and Togodumnus got into his chariot. "You have exhausted yourself for nothing, Cinnamus Ironhand," he laughed in derision. "Caradoc, I will wait for you by the river." As he rumbled away, Caradoc looked at Cinnamus.

"Is this thing real?" he asked quietly. "Will mad Caius come, Cin?"

Cinnamus shrugged in his own cool, inimitable fashion. "I do not know, but the traders would not be panicked by rumor alone. They know something, Lord, and if I were you I would keep Togodumnus and his chiefs here, ready for battle, until rumor becomes fact or sinks under the weight of another wonder."

"Adminius has done this," Caradoc said bitterly. "Sneaking, crawling Roman-lover! He has played on the emperor's feeble mind. If Caius comes and is defeated I will take Adminius and burn him alive on his own funeral pyre."

Cinnamus laughed shortly. "Gladys should have killed him when she had the chance," he observed. "She will be eternally sorry that she did not." He walked slowly and stiffly up the hill, and Caradoc beckoned to Fearachar and got into his chariot, lifting the reins and calling to the ponies. He rolled to the gate, while his mind strayed to the ocean and the port of Gesioracum where Caligula pouted and fretted, and his generals held secret, frantic meetings, trying to decide

112

who should tell the ruler of the world that Albion would greet him with bunched spears, not flower of welcome.

Caradoc persuaded Togodumnus to postpone his departure, but it was not easy. Tog fumed and shouted, cursed and raged, but the chiefs listened to Caradoc, trusting his judgment, and the Council voted Tog down. He sulked for a day, got drunk, then flirted with Vida, went fishing with Llyn, and finally settled down contemptuously to wait with Caradoc. The river was empty. The Catuvellaunian coracles and coastal vessels rocked gently at anchor, the piers were bare of barrels, boxes, sacks, and dogs, and day after day the freemen straggled into Camulodunon from the coast, reporting no sails. Even the weather seemed to hush and pause. The winter wind dropped, the fogs hung motionless in the trees, and the chiefs sat in their smoky huts, polishing swords and spears that already gleamed sun-bright.

Two weeks dragged by. Caradoc and his men sacrificed three bulls to Camulos and went into the woods to propitiate the goddess and the Dagda. But still the ocean lay unruffled by burden of war or troopship, and Caradoc was beginning to berate himself as an overanxious idiot when a freeman came to him in an early dawn, squatting before him in his house. The children still slept, but Eurgain was up, sitting among pillows, heavy-eyed but alert, and Caradoc flung wood on the fire before he dared to order the man to speak. Then he squatted beside him. "The news," he said tersely, and the freeman smiled.

"The news is good," he said, and behind him Caradoc heard Eurgain sigh. "Ships came in the night but they did not bring soldiers. The traders are coming back."

Caradoc felt a great weight roll from him, and he was suddenly very hungry. Beside him the fire crackled with new life, and in the other room he heard Llyn cough and turn over. "And?" he pressed gently, and the man hurried on.

"The traders say that the generals could not dissuade the emperor, but the troops mutinied. They would not cross the water. They said that Albion is a magic island full of monsters and terrible spells, and even for Jupiter Greatest and Best they would not set sail. The traders say that the emperor was furious. He frothed at the mouth and ran about cursing. He had a dozen legionnaires crucified there on the beach, but it made no difference. In the end, the generals were able to turn him around, and he is going back to Rome. Some say he may be deciding to claim Albion anyway."

Caradoc began to laugh. He threw back his head, lost his balance, and fell back hard onto the skins and still he laughed. Llyn woke up and came sleepily to see what had happened, and Eurgain watched her husband with a glad smile, the full-throated, gay sound filling her with weak relief. He had been so humorless lately, with a cutting edge to his words and a new hardness to his decisions that had begun to alarm her. Caradoc struggled to his feet, still shaking. "Monsters and spells!" he managed. "Of course, and worse! Swords and spears and giants! Oh Eurgain, did you hear? Well, let him claim Albion, the poor, witless wretch." He hauled the freeman to his feet and embraced him. "Go to Togodumnus and give him your news," he said. "Now hurry up and dress, Eurgain. This morning we will hunt boar, and tomorrow we will hunt the Coritani!"

CHAPTER EIGHT

THEY ALL HUNTED, feasted, laughed, and drank, and then they went to war. The threat of Rome had been no more than the fangless petulance of a gust of summer wind. Rome had once more tried and failed, and the last restraints fell from the lords of the Catuvellauni. Togodumnus and his chiefs packed up their wives, children, and baggage and left for Verulamium, accompanied by loud music and raucous song. Caradoc made the last plans for his assault on Verica, and then, in early spring when the buds on the apple trees burst into white, fragrant blossom that perfumed the echoing halls of the forest and the sun probed the earth with gentle, warm fingers, he and Togodumnus thundered into action. On a high tide of reckless young strength and bursting confidence they careened across the borders, with their yelling, blood-drunk hordes behind them, and the Coritani wavered, broke, and ran. Verica, after a wild and desperate struggle high above the eastern coast, took ship and fled in anger and defeat to Gaul. It was only the beginning. Throughout that summer the Coritani, bunched together in their northern fortresses, turned at bay and fought Togodumnus with steady ferocity, but Caradoc spent the months of heat chasing this way and that, trying to find the remnants of Verica's kin who had melted away into their forests like handfuls of snow.

In the autumn, when the trees lit suddenly with a fiery, flaunting glory, both of them returned tanned, healthy, and tired, to Camulodunon, the wains and chariots trundling behind them laden with booty, and the herds and flocks of stolen animals before them. There, in the Great Hall, Togodumnus and Caradoc met and flung their arms

114

around each other. "What a summer!" Tog declared as they sat cross-legged by the fire. "Ah Caradoc, I wish you could have seen us! Those Coritani can fight after all. We charged them, we beat them back, we hacked their cheifs to pieces and then chased them into the hills, but they turned on us and gave us a stiff resistance. I nearly lost my head, did you know? A massive chief with bull's horns on his helm leaped upon me from his chariot, and I standing fighting in a dyke. He bore me down but I wriggled free. He swung at my neck, growling all the while like a bear, but ah!" He tossed back his hair and brought his bronze-braceleted arm slicing through the smoky air. "One blow and I cut him nearly in two!" He sighed happily. "What a summer!"

The chiefs mingled around them, telling their own excited tales to each other, and the women chattered contentedly, glad to be settling once more into their snug town quarters. The children ran about the Hall, chasing the dogs or wrestling each other, and the bards sat thoughtfully tuning their harps, their eyes on the cavernous depths of the ceiling as their newest songs took shape in their quick minds. Fearachar brought wine and steaming pork, and there was silence for a while as the lords and their attendants ate.

"Tell me, Tog," Caradoc said, taking a sip of hot wine, "will another season see the Coritani beaten? Can we move some of our people up there next summer, or will the Coritani make treaty with the Brigantians and face us a thousandfold next spring?"

Togodumnus chewed reflectively. "I do not know. The Coritani and the Brigantes do not like one another and are always raiding, but perhaps Aricia will push for a treaty, knowing that I plan to attack her just as soon as the Coritani are subjugated. She would do better to make treaty with us." He grinned. "Then we can take over Brigantia while she is still arguing about her principles."

"She knows that," Caradoc answered. "So she will not treaty with us. I think she will sit down in Council with the judges of the Coritani and they will face us together."

Tog swallowed his mouthful. "Then they are stupid. From what we have heard, Aricia has flung away any principles she may have had, which weren't many as you, of all people, should know. She will speak fairly to the judges, and then if you and I go down in defeat—bang!" He clapped his hands together. "She and that wildman of hers, that Venutius, will be down on the Coritani like thunderbolts, and they will regret that they did not accept our domination." He picked up his cup and drank deeply, wiping his mouth on his sleeve. "And what of the Atrebates?" he asked. "How have you fared?"

"Verica has gone to Rome, as you know," Caradoc replied, "and his people are clever. They hide in the woods and will not meet me in

115

battle. To tell you the truth," he said ruefully, "I have spent my summer chasing shadows. But I think in the spring I will move some of the freemen families into Verica's territory and make their menfolk chiefs. The resistance is so spotty and poor that they will easily be able to handle it—particularly with the goad of enormous honor-prices. Then," he smiled. "Then for the Dobunni. Already they quarrel among themselves, with Boduocus hanging onto the south and the renegade chiefs in the north. It should be easy to turn them all into Catuvellaunians." He and Togodumnus looked at each other smugly. "An empire," Caradoc said softly. "Already we have made a good beginning, Tog. One day the whole of Albion will be ruled by Catuvellaunian chieftains, and you and I will be richer than Seneca."

"They say that even Caesar is not as rich as Seneca," said Tog. "What about the traders, Caradoc? Many of them went home this summer because commerce was not good with all of us away. We will have to do something about that."

Caradoc shrugged. "Let them go. The bigger we are the less we will have to rely on Rome for goods, and when we are big enough the traders will be lured back for pickings a hundred times more valuable."

"Cunobelin would laugh loud and long if he could see us now!" Tog finished his wine and sat back against the wall, and the company began to settle themselves on the floor. "Our names will be feared from one end of the earth to the other. What about the Durotriges, Caradoc, and the men of the west? Shall we save them until the last?"

Caradoc shuddered. "We will leave them. Even Cunobelin did not dare to anger the men of the west, for they fight as though the Raven of Battle lived in each one of them. As for the Durotriges . . ." He frowned. "The Cornovii first, Tog, and then we will see. We must be far stronger if we want to cross swords with them."

Conversation had dropped to a faint murmuring. Cups were refilled, the children taken away to bed, and Eurgain came and sat between Caradoc and Cinnamus. Caradoc put an arm around her and kissed her cheek. "Now we will hear the stories of our summer," he said to her. "Are you glad to be home, Eurgain?" She nodded and put her head on his shoulder, and he called for Caelte. The bard stood, unslinging his harp, and a hush fell. He had taken a spear in his shoulder and still favored it, moving delicately, but his fingers were unscathed, able to coax music like the swift passing of wind in the treetops from his little instrument. He plucked at it, tightened a string, smiled around at the gathering, and cleared his throat.

"People of the tuath," he said quietly. "I will sing to you tonight of Caradoc the Magnificent, and the Dishonoring of Verica."

"My bard has made a song for me that takes an hour to sing," Togodumnus whispered to Eurgain, but she did not look at him, only smiling politely and distantly while Caelte's high, sweet voice rose like the rising of the lark from the meadows of summer.

Caelte, Togodumnus's bard, and the people sang the night away. After the summer had sped before them, blown through their minds on the warm breath of Caelte, they called for the songs of Cunobelin, and Tasciovanus, and still they were hungry. The story of Julius Caesar and Cassivellaunus made them laugh. The haunting, lost lays of their ancestors, now only dimly understood, filled them with passionate nostalgia, and they wept. An atmosphere of emotion-charged poignancy throbbed in the Hall, a billowing, wreathing cloud of pathos that curled around them along with the woodsmoke, and it permeated their souls. The fire was replenished again and again, and the red flames soared on the wings of their melody, sweet or bitter, melancholy or searing. The wine barrels were emptied. Sweat ran down the faces of the bards and their fingers grew hot, but the music took its own power and left them wordless at last, able only to follow stumbling where its rainbow cloak brushed them in its journey. Then Togodumnus shouted, " 'The Ship,' Caelte, 'the Ship'!" and the others took up the cry. " 'The Ship,' oh please master, 'the Ship'!"

Caelte shook his head, his throat raw and his face streaming, but they called all the more and finally he stood, a wry smile on his face. Immediately deep silence fell. " 'The Ship,' " he said huskily and began, and after the first few hoarse notes his voice gained strength in an inhuman, lovely cadence of sorrow.

> There was a ship, her sails were silken red,
> Peaceful she lay, upon a golden sea
> And all about, the graceful seagulls glided, crying.
> He stood like stone upon the deck,
> Like gods of old, the evening wind
> Was in his floating hair, the sun upon his face.
> He looked toward the seaweed-crowded shore,
> The silvered path that wound down from the wood
> Where long the pools of liquid light were lying.
> She did not come, she did not come,
> She lay under the oak trees, dreaming,
> Between her fingers grew the yellow celandines.
> The sun burned out, the stars hung white-bespangled,
> And still he waited, dying in the darkness,

And still she lay, white limbs upon the grass,
Until the seaward night wind filled the whispering sail
And the ocean took him on its murmuring tide.

Togodumnus opened his eyes as Caelte bowed, mopping his fore-head, and sank to the floor. "Aaaah," he whispered. "How good it is to be alive, eh Caradoc? If I had been Cerdic I would have left the ship with my chiefs, then fallen on the village and cut her miserable father into a thousand pieces. Then I would have carried her body away with me and sunk her and myself in the ocean."

"But Cerdic did not know that she was dead," Caradoc said, one ear open to his brother while Aricia twisted in his entrails, lying under the oaks, black hair spread upon the grass and red mouth open under his own. Eurgain stirred and sat up, yawning, and the people began to file out.

"I could sleep until another sunset," she murmured. "But it was a good homecoming." She and Caradoc spoke their goodnights and went out, accompanied by Fearachar, Cinnamus, and a lagging, weary Caelte. But Togodumnus lay on the skins by the fire, dreamily watch-ing the embers darken and fall, thinking of Aricia, and the battles to come.

CHAPTER NINE

IN THE LATE WINTER when the war bands were again preparing to depart, this time to sweep unlooked-for upon the Dobunni and the southern marches of the Iceni, the traders brought word that Caius Caesar was dead. Caradoc listened incredulously to a tale of insanity that had driven the all-powerful Praetorian Guards to an act of brutal murder and turned Rome into a dangerous whirlpool of treachery and betrayals. Togodumnus whooped and danced, twirling his red cloak above his head. "And what did his precious horse, the newest consul, say?" he crowed. "Oh brave and noble guards! I wish I had been there!"

"Is there a successor?" Caradoc asked the man, wishing irritably that Tog would go away, and the trader nodded, his eyes twinkling.

"Oh yes, Lord, indeed there is. The Praetorians were desperate, knowing that if they did not choose the next Caesar themselves they could all die for their presumption. They found him, I believe, cowering behind a curtain and weeping for fear. He is Tiberius Claudius Drusus Germanicus, grandson to Augustus, a mild, book-loving man. It is obvious to all, now, that the Praetorians rule Rome."

Caradoc felt a strange thrill course through him. It tingled in his fingers, prickled across his face, and Cinnamus looked at him enquiringly. "Is he old? Young? Married? What?" He pressed in a sudden urge to know this man, this Claudius, but the trader could tell him no more. Caradoc sent him away, and Togodumnus sidled close, his chiefs with him.

"Now is the time," he said eagerly. "Now we must order Rome to send Adminius and Verica back to us!"

"What for?" Caradoc said, still frowning over the information brought to him, and Togodumnus shook him gently.

"So that the last hope of the Atrebates is dashed, and so that we can get rid of Adminius. With the two of them sitting in Rome, pouring sedition into the ears of all who will listen, we are not safe. Besides," he said haughtily, "this is a good time to let Rome know that we have dignity, that we Catuvellauni are a force to be reckoned with. Let us test this poor, timid little Claudius, Caradoc. Let me order the traitors home!"

"If you like," Caradoc replied absently. It would give Tog something to occupy his mind during the coming months, and it seemed to Caradoc that Rome was in no position to retaliate, even if she cared a scrap about two disinherited chieftains. Caius had sent a flurry of formal, strongly-worded protests to the Catuvellauni when the Roman traders had reached Gaul and spread the word of a new militancy rising in Albion, but Caius was dead, and he no longer mattered. "Be careful that you do not demand from Rome, Tog, if you really want to see Verica and Adminius here at Camulodunon. Be tactful in your request."

"Pah!" Tog said, and swirled away, and Caradoc turned slowly to Cinnamus.

"Come to the practice ground and give me some exercise, Cin," he said. "My body feels old and tired."

"It's raining, Lord," Cinnamus pointed out, but he drew his sword and they walked from the Hall, shedding their cloaks and tying back their hair. For an hour they slashed at one another, slipping in the mud, becoming drenched to the skin, entirely alone there in the shrouded quiet day. Finally, Cinnamus called a halt. He could no longer see his opponent for the water pelting into his eyes and he went off to get dry, but Caradoc stood there on the practice ground, resting on his shield, the aura of unreality still wrapping him in a many-fibered net.

Togodumnus sent off his impertinent demand and waited impatiently for an answer, but winter faded into spring and neither Adminius nor Verica came. Nor did any word from Rome. The battle season opened. Caradoc and Togodumnus fought together this time, for the Coritani had concluded treaties with Aricia and with Prasutugas, chieftain of the Iceni. When the Catuvellaunian spies told this to Caradoc he was surprised, wondering what had happened in the far marsh country after the death of Subidasto, and why the little Boudicca did not captain the tribe. He remembered her vaguely, a brown-eyed slip of a child with thick, waving red hair and chunky hands, and tried to imagine her a woman now, sixteen or seventeen years old. She had been clever, that he did recall. She had accused them all of suffering from the Roman disease, and at remembering it, he smiled to himself. He wondered what she was calling them now.

He and Togodumnus rode north, the summer passing in fire and blood, a summer of unusual heat in which the grass withered to a dirty brown and the streams in the woods shrank to trickles of muddy water. Caradoc fought without appetite, continually afraid that one day he would see Aricia herself, standing in her chariot with her chiefs around her, and here, so close to the rolling marches of her land, he began to dream of her again in the hot, dry nights. But battle followed battle, one red, tired dawn after another, and if she was there among the shouting, boasting, bronze-bedecked Coritani chiefs, he did not see her. The Coritani, their numbers swelled by silent Icenians and huge, bearded Brigantians, held on. Even their women, great-armed and tall, took to the field, screaming strange curses, but still Caradoc refused to let the Catuvellaunian freewomen fight. Gladys had disobeyed him but he overlooked her flagrant disregard for his authority. Gladys had always been a law unto herself, and besides, as she reminded him, she had taken no oath to any chief. She rode by herself, cared for her own belongings, fought where and when she would, and he left her alone.

Autumn closed in quickly, as if the summer had burned itself out before its time, and the Catuvellaunians went home to Camulodunon unhappy with the months of war. Too many freemen had been lost, too little ground gained. Caradoc was resolved to press the Dobunni next spring, instead, and he and Togodumnus stared moodily day after day from the shelter of the Great Hall upon the saturated, puddle-riddled countryside. They had grown tired of the petty squabbles and bloodletting of their chiefs closeted in the huts with nothing to do, tired of the weather which poured out a steady rain and precluded hunting or chariot riding, and tired of themselves and each other. Togodumnus became surlier and more unpredictable as the winter dragged on. He did his best to pick fights with Caradoc, insulting him, and pricking him with the smarting pins of his sarcastic wit, and at last Caradoc, goaded beyond restraint, shouted at him, "Damn you, Tog! Why don't you take your worthless chiefs and go to Verulamium as we agreed! I'm sick of you. I don't want you here any more!" Togodumnus considered it, his head on one side, unmoved by Caradoc's livid face.

"Good!" he said finally. "I think I will. It's not good raiding weather, but raiding is preferable to this stinking, damp inactivity." He swaggered close. "And I may not come back. Think about that, my brother. You've been ordering us all as though you were ricon, you alone, and we do not like it. Besides, you did not lead us well this year, and the chiefs are saying that it is my turn to champion them." Caradoc was speechless. He struggled for words, strangled by his rage, and Togodumnus flung out into the rain, his shield-bearer and his bard trotting behind him.

Caradoc was still angry when Eurgain handed him the comb that night, sitting before her mirror, and he pulled it through her hair with quick, sharp strokes that made her wince. Tog had gone. In a short time he had gathered his chiefs and his freemen and women and had ridden off without saying goodbye, the horses splashing through the mud and the wheels of the wains slithering this way and that. In the end, Eurgain took the comb gently from his cold fingers and threw it on the table, swiveling to face him.

"Why do you glower, my husband?" she said. "You know he will be back."

Caradoc did not move. "I do not think so. At least, I do not think he will be back for the next season of fighting. He wants to face the Coritani on his own, the reckless fool. He will undo all the planning we had done together."

"Well then, let him go. Let him lose his chiefs' respect by making a mess of his campaigns, and then see him coming running home!" She was afraid to tell him what she was really thinking, but that tiny fear passed from her to him when their eyes brushed, and he smiled unwillingly, picking up the comb and drawing it more gently through the lustrous tresses.

"I am sorry, Eurgain," he said quietly. "It is the weather. And you know, of course you know, that I fear Tog's ambition. Once he has the bit between his teeth there at Verulamium, and particularly if he is successful in his battles next spring where I failed, it will be an easy matter for him to persuade the chiefs of his new Council to ride against me."

She bent her head, looking at the long hands clasped tight in her lap, and the comb continued to move, slowly and hypnotically, through her hair. She wanted to laugh, to say—Oh Caradoc, not Tog!—to toss off a light remark, but the moment slid into a longer moment, and the meaning of his words deepened in her mind. He was right. Togodumnus was dangerous. Caradoc had kept him busy, but now there was rain and boredom and the rapid disintegration of an unpredictable mind. She had seen the symptoms before. They all had. She reached up, grasping his arms and, drawing him down, kissed him urgently, as if by her actions she could send his bitter, lonely thoughts back to a place beyond memory. He knelt by the little chair and embraced her, laying his head against her full breasts, but beneath the blind assertion of their passion he could hear her heart beating like the wings of a frightened bird.

Two weeks after Togodumnus had ridden blithely away, Fearachar came to Caradoc as he sat by the fire in his house. The rain had stopped. The sky was low with more moisture, but the clouds were breaking and now and then a weak, apologetic sun bathed Camulodunon in momentary brightness. At the first sign of better weather the children had scattered, Llyn to the woods on his horse, and the girls to the grass before Gladys's hut, to play with her seashells. But Caradoc, bored and depressed, sat drinking, while Eurgain bent over her table, polishing the crystals and humming.

Fearachar nodded glumly. "Your pardon, Lord," he said, "but there is a strange animal waiting outside to see you."

"Oh?" Caradoc did not even smile. Anxiety still pained him. "What kind of an animal?"

Fearachar was disappointed at his lack of reaction. "The kind of animal that says he is a trader but is not. That kind of animal."

Eurgain stopped humming though her hands still moved among her treasures, and Caradoc felt his lassitude begin to fade. "Tell me, old friend," he said softly. Fearachar fixed his loose, heavy-lidded gaze upon the ceiling.

"He dresses like a trader but looks like a patrician. He is too stupid to even disguise his hands. And he's not a common spy. He can't disguise his eyes, either." He chuckled a little at his witticism. "He says he wants to talk to you about the poor trading we've been doing lately, but of course he's lying. Even I could do better than that."

Caradoc sat straighter in his chair, the wine forgotten. He felt his body tense slowly, the way it did before he raised the carnyx to his lips to signal the first charge of battle, and he and Fearachar looked at one another in perfect understanding. "Where are Cinnamus and Caelte?" he asked quickly.

"I sent for them and they are waiting also. A nice, friendly trio they make out there, the trader shivering in the wind and the chiefs spitting him with their eyes. You will not see him alone, will you, Lord? He is probably armed with a poisoned needle, or some such diabolical Roman invention." The doleful face grew even more lugubrious, but Caradoc did not need the freeman's clumsy attempt at humor.

"Of course not!" he snapped, rising and pulling his sword belt forward. "Send Cin and Caelte in first, and then the trader." Fearachar bowed and slipped through the doorskins, and Caradoc spoke quickly over his shoulder. "Go on polishing quietly, Eurgain, and set your memory to work. Remember every word that passes here." She did not reply but he knew that she had heard, and then his men shouldered their way into the room. "Stand beside me," he ordered them. "And listen. I have a feeling." It was more than a feeling. Something rushed to meet him, a premonition, a mind-freezing blast, and as the tall, thin man walked slowly toward him, letting the doorskins fall silently, he saw a hole gape open in the mad whirl of his panicked thoughts. Then his head cleared. Fearachar was right. This was no coarse dog and wine dealer. The eyes were level, full of a calm cunning. The face was long and thin, the nose straight, the mouth sensitive but capable of callousness. The man was dressed roughly. A dirty gray tunic hung on his spare frame, covered by a tattered brown cloak. His belt was of plain, undressed leather, and a simple knife hung from it. The breeches were baggy and mud-spattered. And the hands. Looking at them, Caradoc knew what this strange animal was. He went forward, arm outstretched, and the other grasped it with his thin, supple wrist and elegant fingers.

"Welcome to the tuath," Caradoc said evenly. "May your stay here be one of rest and peace. There is wine and barley cakes. Will you eat and drink before you share your news?" The man's startled eyes met his own, then he laughed, a friendly, warm sound.

"I have underestimated the wit of the Catuvellaunian chieftains," he said dryly. "What trader has ever been accorded a tribal welcome? Well, Caradoc, your chiefs are right. I am not a trader, but I did not want to die with a sword buried in my belly, so I have posed as one." He fingered his long jaw but his eyes never left Caradoc's own. "I will gladly eat and drink with you," he went on. "It is a long way from the river if one does not own a horse."

Cinnamus pushed a chair toward him but he did not sit until Caradoc sank back onto his own, then he lowered himself slowly and began to eat. Caradoc poured him wine and the man's cool eyes flickered over the decorated silver cup before he raised it to his lips. Of course the cup comes from Rome, like everything else about you, Caradoc thought. What did you expect, a ravening horde of barbarians? He refilled his own cup and drank slowly, and his men stood very still, watching. When the man had finished the last crumb of barley cake he turned to Caradoc with a smile, and Caradoc knew that every detail of the room and of they themselves had been noted.

"I will not waste your time," the man said. "I want to speak with you alone."

Cinnamus laughed, a harsh, rude bark of mirthless contempt, but the man seemed not to be offended when Caradoc shook his head. "No chief receives a guest alone," he said. "And no chief discusses any affair alone. All business belongs to the tuath and the Council."

The man shrugged, a movement that stopped just short of disdain. "In that case, I would like your woman to leave. Women have wagging tongues, do they not?" His inviting, sympathetic smile met cold stares. Eurgain gave no sign of having heard, but Caradoc was very glad that it was not Vida who stood quietly in the shadows.

"She is my wife," he said coldly. "She is a full member of the Council, with her own honor-price. State your business."

"Very well. I bring you an offer, and a warning." They waited, and Eurgain's hands were stilled as she brought herself into a state of full concentration, forcing away from her consciousness every thought of her own, as the Druithin had taught her father, long ago. "We in Rome know of your doings, Caradoc," he went on kindly. "We have watched your accession to power within your tribe, and your rapid expansion. We do not deny you the right to live as you wish," he said hurriedly, seeing the dawning annoyance on Caradoc's face, "but we cannot be blamed for worrying when we see our traders idle and the good commerce there once was between Cunobelin and ourselves slipping into chaos. Even so, with you yourself here in Camulodunon, we had little to fear. But now . . ." He paused, drank deliberately, fingered his jaw again. "Now your brother sits in Verulamium, planning your downfall, and it is time to offer you our help."

His words dropped into their midst like bolts hurled from a legion's ballistate, and Cinnamus and Caelte exclaimed in shock. Caradoc sprang to his feet. Only Eurgain remained still, feeling no emotion, registering the words with automatic and cool skill. "Explain yourself!" Caradoc snarled. "What is your source?" and the man waved his arms gently.

"Oh come, Lord," he chided. "We are men of the world. Not all traders are traders. Some are spies, and you know this well. Why should I deny it? My spies came to me from Verulamium yesterday, while I sat in my ship at the mouth of your river. They told me that Togodumnus, your brother, does not intend to fight the Iceni or the Dobunni in the spring. He intends to fight you."

With a monumental effort of the will, Caradoc kept his face blank. He slid back onto his chair, crossed his legs, dropped his gaze so that the man should not see his pain. He was hearing the truth, he knew it. This man's presence here was all the proof he needed. The draft from his door found his legs, and suddenly he shivered with cold. "And your offer?" he managed. The man drained his cup and leaned forward, lacing his fingers.

"Let us help you, Caradoc. You are an honest man, a good fighter, a worthy leader. Your brother is flighty, unstable, and thoroughly untrustworthy. You and I do not want to see him as ricon here at Camulodunon. If that happened, Rome would have to say farewell to her trade, and that would be a great pity. I am empowered to offer you aid. You may have gold, as much as you need to buy help from other tribes. And you may call upon any legion you choose from Gaul, to swell your ranks. The legatus legionis and you would work and fight together until Togodumnus is defeated and trade is safe."

Caradoc felt himself begin to smile grossly, idiotically, while his muscles tightened into one screaming, cataleptic knot. Of course, of course. Oh Camulos, what do I do? What do I say? He forced his mouth to obey him, and slowly he stopped smiling. "What agreement would be arranged?" he asked. The man's hand went to his plunging jaw again.

"There would be a treaty, naturally. Even friends sign treaties to avoid any dispute. There would be a paper, Caradoc. We would promise gold and soldiers. You would promise to promote all trade as well as you could when Togodumnus was . . . defeated." He rose, holding out his hand, and Caradoc took his wrist, sure that the distaste he felt would surge through his fingers. "Think about it," the man said. "And then send me word. My ship is anchored in the estuary and I shall wait there. But do not take too long. Your brother will strike before the trees have come to full leaf." He expected no comment. He smiled again, a trifle superciliously, glanced around the room once more, and was gone. Caradoc sat still, and neither Cinnamus nor Caelte moved either. Eurgain left her cloth on the table and came and sat opposite her husband, her face still immobile and her hands limp. Caradoc spoke to her.

"Now, Eurgain," Caradoc said, his voice low, "repeat the conversation back to me, word for word." She closed her eyes and began to recite in a low, singsong voice, the sound without expression and without pause, and Caradoc, listening, folded his arms and leaned on the table, his eyes on the wine jug. When she had finished he asked her to go over it again. Then he reached out and stroked her cheek. "Put your thoughts to work on your words now, Eurgain. How do you interpret the man?" Cinnamus squatted on the brown skins before the fire, his hands loosely joined, staring into it, and Caelte went and leaned against the wall, his thumbs in his belt and his lively face solemn.

"He is not an equite," she said frankly, "for equites do not do his kind of work. He is a patrician. He is also a truth-sayer and a liar." Cinnamus nodded once, and she went on. "He speaks the truth when he says that Tog is planning to take your head and become ricon this spring. He lies when he offers only aid."

"What else do you divine?"

She hesitated, glancing around at them. "I divine that he showed us only the trunk of a vast network of deep-hidden roots."

Cinnamus laughed. "Eurgain, you sound now like one of the Druithin. But I agree with you. He is no ordinary spy. He is an emissary from Rome. But what is his true purpose?"

Caradoc hushed them then, and sat gazing before him, a frown on his face. He was afraid—of Tog, of Rome, of the decision he must make. If he accepted the offer, then by the late summer Tog would be dead and he would be ricon alone, ruling without challenge. But why should Rome send good soldiers to die on behalf of one small chief living at the ends of the earth? He had dismissed the excuse of the worsening trade situation as soon as it was mooted. Why? Why?

"What indeed?" Caelte said, as if reading the question in Caradoc's thought. "There is no sense to it, particularly as Caligula did not dare to cross the water and oppose us. Is this a new way of conquest, a more devious way?"

He had put his finger on the bruised wound of Caradoc's own fear. Caradoc got up. "Cinnamus, run to the stable and get us horses. Eurgain, go to Gladys. Tell her what has passed here and ask her for her wisdom. Caelte, you and I and Cinnamus will go now to Verulamium, and talk to my brother."

Eurgain protested in shock. "No, Caradoc! If you go without a Druid, Tog will seize the opportunity to kill you and save himself much bloodshed. If you must go, at least send freemen for a Druid!"

"There is no time to sit here while freemen go bumbling about the forests searching for men who avoid us as though we carry a disease," he replied.

"Then let me come with you. Tog will not strike you down before my eyes."

126

"Eurgain," he said patiently, while Cinnamus ran out and Caelte went to summon Fearachar. "If Tog means to kill me he will do it whether you are there or not. But I do not think I am in danger, at least not once he has heard my tale." He kissed her swiftly, absently.

She did not respond, but when he reached the door she said evenly, "Do not forget one thing."

"What?"

"The man said nothing about Adminius."

And there it was. Caradoc felt like a jeweler, fitting tiny pieces of bright enamel onto a silver necklace. All the pieces were there, but he could not make the pattern fit until Eurgain came and gently rearranged the tiles. She knew what she had said. The implications were there, behind the steady blue eyes. She had already faced them and tucked them away under the mantle of her unflinchable assurance, but they flew at Caradoc like driving hail.

"It cannot be," he said after a moment, and she laughed cynically.

"Oh yes it can. How many times has Rome failed to best Albion? Too many times for her vaunted dignity."

Caradoc did not look at her again. He ran out the door, pausing only to tell Fearachar to keep watch for Llyn, then he fled to the gate where his chiefs and the horses waited, muffled against the wind.

They spent two nights sleeping under the eaves of the great oak forest that stalked away beyond Verulamium and into the Atrebates country, propitiating the goddess of the place before they curled up in their blankets. The following evening, when a shy, hesitant rain began to patter on their cloaks, they rode up to the earthwalls of Verulamium. The gate was still open but the gateguard hovered outside, sword drawn, and would not let them through until Caradoc shouted in exasperation, "Look at me man! You know me well enough! I am Caradoc, your lord!"

"Togodumnus is my lord," he retorted sullenly, his surly face full of suspicion, but he moved aside and they dismounted, leading the horses under the gate and up the steep, winding path.

"The freemen have been busy," Caelte remarked in an undertone, noting the crumbled breeches in the wall, which had been hurriedly repaired with fresh earth, the great stones heaped waiting to be fitted where the lip of the defences frowned above them. His companions did not reply, but Caradoc drew his sword. The town was quiet. Smoke streamed from the thatched roofs, and firelight patched golden across their feet as they strode past the doorways. At last they rounded the final bend and found Togodumnus. He was standing cloakless in the quickening rainfall, hands on slim hips, with his attendants behind him. They were watching two chiefs who grunted and slashed at each other in the fading light. He heard them coming and turned, but he did not smile. His chiefs drew their swords, clustering tight around him, their mutters a threatening rumble, and Caradoc and Cinnamus looked questioningly at each other. This strange suspicion was unexpected. At a word the horses were led away and Togodumnus walked to Caradoc, arm outstretched, the words of greeting coming cold and fast, and Caradoc struck his arm away. "How dare you greet me as a guest or a strange emissary, Tog, in my own territory! What is the matter with you? Why all this hostility? I nearly killed the gateguard for his rudeness."

Beyond Togodumnus the two chiefs fought on oblivious, until one of them jumped back with a howl and the assembly shouted excitedly, "First blood!" Togodumnus scowled. "And why do you walk my paths with sword drawn, Caradoc? What are you doing here?" His eyes left Caradoc's face, flicked to his chiefs and back again, and Caradoc tensed, seeing a dozen calculating thoughts go flashing through the agile mind.

"I must speak with you alone, Tog. Do not molest me until you have heard my words." Suddenly Togodumnus chuckled and embraced him lightly. "I will hear, but I may still kill you," he said. "And not alone, of course. News is a matter for all."

"Not this time," Caradoc said, and the smile left Tog's face to be replaced by a huffy offence. "I need to talk alone with you, just you and me, Tog. My chiefs will wait outside with your chiefs, and all swords will be put together in an accepted place. I do not bring news for the tuath."

"What do you bring, then?" Togodumnus spat. The men shrieked, "Second blood!" and Tog swung away, striding to the panting, blood-streaked men who leaned on their shields. "The dog is yours, Gwyllog," he said harshly. "The affair is settled. No more blood." Then he turned back. "Tell your men to lay their swords here," he pointed to the ground, "but my men will not do this. Verulamium is my fortress. Also, you will be searched."

"Has he lost his head?" Cinnamus whispered angrily in Caradoc's ear. "Anyone would think we were Icenians or Brigantians!"

"Stand away, Ironhand," Togodumnus called. "No secrets." He jerked his head at one of his chiefs and the man walked quickly to Caradoc, sheathing his sword.

"Step away, Cin," Caradoc said, and Cinnamus took two stiff, slow strides.

"Search him," Tog called again, and the man bent, his face com-

128

posed, indifferent, his hands roving surely round Caradoc's belt, under his tunic, in his hair. Then he shook his head and went back to his place while Caradoc felt the color mount in his face. He hung on to his temper and gritted his teeth, wishing he had not come. Then Togodumnus waved at him airily and disappeared through the doorskins at his back, and Caradoc followed, feeling utterly defenceless. One word from Tog, and Cinnamus and Caelte would be dead and himself a hostage.

The room was dry and warm, but very dirty. Tog's clothes and weapons lay strewn over floor and bed. An oil lamp flickered, sending a stream of black smoke to the ceiling, for no one had bothered to trim it. A half-eaten piece of pork lay in a pool of grease on the table, and a full jug of wine was beside it. Togodumnus walked swiftly to the table and poured for both of them, but Caradoc had to go and get his own cup. Neither of them toasted. They drained the cups silently, pouring the dregs on the floor for Verulamium's god, then refilled the cups, not looking at each other. Togodumnus flung himself into his chair, waving irritably at his brother. "Oh sit down, Caradoc, and stop watching me out of the corner of your eye. Tell me your business and then go away."

But Caradoc remained on his feet, the door on his right hand and the fire on his left. He held the cup tightly in both hands, searching the thin, handsome face before him and seeing only petulance and a gleam of madness in the light brown eyes. "I have had a strange visitor," he said at length, and Tog did not move. He just went on staring, and Caradoc knew that his thoughts were on his armed chiefs waiting outside and a quick, easy slaughter. He decided to tell it all quickly before Togodumnus's restless body demanded action. "A Roman spy came to me, Tog, a man dressed as a trader. He told me that you are planning war against me this spring. He offered me soldiers and money with which to defeat you." The light eyes darkened in surprise. Togodumnus blinked and sat up. "He said that Rome is concerned for her trade with us, and if you and I fought and I was defeated there would be no more commerce. He said . . . he said that you were flighty and untrustworthy and would be a most unreliable ricon, from Rome's point of view." The last words rushed headlong into the room and flittered, dying swiftly. There was a long, pregnant pause. Then Togodumnus began to smile. The thin lips spread wide, the gleaming white teeth glinted at Caradoc. He began to laugh. He got up and staggered about the room, holding his belly. He came and fell against Caradoc, wrapping his long arms about him, smothering him in brown hair, and still he laughed. Finally he man-

129

aged to control himself. He poured more wine and sat down again, tears of mirth wet on his cheeks, and Caradoc watched him without surprise. He knew Tog's every mood, every impulse to laughter or rage, the one often following the other, and he knew that the only permanence to be found under Tog's erratic, dazzling dances of temperament was his complete instability. No one was safe around him. Caradoc's sense of danger deepened.

"Why do you come rushing to me?" Togodumnus said, still convulsed. "Why not accept his offer, Caradoc, and get rid of me? It is quite true, I was planning to get rid of you. I have even chosen the place where your head will hang. There," he pointed at the door, "beside the skins, so that I can pat it every day."

"You know why I came!" Caradoc snapped at him. He sat down, cradling his wine. "Because I don't believe that Rome cares a bit who is ricon at Camulodunon. Nor do I think that Rome is worried enough about the trade to send a master spy to my gate. There is another reason, but I want to hear it from your lips to convince me that I am not insane."

"Of course you are not insane," Tog said in surprise. "You are absolutely right. Shall I tell you how I know?" He began to laugh again, and Caradoc sighed, but the splutters died and Togodumnus swilled his wine and drank greedily. "Two weeks ago I had a visitor, too, brother of mine. A tall, skinny fellow with long fingers that kept scratching at his jaw and eyes like hailstones. He told me that you were jealous of my popularity with the chiefs and had decided to destroy me in the spring. He offered gold and soldiers, and a paper to sign. I signed it right away."

"Tog!" The intimation of a deadly, brooding doom was with him again, filling his mind with apprehensive fear. He was right. Eurgain was right. At last Rome was turning her iron-lidded eyes to Albion again. "Why did you sign?"

Tog shrugged happily. "I need the gold. Chiefs like to be paid in gold for a war such as ours. As for the rest, well, what is a piece of paper?"

"And then he came to me," Caradoc murmured to himself. Oh, how cunning! How simply—pitilessly perfect!

The amusement went out of Togodumnus's face and was replaced by a cold, serious reflection. "The Romans hoped to drive a wedge between us, that is obvious," he said. "But why this way? Why not simply wait and let us destroy each other?"

"Because we might treaty with each other instead, and then quarrel again, and then treaty again," Caradoc answered. "And Rome does not have the time to wait. She is in a hurry."

130

They looked at each other, a common certainty born between them. "Can it be?" Tog asked softly. "And what of Adminius?"

Caradoc looked at him sharply. His brother was no fool, though he cloaked his animal astuteness with care. "I divine it thus," he said. "The legions will come in the name of Adminius, and conquer us in the name of Adminius, but Caesar will come also, and claim Albion for his own. Rome smarts, Tog. She has decided that this time there will be no defeat, no turning back."

"They will fail as they failed before, all of them, the august fools," Tog sneered. "Julius Caesar failed, mad Caius failed—failure, Caradoc, one after the other. And this Claudius, this meek, book-loving tool of the Praetorians, he will fail also. We are invincible. Let them come. And then let them run away, decimated and unmanned."

Caradoc shook his head slowly, emphatically. "They will not go away, Tog, not this time. They cannot afford another retreat."

"Then we face war. What a pity. I was longing to nail your head to the wall."

They grinned at one another, raised cups, and drank. "Come back to Camulodunon, Tog," Caradoc said. "Bring your chiefs. We will send out emissaries, gather lords. We must send spies to the coast."

Togodumnus considered, his head on one side. "Were you really planning war with me, Caradoc?" he asked with plaintive coyness like a child, and Caradoc denied it, smiling.

"No, Tog. The Roman lied to you. Come home."

"Then I will come. I will ride tomorrow. How long do we have to wait?"

Caradoc looked deep into the quivering red liquid in his cup, and the rain drummed arrogantly on the walls. How long. A week? A season? "I do not know. All I know is that they will come."

He, Cinnamus, and Caelte rode home, sleeping once more under the dripping, twisted black arms of the oaks. Cinnamus had fomented a violent argument as they slopped dismally along the squelching path. He insisted that Togodumnus would not come to Camulodunon. Togodumnus had oathed to Rome and had no intention of aiding Caradoc. Knowing Cinnamus's dislike for Tog, Caradoc refuted him patiently, but then Cin had said, "If he does come, Lord, then slay him in his sleep and be at peace. Face Rome without the fear that Togodumnus's knife should find your back."

Hearing his own desire flay him in the matter-of-fact tone, Caradoc shouted at him, "My honor is worth more to me than my life! Would the chiefs follow a murderer with no honor-price left?"

"At least you should consider it. I will do it for you if you like."

Rage at himself gummed Caradoc's mouth, rage because he was too strong, and too weak, to rid himself of his brother. "Tog knows the danger," he ground out. "He will be prepared. I want him to trust me, or we are all lost. Where is your sense, Cinnamus?"

"Out looking for yours," the green-eyed youth replied tartly, and they rode on to Caelte's low singing and the mutter of the rain.

Back at a shrouded, cold Camulodunon, before he shed his soaking clothes, Caradoc sent for Vocorio and Mocuxsoma. Eurgain had come to greet him, swathed and hooded against the damp, and Gladys waited to hear his news in the Great Hall. He spoke to his men quietly, with Eurgain beside him. "Take five freemen warriors," he said. "Go to the river mouth, and find the Roman trader that was here. Fearachar can go with you. He will recognize him."

"And when we have found him?" Vocorio rumbled.

Caradoc looked up at the endless gray sky, the shining wet roof of the Great Hall. He felt Eurgain's hand under his elbow, the pulse in his throat, the sword lying heavy against his breech-clad leg. Then he grinned, slowly, a wolfish, blood-scenting grimace, and his men found themselves looking into the wily, slit eyes of Cunobelin.

"Kill him," he said.

CHAPTER TEN

THREE DAYS LATER Togodumnus and his chiefs, with their wives, children, and baggage, straggled back to Camulodunon and were welcomed with a night of feasting. Caradoc sent scouts to watch the coast, and the winter plodded on. "How do we know which part of the coast to observe?" Togodumnus had asked him, but Caradoc knew. The Romans would land where Julius Caesar had landed, on the Cantiacan peninsula, and he sent emissaries to the Cantiaci, requesting a joint Council. He also sent men to all the other tribes while the moon waxed and waned, and the rain gave way to hard frosts. Togodumnus went to bed each night with his hut surrounded by sleepless, armed chiefs. He was taking no chances and was quite open in his mistrust, but Caradoc made no move against him. All his thoughts, all his will, were bent on the clash with Rome that he knew would come, and he had no time or inclination to cross swords or hard words with his brother. He ordered regular sword practice for the women, and once more Eurgain and Gladys sparred on the frozen earth, weighed down by the shields he insisted they carry. Llyn was nine now, a short, sturdy boy, and Caradoc ordered Cinnamus to give him a sword of iron. The wooden sword was put away, and Llyn sweated and shrieked happily, slashing at Cinnamus, toppling to the ground, taking scratches and cuts from his teacher's lethal blade with joyous unconcern.

One by one the emissaries returned, and the wind swung into the west, bringing more warm rain and a faint, odorous whiff of spring. The Cantiaci would sit on a joint Council. So would the fierce Durotriges, the Dumnonii, and the Belgae, Cunobelin's old allies. The men of the west, the uncouth Silures and Ordovices, said that they would wait and see what happened. They wanted no truck with Rome, but neither did they want to mingle with the pleasure-loving Catuvellauni. The Iceni, the Coritani, the Dobunni, and the Atrebates, the remnants of Verica's people, all rudely and gleefully refused any aid to the House Catuvellaun, and Caradoc heard the growing number of nays with a mounting despair. He felt that he alone knew what they were facing, and he was afraid. Togodumnus scoffed angrily. "Just wait until Rome runs," he swaggered. "Then we will turn and finish off these stupid peasants. They will be sorry they refused us aid. What did Aricia say?"

"She said she will not be allied with a tribe that sees no boundaries. She hopes that the legions grind us into the dirt." The words came hard. Yearning and bitterness flared within him even as he spoke them, and he felt a kindling in his loins. He wanted to beat her and fling her to the ground, to hear her beg for mercy.

"Then we will do without her," Tog declared. "The obstinate vixen! When I get my hands on her she will cry—Enough!"

"Before the chiefs leave their territories we must do something about the traders," Caradoc said, changing the subject determinedly. "They will have to be rounded up and imprisoned until the battle is over. Otherwise they will be forever running back and forth, taking our plans to Caesar. He must already know that something is afoot. He would not be fool enough to expect to find us totally unprepared."

"I say kill them all," Tog pressed. "If we imprison them we will have to feed and guard them, and we are going to need all the grain and salted meat we can carry if we are to journey to meet the legions." Caradoc saw the logic in Tog's argument, but he was loathe to act so callously. Many of the traders were acquaintances of his, men he had passed the time of day with when his father was alive, and though he did not respect them, regarding them as peasants of Rome with no honor-prices and no morals, he was not so blithely prodigal with human life as was his brother. But he had to agree. The traders must die. It was only good sense.

"You and your chiefs can see to it," he told Togodumnus testily. "I hate useless slaughter."

"Not useless," Tog retorted. "Where's your stomach, Caradoc? I like it no more than you." It was true. Togodumnus liked to kill, but only when there was an element of sport or a matter of honorable gain. There was no sport in the slaying of men who lived by their wits and not by their long, thin knives. So it was done, quickly and secretly.

The lords and chiefs of other tuaths began to arrive for the Council, with their flashy, quarreling wives, their gaudy, patterned cloaks, their bronze helms made to resemble claws or bulls' horns or high, glinting feathers. They were housed in empty huts, in stables and tents, their retainers strutting about, bullying the Catuvellauni freemen and picking fights, and Caradoc spent his time running from circle to circle in the town, pacifying irate chiefs and punishing peasants. Camulodunon became one vast, sprawling ant heap, crawling from morning until night with men and women jealously striving to assert their superiority. They consumed vast quantities of imported wine and they ate constantly, and Caradoc was very glad when the night of Council came.

"It will be like this all the time if we have to fight together," Togodumnus reminded him, mockingly wagging a finger under his nose, and Caradoc wondered grimly how this brawling, shouting mob could ever be persuaded to join any cause. But he need not have fretted. The Council went on all night. The Dumnonii and the Durotriges had brought Druids with them, and the Druids guided the proceedings with calm skill. Joke after joke was told as the air in the Great Hall became stuffier and hotter, and serious things were discussed, but there was no fighting, though many of the chiefs became very drunk. Songs were sung, poems chanted, and there was even some impromtu dancing, but Caradoc, wedged in the forefront between Cinnamus and Caelte, sensed the devious, halting path the Council was taking. The tribes disliked one another, but were all mistrustful of Rome. Though they could slit each other's throats without compunction, steal each other's cattle, and feud among themselves over women or honor-prices, they all shared one fear—slavery. Slavery was the ultimate disgrace, the state worse than that of a peasant. A slave was not human any more. A slave was an animal. The Romans would come and turn them all into slaves unless they resisted, as Caradoc and the Druids pointed out forcefully time and again, and in the end, when another dawn flowed quietly into the town, they piled their swords together and swore unity. It was temporary, of course, and Caradoc could not hope for more, but he watched the gleaming tangle of metal with tired satisfaction.

The tribes went home, and Caradoc settled down to wait. The weather changed again, became mild, and the trees sent forth sticky brown buds. In the meadows, under the shadow of the earthwalls, the pristine snowdrops arched and the air became thick with the strong taunting odors of the stirring soil. The peasants put aside their weapons and took out their plows, and still Caradoc waited, his spies coming to him day after day with nothing to report. He began to wake in the night, an anxious sweat on him, wondering if he had been wrong, and Togodumnus's cheerful sarcasm did nothing to reassure him. Then one of his men came to him, riding wearily through the warm, somnolent afternoon, and slid from his horse to face Caradoc, Togodumnus, and the chiefs clustered in a lazy group upon the slope before the fetid dyke. They rose and greeted him warily, sensing news, and Togodumnus sprang forward.

"Tell us quickly," he said, disregarding the formal offering of bread, meat, and wine. "Is the time here?" The man sank to the long, dry grass.

"It is here," he said. "Scouts from Gaul braved the neap tides to bring us word. Rome is camped on the beaches of Gesioracum. Rafts and sturdy boats wait to carry the soldiers across the water, and the sands are piled high with provisions." He peeled off his dirty, sweat-stained tunic and flung it away so that the wind could cool his body. "It is no expedition, Lords. It is invasion."

Caradoc squatted before him. "How many legions?" he barked.

"Four."

Togodumnus swore loudly. "Mighty Camulos! So many men?"

Caradoc had a sudden and chilling picture of them, swarming like metal-clad insects on the beach. Forty thousand fighting men. Oh, sweet Raven of Nightmares, Queen of Battle, help us now! "Who commands?" he asked huskily.

"Aulus Plautius Silvanus, ex legatus augusti in Pannonia. He is bringing with him his own legion, the Ninth Hispana, and Thracian auxiliaries, also from his Pannonian garrisons. The other three are the Second Augusta, the Fourteenth Gemina, and the Twentieth Valeria. All with their auxiliaries."

Caradoc closed his eyes. Forty thousand men. Togodumnus was

thoughtful, chewing on his lip and studying the ground while the scent of crushed grass wafted around him. The messenger looked up at them, lines of weariness around his mouth.

"There is more," he said. "Geta is coming."

The chiefs stirred and muttered. Caradoc and Togodumnus were silent, but Cinnamus cried out, "Mother! Hosidius Geta! Conqueror of Mauretania! They send their elephants to crush the mice!" Then Caradoc's mood lightened. He smiled up at Cinnamus and rose easily to his feet.

"It is said that elephants fear mice, Cin," he said. "And these elephants are disadvantaged. They will go blundering about in a country they do not know. We, too, have many thousands of chiefs and freemen, and chariots, and bright swords. They come knowing that they have failures behind them. We face them victorious."

Togodumnus muttered something rude under his breath, then he spoke aloud. "We must send for the allies," he said. "The sword count must begin." He stretched luxuriously, breathed deeply, and beamed on all of them. "Then we move! To the coast!"

The messengers went out and the scouts resumed their lonely watch lying high above the empty, wind-swept beaches of the south while the Catuvellauni prepared to empty Camulodunon. An atmosphere of excited anticipation pervaded the town, and the clash of weapons and the thunder of chariot wheels hung in the air. The servants began to pack the wains with food and spare clothing and the women ran to and fro, chasing the children who became infected by the charged mood of nearly hysterical elation, and darted about the busy huts like mad, fluttering sparrows.

Caradoc entered his house one morning to find Eurgain standing in the middle of the sleeping room, her face flushed, and her eyes clouded with preoccupation. A small box lay open on the table, newly filled with her star maps and her crystals. Her tunics and cloaks were piled on the bed in bright profusion, and her jewels lay scattered on the skins, winking and glittering as the firelight caught them. Her sword stood against the wall, a whetstone and a bowl of water beside it, and Tallia moved quietly amid the wreckage of a once peaceful home. He could hear the little girls laughing and talking under the window, but there was no sign of Llyn. Eurgain glanced at him, a frown creasing her smooth forehead.

"Eurgain!" he exclaimed sharply. "What are you doing?"

"Packing, of course," she answered absently. "No, Tallia, don't include the gold and amethyst belt. I would be upset if it were lost or stolen. Put it back. But I will take the three leather ones."

Caradoc advanced carefully, threading his way through the gay

136

debris. "You can put it all away, Tallia," he said. "Eurgain, you are not going."

This time she did not even bother to look at him. "Don't be silly, Caradoc. Tallia, five tunics should be sufficient. Don't forget my short ones, and my breeches. If you neglect to put them in the boxes I shall have to fight in a long gown."

"Eurgain," he said again, more loudly. "You are not going."

Now she turned to him, impatience evident in the angry set of the shoulders. "What do you mean, Caradoc? Of course I am going. All the women are going, and the children, too. It is the custom."

He came and grasped her stiff, yellow-clad arms. "What the other women do is no concern of mine, but you are staying here, in safety, with the girls." Annis paused to listen and Eurgain spoke angrily. For the first time Caradoc saw her cool imperturbability shaken, and a fiery, proud woman blazed out at him as he sought her wide eyes.

"I will not cower here like a trembling winded doe while the other women fight and die! I am a sword-woman. Have you forgotten, my husband? If I do not go I will lose the respect of my sisters, and I will have to battle my way into their esteem once more. What do you fear?" she said scornfully. "For myself, I fear nothing."

"Eurgain," he said quietly, emphatically, "This is not a raid, or a blood feud, or the clash of two warring tribes. We face men who fight day and night, every moment of their lives, like mindless tools of war. And that is what they are. Tools. They have no champion. They are all champions, without mercy and without honor. Either we kill them all or we die. They will not fight as we do. Their tactics are unfamiliar to us and that makes this war twice the gamble."

Her cheeks flamed suddenly like red corals. "But you let Llyn go! And Llyn could be slaughtered by a blind old man with no hands!"

"Llyn does not go to be blooded, as you know full well. He will watch from a place of safety, and learn."

"Gladys will go!"

"Gladys has no husband and no children. Besides, she fights as well as Cinnamus."

"And I suppose that I do not!" The color left her face and her skin became white as chalk. The deep eyes burned like two incandescent caverns, and beneath his hands he felt the rigidity of supreme rage. "What have I become to you, Caradoc ap Cunobelin! A soft, lazy tired servant, living on milk and bread, able only to snore in the sun and bear children? You dishonor me! I will fight you for the right to go! I am a warrior, not a stinking wet-nurse!"

He grasped her shoulders and shook her viciously. "Remember your oath to me, woman!" he shouted. "You will not go, you will not go!"

She wrenched herself free and slapped him soundly across the face. Quick, stinging tears came to his eyes and he stepped backward. "Eurgain," he said. "If we are wiped out and do not come home again then you must fight alone, with none to sing of how you fell in the silent streets of Camulodunon. Can you say that such a fate is without honor? I want all the chiefs to persuade their women not to go, for this very reason. Slavery or death is not only the alternative open to the freemen warriors. It extends to the freewomen warriors too."

"I understand," she said bitterly, folding her arms tight to her breasts. "The men attack, and we defend."

"Yes, that is so, this time."

He went out quickly and Tallia waited, arms full of belts and trinkets, but her mistress continued to stand and stare at the doorway.

The tribes began to assemble and the sword-gathering began. Lords, chiefs, and freemen, farmers, blacksmiths, artists, metalworkers, swarmed over Camulodunon and spilled out into the woods and little fields between the town and the river. By day the forest rang with talk and laughter, and by night the countryside was dotted with the orange eyes of cooking fires. Caradoc had armed the peasants, but as unfree men they were not required to go to war. He gave them weapons only to defend themselves and their huts and farmsteads if the warriors did not come home. For a week the lords and chiefs held Council in the sweet, blossom-heavy air of spring, then they harnessed their chariots, yoked the oxen to the wains, and set out for the coast. The cups of farewell were shared, passing from hand to eager hand, and Caradoc embraced and kissed his wife in the soft, pearly dawn, while Togodumnus paced restlessly in a fever to be gone.

"Remember my instructions," he told her. "If Rome wins through, tear out the gate and fill the hole with earth and stones. Destroy the bridge over the dyke. If the earthwalls are taken, ring the Great Hall with your women. Do not put the children together in any one hut, for the Romans will fire it. Drive them into the woods, send them west. Sacrifice to the Dagda while we are gone."

She listened, a faint, tremulous smile on her lips. Neither of them had slept well. Caradoc had dreamed, terror waking him to sweat and anguish, but there was no comfort in the warm dimness, or in Llyn's loud snores, and he could not sleep again. Eurgain had woken then and they had lain side by side holding each other, talking quietly until Fearachar came to rouse them.

Now she lifted mauve-shadowed eyes to his own. "Go in safety, walk in peace," she whispered, and suddenly they clung together as if it were farewell, and time, feeling their love and bitter grief, faltered

138

and stood still to watch them wrapped tightly in each other's arms, holding the Raven of Panic at bay.

"Make haste, Caradoc!" Togodumnus called. "Already the chiefs are quarreling over who should have precedence on the march." Caradoc pulled Eurgain's warm arms from around his neck, smoothing down her hair with both wistful hands. Then he knelt and kissed his daughters, their big, solemn eyes fixed on his stern face. He hitched at his sword, took one last look at the huts of his town, empty now, cold and forlorn, and strode down to the gate.

For five days the singing, drinking, squabbling horde moved slowly across the countryside, while the apple trees burst forth into clouds of perfumed white blossoms and the trees opened suddenly, proudly, displaying the delicate freshness of their new green leaves to a low, admiring blue sky. They crossed the Thamus, rattling over the narrow wooden bridge, the water flowing slowly and peacefully below them, and the swifts and swallows looping and diving with high cries around them. Each night Caradoc sent out hunters who slipped quietly through the woods and brought back deer and rabbits. He worried constantly about food, for winter stocks were running dangerously low. He and the other lords had brought with them all the grain and salted meat and fish that the wains could carry, but already the wains rolled lighter and men's bellies rumbled, never comfortably full. In another three months the new crops would be almost ready for harvest and the woods would be full of edible green things, but Caradoc, walking from campfire to campfire, watching the men wolf down their rations, wondered how many of them would return to their farmsteads and hill forts to celebrate Samain.

They pushed on, striking for the coast, following the old paths that wandered lazily over the gentle, wooded hills. They waited for low tide and forded the Medway, the chiefs splashing beside their chariots, the freemen goading the frightened oxen with whips and cries. And then at last Togodumnus and Caradoc, with the chiefs of the Catuvellauni, stood upon the white cliffs, with the warm wind coursing through their hair, and looked down at the sparkle of sun on foamy breakers and out to where the coasts of Gaul blurred, a thin gray line misted by distance and the damp hazes of spring.

The scouts had no news. The boats were ready on the beaches of the mainland and the provisions were stowed away, but under Plautius's gray, cool eye the legions still drilled and marched, and the centurions moved among them with curses and blows. The tribes settled down to wait, pitching their little leather tents around the firepits. Gladys tied her sword to her long leg, hitched up her black cloak, and climbed down the cliff face to disappear for two days, meandering alone across the wet, cold sand, singing her melancholy songs of loneliness and magic, and the leather pouch that swung from her belt was soon full of shells and bits of driftwood. The hubbub of the seething host rose above her, but she did not hear it. She sat cross-legged in the sand, looking down into warm, limpid pools and tasting the bitter salt on her white fingers.

Two more days went by, and idleness curdled in the restless chiefs like milk souring under a hot sun. They gambled and came to blows by night. They thieved and fought by day. Caradoc went among them angrily, sword drawn, berating, coaxing, swearing, and threatening while his brother laughed at him cynically and spent his time charging the lip of the cliff in his little chariot, cloak and hair flying behind him, flirting with death again and again.

Then one night a boat nudged the dark shore and a scout struggled up the white, crumbling face of the cliff, Gladys behind him. He came to Caradoc, Togodumnus, and the others and ate and drank slowly, with relish, while the circle of men watched him, and the tension heightened. Finally, when the air was fraught with bursting, silent questions, seeming about to explode, he wiped his mouth, belched, and sat back with a sigh. Gladys poured herself wine and sank down beside Caradoc, and the scout grinned cheekily at them all, his spirits reviving.

"Lord, they will not come," he said. "Once more the soldiers are refusing to cross the water. Three of the legions do not know Plautius and will not trust him when he says that we are only men like themselves. There have been executions, but the mutiny is spreading. Plautius has sent to the emperor for help. Or advice."

Togodumnus whooped, springing to his feet. "What did I tell you Caradoc, you fool! The soldiers have more sense than you. Now we can go home and attend to our unfinished business!"

Caradoc sat stunned, a running tide of exultation washing over him, but even as he looked up at Togodumnus the tide peaked and began to recede, and doubt crept in on its swift wake. He glanced at his sister. She had not moved. Her head was bent, her eyes on the cup held in both thin hands. The chiefs were chattering excitedly among themselves, but Cinnamus and Caelte mirrored Gladys's still thought, and Fearachar grunted contemptuously. "Only a dead Roman tells the truth," he remarked to no one in particular.

Caradoc turned to the scout. "When did Plautius send to Rome? How long ago?"

"Seven days ago. In a week the emperor will be deliberating, and in another week Plautius will have his orders."

140

"Orders!" Togodumnus shouted. "I laugh! A commander who runs bleating to his superiors because he cannot handle his men has lost the respect of all and faces a ruined career, let alone the loss of Albion. And I thought that this Plautius was a man full of authority and power." He began to saunter away, but Caradoc called sharply, "Where are you going?"

"To order my wains packed and my tent struck," Togodumnus shouted back over his shoulder. "Your stupidity is unexcelled, Caradoc." Several of the chiefs rose and began to drift after Togodumnus and one of them, a great, bearded Durotrigan with black hair hanging to his waist, said, "He is right, your brother. Plautius faces disgrace for his failure. The Romans are finished as far as we are concerned." He nodded his shaggy head and went away, lumbering like an old bear.

"It does not smell right," Caradoc said to his men angrily. "It is too easy. I know, I know that they will come."

Gladys answered him softly, a bleakness chilling her voice. "Of course they will come. Plautius is all we have heard, and more. He is a wily man, my friends. I think that he has acted very cleverly in this. He knows that we sit here on the cliffs, waiting for him, and he wants us to scatter. What better way than the rumor of mutiny and a helpless petition for aid to Caesar? He will come. The chiefs must be made to see."

Caradoc rose, and his men rose with him. "Go quickly," he said to them. "Talk to the chieftains. I will call a Council tonight."

"Leave Togodumnus to me," Gladys said. "I think he is past listening to you, Caradoc, but I will make him see sense."

They parted, but already the creak of wheels split the night and angry voices cursed the sleepy, unwilling oxen.

The chiefs attended the Council grudgingly, sitting in the open around the fire, the shushing of the sea an ever present taunt in their ears. Caradoc spoke to them for an hour, striding up and down before them, explaining and cajoling, while Togodumnus sat silently between his chiefs, his head bowed on his scarlet chest, and dreamed of his brother's head swinging impotently from the lintel of his doorpost. The foreign tribesmen did not bother to conceal their contempt for him, this dreamer, this hasty, loud-mouthed Catuvellaunian wolf who had dragged them from calving and sowing to lead them after a lie. Many of them had begun to say that it had all been a trick to confuse them, and that before they could reach their territories the Catuvellauni would descend on them in some wild, wooded valley and wipe them out. But Caradoc's desperate, inspired eloquence rang

141

in their ears and they found themselves agreeing to wait for two more weeks.

The two nightmare weeks went by. The days were pleasantly warm and breezy and in the evenings the sky clouded over and a light, thin rain fell, angling over the cliffs. Gladys went back to the sands, and Caradoc took to sleeping under his wain with Cinnamus and his other chiefs ranged around it. The threats and drunken challenges grew, and he knew that if Plautius did not move promptly the host would break suddenly, and be dispersed. He wondered whether Plautius was waiting also, waiting for his spies to bring him word that his ruse had succeeded and the tribes of Albion had left the coast. His own scouts came to him every day with grim nays—there was no activity outside Gesioracum. He thought of his wife and his little ones now that his woods must surely be carpeted with knee-high blue-bells. The girls would be running under the trees, arms laden with blooms, their high, excited voices echoing under the oaks, while Tallia kept an anxious watch for boar and wolf and Eurgain sat rigidly by the gate, waiting for news. News. The chieftains no longer gathered eagerly around him at the first sign of a scout boat, and even Togo-dumnus kept away from him, trailed by a bored, silent Llyn. Caradoc had forbidden the beaches to him, and he sulked and avoided his father, behaving like a spoiled, younger Togodumnus. Caradoc did not approve, but his mind was too full of anxiety to worry over Llyn's growing attachment to his uncle.

The fourteenth day dawned, and before its light had turned from pink to strong yellow the chiefs began to leave. Caradoc did not try to stop them. He sat on a bluff, his sword beside him, Cinnamus, Caelte, and Vocorio crouched at his feet, and watched as the wains and chari-ots rumbled away and disappeared between the wooded hills. All morning their clamor reproached him, and by the late afternoon the countryside was silent but for the lonely, broken keening of the sea-gulls, the clean, salt-edged air smudged by the smoke of the dying fires.

Togodumnus was the last to go, and he walked to Caradoc, said curtly, "I am going back to Verulamium," spun on his sandaled heel, and went away. I feel no shame, Caradoc thought stubbornly. They will come. But I cannot sit here with a few thousand freemen to face Plautius and his juggernaut. He saw Gladys walking toward him along the clifftop, her cloak over her arm and her dark hair whipping about her face, and he rose slowly, wearily, like an old man.

"Caelte, find Llyn and then get the wains packed and ready to move. Cinnamus, round up whatever scouts are left to us and tell them . . ." He paused. Tell them what? "Tell them to keep to their posts until I send them word, or until they bring me word that the Romans have come."

Gladys approached him. "There is a storm over the mainland," she said. "Far in the east the sea is hazed and it heaves without breaking." She stepped closer so that Vocorio should not hear. "Caradoc, have you considered telling the omens?" Her skin smelt of seaweed. It was tanned to a deep, healthy brown and her eyes were clear as a summer night. "Many of the other chiefs did. They said that the signs were not good, but no one was able to tell them why. Have we a seer still, at Camulodunon?"

"He died, Gladys." The answer came slackly. From somewhere close at hand Llyn's shrill voice was protesting and Caelte remonstrating with humor in his voice. "I have considered such a thing, yes," he finished, "but it is too late now. In any case, we would have to apply to the Master Druid on Mona for a new seer, and you know as well as I that the seers couch their pronouncements in such strange language that the sacrifice hardly seems worthwhile."

"I can read the omens," she said unexpectedly. "Let me try, Caradoc."

He was too tired to be surprised. He sometimes wondered if there was anything Gladys did not know, and he did not doubt that she had absorbed some weird, incomprehensible second sight in her solitary commerce with the ocean. Like my Eurgain, he thought suddenly, remembering the hours she had spent sitting looking out her window, oblivious to all save the minute, nebulous shiftings of her own spirit. "No, Gladys," he said. "We are going home. I need no omens to tell me what I know already."

The Catuvellauni set out for Camulodunon leaving behind them a thousand black, ash-filled pits and many acres of trampled grass, as well as the hopes, fears, and broken dreams of a swift and devastating victory. They went slowly, savoring the growing, brash ebullience of a summer that promised to be hot and long, camping beside the paths, sprawling laxly around their fires in the deep, leaf-scented darkness. Caradoc no longer cared whether Plautius came or not. He was tired, and not even the imminent threat of Togodumnus's war could rouse him from his lethargy.

Then, with a shocking suddenness, two days away from Camulodunon, the scouts found them ambling under the welcome shade of the forest and fell upon them with news that galvanized them into horrified action. The pleasant glow of anticlimax fled and the words sped back down the train from mouth to mouth like groundfire out of control.

143

"They have come! The beaches are swarming with them. Already they are digging in and raising defences for the provisions. The cavalry is still at sea but it cannot be long."

Caradoc sprang to life. "Mocuxsoma!" he bellowed. "Ride to Verulamium. Take a scout with you. Tog must turn back. Gladys, speed to Camulodunon. Tell Eurgain of all that has passed. Tell her we face them alone and she must prepare for a siege. Then stay or return as you choose. Fearachar, from this moment you are not to let Llyn out of your sight." He quickly calculated the distance that separated his tribe from the others, and debated whether to send freemen after them. It would make no difference, not at the first encounter with the enemy. The enemy! He saw himself a youth, laughing with the traders, mad for every new curiosity that they brought, sitting on Eurgain's Roman couch and drinking Roman wine. He knew his change. Regret shook him, then dissolved. Rome was now the enemy.

"Vocorio, choose six of my chiefs. Send them south, west, and north. The tribes will be of no use yet, but perhaps they will come to engage Plautius if he breaks through us."

"We could turn and try to join up with the Cantiaci," Cinnamus said. "The place of Plautius's landing is in their territory. Together we might hold them off until the others come."

Caradoc nodded, thin-lipped, his mind clicking over furiously. There was a chance that the Cantiaci had not disbanded. Of all the tribes, they would know that Rome was here. "Go to them, Cin," he said. "Don't stop to sleep or eat. Take a spare horse with you. Ask them to cross the Medway and wait for us on our side of the river. No use in marching any farther south. We do not want to be caught on the move. Then come back to me."

His chiefs and Gladys scattered, mounting their horses and pounding into action, and Caradoc sat listening to the fading of their dispersion. Then he raised himself, turned, and shouted, "Back, all! The Raven of Battle has come! Back to the Medway!"

Aulus Plautius Silvanus stood on the sand, watching his men disembark. His tribunes clustered around him, the plumes of their helmets tossing in the landward breeze, and beyond them all the troops boiled along the beach, the centurions moving among them. Farther up, where the sand gave way to pebbles and then grass, the standards and aquilae had been planted, and gradually the shouting, seething mass began to separate and gather to their units.

"Where is the enemy?" Rufus Pudens said. "We come expecting to face a horde of screaming savages and we find absolutely nothing. Not even a monster!"

144

Plautius smiled briefly at his senatorial tribune, wondering how Vespasianus was faring. Probably chaffering his seasick, miserable men into some kind of order. A good man, Plautius thought. No more imagination than one of Claudius's precious doves, but a born soldier. Where would the Second Augusta be without his coarse, harsh discipline? "They have gone home," he answered. "But they were waiting." He waved to the south.

"They expected us by the cliffs, or so I hear. The Twentieth will know by now."

A shrill, frightened neighing split the air, and the men turned to watch the first of the horses led ashore. The praefectus alae stood, hands on hips, and his men struggled to pacify the plunging, wild-eyed brutes. Already order was rapidly being established, and inland, just out of sight, they heard the soldiers begin to dig the trenches that would become the perimeters of their first camp. By nightfall the earth would be pulled into walls, the towers erected, the tents laid out in neat rows, and the officers would sleep on their own cots. Plautius listened to all of it with great satisfaction. So far, so good.

"Pudens," he said, "Find me the primipilus. I want to know how many men have been incapacitated by the storm. And see that guards are posted well inland. To work, gentlemen. How I would like a bath!" They laughed dutifully and turned away and he sighed, his gaze traveling the calm, sparkling ocean, the sun-drenched, stirring grasses. In spite of the activity going on all around him he felt a deep peace. Before the sun set, word would come from Vespasianus and from the Twentieth, and in the morning they could begin their march. He was glad that it was he standing here sweating in the sun, and not Paulinus, who was even now on his way through the mountains into Mauretania. He could find no reason for his happiness. It was just there, like the wind and the waves. He wondered how Vespasianus's emissaries were getting on with the Atrebates and their new chieftain, Cogidumnus, who had offered their aid against these two foolhardy Catuvellaunian brothers. He thought briefly of the sulky, intractable Adminius, still sitting in one of the boats, and derision curled his lip for a moment. He would have his uses, but Plautius despised him. The primipilus coughed politely at his elbow and Plautius at last brought his thoughts back to the present. There was much to do before he could settle down in his tent to a little reading. Julius Caesar's *Comentarii* nestled snugly in his knapsack.

CHAPTER ELEVEN

CARADOC AND THE CATUVELLAUNIAN CHIEFS wended back the way they had come. Many of the women who had traveled to the coast with the wains had decided to join Eurgain in defending their town and had taken their children back with them, but Gladys returned, catching them up just before they crossed the Thamus. They camped briefly on the farther side of the river, high out of the tide's inexorable reach, then pushed on quickly and came to the Medway at noon of the next day, Scouts passed in and out of the camp, bringing Caradoc detailed accounts of each movement of the enemy. In the middle of that night Togodumnus arrived, his men tired and hungry, for they had slept only briefly, curled in their cloaks beside the path, and had not stopped to light fire. Togodumnus did not apologize for his flagrant bad manners of the days before, but sauntered cheekily into camp, greeted his brother, and called for meat. Llyn left Fearachar's side and ran to his uncle, throwing his arms about the slim, tight-muscled waist, but Caradoc ordered him sharply back to his place and told him to stay there on pain of a drubbing. He did not want his son to blithely follow Tog into the heart of battle, and he knew that this was what Llyn wanted to do. Later he told Fearachar that he was to use force if necessary, but Llyn was not to trail after Togodumnus any more.

At dawn a scout came, warning them that the legions, which had landed in three different places along the coast in an extremity of caution, had now joined forces and were on the march. Caradoc left his meal hastily and melted into the white morning mist, with Cinnamus and Caelte beside him, and soon the Catuvellaunian host followed, and began to spread out along the bare, level banks of the wide river, moving like wan, gray ghosts, silent in the clinging mist. Caradoc went up and down the lines, going from chief to chief, advising and admonishing. The chariots rolled between them and the water, their warriors and drivers swaying, but strangely there were few sounds. The damp chill of early morning enveloped them all, dulling thought and senses, and the warriors and freemen stood or squatted, wrapped in their own private, anesthetic dreams. Cinnamus had told Caradoc that the Cantiaci would come, but that they would sweep wide and find the fords to the south so as to avoid the Roman column, and could not be expected to arrive before noon. Caradoc heard, weighed, and shrugged. He and his men could surely hold the river until noon. He went back to Fearachar and Llyn.

"Take the boy," he said, "and go back toward the hills. Climb a little before you turn to watch, but choose your line of escape before you settle, my friend. And you, Llyn," he said, taking his son's hands and speaking sternly. "If you leave Fearachar's side I will take your freedom from you in Council and you will become his slave forevermore. Is that clear?" Llyn blanched and nodded solemnly, and he knew his father did not speak idly. Caradoc kissed him and sent them away, then he went and sat on the damp grass beside his chiefs, huddled in his warm cloak.

Already the mist was thinning, turning from pallid gray to the palest golden, shredding slowly, and he sat with head bowed, thinking of Eurgain and their cozy, laughter-filled house, and of Cunobelin, who in all the invisible nets of his ambition had never dared to snare a Roman army. But he thought also of his own moment of fear, of the feeling that would come soon when he sounded the carnyx and his chariot would begin to roll. He already felt it creeping over him, tingling in his limbs and filling his mouth with the taste of metallic sourness, and he rose abruptly and began to walk the lines again, hearing the muttered spells, the faint, guttural curses, and the pledges and pleas to Camulos. They had made the sacrifices yesterday. Many in the host had demanded a human victim, but Caradoc, not yet free completely of the years of Roman influence, though he did not know it, forbade the sacred knives. Besides, there was no Druid.

He found Togodumnus deep among his own chiefs, leaning on the spokes of his chariot and humming softly, but there was nothing to say, nothing at all. They looked at each other without rancor, then they embraced affectionately and Caradoc went back to his post. He tied back his hair and put on his helm, working it snugly against his head, then hefted his spear and loosened his sword in its scabbard. He removed his silver and bronze bracelets and put them in the pouch at his belt. His slow, nervous fingers found the golden torc at his neck and he stroked it for a moment, pride stiffening his spine. Catuvellaunian wolf! They shall feel my fangs this day, he thought. Then he picked up his shield, and as he slid his arm into the leather straps, the mist suddenly shook, dissolved, and blew away, and a gentle morning sun beamed down upon them, firing the sluggish water.

Then he saw them. It was as if they were black rocks, or a great hard wall of adamant sunk viciously behind the covering cloak of the fog by the hammer blows of some angry giant, or . . . his heart missed a beat and then began to thud within him. Like thousands upon thousands of stiff, motionless gods of doom carved out of stone, waiting for a word of magic to release them from the holding spell. The Catuvellaunians sprang to life. Their shouts and curses rent the

147

air. They howled, they screamed, they drew their swords and beat upon their shields, and still the Roman forces did not move. Only the horsehair plumes on the mounted officers' helmets danced gaily in the breeze.

"Jupiter!" said Pudens. "I have never seen such a sight! And listen to them! Are they drunk?"

"Some of them perhaps," Plautius replied, "but their noise is ritual, Rufus. They beat the demons of death away and they also intend to frighten us." He gazed across the river, watching the gaudy, screaming mob. How far? he thought swiftly. A quarter of a mile?

Beside him, Vespasianus grunted contemptuously. "Barbarians! And so few of them. Julius Caesar was right. They must be war mad."

Plautius turned to the heavy, red face. "Remember what I told you all last night," he said. "Their first charge is most to be feared. They pour all their effort into it. And do not forget what I said about the women!"

Vespasianus chuckled hoarsely. "Our men are not likely to care which sex is behind the swords. And as for a charge, there will be none today, poor fools."

Plautius took a last, sweeping glance around at the flat, peaceful river valley, the sun streaming to mingle its warm rays with the turgid water, and the trees smudging into distance behind it. Then he straightened. "Vespasianus, get the Thracians into the water. Sound the incursus."

The men around him saluted and scattered and the strident, harsh notes of the trumpet ended the dreamlike quiet of the summer morning.

At the sudden shock of a trumpet's call Caradoc swung into his chariot and Cinnamus gathered up the reins. They rolled forward quickly, the chiefs running behind, spears raised and swords drawn, their clamor a constant, terrifying din, but when they reached the bank they stopped incredulously. There were soldiers in full armor in the river, swimming strongly, and behind them troops splashed into the shallows and struck out, hundreds of them. The river was full of bobbing, iron-clad heads. "They will flounder for sure, the idiots!" Caradoc heard Caelte shout. "The river is too deep and there are strong currents!" But Caradoc felt his heart sink. The men who were now almost halfway across were not Roman. They were auxiliaries, Batavians or Thracians or both, tribes renowned for their water skills.

"To the river!" he shouted. The bronze carnyx glittered suddenly in the upflung arm, its wolf's claws grasping its gaping mouth, and its wolf's fangs snarling to meet his own as he put it to his lips. He blew, and the company howled and began to run. "Camulos and the Catuvellauni!" he called, his voice rising strong above the chaos. "Death or victory!" Then he flung the carnyx to the floor of the chariot and they galloped at full stretch across the dry, cracking mud flats, the wind singing keenly in their ears.

The auxiliaries reached the bank and struggled out of the water to meet the brunt of the first mad onslaught. They went down like stricken boars, their blood suddenly, vividly pooling out and spreading on the water, but the second wave and the third gained the shore and rose to fight. Caradoc, out of his chariot now and swinging his blade, Cinnamus beside him, sensed a strange reluctance in the grim, expressionless faces that reared before him. The soldiers did not want to give battle. They were dodging blows, running this way and that, pushing for the rear, and suddenly Caradoc knew why. A scream of terror split the air and then another, the high, mindless outcry of animals in pain, and he turned with an oath and a bitter shout. The legionaries were hamstringing the chariot horses, darting in under the wide blows of the chiefs to slash quickly and run away again, and one by one the gallant beasts fell to their knees, their eyes turned back in their brown heads, the chilling, inhuman sound of their agony filling the ears of their masters. But Caradoc had no time to feel outrage at this cowardly attack. The flats were swarming with soldiers and more were coming, rising from the river water flooding from them as they came, and he turned from the useless chariots, a fierce bloodlust welling within him. He saw Gladys beside Caelte, both hands grasping the hilt of her slimed sword, her feet planted sturdily apart. She swung, but he had plunged with a snarl into the mess of seething, leather-clad Roman bodies and did not see the blow go whistling through the hot air.

The legionaries swam across the river like black flies and Plautius sat on his horse and watched. The resistance had been more sustained than he had expected, and accordingly he prepared for a long day. Soon the soldiers were across in sufficient numbers to form battle ranks, and hour after hour the solid, almost impenetrable wedges of men beat back the enraged Catuvellauni with their simple but devastatingly effective ploy.

Caradoc, sweating and filthy, caught in a sudden, welcome lull, watched as the front line retired and the second came to take its place, each man stepping smartly forward while the front rank rested far back. They fought without heart, without emotion, these Romans. Their faces remained blank, their arms moved with tight precision, while his chiefs hurled themselves against the cruelly studded leather

149

shields with heroic recklessness, again and again. He turned back into the melee, then saw something that stopped his breath and brought a shout of unbelieving joy to his lips. The whirlpool of battle that had spun away from him had revealed an avenue of clear ground leading straight to Hosidius Geta as he sat calmly on his horse, surrounded by his protecting cohorts, and Caradoc looked wildly about him.

"Royal War Band! To me!" he shouted urgently, and his train came speeding out of the mass of struggling men. Other chiefs had seen the opportunity that would never come again and they fell in behind Caradoc, rushing up that sweet, open pathway. Togodumnus joined them, bloody and grinning, and together they charged. "Not dead!" Caradoc yelled. "Take him alive!" and the startled cohorts tumbled to close ranks around the general.

Plautius, watching from his vantage point, saw the pattern of engagement suddenly break up and swirl in another direction, and, astonished, he saw Geta islanded by a sea of jubilant, bright-clad chiefs, his cohorts in confusion. "Mighty Jupiter!" he exploded. "Rufus, have a left swing sounded and be quick!" The trumpets blared, two embattled centuries answered promptly, wheeling in tight precision, and the bitterly disappointed chiefs found themselves edged farther and farther from their almost defenceless target.

"A good gamble but evil luck!" Togodumnus shouted. He and Caradoc saluted each other ruefully and parted and Plautius saw his friend come galloping along the riverbank, cloak flying and plumes dancing.

Geta reined in and blew out his cheeks. "A tight moment, Aulus! What a prize I would have been to them. They would have bargained us right off the island!"

Plautius laughed. "Hosidius, you're getting old."

The Cantiaci came at last, rushing screaming into the fray, putting new heart into the beleagured Catuvellaunian warriors, and the sun westered slowly, sinking at last beneath the reek and fume of battle. Finally, when it was too dark to tell friend from foe, the armies broke off, retiring to campfires, staggering with weariness. Not all the legions had crossed the river. The soldiers of the Second still waited on the farther shore with their commander, Vespasianus, pacing before them, and when nothing could be seen but the red twinkle of the watchfires, Plautius sent for him.

"Take your men, all of them," he said. "Go south and try to find a ford lower down. It may be that we can encircle the barbarians and have done with this indecision. They fight well, don't they?"

150

"By Mithras!" Vespasianus replied, a grudging admiration tinging his voice. "They fight as though they were possessed. I am no longer disposed to pity them." He saluted and rode away and Plautius turned wearily to Pudens. He needed sleep. Tension ate at him, etching the lines around his thin mouth still deeper, but he knew from past experience that he would lie awake until the dawn, his strategies going round and round in his mind as he examined each one and searched for the flaw, the hidden mistake.

"Rufus, bring me the barbarian," he ordered. "It is time for him to prove his worth."

Pudens nodded and disappeared to return some minutes later with his reluctant companion. Adminius looked surly and afraid. The clean, handsome lines of his face, the cleft chin of the House Catuvellaun, the wide eyes and broad nose that he shared with his brothers were becoming blurred, softened with age, and he had a loose, unhealthy look. The years in Rome had put fat on him, and the idleness and frustration of his life had embittered him.

Plautius did not meet his eye. He was afraid that his distaste would show. "Now, sir," he said crisply. "I want you to cross the river. Go quietly among your kinfolk. You know what to say. They will be tired and dispirited tonight, and your words should bear fruit."

"What if they take me and kill me?" Adminius said plaintively.

Plautius smiled. "I do not think they will. Not if you choose the right ears for your . . . sedition."

"It's useless," Adminius said sulkily. "They hate me, all of them, and they will hate me all the more now, for bringing the might of Rome down on their heads."

"But Adminius, you led the emperor to believe that your tribe could not wait to shake hands with Rome and welcome you back," Plautius said gently. It was too dark for Adminius to see the sarcastic glint in the gray eyes.

"It is true," Adminius protested vehemently, "but not in the middle of a battle, sir!"

"If you are successful the battle is over," Plautius reminded him. "You know what to say, Adminius. Now go." The words ended heavily, and Adminius saluted shortly and vanished.

Caradoc lay beside the fire, too tired to wash or eat, though Fearachar had offered him goat's flesh and barley bread. Cinnamus sat beside him wrapped in his flower-patterned purple cloak. He was polishing his great sword, a cup and a jug of wine at his knee, and his golden braids shining in the warm glow. Llyn was curled close to the fire, fast asleep, with one grimy hand under his brown cheek and his cloak over him. Beyond him sat Gladys, her head bowed and her arms folded on her green chest. She had not spoken since the dusk and Caradoc knew that she suffered, her longing for the healing quiet of the lonely ocean wounding her. But he was too weary to care. Togodumnus had come to him, boasting of his tally, but Caradoc, lying prone with grass under his sweat-bedraggled hair, his muscles burning and his right arm and hand almost numb, had sent him away with sharp words.

The subdued rise and fall of many voices filtered through the dark trees around them, and Caradoc stirred and sat upright.

"How many have we lost, Cin?"

Cinnamus spoke without looking up, his hands busy. "I do not know, Lord."

"Can you not make a guess? A hundred? A thousand?"

"Oh Mother, Mother, I do not know!" Cinnamus snapped. "All I know is that the chiefs are almost done and the Romans are fresh as spring daisies, and the morrow will bring an unknown fate."

Caradoc fell silent. He needed to sleep, if only for an hour, but something knocked at the back of his mind—an insistent, unwelcome pulse of warning. It had no shape, no coherence, but he felt that there was something he should know, something he had overlooked. The unblooded legion across the river, waiting in the darkness, bothered him. Why had Plautius withheld it? What new horror was he planning? The shrieks of the tortured horses rang again in his ears. He thought of Eurgain, sweet, sane, blue-eyed Eurgain, and of his little girls, dimples and blowing curls, but the pictures in his mind had no substance, like the wraiths of a dream. He sighed, troubled, then fell back onto his side and slept.

One hour before the dawn he woke, cold and stiff. His cloak was soaking with dew and he rose and carried it to the fire, and stood shivering while it dried. The woods were full of morning noises, of the first drowsy bird calls and the spasmodic, disgruntled murmuring of sleepy, hungry men. Llyn was awake, sitting cross-legged on the other side of the fire and chewing thoughtfully on dried beef, a cup of water by his knee. Caradoc greeted him, and Fearachar moved from his perch on the lowest bough of the overhanging oak and went to bring him meat and beer.

"What did you think of the battle yesterday?" Caradoc asked Llyn. "Were you afraid?"

The round, dark eyes met his scornfully. "Of course not! The Catuvellauni are afraid of nothing and no one. But I couldn't see much, father. Fearachar made me lie down and peer over the edge of a hill."

152

"That was wise of him."

"Will we defeat the Romans today?"

Caradoc handed his cloak to Fearachar and took the food held out to him. He still was not hungry but he forced down the tough, unappetizing mouthfuls. "I do not know, Llyn. Perhaps. Now you and Fearachar must leave, for the sun is rising and there is work to do."

"If you do not beat them today, Father, I think that I will go home," he said, getting up obediently. "It is good hunting weather and my dogs will be looking for me."

Suddenly the meat tasted to Caradoc like the bark of some old, sick tree, and he spat it out. "That is a very good idea, Llyn," he said gravely. "Why don't you go now? If you hurry you can be with your mother in three days."

Llyn shook his head. "Not yet, father."

"Farewell then. Be obedient to Fearachar."

The man and the boy walked away into the mist and Caradoc slung the cloak that Fearachar had handed him around his shoulders. The sun was up. The mist lay only on the ground, and above, through the lacy-green, fluttering branches he glimpsed a bright sky. Good hunting weather. He smiled with wry pain and drank his beer, then struck out through the wood, moving silently, keeping low, hugging the shelter of the biggest trees. At last he came to the edge and dropped to the ground, slithering easily through the long grass. He halted, and peered out.

Across the river the brown mud flats were deserted. The legion had gone. Panic seized him. Where were they? The hairs on the back of his neck crawled. Between himself and his own side of the water the Romans were up, forming ranks, readying themselves for another day of slaughter. They had piled the dead in great heaps away from their fires, but here there was no sign of any wounded. Caradoc hastily wriggled back the way he had come and then took to his heels, pelting through the dense brambles and briars. Where, where, where? He tied up his hair as he ran, and burst into his own camp to find Mocuxsoma and Cinnamus searching angrily for him, and the chiefs harnessing their chariots.

"Where have you been?" Cinnamus panted. "There is news."

Mocuxsoma shouldered forward. "Lord, your brother has been here in the night. He slipped past the guards and went among certain chiefs and their freemen. Half our force has gone."

"What do you mean gone? Gone where? What has Tog been up to?" His heart was still pounding and his throat was dry.

Mocuxsoma stamped on the ground. "Not Togodumnus. Adminius! He has enchanted the men away. Now they fight beside Rome!"

153

The words struck Caradoc in the deepest part of his soul, igniting his whole body in a sudden, flesh-searing explosion, and he flung back his head and roared like a wounded boar, his eyes closed, his voice screaming. "May Camulos split his belly and spill his guts before his eyes! May Epona trample out his brains! I curse him! In sleeping and eating, in hunting and feasting, I curse him! Taran burn him! Bel drown him! Esus strangle him!"

Cinnamus went to him, touching his arm, but Caradoc threw him off, the pain of betrayal ripping through him, becoming a torrent of despair. The tuath was forever disgraced, and all the worry, the sleepless nights and careful planning, all the suffering—all, all for nothing.

Rome would be victorious. It was the end.

Caradoc winced against the belief that their life of freedom had been shattered, but after a moment the pain receded and a new, pitiless stubbornness began to harden within him. Something of himself, some vestige of his youth, some boyish innocence that still believed that honor was all had gone forth with the howling of his anguish, and he felt the red-ringed, bleeding hole that its passing left within him.

"Tell me," he whispered, his voice trembling with intensity. "What were the magic words this animal used to lure good men into slavery?"

"He told them that we had no chance. He said that the Second Legion even now surrounded us, deep in the woods, and in the morning we would be wiped out. He said that if they surrendered they could go home to plant, and breed cattle, and there would be good trade as before."

"Mother." It was a word of utmost, soul-emptying contempt. Caradoc sat down suddenly and the two chiefs sat with him. The remaining chariots should now be rolling toward the water, but Caradoc waited in his timeless moment of hell, unable to think or feel.

"Lord," Cinnamus said. "I am sorry, but there is more. Will you hear it, or shall my mouth be stopped?"

More? What more could there possibly be? The knife could turn no more. There was no more blood to flow. Yet he said, "I will hear it."

"In the night the Dobunni came. Boduocus has been promised his old boundaries and he will fight against us, for Plautius. The Atrebates are here also. They have a new ricon, approved by the emperor, one Cogidumnus. We have lost all." Cinnamus spoke in a monotone, his voice not betraying any emotion, but the strong hands hidden under his cloak pressed together as if hanging onto life itself.

And I slept, Caradoc thought, his mind calm now, hiding from his rage and bitterness. By the Great Mother, I slept. The earth has split

154

under my feet, the sky has fallen about me, and . . . He turned around quickly to find Mocuxsoma. "Does Togodumnus know all these things?" he asked.

"I do not know, Lord," Mocuxsoma replied, shaking his head.

"Well find him and tell him and bring him here. Run!"

He and Cinnamus sat in silence. Tog and I have sown these seeds and the crop has sprung up a thousandfold, Caradoc thought. Raids, insults, murders, and all the time the steady push—outward, always outward. If I had been ricon of the Atrebates, what would I have done? The answer came without hesitation. I would never have sold my people into slavery. I would rather have offered myself to the sacred arrows.

Togodumnus came leaping down the path, his chariot behind him. His face was ashen. "No words, my brother!" he shouted. "First we must kill Plautius, then Adminius, then this Cogidumnus, then Boduocus!"

Caradoc laughed, in his face rudely and loudly. Slowly, wearily, he got to his feet, put on his helm, and walked to his chariot. He picked up the carnyx. "I love you, you poor mad fool," he said. He blew one long, harsh blast and the remaining chiefs came out of the trees. They were grim-faced, their eyes, filled with impending death, looking toward Caradoc with reproach.

"A red morning!" he shouted, grief choking him. "A blood morning! We ride in honor, my brothers!"

They picked up speed, thundering out of the wood and onto the flat land beyond, while the incursus sounded and the standards of Rome surged to meet them, but there was no hope. The legions were before them, the Dobunni and the Atrebates to the right and left, and they crashed headlong to meet their doom, crying, howling, their swords held high. Valiantly, the Cantiaci swung in behind them. Caradoc dismounted and ran, and a tall warrior swung to meet him—a Catuvellaunian, brown-haired, his dark blue eyes now bloodshot. The tears ran down Caradoc's cheeks as they hewed at each other and the warrior fell to the ground. Who will purify me from the blood of my people? he thought, turning, and suddenly a great, terror-stricken cry went up from his men. Caradoc looked. Behind them all, out of the woods, poured a host of iron-clad legionaries, fresh and vigorous, and the wail of fear grew and swelled into panic. It was Vespasianus and the Second, muddy, wet, triumphant. Everywhere the Catuvellauni began to cast away their weapons, running here and there, and the Romans and their own countrymen flowed over them and cut them down like rabbits.

155

"Stand and fight!" Caradoc screamed, but they were seized with the animal terror of death and did not heed him.

Cinnamus ran to him, dodging the wide slash of a Dobunni sword. "Run, run, Caradoc!" he shouted. "Back to Camulodunon!"

Suddenly Caradoc found himself doubled over and running, running, darting, stumbling, caught in the confused uproar, his chiefs running beside him. They gained the shelter of the trees but kept on, their breath coming in gasps, their sides searing with pain, and all around them, in the sun-dappled drowsiness of a summer morning, the Catuvellaunians fled.

"Llyn!" Caradoc blurted, but Cinnamus urged him on. "He and Fearachar have gone," he managed, and still they ran, their legs aching, their lungs burning, hot and dry, their limbs pumping with waning strength, surging, stumbling forward until the noise of the carnage faded and the trees stood tall in the gentle silence and at last they fell to the wet grass and lay with eyes closed, no longer caring whether they lived or died.

For two days they stumbled through the wood. One by one other chiefs joined them, tattered shocked survivors without horses, food, or weapons, stunned and incapable of words. Together they trudged along the paths that had seen them pass before, gaily bedecked, their horses' harnesses ringing and their spirits high.

Near dusk on the second day they rounded a bend and saw another group, five or six chiefs sitting on the bank, heads and hands hanging, a crude litter lying before them on the path, two branches with a cloak slung between. Suddenly Caradoc's heart constricted, and he ran forward, his legs shaking with the effort. He came up to the litter and knelt, and Togodumnus slowly turned his head. Blood was matted in his long brown hair and caked about his mouth. One shoulder was a mess of bone and pulpy flesh, and Caradoc, lifting the covering cloak with nerveless fingers, saw deep wounds about his chest, his hip. He was lying in blood, steadily oozing blood that spattered the earth like bright coral and stained Caradoc's hand as he let the cloak fall back. Tog's face was gray and old. The spider lines of laughter about his eyes and mouth had become the caprices of a swift-drawn knife, deep and pitiless. He opened his mouth to speak and a slow bubble of blood welled between his teeth and burst to trickle down his cheek.

"Caradoc," he whispered. "Who would have thought that it is so hard to die? Ah, Mother, it hurts, it hurts." The black, bruised fingers found the ragged edge of Caradoc's sleeve. "I spit on death." He tried to laugh and another gobbet of dark blood spewed from his lips. "The mighty Catuvellauni are no more. I am glad . . . glad . . . to die now.

156

Fire me high, my brother, fire me well." A great spasm of agony gripped his face then, the muscles slowly tautening and the eyes widened, filled with a lonely terror. "I do not think that I can bear it."

Caradoc could not answer. Late sunlight streamed onto the path, shafting down in golden glory, and the birds whistled and piped in the green-halled vastness around him, but he could think only of the free-dancing, wild-leaping spirit now huddled before him, maimed and broken. The eyes that tried to focus on him were full of incoherent sadness and a new, dark knowledge, but Togodumnus's indomitable, flaming spark of life fought on. He tried to speak again, but his strength failed him and he gasped, struggling for breath. Caradoc rose. "Pick him up," he ordered, not ashamed of the tears that poured down his face. They went on, Caradoc pacing beside the litter, Cinnamus behind him, and the other chiefs walking silently in the rear.

When the sun had gone and the chill of evening rose from the ground they stopped, hunger gnawing at their empty bellies. Caradoc spoke sharply to the litter-bearers who stumbled in their faintness, but Cinnamus said, "It does not matter, Lord. He is dead." Caradoc fell beside the shadowed form and took hold of the limp hand, covering it with his own and leaning over the bloodied face. Togodumnus gazed past him into the star-studded sky, a slight, serene smile on his lips, and Caradoc cast his cloak over his face and sank to the ground, weeping quietly. The chiefs sat or lay in silence beside the path, watching the last ricon of the House Catuvellaun mourn for his kinsman.

They reached Camulodunon late on the fourth day, bearing their burden. The first gate had been deserted, and stood wide, but the gateguard of the second saw them coming, straggling like sick cattle across the dyke, and he ran for help. Men and women came rushing from the huts, spilling out of the gate, welcoming them with cries and tears, and taking the litter from their weary arms. Eurgain, hearing the commotion, stepped out of the Great Hall with Gladys beside her. The filthy, staggering group of men climbed slowly toward her and she waited, her eyes frantically searching and her hands pressed together. Then she saw him, his hair tangled about his thin face, and his eyes black holes of suffering. With a shout she flew toward him and fell on her knees, embraced him, felt his quivering hands on her hair. "Eurgain," he said. Then his legs would not hold him anymore and he sank before her and wrapped his arms about her. They clung to each other eyes closed, while the first shocked wailing began for Togodumnus and the gate was swung shut and bolted fast.

157

At last they rested in the Great Hall, sitting ranged about the walls, heads lolling back in an exhausted indifference, watching the servants scurry to stoke the fire and carve meat for them from the haunch of roasted beef. Caradoc, too, rested against the wall, but his eyes had closed as soon as he had sat down, and Eurgain sat quietly beside him, her arms folded on her knees. Gladys came gliding across the floor to squat before him, but neither woman spoke. The Hall was hot. Sun beat down upon it, and the fire sent a suffocating mixture of smoke and sizzling fat drippings out into the dry air. Every now and then Caradoc shivered and drew his cloak tightly around him. At length Fearachar ran up, bearing a platter heaped with meat and bread, porridge, and boiled peas, and a jug of beer. Caradoc stirred, opened his eyes and sat up with effort as Fearachar set the plate before him. He began to eat, slowly, carefully, even though he was famished, but he drained the jug in one long gulp and Fearachar left again to refill it. A low, halting spatter of conversation began around them as the chiefs, revived by food and drink, talked to their freemen, and Caradoc felt his blood begin to flow again sluggishly, unwillingly, and his head began to clear. He mopped the last of the gravy from his plate, loosened his cloak, and turned to Eurgain.

"Llyn?" he asked, his eyes anxious and his voice still not strong.

"He returned last night with Fearachar. He and the girls are with Tallia in the house."

He nodded gratefully and then the starved, hollowed eyes left her and found Gladys. "And you? How did you return home?"

"I found a cavalry soldier in the woods, Caradoc," she answered quietly. "He was wounded. I killed him and took his horse. What happened there by the river? How was it that we dishonored ourselves?" Her tone was wondering, bereft of bitterness. The time for recriminations, regrets, or anger was long past, and she, like the remnant of the cowed, puzzled Catuvellaunian tuath, hung suspended in stunned hopelessness. Caradoc answered shortly, scarcely aware of what he said, his head buzzing for want of sleep.

"We were betrayed by one of our own kin, we were tricked by the enemy, we were set upon by our own countrymen. Is it any wonder that even Camulos and the goddess deserted us? We were not dishonored, only outnumbered and surprised. We will fight on." Outside, the wails and keening of Togodumnus's mourners came to him, rising and falling, a fitful, stricken wind, and his mind pressed with the plans and decision that had to be made.

Eurgain began to speak rapidly, her eyes filling with angry disagreement, but he lifted a finger and put it to her lips, rising stiffly,

158

standing with one shoulder against the wall. His legs still felt like straw husks.

"I call for Council!" he said, and the talk died away. "Slaves depart, the rest of you come close. I cannot find the strength to raise my voice."

All gathered around him and he surveyed them grimly, pity and rage filling him. They looked like a pack of sick, emaciated, and mangy wolves, tamed by hunger and hardship, but their eyes raised to his face in trust. Faintness swept over him, but he fought it down, the new, callous stone of calculation and determination heavy in his breast. "I will not speak of the unspeakable," he said, "nor of the passing of my brother. We are the Catuvellauni. We do not surrender. The tuath shall fight until the last of us falls. If anyone wishes to leave Camulodunon while there is still time, and flee into the west or go to the Druids on Mona, I will not deprive him of his honor-price or decree him a slave. Are there any who wish to go?" He stopped speaking to gain strength but no one moved. No eyes dropped guiltily, no hands quivered in sudden betrayal, and he felt a weak, pathetic surge of renewed pride waft toward him from the cavernous, desolate eyes that met his own.

He began again, his voice filled with cold decision. "Then we will prepare for another fight. I want the gate torn down and the hole filled with earth and stones. Is Alan here?" His farmer freeman stood. "Alan, see that all the cattle, the others, as well as mine, are driven into the woods to the north. Set a few peasants to guard them. If necessary they will all be slaughtered. I want no Romans feasting on my honor-price." Alan nodded and sat down again. "Vocorio, you and your freemen find all the farmers and peasants you can and bring them within the defences. Most of them will have hidden themselves in the woods, but round up those who will come. There are plenty of empty huts." Images of the chiefs who would never ride home flitted quickly across his mind, but nothing could help them now and he did not want the survivors to think back on them and their fate, not yet, and so he let the sorrowful picture go without speaking of it. "Mocuxsoma," he called, returning to his vision of what had to be done. "Burn the bridge across the dyke. Do it immediately. The peasants can cross on logs. And all of you, scour the town for weapons. Anything will do as long as it can be used to kill Romans. But for now, go home and rest this night."

He wanted to say more, to talk about glory and honor, but even his thoughts had an empty, mocking ring and he dismissed them, sinking once more to the skins. He felt nauseated with weariness and with the

159

unendurable tragedy of the past few days. Fire me high, Tog had said, fire me well. Pain stabbed at him as the words came back to him in Tog's own faltering voice. Tog. Feckless you were, and lawless, digging into the rich basket of life with both eager, greedy hands. Yet, I loved you. You were linked with the high stars, blown gloriously, impulsively on the winds of the heavens while I . . . He looked down at his filthy, shaking fingers. While I am chained to the earth and my hands will never touch a star. Only a sword. Only a bitter, cruel sword. He battled his emotion, swelled now by his exhaustion, and he finally looked up. The Hall had emptied. He forced himself to look at the two women who waited.

"There is no hope, is there?" Eurgain said.

"None at all," he replied brutally. "We are finished as a tuath and as a free people. Eurgain, I want you and the children to go into the west. I will send Caelte and his freemen with you, for I do not think that we shall ever again sit here in the nights and listen to his songs."

She had been expecting just such a request and she replied emphatically. "No, Caradoc. This time I will not cower behind my children. I do not want to pass into the west, knowing that none but I and my family are survivors of the great Catuvellauni. Such loneliness could not be borne." She took his hand and kissed it and Gladys looked away, feeling a great isolation engulf her for the first time in her life. "If we are to die, my husband, then let us die together. I love you and will not live out my life without you and among strangers." He kissed her, too tired to argue, but warmed by her words, and they rose together and went out of the Hall, leaving Gladys sitting in emptiness, her sword heavy about her waist, and scalding, salt tears burning her brown cheeks.

So the last warriors of Camulodunon prepared for their end. They worked quickly and grimly in a town whose once cheerful, light-filled huts stood silent and waiting, whose paths and open spaces lay forlornly silent in the thick heat of the summer afternoons. The rites for Togodumnus were held in the same drugged, resigned quiet, and the crackling of his pyre was the only sound for a day and a night while the sky clouded over, great thunderheads moving majestically in from the coast to bulk heavily above the town, and lightning flared spasmodically over the ripening fields. Caradoc felt nothing as he thrust the torch into the dry brushwood on which his brother lay. There was no room left in him for grief or sorrow, and he could not speak of the youth that had been, for the days of raiding and light-hearted stealing, of drunken pranks and half-earnest sparring, belonged to another age. Once there had been two brothers, growing up under a mighty

160

ricon, with friends and cattle, with loves and hates, but they had no reality, they belonged to one of Caelte's songs, to part of an old, sweet dream. No one wept as the flames caught hold and began to feed. All of them, the chiefs, their women, the sullen Trinovantian peasants, heard in the roaring fire the hot and pitiless words of their own coming deaths, and they stood dumb and passive, as if seeing their own bodies consumed.

The gateway was blocked, the cattle driven deep into the woods, and the peasants housed unwillingly by dead men's hearths. The country and the river lay deserted. And still the Romans did not come. Gladys took a coracle and disappeared one day, alone, leaving no word. Llyn wandered in and out of the Great Hall, up and down the paths, morosely scuffing the dry dirt, and the little girls played desultorily with Gladys's seashells, while Tallia sat in the shade. Eurgain and Caradoc walked the walls day after day, blonde hair and dark mingling on the hot winds, choked with words they could not say. Cinnamus crouched in the lee of Camulos's shrine, polishing the sword that already gleamed fever bright, murmuring incantations over and over to the god that brooded angrily within, and Caelte, his gentle, humorous face serene, stood outside his hut and strummed his harp, making new songs while the sun drowsed in his music and watched his long, supple fingers move in its light.

Gladys returned after a few days, and with her came a scout, one of the few left to watch the legions. Caradoc and Eurgain, standing high above the valley, saw them come and scrambled down to greet them as they slipped through the slit that had been left in the wall.

"They are waiting for the emperor, for Claudius himself," the scout said without preamble. "They are camped in the woods not five miles away, and Plautius is fuming at the delay but dares not move until the party from Rome arrives. In the meantime he has sent Vespasianus and the Second against the Durotriges."

"How long?" Caradoc interjected.

The man shrugged. "How should I know, Lord? It has been two weeks since the message went out. Perhaps another two."

"And then?"

The scout looked at them curiously. There was something so fatalistic, so immovable about their faces, that he scarcely recognized them. Caradoc had a hand on his lady's shoulder, but it rested lightly, almost confidently, and she looked before her with eyes that were clear and untroubled. He felt a strange respect, as though the two were gods above all fear and uncertainty, and he shuffled, aware of his own mortality. "Then the emperor himself will lead the troops to an easy, safe victory, and the legions' aquilae will ring the Great Hall."

Caradoc and Eurgain remained motionless when he had finished, still showing no emotion, and Gladys left them and strode away toward her own spartan hut. At last Caradoc smiled, a whimsical, warm smile that lit his face with sympathy. "Go to the Hall and eat. We cannot spare much but there should be meat at least. Then sleep, and return to the forest. If you are wise you will not come back." The scout nodded curtly and went away, climbing the steep path with weary feet, and Caradoc turned to his wife. "The news does not alarm me," he said. "Indeed, Eurgain, I can feel nothing. In two weeks we will be dead and Camulodunon in flames, yet I look at you and my heart laughs. Why?"

She faced him and cupping his lean jaw in both of her hands, kissed him on his mouth with cool, steady lips, and then, rising on tiptoe reached to touch his eyes. "Because there is nothing left to face, no unknown," she replied lightly. "There is only you, and me, and the sunshine, and death." They stood for a long time with their eyes closed, pressing against each other in the deep shadow of the earth-wall, while above them the swifts darted, crying joyously in the free blue sky.

CHAPTER TWELVE

THE TIME PASSED SLOWLY. Claudius and his entourage lay seasick on a stormy ocean while the Catuvellauni waited almost listlessly with nothing to do. There were no fights or petty squabbles, for there was not even anything to quarrel over, and the men and women withdrew into their last dreams, sitting in the sun or walking slowly, wrapped in a drugged peace.

Only Gladys was restless. She got on her horse and rode in turmoil around and around beside the dyke like a newly trapped deer or a young boar at bay. Her life suddenly seemed to her to have been worthless and useless, a journey never begun. Fiercely, bitterly, she did not want to die, but honor was all she had lived for, and now she knew that only by dying could the years behind her be proved to have been of value.

In an early summer dawn of silence and cool, still air, the Catuvellauni rose to find their town ringed with a dense mass of helmets and studded shields. They were not alarmed, and they buckled on their swords calmly, took their spears, said their last farewells quietly, and moved to their appointed places, breathing deeply in the sweet morning.

Caradoc gave Tallia a knife and herded her and the children into the Great Hall. "When the Romans can be heard on the path below," he said, "kill the children. You will know that I am dead, and Eurgain with me. Farewell, Tallia." Llyn flew at him, hugging him and shouting incoherently, beating at him with balled fists like little stones, and Caradoc took him firmly by both wrists and forced him back.

"Llyn!" he said sharply, though he wanted to gather his son into his arms and cry with him. "How does a Catuvellaunian chieftain die?"

The boy raised a flushed, tear-strained face. "He . . . he dies like a warrior, without fear."

"Even so." Caradoc did not trust himself further. He tore away the pleading, clutching fingers roughly, and turned to the girls who stood silently watching him. He knelt and kissed them, hearing the sound of the incursus and then Cinnamus shouting "Lord! Come!" from without. He dared not look again at the tiny, bewildered little group, and he drew his sword and ran outside.

Cinnamus, Caelte, and Eurgain joined him as he came. Already a clamor rose from the walls, and below he heard the sharp, clear orders barked as the legions surged forward to lay wide planks over the dyke. Halfway to the stopped gate Gladys joined them, her arms bare but for her silver, her hair piled haphazardly on top of her head and already loose, her eyes still swollen with sleep. Together they reached the top of the wall and peered over.

The valley below was swarming with soldiers, and Caradoc's sweeping glance took in a little knot of men far back, standing on a knoll and watching. He pointed. "That must be the emperor, curse him! Where is Plautius? And what is this?" The ranks parted directly below him and he saw something being wheeled forward.

"Ballista, Lord," Cinnamus answered coolly. "They will weaken the walls and the soldiers will tear a hole. Then they will pour in like water through a breached dam." Even as he spoke a dull boom reverberated through the air and the ground shook beneath their feet.

"We cannot fight, not yet," Gladys said, the frustration and venom in her tone causing Eurgain to look at her sharply. "We must sit up

163

here like stupid pheasants in a tree, and wait to be struck down." She looked along the curve of the wall, where the chiefs stood resting on their spears, their women beside them, splashes of scarlet, blue, and yellow. "Like stones, like dead, useless branches," she spat. "We should leap the wall and die quickly."

"Peace," Cinnamus said easily. "You sound like Vida," and incredibly, wonderfully, they laughed, the swift ripple of mirth reaching the soldiers beneath them who paused to look up. In that moment Cinnamus coolly leaned out and threw his spear, and one of the men below crumpled backward. His fellows raised their shields again and went back to their digging, while the ballista let fly with a crack and a whizz and the stones from the peasants' slings clicked and rattled.

"Where is Vida?" Eurgain asked.

Cinnamus shrugged. "She is still in bed," he grunted. "She will come when she is ready."

For a moment Caradoc was back in the Great Hall. The fire leaped merrily, voices rose and fell, the meat spat and smelled delicious, and he, Tog, and Adminius raised their cups while Cunobelin swayed to Cathbad's music and Aricia and Vida argued and shouted, their black heads together, their black eyes flashing and their hands flying through the smoky air like the ashes spiraling to the roof. Eurgain put a hand on his arm, and he was recalled to himself by her touch.

"What about fire, Caradoc? Have you forgotten . . ."

He clapped his hands to his helmed forehead in exasperated disgust. "Fire! Of course! Caelte, run and find Mocuxsoma and the others. Begin tearing down the kennels and the stables. Cin, find Fearachar and tell him to bring us fire. What is the matter with me? I feel as though I have been in a deep sleep." His chiefs quickly ran to do his bidding and he, Gladys, and Eurgain crouched against the wall, feeling the vibration of the siege machine quiver in their feet and the rocks and hardpacked earth under them crack and loosen.

Vida sauntered over and sat beside them, yawning, her face pale, blinking in the strong daylight. She was dressed in one of Cinnamus's simple tunics, but her legs were bare, and her feet were unshod. Her sword was held in one languid, uncaring hand, and two knives were thrust into her belt.

"Vida, where is your shield?" Caradoc asked.

She yawned again, then grinned at him, her big white teeth flashing in the sun. "I lost it to one of my husband's freemen last night, Lord—at the gambling." Caradoc was angry. He began to lash at her, words of anxiety, but Fearachar and the other chiefs came running, arms full of wood, and he rose.

164

"Make a fire here," he commanded. "Pile on the wood. Get anything that will burn. If we can hold the soldiers back for a time it will be something." They all hurried to fling brush, thatch, sticks from the walls of the huts, planks from the stables, on Fearachar's fire, and soon it began to roar, the flames pallid in the sunlight.

The ballista hummed. Beneath them, the soldiers doggedly picked away at the wall, and the other chiefs, seeing what was in Caradoc's mind, ran to take their own brands from the fire. Soon a hundred fires flickered, a ring of heat around the lip of the defences, and the heaps of wood grew beside them. Caradoc was satisfied at last. With a shout he grasped a burning brand, leaned over the edge, and dropped it. A scream went up below him. Gladys stamped her foot. "Right in the face, by the Mother! At them, Eurgain!" And Eurgain and Vida began to drag wood from the fire while Fearachar fed it.

All that day the Catuvellauni kept the legions from the walls, until the wood was gone from the kennels, and the stables, and all the huts of the freemen's circle. Claudius, who had been watching greedily from his little hill, began to sweat under the noonday sun, and he called for his canopy, and sat under it, wiping his brow. Plautius finally ordered in the tormentae and the scorpios, and the chiefs began to fall from the walls, pierced by arrows as they stood to cast their fire downward, but the rain of orange hail did not stop, even though several of the fires, their tenders now dead, had gone out. Plautius ordered again, calmly, almost regretfully, marveling at the desperate tenacity of these uncouth people, and a great cry went up from the Catuvellauni. Flaming arrows now flew above them, burying deep in the dry, summer-parched thatch of the remaining roofs of the chiefs' circle, and the huts burst into bright conflagrations, red against the slowly deepening, late afternoon sky.

"Caradoc, the children!" Eurgain screamed at him. "The knife is one thing, but I will not have them burned alive!"

Caradoc paused, wiping the sweat and grime from his eyes, and looked up. The Great Hall was untouched, rearing tall and proud against the gathering clouds of evening, just out of reach of the range of the scorpios. "I need you here, Eurgain," he said shortly. "The Hall will stand until the walls crumble." She thought for a moment, nodded grimly, and went back to her work, her blonde braids gray with ash, her hands swollen and burnt, her arms bleeding from a hundred scratches.

Night fell, and Plautius ordered the retreat sounded, well pleased with the day's progress. The walls of the town were now so weakened that his men could pull them apart with bare hands, and the enemy had lost many men to the arrows of his scorpios. He stood beside a sleepy, grumpy emperor and watched the fiery destruction of Camulodunon. The tormentae had done their work well. The whole town was ablaze, all but the large, wooden building at the summit. It still stood defiantly, a black, flame-shadowed bulk, mocking him, but in the morning, when the fires would have eaten themselves out, the legions would at last be able to go in and they could complete their slaughter.

Somehow, in some strange, twisted way, he was sorry that it would all be over. He would have liked to meet this Caradoc, the chief whose determination in the face of certain defeat had kept his men fighting like lost demons. He would have liked to have shared a cup of wine with him, to have talked pleasantly of tactics and deployments over a good dinner. Already he felt the mystery of this land. It whispered to him as he lay in his tent at night, and it taunted him as he rode through its dense woods, a land full of spells and subtle, luring magic.

The cooking fires of his troops sprang up around him like sparks dropped from the colossal inferno that raged before him, and he thought of the tall chief he had glimpsed standing on the wall, bronze helm glinting in the sun, but Claudius spoke to him, a whip of annoyance in his voice, and Plautius sighed and bent to answer. He was not so sure now that he was more fortunate than his colleague Paulinus.

The chiefs sprawled sweating in the Great Hall, gnawing on chunks of cold meat and drinking the last of the beer as they listened to the steady wind of flames that was burning their town to ashes. Caradoc, sitting beside Llyn, with the little girls in his tired arms, felt a pang as he looked at them. So few had left. So few. Eurgain sat with her hands in a bucket of cold water, her eyes closed, and Gladys, her head sunk on her breast, was hunched against the wall, her naked sword resting across her knees. Vida and Cinnamus lay side by side on the skins and seemed to be asleep, and Caelte, who had recovered his harp from the corner where he had hidden it, sang softly to himself, seemingly unmindful of the angry red weal of a burn that snaked along one arm.

Caradoc knew that he should order them all out again to watch in case the Romans breached the walls under cover of darkness, but he did not have the heart to do so. Let them rest. What was the point of a sleepless night when here, for a time, they could forget their last tomorrow? Caradoc noticed that no one had crawled to the welcoming shadows of Cunobelin's corner. The old warrior's spirit still brooded there and would until the Hall fell in ruin, and Caradoc smiled in spite of himself.

"Caelte," he called. "Sing us a song!"

There was a shocked silence, but Caelte's kindly face lit up in answer. "What would you hear, Lord?" he asked.

Not of victories, Caradoc thought quickly. Not of raids or conquests. There must be no tears tonight. "Sing to us the song my father would not let Cathbad sing all those years ago, if you remember it. Sing the 'Lady of Togodumnus the Many-Handed, and the Twelve Lost Cattle.' " A ripple of cracked, mirthless chuckles spread and Cinnamus sat up as Caelte struck a jaunty lilting chord and began to sing, the music slowly kindling the dull eyes that filled the Hall.

> Togodumnus crept out in the deep, dark night,
> He took with him no chief.
> He wanted no man to spy him out—
> Togodumnus was a thief! . . .

Caelte tapped his foot, his cheeky lyrics bringing smiles to the company, and they began to sway and hum under their breath, forgetting the desolation around them. When he had finished they applauded warmly, and Cinnamus shouted, "Ah, Caelte, what a good song! The best song you have ever composed! Sing it again!" So he sang it again, and they sang snatches of it with him, their quick ears picking up the words, and Caradoc, his heart lighter, glanced to the corner and fancied that he felt two spirits watching there, the heavy, cloying emanation of his father, and a merry, capering Tog.

Caradoc gently laid his sleeping daughters beside him on the skins while the Hall quieted down, and Fearachar came with cloaks to cover them and Llyn who was stretched out by his mother, already dozing. Caradoc sat back against the wall and Eurgain moved over to sit beside him. He put an arm around her and her head found his shoulder.

"How are your hands?" he asked softly.

"Better," she answered. "But there are many blisters. If I want to swing a sword tomorrow I will have to bind them tightly."

"It is not too late to leave," he said after a moment. "I could let you and the children over the wall on a rope."

"Oh, be quiet," she murmured, and at last he laid his head on hers and fell asleep.

CHAPTER THIRTEEN

SOMETIME IN THE NIGHT, in the middle of a nightmare, Caradoc felt a hand on his arm. He was standing above a rocky valley, and the oppressive, sticky atmosphere, fraught with terror, turned his bones to sodden wood. Behind him waited a group of strange, unknown chiefs. A black spot appeared in the sky, grew rapidly, and became the Raven of Battle speeding toward him with a rustle of black wings, and just when his breath grew shorter and the sweat began to pour down his face, he felt one of the chiefs take his arm. He shouted aloud in shock, reaching for his sword, and sprang to his feet to find himself in the Great Hall, Eurgain struggling up beside him, and Cinnamus swaying blearily toward him, fumbling with the knife at his belt. One lamp burned, and around it the shadows were thick and black and utterly still. Outside, the roaring of the fire had died to a fitful crackling, and light rain pattered on the roof, while now and then the thunder rumbled discontentedly.

Caradoc came fully awake. A tall figure stood before him, hooded and cloaked. Nothing of the face could be seen. There was only a deeper blackness within the long oval of the hood, and Caradoc, his mind still teeming with the vivid images of his dream, cried out and raised two crossed fingers. In the unseen depths of the Hall the chiefs stirred, whispering, and blundered toward him, and Gladys strode under the lamp, her sword already raised high. As the Catuvellauni crept closer, peering in the dimness, the figure bowed, put a hand to its head, and folded back the hood. Black hair rose stiffly in a great crest from the forehead high above the two black, sharp eyes, and a black beard bushed around the hidden mouth and fell into riotous curls upon the massive chest. The hand moved to the beard and parted it, momentarily revealing a plain bronze torc, and the thick fingers then extended in greeting and Caradoc stepped forward to grasp the wrist. Gladys still held her sword above her shoulder and Cinnamus's hand stayed on the hilt of his knife.

"No words of welcome to your Hall, Caradoc ap Cunobelin? Am I not bidden to rest in safety?"

Caradoc withdrew his hand. "There is no longer any safety within my walls, freeman, nor can I offer you anything but old, cold beef and the barrel's dregs. I do not speak the words of hospitality until I know whether I face friend or foe."

The man gazed around at the listening chiefs. "At one time the proud Catuvellaunian tuath and its Roman friends would have re-

168

garded me and mine as foes," he said, "but it seems that certain friends have had a falling out and the tribes of the lowlands tumble over each other to snatch up the pickings. What shall I be to you, ricon without a people. Friend or foe?"

"I do not want to play the game with you, stranger," Caradoc snapped. "There is no longer any time or place for such pursuits. If you want food and drink, that I will offer, such as it is. If not, state your business. Where are you from? How did you pass the Roman sentries?"

It was the question uppermost in all their minds. This man might be a Roman emissary. Gladys and Cinnamus did not move, and Eurgain slipped quietly and unobtrusively to stand over her children. The man laughed.

"On my belly! The Romans have worked much harder than you, digging into your fine walls for hours on end, and the night is old. The sentries' eyes are heavy. Now for my business." He undid his cloak slowly, so that all could see the grass stains on his brown tunic, and he loosened his belt, and sank to the skins with a grunt, the others following, all but Gladys, Cinnamus, and Eurgain. "I have come to take you all away with me, those who will come, of course. My men wait for you in the woods, with horses."

A stunned, unbelieving silence greeted his words, and a glimmer of understanding flashed across Caradoc's mind and was gone. "Where are you from?" he repeated, motioning for Cin and Gladys to put away their weapons.

The man clucked impatiently. "You know where I am from," he said. "We waste time. I am a man of the west. The Silures are my tuath. I have orders to bring you, Caradoc, and all your family and your chiefs to my country."

"Why?"

"Because you will all die tomorrow if I do not. You know this. There is absolutely no hope of any reprieve. Even your own people fight against you, and with your death goes the last resistance of the lowlands. You have always been soft, you river lovers," he went on derisively. "How wise we were not to trust you! Look at you! The Atrebates surrendered, the Dobunni surrendered, the Iceni, the Brigantians, the Coritani, the Cornovii, ready to sue for peace without raising a single sword! And the Durotriges were defeated."

Shock tingled in Caradoc's fingers. So Vespasianus had returned victorious, just like that. Mother! It was not possible! The Durotriges were the best fighters, the wildest, most tenacious tribe of them all! Except . . . He looked at the Silurian and realized the answer to his own question. Except for the men of the west.

169

"You dug your own grave with your rapaciousness, Caradoc ap Cunobelin, you and your mad brother, and the tribes have turned against you. The Romans will toss you into the earth tomorrow, and the captured Trinovantian peasants, your slaves, will shovel the soil over you. My lord has been advised to rescue you, though it was against my wishes. I spoke in the Council, but the Druid spoke too, and my voice went unheeded." He grinned maliciously. "It seems that you are needed in the west. Perhaps as an offering to Taran or Bel."

The chiefs began to mutter among themselves, but Caradoc caught their sly, sidelong glances and his heart sank. Here, on the edge of eternity, facing annihilation, came a gift from the goddess, a chance to go on living, and suddenly their pledges of honor seemed a tawdry exchange for the hope of one more breath. He glanced at Eurgain as he turned to address the Silurian, but seeing the new hope light in his wife's eyes, he stayed his eyes on her and kept his voice loud. "I have sworn to defend my birthright to the end, and my chiefs with me. I will not go as a slave and an outcast into the west, carrying with me a load of shame, while the Romans tear down the shrine and plant their aquilae on sacred ground."

The man snorted rudely. "Rubbish! They will do those things anyway, you fool, as soon as your body is flung on the dungheap with the rest. Besides, I swear on my honor, on pain of forfeiting my honor-price, that you are not needed to haul wood and draw water. The Druithin have a use for you."

Of course! Caradoc thought frantically. Mother, I know, but how do I know? There is something to remember, I must remember. But the remembering did not come. He shook his head. "This is my tuath. I will not go."

The chiefs pressed forward shouting angrily, all but Caradoc's own train. "Call for Council, Lord! We must all decide!" and the man sat back, smiling.

Caradoc kept silent, but then Eurgain stepped forward, her color high and her mouth set in a firm, rebellious line.

"It is time for Council," she cried. "All slaves depart. All freemen draw near." Caradoc jumped up but it was too late. She met his eye with a defiant glare and sat down taking Llyn's hand, and he knew he had lost. Wild rage took him but he could only stand and shake with it, as one by one the chiefs leaped to their feet and voted to go. It did not matter where. Many of them had already decided to escape with the Silurian and then forsake him, heading north or southwest, to the coast, running anywhere but free, free, and only Gladys did not speak, watching them all with a twisted grimace of pure contempt.

She had already made up her mind. She did not want to die, but she had never run from anything or anyone and she was not going to begin now. She had no one to love, no ties to bind her, no one to mourn for her and eulogize her in song. All she had was her honor and her stubborn will, and she knew that if she ran she would leave even those things behind and become nothing. Her thumb found the edge of her blade and she drew it back and forth, feeling its sting.

Finally there was quiet. "What about you, Cin, and you, Caelte?" Caradoc said, holding his temper forcibly in check. "Fearachar? Vocorio? Mocuxsoma? You have a right to speak also." Fearachar struggled to his feet, his loose jowls quivering and his mournful, hang-dog eyes sorrowful.

"I will stay with you, Lord," he groaned. "I always knew that I would come to a violent end, but it does not matter. What is the final misery in a life of misery?"

He sat down and Cinnamus rose, his eyes on his wife who stood against the wall sneering, her hands on her curving hips.

"I stay," he said shortly.

Caelte brought his hand smashing onto the strings of his harp, and a loud, discordant twang filled the room. "I, too," he said, and then Vocorio and Mocuxsoma nodded.

Caradoc took a step and looked down on the rest. "I cannot gainsay the Council," he said bitterly. "You are free to go as you have always been free in my service," but the Silurian was rising, his fleshy hands waving.

"No," he said firmly. "If the Lord and his men will not go, then my orders are to leave all of you." An uproar of angry shouts and shaking fists greeted his words, and several of the chiefs turned on Caradoc, who drew his sword and backed against the wall.

"Idiots!" he called. "If you wanted to go why didn't you just slip over the wall!" He swung the blade and the men retired.

"That was before Council," someone said in an undertone. "Are we not men of honor?"

Caradoc felt like spitting in his face. Honor! By the Mother! Eurgain came close to him and put her hands on his shoulders, her eyes strained and her mouth trembling.

"My husband," she said, her voice low. "All of us were prepared to die with you, but the Dagda has sent a chance of escape. Think well. It is good to die for honor's sake, but is it not better to flee and then to turn and fight again? I know why this man is here. The Silures need you. You know the Romans as none of their people do. You can win the trust of their chiefs. Men follow you. Oh, Caradoc, please, please listen to me. I am not afraid to die. None of us is. But to die without reason, to throw away our lives in pride and stubbornness, this is not our way.

If you stay then I and the children will stay and we will perish, but would you not like to see the sun set over the mountains of a free country and know that you live to fight again?" Tears shimmered on the long blonde lashes, and she dropped her hands and clasped them tightly together.

He looked at her for a long time. All his training, all his upbringing urged him to draw his sword and set about them. Before this, before his betrayal by his own people on the battlefield, before his brother's death, honor had meant the sacrifice of everything else, but now his men had forgotten their honor, and suddenly he knew he could not blame them. Everything else had gone. Only pride remained, and pride, to a broken, dying tuath, was too expensive. He knew what Tog would do. Tog would kill the foreign chief and perhaps a few of his own men, and then stay lightheartedly to die. But then, Tog had been crazy. And what of you, my father? he asked in his mind. What would you have done? And again, he knew. Cunobelin had always walked the middle road, and that was why the Catuvellauni had become the greatest tribe in the lowlands. Caradoc sighed inwardly. Cunobelin would run away and live to smite his enemies again, but Caradoc, seeing his own struggle mirrored in the blue-clouded, pain-filled eyes of his wife, feeling her steady empathy, knew that whatever he did would bring guilt to torment him. Honor or life? Die like a warrior or sneak away, leaving the peasants to be slaughtered?

"Hurry!" the Silurian urged. "The moon is setting and soon the choice will be taken from you."

Reluctantly, Caradoc sheathed his sword, picked up his cloak, and looked around disdainfully at the eager, watchful faces. "I will come," he said.

The men sprang to life, cloaking and hooding themselves, thrusting their few treasures into their tunics, and Eurgain went to gently rouse the little girls. Fearachar spoke to Llyn, taking him by the hand, and Caelte thoughtfully wrapped his harp, and then they all moved toward the black hole of the doorway.

Only Gladys stayed where she was, leaning against the wall, her sword point in the floor and her head hanging.

Caradoc ran to her. "Gladys, sheath your sword. Be quick!"

"I am not going," she said, raising her head wearily.

He wanted to slap her, to shake her, to draw his knife and put it to her throat and push her out of the room, the barbed lash of his own faint-hearted decision blooding him, and the undisguised scorn in her eyes a goad to his guilty rage. His head had said Go, but his heart still throbbed with the urge to stay. "You must!" he said, shouting at her. "There will be no one left! We can go on fighting, Gladys!" He took her arm, dragging her away from the wall, but she let go her sword and struck his hand away.

"Someone must be here when the peasants wake," she hissed. "Someone must lead them, someone must put up at least a token resistance. Never before have the Catuvellauni abandoned a stronghold without defence!"

"Gladys," he replied quickly, while the chiefs shuffled at the other end of the room. "Our father himself would tell us to run if the opportunity came, for never before have we faced the might of Rome. We gave them battle on the banks of the Medway. We held them off for nearly two days. Who else could have done that? We did not dishonor ourselves then and we do not dishonor ourselves now. We run in order to preserve our heritage."

"What heritage?" she sneered openly, tears pouring down her sallow cheeks. "For a hundred years no Catuvellaunian chieftain has been bested by Rome, or anyone else, until now, and now our heritage has dwindled to a handful of cowards."

He looked at her speculatively for a moment. "This is not like you," he said at last. "You of all people have always kept a clear head. You know what Cunobelin would do, and you would have advised him to do it, so why this sudden blindness?"

Her shoulders slumped and she held out her hands. "My fingers are soaked in blood, Caradoc. I cannot wash it away. It is not Roman blood, for Roman blood is thin and cold. This is the blood of my kinsmen, my friends, hot and strong, and the stains will not go away." She turned to him, tendrils of dark hair curling on her wet, high forehead, and her eyes were full of a suffering he could only see but never feel. "Do you know who I killed, Caradoc?" she said, laughing, the sound coming out breathy and abrupt, strangled. "Do you? I slew Sholto as he swung beside a Roman soldier, before he could cleave Togodumnus in two. What madness took them, the traitors? You and I, all of us, were forced to dishonor ourselves by killing our own tuath, and I dream of their blood streaming around me and I cannot rid myself of the vision of Sholto's eyes as he went down under my blade. I must stay. I must retrieve my honor somehow."

Aching with pity he gathered her into his arms. "Gladys, Gladys, do you want to die?" he whispered. "All of us are guilty of this blood. None of us will ever be clean, but perhaps the Roman lives we can yet take will help to wash away that stain."

She rested against him, her thin, tight body tense, but then she pulled free and bent, picking up her sword. "How do you cleanse a soul, my brother?" she asked him. "Yes, I am ready to die."

He saw that she would not be swayed. The others were calling to him, their voices sharp with panic, and he kissed her on her forehead. "Farewell, my sister," he spoke softly.

"Go in peace," she whispered back, turning away deliberately as he ran to the door, his tears coming slowly, hurtfully.

The Silurian motioned to his followers as soon as Caradoc joined them. "Follow me," he said curtly. "Keep low and do not speak." He vanished into the darkness and they crept after him, moving silently through the warm curtain of rain and the gusting freshness of the night wind. He led them down the path that ran to the now impassable gate, crouching swiftly, blending as only he could with the wet darkness, and they hurried after him, gliding unseen between the warm, smouldering heaps of ash that had once been their homes.

Caradoc, a child in his arms, still wept, but his spirits began to rise as he felt an end to the weeks of living with the certainty of death. It was good to be doing something, to be going somewhere, to be able to look ahead without flinching. He would not mourn Gladys and her fate. Each freeman and freewoman had the right to choose death, and if that death was honorable, no tears were expected. Tears were spent on memories, not remorse. Each independent member of the tuath dictated his own fate, and so it was right.

The Silurian veered suddenly, dropped to his belly, and slithered away, Eurgain behind him, and Cinnamus with little Eurgain in his arms behind her. Caradoc, on elbows and knees in the mud, the rain soaking his back, looked up. The wall loomed ahead and lower down. He shifted his daughter's weight and she whispered, "Father, put me down. I can crawl." He nodded, gesturing, and she disappeared before him. There was no sign of the peasants. They would be crowded into the few huts still standing behind the Great Hall, probably asleep, and he felt a surge of guilt but quickly beat it back. They were nothing, only peasants, little better than cattle or slaves. But unlike slaves, they are men, his mind retorted. He groaned and crawled on.

At length, the man stopped. They were right against the wall now, at its foot, in a hollow of dryness that the rain could not reach. He waved silently, pointed to a rock, and put his thick arms around it. Two chiefs crawled to help, and with surprising ease the rock moved, came loose, and they eased it outward. The man vanished for a moment, wriggled back and waved them on, and they squeezed after him. Caradoc, pushing his way after little Gladys, found himself suddenly outside Camulodunon, in a place where the wall snaked back on itself and made a sheltered, hidden corner. The valley was shrouded and quiet. The Roman cooking fires had long since been put out, but Caradoc, his ears straining to reach what his eyes could not, fancied that he heard the low voices of sentries off to his left. Now for the dyke. Must they swim? The last chief emerged from the hole and the Silurian motioned to them, striking out once more into the drizzle, running low down the grassy bank before the dyke. With scarcely a ripple he slid into the black, oily water and began to swim, and Eurgain followed after, her tunic billowing about her on its surface for a moment like a gray sail. Caradoc picked up little Gladys and swung her onto his shoulders. She was exposed now and any soldier who happened to look their way with sharp eyes could have seen her, but she was still under the shadow of the wall and the chance had to be taken. In another moment Caradoc was in the water. Gladys slid to his back and clung to him with frightened fingers and he fought his way across, the cold of the water shocking to his bones even though it was high summer. The Silurian had already pulled himself up onto the farther bank and was crawling away, with the muffled, almost invisible line of men and women after him. Caradoc tumbled Gladys onto the bank and climbed out of the water to see Cinnamus waiting in front of him. Suddenly Caradoc had an idea. He turned to the chiefs behind him. "Here, Vocorio, take care of Gladys. Cin, give Eurgain to Mocuxsoma," he whispered, and the chiefs took the children without a word and passed on. Caradoc then went close to Cinnamus and put his mouth to the other's ear. "Adminius," he said. "Where do you think he is?"

Cinnamus shrugged. "There are thousands of tents out there," he whispered back. "Any one of them could hold him."

"But wouldn't Plautius want to keep him close by? I would like a chance at him!"

Cinnamus pondered briefly, then shook his head. "It is too great a chance to take, Lord. We might find him but it would take too long. He is probably well guarded. No, we must leave him to the demons."

Caradoc had to agree. It was only a thought, but it had brought him a spurt of pleasure. More than anything else, he wanted his brother's breast under his knife. He and Cinnamus crawled on.

In half an hour they had passed clean through the neat, precise lines of the enemy tents. The Silurian had chosen a good time to make his bid, for it was the hour when time seemed to slow, when men slept heaviest, when the sentries' spirits were at their lowest, their heads thick with the need for rest. In two hours the dawn would come, bringing an end to the haphazard, sprawling Catuvellaunian empire. Claudius snored, lying on his back in his spacious, silk-hung tent. Plautius dozed uneasily, worry still dogging his thin dreams like a cloud of mosquitoes, and the Catuvellaunian chiefs gained the cover of the dark woods at last and straightened with relief. The Silurian did not pause. He plunged in under the rustling branches, moving in a half-run, half-lope like an animal, and the others followed. Caradoc knew where they were. He, Tog, and Adminius had used this path many times on their way north, riding out to raid, and memories curled about the trunks of the trees and drifted in the long grasses under his light feet. But the man left the path after a mile, running straight into the brush where the dark brambles hung heavy with beads of moisture. Further on there was another path, Caradoc knew, that would have taken them into Dobunni country, but this man of the west obviously wanted to travel on the border between the Atrebates and the Durotriges. Caradoc looked ahead and saw that Llyn was failing, walking with one hand clamped to his side while his feet stumbled beside Fearachar. Just then they were challenged by a group of men on horses. They all halted, panting, and the Silurian went forward. Caradoc counted five, perhaps six riders, but he could not be sure in the gloom. The Silurian spoke to the horsemen rapidly, then turned and beckoned to Caradoc. Unconsciously, and from long habit, Caradoc drew his sword and then started forward. Cinnamus and Caelte swung in beside him, and together they walked noiselessly to where the black beasts pawed the ground, their harnesses muffled. A tall man dismounted and strode to meet them, his step long and purposeful. His hood was up, and silver gleamed on his wrists as he held out his hand.

"Greetings, Caradoc ap Cunobelin," he said softly. "So we meet again. I told you that the day would come when you had need of me." Caradoc took the thin wrist, feeling a jolt go through him as he did so. Above them the waning moon came out for a moment, leering through the trees, the pallid face of a drowned man, and the stranger raised his hand in a curious gesture, half-greeting and half-command. "Remember," he ordered softly. Then he pushed back his hood and Caradoc found himself gazing into a lean, bearded face dominated by two bright eyes that watched him steadily. "I am Bran," he said, and suddenly Caradoc was back in his room at Camulodunon and it was late, a dark night, and a Druid sat before his fire, the flames casting grotesque shadows on the walls. The fear that he had felt then came back, a tide of rootless anxiety, but now it was muted, faded with the years if disillusionment and dangers in between, and even as Bran smiled it flickered and was gone. The two men stood looking at one another, while around them the forest was hushed and the men, Silurian and Catuvellauni, blended quietly with the black tree trunks and waited.

Bran had not changed, Caradoc thought. The beard was thicker, perhaps, and crisper, the cheeks more drawn under high bones, but the voice was still compelling, vibrant, and the eyes still caught him in their black points and held him prisoner. But Bran, searching Caradoc's face, felt himself overwhelmed with pity and admiration. There was suffering in the wide, dark eyes and the lined mouth, but it was held tightly in check, and the hard, emotionless stubbornness that Bran had merely sensed in the lad all those years ago was now stamped clear for all to see. The sensitive lips were thinner, held in a grim line, and would smile only unwillingly. The high, proud forehead was furrowed by two great, slashing lines. For a moment Bran wondered if the budding clear-sightedness he had seen on that night had been extinguished by Caradoc's bitterness, if the stubbornness had become only a reckless, suicidal hatred, but then Caradoc smiled slowly, his eyes narrowing, and Bran knew that his own intuitions had not played him false.

"Yes, I remember you," Caradoc said evenly. "I remember very well. You sat in my chair and prophesied, Druithin, but I was young and stupid and full of pride, and would not listen. I will not thank you for snatching me from the gladiae of Rome, for you have brought me and my kinsmen only the sorrow of division and the agony of dishonor, but I will ask you—what do you want of me?"

"You know what I want, Caradoc." The bronze rings tied in his hair glinted as he replied. "The Silurians would have left you to die. They care nothing for you or Rome or anyone but themselves, but I spoke and they listened. I want you to put yourself in my hands. The Romans can be beaten, but not until the tribes sink their differences and move as one." He stepped closer. "I want you to be the arviragus, Caradoc."

Caradoc laughed, a harsh, croaking bark. "You are mad. The last arviragus of the people was Vercingetorix, and though he led two hundred thousand warriors, yet he was flung into the dungeons of Rome, living in darkness and filth for six years until Julius Caesar paraded him around the forum and then had him strangled like a sick animal. The Gaulish tribes remember him, but they fight no longer."

"Yes, he failed," Bran said, "and we may fail also, and you, Caradoc, may end your days in the dungeons of Rome, emerging only to humiliation and death. But think carefully, as I have thought over the years. There is only one choice. Fight on, or surrender."

"Then there is no choice. I deserted my peasants, Bran, and my sister, and my Hall, because only thus can I live to draw my blade again. But I do so with no hope. Your dream is foolish. The men of the west will never unite."

Bran went on staring at Caradoc through the dimness, while the moon was veiled once more and the rain began to fall. "Caradoc," he said, finally breaking the silence, "I am no seer, as I told you once before. Yet you are wrong. The tribes can be drawn together if the right man counsels them, a man with the power of reason, a man who can inspire loyalty. I do not dream. I think." The fruit has ripened on the tree, he thought, and now we have plucked it before it could fall to the earth. "Will you attempt this thing?" he asked.

Caradoc's gaze left the Druid's to find the leaf-strewn ground at his feet. Arviragus. No, it was impossible. But better to pursue the impossible than to turn and die at Camulodunon, or even to gather the few chiefs he had left and to fight the legions alone. The Silures intended to resist Rome to the bitter end, that was obvious, but what of the Ordovices, the Demetae, the Deceangli, the other tribes of the west? He was not a child any more, he did not shudder when their names were mentioned, but he still felt a vestigial reluctance to pass into their ragged, snow-shrouded mountain fastnesses. They would fight on, he thought, with or without him and his chiefs, for no commerce with Rome had softened their swords. He looked up. Bran had not moved, and the black eyes still regarded him almost indifferently. Caradoc knew that he had made his decision, knew what he must say, but all at once the words stuck in his throat. He knew that an arviragus was not like other men, and that if he agreed he would become something unrecognizable even to himself. He felt alone, imprisoned by the darkness, and by the cool rain that trickled down his neck and dripped from the hem of his cloak, and he sensed the wights and demons who were standing behind every tree, watching him, their pronged, horned helms monstrous in the poor light. The weight of his choice seemed to stretch before him with more consequences, more infinite, twisting roads of fate than he could comprehend, and it bore him down. He swallowed, meeting Bran's eyes, and the current of strength seemed to flow once more from the older man and he squared his shoulders.

"I will come," he managed huskily and as he said it, he thought he saw pity or sympathy flit across the lean face.

Bran nodded, turning abruptly to his men. "Good. Jodocus, bring up the horses. We must ride swiftly if we are to put many miles between us and this place before the battle is over and the Romans turn to seek you." He issued more orders, then swung back to Caradoc, who had not stirred. "How many chiefs did you bring?"

"About one hundred."

"Your family? Your son?"

"Yes." The questions were sharp, businesslike, and Bran left him, striding to where horses were being led from somewhere in the dimness behind the morose and silent Silurian chiefs.

Caradoc went to his men. "We will go with them," he said. "Cin,

178

you take little Gladys on your horse. There are no wains. I'll take Eurgain. Llyn, you can ride, but remember that if you tire and fall off, no one will stop. Would you rather sit behind Fearachar?"

Llyn was shivering, his cloak pulled tightly around him, but he answered arrogantly. "Of course not, father. I will not tire, and I will not fall."

Caradoc nodded and walked to where Eurgain stood. Her hood was back. Her fair hair was plastered to her face, her breeches clung sopping and cold to her long legs, and the blue eyes flew to him, smoky gray with fatigue and stress. He kissed her, pushing the wet hair from her cheeks. "They want me for arviragus," he said. "They want me to unite the tribes, but if I can only fight beside the Silurian chiefs I will have accomplished something. What do you think?"

"If the Druid did not believe that you could do it he would never have spoken for you or come all this way," she replied. "It is worth a try, my love."

"You know what it will mean."

"Yes, I know." She unwrapped her arms and embraced him. "Be glad, Caradoc. We are still free, still alive. What other days of unlooked-for hope wait for us under the shadow of the mountains?" Her voice shook with something, excitement or fear he could not tell.

"I think in spite of everything you will be happy to see these mountains," he chided gently, and she stepped away, snuggling her arms inside her cloak again and smiling at him.

"I feel a great peace," she said. "Here we are, cold, hungry, without tuath or tribe, while all around us the world has gone mad. Yet at the thought that I will at last see the land I have heard of only in tales, my heart pounds as it did on the day we shared the cup of marriage!" There were other truths behind the words. Be cheerful, she was saying, have courage. We belong to each other whether the world ends or staggers on. He answered her smile, the grim, pure line of his mouth curving for a moment, then he left her and mounted the horse standing ready for him as Cinnamus and Caelte swung to ride beside him. Fearachar handed up little Eurgain and he settled her before him, her head against his wet chest, her eyes half-closed in utter weariness. "I'm hungry, father," she murmured, but he did not respond, knowing that she would sleep for many hours yet, and their fast would not be broken until well into the morning. Looking back he saw Llyn pick up the reins of his mount and Fearachar nudge his horse close to check the harness. Then Bran turned, raised a white-clad arm, and they began to move. Caradoc eased his daughter's weight closer into his shoulder. The west, he thought. There is magic in those words, spells of fate and deep rivers of mystery. I have changed, already I feel it. Farewell, Gladys, my sister. May the wine of the next world bring you forgetfulness and peace. Farewell, Camulodunon, tortured ruin of my heedless youth. Ah, Cunobelin, Togodumnus . . . Togodumnus . . .

He looked back. The night was already thinning. The path behind him wound about the bole of a great, gnarled oak and vanished. The trees closed in and made a wet, green wall, clothed in the first mists of morning. You cannot go back, they whispered to him. The way is no longer open. Those days are over. He turned again, kneed his horse, and vanished like a gray ghost with the fleeing shadow of the night.

CHAPTER FOURTEEN

GLADYS SAT ALONE in the Great Hall listening to the thrumming of rain on the roof. She sat hunched against a wall, her knees up, and her arms wrapped about her legs. She was crying quietly, while through the vents far above her in the thick darkness a capricious summer wind moaned. One lamp still burned, high and lonely, but the far reaches of the echoing room were shrouded in blackness, and she could only sense the tall, carved pillars marching across the empty floor, the cold hearth, and the great shields and crossed spears still hanging where they had hung for years beyond counting. The soft noises of a night almost spent served only to make the stillness in the deserted Hall more poignantly endless. No fire would ever again roar its warm, friendly greeting to tired chiefs who gathered around it, sniffing the meat, chattering of the raid that had ended well. No chieftain would ever again rise from his place, with the light glittering on his golden torc, and his bronze bracelets and brooches flashing as he flung out his arms and shouted for Council. The Hall was a shell, an empty cup from which the sour dregs had been poured, never again to be filled. Gladys felt it complain, moaning gently in reproach and resignation. It was settling into its dreams of days gone by while the unseen tendrils of nostalgia writhed from the corners, mingled with the strange leaf patterns of the dead Trinovantian craftsmen, curled about her with vines of memory and passionate regret.

"Mother," she whispered into the sad quiet, "Mother." And the whisper ran around the walls and came back to her, bringing with it dead voices from the past, dead faces, gone, all gone. She caught a mouth open in a great shout of laughter, a shy, quick smile, a contemptuous, tossing head, and then the eyes of Sholto, wide with shock, filling with an astonished pain and reproach like the sudden rush of water when a dam gives way. She groaned, putting her forehead to her knees. I ache, she thought. Mother, how I ache! Come dawn, come death, I cannot live another hour with these memories. Her eyes throbbed and her face burned with the dry roughness of weariness and too many tears. She began to doze, hearing the last lamp crackle and go out, hearing the rain ease, and sensing that the dense darkness of the Hall was thinning. She slept a little, lightly, dreaming that she was lying on the edge of the ocean. The little waves were washing around her, licking her face and the tips of her outstretched fingers, and through the cool sand came the pulse of the rumbling surf. She woke suddenly, refreshed, and stood and flexed her stiff limbs, aware that the rain had stopped and pale new sunlight crept apologetically under the skins of the doorway. She buckled on her sword, went to the water barrel and plunged her face and hands into it, then pushed the skins aside and looked out on the morning.

The fires had died. Only sullen, impotent embers glowed where the huts and houses had been, and the sun fell bright through air no longer murky with smoke. She saw beyond the wall to where the Romans were already astir, cooking their wheaten porridge and squatting easily in their thick short leather tunics, their legs bare and their iron helmets lying in the grass beside them. The centurions moved among them with swagger sticks tucked under their arms, and the optios strode behind. Before Gladys turned away she saw, far back, a group of cavalry officers go by, the sun glinting from their polished harness, the plumes on their helmets bouncing gaily. She walked around to the rear of the Hall, and moved from hut to hut, greeting the peasants who stared at her darkly and muttered as they felt their empty bellies grumble. Then she went back and sat before the door, her eyes on the rinsed blue sky, and her skin warmed by the sun. Presently the peasants came to her. They were barefooted and sturdy and they squatted in front of her with questions in their eyes. She tried to count them as they filled the large open space and flowed between the heaps of dead ash. Two hundred? Three? She wanted to laugh. She rose at last, raising an arm for silence, while beyond them a trumpet blared and the soldiers put away their spoons and dishes and reached for their helmets and weapons. She did not mince words. "Trinovantians!" she called. "My brother and the chiefs of my people

181

have left Camulodunon. They go to fight in the west. They have left me to lead you this day."

An explosion of rage greeted her as she knew it would. The peasants got up and surged toward her shouting, with sallow, dark, contorted faces. Hunger and fear fanned their anger at this betrayal, but she stood her ground, shouting for silence again and again until they ringed her, still muttering but no longer yelling, a menacing, seething mob. "They will come back!" she lied but her voice carried no conviction and a tall, muscular man pushed his way to the front. His black hair was tangled, his arms were scarred and bare, and his hands were like twin clubs.

"They will not come back," he sneered contemptuously. "Cowards! The Catuvellauni at last are showing what they are. You should have gone too, Lady, and saved us the trouble of killing you before we go ourselves. Did you think that we would stay and fight for you?" He spat at her feet. "My father was a chief, and his father before him, until Cunobelin came and took away his torc and dishonored him by making him till the soil. Now the Catuvellauni are destroyed, and once more Camulodunon belongs to us."

"Listen to me, you fools!" she shouted. "If you want Camulodunon back you must fight for it. The Catuvellauni were hard masters but the Romans will be harder. They come to enslave you anew. Stay and fight! Then even if we are conquered we can still say that we were not defeated without honor. I give you back your freedom! I give you back your honor-prices, all of you! I swear by the Mother, by Camulos, by the goddess, that if you stay and we are victorious you will once again be masters of this land!" She lowered her eyes and her voice to the burly, glowering man before her. "Come and stand beside me," she said. "If you are a chief, act like one, fight like one, and if it is to be, die like one." He stood there chewing his lip, and seeing his indecision, she pressed him desperately. "If you have any honor left, you will fight. If not, I will fight and die alone and you will be proved to be what Cunobelin called you—stupid cattle!"

His eyes suddenly flared. He grunted like an irritated bull, then he took one step and stood beside her. "We will fight!" he said. "If we win we will sacrifice you to Taran and take this place for our own. If not . . ." He grinned at her. "If not, we will die as warriors."

Impatience tugged at her. She unsheathed her sword. "I agree," she called. "Spread out now. Climb the walls. Take your slings. The soldiers will be ready to break through today and you must keep them from breaching the walls. I have no food or beer to offer you. Everything is gone. But if you win you may feast on Roman food tonight."

They ran then, unwinding their slings, spreading out as they began

182

to scale the walls, and she left the belligerent chief and walked to where the gate once stood, feeling no shame at having used them. She knew that they would never inherit Camulodunon, and neither would she, but at least their blood would be spilled with honor, and they had lived without honor for more than forty years. How have they borne it? she wondered, slipping her arm into her shield while beyond her the incursus sounded and the troops surged forward with a great shout. I have been without honor for only a few weeks, but already I am half-dead with the load of my guilt.

Above her she saw the Trinovantians pulling stones from the rim of the wall, fitting them to the leather slings, whirling them and letting them fly, and she heard cries outside, and angry curses. But she knew that for every Roman struck there were fifty to take his place, and soon the wall would crumble. Already she heard the grate of spade and pick, saw the earth move in a dozen places, while the deafening cacophony of war battered in her ears. Then directly in front of her a hole appeared, a spade rang on rock, withdrew, and a hand began feverishly to tear at the loose earth. She ran forward, coolly raised her sword, and struck the fingers from the palm. She heard the man scream but immediately more hands were there, and to her right and left more holes were widening, as though rabbits had gone mad and were burrowing in a frenzy to reach the air. Above her the sun beamed down, filling the beleaguered town and all the valley beyond with a dazzling, blood-warming heat. High beyond sight two larks trilled and piped, but Gladys, in a final, drenching sweat of momentary terror, hewed at the first head to appear almost at her elbow and then swung desperately, as behind her the legions began to pour into Camulodunon. The peasants had retreated from the walls, fighting with knives and fists and teeth, a ferocious madness on them, dying without sound, and Gladys turned and fled back up the path to the Great Hall and the shrine of Camulos, her feet matching the rapid thudding of her heart. She whirled at the door to the shrine, flinging her shield away. Snatches of old prayers and incantations flitted through her mind, and she stood panting, leaning on her bloodied sword, and watched the rape of her home.

The battle raged fiercely, still two circles from where she stood. The peasants, men and women, did not fall back. She saw them die, still in the same awesome, strange silence, pierced by swords, impaled by spears. And now there were officers in the forefront, moving ahead of their men, and Gladys watched it all, encased in an armor of fatality that detached her from the scene. Time had run out. Time had played with her for a while and then grown tired, moving on to sport with others, and she was left to die in a weird, cold place where every

183

remaining breath was borrowed from the years before. The soldiers were hunting now, no longer faced with a foe, and the peasants who remained died alone, surrounded by the enemy. The officers came on, but slowly, looking about them, and Gladys straightened, raised her sword to rest against her neck, and drove all thoughts from her mind.

Now they came, toiling up the path with red faces, and swords held close to their breasts with bent arms. She felt herself grow calm. They saw her and rushed forward, shields swinging to cover them, booted feet crunching in the loose stones, and she raised her sword, grasping the hilt in both hands, and leaped to meet them. There was a moment of confusion. She was ringed by swords, stabbing in and out like sharp tongues of fire. One man went down, his leg severed below the knee, and she slashed again, her sword striking a shield with a force that stunned her. A shock ran up her arm and it went numb, but she tugged her blade free, turning to meet the soldier behind her, lunging with a cold detachment while her body danced like wildfire. He ducked, throwing himself forward behind his shield, and the cruel bossing caught her in the ribs, knocking the breath from her as his sword jabbed for her belly. She jumped backward desperately, hearing a sharp, shouted command. She was sensing the men who closed in at her rear where she was defenceless, staggering without balance, and her shoulders tensed against the blow that must come. But it did not fall. Strong arms went around her, one about her neck, grinding her against a hard iron breastplate, one over her own arms, encircling her. She struggled maniacally, screaming with rage. She kicked backward, and her imprisoned hands scrabbled for the knife at her belt, but the inexorable grip only tightened and she felt the blood begin to leave her head. Blackness swam before her eyes and the sounds of the shouting around her began to fade. Her legs gave way.

"Don't strangle her, Quintus," she heard someone say. The voice floated to her from miles away, drifting over a heaving ocean where dead men rocked. "You have a handful of royalty there. Plautius will want to see her." Suddenly she felt herself dropped like a heap of dirty tunics, and the sword was wrenched from her hand. Someone undid her belt roughly, pulling it free, and hands moved over her, checking for more weapons, but she could not move. Her sword arm tingled and throbbed. Her head swam. She could only lie there, eyes closed, while the man with the severed leg went on screaming. "Where are the stretcher-bearers?" the same voice said irritably. "It is all over, there is nothing left to do, they should be here." She wanted to open her eyes but the effort was too great. She lay there listening to the bustle around her, trying to breathe deeply while her head cleared and she felt strength seep back to her legs.

Presently there was the sound of running feet, and a moment of quiet, then the screams began to recede and at last she was able to open her eyes. She was lying against the shrine of Camulos. Above her, one hand on his hip and the other resting on the vine stick under his arm, stood a centurion. Beside him was his optio, a wide chunk of a man with the thick arms and craggy, twisted face of a wrestler. He still held her sword, and her knife now rested in his belt. Beside him, so close that had she stretched out her hand she could have dabbled her fingers in it, was a pool of bright blood where the wounded man had lain. Good! she thought. I hope the rest of the leg falls off and the stump goes bad and he dies in agony. The centurion glanced down at her and then motioned to his second.

"She has recovered, Quintus. Set her on her feet but watch her carefully. Tricky as weasels, these barbarians." Gladys found herself hauled unceremoniously to her feet. Her legs were trembling, and where the shield boss had struck her breast, she was so bruised that every breath was an experiment in pain. But she folded her arms and stared straight at the centurion while the optio hovered behind her, his hand on his knife.

"Who are you?" the officer asked. "I know you are royal. Loaded down with silver you couldn't be anything else. What is your name?" She did not answer.

"She probably can't understand you, sir," the optio said. "Can you speak her language?"

The centurion shook his head, uneasy under Gladys's dark, hostile eyes. "No. Now what shall I do with her? Plautius will want to see her but he'll be too busy for some hours yet. The gate has to be opened and a place prepared for the emperor. Find a couple of soldiers, Quintus, and put her in the shrine for the time being." Quintus saluted, and the centurion, after another hesitant, sweeping look at his prize, went away. The optio took her arm.

"In here," he ordered. "You!" Two passing legionaries stopped and saluted. "This prisoner must be guarded. You can see to it." He pushed her into the shrine and went away, and the two grumbling soldiers took up their posts on either side of the low, narrow door.

"So much for a mug of wine and a rest," one said. "I suppose we must stand here until Quintus remembers us, which won't be for hours. Got your dice on you?"

"Let's have a look at the prisoner first," the other suggested, and they turned to the doorway. But Gladys, hands pressed to her ribs where the pain seared her, fronted them.

"This is a holy place," she said, her voice flat. "If one of you puts his dirty foot over the threshold the god will curse you. Your belly will

185

begin to burn. Your head will ache until you plead for someone to cut it off. And demons will pursue you night and day and drive you mad with terror." They backed away, superstitiously awed as every soldier was when faced with strange gods, and Gladys sank to the ground.

In the dimness Camulos squatted, scowling at the doorway, big hands resting on his fat belly, the lobes of his ears looping up to envelop his bellicose head. Gladys smiled wearily at him. "Where were you when I needed you, Camulos?" she murmured. "Were the sacrifices not pleasing to you? Are you tired of serving the Catuvellauni?" She lowered herself, lying on her side, but whatever she did, her bruised ribs cried out with every indrawn breath. The boss had struck her with such force that her tunic had been driven into the flesh, but she did not try to loosen it, knowing that the pain would only become worse if she did. It was cold in the shrine, and dampness rose from the dirt floor and chilled her until she began to shiver. Her sword arm had no feeling in it and would scarcely obey her. There was a piece of cloth lying across the god's feet where offerings were placed, and finally she crawled over and took it, bundling it up and placing it beneath her head. The soldiers outside were sitting on the threshold and she heard the rattle of dice and their uncouth laughter. She tried to relax, closing her eyes and thinking of her brother, who was surely now far into the forests, along with her little nieces, armfuls of soft, sweet flesh. But it was for her beloved sea that she longed, and she wanted to crawl into a cave with her hurts and her grief and lie there until the solitude of a deserted summer shore could heal her. She missed the comforting coldness of her sword beside her, and without her voluminous cloak she felt naked, but she slept. The morning turned into afternoon, and the summer sun began to drop slowly and heavily to the horizon.

She awoke in a sweat, her heart thumping and her head thick, to the sound of loud voices and she sat up carefully, while every muscle protested. "Go in and get her!" she heard someone order impatiently. "What's the matter with you?" And one of the soldiers answered sullenly.

"The god will curse us if we go in. The woman said so."

"Oh she did, did she? So she can speak a civilized tongue after all! Well, well! Quintus, go in and bring her out. You two, go down to the camp." Gladys rose shakily, clinging to the wall, trying not to breathe for the agony of it, and the huge optio darkened the doorway. Before he could step within, she walked toward him, willing her feet to obey her, and he snapped his fingers.

"Hurry up! The commander is waiting!" She came slowly into the sunlight, blinking, and for a moment stood looking out over the town.

186

Long shafts of evening light lay peacefully over the valley, and smoke from the Roman cooking fires spiraled straight into the drowsy air. Below her a busy horde of soldiers labored on the earthwalls and the level of the defences had already shrunk. To her left, men came and went, and baggage stamped with the imperial eagle lay piled about the door of the Great Hall. From within came the crackle of new fire and the laughter and talk of the emperor's servants. She felt bewildered, lost, as if she had gone to sleep only to wake a hundred years hence in a different age, with nothing familiar to hold to. Quintus tugged at her arm, guards formed about her with the centurion leading, and she began to walk, her head high, vowing grimly not to faint. They passed the Great Hall, turned left, and followed the path that ran to the very summit. At last Quintus halted her outside Caradoc's gray stone house. No! she thought in panic, not here! But the centurion had already gone inside, and presently he came out again, nodding to her. She stepped past the doorskins, with the centurion behind her, and halted. Three men looked at her with a frank, open interest and she stared back, seeing out of the corner of her eye the familiar, homely things, which brought a lump to her parched throat. Eurgain's box lay on the floor in a corner, open and empty. One of her silver drinking cups stood on the table beside the brown, folded hands of the commander, and down by the hearth, where a fire blazed, lay one of Caradoc's cloaks, the one striped with red and blue and fringed in gold thread. Tears sprang to her eyes but she sternly fought them back, wanting to snatch up the warm, soft garment and bury her face in its gay folds. But something of Eurgain still lingered here. A whiff of peace, a sane comfort, and Gladys felt her spirits rise with the little spurts of flame that twinkled in Eurgain's copper lamps. She stood straighter.

"Thank you, Varius, you can go," the commander said, and the centurion beside her saluted and went out. In the moment before he spoke again, Gladys studied him. A man in early middle age, she thought, his black hair sprinkled with gray and cut short. The face was long and thin, the nose slightly hooked, and the chin clean and decisive. His mouth in repose was hard, a slash across his face, but when he spoke it broke into lines of gentleness. He was immaculately dressed. His white linen shone, and the drapings of his short cloak were fresh and stainless. The fastening on his shoulder gleamed and so did the thick bronze arm bands about both wrists. On the index finger of his left hand he wore a massive gold seal ring. At last her wandering eyes found his own and a jolt of recognition went through her as though somewhere, sometime, in a place before memory or consciousness, she had looked long into their depths and had now found a part of her own self. They were blue-gray, speculative eyes, full of an objective perception, deep with a knowledge of the world and himself, but telling her also that this man was a mystery, who kept his thoughts to himself, a man of quiet self-containment. With difficulty, with a strange, bewildering gladness, she tore her gaze from him and glanced at the others. A large, red-faced, ugly man stood beside the table with his hands behind his back. His massive, bronze-plated chest was thrown out, and the iron-stripped apron around his waist hid thighs like boulders. Off to her right, a young, cheerful-faced man rested one sandaled foot on Caradoc's stool and met her eyes with undisguised curiosity. She looked away.

"What is your name?" the commander asked her. She stared into his face and did not reply, and his hands tightened about each other. "What are you called?" he repeated, and she met his steady look coldly.

"I give my name only to my own people."

"Where are your chiefs? Where is your ricon?"

"Dead."

He shook his head firmly, and when he spoke again the level, cultured voice was sharper. "No, they are not. No chiefs lie among the bodies, and I myself checked the prisoners. Where have they gone?"

The soft lips remained firmly closed and Plautius regarded her in the silence. He, like the centurion, had no doubt that she was a prize, a member of some ruling house. Her bracelets were all of silver, the hem of her tunic was rimmed with gold thread, and the two necklaces that hung from the brown throat were silver filigree. The centurion had told him that her shield was studded all over with red coral and sprinkled with pearls. But who was she? What chief could be coerced into submission because Rome held this woman hostage? A husband? A father? No, not a father. She was well past her first youth, though the slim body could have belonged to a stripling and the dark hair fell in a glossy shower down her back without a trace of gray. The face was already traced with lines, fine meshes around the big eyes, faint tracks from the small nose to that cool mouth, but those eyes . . . He frowned unconsciously, annoyed with himself. This was no time for idle philosophizing on the endless permutations of the barbarian character. Yet there was familiarity in the face and a hidden tension, manifested in her very stillness, a tension borne of long years of some kind of discipline. He had seen it before in the faces of men who had devoted all their energies to art and withdrew into themselves. He looked back at her to see the color draining from her cheeks. She put one shaking hand to her breast and swayed, and he spoke quickly. "She's hurt. Rufus, give her the stool." The young man left his perch

188

and carried it to her, she sank onto it and they waited, Vespasianus shuffling and breathing heavily, obviously impatient to get the business over and move on. Then she raised her face, and the color was creeping back.

"You ask me where they have gone," she said, holding her bruised ribs, the faintness of hunger and exhaustion still threatening to pitch her into oblivion. "And as it can make no real difference now, I will tell you. They have gone to gather new forces. They will fight you again, Roman, and again, until you crawl back to your dungheap and leave us alone." The insult was ignored. Pudens raised his eyebrows and smiled, and Plautius left the chair and came to stand before her.

"Where have they gone?"

"I have told you enough." She spoke his native tongue with a pleasant, lilting accent, her voice deep for a woman, but soft, soft and compelling, and he found it hard to remember that she was a warrior, and that many of his men lay dead or wounded because of her.

"Why didn't you go with them?" he probed more gently than he had intended, and she looked up at him sadly.

"It was . . . It was a matter of honor." Vespasianus muttered something and sat on the edge of the table, and Pudens leaned against the wall, arms folded, his smile broadening. He found a respect for her growing in him. Plautius thought for a moment and then went on.

"Lady, I must know where they have gone, surely you understand that, and so I will keep asking you. How many chiefs left this place? How great is the force?"

"Not great—yet," she said. "But it will grow. And if you think to keep me here as a hostage in order to draw them back, forget the idea. My brother would rather see me die than surrender himself to you."

"And you yourself? Don't you want to live?"

She shrugged and then cried out in pain, mastering herself immediately and answering with pride. "Life without honor is nothing. I will die if necessary. There is nothing left to live for."

And yet you do want to live, Plautius thought. You do not know it yet, but you do. You are full of misery, lady, and dreams, and strange, unfulfilled yearnings. I see them all behind those dark eyes of yours. He walked to the door and called, and Varius returned and saluted. "Find a hut for the lady," Plautius said. "Send my surgeon to her, and food and drink, but keep her well guarded." Varius nodded and stood waiting and Gladys rose slowly and went to him, passing through the doorskins without a backward look. Plautius turned to his men. "Well?" he said. Vespasianus grunted.

"What a primitive idea these people have of firmitas!" he replied. "Give her to Quintus. He'll soon wring the truth from her, before it's too late to round up the chiefs." Plautius had a thought, then rejected it.

"She would not speak, and in any case it is already too late to make any difference now. Honor is all she lives for. Who is she, Rufus?"

Pudens left the wall and came to stand with them. "She mentioned her brother. We know that the younger brother is dead and the older one here with us, so it must be Caradoc who has slipped off with the remnants of his men. Cunobelin had only one daughter, sir."

Plautius nodded. "Gladys, I believe. Quite a prize for us, gentlemen! She should have gone with her brother." But even as he said the words he was suddenly glad that she had not.

She was put in a hut in the first circle that had escaped the ravages of the fire, though the outer wall was scorched black. Plautius's surgeon came to her, a brisk, efficient man who ripped the cloth from her ribs with no comment, slapped a cold salve and a bandage on her, and told her that her arm would heal and the feeling would come back, but that it would take some weeks. She was brought a soldier's meal—broth, leeks, beans, and barley porridge, and wine diluted with water—and she wolfed it down while the man left her and returned with her clothes rolled up in a sack. All her jewels were gone, resting now in the packs of the legionaries. She begged for her sword and her knife but the man just laughed in astounded contempt and went away.

Three days later Claudius, with the arrogant insurance of the Moesian Eighth Legion, made his triumphal entry into Camulodunon.

CHAPTER FIFTEEN

THAT NIGHT, after the fanfares and the ovations, the sacrifices and pomp, the emperor and his officers gathered in the Great Hall to celebrate the victory. Plautius, in full and glittering regalia, reclined on Claudius's right in the place of honor, and listened to Claudius's brusque comments on his plans for the future of the new province, the state of his delicate health in this contemptible climate, and his promises of promotions and rewards. Plautius's mind roved among the retinue gathered about the royal couch. Claudius is no fool, he mused, hearing the roars of masculine laughter go echoing to the roof as a servant bent to fill his cup. He has brought all his enemies with him. The thought made him smile. Here they all were, the Gallic senator Valerius Asiaticus, a contender for the purple after Caius's murder, a man who could still harbor a lingering ambition beneath that grizzled gray skull. Crassus Frugi, whinnying with horselike laughter, his big teeth exposed while Rufrius Pollio, commander of the elite Praetorians, calmly finished his joke, his eyes, as always, on Claudius. Frugi was married to one of Pompey's descendants. What was it Seneca had said of him? Plautius sipped the wine slowly, savoring its dry bite. "A man silly enough to be a possible emperor." A man of power also, and Claudius was busy trying to placate him and his illustrious house. He had married Frugi's son, Pompeius Magnus, to his daughter Antonia, but did not trust the son any more than the father. Magnus lay on his couch and watched the company with shrewd, heavy-lidded eyes.

Claudius turned away from Plautius to speak to Galba, and there, Plautius thought, is a man worth listening to. The emperor puts his trust in the right hands, but warily, for Galba rolled in money, Galba was a fanatic, devoted to his duty and the physical prowess of his legions, driving his own body with the same nerveless, humming energy that he demanded of his men. He was here to assess the situation in Albion, and to pronounce. He and Plautius had spent hours together discussing Plautius's future course in this wild, furtive, outlandishly lovely country, but Plautius, though recognizing his vast experience and superior tactical knowledge, did not like him. He could not believe that behind the flaming, forceful drive of the man there was no secret, hidden ambition, and perhaps Claudius doubted also, and kept Galba in his constant company. Galba, two years ago, had calmly crushed the warlike Chatti in Germania and took the subsequent adulation as his right. But most of all, Galba was connected to the old Empress Livia, and Claudius never forgot it.

Plautius met the eye of his relative, Silvanus Aelianus, and they smiled at each other, lifting their cups in silent, mutual toast, and Plautius, drinking, thought—you too, Silvanus. Is it a curse or a blessing to be related to Caesar? "Oh a curse, a curse, my dear Aulus," he could hear his aunt complain, the aging face puckered in distaste. "Can you imagine being made love to by a man who dribbles when he becomes roused?" and Urganilla's painted lips would pout. "Then he becomes offended because of my lovers. Well, really. What could I do?" Plautius grinned at the remembering. Claudius had divorced her, both of them hugely relieved, but then Claudius had dónned the purple and Urganilla had howled, not at her lost status but in fear that the career of her favorite nephew might be ruined. She need not have worried. Claudius was just. He saw the potential in Plautius and acted accordingly, and since that time he and Plautius had, by tacit agreement, never mentioned Urganilla. Claudius had Messalina now, and Plautius wondered whether he ever missed the petty nagging of his aunt. Messalina did not nag. Messalina smiled, and men's fortunes were made or broken on the strength of the whims beneath that smile. At least Urganilla had had no great ambitions.

"What a dark, stinking hole this is, eh Plautius?" Claudius had turned back to him and he shook his mind free of reverie. "When I am gone, burn it down. It reeks of stale pork drippings and magic. I think we will have a temple on the spot, to myself, of course. At first it will hearten the soldiers and later when the barbarians have begun to acquire some civilized habits, it may serve as a focus for their otherwise depraved religious instincts. What do you say?"

Plautius glanced at the emperor and away again. The face was fine, noble, a true patrician face, but Claudius's nose had begun to run again and little gray bubbles of foam had gathered in the corners of his mouth. "I think that would be wise, sir," he replied. "The peasants have begun to creep back to their farms now, and every day more of them leave the woods in search of food. I can have them put to work. It will keep their minds and bodies occupied."

Claudius smiled. "I do congratulate you, Plautius. A brilliant campaign. I have decided to name my son Britannicus after my new province when I get home. I must say I am looking forward to going home. Triumphalia ornamenta for Vespasianus and Geta, and the salute of the senate for me." He smacked his lips and lay back. "I hear we took an important prisoner," he went on. "A barbarian princess. Have her brought in, Plautius. I want a look at her."

Plautius rose reluctantly, and Claudius, seeing his hesitation, waved a heavy, bejeweled hand at him. "Don't be afraid that she may insult my Divine person. She can say anything she likes to me and I shall be vastly amused. I feel expansive tonight. You did say," he leaned forward anxiously, "that she spoke Latin?"

"Most of her tribe speaks our tongue," Plautius replied. "The traders say they are most proficient in it." Claudius was unaware of the mild rebuke. He liked and admired Plautius and he merely smiled and shooed him out, his head wobbling with excitement on its stalky neck.

Plautius strode from the Hall and sent two soldiers to fetch Gladys from her hut. He did not trust one man alone, not since he had seen her sword, bloody and notched. He waited patiently, looking at the star-strewn beauty of the night sky, the thousands of pricks of red light on the valley below, and he felt enormous contentment. Life was good. He was high in favor, his invasion had gone well, and soon Claudius would take his powerful, sophisticated retinue and return to Rome, leaving him, Plautius, to carve a province out of this wild land. Pannonia had been a challenge, but this . . . This would be like jumping into the arena to face a hungry lion with only a knife between himself and disaster.

He heard them come and he turned. She was swathed in a long, flowing cloak, black, he thought though he could not tell until she stepped into the light of the torches, and her dark hair mingled with the folds of it so that it seemed to him she was hooded as well. Starlight and firelight glinted on her pale face, giving it an ethereal, unearthly beauty, a softness that he had not seen there before, and he almost bowed and held out his arm. The eyes sought his without pleading or fear, and he gestured the soldiers away and spoke to her politely.

"Are you recovering from your hurts, Lady? Do your ribs still ache?" She nodded once, faintly, and did not reply. "The emperor has called for you," he said. "Do not fear him. He is curious, that's all. Come in." She smiled then, a sardonic, knowing twist of the mouth that made him feel like a fool. He turned swiftly, and she followed him.

Gladys stood on the threshold, shocked into momentary immobility by the change that had been wrought. Her eyes flew from wall to wall, darted among the now silent, staring company, but still she could not absorb it and adjust quickly and calmly, as Eurgain would have done. The dirt floor was covered all over with soft, thick carpets of blue and yellow. The fire burned, but in a huge grate raised high above the hearth. Torches flared about the walls and on every pillar, their yellow light reflecting from the gleaming breastplates, the gold cloak clasps, the bronze arm bands of the men who filled the Hall. Couches had been drawn up in a wide semicircle, brocade and damask sweeping from wall to wall, and in the middle was a table hung with bright cloth, laden with strange fruits, golden flagons, dishes piled with food that she could not begin to identify. She was suddenly shy, overwhelmed by the inquisitive, worldly eyes of the Roman aristocracy fastened on her in amusement and scorn, but she drew herself up regally and walked forward, following Plautius's tall back. He stopped, bowed, and stepped aside. "The Lady Gladys, sir," he said and went back to his couch, and Gladys looked into the most powerful face in the world.

At first she was impressed. He was tall even when seated. His forehead was high, crowned with thick gray hair cut short across his brow and below his ears. His nose was broad like Caradoc's, but the nostrils spread, and around them deep lines curved that gave him a cruel, sullen look. His mouth was large, well-determined, but again harsh lines marred it, made it petulant and capricious. The eyes that now were hungrily regarding her were fine, intelligent, and steady, even kindly. But Gladys felt a flash of pity, for the emperor was slobbering, wiping the spittle away now and then with a white cloth, and nothing could disguise the tremor of his head. He held out an elegant hand and the purple cloak fell back. "Come closer," he said and Gladys obeyed, trying to remember all that her brother had said about this man. He was a coward. He lived in continual fear of poison and betrayal. He was a genius, a historian, a great and learned reader. He was a tool of his Praetorians, his freemen Greeks, and his women. "We salute your bravery, barbarian woman," he went on. "You fought well, or so I have been told. We are not vengeful men, Gladys. We bring you and your people a new peace and prosperity. For many years your countrymen and ours shared good trade and we have become as brothers. So, like brothers, let there be continued cooperation and growth together. What do you say, eh?"

Gladys did not know whether to burst into astonished laughter, or spit in his face, or burst into tears. Sholto . . . Tog . . . She felt the lump form in her throat. Tossing back her hair she fought it down. "My town is in ashes," she said huskily. "My brother is murdered, my people are scattered. I have neither honor-price nor position left to me. Even my sword has been taken from me. And you dare to speak of peace and cooperation." She could not go on. More words would have brought tears, and she would rather have died than afford these spotless, superior lords the sight of a sword-woman in public disgrace.

Claudius considered her, his head on one side. "Delightful accent," he said at last. "Well spoken, for a savage." Plautius held his breath. Why am I caring? he thought, amazed at himself. How many barbarian men and women have I seen brought to their knees before the imperium? Let them all humiliate her. It would do her good, stubborn female. But he felt his fingers grip the cup even tighter and was unable to relax them. Claudius was in a merry mood now, but he was less stable than he used to be. He might order her execution if the game palled. "Rome is here," Claudius said affably, "whether you like it or not, my dear, and before long you will like it, we are sure. Come and drink with me." Plautius tensed still further, hoping for her sake that she would bend that arrogant head, smile apologetically, and take the cup from the servant's outstretched hand. But he was hoping for his own sake that she would not. She had eyes now only for the emperor. They stared openly at one another, taking a measure, then Gladys stepped forward, an enigmatic smile on her face.

"And who will taste my cup?" she said quietly.

Deep silence descended as the implication of her insolent words sank through the cheerful, victory-flushed company, and Plautius wanted to stand and applaud. He actually felt his knees stiffen, then he bent his head to hide his action. The fire danced merrily on, the only sound in that warm, hushed place, then Claudius snatched the cup from the servant's fingers and turned it upside down, and the red wine splashed onto the carpet.

"Go away," he said, his reedy voice trembling. "Go away!" Gladys looked slowly around at the still, heavy faces, now full of hostility and a new respect, then she spun on her heel and glided out the door. No one spoke. Claudius's heavy breath rasped into the thick air and he turned to Plautius, his nose streaming. "If they are all like that," he said, suppressed rage flooding his face with color, "then we might as well exterminate them."

But they were not all like that. By noon of the next day embassies began to arrive in Camulodunon, riding up to the gate in their bright cloaks and glittering bronzes, looking with uncomfortable amazement at the transformation that met them. All that remained of the great defences was a little wall, hardly breast high, a pleasant place to stand resting and gazing out over the river valley. The mounds of ash and rubble were being cleared away, and the officers' tents ringed the Great Hall in severe, pristine circles. Before the Hall, flapping idly, the standards and the tall, bronze aquilae of the five legions were clustered, guarded by motionless soldiers. Everywhere there was motion. Messengers came and went, troops wandered about, the auxiliaries sat in the dust and gambled. Claudius and his retinue, and the officers of the legions, sat in the Great Hall to receive the formal surrender of the subdued chiefs who filed through with their shield-bearers and bards to bow and squat before them, anxious only for peace. The brutal crushing of the once powerful Catuvellauni had awed them. All they wanted was treaty and then the long, relieved ride home.

Gladys, pacing back and forth in her dark hut, heard the ring of their harness and the sweet familiarity of their common speech, and she went to the door. "Please let me out," she said to her guard. "I want to speak with the chiefs. I will not run away." He looked at her doubtfully, shaking his head. "I will have to get permission," he said. "Wait until my relief gets here in another hour, and I'll ask my tribune. But he'll say no." She retired, pacing slowly again from bed to door and back, ignoring the now faint twinge in her ribs where the big black and purple bruise was shrinking. She listened with straining ears to the snatches of conversation outside. She heard the guard change, and she went and sat in the little chair, folding her arms, beating back the feeling of suffocation that the dimness and stuffiness of the room brought to her. A dozen mad visions fluttered through her mind. She would slip away and steal a boat, and run free on the sand in the hot sun. She would disguise herself and ride out with the chiefs. She would overpower her guard and take his knife, and rush into the Hall and kill the emperor. But then between her and her frustration came those eyes—steady, smoky, full of sternness, and she hugged herself tighter and closed her own eyes, a new restlessness joining the others.

The doorskin was pushed back and she rose quickly. There were epaulettes, and colored horsehair in the curved helmet. It was a tribune. "You have a request?" he asked her briskly, and she nodded.

"I want to walk about a bit, take exercise. Please give me permission." The word "please" came hard to her tongue but she was beginning to realize its advantages. He stared at her, thinking.

"If you were an ordinary prisoner I would deny your request, but you are not. I must consult the commander." Then he was gone and she sank to the bed again, hoping that Plautius was not still in the Hall with the emperor, for surely Claudius would immediately deny the request. She smiled to herself, remembering his affronted face. It must have been a long time since anyone had dared to insult him. She heard more voices, the tribune's, the respectful response of the saluting guard, then Plautius himself shouldered into the room, bending his head under the lintel as he came, filling the tiny, dark space with his calm authority. Her heart suddenly leaped and she found that she could not meet his eye.

"You want some sunshine, Lady," he said gently. "I am sorry, but you are much too valuable a prisoner to be allowed to wander about. My men are all busy today, but if you care to wait until this evening I will allow you to walk around the Hall." Gladys stepped to him, putting a hand on his bare arm, only the shreds of dignity clinging to her, and her eyes filled with tears.

"Sir," she said, her voice trembling. "If you keep me a moment longer in this darkness I shall go mad. I will swear by all my gods, by the price of my honor, that I will not try to run, but please, let me out!" He paused. She smelt of clean things, wind and sun, cut grass and dewy, blowing flowers, and her hand was warm on his wrist. With a mixture of irritation and eagerness he sought her eyes, saw them blurred with the tears, and thought to himself, What does it

196

matter? An hour in the sun is nothing, and the emperor need never know. He disengaged his arm politely.

"It is against my better judgment," he said, "but if you like you can take your guard and walk a little. Stay away from the gate and the wall, and if you try to escape the guard will have orders to kill you immediately." Her smile lit her face and he smiled back. Then he was gone, the tribune stalking after him. She heard him speak briefly to her guard, then she snatched up her cloak and went into the sunshine.

For an hour she wandered about Camulodunon, drinking sunlight, watching the hustle, approaching the chiefs who clustered together down in the third circle with pleading hands and a glad smile. So familiar, the garish patterns of scarlet and blue, the yellow and black chequered tunics, the long, untidy red or blond hair. For a while she did not care that these were men come from chieftains without honor, chieftains who were willing to sell their people without once drawing sword. They spoke to her warily, eyes flicking over the stolid, sweating soldier by her side, shaking their heads in answer to the one question burning in her, "Is there news from the west?" She found herself near a face she thought she recognized, a tall chief, black-haired, standing a little apart from the others as if he were ashamed of them and himself. His orange cloak folded about his booted feet and his hand was on the hilt of his heavy sword. The scabbard was finely wrought, bronze that sparked, figured all over with tight, never-resolving curlicues that flowed from the mouths of tiny, grinning wolves. About his neck, falling on his blue breast, were necklaces of some shiny black stone, and the same stone fastened his cloak and glinted mysteriously in his hair. Then she placed him, mounted on a black horse, his animal eyes fixed on Caradoc as he embraced Aricia on that damp, cold morning when she had ridden away into the mists with her red-bearded chieftain. She greeted him with respect. "A good morning to you. I am Gladys, sister to the Ricon Caradoc of the House Catuvellaun."

His expression did not change. His eyes remained cautious and haughty, but he answered her with the same politeness. "I am Domnall, chief to Aricia of the House Brigantia. What do you want of me?"

Her guard touched her shoulder. "Speak Latin, Lady," he warned her, obviously ill at ease, and Gladys switched to it, speaking slowly and carefully, believing that this man would have little knowledge of the Roman tongue, but to her surprise she found that he had mastered it quite well. That, more than anything else, told her how the years had treated the wild sheepherders. Aricia had been making good her vow to turn them all into Catuvellauni.

197

"I want news of your ricon. How is she?" He considered well before he told her. He does not want to lie, she thought with quick intuition, but neither does he want to seem disloyal. Oh Aricia, what havoc have you been wreaking on your proud people?

"She is in good health, Lady. We have prospered as a tuath since she returned to us. She has brought in much trade from Gaul and Rome and we are richer than we ever dreamed." The deep voice was emotionless.

"And what of her husband, Venutius?" Domnall gave her a penetrating look.

"He is well also," he said, and abruptly turned away. Gladys left the colorful little knot and began to stroll around the first circle, ignoring the long, curious stares of the officers who sat outside their tents. Domnall had told her much with his few words. Aricia had ordered surrender, Aricia had sent the delegation to make it formal, almost certainly against her husband's wishes. Venutius would favor a policy like Cunobelin's, the neutral middle way. Or had he seen that the middle way was no longer possible? What would have happened if Caradoc had married Aricia instead of using her, and had faced Plautius with the combined armies of the Catuvellauni and the Brigantes? So many ifs, so many useless, dead avenues of speculation. She stopped in the middle of the path, closing her eyes and raising her face to the sun. I am alive, she thought unbelievingly. Against all odds, I live. The sun warmed her blood, fell hotly on her cheeks, and a happiness greater than she had ever known swelled within her. "Time to go back," her guard said at her elbow, and she turned to him with an infectious, youthful smile.

"Yes, yes, I know. Will he let me out again, do you think?" The man shrugged, embarrassed at her sudden change of mien, and together they began the climb to her hut.

Three days later Claudius and the unnecessary Eighth Legion under Didius Gallus left Camulodunon. Vespasianus and Geta went with him, for they were to parade with him in his triumph and receive laurels at his hands for their part in the invasion, and Plautius and Pudens bowed them all to the boats with relief. Claudius had left Plautius with a list of injunctions. "Conquer the rest," he had said airily, but Plautius had known that the emperor did not mean it. Spread out, he had ordered, build roads and forts, consolidate. He had appointed Plautius as First Legate of the Imperial Province of Britannia, a post that followed almost automatically from his command of the invasion forces, and he had spoken again of the temple he wanted on the razed site of the Great Hall. Plautius had listened absently, regarding the erection of the temple as the least of his worries. The merchants and traders were already flooding the captured territory, and he knew that after them would come the land speculators, the usurers, the adventurers and beggars and offal of the empire. While Claudius rambled on, Plautius frowned over his wine, wondering how many beneficiarii and speculatores he would need to maintain some kind of order as the boundaries of peace were pushed back and his greatest worries would be with civilians.

At least he did not have to worry about setting and handling taxes. The procurator would soon arrive, with his staff. Plautius wondered who it would be, then decided that it did not matter. He was used to handling procurators. Tact, dignity, and gentle persuasion, that was all it took. Besides, he himself was in such high favor that he need not fear the sealed dispatches that always went direct from the procuratorial offices to the emperor himself. He liked Claudius. They had spent many hours together discussing the latest books, and Plautius was always amused and touched to see his emperor forget his fears for a while and grow excited and expansive over Seneca's latest dry, witty pronouncements. But now, listening to the emperor expound on the dimensions of his temple, he was very glad that he would soon be left in peace to get on with his job. Claudius had made that job very clear. "We have a duty to assimilate these barbarians," he had said earnestly. "This is Rome's mission to the world, Plautius. They must be civilized for their own good and for the commonweal. They will live to bless the gods of Rome."

Everyone knew that Claudius wanted to see every barbarian wearing a toga. Seneca had made Claudius's odd ambition the joke of Rome. But Plautius had been touched by his emperor's transparent goodwill. He was a liberal, fair man, and though his physical defects distressed and titillated those around him, Plautius could see beyond them to a man wounded by a harsh childhood without family affection—a dreamer, a shy reader propelled unwillingly into the glare of divinity. But Claudius was fast becoming something else, and Plautius pitied him. He was anxious to be gone now, fretting continually about what Vitellius was doing in Rome during his absence, and the more upset he became the more his hands shook. Plautius and Pudens exchanged rueful smiles as the imperial barge, with a great fanfare of trumpets, floated out of sight down the river. They were also pleased that the emperor had taken with him all his polite, predatory enemies.

In the late afternoon, Plautius sent for Gladys. He was not sure why he did so, but somehow in the peaceful lull between Claudius's departure and the new duties that waited he wanted to see her. She came quietly, as self-composed as she had been on the night when she had bested the emperor, and she stood before him in the Great Hall, waiting without impatience, the low, yellow sunlight streaming under the doorskins behind her. Vespasianus's brother Sabinus, and Pudens, were engaged in paperwork, heads together over a table piled with scrolls, their secretaries waiting to take notes, and they barely glanced at her as Plautius dismissed her guard and beckoned her closer. "Come and sit," he offered, but she shook her head, standing before him, hands hidden in the sleeves of her green tunic. "Have you any complaints?" he asked. "Have you enjoyed your walks?" He thought she looked better. Her cheeks had more color, her eyes were free of the cloud of pain, but that strange tension was still with her like a permanent aura.

"I have enjoyed them more than you can ever know. Thank you," she said. "But now I would like to test your goodwill with another request." Plautius sat back and crossed his legs, and she read a pleased smile in the austere eyes.

"I have already allowed you more liberty than I ought," he replied, "but ask if you like. I can always refuse." She took one gliding step.

"Sir, let me walk by the ocean." The inflection of her words rolled back a screen for him, and a new corner of her carefully concealed personality peeped out. He was intrigued.

"Why? You are presumptuous, Lady. You can walk the town every day. Why do you need the ocean?" He had placed an unerring finger on the mystery of her life that even she had been unable to solve, and she quickly shrugged, lifting one shoulder to dismiss the question before he began to probe too deeply.

"I am unaccustomed to a cage, sir, and even Camulodunon can be a cage to a captive bird that is big enough!"

He sat looking at her, knowing that he should refuse. She would be too hard to guard on the lonely, open stretches of beach, and besides, what might she ask for next? Her weapons returned to her? He glanced back at Pudens. "Tell me, Rufus," he called, "when is that shipment of goods due for the troops?"

"It should have arrived this morning, sir," Pudens replied, not looking up, and Plautius looked back at Gladys.

"I take too great a risk, letting you journey to the estuary with only your guard," he said, "and if you escaped, the emperor would be very angry with me. You are still worth something, Lady."

"I have told you before," Gladys said. "My brother will never cooperate with you, even if it means my death. If you like, I will swear an oath not to attempt escape." He shook his head, his smile broadening.

"I do not think such an oath would be binding on you," he said, "or am I wrong? Isn't there a time limit on oaths sworn to an enemy?"

She did not reply and he saw her shoulders droop. Then he emptied his cup and rose. "I want to check on the baggage that arrived today," he said. "I could wait until it is unloaded here, but I wouldn't mind a stroll on the beach myself. I will come with you." She smiled then, that strange, sourceless happiness blossoming like a spring flower on her face, and he shouted for his orderly. "My cloak, Junius, and my helmet. Lady," he walked to her as the servant entered, cloak over his arm and shining helmet in his hand, "do not be deceived. My days in the ranks may be over, but you would find me more than a match for you if you tried to run!" Her smile widened. He took the cloak and helmet and together they left the Hall, walking down to the new gate in the bee-busy afternoon.

They rode slowly through the dappled green woods, the quaestor, two centurions, and three soldiers with them. The men chatted desultorily, and Plautius, acknowledging the salutes of the passing legionaries who came and went between town and river, relaxed on a tide of monumental well-being. Gladys did not speak. She rode easily, her eyes wandering in the trees, listening to the echo of bird song and the mild fluttering of the breeze in the ferns and leaves, her thoughts on Caradoc. Had he come this way? Where was he now? The thought that he believed her dead sent a pang of remorse through her, but it could not dull her mood. They rounded a bend and the river flats lay before them, brown water flowing slowly under the sun, boats drawn up to the pier and rocking gently, and she dismounted. One of the soldiers took her horse and she, Plautius, and his men clambered onto a barge. "Cast off," Plautius ordered and they swung into the turgid current, the stiffer wind off the water blowing away the heavy forest scents and bringing to her a pungent whiff of the sea.

The estuary was busy. Beyond the sodden marshes where the river dawdled out to linger before it trickled into the ocean, a camp had been set up, white tents and earthworks, and the bay was full of the slim ships of the newly formed Classis Britannica. Gladys could make out sailors leaning over the sides and enjoying the sun, and the gay standards and pennants of the ships ripped frantically in the onshore breeze. Their barge came to rest against a new, solid pier, and the sentries ran to make it fast, stiffening and saluting as Plautius and the officers got out, with Gladys following. Shouts and the clamor of unloading came from the beach, and an officious soldier approached Plautius, worry creasing his brown forehead, a slate in his hands. Plautius turned to Gladys. "Where do you want to go?" he asked, and she looked up to where the stark, bird-circled cliffs rose from the bay and gained height, their shoulders grass-covered and their feet planted among black rocks.

"Around that curve there is sand and pools and silence," she said. "Let me walk there."

He nodded. "Quaestor, see to the tally. I will come too."

Gladys spread out her arms in pleading. "Oh sir, let me go alone," she begged, but impatiently he brushed her off.

"What kind of a fool do you take me for?" he snapped as the quaestor took the slate, already preoccupied, his eyes on the mountains of sacks and boxes by the water. She turned away, Plautius moving behind her while the quaestor strode under the shadow of the ship.

The yells of the officers, the grunts of the perspiring soldiers, the crashes and thumps slowly faded. She took off her sandals and laid them on a rock, putting her cloak over them. Then she straightened and drew a long breath, and shook her head as the wind found her hair and sent it floating out behind her. The breakers boomed as they rolled toward her and collapsed in white fury almost at her bare feet. "Plautius, don't be alarmed," she called. "I am going to run!" She saw him nod, his face shaded under the helmet, then she pelted down the sand, her arms wide and her eyes squinting in the blinding glitter of sunlight on blue water. The curve of the bay narrowed but she did not slow. She turned in a shower of sand and careened back, her breath coming fast, her heart beating strongly, and a mad gaiety tingling in her fingers and hot, bare toes. Plautius watched her, amused, with his arms folded over his bronze breastplate, and she came up to him and stood, hands on knees, panting and laughing at him.

"Now I will walk!" she puffed. "How hot you look! Take off your helmet and your armor! You do not need defence from me. I have no knife!" He gestured to the top of the cliff. "I might be shot at from up there," he protested, and she laughed at him again, her eyes slitted and her black hair whipping about her shoulders. He removed the helmet, unbuckled the breastplate and let it fall, and the hot wind ruffled his gray-sprinkled hair with dry fingers. She turned away and walked down to the water, squatting, catching a wave in both hands and raising it to her nose, putting her tongue into it, and rubbing wet palms over her face. He stood behind her looking down on the thin curve of her green-clad back, and the tangled, falling hair. She was all innocence today, making him feel worn and old, and a tenderness flooded him. He wanted to hold her in his arms like a mother cradling a wounded child, but she reached out to catch a piece of seaweed that went floating by and the sleeve of her tunic fell back. Her arm was scarred and pitted with dozens of white, puckered sword slashes, and once more he felt confusion.

She rose, and together they explored the beach. They stood ankle deep in the warm, translucent pools left by the tide. They teased the irritated crabs that vainly rose up on their silly legs and clicked at them with offended claws. They pried the mollusks loose from rocks festooned in gray, rotting weeds, and Plautius scraped out the juicy, strong-smelling meat, offering it to her on the point of his knife, smiling at her, and she found herself suddenly laughing over nothing like an idiot. Then, when the sun began to drop toward the cliffs and the light that streamed over the water no longer blinded them or made them sweat, they sat side by side, their feet buried in wet sand, and fell silent. The gulls wheeled above them, crying. The wind veered and began to gust from the summit of the cliffs, and down where they were there was a sudden lull. They watched as the sun behind them opened a wide, scarlet pathway, a water road leading to the dark blue, far horizon and their shadows mingled. Gladys looked out upon the ocean now slowly changing from bright blue to a somber, cool gray. Ah, freedom, freedom, she exulted, boundless wealth of my soul, and she turned her head to find him watching her. All at once freedom seemed to dwindle, shrink, and become contained in those crinkled eyes that held within them the color and mystery of the sea. She looked away quickly, but now the ocean only reflected his steady, gray gaze, and its depths flung back at her his thoughtful face. She sighed. What is freedom?

"I am grateful for this," she said. "I do believe I am fully healed."

"I am grateful, too," he said simply. "I needed a few hours of peace."

"What are you going to do with me?" she asked him, her eyes fixed on the horizon where evening clouds were forming, and he followed her gaze.

"There are several possibilities," he said evenly. "I could send you to Rome as an important prisoner of war and you would be paraded through the streets in chains. I could keep you here as an encouragement to the remnants of your people to cooperate without fear. I could kill you and send your body to your brother." She did not stir.

"And what do you *want* to do with me?" she pressed.

"I don't know. You could be useful, but without your cooperation you are just a nuisance. I should send you off to Claudius and forget you." Something in his voice warned her not to argue and she changed the subject.

"Where is Adminius?"

"Your brother? He has gone on a little tour with one of my cohorts in an effort to reach the chiefs and people still living in the woods. I also sent him to Cogidumnus and Boduocus. He is proof that Rome is not bent on the destruction of the tribes. He will return in two or three days. Do you want to see him?"

"Keep him away from me!" she exploded. "Slave! Stinking Roman pig! I disown him! I have only one brother!"

She had begun to tremble and her voice held such anguish that he was embarrassed. "Tell me about your brother," he said quietly. "What kind of a man is he? You know I saw him once, standing on the earthwall, and something about him made me want very much to meet him."

"Not kill him?" she snapped, her mouth twisted and her color still high. Then she loosened, drew up her knees, and began to studiously trickle the warm sand through her fingers. "I am sorry. I find my position extremely difficult, and moments such as this only serve to make my future look more dark. About Caradoc." She smiled, a lingering, gentle smile of reminiscence and love. "He is upright, full of honor, a great warrior. Men count it a privilege even to be his enemy."

"It is a privilege to me," he said softly, and she turned to the lean, stern face.

"Is it? How can you, a Roman, understand that an enemy may be loved even while your sword cleaves him in two? How can you, with your disgust for us and our barbarism, begin to know the meaning of a warrior's honor?"

"I feel no disgust for you or your people," he said. "I, too, live by honor. It is simply interpreted in a different way. I do my duty and am proud of it, and if my duty included atrocitas for the sake of my emperor, then I would order it. But Gladys, I prefer swift battles, and then a slow, peaceful transformation."

"Well, you will not get it here!" she retorted.

"Why not?"

"Because the tribes value one thing above all others, and that is the one thing Rome can never promise, pay for, or bestow. Freedom. Freedom. You will never kill all resistance no matter how many years you squat here in Albion, let alone turn the warriors into Roman citizens apart from a few weaklings like Cogidumnus, because death is always preferable to slavery, and freedom is the jewel beyond all price."

"How like a bird you are indeed," he said. "A poor, struggling bird with wings cut and claws filed. I wish that I could set you free."

"It is easy enough," she answered lightly. "Open the door of the cage and let me go."

"Where would you go?"

"Into the west. What difference can the detention of one aging, miserable freewoman make to the great Roman war effort?" She turned her face away to hide the beginnings of tears, so close to the surface after days of physical stress and mental torment. The sun finally sank, picking up its red skirts and hiding them behind the cloak of the cliffs. Twilight descended, a dim, warm shadow, and in a sky still tinted with melancholy light the first stars appeared, faint and pale.

"You underestimate your value," he reminded her, tactfully ignoring her struggle to contain herself, and she shook her head emphatically, lifting the hem of her short tunic to dry her face.

Then she turned back to him. "My only value lay in Caradoc's willingness to surrender to you, but I know he would never do that. Would you? He has the chance to go on. He will not give it up in exchange for seeing me again." They stood then as if by unspoken agreement, and began to wander back to where her cloak and sandals and his helmet and breastplate lay, a black huddle on the rock. It seemed to him that he had shed them years ago. When they reached them Plautius took her cloak and laid it gently around her shoulders and she thanked him briefly, turning for a last look at the placid, star-silvered water and the empty sweep of rock-strewn beach. The ecstatic, sparkling child was gone. Plautius, a hand under her elbow, his eyes scanning the sharp profile as she looked back, felt the guarded dignity of a royal captive wrap her again. By the barge his officers waited, torches lit in their hands, and the aft light on the tall seagoing ship cast red ripples that danced on the water. He felt her move away from him, lifting her elbow from his grasp, and he realized that he had been gripping her too tightly for politeness. He adjusted his helmet.

"Lady," he said as they neared the boat. "Will you have dinner with me and my staff tomorrow night in the Hall? I can promise you good conversation, a few jokes, and of course a change from a prisoner's diet!"

"I do not wish to sit all evening and be stared at!" she retorted, but she was smiling, the silver at her throat glinting as her breast rose and fell.

"I will order ten lashes for the first man who raises his eyes to you!" he promised and she laughed suddenly, pitifully, the humor catching in her throat and turning to sadness, dimly aware of the new course her life was taking, a new thread waiting to twine about her. In the boat she sat far apart and silent, already fighting a future that promised only more sorrow.

Pudens himself came to fetch her when the broad blade of sunset still blooded the horizon. He was dressed in his toga, the white linen folding softly about his legs, and he bowed to her and offered his arm.

She stepped from the hut, with Eurgain's long blue tunic swishing about her. Her hair fell clean and shining, and her little remaining silver was polished and bright. Plautius, in his explorations, had come across one of Eurgain's tiring boxes shoved under the bed, and in it had been a tunic and a thin silver circlet. He had sent them to Gladys in the morning and she had sat for a long time, fondling the cool, regal gown. It smelt of friendship and happiness, bouts on the practice ground, and drinking together in the Hall while Llyn chased his sisters and Caelte sang softly. She put it aside, determined not to wear it, but it lay on the bed all day, reproaching her as Eurgain herself would have done, and she paced before it, her eyes never leaving it. If she put it on she would be admitting something to herself and to Plautius, something unlooked for and unexpected that as yet she could not face. If she went to the Hall in her worn, war-torn green male tunic she would be saying something else, something that would take the fragile, delicate growth of a spring flower in the middle of her winter and crush it forever, leaving her frozen in the grip of her self-made isolation. In the end she stripped, washing in the hot water the guard brought to her. Then she slipped Eurgain's tunic on, tying it with her own plain leather belt, and setting the circlet on her brow. You are a fool, she told herself. You are more crazy than Tog ever was. She placed a hand on Pudens's arm and walked slowly to the Hall.

Candlelight and firelight spilled out to meet her, and in the doorway Plautius stood waiting to receive her, imposing and foreign to her eyes in his snowy toga bordered with senatorial purple. The hand he offered to her was heavily ringed and his wrists were covered by embossed arm bands of gold. He inclined his head. "I will not insult you, Lady, by welcoming you to your own Hall," he said. "Let me rather welcome you to the company of my friends and my table. It occurred to me in the night that perhaps my invitation would seem like a new ploy to gain your support. What I could not win by coercion I might succeed to by a kinder, more devious route, eh?" He smiled. "If I gave you that impression I apologize, and deny any such intent." She took his metaled wrist, thinking how grossly, how finally Tog and Caradoc and all the others had underestimated the Roman mind. There had to be more to men that made them masters of the world than the unexcelled ability to wage war, and she understood how Plautius had come to be a senator, a general, a much-loved and respected man. She swallowed. Forgive me, my brother, she thought. Forgive me, Cunobelin, true father, forgive, forgive, members of my Council. She spoke slowly, her words almost drowned by the laughter that gusted from the Hall and the rattle of dishes and cups.

"Welcome to this Hall," she said, her grip firm. "May your stay here

206

be one of rest, and peace." For a long time he studied her face, seeing a proud submission there, the promise of a gift, and he was profoundly moved. He knew that the words were not for Rome but for him, yet in declaring him formally safe from her she was also facing the final ostracism of her tribe. He slid his hand back and took her fingers in his own, finding them warm and firm.

"Enter," he said gently and she followed him while the men in the room fell silent and rose to their feet, cups in their hands.

After that night, Plautius allowed her to walk free. He was busy again, closeted night after night with his officers, and soon Gladys stood by the gate and watched the legions march away, the Ninth to the land of the Coritani on the borders of Aricia's country, Sabinus and Vespasianus's Second to the southwest to put down the fresh stirrings of revolt among the Durotriges, and the Fourteenth and the proud, independent Twentieth toward the west. Camulodunon emptied but for the members of the commander's staff, for the soldiers who were left to build more permanent housing for themselves and to defend and maintain the town, and for the Trinovantian peasants and Catuvellaunian freemen who had scattered, only to come creeping back under Adminius's persuasion. Plautius had them put to work. The legions were moving slowly, conscripting local labor to build roads as they went, and the speculatores and beneficiarii already clattered over the smooth cobbles on their swift horses, carrying dispatches to and from Camulodunon.

The Great Hall was finally burned to the ground. Gladys stood and watched without emotion. All the farewells had been said, all the memories, bitter and sweet, had been felt and dismissed, and she waited now for the hollow places of her soul to be filled with another reality. When the ashes had cooled, Plautius ordered the site immediately cleared and leveled, and the new procurator, the architects come from Rome, and the officers gathered to discuss the erecting and financing of Claudius's temple. Taxes, both annona and tributum soli, were set and they were harsh, for Claudius had refused to provide funds from his own treasury for the building of his temple. The money and labor had to come from the peasants who were even now threshing and havesting their crops and preparing their cattle for winter. The peasants were outraged, not so much at the corn tax or the cattle that were driven from their fields as at the slave chains that fell about their necks and the optios who stood over them with whips as they labored over the charred remains of their freedom. Blood was shed, and cries went up, for a slave was less than a man. A slave was without rights, soul, or voice, but Plautius calmly ordered public floggings and executions and the grumbles died. The only resistance left went underground, into the fierce spirits of the naked, sweating peasants and once-free tribesmen. Gladys, walking by them of a morning, was pierced by the smouldering, dumb hatred in their black eyes. Guilt, held at bay in the lull after her capture, returned to torment her, and she again felt dishonored, reading in those suffering eyes a deep contempt. She should have been there beside them, sinews cracking, lungs straining, instead of lunching with Plautius in his tent and discussing the merits of Roman art. But though she was less of a prisoner than they, her hands were tied. I stayed, she told herself again and again. I fought to the end. I held tight to my honor. But she felt the muscles of her sword arm grow limp from disuse and her body soften with too much good food and too much leisure. She despised herself. She requested sword practice from Plautius and he agreed. He came to watch, an amused smile on his face as she circled and slashed at a disgruntled Varius, appointed by his commander to keep the barbarian princess happy. Once or twice she could have killed him but did not. She was not afraid of the immediate, final reprisal that would come, but she remembered her tribal promise to Plautius and something in her was repelled at the idea of betraying his trust in her.

One day, sitting and panting after a stiff bout in the shade of one of the new houses that now fronted the path to the gate, her sword beside her, she felt something in the dirt under her hot hand. She scraped absently at the earth and it dribbled away revealing a leather sling, coiled in a knot, brown with old blood. She quickly tucked it out of sight under her belt, not knowing why she did so. The soldier from the armory, which now squatted sturdily beside the stables, the hospital, the grain storage sheds, and the new barracks where the last circle had sprawled, came for her sword and she handed it over, rising wearily to seek water. A sling was of no earthly use coupled with her self-imposed truce, but she took it to her hut and cleaned it anyway, rubbing it with oils and wondering whose blood had spurted over its soft, brown hide.

Two days later she knew why Camulos, who now stood behind the stables, had given her the weapon. She had taken a coracle and drifted down the river, hugging the bank to avoid the laden barges that plied daily between the coast and Camulodunon, and raising a hand now and then in answer to the shouted greetings of the soldiers who stood beside the piled goods. Half a mile from the estuary she grounded her little craft, pulled it high, and left it, striding toward the lip of the cliff over rolling, grass-covered hills, breathing deeply and gratefully as the fresh landward wind buffeted her. She had given up sailing right to the estuary, for it was now a busy, noisy place where

ships came and went, where soldiers gossiped with the inevitable traders and the sands were always full of cargo. Now she walked farther
to where the cliff fell sheer to the rocks and the boiling surf below,
and already her feet had made a faint track in the long grasses. She
would tie up her tunic and clamber down the dusty, crumbling side
without fear, coming to rest in silence and peace where only the cry
of gulls and the crash of the breakers spoke.

On this day she crested the last humping roll of hill before the land
broke off into blue sky, and she saw two men standing on the edge,
talking. Immediately she dropped to her stomach, lying still in the dry
grass, surprised at the mindless reaction of her body. She had nothing
to fear anymore from Romans. All the same she lifted her head with
caution, peering through the waving stalks of grass. Then a strange
thrill went through her and her fingers clenched. One of the men was
a soldier, a centurion, vine stick held languidly in his hand, sun glittering on his iron-stripped skirt, but the other . . . The other man was
Adminius. She craned her neck, eyes straining. There could be no
doubt. The light brown hair billowed toward her, the tunic was scarlet and yellow, the long sword clung to his breech-clad leg, and as he
turned to say something to the soldier beside him she saw the broad,
thick nose and the cleft chin of her father, but here it was a caricature
of the features she had loved. Adminius was running to fat. His years
in Rome had softened him, and bitter thoughts of treachery and
revenge had eaten into the fair face, giving it a surly, crabbed look.
Cunobelin's unrivaled cunning was there, too, as it was in Caradoc,
but not tempered by Caradoc's sensitivity. Gladys felt sick. She knew
that Plautius had kept them deliberately apart out of respect for her,
but now here he was, alone but for a solider, here in her hands. She
pulled the sling out of her belt, thinking of the last time she had seen
him, there in the dim stable harnessing his mount in a furious rage.
He had flung his torc at her, grazing her cheek. I should have killed
him then, she thought, but I suppose it has made little difference.
Claudius would have plotted his invasion anyway, and Plautius would
have come, and I would still be carrying with me the fiery brand of
my tribe's dishonor and my own guilt. Sholto died again before her
eyes but she blinked the vision away, feeling around her cautiously. A
stone, she prayed, eyes closed. Camulos, you put Adminius within my
grasp. Now give me a stone. She forgot her new contentment, she
forgot her still-nebulous dreams of imprisonment in the circle of
Plautius's strong, inviting arms. She was a sword-woman stalking an
enemy, all effort tensed on the kill, and the man gesturing expansively, laughing as the centurion spoke, was not her brother. Her
fingers closed about a stone, round, smooth, too small, but it would

have to do. She knew that she was not proficient with the peasant's weapon and all she could hope to do was topple him over the edge. She shook out the sling and fitted the stone snugly within it. What if I hit the soldier? she thought. Then I must face Adminius with bare hands and die. She shrugged off the consequence. Mother, keep them talking, keep their eyes seaward, she prayed as she rose slowly. She swiftly raised an arm, began to swing the sling, gauged the direction of the strong wind. Die, you miserable wretch, she thought as the sling whizzed faster. No clean slaying for you. Die in shame. She let go and dropped out of sight, but before she began to wriggle back to the covering shelter of the trees along the riverbank she waited to see whether fate had been with her, her lips drawn back, teeth clenched. The stone struck. Adminius cried out, his hand flying to his neck, and even as he flung out an arm to steady himself he lost his balance and his feet slipped. The centurion leaped forward, grabbing at his tunic, but it tore away, and the scream that ripped the sun-drenched summer air was more sweet to Gladys's ears than the loveliest song Caelte had ever sung.

At last, at last, she exulted, sliding on her belly through the grass as the centurion dropped his pitiful handful and began to run shouting along the clifftop. I am clean, I am avenged. Take heed, Tog, and all you noble dead. She reached the trees and forced herself to walk slowly along the damp turf beside the water until she came to her coracle, got in, and picked up the paddle, dropping the sling into the river. The sun beamed down, dappling the limpid depths, and fish flicked away like cold shadows to hide in the waterweed as her boat moved upstream. She would go back to Camulodunon. She had no need of the ocean's balm this day.

Plautius kept his opinion about the cause of the Catuvellaunian chief's death to himself. He questioned the centurion briefly, listening to his story with an inward smile, then he sent for the river guards and enquired when the Lady Gladys had taken out a coracle that day. His knowledge of her and his growing intuition about her did the rest. The soldiers were saying that an insect had stung the barbarian in the neck and he had swiped at it, lost his balance, and fallen, and the story was a two-day wonder. Then Vespasianus returned from Rome and the legionaries found other topics of conversation. Plautius let the matter drop. He knew the necessity of using traitors and informers. He had done it many times in the past, but always with an almost physical distaste, and he was not sorry that Adminius was dead. He had outlived his usefulness to Rome in any case. The invasion had been so decisive that he had not even been needed as a puppet king. The act had not been murder. To a Catuvellaunian sword-woman it had been retribution, and Plautius knew that Gladys would not kill again in the same way. From then on he never once referred to Adminius in her presence, and by this she knew that he understood.

He took to accompanying her every evening when she floated to the beach and strolled beside the dark water, the cares and decisions of his day somehow shrinking into a new proportion under the influence of her calmness. Summer was almost over. The early mornings were soaked with a fine, white mist, the evening air held a nip, and day after day the migrating birds rustled overhead in piping black clouds. Preparations for winter were going ahead well. The Ninth had built an encampment on the Marches of Brigantia and were preparing to enter winter quarters, their front secured by Aricia's promises of co-operation. Vespasianus had rejoined the Second, now in snug temporary barracks, while the Durotriges smarted, cowed after more than a dozen new defeats. Vespasianus had already begun to plan his push northwest in the spring if all went well. The Fourteenth and Twentieth were still moving uneasily through Cornovii country, all too aware of the proximity of the men of the west, but all seemed quiet.

Plautius knew that he must soon begin a tour of his legions, but in the days left to him at Camulodunon he lingered, walking beside Gladys, often in silence. Both would be cloaked against the night chill, watching the moon rise pure and clean to silver the quiet water, and standing by the gray, bubbling foam while the stars came out to shine, netted in the motionless clouds of a tranquil sky. When he finally kissed her, deep under the shadow of a rock that leaned over them and smelled of salt and age, it was with an unselfconscious artlessness, as though he and she, the sand, the cliffs, the ocean, were all linked by ties of a sweet and ancient innocence. Her lips were soft and cool, fitting his easily and naturally, and she tasted of dry wind and herbs. He felt little passion. He wanted only to touch her long hair, feel with his fingers the clean contours of her face, hold her fresh warmth to him under the shelter of his cloak, knowing that with this woman life could be rich and full. He took her cloak and spread it on the gray sand and they sat together, his own cloak enfolding them both, and her hands cool in his. He spoke to her quietly of his estate on the hills outside Rome, and of the marble stillness of his halls in the drugged heat of a midsummer afternoon. He told her of the shady wet greenness of his garden, with the little wrought-iron gate under the spreading plane tree, where one could lean and look out upon his dusty vineyards, and beyond them to the wide reaches of the Tiber and the towers and rearing columns of the city. He told her of the sun lying long in the empty rooms, of his study lined with books and scrolls, of his years governing in Pannonia away from the place he loved. Albion was his last active post. In five years, or six or seven, he could return to Rome with honor, to his grapes and his horses and his beautiful, quiet house. He made no request of her. There were no unspoken questions. In a while he stopped talking and put his arms about her, drawing her to him, and the ocean crashed at their feet, speaking to Gladys of a new freedom.

Summer, A.D. 43

CHAPTER SIXTEEN

*A*s SHE HEARD the shouting and cheering begin, Boudicca lifted the sleepy, replete baby away from her breast, wrapped it swiftly, handed it to Hulda, and ran outside. The afternoon was hot and drowsy. Beyond the town the forest stood motionless as if dazed with the weight of stifling air, and the marshes were silent under a high and burning sun. She saw her husband leave the cool shade of the Council hall with his train and begin to move toward the gate, and she hurried to catch up with him, snatching her sword from its resting place before the doorskins and buckling it on. Seeing her coming he stopped and waited for her.

"What is it?" she called to him. "Why are the people so excited?" She came up to him flushed, the sun drenching her bare, bronzed arms, her copper-colored hair, her brown, freckle-flecked face. "Is the sky about to fall on us?"

Prasutagas smiled at her fiery, unkempt anxiety, and Lovernius the bard acknowledged the old, proud joke with a rattle of his gaming dice and a shrill, tuneful whistle. "Some would say yes and some no," Lovernius answered her. "It depends in what light you see the return of our embassy from Camulodunon. Of course, it depends also on how you see the embassy itself. You, Lady, may expect the sky to come crashing down at any moment, while you, Lord, are full of joy at how high and clear it is."

"Save your wit for the Council fire, Lovernius!" she said rudely. "Prasutagas, is it the embassy?"

"I think so."

212

They turned and walked toward the gate where a growing crowd had gathered, eyes fastened on the figures of three horsemen that wavered and danced in the heat haze to the south, and Prasutugas was cheered as he shouldered his way through them, bard, charioteer, and wife behind him.

"Peace for us all, Prasutugas!" someone called gaily. He nodded and waved, carefully keeping his eyes from Boudicca, who had come to stand beside him and was gripping his naked forearm.

"Are there any Romans with them?" she breathed. "If they have brought the enemy back with them I shall shut myself away, I shall refuse them hospitality, I shall . . ."

"How is my daughter today?" he cut in gently, pointedly, and she let go of him, her hand dropping to the hilt of her sword. "Does she suckle well?"

"Sometimes, Prasutugas," she replied tartly, "I think I hate you, for you have no intuition and certainly no intelligence."

He planted a swift kiss on the tip of her small nose. "Good, good," he teased her. "I shall enjoy being hated by you, for then you will leave me alone. I am the most wife-ridden, nagged man in the tuath, and everyone knows it!"

She looked across at him, meeting his blue, smiling eyes, and then suddenly leaned her tousled head against him. But before she could speak a roar went up from the people and she straightened to see that the flickering shapes had become cantering riders approaching the gate, their blue, yellow and scarlet tunics pasted wet to their chests, their breeches fluttering from their hanging legs. When they had come within earshot they drew their swords and held them high, and in a moment they had drawn rein and the crowd flowed swiftly around them. The nearest chief flung his sword at Prasutugas's feet and the tip of it thudded into the dry earth.

"Success, Lord!" he panted, sliding from his mount's back. "We have much news, all of it good, and the Iceni are safe!"

"Peace?"

"Peace!"

The cry was taken up. Peace, peace, the people shouted as Prasutugas, his train and the members of the embassy began to move into the town. Only Boudicca walked with a stiff back and a glowering face.

"Did the sky hurt your head when it splintered around you?" Lovernius whispered in her ear. She swung around to strike him but then did not dare. His eyes were full of sympathy.

"From now on, shut your mouth, Lovernius," she murmured. "If you have felt the sky cracking around you own ears, keep it to yourself."

The hall was blessedly cool and dim, a shadow place with its huge shields frowning from the walls, its ancient swords that in winter reflected the light of Council fires, its massive chains from which the cauldron hung. Men and women pressed excitedly through the doorway to sit on the skins or stand, and Prasutugas, Boudicca, the embassy, and the others went down near the now-cold hearth. Beer was brought and they drank thirstily, the travelers gulping down two and three mugsful. The leader of the embassy wiped his mouth carefully on his tunic and relaxed with a sigh, while a servant threaded his way through the packed bodies bearing cheese and bread, and fresh, steamed fish.

"Well?" Prasutugas demanded. "Did you speak with the emperor? What did he say? Does he accept our offer of cooperation?" There was a hush throughout the hall as the people strained to catch the conversation.

The man took a loaf from the proffered tray and tore it apart. "We met with the emperor," he said slowly, proudly. "He is a very great ricon and his hospitality is boundless. He fed us strange dishes and gave us sweet wine to drink, and talked very fair, but his words were of all the fine things that would come to us and we quickly understood that our business was not with him but with the man who beat the Catuvellauni. There were many other embassies present, who also ate at the emperor's table, and he was so polite that we felt no stain upon our honor at any time."

Boudicca snorted and began to speak, but Prasutugas said quickly, "Tell me what has happened at Camulodunon. Were there many soldiers? What of the Catuvellauni? What has become of them?"

The chief stopped chewing. "There are soldiers everywhere, but they treated us with respect. They have leveled the earthwalls, and most of the town was burned. As for the people, they are already hard at work for their masters, and very fitting it looked. How pleased I was to see those sons of dogs sweating with picks and spades in their hands instead of swords!"

"And Caradoc?" Boudicca could contain herself no longer. "Is he dead? Taken? What?" Prasutugas looked at her curiously, wondering at the catch of plaintiveness in the deep voice, and those in the crowd who had lost members of their kin in the wars against Cunobelin's sons craned nearer. The chief signaled for more beer.

"Caradoc and many of his closest chiefs ran away. Some say that the god of the Catuvelauni carried them over the walls to safety in the forest, but the strongest rumor is that he has gone into the west. He left his peasants to be slaughtered and his sister to be taken prisoner,

214

coward that he is. But what else can one expect from a Catuvel-launian?"

The eager crowd murmured their assent but Boudicca sat very still, remembering the brown-eyed, tall young man who had set her on his horse and galloped with her through the shedding trees in the crisp, sparkling winter air. She had felt his kindness as an impersonal, in-different thing then, with the swift knowing of a child, and her pride had been stung at his loud laughter, his disdain of her father. That disdain had fueled her anger when she had taken to the field with Subidasto against the two arrogant young Catuvellauni brothers. But now, as she felt the air in the hall grow warm and stuffy, and listened to the chief speak so easily and glibly of the end of her tuath's free-dom, she remembered Caradoc's impatient, sure grip on the reins that had kept her secure and the way a path had opened before him so smoothly through the excited, seething cattle owners by the river. So he had gone, he had escaped. A thrill of gladness ran through her. He had not capitulated to Rome after all. In the end his honor had been worth more than the honor of her own husband and her tuath, and the once-corrupt Catuvellaunian had been through the fire and had emerged—as what? Why had he gone west? What spell had caused him to sacrifice blood kin? She did not believe for a moment that he had run away.

"I saw his sister," the chief was continuing. "She was walking about the town with her guard and talking to other chiefs, but she did not approach us. No one knows why the Romans have not executed her." His lip curled in spite. "Perhaps she will be sent to Rome and torn to pieces in the arena."

Prasutagas felt his wife begin to fidget, her annoyance mounting. "So Caradoc has left the lowlands," he said. "Well, what of Plautius? What agreements did you make? Will he leave us alone in exchange for our submission?"

"He will not molest us as long as we make no war on him, but we must allow roads through our land if he sees fit, and perhaps a garri-son. The emperor is offering a gift of gold to all the tuaths that desire peace with him, and with the gift goes his most honorable word that we will be left alone."

Boudicca sprang to her feet, her hair flying. "Bribery!" she yelled. "Call it by its proper name and do not tiptoe around it with such reverent awe in your voice! This so-called gift of gold is nothing but a bribe and comes without the sealing of the pact of friendship. Do you really believe that Claudius gives gold and promises in return for nothing more than smiles? What chief could offer these things and ask for nothing and not be thought a fool or criminal? You make me ashamed, all of you," she glared at Prasutagas, "and afraid, also. What seeds of ruin are you sowing?"

"Sit down, Boudicca!" someone shouted. Another voice boomed out, "No more war!" The call was taken up. "No more war!" the chiefs and their women began to chant, and after one sweeping glance over their stubborn, determined faces she stamped her foot, shook her fist at Prasutagas, and marched outside.

He found her an hour later, sitting moodily on the bank of the river with the shadow of the copse at her back and her bare legs dangling in the cool water. He quietly took off his sandals and his sword and lowered himself beside her, gasping as his sweating feet touched the slow-washing shallows, but she kept her head averted.

"In two days a Roman called Rufus Pudens will be here," he said after a moment, "with his escort. He is bringing us the gold, and papers of agreement to sign."

"Can you read Latin?" she shot back at him, her gaze still fixed on the white sparking of sun on bright water.

He put his hand to her cheek and forced her to look at him. "Boudicca," he said softly. "Do you remember how the chiefs carried the headless body of your father home, and we walked through the night crying and wailing beside his bier while the rain pelted down out of the blackness? Do you remember how Iain slew the tall Catuvellaunian warrior who had hacked off my arm and was waving it about his head and roaring with laughter? Can you forget how you screamed and raged at Lovernius because he told you that I was going to die? Such agonies, such raw, searing memories! Do you want those things to go on happening all your life?"

She pulled away from him, stood up in the water, and stepped out until the current swirled frothing about her brown knees. Bending, she scooped up the water and splashed it on her face, then folded her arms and looked at him. So young, so serious, the open, guileless vulnerability of him pierced straight to her heart.

"We fought the Catuvellauni as a free people," she said harshly. "In the end we may have lost, we may have won, we may have made a peace and then turned on the Coritani and made war again. This is how it has always been. But then the Romans came, and Caradoc begged help from us, and out of maliciousness we refused, because the people could not see past revenge to the deeper danger beyond."

"That is not the only reason," he reminded her. "The people had grown tired."

"You persuaded them that they were tired!" she shouted. "You spoke to them of peace forevermore, and they elected you ricon over me in exchange for this peace, but the price, Prasutugas, the price! For the dishonor of the Catuvellauni, for Roman gold, for peace, you have secretly taken their souls away from them!"

"What nonsense you talk! We want change, all of us. Are you glad that your father lies buried without his head? Are you happy that the sleeve of my tunic hangs empty and my wound still drags me to the earth with pain? I do not understand you, Boudicca. What do you fear?"

She pushed back her red hair with both wet hands and then gazed past him to where fat cattle grazed in the long, lush grass and the grain was ripening to a heavy gold in the fields. "I do not fear Rome for herself," she replied slowly. "Nor do I fight you, my dear one, because I am ignorant and mean of mind. The people want change, but they do not realize that the change will not be outside themselves but within. Something will be lost to the Iceni, Prasutugas, something precious, and though I myself do not yet know what it is, I feel it, feel it deeply, and know that once gone it can never be replaced." She flung out her arms. "Already the Druids have gone away, and soon the gods will no longer speak to us. It is death that comes to the Iceni. Can't you feel it sliding closer?"

"No," he offered calmly. "No, I can't. You are carried away with your own sense of doom, and how you love the sound of your own voice! I think that if you had no one and nothing to battle, you would hold up your mirror and scream at yourself instead."

"Idiot!" she said hotly. "My father was right, the invoker was right. I should never have married you. This year has been a trial for me, and I think that now I shall take another husband."

He burst out laughing. "Any other man would have beaten you into silence by now, and then slit his own throat out of boredom."

"Well, I would rather face fists than your endless humoring and cowlike acceptance!"

He bent his head and made as if to rise, but then suddenly threw himself forward, still laughing, and caught her unprepared. His good arm shot out, catching her around her neck. She lost her balance, and together they fell into the deeper water with a splash and a shower of spray. He swiftly changed his grip, pushed her to the gravel bottom, and held her there while she kicked and clawed at his breeches, then reluctantly he released her and flung himself just out of reach, grinning while she floundered and gasped. "Boudicca," he called, while she found her breath.

"What what what!" she shouted in a rage, still coughing. "Andrasta, how can a one-armed man pinch in so many places at once?"

"I love you very much. Give me your hand." He gripped her fingers tightly and for a moment they stood, clothes plastered to their strong bodies, red and blond hair matted on their cheeks, water shining on their faces and arms.

They scrambled up onto the warm earth of the bank. "I do not take you lightly," he said. "There are two wounds that plague me. One is seen by the world but the other is my pain at your unhappiness and my constant care for you."

She relaxed against him and her arms crept around his neck. "I love you also, Prasutagas," she whispered. "Oh, how I love you! More than my kin, more than my love for the people, I love you. What is existence without you? For your sake I will give hospitality to this Roman, this Pudens, and smile and be agreeable, but my smile and my outstretched hand will be only for the love I bear you."

He kissed her gently, their many and often wounding differences submerged for a while under the love that had taken them both by surprise.

She stood up, pulling the heavy, wet tunic away from her legs. "I must go to my duties. Ethelind will be crying again and Hulda will be walking her up and down and getting angrier and angrier." She lifted the hair from the nape of her neck. "How hot is it! I can't remember such a scorching summer! I suppose the Romans will be congratulating themselves on having found a new province that promises to be as fruitful and pleasant as their own country." She snorted. "Let them wait until the snow comes! Then we shall see."

He struggled to his feet and stood looking at her, knowing by her sudden lost, pensive air that her thoughts were on Caradoc and the mystery of his disappearance. He picked up his sandals and sword and moved away. "Shall we sleep under the stars tonight?" he asked. "We can bring blankets, and lie beside the river. Ethelind will not stir until the dawn."

She came to herself and grinned at him. "If you promise not to roll me into the water when it is time to get up! I may catch a chill and have to take to my bed. Then you will have to receive the Roman by yourself."

"And how disappointed you would be!" Together they strolled back through the green, listless dimness of the copse, and long before she reached the door of their hut Boudicca could hear the baby's thin, hungry wails.

That night they carried their bedding out onto the tall grass that grew beside the river and sat watching the lingering summer light fade slowly from the sky, and the white stars come out to hang low and glittering over the marshes. The soft darkness was full of the noises of warmth and life. Frogs burbled in the mud, insects rustled and clicked around them, and away in the forest the owls hunted, and the myriad small, unnameable things uncurled beneath the trees' close protection and made of the night a friendly, many-hosted time. The two young people talked quietly and without strain of simple matters of the heart and the day-to-day concerns of the tuath, but they did not speak of the future. For them the night was precious, a time of rest which they had learned to hold fiercely for themselves alone, hours which contained only the companionship of privacy. Prasutugas forgot the grinding worries of a tribe whose welfare revolved around him like a great, weighty wheel. Boudicca pushed aside the creeping terror that seemed to her sometimes to be like a noisome choking sludge which drowned all joy. The future was for the sunlight, linked remorselessly to actions and decisions where each was forced to become what he was not. Only here, beside the silver lullaby of the river flowing calmly by forever, under the flaming silence of star fire, could they remove the cloaks of necessity and care. They sat huddled under the blankets, heads together, murmuring and laughing. They made love and got up to drink from the clear, cool river, and loved again, and though they did not sleep they wandered back to the gate refreshed when the coming of the sun was only a grayness in the east and the wind of dawn poured a steady, crisp air around them.

The day was hot again, and sultry. Cattle stood in the river with hanging heads, while the naked children splashed and shrieked around them. Horses walked slowly with tails swishing at the clouds of flies. The people sat in the shade of their huts, and only the few slaves were busy about the Council fire that had been kindled outside the palisade. Even the tradesmen, the blacksmiths and weavers, the tanners, the jewelers, and the clothmakers, left their tools and congregated by the water to gossip desultorily or drowse. Prasutugas, all his thoughts fixed anxiously on the Roman delegation even now wending its way to the borders of his land, walked the paths of the town with Lovernius and Iain, all three sweating and silent. Boudicca spent the morning riding among her cattle and her fields, talking to the peasants and freemen who worked for her, looking bitterly and sadly at her honor-price and wondering how much of it would end up in the bellies of the ever hungry legionnaires. In the afternoon, dispirited and oppressed by the heat, she went to her bed and slept with the baby in the crook of her arm.

Evening brought an illusion of coolness, and after a subdued meal eaten in the open and a word with her husband she walked alone to the forest, her feet bare on the dry earth, and her cloak slung over her arm. The grove of Andrasta lay deep within the trees, at the end of a path that had already narrowed through disuse, and to her distress she found that once or twice she had to push aside arching brambles or step over straggling encroachments of nettles. No sacrifices had been offered that summer, not since the Druids had vanished, and as she walked, Boudicca thought of the gatherings of chiefs and their women who had crowded to beg spells and make incantations here before the chariots had rolled south to face the Catuvellauni. Her father had bowed his massive head with the others, that head which lay hidden somewhere, the skull bleached white by now, or else hanging lonely and forgotten against the lintel of some deserted Catuvellauni hut, and Prasutagas had taken his great sword in both life-filled, mighty arms and had swung it through the air, laughing, to show her how sharp Iain had made it. He had sliced through a leaf fluttering past him. No, she thought, eyes squeezed shut for a moment while her body moved along the way she knew so well. No, I do not want to return to those times. He is right. If the tribes had decided at some Samain Council to give up warring and to live in peace forever, how good and rich life would be now! But for Rome . . . It is not the same . . . It is as if we steal the object of our fervent desire instead of paying for it honorably, and the joy of its possession will turn to loathing and self-reproach.

The grove lay still and secret, lit dimly by the heatless rays of the new-risen moon, the shadows of a thousand branches black-chequered over the semicircle of the roofless wooden shrine and the dark stone altar. Andrasta sat cross-legged beside it, tall and thin-shouldered, her eyes closed, her mouth parted a little, the moonlight touching her winged helm and the writhing snakes of hair that escaped from under it. Her arms, thin and formless as hazel sticks, rested beside her knees, and in each upturned palm a silver-chased skull gazed vacantly into the gloom. Boudicca glided forward, but even as she stood before the face that was forever closed behind the lidded eyes, she felt the absence of magic in the grove, the pathetic, desolate emptiness of the place. The power had gone. The Druids had felt the winds of change begin to blow within the Iceni, and they had cursed the people with warnings, but the people had turned their faces to this new wind and their backs upon the invoker and the sages, and when they had turned cautiously around to see what would happen next, the Druids had melted away and their curses had seemed mean and void of strength. If you dance with the demons of Rome you will pay with everything you have and more, the Druids had said. But Prasutagas had shown the calm stubbornness, which had at once attracted and repelled Boudicca, and the war-weary people had braved Andrasta's wrath and formed ranks behind him.

"Where is your anger, Queen of Victory?" Boudicca asked her

quietly. "Where is your vengeance?" But the stillness was calm, dumb, and the night untroubled by whispers. Boudicca stood there helplessly, knowing the uselessness of prayers and invocations. She had not believed that in the end her husband would surrender to Rome, but now Rome was coming to fill the darkness the Druids had left with a blacker presence, and she could do nothing.

Suddenly a twig snapped behind her, and the dry grasses stirred. She turned. Lovernius stepped into the moonlight, a bundle in his hands, and for a moment they smiled at one another ruefully. Then he came up to her and spoke.

"I thought you were Hulda," he said. "I did not recognize you, Lady." There was caution in his voice. "I have not been to make an offering all summer." The words could have expressed contrition at his laxness or an acceptance of Andrasta's slide into oblivion, and he watched her carefully.

"What have you brought?" she enquired evenly, as he unwrapped his gift.

"Some money. A silver bracelet that was part of my mother's honor-price. And a knife." Moonlight gave the pearled hilt a gleaming luster, and garnets glimmered on the little scabbard. She swiftly scanned his face and then ran an admiring finger down the heavy, encrusted edge of the scabbard.

"It will do no good, Lovernius. She will not receive the gifts. The Druids have bound her with spells, and nothing we can do will rouse her to our will."

"Nevertheless, I will offer them, and I will keep bringing her what I can."

She watched him lay the bundle on Andrasta's knees, listened to the words of debt, but she knew that the goddess was no longer impelled to honor the present with a service, and she slowly swung her cloak around her shoulders and prepared to leave the grove. "We are alone, you and I," she said flatly, gruffly, as he scrambled to his feet. "Tell me, singing man, out of your wit, what shall I do?"

"The same thing I shall do," he replied simply. "I shall go on singing to my lord of his triumphs and mistakes, and you must raise your child and tend to your honor-price."

"So that in the end the Romans can take both? I want to go away, Lovernius. I want to run into the west."

He searched her eyes for a long time, and then gently took her hand. "You do not really want to do that," he said. "You love him too much to leave him defenceless. Have courage, Boudicca! Our time will come. We must wait."

She turned away and together they filed back onto the path. "I am not good at waiting," she answered him at last. "I have learned many things in my short life, Lovernius, but patience is not one of them!" She spoke gaily, her mood of depression lifting, and he spoke in the same vein.

"If you would spend more time with your mouth shut and your eyes on the stars, and less with your head down, charging at everyone and everything like a mad bull, you would learn it!" he quipped, and she laughed.

"Make me a song to remind me," she called back over her shoulder. "And come and sing it to me every day. Prasutugas would reward you handsomely for teaching me to curb my tongue."

"No, he would not!" he replied. "He is besotted over you as you are over him!"

She chuckled again but did not comment, and the town's firelight beckoned them as they left the trees and ambled slowly toward the gate.

Rufus Pudens and his escort of tribunes and infantry arrived late the following afternoon. They were greeted riotously by the townspeople, the farmers from outlying areas, and many traveling tradesmen and drifters who had gathered for a look at the new masters of Albion. Prasutugas and Boudicca stood at the door to the council hall with their train, a splash of vivid, motionless color in the jostling, shouting mob. Prasutugas had donned his high bronze helm and had left his hair loose, and it cascaded over his shoulders in golden waves. His ceremonial sword hung from his enameled belt, and his one arm rested along the jewel-strung shield that had been his father's, and his before him. Boudicca waited demurely at his side in her soft yellow tunic. Gold bracelets tinkled as she clasped and unclasped her blunt fingers, and on her head was the gold circlet studded with amber that had been a wedding gift from her husband, but circlet and stones were lost in the bright hair that curled and frothed to her waist.

"Remember," Prasutugas whispered to her out of the corner of his mouth. "I forbid you to lose your temper today. If you do I will punish you, and this time I mean it most seriously."

"I promised, I promised!" she hissed back at him. "Andrasta, love has made a fool out of me! Oh look, Prasutugas! Here he comes! Such gleaming assertion, such dazzling might! It is not too late to change your mind, you know. And who is the tribesman with him?"

"Hush!" He nudged her and then stepped forward, for the tight, armored group of soldiers had wheeled to a halt by the gate at a short word of command, and a silence had fallen among the admiring crowds.

Pudens dismounted together with his tribunes and swung onto the

222

path that led straight to the hall, and in spite of herself Boudicca felt a thrill of approval at the smoothly folded scarlet cloak, the shining breastplate, the plumed, glittering helmet. A clean order and discipline radiated from the sure, upright stride of the four men, the back-flung set of their shoulders, the free tilting of their heads. With them came a tall, burly chief clad in a sleeveless, vivid blue tunic. Bracelets bit into the bulging flesh of his upper arms and a plain iron sword thudded against one long, thick leg. His hair was soft brown, graying a little above his high forehead, and as he came nearer, Boudicca saw his face more clearly, a face that could have been handsome, alive with sensitivity and humor, if only it had not been stamped with sulkiness and petulance. I know that man, Boudicca thought to herself incredulously. I have seen him before. Prasutugas suddenly felt as though he and Boudicca were children caught out in some forbidden game by stern, disapproving adults. The Romans came up to him, removed their helmets, and he passed his shield to Iain and extended his arm.

"Welcome to this tuath," he said warmly. "Food, wine, and peace to you."

Rufus Pudens took the proffered wrist. "I thank you, Lord, in the name of the emperor," he responded gravely. "It is a great pleasure for me to meet with you personally at last. This," he said, indicating the tribesman with a small gesture, "is my interpreter."

The chief rapidly translated Pudens's words, then added, "My name is Saloc. The noble Pudens has some facility in our tongue, but not enough to make his meanings clear to you. That will be my honor." He stepped back, took her husband's arm briefly, then turned his attention to Pudens, who was holding out his hand to Boudicca and waiting.

Prasutugas introduced her quickly. She hesitated, her eyes fixed mutinously on the toes of the Roman's sandals, pride and loyalty vying furiously within her, then slowly her hand came up and her glance with it. She felt, not the cold, cruel tentacles of her imagination, but a smooth, live grip of friendship, and smiling eyes shone at her out of a boyish, eager face topped by a fringe of black hair. She managed to smile back but the words of graciousness would not come and in the end Pudens, seeing and understanding all in a flash, let her go and introduced his tribunes. The formalities were over for the moment, and Prasutugas bowed them into the hall. A small fire had been lit in their honor, with skins placed around it, and they all sat in the cool shadows with a sense of relief, reaching for the wine that Prasutugas had ordered for the occasion, but Boudicca cradled her jug of mead and kept her face composed. The rest of the afternoon would be spent in polite talking about nothing, and she steeled herself against the waves of resentment, knowing that in the evening, after the feast, she would need all her control to stay quiet when the business came into the open. The men drank and conversed easily, Pudens adroitly keeping away from any hint of war, occupation, or Roman demands, while Saloc interpreted with automatic, detached skill, and Boudicca found herself listening with interest to an account of the Roman ways of hunting and farming. Then Prasutugas began to talk of his precious dogs and offered the Romans a tour of the kennels and other areas that might be amusing. They all trailed back into the weakening light of a sun that was westering slowly, and were followed as they walked about the town by crowds of chiefs and freemen who listened to the hard, exact Roman speech with awe and some uneasiness. Later, with the last red light of the day, they gathered by the big fire that roared cheerily outside the gate and they mingled with the commoners, feasting and drinking, watching chiefs spar and wrestle and race their chariots around the torch-lit palisade. At one point, to her horror, Boudicca found Pudens beside her, wine in hand. It was too late to edge away from him and she clutched her mug to her breast and faced him resolutely.

"You have a daughter, Lady?" he said haltingly in her own tongue, his voice raised above the merry din around them. She nodded briefly. "What is her name?"

Her name is offered only to her kin, Boudicca wanted to snap, but she answered meekly, "Ethelind."

"That name has music. I am very fond of children. I have many nephews and nieces at home who ply me with requests for gifts every time I return to Rome, but I don't mind." He smiled at her. Were you also fond of the little ones you Romans slaughtered in Gaul? she wanted to sneer, but somehow that face was too open, too exuberantly youthful, and she could not.

"Have you a wife?" she asked him curtly, and he shook his head.

"No, not yet. At the moment I am wedded to my career, as they say, and my career is a jealous and time-consuming mistress. It does have its rewards, though." Immediately he saw his mistake. Her eyes darkened and her mouth turned down at the corners. He thought quickly of turning the conversation but decided that she was not one to be softened with light words, so he said gently, "I am sorry. But I cannot guard my tongue all the time and I am only a beginner in your language. You hate us, don't you?"

Her head came up. "Yes," she shot at him. "I do."

"Then it does no good to say to you that in a few years, when you have got to know us better, you will at least forget to hate and perhaps only dislike us a little. I admire your honesty, Boudicca, and though you may not believe me, I understand it. I have met only one other woman with this regard for honor."

"Caradoc's sister."

"Yes," he said in surprise. "If it is any comfort to you, she defied the emperor himself."

"It is no comfort," she retorted harshly. "For the emperor still did not go away."

They both drank quickly, self-consciously, then without another word he bowed to her shortly and left her.

While the freemen still quarreled and laughed and the fire still leaped high, its red and orange flames alive against the soft blackness of the sky, the Romans and Saloc, Boudicca, and Prasutagas and his train, went to the hall and settled by the hearth. Lamps had been lit and their glow lighted the formal, ceremonial dimness. Servants moved quietly to and fro, anonymous and unobtrusive, replenishing the fire and bringing more wine, and when they had finished Prasutagas motioned them out and turned to Pudens. Silence fell. Boudicca unbuckled her sword and placed it carefully before her knees, and Lovernius and Iain followed suit.

Pudens cleared his throat and spoke. "First I must again thank you, Lord, for your hospitality, and for the wisdom that prompted you to seek peace with us for your people. I believe without question that because of your courage in seeking his path your tribe will revere your memory as a true father and guide to them. Let there be no words of surrender or conquest between us. Rome wishes only good things for you so that together we may become friends."

Saloc echoed the words in the mellifluous rise and fall of Boudicca's tongue, and Boudicca felt a great sadness begin to seep through her. She had prepared herself to fight anger, but this creeping grief startled and horrified her and she thought, Ah no! I must not weep. Above all, I must shed no tears before the foreigners.

Prasutagas lifted a hand, his young face furrowed with the weariness of the late hour and the strain of the occasion. "Sir," he said with a trace of humor, "I look to you to be scarcely more than a child, but that is because among your own people, childhood is prolonged and your children are sheltered. I am a man, I am ricon of my people, and I beg you not to tread the fringes of my honor by speaking to me as though I were slow of understanding. Let us not waste the hours of sleep with fine but empty words. Rome has conquered. I do not want to fight Rome, and neither does the tuath. As for friendship, that may come but for now let us talk of terms."

Saloc smiled faintly as he interpreted, and the tribunes grinned ruefully into the fire. Pudens sat looking at Prasutagas, taken aback for a moment, then his glance slid to Boudicca and noted her quivering lips, the rapid blinking of her eyes. He squared his shoulders against a fleeting breath of shame.

"Very well," he said loudly. "I am glad, Lord, that I do not have to couch those terms in pretty language. Some chiefs are so touchy!" He smiled. "The terms are thus. The Divine Claudius gives gold to you. It is a gift, a token of his good will. As a pledge to Rome of your own honesty and fair dealing you will swear oaths not to bear arms against any citizen of Rome. If you have grievances in the future you will bring them to the courts at Camulodunon. You will also allow a small garrison to be built here, near the town, and posting stations every ten miles along the road that will be built to the garrison. Later, if all goes well, there will be another road."

Again Prasutagas raised a hand. "I want no roads cutting across my people's fields. No oaks are to be felled to clear the way for such roads, either. How many soldiers will man this garrison? What authority will they have over us? I will allow no interference with my rule, Pudens."

Rufus nodded. "The roads will be built along the existing paths. I have ridden them here, coming up from the south, and they need little changing. The garrison will hold eighty to one hundred men, depending on the state of peace in the province from year to year. The commander will have no authority whatsoever over your internal affairs, Lord. He will be concerned only with keeping the peace, and he will be invaluable to you as an intermediary between yourself and the governor."

"That depends entirely on what kind of man he is," Boudicca spoke up sharply. "If he is a barbarian-hater he could make our lives a torment."

"That is true," Pudens acknowledged. "Therefore I will request that he be sent here on probation. If after six months you are not satisfied with him, the governor will replace him."

"Why do you want a garrison here?" Boudicca persisted. "Icenia is surrounded on three sides by the ocean, and to the south there is only land that Rome already holds tight. You want to spy on us, don't you?"

Carefully Pudens lifted his cup, put it down, poured into it from the silver jug at his elbow, then, having given himself time to think, he answered her. "I must presume, Lady, that you are no child either. Your people want peace at the moment, but what of next year and the one after that? Surely you understand that Rome must protect her own interests by making sure that no disaffected elements rise within your tuath and turn your husband's good work into chaos in the future. The commander will not spy on you, but he will be always present to make sure that there is never any need to do so."

"Well, you are honest in this, at least!" she snapped. "But as I see it, Icenia will be in the hands of one man. If he is fair and just all will be well, but if not, we are prisoners. We will not be able even to reach the governor's ear."

"You presume that men are either all evil or all good," he said with a smile that was almost indulgent, "and of course Romans are all evil, and if they are not then they hide their wicked hearts behind a mask. Your fears will soon be seen to be unfounded, Lady." He returned to Prasutugas. "There is also the matter of tribute." Boudicca let out a long breath and her husband's face hardened. "I cannot tell you with any certainty what the taxes will be, for the procurator has not yet arrived from Rome. But he will visit you and assess your land and the numbers of your herds and flocks. You are very wealthy, Lord, and your taxes will be high," he warned.

Prasutugas kept his eyes on the glowing depths of the fire, wondering at Boudicca's stillness. She had slumped back into the shadows but he felt her distress. Where is her rage? he thought to himself anxiously. Where the flood of barbed questions?

"I will pay the taxes," he said slowly. "We can afford this, in exchange for peace. But I absolutely refuse to allow any Icenian freemen or women to be taken as slaves, nor will I send levies of my young men for the legions or the arenas. I cannot bargain with you on this, Pudens."

"I understand. You still do not quite believe, do you, the Rome is kind? I will tell you the truth, Prasutugas. No free people will be taken as slaves, but I can make no promises about the levies. Rome needs healthy young men, and Albion has them in abundance. I think that in this you will have no choice."

His voice was firm, hard, and Prasutugas answered bitterly, "I see that we have no choice in anything. Yet I will not complain. I thirst for a life of contentment and growth for my people. The price is high, yet we will pay it." Still Boudicca did not comment. She, Lovernius, and Iain sat hunched in the darkness, but Prasutugas felt her agony like a smothering weight. His head ached and he felt older than his years. "I have a request to make of you," he said. "I have heard that the philosopher Seneca is a very rich man, and is willing to lend his money to any who can afford to borrow from him. I and some of my chiefs wish to borrow."

Boudicca jerked upright. "No, Prasutugas!" she cried out. "No, no! We do not need this money! Such a debt is without honor, and who will stand as surety for you if you cannot pay? Who will make the promises?" Saloc began to translate her words but she silenced him with a vicious oath. "My husband," she pleaded softly. "Already we swim desperately, afraid lest the waters close over us. Leave all as it is. Ask for no more, or we will drown."

He turned to her and grasped her hot hand in his own. "My love," he whispered, near to tears. "Can't you see that I am doing what I can to save the people? The money will soothe the pain of transformation. It will quicken the time it takes to put the tuath on Roman feet. For the Catuvellauni the time was long, a hundred years of slow weaving, but for us it must be now, today, this year, a swift slash to sever all the yesterdays, and then a slow, easy healing. I know what I am doing. I am killing, I am murdering, so that something else can be born. Understand! Please, Boudicca, do not fail me now!"

Pudens and his men sat with lowered heads, fidgeting with their cups, the raw, unselfconscious emotion in Prasutagas's words making them squirm inwardly with embarrassment, but for a while the two did not care that they were present.

Boudicca rose, took a step, and then knelt before Prasutagas, putting her head onto the warmth of his chest. "Help me," she whispered. "I want to do what is right. I cannot bear what is happening tonight, I cannot bear it, Prasutagas, and I am the first you kill." His arm closed around her and he put his cheek against her hair, but he had no more words to say to her and in dumb unhappiness they swayed together, then he pushed her gently away. She rose, signaled to Saloc to continue, and went out of the hall without another glance at any of them.

When Prasutagas finally came to bed she was still awake, lying on her back with her eyes on the ceiling. Beside her, in its cradle, the baby slept deeply, and one lamp burned on the low table opposite the door.

"He is leaving in the morning," he said. "Aricia and Venutius are expecting him in Brigantia. I have arranged the loan, Boudicca, on behalf of myself and the other chiefs who wanted it." He looked toward her for comment but she said nothing. She did not even blink. The eyes went on staring, and in the end he stretched himself beside her with a groan of pure exhaustion. "I am too tired to even undress myself," he sighed. Before long his breathing deepened and he relaxed against her, but he did not feel the tears that trickled over her temples to wet his tangled hair.

After a polite but hurried meal eaten in the hall, Pudens and the soldiers said their farewells. None of them had slept well. Their faces were gray in the strong summer morning light, their eyes bleary, and

228

Boudicca looked as though she had not rested at all. Saloc, who had been oddly attracted to her, tried to engage her in small talk while her husband pointed the tribunes to the northwest tracks, but she edged away from him and refused to take his hand. Finally Pudens mounted, the infantry formed ranks, and at a brusque command the little cavalcade set off toward the forest. For a moment Boudicca watched them go, new sunlight glimmering softly around them, then suddenly she picked up the hem of her tunic and raced after Pudens. He glanced back and saw her coming, and he reined in his fretting, impatient beast. Panting, she grasped his leather-shod heel.

"'Let me remind you of one thing," she said hoarsely. "Even dogs have dignity. Do you understand me?"

He gazed down into the freckled, chestnut-haloed face for a long time, feeling those capable, tough fingers bite into his ankle, seeing the mingled pleading and defiance in the mauve-shadowed eyes. He nodded curtly. "I do." She let go of him and he wrenched on the reins and cantered after his men, and she walked slowly back to Prasutugas.

"What did you say to him?" he asked curiously, and she shrugged.

"Nothing very much. I simply wanted to know if he was fond of dogs."

CHAPTER SEVENTEEN

BRAN REINED IN HIS TIRED HORSE, dismounted, and strode back to Caradoc, who sat still, Cinnamus and Caelte beside him, and Eurgain behind. "We have arrived," Bran said. "Leave the horses here, they will be attended to."

Caradoc slid from his mount and gently set Gladys on her feet. The child was ill and shivered continually. She whimpered as she felt the sodden ground quelch under her boots and Bran, bending and peering into her flushed face, scooped her up and walked away. Caradoc stretched, loosened his sword, then ordered Cinnamus to take Eurgain and follow Bran. He looked around him. There was not much to see. The night was very dark and rain poured down in a chill, never-ending curtain. It had been raining for five days, and Camulodunon lay three weeks behind them, back where the summer was hot and dry and a man could stand on the hill by the Great Hall and see for miles over the forest and the river. He could not see them but he could feel them here, the mountains, rising from low, tree-clad foot-hills, ragged heights bare of snow in the fleeting warmth of summer. He felt uneasy, knowing that they were there. They dwarfed him.

For a week they had ridden hard during the day and half the night, through tinder-dry woodland, beside warm streams, sleeping with their faces to the stars and their cloaks flung from hot limbs. But gradually the weather had changed. Summer did not hold the west for long. The party began to climb imperceptibly, the ground rising and falling in long, thickly treed troughs, but always rising more than it fell, and one day the rain came. At first it was pleasant, a cool, cleansing draft after the summer heat, but as they rode on the rain became heavier, colder, and the children sneezed and huddled deeper into cloaks that were never quite dry. Bran and Jodocus led them confidently, oblivious of the weather, and they saw no man in all the miles lengthening between them and their familiar country. Some-times there were little fields hewn out of the forest's greedy fingers, crops standing yellow and tall, splashes of color and order in an otherwise wild land, but the peasants who tended the fields had van-ished. Only the animals watched them with hidden, bright eyes as they passed along the hunting paths as furtively and swiftly as the wolves themselves. At night Caradoc heard them crying far away, a chorus of howls and yips that froze his blood, for the moon was nearing the full and magic ran strong and deep under the dark, dripping trees. More often than not the company did not know the names of the goddesses whose woods they crossed and they could not placate them. Only Bran and Jodocus were at ease. They sat talking softly together at night, sitting cross-legged by the fire that hissed as the raindrops steamed in it, black beard and gold wagging in the flickering light.

Then the morning came when Eurgain woke early, rose from the mossy ground under the oaks where they were camped, and stepped through the trees to where pale light was flowing. For a moment she stood unbelieving, her cloak bundled against her breast, and she whirled and ran back, taking Caradoc by the shoulder and shaking him urgently. "Get up, get up," she whispered. "Come and see!" He came awake immediately, grabbed up his sword, and ran after her. They broke through the edge of the wood and she pointed, hardly able to speak for the excitement bubbling within her. The trees ended abruptly and right at their feet the land fell away, sloping steeply in a long, running curve that ended on a wide valley floor through which a river snaked, red in the morning sun. The valley bottom was patchworked with golden, cropped fields. Two miles away they could look across the chasm and see the land struggling up again like the crest of a huge, frozen wave, but it was not the valley that made Eurgain's voice tremble. Far beyond, over the scrub that lipped the other side of the valley, was a marching line of hills dressed in forest, crowned bare like the knobbled spines of sleeping monsters. And farther back still, so far that they seemed to drift on a sea of pink mist, were the mountains.

"Ah, Caradoc, to see them, to actually see them!" Eurgain breathed. "What strange rocks and crystals lie hidden there, waiting for me to discover them! I could only dimly sense their secrets, sitting at my window at home, but here they have a voice!"

"They sing a song of promises to you, beloved," he said. "But take care. Do not give them your heart. You will be very lonely if you do." She turned and smiled at him, kissing him on the mouth and laying her tousled head against his neck.

"Are you jealous, Caradoc?"

"Perhaps. There are many things far stronger than another man that wait to take a wife's love away from her husband." She raised her head.

"And what of the things that divide husband from wife? You from me? How many more times will I hold you in some quiet, peaceful place such as this, far from councils and war and all the other things that claim you? Oh Caradoc, I wish that fate had not seen fit to choose this way for you. I love you. How can I live, wondering, not knowing from day to day whether you live or die?" She seldom let down her cool guard, even to him, and he held her tightly. There was nothing to say. The very pores of her body were better known to him than his own, yet after ten years of marriage she could still surprise him, still intrigue him with glimpses of a character that ran infinitely deep, each layer carefully covered over with a mystery of which he would never tire. He took her hand and led her quietly in under the trees, away from the still sleeping camp, and the brief moment of watery sunlight went out as the day's rain clouds began to gather.

To Eurgain's disappointment, they did not enter the mountains. They picked their way onto the valley floor and then turned south, riding beside the river. For two days they followed it without sheltering trees, defenceless under the rain's fierce lashing. Then they forded it at a place where it widened into a shallow, rocky pool. Caradoc thought that he could catch the tang of the ocean mingling with the river's dank odor and the smell of sour earth, and with a queer twist of the heart he thought of Gladys's cave, its dry dimness empty now forever. Then they clattered up the farther bank and pressed on,

231

skirting the dark foothills that bulked sullenly on their right. In another four days and half a night they had arrived.

Caradoc waited while Eurgain dismounted stiffly and came to him, then they followed Bran, and the silent Catuvellaunian chiefs straggled behind. The village was small, three or four circles of round, wooden huts with thatched, sloping roofs, but the huts themselves were large and spacious, each with a low gate followed after a few steps by doorskins. At the gate to the largest hut a man waited, uncloaked, and as Caradoc walked forward the man spoke, holding out his arm. "Welcome to this hall," he said. "If you come in peace, then stay in peace." Caradoc's cold, wet fingers found the other wrist, strong and warm. "I am Madoc, of the House Siluria. I apologize for the rain. Our summer is almost over, and between it and the autumn there is always a period of turbulence." He withdrew his hand and turned, bidding them to follow, and they stumbled after him, eager faces and hands reaching out to the room's welcome heat.

Slaves waited to take their sodden cloaks, small, dark men with blackbirds' eyes. In the center a huge log fire crackled, its smoke hanging thick about the airy ceiling, and Caradoc, shedding his cloak and going to the fire, felt as though he were in a big, pleasant tent. Madoc drew his knife and hacked part of the haunch from the pig that turned slowly over the flames, handing it to Caradoc, and easing him to a place on the skins. Another slave brought dark, strong beer and a dish full of new peas, green and juicy. Llyn and Fearachar had entered, the boy swaying on his feet, blinking in an effort to keep his eyes open, and Madoc beckoned them over. Caelte had not waited to be invited. He was already settling himself by Caradoc's knees, and his glance flicked over the company. About forty chiefs squatted on the skins, with the remains of their meal on the floor in front of them. Their gaze went unashamedly to the bedraggled, dirty foreigners. Little Eurgain was already asleep, too tired for food, rolled in a dry cloak against the wall, but of his wife, his other daughter, Cinnamus, and Bran there was no sign. Madoc, seeing his anxious, roving glance, gently pushed the dish closer to him. "Eat. Eat! The Druid ministers to the little one. A fever is a small thing for him to cure with his herbs, and with good sleep she will be well by the night after tomorrow." Caelte met his master's enquiring eye and nodded.

"They have gone to another hut," he said. "Eurgain went too," and Madoc chuckled.

"You do not trust us fiends of the west! Well, you will learn. And *you* will learn also!" he roared at his still-staring, silent men. "Where's my bard? On your feet, man, and sing! The foreigners are hungry and tired and there will be no Council tonight." His odd, stiffly frilled hair seemed to bristle at them, and he lay back on his skins with a grunt and closed his eyes. "Food and sleep, and then war, eh Catuvellaunian? I hope you are worth all the trouble we have taken over you, as the Druid says you are." The bard tuned his little harp and cleared his throat, and Caelte's eyes began to shine in the firelight. Presently Cinnamus and Eurgain pushed back the doorskins and slipped to Caradoc's side.

"She is better," Eurgain whispered. "She sleeps. Bran is still with her." Then real exhaustion descended on Caradoc, and he wrapped the strange-smelling cloak around him, put his head on his knees, and fell asleep.

Some time during the night, when the fire had died to red embers and the chiefs had all gone, Jodocus roused him and he staggered after the silent man, still too weary to care where he laid his head. He had a confused impression of new fire, long shadows, and an inviting, well-draped bed, then he dropped the cloak, pulled off his tunic and breeches, and fell beside Eurgain. Drowsily she covered them both and went back to sleep, both of them lulled by the steady patter of the rain.

In the morning they woke refreshed to sunlight. Fearachar was already up, tending the fire and laying out clean clothes, and the beds that the children had slept in were empty. Caradoc heard Cinnamus and Caelte's low voices outside and he got up, splashed in the basin on the table beside the bed, pulled on his clothes, and after kissing a still-somnolent Eurgain, he went out. His chiefs greeted him, and together they looked upon Caer Siluria. The village lay in a small valley, beside a river. To the west the foothills rose again, and the tips of far-off mountains could be seen. To the north the valley meandered with the river, heavily wooded, and though the mountains they had seen above the big valley were not visible, their knees were, humping in the east, swathed in white mist. "Mother!" Cinnamus said. "A pretty place to die in! The enemy only has to seal off the mouth of the river and these stupid people are trapped like rabbits."

"They are far from stupid, Cin," Caradoc remarked. "This village is close to their fields and to water. They have flat land for their cattle and sheep. And you can be sure that the chiefs know every path that winds about the hills and climbs into the mountains. At the first sign of trouble they could melt into that gloomy wilderness and never be found unless they chose to be."

"Of course," said a voice at their elbow and Madoc sauntered into view, hair spiking to the sky, his red tunic glittering with necklaces and his arms weighed down with bracelets. "So you are at last awake, Caradoc. You have missed the first meal of the day, but it does not matter. It was only bread and apples. Come. I will show you the caer."

His bard and his shield-bearer, who carried an enormous weight of leather and bronze tooled over with trumpet whirls and long horse faces with closed eyes, swung in beside him, and they all strode through the huts, which were full of the smells of cooking and the laughter of women. Dogs and children came out and ran beside them barefoot, their tunics hitched above bony brown knees and their hair stringing to their waists. Beyond the last circle Madoc halted. "Here are the stables," he said, pointing. "We keep few horses, for they are useless on the high passes, and we do not bother with chariots. Looking around you, you must see why." They did. No chariot could ever navigate the winding, rocky paths of the foothills. "Over there," he turned and waved an arm, "down along the valley, two days' march away, is another of our caers, and between there are many farms. We do not like to huddle together in one big mass like you Catuvellauni," he said with a sidelong glance. "We prefer to live and fight on our own. Each chief lives on his farm with his peasants and slaves, and each chief has the right to speak with equality in Council. The Druids have the last word. After me, of course!" He chuckled, a dry, gasping bark, and his men smiled dutifully.

"This valley, though narrow, cuts a long way between the mountains, and most of our people have settled along it, but we at this end seldom hear from our freemen and brothers at the other end. We trade a bit, by boat. As for the rest of us," he grinned at Caradoc, showing yellowing teeth in the black beard, "we are scattered through many little valleys hidden up there." He waved again airily at the ragged tips behind him and Caradoc's heart sank. Madoc gazed at him, the twinkle in his eye telling Caradoc that he knew very well what was passing through his mind. These people could never be united. They might be able to fight like a thousand demons but always with the arrogance of invincible independence, when and with whom they chose.

He looked at Madoc, his belly empty and his spirits low, and Madoc nodded and came closer. "We have quite a task ahead of us, my friend," he said in a low, rumbling purr. "I listened to the Druid when he spoke of you because, well, I can lead my chiefs to battle, there is no greater warrior than I, but up here . . ." He tapped his stiff hair with one stubby finger, "Up here I am stupid. Yes, I, Madoc, chieftain and mighty swordsman, admit this to you, foreigner. I have not the brains for such work as we plan. So I send, and you are delivered. In a while the Council will begin, and you must say the words that will cause my chiefs to listen to you. If you do not you might as well go away. I can make them hear, but I cannot make them obey if they do not want to." His voice dropped lower, a buzz in Caradoc's ear. "Say nothing of the Druid's dreams of an arviragus rising. I think he is a fool where this is concerned and I see that you do also, but it just may come to pass at the proper time. First, gain the trust of my chiefs. Then travel, Caradoc, with me and the Druid, into the little valleys of which I spoke. If we can rouse all of Siluria we will have done a great thing."

Caradoc looked into the sparkling dark eyes with a new respect Madoc was no wild mountain man after all, and behind the wide, rough manners, the garish jewels, the boastful, stalking walk, lay a powerful, cunning chief. Cunobelin had taught his sons to fear only the men of the west, and now Caradoc knew why. Madoc was Cunobelin, a Cunobelin without Rome's tempering influence, and Caradoc knew that he was seeing his father as he could have been, a pure, unadulterated warrior. A strange new pride uncurled in him and the dimensions of the knowledge he had of his ancestors expanded. He had called his task impossible, but what if it were not? What if he could indeed rouse these brilliant, uncouth fighters into a common aim? Bran believed that he could. He smiled at Madoc, and clasped the other's shoulder.

"I understand," he said. "Yes, Madoc, together we will do a great thing." A tiny thread of approval began to be spun behind Madoc's eyes, still as fine as gossamer, and he fingered his beard and grunted.

"I think we have already begun," he said. "Now let us walk a little farther. I have one more thing to show you." He strutted away and they went after him, past the kennels of the hunting dogs and the smoking potteries. The children had become bored and had left them to run screaming and laughing down to the river. They plunged straight in, though the morning was cool, and they swam strongly against the currents, brown, red, and black heads bobbing together, but Madoc lead the chiefs away from the water and stopped finally outside a plain, freshly thatched hut.

"Freeman, are you there?" he called, and the doorskin was thrust aside. A young man greeted them absently, tools in his hands. "Bring out your work," Madoc ordered. "I want these men to see it in sunlight," and the youth left to reappear a moment later with something wrapped in a cloth that he carried gently. He squatted and began to unwrap it and they knelt down with him. He lifted it up in loving, in gentle fingers, caressing it as he did so, and Caradoc, Cinnamus, and Caelte gazed at it in astonishment. It was a gold necklace, obviously unfinished. "He is making it for one of my wives," Madoc explained. "What do you think?" Glinting snakes writhed sinuously, their hooked fangs lengthened, gliding, becoming the stems of strange, languid plants whose flat leaves were drawn out in their turn to become smooth fluid curves. The eye could follow, but never discover where snake ended and leaf began, or where leaf ended and curve flowed into fang. Caradoc touched it with awe, the power of it driving to the heart of him and waking an old, long-forgotten response. It reminded him of the carvings on the pillars of the Great Hall and of the cloak-bronzes and arm bands of Aricia's chieftains. But beside them it was alive, full of magic, whole and vibrant as though the carving on the pillars had been only lifeless reflections of this hidden, burning reality. Madoc was pleased at their silence. He glanced at them slyly. "Bring out more," he commanded, and the silent young man brought a silver cloak brooch, a wolf's head, its hungry, predatory eyes following Caradoc's own. Between its teeth was the tiny head of a man, the hair curling around the fangs and dripping like solid blood from the mouth, and in the silent scream of the man Caradoc glimpsed another head, a wolf's. Yes! he thought excitedly. Yes, yes, oh yes!

"More," he whispered, and the youth shot him a keen glance. He brought a great pile of precious things, rings, brooches, bracelets, bits and harness for horses, circlets for a lady's head, anklets for her feet, all seething with images, live nightmares, summer dreams, a profusion of visions. Caelte's wandering hands touched wild music.

"You made all these?" he asked, and the youth nodded once.

"I did." He began to gather them up.

"In my tuath," Caradoc began, and the young man stopped what he was doing and gave him a frosty, bitter smile.

"In your tuath," he said coldly, "my works would have been trampled disdainfully in the mud and I would have been driven away." He gathered his treasures carefully in his cloak, and Madoc laughed.

"Baubles!" he roared. "Pretty playthings for my ladies and my chiefs who pay and pay, and you, my fine wolfling, get rich! Aaah, but you speak to their wild hearts with your genius." He rose. Caradoc turned to say something to the youth, wanting to tell him how he had squatted as a proud chief and had risen humbled, but the space before the plain hut was empty. He and Madoc walked back side by side.

"You have gold here," Caradoc said, and once more Madoc chuckled.

"Yes," he replied. "Up there, in the mountains."

The Council hut was full and the fire burned brightly. Madoc led them to their places, slaves brought them food and beer, and Caradoc ate quickly, still not knowing what he would say to these suspicious people. He noted that here the precedence of seating was rigidly upheld. Eurgain and Vida sat together with the other chiefs' wives. Tallia sat among the freewomen. Llyn chatted away to the sons of other chiefs, and the Silurian men, with shield-bearers and bards, ringed the walls. Only Bran wandered where he would in his white tunic, stopping here and there for a word or a joke. Presently he came and squatted before Caradoc. "Your daughter's fever has broken," he said, "but she stays in bed for one more night. Have you decided what you must say?" The brown eyes were calm, and Caradoc shook his head.

"Not yet," he replied tersely, and Bran got up and went to Madoc, pushing his way through the jostling chiefs who were not yet seated. Caradoc noticed something that he had been too tired to see last night. The hut was ringed with severed heads. Where the tall wall swept in a circle from post to post, just under the angle where the roof began to rise, they were hung, tied by their long hair, eyes shrunken in deep sockets, skin dried and withered, lips drawn back from leering teeth. Jodocus, who was seated next to Cinnamus, saw Caradoc's glance and leaned across.

"All taken by the chiefs you see here," he said proudly. "And most of them were chiefs themselves, Ordovices, Demetae, a few Cornovii. You see that one?" He pointed up to a massive head, black hair, a stump of bone gleaming beneath the thick neck. "He was an Ordovician champion. Madoc fought him and killed him, and we drove many cattle through the passes that day!"

"Mother!" Cinnamus hissed. "And you want them to fight side by side?" Caradoc said nothing. Across the room Eurgain caught his eye and smiled at him, and over by the door two chiefs were fighting, swords ringing, the disputed place lying empty. Madoc rose, lifted an arm, and silence fell. The chiefs retired, arguing heatedly under their breath, neither one willing to take the place, and they went and stood against the wall.

"Council is called!" he boomed. "Slaves depart." The slaves filed out, the gate was shut, and Caradoc put aside his dish and cup, unwillingly loosening his sword belt and placing it before him on the skins as the other chiefs were doing. "Bran," Madoc went on after a moment, "do you want to speak?" Bran rose, tucking his hands into his long sleeves, his golden, gray-flecked hair shining in the firelight.

"'I have nothing new to say," he said quietly. "But I will remind you all that the Catuvellauni have fought the Romans and we have not. Listen well to them." He sat down.

237

"You all know why I have brought Cunobelin's son here," Madoc shouted, "and now you must decide for yourselves whether what I did was right. Speak, Caradoc."

He went to his place and Caradoc rose reluctantly, his mind still blank, his eyes traveling slowly over the hostile, jealous faces fixed on him. A hundred images paraded through his thoughts, conjured from the past, and he sought among them one point of contact, one link that would join these chiefs to his own experience. He was silent, looking at his booted feet, and a restless whispering began. Then he raised his head.

"Men of the west. You call me Cunobelin's son and make it an insult. Cunobelin was a trader with Rome, Cunobelin gave Rome a foothold in this country, Cunobelin had dreams of conquest that included you, and if he had lived you would have faced him, and all the might of my tuath. So you sneer at him and at me, looking at me and seeing a man stamped with the corruption of Rome. Yet who was it that faced the legions almost alone, while you and many other tribes refused us aid? I did, my people and I, and because of it the remnants of the Catuvellauni are now slaves. When you wish to curse me for a Roman-loving foreigner remember that you did not answer my pleading and now Rome floods the lowlands like poisoned water, turning what was there into a twisted wreckage of tribal life.

"Cunobelin was a great man and I am proud to be his son, but Cunobelin did not see Rome for what she is. That was his greatest mistake. Silurians, it was not mine. I saw, I knew, I refused treaty with Rome, I gathered my chiefs and fought for my territory and I lost. If any of you still hesitates to trust me, think of the battle at Medway and the killing of my brother Togodumnus. I am no longer chieftain over many people. I have no tuath, no honor-price, no riches. But I still have the one thing more valuable than all those things. My freedom." There was not a sound. The eyes still cut him with their hard, merciless glare. He had almost accused them of cowardice, and that they would not tolerate. But he went on, the words flowing more easily, a confidence rising in him with a new power, and Bran sat back, smiling under his hand. The Silurians would soon have a new chief, though they did not yet know it.

"What do you fight for? What do you fear above everything else? Slavery. The taking of your souls from you. Here you are free. You come and go as you will. No man tells you what to do. You own the river, the valley, the mountains. You fear nothing. Here, in your country, is the heart of freedom, and for many years you have disdained to traffic with the tribes who were selling their freedom into Roman

238

hands in exchange for wine and jewels. Your freedom cannot be sold. But it can be taken from you."

He almost shouted the words at them and they sat straighter, the contempt in their eyes fading into a guarded interest. How innocent they are, he thought desperately, sitting here so smugly, never seeing beyond their mountains from one year to the next, wrapped in their pride and their prowess. "The Romans plan to take it from you," he said softly. "Even now they are spreading out, building forts, striking ever deeper toward you, and they come determined this time not to fail. They will not give up or give in. Your days as a free people are numbered."

One of the chiefs jumped up. "The mountains will stop them!" he yelled. "They stopped old Cunobelin!"

Caradoc grinned ruefully. "Cunobelin feared you and his fear stopped him," he answered. "The mountains will not stop Rome. She has fought in mountains before, and won. She will creep right up to their feet, consolidate, explore, and then find you and wipe you out."

Another chief struggled to his feet. "All we need do is gather the war band, march into the lowlands, and give the legions battle," he snapped. "We will send Rome running back to the coast. Perhaps we can challenge their champions and defeat them and take their heads, thus saving ourselves much trouble." He sat down amid a pleased murmuring of assent and Caradoc sighed inwardly, seeing the iron-clad phalanx of the Fourteenth driving into his warriors who died before they could find a chink in that solid, faceless mass of discipline.

"Believe this," he said forcefully. "If we attempt to meet Rome in pitched battle we will lose. The Romans fight differently from us. They have no champions. Each man is a champion. Never again must the tribes make that mistake. There are other ways of dealing with Rome."

"We know," another chief said with disgust. "Slinking through the woods, striking in the dark, and slinking away again. That is not for warriors."

Caradoc lost his temper. "What do you value more," he shouted furiously, "your freedom or the empty respect of the tribes? If you want to give your country to Rome then go ahead and take the chiefs and ride out. None of you will ever come back!" He stamped. "Listen to me, you fools! Roman soldiers have no minds! They fight like demons, they do not fall back, they have been trained and disciplined until they obey orders as the dogs obey whistles, without thought or emotion. Their officers are seasoned, clearheaded, clever men who make no mistakes. Do you hear what I am saying? Do you understand? If you want to defeat Rome you must discard every lesson you have ever learned about how to fight, and you must learn new ones, from me. Be thankful that you do not have to learn them, as I have done, at the hands of the enemy! You are the only people left to fight, you and the Ordovices, the Demetae, and the Deceangli. If you fall Albion falls, and the Roman night will descend forever. Put yourselves in my hands and dare your last chance, or cast me out and die."

He picked up his sword and belt and strode away through them, and even before he had let himself out the gate a cacophony of angry shouts and heated, rapid talk mushroomed. He smiled wearily to himself. They would never accept him. He heard Cinnamus and Caelte come running and together they went to the river, sitting on the bank in the pale, almost heatless sunshine. Caelte, at his master's order, got out his harp and sang, but Cinnamus flicked pebbles into the water and refused to listen, and Caradoc, chin on knees, thought with a formless excitement about the young artist and his marvelous magic.

The Council went on all day. Eurgain, Llyn, little Eurgain, Vida, and the other Catuvellauni finally left the hut, telling Caradoc of the furious quarrels going on within, and they all gathered by the river and spent the day sharing stories of the past. They all felt alone and homesick in this strange place, except Eurgain. Bran had promised to take her into the mountains and she sat beside Caradoc smiling to herself, placid and self-contained, with Caradoc's arm around her. Cinnamus and Vida quarreled desultorily. Little Eurgain lay beside her mother and made daisy chains. Llyn went off to find the other boys, Fearachar trailing him resignedly, and then, when the afternoon began to borrow the chill of evening, Madoc and his train came swiftly to them over the grass. He was smiling. Caradoc rose at once, and Madoc threw a big arm around his shoulders. "They have agreed to follow your way," he said, "but they want me to tell you that they reserve the right to disobey you if they choose."

Caradoc exclaimed in disgust and Madoc withdrew his arm and shook a meaty finger. "No, no," he said, "it is a good thing. This way when they do choose to obey you it will be out of love, and they will fight better. I know them. They also say that your son must be initiated into this tribe when he comes of age."

"No!" Caradoc shouted, shocked into rudeness. "Never, never! Llyn is of the House Catuvellaun, and a Catuvellaunian he stays!"

"You must agree," Madoc said softly. "It is a form of security for them. Besides," he gasped with cracked laughter. "He may never come of age."

"Oh Mother," Cinnamus said softly. "How glad I am that I have no children!" Caradoc glared at them all, disgusted, but Madoc smiled and took his arm.

"Come and eat, all of you, and talk with my chiefs. We live in terrible days, my friends, and must meet the needs of each moment with minds uncluttered by the past." Caradoc followed him, trapped in bitter awareness that he spoke the truth. Why me? he thought angrily. Why this fate for me and mine? The hut was warm and the odor of roasting pig wafted toward them. They entered, heads high.

Caradoc, his train, and some of his men, together with Bran and Madoc, began the task of traveling throughout Siluria, visiting every hamlet, every farmstead, every proud, impatient chief, and summer fled, autumn riding victoriously over the country with red sword drawn. The trees along the river valley and on the hills were blooded, flaming suddenly red and gold, and for a few weeks the sky cleared and the sun shone hot and strong. Caradoc worked on, arguing far into the night, shouting, pleading, answering the same objections, countering gently the same blind, arrogant ignorance, sitting outside rough wooden palisades, crowded into tiny, stinking huts, leaning on stone walls in cold winds. And always, always, there was the terror at his back and in his mind, of Rome spreading slowly toward him while he wanted to take these recalcitrant men and shake them until their teeth rattled and to shout, Time! Time! No time!

Eurgain did not see him for weeks on end and when he did return to her it was with lines etched more deeply in the weather-beaten face, eyes harder and more cunning, mouth grimmer and less able to break into smiles or laughter. She would lie awake in the cold hours of darkness, listening to him moan and cry out in his sleep, aching with a deep sympathy and feeling a new impotence. He would conquer or he would snap, and she could only hold him in the warmth of her arms, give him forgetfulness for a while, allow him to penetrate her body with the harsh sword of his frustration. He took Llyn with him everywhere and the boy seemed to thrive on the hardships, riding along with a song on his lips, and Caradoc, thinking of Togodumnus as he watched him, was comforted.

Autumn was gone in a night. A cruel, knifing wind sprang up, tearing the crisp leaves from the trees and dashing them to the ground. It brought the icy rains of winter, and for the first time

Caradoc felt some hope. He and many of the chiefs had been flung together and had learned a wary respect for each other. The Silurians were seeing Caradoc's driving, selfless single-mindedness, and they now supported him in his verbal battles with the suspicious, lonely chiefs on the farms and pastures, lending a weight of their approval that was worth more than all Caradoc's eloquence. The rain halted all travel, turning the tracks into gray quagmires, and the chiefs feasted and quarreled among themselves while Caradoc rested in his hut with Eurgain, glad of the respite.

He had begun to take on the color of his new tribe, cutting his hair shorter and washing it in lime so that its natural color began to fade to blonde and it crested from his furrowed forehead like a horse's stiff mane. He put aside his Roman bronzes and had the young artist make him new ones, promising payment in kind, not in coin. The Silures had no use for coinage. Their wealth was in their sheep and cattle, and Caradoc had been told that he would have to see to gathering the tangible side of his new honor-price himself. That meant raiding, but raiding was the one thing he wished to avoid. The time was not right and besides, he could not urge unity on the one hand and then go out and kill the very people he wanted the Silures to placate. He told the artist that payment would come in the spring, and the youth shrugged and nodded. He did not need wealth, but payment was a matter of honor. Madoc stood surety for Caradoc with the artist. Caradoc did not like the arrangement, for if he defaulted on the promised payment Madoc would suffer, but he wanted those new bronzes with a perverse, avid thirst.

Eurgain watched the changes with understanding but she pointed out to him the futility of an attempt at any permanent assimilation. "We are different, my husband," she told him gently one night, sitting on her stool while he combed her long hair, one of the few things he did that still brought him peace. "We will always be different, no matter how often you lime your hair or however many new bronzes you sport. Outwardly we can return to the ways of our ancestors, deny Cunobelin and Tasciovanus and all the years of truck with Rome, but whether you like it or not, those years have changed us." He did not answer and the comb continued its steady journey through the dark blonde waves that fell almost to the floor. She touched her breast. "In here we cannot go back, though our roots reach deep."

He grunted noncommittally. "We can try" was all he said.

The rains ceased, the ground hardened with frost, and Caradoc resumed his harrowing rounds. He wanted the Silures to be melded into one fighting force by the summer, but the attitudes of centuries could not be altered overnight, and for every chief who greeted him as

242

a brother there were three who told him to his face that they could defeat Rome with a flick of their cloaks whenever they wanted and they did not need him.

Madoc, however, was pleased. "You have a gift there," he commented. "A persuasive tongue. The chiefs may scorn you but you make them listen, and they will think on your words. Do not be discouraged. We have plenty of time."

It seemed that after all, they did have plenty of time. With the first wet, cloying snowfall, scouts rode into the caer with news for the Council. Caradoc sat in the warm Council hut with the others, sword before him, and heard how the legions were quartered for the winter and would do no more campaigning until the spring. The Ninth had halted their road-building in Coritani country. The Second was mopping up the Durotriges and would quarter there, and the other two legions, with Plautius himself, were nesting cozily with Boduocus and his Dobunni. The lowland was quiet, but none of the chiefs failed to note that the Dobunni territory abutted their own.

Then the scout turned to Caradoc. "I have news for you, Caradoc ap Cunobelin. Your sister Gladys is alive. The Romans hold her prisoner but treat her well, or so I have been told. I have not seen her myself."

He turned away and spoke of other things while Caradoc, on a tide of unreality, felt the shock of the words race through his veins. Gladys alive. It was not possible! She had been so determined to die, so sure of the fate that awaited her. What had happened? His quick mind explored avenues, discarded, came up unsatisfied. Why had Plautius not used her to gain his own submission? Not that he would have surrendered, the idea was inadmissible, but at least there should have been envoys, Druids perhaps. He felt warm and happy knowing that she lived, and some of his guilt was lifted from him, but behind the news was a mystery, and his joy was tempered by anxiety. What did Plautius have up the short sleeve of his pristine, spotless tunic?

That night he lay beside Eurgain, unable to sleep. The hut was quiet, the children cozily asleep, but he stared into the cone of the ceiling thinking of Gladys, of Plautius, of the swift and orderly dispersion of the legions. The Ninth was with the Coritani. And beyond that Coritani was Aricia. Would Aricia fight? He did not think so. Far more likely that she would force treaty on her rough tribesmen. Aricia went with the falling of the dice. Aricia would never be without her creature comforts.

He found his thoughts circling her, the black, foreign witch, with her jutting young breasts, her perfumed hair, the long, lithe beauty of her strong legs. He closed his eyes. How old would she be now? Twenty-four or five, maturity heading into swift middle age. Had she changed?

Did she ever think of him wistfully? He doubted it. If she thought of him at all it would be with a thwarted bitterness.

He sighed, moving under the blankets, hot with his restlessness. . . . A hole that would never be filled . . . But the hole is filled, witch, filled still with fire even here, even now. It was easier to picture her among these men of the west. Her own tuath must be much like this, wild, intense, full of the essence of magic and spells, and her own particularly virulent spell came often to taunt him in the many weary, unguarded moments when he had no reserves of will or energy left. He felt for his wife's fair hair, wound it around his fingers, and turned on his side toward her, but tonight her aura of tranquillity did not reach as far as the feverish turmoil in his soul.

The snow melted under torrential, freezing downpours, and once more Caradoc and the others were forced to stay in the town. Samain approached. The chiefs went out with their freemen to find their cattle and drive them to the river for the slaughter, and Cinnamus took to fighting. For months he had keenly felt his own and Caradoc's poverty, and now, with the coming of Samain, the taunts of the Silurian chiefs became more immediate. The Catuvellauni had no cattle to slaughter. The Catuvellauni lived like parasites off the good-will of their chieftain and the Druid. Cinnamus could bear it no longer and one wet day he rode into the town shouting with delight, blood streaming from a wounded shoulder and mingling with the steady rain. He drove ten head of shaggy cattle before him. Caradoc ran to him in alarm and Cinnamus jumped down while the cattle jostled and lowed impatiently. "Cin, what have you done?" Caradoc said urgently, and Cinnamus cut him short, the green eyes alive with success, the sharp face wreathed in smiles.

"No raid, no raid, Lord," he assured Caradoc, fingering his shoulder. "I challenged a chief to combat, for he insulted us, and he, in his pride, offered me ten beasts if I won. Of course he intended me to be dead." He wiped the streaming water from his face and pushed back his dripping hair. "He did not know that I am Cinnamus Ironhand, but ah, Mother, what fighters these men are! I put forth all my skill and won only by a hair's breadth, but how good it felt to wield blade again! These chiefs are all worthy of the name Ironhand! And he was full of honor. When I had him down I decided not to kill him though he urged me to do so to save himself from shame, and see!" He waved at the cattle, then yelped with pain. "We have cattle. Not many I know, but perhaps enough for the winter." Caradoc did not know what to say. He embraced his shield-bearer, and Cinnamus left the freemen to corral the beasts, whistling as he strode away to find Vida, and dressing for his cuts.

244

On Samain Eve the rain stopped, the clouds folded limply and sailed away to the north, and the moon shone full and cold on the stark hills. Caradoc and Eurgain wrapped warmly and set out with the chiefs for their sacred place, leaving the children with Fearachar and Tallia. The town emptied, the people gliding silently one by one away from the river and up the wooded slope of the nearest foothill. Caradoc and Eurgain followed, flanked by Cinnamus and Caelte, and the old fear flicked at their heels, intensified by the wan shadows cast by the pale moon and a destination that was unknown to them. They entered the woods bunched together, while the Silurians passed ahead of them with scarcely a rustle, and above them the winter wind sighed through branches that rubbed together like the bony fingers of evil old men. They climbed steadily along a faint but unmistakable path, not daring to whisper to each other for fear the demons would notice them, and presently the trees began to thin. Lights flickered, the dancing corpse-lights of the dead, and Eurgain's hand stole into Caradoc's. The light grew stronger and they found themselves on the crown of the hill, in a bald, grassy space where the wind whipped at the torches. In the center was a single stone, its black shadow feeling for their feet, and they circled it warily, moving in the direction of the sun's path with almost automatic skill, remembering suddenly old tales, old songs, and the rites of Samain long since forsaken by the Romanized Catuvellauni. Still the silence, like the moonlight, lay heavy and deep. Bran and the invoker stood by the stone, motionless in their white robes now dulled to silver in the night, waiting while the last tribesmen straggled in, and Caradoc, looking around, saw the wooden stakes surmounted by bare skulls. All were old, all tilted drunkenly, but one was naked, its fresh-whittled point now waiting for its bloody crowning.

The last chief circled the stone and stood wraithlike, and the invoker stepped forward, his arms raised, and his robe falling back from silvered wrists. "Gods of the woods, gods of the water," he sang softly, "Belatucadrus, Taran, Mogons, stay your hands this night." A murmuring sigh went up and the wind gusted through the trees around them as if in answer. "We offer blood. Drink and be satisfied, and leave us in safety." Again the people murmured, a rising swell of incantation that died away into a whisper. While the invoker continued the rite, two chiefs, Madoc and Jodocus, came within the torches' light, with a naked man between them, the fading summer tan of his arms and legs in startling contrast to the pastiness of his chest and buttocks. They led him to the stone and turned him so that he faced the company, and though Caradoc strained in the leaping glare he could not read the impassive face. Black hair fell to the elbows, and Madoc came with rope, tying the hair back gently while the invoker sang on. Then suddenly there was silence.

"A slave again," someone complained softly behind Caradoc. "It should have been a chief this time."

Caradoc swung round. "Next year," he said, his voice low, his eyes narrowed, "I will give you a Roman." He turned back. Bran walked to the man, taking a long knife from his sleeve. For a moment he spoke quietly to the victim, and Caradoc saw the doomed man nod once, quite composed, then he turned around, leaned against the rock, and closed his eyes. Caradoc thought that he saw the brown knees tremble. Madoc came forward, and Bran handed him the knife. Without pause Madoc strode to the slave, swung the knife, and plunged it deep into the white, defenceless back. A cry went up as the body fell twitching, blood gushing from nose, mouth, and wound, but the invoker and Bran squatted coolly, watching the death throes carefully. Would the winter be without want or disease? Were the gods appeased?

At last the jerking, quivering body lay still, a limp white bundle, and Jodocus drew his sword and cut off the head in one mighty stroke, picking it up and driving it onto the stake prepared for it. Bran spoke. "The winter will be long and hard," he said, "but this year we will not go hungry and the demons will take no man tonight. Thus says the invoker." He took the bloodied knife from Madoc and slipped away, melding with the shadows under the oaks, and the people left the hilltop, saying nothing, hurrying to their huts for fear that the invoker had misread the signs and already the unslaked demons padded through the wood toward them.

Caradoc, the last to leave, looked back. The torches were guttering, and as they died the moonlight strengthened, pouring white and joyless into the clearing. The stone stood like a watchful finger of doom, and blood trickled black down the wooden stake and pooled in the earth beneath. Wind troubled the long grasses. He turned and hurried after Cinnamus.

The next day, in another shrine deep in the woods, a white bull was sacrificed. There, fire burned on a stone altar and the Dagda squatted bluntly beside the Silurian tuath's own god, a tall, skinny idol with three hands and three long faces that looked apprehensively into past, present, and future with deep-hollowed eyes. There was no mistletoe that year. Bran and the invoker had wandered far seeking the holy white berries, but they found none and the altar was bare. The soft white hide was flayed from the dead beast and the flesh was carved up for the Druid's use. The people went back to the river and

246

watched while all day their cattle were slaughtered, the hot stench of blood enveloping the town. Caradoc was forcibly reminded of the Samain when he, Tog, and Aricia had taken the dogs without permission and then lost them in the gentle Catuvellaunian woods, and he thought how here he would not have been so foolish. The woods of this country were wild, lonely, alive with malevolent powers, teeming with wolves and often bears, and no man who entered them on Samain Eve, other than to make the spells, ever returned.

The season dragged on, long and hard as the invoker had promised. Snow fell on snow, sealing off the valley. In the lowlands it rained and stormed without cease and the few scouts who managed to struggle through the choked foothills or brave the sea route told them that nothing was moving. The peasants and few chiefs who were left were almost starving, for Rome had taken much of their autumn harvest to feed the legions, and in the end Plautius was forced to ration the grain and feed native as well as soldier. Spring was late and came in wet. The snow melted under the battering of torrential rains and the river rose to ominous heights, but at last the clouds drew back, the sun shone, and the ground began to dry.

Caradoc and the others resumed their journeying. The Silurian chiefs were disappointed. They had expected an early mustering of warriors to fall on the legions with the bursting new life of spring, but Caradoc was more determined than ever that no strike be made until he could confidently command all the mountain tribes. A premature attack would mean disaster, and the end of his efforts. Stubbornly, doggedly, he and Madoc visited the farmsteads and summer huts of the chiefs who had refused him their allegiance the summer before, and he found them less sullen, more willing to listen. It was clear that Plautius had no intention of moving against the west, not yet. His hands were full with consolidation, building roads, setting taxes with the surrendered ricons, and erecting more permanent forts than the uncomfortable temporary winter quarters of all his men. From his headquarters at Camulodunon he and the procurator went out with their staff, satisfied to see the embryonic province begin to grow.

Caradoc began to build a network of spies. He chose freemen, not chiefs, who scorned such work and who would have drawn attention to themselves with their limed, bristling hair and their strutting walk. At first he sent them out as they were, some to settle quietly among the peasants of Rome's client kingdoms—the Atrebates, the Iceni, the Brigantes, the Dobunni—some to live in the woods of the Coritani and the Durotriges. He promised them a new status if they worked well and were able to survive for two years. They were eager to learn from him, coming to his hut while he spoke to them of the ways of the foreigners and the habits of the Romans, and they left the caer with the prospect of chieftain status bright before their eyes. But in that first heartbreakingly tentative year many were lost to the soldiers, to wild animals, to suspicious, nervous peasants, and to their own loneliness. Caradoc knew what he was doing to them. Without chiefs to defend them and land to feed them, they were cast adrift, and only the more enterprising established themselves as refugees expelled by the barbarous men of the west, as part of some chief's honor-price, even as young Druids. He callously disregarded the cost. It had to be. He felt deeply that this was a year of beginnings, a year when many seeds had to be sown in ruthlessness if the fruit was to be victory, and spring became summer while the Silurian freemen slipped over their borders and vanished, many of them forever.

Eurgain and Bran took the journey to the mountains that he had promised her. They were gone for two weeks while Llyn and Caradoc were traveling the coast, and Eurgain returned with pouch full of new crystals and her eyes dark with new mysteries. She and Bran took to lying out under the stars. He would point out to her the lofty, ageless constellations and their meanings, and she would dream spellbound as the heavens wheeled by above her, locked in a wonder and delight that was linked to her absorption with the mountains. When he left with Caradoc and the others, striking north to the wary freemen who lived in constant fear of raids on the border with the Ordovices, she lay on the cool, dry grass alone, staring unblinking and wrapt, while her soul leaped to the sky and danced riotously among the living crystals.

Caradoc saw little of his daughters. They had many friends now, Silurian friends, children who played roughly, ran like a mad wind, shrieked and fought with each other and swam like brown fish, and they needed him less and less. Sometimes, watching them tumble by the river, their ragged hair flying, feet bare, and tunics hitched free of wet, muddy legs, he felt a great remorse. They were the daughters of royalty. They should have been enjoying the riches and comfort that a great honor-price and many servants could bring. Their arms should have been laden with silver, their heads circled in gold, their tunics bordered with rainbow fringes. They should have been riding noble horses harnessed in tinkling bronze, surrounded by chiefs. The pain of their loss had become a physical gnawing in his breast. He had nothing, only his wits on which to live, only his visions on which to feed his deprived children. He heard their laughter but was not comforted.

CHAPTER EIGHTEEN

*A*N EMBASSY RODE OUT OF THE HILLS and down into the town. Cinnamus saw them first and he clambered from his perch in the apple
tree and ran to where Caradoc, Caelte, and Madoc sat in the sun. They
had returned from the north the day before, leaving Bran to journey
on to meet with the chiefs of the Ordovices. The time had come to meet
them in Council, and Bran was to spend the coming months with
them, dropping his soft persuasions into their hard ears. Cinnamus
came up, green eyes glinting. "Guests, Lord. By the Mother, we have
had no guests in months!" Caradoc and the others rose, hands going
to their swords, and Cinnamus stood beside his master, watching the
six horsemen come cantering over the smooth turf. Madoc nodded,
and Jodocus drew his sword and went to challenge them as they reined
in, and his shield-bearer and bard closed in beside him.

"Who comes to this tuath, friend or foe?" Jodocus called, and the
tallest rider leaned forward on his horse's shoulders as if too weary to
sit upright. "Have you a Druid?"

"No Druid," a deep, firm voice answered, and Caradoc stiffened.
He knew it. It awoke waves of an old fascination in him but he could
not place it. "We could not find one. But we come in peace, trusting
your justice, men of the west. We seek the Catuvellaunian chieftain,
Caradoc ap Cunobelin."

"Throw down your swords." The other mounted men began to
mutter angrily but the tall one reached to his belt and it and his sword
went thudding to the grass, and the others reluctantly followed suit.
"Now dismount. Keep your hands from your tunics." Jodocus called
again and the men slid from their mounts and stood waiting.

"Who are they?" Madoc growled in Caradoc's ear. "Do you know
them?"

Caradoc shook his head. "Perhaps. I am not sure." He jerked his
head at Cinnamus and Caelte, who drew their swords and strode with
him to where Jodocus, his hands on his massive hips, was surveying
the visitors with no pretense of good manners.

"You break the laws of hospitality," the tall chief said sharply, and
Jodocus growled, "In these days the laws of hospitality must give way
to the laws of survival." Caradoc came to a halt, hesitated, took another
step. There was red hair, a curling red beard, eyes that raced over
them all like the eyes of a thing of the wild. He went forward with his
arm outstretched, feeling himself seventeen again, full of pride and a
haughty, supercilious superiority, full of a reckless shame.

"Venutius," he said, and the short, strong fingers closed about his wrist.

Venutius smiled. "Caradoc. I am glad to find you at last. So many rumors have been whispered among the tribes this winter. Some said you were dead, some said that you had fled to Mona, but I knew you would be here." With one friendly, encompassing glance he took in the stiff mane of hair, dark at the roots, blond at the tips, the enigmatic native art about the corded wrists and neck, and hanging on the scarlet chest, and the prematurely lined face from which the glow of youth had been seared. His eyes brushed Caradoc's, registered a stubbornness, a smouldering cunning and obduracy that had been lacking all those years ago. Caradoc smiled.

"Pick up your swords and buckle them on," he ordered and they did so gladly. He led them to Madoc, who waited patiently, arms folded on massive chest. "This is Venutius, chieftain of Brigantia," he explained, and Madoc's arms loosened, the hand went out, but the face did not relax into a welcoming smile.

"I take your wrist in greeting," he rumbled, "but I reserve a full welcome. It is said that your ricon has opened her borders to Rome with an eagerness that does you no credit, and so I do not apologize for my rudeness." He looked from Venutius to Caradoc, quickly noting the same air of indefinable strain on the bronzed faces, the same hidden wounds in the dark eyes. Then he turned abruptly and led the way to the Council hut, the Brigantians striding after.

Inside they shed their cloaks and settled themselves against the wall under the mirthless grins of the smoke-grayed severed heads, and Madoc, Caradoc, and their chiefs sat also, as the slaves skewered fresh pig onto the spit and freshened the fire. Beer was brought and they all drank silently, pouring the dregs politely onto the floor for the Dagda and the goddess. Eurgain and Vida came and squatted with them and Venutius looked at them, recognized, and looked away, his heart full of the chill morning when he had taken his black-haired, grim-lipped little ricon away from them. I should have left her there, he thought viciously, or slain her in the forests or when she was ill, feverish and defenceless in my hands. Cursed bitch. Now we sleep under her holding spell, and the once-mighty tuath is a wreck of lost dreams and servile, dishonored people. Cartimandua, fair slayer of men's souls!

They spoke of inconsequential things, the weather, the new disease that was attacking the breeding stock. The peasants were saying that Rome had brought it, but Madoc thought it had come with the unending dampness of the winter. Brigantian, Silurian, and Catuvellauni

250

drank again, the conversation lapsing into moments of brooding quiet while the slaves laughed and hurried about the huge hut and the dishes set up a friendly clatter.

One by one other chiefs and freemen drifted in, lured by the rumor of guests, and came to stand or squat, listening to the talk with greedy ears. The pig browned and crisped, its aroma floating with the smoke to tantalize the hungry, weary men. Caradoc felt that if only he closed his eyes he would be at home in Camulodunon, Cunobelin's Royal War Band around him laughing and squabbling—Aricia, her dark eyes flashing, Gladys folded deep into her cloak and watching reflectively, his Eurgain responding to Tog's rough teasing with a flush of color in her cheeks and a placid smile on her gentle mouth.

Venutius was talking of the fierce, destructive tides that had raced up his tuath's river that winter, his voice firm, the cadences rising and falling in and out of the general clamor, and Caradoc realized dismally that the past could not be wiped out, even as Eurgain had said. Homesickness rolled over him, tinged with poignant, full-bodied memories, and he would have given away his honor, his sword, even his children, to be back there with his father and his friends, to be lusty and impetuous and untroubled, to be young again. He knew then that Catuvellauni he was and Catuvellauni he would remain, forever.

Madoc rose and went to the pig, snatching the knife proffered to him by Jodocus and hacking the choice portions of haunch for the guests, then all the company helped themselves and sat eating, while Madoc's bard sang and the children finished quickly and ran outside to play in the warming sun.

Finally Madoc threw aside his dish and leaned back on one elbow. "Is your business for the Council?" he asked Venutius, and the other paused, considering.

"No, it is not," he said slowly, "although you have the right to discuss it in Council. That is for you to decide. I would rather state it only to you and to Caradoc."

Madoc's shaggy head nodded. "Then we will walk by the river together." He struggled up and Caradoc and Venutius rose too, following him into bright sunshine and the air that wafted to them the tang of rising sap from the forest. They passed the three circles of huts, the artist's home, the kennels and potteries, and strolled at last in deep grass beside muddy water that rushed by them. The melted snow of the mountains and the spring rains carried driftwood, dead wolves, and bloated mountain goats, all the debris of the foothills. Beyond them the forest steamed, tinted with an almost imperceptible blur of soft green, and the mountain heights were lost in the humid haze. The chiefs straggled behind, Cinnamus with naked sword, his green, hard eyes on Venutius, his mind full of the black witch he had always despised, and Caelte whistling tunefully as he turned his face to the white glory of the sun. "Now speak," said Madoc. "What do you want of us?"

"I have heard," Venutius said softly, "that men from the west are leaving their mountains and new peasants are taking over lowland farms deserted by the war. I have heard that in the towns there are new freemen who speak and dress as members of the various tuaths, but are not. I have heard of unwary Roman soldiers found headless within spitting distance of Camulodunon. Have I heard aright?"

"That depends on why you want to know," Caradoc said smoothly. "In times like these men's fears often turn innocent happenings to imagined threats, and make into mountains the most innocuous mole-hills."

"I am no pawn of Rome," Venutius flashed angrily. "Give me no smooth words of caution, Caradoc! I come to you with honor unstained!"

Caradoc took his arm and swung him to a halt. "Unstained?" he hissed. "How can that be, when your tuath has welcomed the Ninth with open arms, and your ricon drinks with Roman officers who already plan roads and posting stations through her land? Is there one Brigantian chief left who dares even to speak of honor? Roman ships ply your coast, not only traders but also vessels of the Classis Britannica, and has not your ricon already begun to build a great Roman house, designed for her by the legion's architect? And to think that once you sheepherders accused me, Caradoc, of toadying to Rome!" The biting words stung with contempt, lashing Venutius.

"So it is true," Venutius said, his leathery face staining brick red. "How else could you know so much of the business of my people? Oh Caradoc, how sly and secretive you have become." He lowered his voice. "Send me your spies. I will give them cattle and sheep to herd, I will take them in my train and they can move among my tribe with words I dare not utter myself. Send them, and tell them to stir up the faint and dying hearts of my chiefs. Ah, Caradoc." His voice broke. "How can you understand? She has bewitched them with promises of riches and ease, and they follow her like puppies, panting to please. She tells them that Rome brings peace and prosperity, and an end to the fear of other tribes, and she has made them forget that they cared more for honor than for life."

"Why don't you rally them yourself? Your chiefs have a reputation for ferocity and your boundaries encompass most of the north. You could repulse the Ninth without too much trouble, before it becomes too deeply entrenched."

Venutius gazed in the direction of the river. "Because I have sworn allegiance to her, and my oath must stand," he said quietly, and it was then that Caradoc knew. Venutius still loved his treacherous, spellbinding wife, and he burned day after anguish-filled day on the pyre of her rapacious greed yet was unable to face the cold darkness of a life without those flames. "I will give aid to the spies," Venutius went on, "but you must understand that if my ricon's men find them out I cannot defend or acknowledge them and they will have to die at her hands." His eyes snapped back to Caradoc. "This only I can do. I can lay a scent, I can keep memories alive, I can prick the spirits of my chiefs with the sword of a lost honor, if you will help me."

"Strange idea of honor you have, Brigantian," Madoc burst out angrily. "You are too cowardly to do what my Silurian freemen will do, and you call it honorable! If you hate your ricon so much then lop off her head and drive the Romans out yourself!"

"I cannot," Venutius whispered, "I cannot," his voice like the death sigh of a hunted deer, and Caradoc deliberately turned and began to walk again, Madoc and the others following.

"I accept your offer, unsatisfactory though it may be," Caradoc said. "I will send more spies. But what will you do, Venutius, if the swell of revolt grows and the chiefs wake from their holding spell?"

Venutius's lips tightened. "I do not know. You ask me to predict the secret surgings of my soul, and that is impossible. One day at a time, Catuvellaunian wolf!" They smiled at one another in rueful understanding and paced on, the sun hot on their backs, their swords rattling in their jeweled scabbards.

That evening, after the feasting, when Venutius had retired to the guest hut and his chiefs, apart from his bard and shield-bearer, had curled up in their cloaks on the ash-strewn floor of the Council hut, Caradoc handed Eurgain her cloak. "Go to Venutius and talk to him," he said. "You and Aricia grew up together. It will be quite natural for you to want further news of her. Make him speak of her, my love. I need to know just how deep the Roman penetration has been, how strongly Aricia holds the reins of power, what chink there may be in her armoring. Brigantia is in an ideal position for Plautius to launch an attack on the west if he so desires, and the spies are not yet well enough established with the Cornovii to bring me all the information I want." She settled the cloak around her shoulders, withdrawing her hands into its blue depths and looking at him coolly.

"The spies in our country tell us that the emperor ordered Plautius to strengthen, to consolidate, not to expand too far north or west until he has secured the lowlands. I do not think that he will strike against us here for at least another two years."

"Unless he has provocation. And provocation, dear Eurgain, is just what I intend to give him, provided I can come to some agreement with the Ordovices next summer. Then the paths through Cornovii country and into Brigantia will be of the utmost importance."

She nodded calmly. "But even so, Caradoc, between now and then the situation everywhere could have changed enormously. Are you sure that you send me only to extract tactical information?"

"We have been married for a long time, Eurgain," he replied quietly, with a firmness he suddenly did not feel. "And I have never taken another wife, nor wanted to. That should answer your question."

"It should," she said lightly, coming to plant a swift kiss on his lips, "but it does not. It tells me only that my husband does not like to lie, and so dissembles with care." The cornflower eyes darkened in quick jealousy, and as always when she thought of Aricia and the strange fascination she held for certain men she yielded to it, let it wash her for a moment, then stoically pushed it away. She had no wish to own her husband body and soul as Aricia had wanted to do, though Aricia had not loved him. She loved a man, a whole, independent being, and she respected him because she could sway him but never make him bend. But sometimes, as tonight, watching the play of hurtful, lustful memories on his face, she ached with a dull, heavy despair that the years had not healed, even as they had not healed the wound in Caradoc. Somewhere deep within him was a place from which she was barred, a place where Aricia nestled sleeping, waiting for an event such as the coming of Venutius to wake and stretch and send waves of misery through them both, and it would always be so though they loved each other in their way. She sighed. "I will go," she said.

Venutius's bard stopped her at the doorskin, his arm reaching from post to post, and he asked her sharply what her business was. "I am Eurgain," she explained patiently. "I was once a friend to your ricon. I want only to enquire of your chieftain how she is doing. Please ask him if he will see me." She lifted the cloak, spreading her arms wide. "I come unarmed. I bear no sword or knife." He bent his head under the lintel and she waited, back to the door, eyes on the star-strung heavens held in silver veils of wisping cloud. The moon rode serene, the air was mild and still. She breathed deeply as Bran had taught her to do, opening her mind and heart to the peace of the night, imagining the fears and uncertainties of her life flowing from her on her outward breath, then she turned and entered the hut while the bard held the skins back for her.

Venutius rose from his stool beside the dead hearth. He had removed his weaponry and was clad in a short green tunic, and his legs and arms were bare. He had unbound and brushed his hair, and it lay on his shoulders like a soft, gleaming hood, the red waves imprisoning the lamp's faint light. Eurgain allowed herself a second of vision, Aricia in his arms, her black hair tangling with his red, mistress and slave, enchantress and victim, locked in passion. Then she removed her cloak and smiled. "I am sorry to disturb you," she said, "but I wanted to talk with you quietly. Aricia and I knew each other well, long ago. How is she?"

A shadow passed behind his eyes. He smiled back, waving her to the chair, and she thought for the first time how handsome he was. He poured beer for her from the jug, pushed it toward her, and sat back on the stool. He remembered her, of course. The silent one with the perceptive eyes, the thinker, the visionary with the streak of mulish common sense. He remembered the other one too, older, dark, also silent but with an edge of tension to her, a danger. Strange, he mused, watching the long, clean fingers curve about the cup, how much I do remember of those fleeting days. The last days of my happiness. Perhaps that is why. So few memories from the years between are ones I wish to dwell on. "Tell me, Eurgain," he said, twirling the bronze cup slowly in his hand, "did your husband send you to me?"

She laughed, startled. "Yes, he did. I must not lie to you. But I think I would have come in any case. We have had so little news of Aricia since you took her away from Camulodunon."

"And most of the news has been bad," he finished for her brutally. "You need not spare my feelings, Lady. I have very few left to be spared. She has killed them all."

"Aricia always loved her comfort," Eurgain said awkwardly, trying to maintain a polite composure, "yet there was great affection between all of us at Cunobelin's town, and the closeness of family. It was a shock to her, Venutius, when she had to leave."

"All that was eleven years ago. I do not wish to talk about the past. What is the use? She came, she hated us, she used us, and we, like our own stupid sheep, stumbled after her. At first it was wine and trinkets. Where is the harm, she said, in using our surplus hides to bring wine to the chiefs? We obeyed her because we had oathed to her and she was the daughter of our dead lord, and where indeed was the harm?" He drank a little and then gazed morosely into the cup. "I married her. She was sixteen. She wore white flowers in her hair and my wedding gift to her around her neck. 'You and I, Venutius,' she said, 'You and I. Together we can raise Brigantia higher than the Catuvellauni!' I did not understand then what she really meant. How she must have laughed at me! Oh Sataida, Lady of Grief, I did not marry a woman, I married a demon!"

Eurgain sat very still while the man before her struggled in the grip of a torrent of bitterness. Her calm assurance and her friendly silences often welcomed confidences, that she knew. She had been useful to Caradoc in the past because of it, but she had not invited this bloody self-inflicted agony and she was aghast. You would be like this, my husband, she thought, if you had married her instead of proud Venutius. Did you see it? Did you know?

"You say you were her friend," he went on more evenly, "but she was not yours, Eurgain. You know that, don't you?" Their eyes met, tentatively held, acknowledged the thing they had in common, and she nodded once, the light sliding up her smooth blonde braids.

"Yes, I know. I know it all, Venutius."

"Yet I love her still," he went on softly, a wondering tenderness in his voice. "When she calls for me, I run to her. I know her for what she is and I can come here seeking her downfall. But in the midst of my hate, I love."

They sat in silence, bound by a shared sorrow that went beyond convention and beyond words, then Eurgain changed the subject. She felt herself trembling with emotional weariness, her nerves, beneath the impassive face, screaming for flight. "Is Rome building within your borders?"

He gulped his beer, folded his arms, and answered her easily. The moment had gone. Once more he was the half-wild, fierce son of the hills she had met all those years ago. "Not yet. A fort is nearly completed to the southeast of us, just within the Coritani border, and the soldiers and officers come and go freely to my ricon's house, but as yet no roads have been laid across us. Where would they go? Plautius is not ready to face the far northerners—or you! He will use us as his friendly wall, with my ricon's glad consent. He has sent her rich gifts. He will not take her lordship from her, that he has promised, as long as she cooperates, and of course she does so, eagerly."

"What of your people?"

"They obey her in silence. They believe that it is too late to do anything other than bow to the inevitable. Some chiefs and their freemen grumble in secret. They blame me, and with cause, for the loss of their honor, but as yet they do not see that they have also lost their freedom. I want the Silurian spies to convince them of that. As for me . . ." He spread his hands, and jet glinted wickedly up at her from the stubbed, scarred fingers. "I am twice a slave, yet I will do what I can."

256

She rose then, ashamed of herself for coming in cold blood in an attempt to deceive him, ashamed of Caradoc's necessity. "I am sorry, Venutius," she said softly. "The times are evil, and I have only made them more so by coming to you tonight."

He stepped to her side and kissed her cold hand. "No, not you, Eurgain. In you Caradoc has his greatest treasure."

She smiled. "Go in safety, walk in peace."

"You also, Lady."

She withdrew her hand and left him, walking quickly to her own hut with her cloak slung over her arm. Her face burned in the cool night breeze and the scent of blossom newly born wafted around her. Somewhere close by a nightingale trilled and warbled a song of heartbreaking, unintelligible loveliness, but her thoughts were turned inward. She entered the hut, flung the cloak on the chair by the door, pulled off her tunic, and undid her hair. Caradoc watched the sharp, angry gestures from the shadow of the bed.

"Well?" he said finally, and she ripped off her breeches, not looking at him.

"He is a good man, and honest, but do not trust him until he has been proven. He is torn."

"That is all?"

She strode to the bed, her nostrils flared, her eyes huge and gray. "That is all. I don't want to talk about it any more, ever. And don't touch me, Caradoc. I feel sullied enough tonight."

Venutius and his chiefs went home, slipping away from the valley one pearly red dawn, and two days later the Silurians celebrated Beltine. The trees opened suddenly to a full, shining green glory. White blossom drifted from the apple trees and snowed scented petals through the forest halls, which echoed all day with bird song, and the dry gray bones of the cattle slaughtered last Samain were piled into two huge bonfires. The breeding stock, the new young calves, were driven protesting between them, rolling their eyes and bellowing in fear as the smoke enveloped them. In the evening the people of the town danced with their hair and necklaces flying. Their eyes sparked in the leaping orange glow of the fires, and they sang the old songs as the beer barrels emptied. All night the festivities went on. Children shrieked and played in the shadows of the huts, running in and out like demented candles. The chiefs shed their tunics and wrestled in the grass, sweat gleaming on their muscled bodies, bronze and golden torcs licked by the light from the bone fires. In the end they slept, some going to their huts, but most curling in their cloaks and lying contentedly in the grass, lulled by the rustle of the wind in the trees by the river.

Late in the morning Fearachar packed Caradoc's and Llyn's gear and the chiefs set out again, this time going west to Council with the Demetae. Their ricon's curiosity had been piqued by rumors of the foreign chieftain who had already many of the stubborn Silurian warriors eating out of his hand, and his emissaries had come to Madoc with the melting of the snow in the high passes. Eurgain had begged to go, too, this time, longing to summer among the rugged freedom of the peaks whose teeth ripped at the sky and whose winds blew steadily day and night, unscented and unsoftened by wood or grass. But Caradoc had refused.

"The Demetae are an unstable, suspicious people," he had said. "No friendly Silurian Druid has been among them, preparing the way for us. When I go to the Ordovices next summer you can come." She argued and pleaded in vain. He simply set his lips in a thin, uncompromising line and shook his head. She kissed him goodbye, hugged Llyn, who suffered himself to be embraced with barely concealed irritation, then stood and watched them all disappear over the breast of the hill, blue, scarlet, and yellow cloaks billowing together like the fanned plumage of some huge, exotic bird.

He did not come back until the first snows of winter fell, and when he did she was appalled at the change in him. His flesh had shrunk to his bones so that nothing remained but the iron-hard muscles. He was gaunt, restless, unable to eat, unable to sleep until dawn came pale and cold under the doorskins of their hut. He spoke little to anyone during the day but when he did sleep he muttered continually, tossing to and fro, and she lay beside him rigid with worry, seeing the growing obsession of his vision gnaw away his spirit. He thought and spoke of nothing but Rome and the coming confrontation, and he fretted continually at the western tribes' petty quarreling. Unity was his invisible standard and its weight had lain along his spine as he struggled over the mountains and flogged himself and his men from village to village. Eurgain went to Cinnamus with her anxiety. She found him in his hut stretched out on the bed, his helm, shield, and sword on the floor beside him in a welter of polishing cloths. He sat up when she entered. His own face was thinned by days of privation, and the glossy crystal shine of the green eyes was ringed in new lines. She sat on his stool. Vida's tunics lay piled by the fire but she was not there.

"What happened this summer, Cin?" she asked him peremptorily, and he flexed his stiff limbs and swung from the bed, going to the fire and tossing new wood on it, standing before it.

"The Demetae nearly drove him mad," Cinnamus replied. "Mother, what a tuath! It would have been better if Bran had been with us but as it was we had to sit for hours in Council while they strutted about, flaunting all the raids they had ever taken against the Silurian chiefs, doing their best to make us all lose our tempers. The walls of their Council hut are festooned with Silurian and Ordovician heads. I have never seen so many trophies. But their jewels are beautiful and their women fierce, and if Caradoc can win them the Romans will have to look to their precious laurels. He fought three of them, Eurgain, killing one and badly wounding the others."

"What?"

Cinnamus grinned engagingly at her. "They listened to him because their chief had wanted to hear him, but they wanted to see how great a warrior he was before they settled down to seriously consider his words. They judge no man on words, Eurgain, only on deeds. Oh Mother! What fights they were! I do not think that Caradoc intended to kill the chief but he lost his temper. He was tired with all the stupid boasting and talking. The Demetae unstopped their ears after that, I can tell you! They have promised to attend a joint Council, but not before Madoc agreed to cease raiding them. He did agree, but he had a lot to say about the Silurians' own losses to them."

Eurgain sat quietly for a moment, her head bent. Then she said, "What is the matter with him, Cin? He takes no joy in anything. He will not allow himself to relax. I see him changing every day and I fear for him."

Cinnamus sobered. He came to her, squatting before her loosely, and he took her hands in his own. She raised her eyes to the well-known hard mouth, the beaked nose, the spring-green eyes that could melt with love and laughter or turn to stone, and she felt something within her crack like frozen water. She was tired of tension and worry, tired of lonely days and empty nights, and she put a hand to the cascade of waving blond hair before her, wanting gentleness, warmth. He slowly gathered her into his arms and held her strongly and she sighed.

"He has cut himself off from all of us except Llyn," he said. "And only one thing keeps him going—the dream of one day becoming the west's arviragus with the tribes united under him and thousands of warriors moving as one to drive Rome into the sea. He believes himself to be Albion's last hope, Eurgain, and I believe it too. So do Madoc and Bran and the Silurians. And he is homesick. He hates the mountains. He longs for the gentle Catuvellaunian lowlands. We are in danger every day as we journey—from hunger, the weather, wild chiefs and wilder animals, from the winds of the passes as we crouch against the rocks. For myself I do not care. I have fought most of these things all my life and have never had a great position to lose or overmuch cattle to fill my belly. But my lord has lost a kingdom and found a deadly vision, and he struggles to accept, to adjust. He knows, we all know, that we can only go forward. There is no going back." He kissed her forehead, intending the gesture to be a signal of finality, but somehow he found his lips straying into her hair and he felt her arms move slowly to encircle his neck. He knew he ought to pull away, and indeed he thought he had begun to do so, but instead his hands grasped her shoulders and his mouth slid across her temple and along the curve of her cheek to fit itself softly against her own. She did not start, though for a moment the lips beneath his own quivered, then slowly opened and she sank toward him, leaving the stool to topple and roll away. Her hands cradled the back of his head as he released her shoulders and lowered her to the skins, keeping his mouth pressed against her own, but when he raised her tunic she let him go and her arms fell to her sides, feeling his mouth move to her neck. Strange kisses, she thought, yet not so strange. Hands with a touch my body does not recognize though I have known them since my youth. Ah Cinnamus, love me! Let your body tell me that I am still who I think I am! He entered her tenderly and her flesh, still wondering at this unknown other flesh that nevertheless had the warmness of familiarity, did not recoil. The rhythme of another life, she thought again, lapped in his gentleness, feeling the hard knots of anxiety and misery slowly untie within her. Tell me, Cinnamus my dearest friend, tell me! Heal the wounds! She rose with him on the tide of his own passion, lying under him, enfolded by his unspoken response to her loneliness, giving to him her need and her thanks. When he had ceased to move against her he did not release her immediately. He propped himself up on his elbows and smiled down at her, kissing her with that same careful gentleness, and only when he had coaxed an answering smile did he rise and help her to her feet.

"Next summer we treat with the Ordovices," he said, as though nothing had happened. "The last test, and the greatest. Then we will see."

"I will come with you then," she replied evenly, though she was trembling. "I can no longer wait here in idleness while my thoughts run from my grasp to follow where my body cannot go. I was wrong to let him take these burdens without me. I too want to go back, Cin, but not from any love of Camulodunon. The mountains satisfy my soul. I wish only for a husband whole and carefree again, concerned with nothing but raids and honor-prices."

"That day will come, Eurgain, do not fear." He tried to cheer her, but her lip curled and her face was suffused with bitterness.

"I do not think so," she said, straightening her tunic and moving to the door. She made as if to leave but then turned back, hesitating, one hand on the doorskins. "Cinnamus, I . . ." she began, but he cut her short.

"Do not think about it, Eurgain," he said. "It was not a matter of dishonor, to yourself or to Caradoc, and Vida would understand, if I chose to tell her. It was a matter of comfort, that is all."

"Yes," she answered slowly. "I know. Comfort. I am so tired, Cin." She left then, and the doorskins whispered shut behind her. Cinnamus lifted the stool and stood looking at it, but after a moment he set it back in its place and picked up his helm and a clean polishing cloth, whistling and smiling to himself.

For three summers Caradoc had been constantly on the move and now his spies came to him with messages that whipped his impatience to a frenzy. Roman civilians were pouring into Albion in a steadily increasing stream, still mainly traders and adventurers, but also more women, officers' families, people bent on settlement. Many of the roads were completed, and the speculatores cantered along them bearing dispatches from posting station to fort, and the wains rumbled, full of grain and wine, strange new seedlings and plants for the homesick settlers trying to turn their wooden homes into Roman estates, plate and hangings, provisions of all kinds for the legions. The once-mighty hillforts like Camulodunon were becoming peaceful Roman towns, transforming slowly, their straggling, mean huts giving place to blocks of smart wooden houses, shops, and baths. At Camulodunon itself the temple to the Divine Claudius rose block by monumental block, paid for by cowed freemen who no longer ran with angry protests to chiefs who could do nothing. The gangs of chained Trinovantian and Catuvellaunian laborers paid for it in blood. But none of these things drove Caradoc to the point of recklessness. Other news did that.

A scout stood before him and reported without emotion how the first shipment of young tribesmen had left Albion, bound for Rome to be trained to fight in the legions, and more would follow regularly. Rome knew that a great deal of the wealth of the new province lay in its uncouth warriors, tall, healthy, and fearless, and in vain the chiefs and sword-women stood on the shore, weeping and cursing. Their brothers and lovers were never seen again by the tribes.

Caradoc listened coldly, his mind clicking over behind the white-hot wall of compulsion that always seemed to stand between himself

261

and his people, thinking of Llyn with a sudden, fierce protectiveness. Llyn was eleven, stockiness giving way to the gangling, easy grace of Togodumnus, not yet blooded, not yet a man. Caradoc saw him with the Roman slave chains about his neck and then in the ranks of some legion's auxiliary somewhere, hardened and changed, his quick wit and fearless laughter gone. He thought also of other reports, closer to the caer. Roman patrols had been seen too close for comfort, moving through the dense forest where the Dobunni territory ended and the Silurian began.

Caradoc knew that he had almost run out of time and he did not wait for winter to relinquish its grip. He called a Council. As he had expected, the Silurian chiefs oathed to him to a man, flinging down their swords before him, greedy for action at last, and he, Cinnamus, and Caelte, together with Madoc and Jodocus, led them out of the valley going east. They slipped through the empty, bare forests with nothing but their weapons and as much food as they could carry on their backs. They had learned his lessons well. They kept away from the new fort where Boduocus warmed his old hands at the fires of Rome. They lay concealed in the bush beside the new road that ran south to the fort in Belgae country, picking off dispatch riders, ambushing small patrols, capturing food wains while the last rains of winter washed the bright colors from their cloaks and the cobbled road clean of Roman blood.

His actions caused no more than a small ripple among the conquerors of the lowlands. He was careful not to pressure the Second Legion too hard, for he did not want to bring the full force of Vespasianus down on his head before he was ready. The Ordovices waited for his coming and the last knot had to be tied. Irritated, Vespasianus doubled the guard on the wains and alerted the patrols, sending a report to Plautius at Camulodunon, but as yet there was no cause for alarm. A few chiefs, desperate with starvation, had had the temerity to attack his men and eventually they would die. That was all. But Plautius, reading the scroll beside the window of his new headquarters through which the winter sun pooled weakly, felt a stirring of intuition. The men of the west, and Gladys's brother. It had to be. He again felt a quick desire to know this man and he handed the scroll to Pudens to read. He sat at his desk with fingers pyramided to his chin, thinking. "Will you order counterattacks, sir?" the young man asked him. But Plautius, after a moment, laid his ringed hands flat on the desk's smooth surface and shook his head.

"No, not yet. Too soon, and besides, it's still winter. I think I will wait for the spring and see what happens. Answer the dispatch for me, Rufus, will you?" He took up his helmet and cloak and went out

262

seeking solitude in which to think, but there was nowhere in Camulo-dunon to go nowadays to escape the noise of industry. He might as well have been in Rome.

On the last foray of the season, when the wind already blew warmer and wildflowers pushed determinedly through the slush, Llyn went missing. Caradoc and the chiefs had sprung upon a century not knowing that behind the soldiers an alae of cavalry rode, and the little battle that ensued was hot and vicious. Llyn and Fearachar had remained hidden, as usual, lying behind brambles that choked the hill from which the chiefs had attacked, hearing the shouts and cries, the clash of swords and thud of shields, but not able to see much for the misty drizzle that whitened the morning. Down on the road Caradoc and his men fought grimly back and forth, while the Roman centurion barked his orders and the soldiers tried to form ranks, confused by the suddenness of the onslaught. There was an impasse and for a while the Silurians began to gain the upper hand, but Caradoc's sharp ears picked up the clatter of horses' hoofs and he ordered a retreat.

Without a question the chiefs and freemen turned and ran, melting into the mist and the trees, but this time the Romans, emboldened by the arrival of the cavalry, gave chase, and the tribesmen found them-selves hunted relentlessly. Under the shrouded, dripping trees they turned singly at bay or ran on silently to the safety of the pathless depths, and not until Caradoc, Cinnamus, and Caelte had crossed the river did Caradoc think of his son. Then he sped among the men straggling to safety, searching for Fearachar. Cinnamus stopped him. "It is no use, Lord, until all the chiefs have returned to the caer and a count can be taken," he said and Caradoc angrily agreed, a wildfire of fear raging in him. Llyn was his talisman. Llyn was his comfort, his charm against despair, and if Fearachar returned without him Cara-doc would have his head. He went straight to the Council hut and paced before the gate in the rain. The chiefs went by him one by one seeking warmth and food but no Fearachar padded lugubriously into sight. Eurgain came to him, begging him to change his sopping clothes and to eat. He refused brusquely so she walked with him until Madoc came to tell him that there were no more living men left to be counted. A silence fell on the little group, then Caradoc sprang to life.

"Cinnamus, round up our chiefs, the Catuvellauni. Madoc, I must take the few horses you have. Is the patrol still seeking us?"

"No. The officers came to their senses and ordered their men back onto the road. The scouts tell me they have moved on, sadly short of men, though."

"Good. Eurgain, where are you going?" She was hurrying away and shouted over her shoulder, "To get my sword."

"No!" He ran after her. "No, you are not. Stay here. What can you do in this cursed mist?"

She flung round and faced him, two spots of color flaming in her pale winter cheeks. She yelled at him at the top of her voice, driven by more than she could stand. "And what do you think you can do? Damn you, Caradoc, I will not be told no by you again! I am not your chattel, I am a free sword-woman! I will come and go as I please. By Camulos!" She was screaming now and Madoc and the gathered Silurians looked at her in awe, but a tiny, approving smile played about Cinnamus's mouth. "Are you still so much of a Roman that you would keep your woman put away in her house like a piece of pretty furniture? I did not put on a slave chain when I married you and by the common law I can leave you whenever I like!" She dropped her voice. "And sometimes I think that I would like to leave you," she said huskily. "I have become no more to you than a convenience."

For a moment more she glared at him, standing tall, her breast heaving, and her hair plastered to her face and snaking over the sleeves of her orange tunic. Then she whirled and ran in the direction of their hut, calling to Tallia for a dry cloak and her boots and sword belt. Stunned, Caradoc watched her go, then he turned to where the horses were already being led toward him. His face was white and a pit of hopelessness was opening before him. He mounted quickly and gathered the reins into his hands, sitting motionless and gazing at the ground while the chiefs followed suit and Eurgain came back, blue cloak trailing the ground, hair bound up, sword clanging against her boot. She passed him without a glance. He peered into the pit, a vertigo making his head spin. Llyn was dead. He had lost Eurgain. The Ordovices would refuse him aid, and so would the Demetae. Then a shred of humor came to him, a cleansing shaft of steady wholesomeness like white sunlight at the end of a tunnel. Surely Llyn was lost, not dead. Eurgain could be courted and won again. And the Ordovices and the Demetae would oath to him, he knew it. He blinked and looked behind him to the waiting chiefs, quelling the bubble of laughter that threatened to become an unrestrainable, hysterical outburst. He raised an arm. "Ford the river and spread out!" he shouted. "Go in twos! Search the forest up to the road, and then return!" He dug his heels into his horse's belly and cantered into the mist.

Cinnamus and Caelte rode with him and together they traversed the forest, now full of a gloomy, cheerless light. The mist thinned as

264

noon passed. They followed the paths and found nothing, not even the trace of a passing, so they dismounted, tethering their mounts and moving through the trackless undergrowth with their swords drawn. As they neared the road they began to stumble across bodies lying hidden in the long grass and sodden leaves and they methodically stripped them of their precious weapons as they went. They were hoping that the goddess of the forest would see their action, know that the weaponry was for her, and send Llyn to them. Caradoc walked in an introspection that deepened, while Cinnamus knelt now and then and studied the dewed forest growth. Togodumnus had knelt in the same way in the lovely Catuvellaunian woods as they searched for Cunobelin, and a superstitious dread took hold of Caradoc so that he had to force himself to look in the face of each obscene, outspread corpse they found, seeing his father lying there under each tree, neck snapped, gray hair floating in the grass. When Cinnamus spoke it was with Tog's light, quick tones, and each white, still face seemed more lined, more cunning than the one before.

At last Cinnamus knelt, then gave a low exclamation. "Here! Look, Lord! Fresh tracks, a Roman cavalry mount, lightly loaded, one shoe cast and another coming loose!" Caradoc bent, seeing the faint indentations in the wet earth. "That is obvious," he snapped, "but no use, Cin. We do not seek a lost soldier. Let the chiefs find him and kill him."

"You do not listen, Lord," Caelte interrupted. "The horse is lightly loaded. It may be carrying a soldier's gear, or it may bear a boy."

Caradoc straightened. "Of course. It is a slim hope, but we must seek this beast. Cin, you track. You are better at it than I."

They went slowly, and Cinnamus paused many times to examine the tracks. Above them, beyond the sullen clouds that blanketed the forest, the sun began to swing into the west. For an hour they plodded on saying nothing, alternating between surges of hope and despair at precious time wasted, then Cinnamus stood upright, his eyes clouded with puzzlement.

"This rider is certainly lost," he said. "We are traveling in a circle, Lord. Had you noticed?" Caradoc had been too abstracted to notice, but now he sighed. "You are right. How far are we from our starting place? Can you tell?"

Cinnamus pointed. "We have almost arrived there. Through those trees, behind the two oaks that have twisted together, is our beginning."

Caradoc cursed, but dared not berate the goddess of the forest. "We can only hope," he snarled bitterly, "that the other men have had more luck than we. There is no sign of horse or rider, which is a good fortune, for if I met another Roman now I would tear him limb from limb."

Suddenly Caelte flung himself to the ground and as if at a signal the others followed, all talk forgotten. "What?" Cinnamus mouthed, and Caelte pointed. A flutter of gray movement, a brief scarlet flash, then Caradoc was on his feet and running, crashing through the branches like a wounded deer, shouting and calling Llyn's name. Cinnamus and Caelte followed.

Llyn was sitting astride a huge gray cavalry charger which still had a soldier's pack slung across the broad withers. He sat with reins limp in his small fingers. He was cloakless and bootless. His red tunic was in tatters. One sleeve had gone and he was splashed in blood from knee to shoulder. He watched them come almost without recognition, eyes glazed in a face riveleted by tearstains and grime, brown hair tangled and full of twigs and thorns. Caradoc fell forward, then came to a halt, shocked for a second into immobility.

A head swung against the horse's shoulder, pale eyelids half closed in death, eyes black and dull in blood-rimmed sockets. The nose had been crushed. Dried blood caked the open mouth and the ragged, severed neck, and a rope passed under the chin and up around the forehead over the short, wet, dark hair. A Roman.

"Mother," Cinnamus whispered. Caradoc felt the blood drain from his face, then he recovered and lunged forward, gladness spilling over into arms that lifted of their own accord. Llyn turned his head slowly and looked at Caradoc; then the frozen, blank little face began to pucker, and he fell from the horse into Caradoc's embrace.

"Father! Oh f . . . f . . . father! He killed Fearachar and I stabbed him from behind and cut off his head. It took a long time. I . . . I . . . was lost, I could not find the way, father . . . father . . . ! He buried his face in Caradoc's neck and babbled incoherently while the other men stood silent. Caradoc hugged him fiercely, feeling his knees weaken with relief and terror, then he set him on his feet, soothing him with words that were no words, reading mingled horror and grief in eyes that were supremely, pridefully dry. A warrior did not shed tears of fear and Llyn had wept to the towering trees but would not break again. The thin, brown lips shook uncontrollably, the mouth would not be still, but the square, cleft chin rose high. "I brought his sword with me, Fearachar's sword, but I could not lift him to set him on the horse." His face grimaced with the effort not to cry afresh and the eyes pleaded, Father, help me not to disgrace myself. Caradoc put a hand to his own neck and slowly removed his bronze torc.

"Llyn," he said, his voice husky with emotion. "You are blooded.

Not with a formal raid, not in the company of your train, not at the proper age, but alone, unaided, in defence of your friend." He lifted the wet hair and set the torc around the small neck. "As ricon of the Catuvellauni I make you warrior, freeman, and give you my blessing. Will you now oath to me?" Llyn raised his eyes and in them Caradoc read the final death of any innocence the lad might have had. Great pain was there, and fear still, but no cheeky glint of boyishness. Llyn had become a man. He pulled his sword from its scabbard, hardly able to unsheath it for its length, and he flung it at Caradoc's booted feet.

"I will," he said.

"Will you fight for me, swear for me before the Druids, and serve me to the death?"

"I will. Will you protect me and my honor-price, swear for me before the Druids, and loose me from my oath as is my right, if I desire it?"

"I will. Llyn ap Caradoc, you are now a Catuvellaunian chief." He picked up Llyn's sword and handed it gently back to him, wondering what Madoc would say. There would be no Silurian initiation now. But surely Madoc would understand and forgive, for the circumstances were unusual, to say the least. "Now go with Cinnamus," he said quietly, "and ride my horse back to the caer. I will ride this one." Gratitude sprang to the pale face but Llyn hesitated, stepping close to his father and taking his sleeve.

"Lord," he whispered. "It was not like killing a boar, no matter what I told myself. I do not think that I can do it again."

Caradoc wanted to cry out in pity. He put a hand on Llyn's cold cheek. "Don't think about it now," he said. "I shall not call on you to fight with the chiefs for a long time yet. Be at peace." Llyn nodded faintly and walked unsteadily to where Cinnamus and Caelte stood, still dumbfounded, and Caradoc mounted the gray. He looked down on the lifeless thatch of bloodied, black hair. He looked ahead at his son's straight back. Suddenly a wave of acrid bile filled his mouth and he spat, a dark stream of revulsion. Then he kicked at the horse and followed his men.

Eurgain had returned and was waiting on the bank of the river, motionless in the folding blue cloak. She saw them come splashing slowly across the ford, three weary men and a scrap of a boy, and she walked toward them, her hands clenched into hidden fists under the cloak. Llyn slid from the horse and she bent and kissed him, seeing the bloody fingers, the caked tunic. "I am glad you are safe, my son," she said evenly. "Now go to the Council hut and eat. Then Tallia can find you clean clothes." He nodded faintly and left them and she turned to Caradoc, her eyes widening at the sight of the huge charger and the head dripping with water. "Was there trouble?" she asked, and Caradoc dismounted. The stable slaves ran to them and he relinquished the reins, while Cinnamus untied the head and laid it on the ground. Caradoc shook his head.

"Not for me," he said shortly. "This head is Llyn's. I will tell you later, Eurgain, but now I need fire and food." He brushed past her, leaving her looking down on the trophy, her heart pounding painfully in her chest.

In Council that night Madoc roared with laughter when he heard of Llyn's escapade. Caradoc was now so firmly in the Silurians' favor that they agreed not to insist on Llyn's initiation. They all sat in the warm, firelit hut while muic floated with the sweet woodsmoke and the beer was passed from hand to hand. The head, now washed and tidied, was brought to Llyn, but he put his hands behind his back and flushed, the lamplight lying golden on the torc about his throat.

"Actually," he said, "I don't want it."

"But it is your right!" Madoc said, pushing it forward. "It is the proof of your manhood. Better than cattle, eh Llyn?"

"I would rather be a child again, and have Fearachar beside me," he insisted. "You can have it, Lord, if you want it. Put it up beside the others."

"But I did not take it, nor did any of my chiefs. It does not belong to the Silures." Madoc was mystified. He breathed heavily, the thick brows drawn together in bafflement. No Silurian child had ever brought such an honor as this to the tuath, and Llyn's attitude was incomprehensible to him.

"Then give it to the goddess," Llyn said definitely. He sat down beside his father and Madoc shrugged, handing the head to Cinnamus, who put it against the wall beside him. What odd people these Catuvellauni were. They fought like devils when they had to, and loved their honor like good freemen, but they were too full of womanish sensibilities. They had probably lived too long under Rome's enervating influence. But in spite of everything, Madoc had only respect and admiration for them.

Fearachar's body was found lying amidst a thicket of brambles, the ribs stove in by a shield's cruel boss, the arms, neck, and face a mass of sword cuts and one deep hole under the right breast. It was carried back to the caer with great solemnity and Llyn himself, with Cinnamus's help, washed it and dressed it in a fine, gold-embroidered tunic, laying the notched sword on the breast, putting a chieftain's helm on the brown locks. Caradoc purchased a simple bronze torc

268

from the artist and set it on Fearachar's neck. "Once, long ago," he told Llyn, "Fearachar was a rich chief with a great honor-price. But he and his family began a blood feud, Llyn, over a woman, and he lost it all. Now he has bought it back."

They did not bury Fearachar in the Silurian way. They built him a tall pyre and laid him reverently upon it, and while the flames crackled and leaped upward Llyn himself stood by it and gave the eulogy, tears pouring down his face. The songs were sung, the memories brought forth, and all the Catuvellauni paid homage to a man who had been, under a doleful, wry exterior, an honorable and trustworthy chief. Then they gathered up the Roman arms taken from the bodies of the slain, and Llyn took the head, and they went to the well that lay deep and still within the arches of the wood, now fully leafed and strongly scented with spring. There they cast the treasures into the scummed water and Llyn saw his trophy sink slowly, taking with it his childhood. He knew that the sweat and terror of his blooding would stay with him for the rest of his life, but now the memory was muted, overlaid with the grief of the passing of his friend and guardian, and he went back to the funeral pyre and took out his sword and stood before the flames, still crying. He remained there all night.

A week later Bran returned, thinner than ever. He and Caradoc sat by the river in the warm sun and he told Caradoc that the Ordovices were at last willing to listen to him in Council. "But we must go at once," Bran warned him. "If we wait too long they will change their minds, and my brethren and I do not want that." He fixed his piercing gaze on the other man. "Are you ready to fight, my friend?"

"I am, but even if I were not, the time for preparation is almost over. If we wait too long the people of the lowlands will have forgotten their freedom, and no sword will be able to rekindle that desire."

"Will you bring Eurgain with you this time?" The question was placed lightly but Caradoc turned with eyes full of suspicion. Bran had sought out Eurgain as soon as he returned. He had brought her new crystals and a star map made especially for her by the master of the Druithin on Mona. Walking to his hut, Caradoc had heard her delighted laughter, a carefree, uncomplicated, happy sound that was no longer shared with him. He was not jealous. One was never jealous of a Druid for they seldom took a sexual interest in women. But Caradoc remembered what Eurgain had said about the many things that could separate husband from wife, and he felt himself guilty. His work had to be done. No one else could do it, and that she understood. But she had never understood why he had left her alone instead of taking her with him, and he knew now that he had been wrong to try to shield her from the dangers and weariness of his missions. Now he met Bran's eyes with the uncomfortable feeling that the Druid knew what he was thinking.

"If she wants to come," he said noncommittally.

Bran looked away, across the quiet water. "Caradoc," he said. "If you do not take her you will lose her. She is a proud and talented woman, wasting in idleness. She could be of great use to you. She loves you as she always has, but if she feels that you have no more need of her she will gather her belongings and slip away some night, to carve another destiny for herself."

"I know," Caradoc replied simply. "But I have been too bone tired to consider the matter. A life such as ours brings many deaths, not all of the body. There are parts of me that are dead, Bran, and nothing will ever restore them. I teeter on the brink of madness. I am driven. I cannot rest."

"Take heart, Caradoc. Only a little longer. We face the final task before our destiny comes to float us away. If you are elected arviragus, have you plans?"

Caradoc rose. "One thing at a time, Druithin! It will take a mighty spell indeed to turn these western men into one tribe, and me into an arviragus!"

Bran rose also, and smiled. "But the spell has been cast," he said. "You have been weaving it yourself, for three years."

CHAPTER NINETEEN

N O SILURES WENT NORTH to the Ordovices. Caradoc left Madoc and his men to harry the Roman patrols through the summer, and only Bran and the Catuvellauni set out for the high mountain passes. They went on foot and all of them, even Eurgain, carried their needs on their backs. They had changed so greatly that not one of them thought twice of bearing these burdens they would have scorned to take up at Camulodunon.

The early summer was mild and settled, and to Eurgain the winding track, steadily meandering higher and higher through flower-sprinkled meadows, beside cold, rushing streams, taking them along the crest of bald hills from which the whole of the west lay under their feet like a shimmering mirage, brought hours of a still contentment. They camped each night in the lee of a hill, or beside a river, or in the shelter of the rocks that had tumbled from the heights above to be trapped by the clinging fingers of strong mosses and grass. They lit their fires and cooked their prey, drinking icy water, singing and laughing. Only Caradoc was silent. He knew what the mountains could do to a man if the weather changed and his thoughts flitted between the screaming winds of the gorges still to be traversed and the coming Council with the Ordovician chieftains. Bran had told him nothing about them. He had merely smiled. "You will never meet their like again" was all he would venture. And Caradoc brooded in the folds of his cloak while Llyn gathered wood with Cinnamus, and Eurgain and Bran scanned the heavens to the soft singing of Caelte. Every day was like a festival day, Beltine or Imbolc, and the weather held, and the moon waxed round and silver.

In a week they had crossed the invisible border which lay in a valley between gray, broken cliffs and they began to climb again, now in country that only Bran had traveled through. A wind sprang up, veered to the north, and black clouds sped toward them on a howling gale. Up there, where trees clung precariously to the sides of steep canyons, where only herbs and lichens grew, summer was a faint, apologetic dusting of momentary green between the torrents of melting snow in the spring and the gales that brought more snow after the brief calm of autumn. The track to the passes was narrow but clear, used by raiding parties, scouts, and Druids carrying messages, and they made good speed. Eurgain fell to wondering what irrational fear lay behind Caradoc's insistence that she stay in the town as she strode easily after Llyn. But Cinnamus, Bran, and the others knew that this journey was the simplest part of their trek. The exhaustion and the dangers came when they had received a Council's permission to visit the isolated, palisaded farmsteads to which no tracks conveniently ran, crouched in country where a man could lose his way and leave his bones to bleach in wind and sun. As they climbed higher they had to slow, for the way was often blocked by boulders and the track dwindled in many places to a thin ribbon, but within a day the passes had been left behind and the Ordovices' territory lay below them. It was ragged, with rock-strewn slopes and heavy dark woods, a country deserted by all save the plaintively calling curlews and the wolves.

In three more days they crested a long, rolling slope and found themselves looking down on a village. The round huts were of stone, and smoke spiraled from the beehived roofs. Along the little valley, sweeping around the circles of huts, were tiny, fenced, patchworked fields splashed with the brilliant green of new crops, and beyond them herds of cattle and sheep grazed beside the river. Bran hitched his pack and started down the slope, heading for the bridge that spanned the narrows, and the silent company straggled after.

"You can almost smell it, can't you?" Caelte whispered to Cinnamus, and Cinnamus nodded, lips compressed, eyes on the huts rising to share the horizon. He did not need to ask what Caelte meant. Magic lay so thick on the valley that he imagined he could see it as well as smell it, thin clouds lying above the water, curling around the huts, wreathing from the darkness of the trees that covered the valley sides. It was late afternoon. They reached the bridge unchallenged. Then from under its shade three men appeared, swords drawn, massive shields at the ready. Two of them wore curiously pronged helms, and the face of the other was covered by a mask of beaten bronze, a wolf's face, the ears laid back against the man's own long black hair, the pointed muzzle covering his mouth. From its glitter two black eyes flicked over the company, as hard as stones.

"Wait here," Bran said in a low voice, then he walked quickly across the bridge, with his arm outstretched. "Aneirin! Gervase! It is I, Bran. Sine, I come with immunity for the Catuvellaunian chieftain Caradoc and his men. Will you grant it?"

They took his wrist in turn, greeting him calmly, regally, and with surprise Eurgain heard a woman's voice coming from beneath the wolf mask. "We will grant it. Bring the foreigners over."

Bran turned and waved and they filed across the bridge, then Bran went to Caradoc. "Lords, this is Caradoc ap Cunobelin, come to address the Council. Caradoc, this is Aneirin, Gervase, and Sine, chiefs of this tuath."

They extended brown arms laden with silver and bronze toward him, then to his men, and Eurgain, grasping Sine's thin, strong wrist, felt the woman's cool, enquiring eyes travel over her. She met the quick scrutiny boldly and had the pleasure of seeing the eyes drop.

"The lord will welcome you properly," Gervase said. "Please follow me." They went with him up the bank, across a smooth, grassed meadow, watching how these people did not swagger as the Silurians did. They glided surely, heads high, limbs easy and relaxed, in a pleasing, fluid motion like deer loping gracefully across a field, but somehow their very symmetry was menacing, and Caradoc knew that they could turn and kill with lightning speed, still with that inborn elegance. They passed between the stone huts from which curious children peeped and barking dogs ran, then turned to the rear of a building and were blasted suddenly by the hot odor of molten metal. There were kennels, but no stables. With legs like those, Eurgain

272

thought, watching Sine's long, breech-clad limbs swing, they surely do not need horses.

The Council hut stood in the center of the village, surrounded by a low stone wall. At the opening three more chiefs waited, swords sheathed, slings wound around their enameled belts. Two of them were helmless but the tallest one had a thin circlet of silver about his brow. The late, soft sun lay golden on their bronze brooches, their golden torcs, their jeweled arms, and gaily patterned cloaks. It gleamed on black hair that was smooth as ravens' wings. Bran led them to a halt.

"Caradoc, Ricon of the Catuvellauni, has come, Lord," he said briefly, and the man in the center bent his gaze on Caradoc. He was taller than any of them and built like a healthy oak, straight and solid and somehow satisfying to regard. His eyes were set wide and were full of a clean, open severity. Indeed, his whole face reflected wisdom and austerity from the stern mouth to the high forehead. If this man can be won to me, Caradoc thought, I will never need to worry about treachery or deceit from him. Something of the same character was revealed in Cinnamus; an open freedom of trust and honor coupled with the ability to kill well if need be. There was something else in the face, too. A nobility, the touch of innocence that Caradoc had never seen before in his life. He felt that he was in the presence of an enigma, a spellbinder, and he could do nothing but stare rudely at his host.

The chief smiled warmly and held out his arm. "Welcome to my tuath, Caradoc ap Cunobelin. If you come in peace then peace be upon you. Enter, and eat. There is meat, bread, and beer." He was exquisitely polite and Caradoc had to forcibly remind himself to be on his guard. These men were legend among the tribes, and while the others were blatantly, virilely excellent warriors, the Ordovices' strengths were hidden and ran much deeper. He took the proffered wrist. "I am Emrys, chief of chiefs. This is my bard Cerdic and my shield-bearer Ninian."

Caradoc answered with the formal words of thanks and introduced his train, and when Llyn stepped forward Emrys's dark eyebrows rose. "I did not know that the Catuvellauni blooded their boys so young," he remarked, seeing the torc about Llyn's neck, and Caradoc said quickly, "We do not. We wait for the proper age. But my son performed a deed of great bravery and I awarded him his manhood."

"Indeed? Then he shall be accorded a chief's place in the hut. Come within." He slid between the doorskins with the same lithe fluidity and they all followed.

The hut was full of light and the Catuvellaunians, bracing themselves for the usual stuffy dimness of the many Council huts they had entered, blinked in momentary confusion. Then they saw why. The circular stone wall ended well below the sloping overhang of the thatched roof so that at any time of the day sunlight and air might pour into the room and the smoke might drift out. Trophies were slung together in threes and fours on the roof supports. The fire burned in the center, its flames battling the shafts of soft, late sunlight, and six chiefs sat cross-legged on the skins, seemingly sunk in thought for they gazed at the ground or into the fire and reflectively lifted their cups to drink. When their lord pushed through the door-skins they rose, graciously greeted the Catuvellaunians behind him, then went back to their silent musing.

"Sit," Emrys said. "When the sun goes down we will feast. Are you hungry now? Would you like cheese or bread?"

The servants did not wait for an answer but were already moving, carrying small tables to the strangers, placing platters on them. Caradoc noted that Bran had been served first, with a deferential respect. Emrys had folded himself a little apart from the travelers, his train nearby. The lady in the wolf mask went down beside him, her long legs stretched out before her. Caradoc wished she would remove her cover, wondering whether it concealed a face disfigured by disease. He drank his beer and sank his teeth into the strong cheese.

"I have never before met foreigners from the lowlands," the wolf lady said. "Tell me, is it true that the freewomen of the Catuvellaun no longer know how to wield their blades and they now wear them only for show?"

Caradoc tensed. He knew this game only too well, having been forced to play it in Council with the Demetae. But this time the insults that would slowly grow more pointed would not be aimed at him, and he wished he had left Eurgain with the Silures. She stirred beside him, put down her cup, and folded her arms.

"It is not true," she answered mildly. "Perhaps, Lady, the Ordovice freewomen wish to delude themselves into believing they have no equal in swordplay, and so delight in exaggerating certain rumors."

"H'm." Sine lay back on one elbow. "But is it not a fact that once a Catuvellaun freewoman has given birth to three children she loses interest in her honor and hangs up her sword?"

"Bitch," Caradoc heard Eurgain mutter under her breath. "You must ask the Druithin if you want to know the difference between fact and seeming fact," she said aloud. "I suggest to you, Lady, that you ask Bran without delay. You obviously need help in divining this difference. The Catuvellaun freewomen are the greatest sword-women in Albion, for they know how to combine the gentle art of child-rearing with the noble art of war. The women of other tribes are not so well-rounded. They give all their attention to fighting, to disguise the fact that in their womanhood they are deficient."

Sine was quiet for a moment, acknowledging the blow and considering her next attack. Eurgain appeared unconcerned, and in the silence she ate a little and raised her cup, but Caradoc felt her aura of concentration like a bubble of ice.

"Such a balance is admirable, if it can be achieved," Sine remarked. "But the Catuvellaun women have not achieved it, and their children have blunted their swords. Only the Catuvellaun warriors met the invading legions of Rome. The women stayed at Camulodunon, huddling around their offspring."

The gloves were coming off now. All in the hut listened avidly, not stirring, the Ordovice chiefs smiling, their mouths open in anticipation. Caradoc could have broken in to point out that Catuvellaun women were obedient to their oaths and he, as ricon, had ordered them to stay at home, but to do so would have been to transgress the rules of the game, and he sat with lips clamped shut.

"Catuvellaun women do not need to prove their bravery in foolishness, nor do they feel impelled to strut and boast and provoke others into a show of arms out of doubt in their own ability," Eurgain returned. "It was better for the women to defend the town if the men were defeated, rather than to rush into battle and leave all to be burned, and we are sufficiently sure of our own power, Ordovice Lady, to feel no need to explain our stand. It is nobler to die in defence than to live in victory. Your pride is blind arrogance, and your honor is only unstained because here in the mountains it has never been put to the test. You Ordovice women remain unblooded."

"Do you call me a coward?"

"No. I only call you ignorant and ill-mannered."

Emrys raised his eyebrows. No tribe was as polite as the Ordovices but the game had taken a swift turn and the challenge would not be arrived at gently, couched in the right language.

Sine swung to her feet. "But I call you a coward, Catuvellaun nursemaid, and I will wager my life to prove that your honor, like your sword, is rotting away."

"Do not accept," Caradoc whispered to his wife, but she was already rising.

"This is not your business, Caradoc," she whispered back fiercely. "Even if you care nothing for my honor, which seems to be the case, I care. If I do not fight you may as well scurry back to Madoc." There was disgust in her tone and he said no more.

"Do not kill the lady," Emrys called to Sine. "She is our guest."

Sine smiled down at him. "I may or I may not, depending on how well she fights. Come outside, mother of three. Can you draw your sword?"

Cinnamus rose with Eurgain. "I have been told that they fight in one long, continuous dance," he murmured in her ear. "One action blending into another. Remember that."

"Thank you, Cin." Eurgain strode from the hut after Sine, and all the chiefs straggled after her.

Emrys came to stand beside Caradoc. "Your wife's shield-bearer did not come with you," he observed, and Caradoc answered curtly, "Eurgain has no shield-bearer in her train." He thought of adding that Eurgain had no shield either but he wanted no conversation just then and he went to the warm earth, squatting with Cinnamus and Caelte as the two women shed their cloaks.

Bran stood apart, with his arms folded and his eyes on the slowly reddening sky. Like Caradoc, he knew that if Eurgain was defeated the door to western unity would close, politely but firmly. He was anxious for Eurgain but his thoughts were fixed on the larger concern, while Caradoc could think only of his calm, terse wife lying bloody under the sword of this strange, ferocious woman. Cinnamus watched Eurgain with a professional eye. She was glancing over the terrain, and he was pleased she had noticed a slight slope and how the setting sun sent its light angling over it. Sine gestured and her shield-bearer ran forward, the enormous bronze weight in his hands. Like her mask, it was figured into the shape of a wolf's head, but its eyes were two chunks of yellow crystal. She took it, wriggling the leather thongs onto her arm, as Eurgain stood, feet apart, both hands resting on her sword's hilt.

"What is this, Wolf Lady?" Eurgain called. "Do the Ordovice women always hide behind their shields?"

Cinnamus chuckled. "She is wily, Lord," he whispered to Caradoc. She and Gladys had never used shields, and without hers the Ordovice lady would be thrown off balance.

Sine paused, her eyes flicking across at Eurgain, as Eurgain steadily stared back, only her fingers betraying any tension. I wish you would take off your mask, she thought. I wish that I could read your face, know whether the lack of a shield will slow you down. Sine shrugged and pulled her arm from the thongs, handing the shield to her chief. "It is all the same to me," she shouted back, but Eurgain heard a tremor in the words.

"If you wish, you may fight with the sun at your back," she offered. "I do not mind." Now move, Lady, she thought. If you put the sun behind you, you will be standing on the slope. The rise in the ground

276

will keep the light from my eyes and you will have to slash at me uphill.

"How confident you are!" Sine sneered, taking three steps so that the sun struck her green shoulders. "Would you like to hand me your sword also?"

Eurgain did not reply but lifted her weapon to her husband and then to Sine, confident she had taken every advantage to herself. She was tired and in a strange place, and would have to work quickly to stay alive, but when her opponent saluted her she realized she was happy.

The watching chiefs stopped chattering and silence fell. The two women closed, Eurgain with both hands grasping her hilt, her sword high, Sine visibly unsure of what to do with her naked and weightless left arm, her mask sparkling gold and red as she moved. Eurgain did not wait for her to decide. The blade left her shoulder, came whistling in an arc, but it was a testing stroke, a slow feeler, and Sine easily stepped to avoid it. Eurgain followed with a back-handed swing, strong enough to bring her to the brink of unbalance. And then Sine struck. Those watching saw her left arm move out and her sword glide in. Her knees flexed with a slow elegance that bespoke rigid control, and as her body eased forward she seemed to fall gracefully into the reach of Eurgain's sword. Eurgain lunged for the long neck but the sword was in its place and speeding to her shoulder, a hawk falling from the sky to its prey. Eurgain let go one hand, brought her sword upright, and sent it crashing sideways. To draw back would have been to lose her arm. The blades screamed along the length of each other and Sine's body bent like a bow as she fought to keep the sword in her grip. Eurgain backed away and poised for another sweep, expecting Sine to straighten, but Sine, still bent, her left arm high, seemed to ripple in under Eurgain's high stroke and Eurgain once more had to deflect a slash that would have cut her in two. Sine's body seemed to move in a slow, elegant dance, without music or formal steps, one lithe stance blending with the next as she adapted effortlessly to the fortunes of the encounter. She seemed disconnected from her sword as it wove its own clean, rapid pattern of death, a pattern Eurgain began to see. It did no good to focus her attention on the body; it was the other, faster dance that counted. She began to see something else, also: without her shield, Sine's balance was upset, her movements too swift, almost uncontrollably so, her blade arriving at its appointed place before its point of contact. The slope of the land further aggravated Sine's tenuous balance, and Eurgain began to time her own strokes to fall more slowly, with less force but more direction. Her wrist and legs began to ache under the strain, but she heard

Sine's ragged breath and knew that she too must soon fight at a standstill. Sweat ran into Eurgain's eyes but she dared not blink it away. Sine was upon her again—cut up, slash down, parry, and disengage, as the minutes went by. Sine's new offensives lacked power, the sound of blade striking blade became a sullen slither of metal on metal. The sun slipped to the horizon as their feet slowed and their movements disintegrated to drunken staggers. Sine stumbled suddenly, and, unthinking, she covered her breast with her left arm as she went down on one knee. Eurgain summoned up the last of her strength and leaped but she was met by an arm that swung desperately for her ankle. She aimed a blow, but, weary, her arm played her false and the blade swung wild. Pain flamed up her leg. A sigh rippled fast around the circle of watching chiefs as Eurgain sank to her knees, gripped her hilt in both shaking hands, and raised her sword high. In the second before it fell, Sine rolled away and rose up, her own sword held out, but neither woman had the strength to make another blow. Blade smashed against blade, lowered, and dropped in the grass. The combatants knelt facing one another, panting and trembling, sweat pouring from them.

"Take back your words," Eurgain croaked.

Sine swallowed. "No." Eurgain fell forward, her hands grasping for Sine's throat, but Sine toppled sideways, her fingers entwined in Eurgain's fair hair. Neither woman moved. They lay weakly in the grass while the onlookers waited breathlessly.

Eurgain released her hold on Sine's neck and Sine, still fighting for breath, tore off the mask and cast it onto the ground beside her. Eurgain stared at the sharp, cleanly contoured face, dominated by a pointed chin and two black eyes. It had a wild, animal beauty—a brown complexion like still water, a thin, delicate nose—but there was no softness in its keen curves or in the hard glitter of the big eyes.

"Perhaps we will fight again, Eurgain," she said, wiping her forehead on her tunic, "but let it be side by side next time. I think that I am a better warrior, but you make up for your physical lack in a devious and lethal mind." Eurgain struggled up and looked into the newly exposed face of her opponent. "We will be friends?" Sine asked, accepting Eurgain's examination. "Yes," Eurgain replied, still searching the other's eyes. "We will."

They both stood, swaying, and then together turned to stagger through the chiefs and into the Council hut.

In the ensuing days Caradoc found yet another dimension to this reality. The Ordovices were a silent, thinking people. They smiled often, slowly and reflectively, but they seldom laughed. They settled their quarrels by the sword and always to the death. At their feasts there was little talk. The men and women would sit eating and drinking, watching the bard as he played and sang with eyes that held a thousand spells and a thousand mysteries. They listened to music that was hauntingly, frighteningly beautiful, a wild, undisciplined cascade of abandonment that did not thrill the senses but incited the soul to a ferment of longing. Caelte spent hours in the company of the bard, perpetually excited, jolted from his warm, sunny security by a new truth. And the whole valley was possessed by magic, as though reality flowed perilously close to another world and sometimes mingled with it, like the terrible, wonderful patterns and faces on the chiefs' jewels, savage or trancelike, expressing the duality of waking dream and sleeping life that was the pure core of the men of the west.

Eurgain blended immediately, as Gladys would have done. She and Sine, Emrys's wife, soon took to eating and spending the days together, clambering up the steep hillsides, hunting boar, and crossing swords on the practice ground, while Llyn repeated the story of his blooding over and over again for the admiring sons of the tribe, and Caradoc, Bran, and the others sat in Council.

Here, at the last, Caradoc was forced to call upon all his skill. In spite of their labyrinthian introspection the Ordovician chieftains and freemen were obstinate, clever men. Caradoc found that he did not want to accuse them of cowardice as he had Madoc and the Silures. The charge would have been preposterous. He could speak only of the forts and posting stations creeping closer year by year, of the once-free men who now wore slave chains and labored on roads and in fields they had once owned, and of the ships full of the flower of the tribes, young men who would never ride free in the forests again. The chiefs rose politely, spoke quietly, listened attentively, but Caradoc felt the barrier between them grow higher. They simply did not need him. They were isolated in more than body. They were isolated in spirit.

Then, one night, after six days of fruitless talk, out of sheer desperation, he told them bluntly that if they did not accept his advice, if they did not join with the other men of the west, their goddess and the Dagda would desert them and their tuath would become a place of disease and death. They sat up immediately, their eyes going to Bran and Emrys, and the latter looked at Caradoc with wonder, rising. "Bran, is this true?" he asked. "Speak now, and either refute this man or give us truth. What do your brethren on Mona say?"

Bran rose and Caradoc sat down, sweat beading on his forehead and trickling past his temples. I think I have done it, he thought breathlessly. But how? Where did that idea come from?

"Freemen!" Bran said. "You all know the old law by which you live.

Worship the gods, do no evil, maintain your honor.' You have heard from the mouths of refugees who flee to the holy island through your country how the Romans seek to destroy our gods and enslave us, and how they have sworn to kill every Druid. Can any of you doubt that Rome must not be allowed to remain in Albion? And who is left to drive them out but you? Can the gods be made to serve a people who can only worship them in slavery? It would be an affront and the Dagda would flee from you. How can you maintain your honor with slave chains around your necks? Go to your seer, your invoker, your goddess as your brothers have done, and learn that my brethren order war to preserve the service of the gods. You know me, freemen! You trust me. I know you, and your fears. Caradoc is not a ricon without a tuath, seeking to take power from your chief. He comes to offer himself as arviragus for a while, leading free people until the oppressors are cast out. Then he returns to his own people, as is the custom. But you must decide for yourselves in open Council, and let me warn you. Refuse Caradoc aid, and shut your eyes and ears at your peril. The Romans will come here, to this valley, and kill the chiefs and take the women and children for slaves, and the Dagda and the goddess will fold their arms and look the other way." He stopped speaking and sat down and a deep silence fell, full of bewilderment and suspicion.

Then Emrys rose, his calm, stern face resigned. "We know in our hearts," he said slowly, "that Bran's words are true, yet we will ask of the Dagda and the goddess. And while we ask, Caradoc may journey in our country, as he has done among the Silures and the Demetae, for I am lord of a scattered people. Then we will hold a greater Council, calling all chiefs from the hidden valleys, and make our decision. Does any freeman disagree?" Heads were shaken, but dubiously, then Gervase spoke for them all.

"If the Catuvellaunian can conquer the mountains then he can lead us," he said. "For we are the mountains."

When Caradoc would look back to the days that followed, the memories would be clouded, obscure, as though his mind had compartmentalized them and then shut the door, and the only remembering came with thoughts that escaped from under its protecting rim. He was a haunted, driven man, he and Eurgain, Bran, and his chiefs clambering among a desolation of cruel rock, wandering lost for days beside cold streams that ran through deep, sun-starved gorges as silent as death, and they were often hungry, always weary. The Ordovices had refused him a guide.

"If you cannot best the mountains you are not one of us," Emrys had said, not unkindly, and so Caradoc and his little band had set off alone into the wilderness, leaving Llyn as a hostage. "Pardon us," Emrys had explained firmly but politely. "He must stay. It is the custom, as you know." They knew, but Caradoc, worn down to the bare bones of his reason, had to shoulder this new anxiety. He missed Llyn, his cheerfulness, his comfort, his company, and felt that his luck was slowly deserting him. Eurgain would have shielded him from the hardships both within and without himself, but the wall of misunderstandings and resentments had been growing between them and he wordlessly resisted her attempts to help him. He knew that he was alone, his future hanging by a thread, and Eurgain withdrew into herself, all her energies spiraling inward as she faced the test of the mountains. She heard their challenge, she believed that his journey was a part of the testing of her own honor, and at night she lay in her blanket, taut with fascinated fear and a strange, warm thrill, as she listened to the siren voices of winds soughing in the rocky funnels and hidden crags around her. She was happy in spite of everything, muscles and mind stretched gloriously to the limits of their endurance, and she proudly put away thoughts of her failing marriage.

They stumbled across many farmsteads tucked into the folds of grassy slopes where the teaks swooped down before rising afresh, stone huts ringed by stone walls enclosing granaries and workshops. They were inhabited by silent, tall chiefs and their peasants and families, who welcomed them with the words of hospitality and fed them, and who listened to him gravely, without comment. When their nights were spent in the shelter of these chiefs Caradoc always set Cinnamus or Caelte to guard, for he knew that in spite of the immunity Bran brought them, some Ordovician chieftain might decide to slay them all and take their weapons, and Emrys would conclude that they had perished in the trackless wastes of his country. When he left them they would give him directions to the next farmstead, tell him to go in safety, walk in peace, all with the magnificent aloofness of their mountains. Then Caradoc would set off down their valleys, among their shaggy cattle and indifferent, staring sheep, still not knowing whether his words had even been digested.

Autumn found them still wandering in the northwestern reaches of Emrys's territory. The hot summer wind gave way to a sudden, deceptive calm before the howling gales of winter, and when they rose each morning their blankets were stiff with frost. Now they spoke little to each other. It was as if the mountains pressed down and around them, hanging from their necks like ugly, misshapen jewels, and each unnecessary word was an effort that made them consider twice if it were worthwhile.

Caradoc said nothing at all. In the mornings, when Cinnamus went off to hunt and Caelte laid the fire, Eurgain and Bran would exchange a few words on the weather, the cooking to be done, the miles to be covered. But Caradoc sat apart, his legs crossed and his thin hands on his knees, his empty eyes gazing at each new horizon. If they spoke to him he often did not hear them. He was reaching a crisis, though he did not know it. Bran knew it, but he also knew that he was powerless to aid. The fire must be entered, the dross burned away if Caradoc was to emerge an arviragus, even though nothing might be left but a flame-scoured hulk.

Eurgain was almost past pitying or suffering for him. In self-defence she cut the living cord of love between them and nursed the maimed stump quietly, asking and giving nothing until the time when he returned to himself. It seemed that with his utter silence a new force pulsed through his arguments to the isolated Ordovicians, as if the gathering in of his thoughts produced a more potent spell. Sitting in dark huts, on wind-swept hillsides, in the shadow of great boulders, Eurgain listened intently with her eyes on the strange families who gathered to hear him. Her clean intuition told her that they were moved, even as she was time and again, as the strong, stirring words poured from her husband's twisted mouth and struck them all.

As for Caradoc himself, he found that all his extraneous thoughts were killed before their birth and only one thing dominated his dreams and his waking hours: the coming clash with Rome and his own calling to lead the tribes. Sometimes, in the one sweet, unguarded moment of the day when he was emerging from sleep to the consciousness of a burdensome reality, he wondered whether perhaps Bran was secretly drugging him in order to produce this screaming, mind-burning obsession. It was not an impossibility. When it came to hatred for Rome, the Druithin were ruthless. But Caradoc dismissed the idea. Bran was an old friend. Bran would have told him. Or would he?

Then one evening they broke through a stand of trees guarding the foothills to the peak they had just struggled across, wading through crisp red and brown leaves that sailed about them on the new coldness of a merciless wind, and they came upon a village. It nestled cozily with the wood to its back, and beyond it was the sea. They all paused and drew deep breaths of the salt-tanged air, and watched gray breakers curl and fold toward them. For the first time in weeks a peace stole over them and they looked at one another with an abashed, puzzled embarrassment, as if they had been in a deep dream all this time, or under a holding spell. Cinnamus sighed. "Mona, holy

Mona," he murmured. "What strange and marvelous things I have seen since I left Camulodunon!" The island lay calmly, a black, hazed bulk three hundred yards from where they rested, and Bran raised an arm and saluted it.

"Soul of the people," he said quietly. "The heart of freedom. Come. Let us go down and find fire and food. These chiefs know me, and the village is full of my brethren. We can sleep tonight without fear." They shrugged their tattered, faded cloaks higher on their shoulders and walked down the slope behind him.

That night they stayed in the village, resting, eating, and nursing tired bodies. The chiefs of the village were used to battered, defenceless strangers. People straggled in at all times of the year seeking the sanctuary of the holy island, beaten and hopeless, bringing nothing with them but tales of Rome's brutality and a need for peace. Caradoc was received kindly and he spoke to the Council, telling the people of his vision, and they understood. They, unlike their ricon far away, had a very good idea of what the domination of Rome would mean to the men of the west and they gave Caradoc the first open, unstinted support he had received since he left Madoc and the Silures. He relaxed. He slept well. But he and Eurgain remained strangers, looking at each other with eyes that prisoned the sweetness of the past and could not put the key of love to the lock of a lonely, painful present. She was too proud to face a rebuff, and he was too preoccupied to care.

In the morning they crossed to Mona. The wind was high and cold, fretting the narrows into boiling white spray, and the island itself alternately gleamed green under the sun and was plunged into a brooding gloom as the big gray clouds raced over it. The fishing boat yawed and bucketed and Caradoc and the others clung grimly to the sides, their faces and hands soon slick with salt water, but within a very few minutes the two taciturn Ordovician fishermen were stepping into the knee-high shallows and the boat was beached. Cinnamus knelt and kissed the sandy, sloping shore, Bran gave his hand to Eurgain as she struggled to keep her footing in the hissing undertow, but Caradoc and Caelte strode together to where sand became pebbles and then grass. Far to the right, beyond the oak groves that pressed close to the beach, the land rose, still thickly forested, but before them lay softly undulating fields glinting golden with uneven stubble between the tree trunks. Here and there smoke rose from the roofs of many huts and houses, then was whipped into nothingness by the steady gale. From where he stood, Caradoc could sense movement in the woods. The voices of children came to him, twigs crackled underfoot, the laughter of women filtered from the verges of the little fields, and he turned to Caelte.

"There is peace here," he said. "A spell of contentment that could persuade me to forget my duty and sink under it like a stone dropping through water."

"I know, Lord," Caelte replied. "I feel that I should sing, but I have no song. How far away is Madoc, and Emrys, and the dark stain of Rome!"

Not far enough, Caradoc thought, his eyes watering from the sting of the wind or a long-forgotten uprush of emotion, he could not tell which, and then Bran, Cinnamus, and his wife joined him and they all followed Bran along the path that ran narrow but sure through the oaks. They did not hurry. They walked steadily, their eyes never still, for many other paths branched from the one they were treading and each seemed to beckon in friendly understanding. One track, running straight to a treed hillock, gave Caradoc a glimpse of a stone altar, a ring of wooden stakes with carved boar and human heads upon them, and another ended at a palisade, with the roofless walls of a shrine visible and the quiet, folded form of a Druid sitting before the gate. After a mile the trees gave way to more fields, and the travelers could see how, though the forest curved and swept this way and that, the gently rolling land was heavily cultivated. The crops had been harvested, and now women and children gleaned, their backs bent and their cloaks spread high in the wind. They straightened and called greetings as the group passed, and many bowed to Bran, but only Caelte answered their gay words. Cinnamus was lost in wonder, setting his feet down carefully on the sacred soil, and Eurgain marched with her arms folded and her chin high, conscious of her husband's dour, preoccupied glare. For two miles they trudged through stiff yellow stubble, under the branches of the leafless oaks, past huts full of the homely smells of cooking and the murmur of voices, then they came to a river. It flowed slowly, a wide, green expanse of marshy, bird-clouded water, and huts straggled along both its banks to form a town. Beyond it the land continued flat and golden, but far to the northeast Caradoc saw it begin to rise, to hump, then to be lost in a forested haze. Bran halted.

The Council hut was large, wooden, and protected by a high palisade that was in turn ringed by more of the wooden stakes carved at their summits into solemn, self-contained faces which gazed out over the heads of the passers-by with stolid indifference. At the low wooden gate of the palisade two chiefs stood guard, spears upright in one hand and swords drawn in the other, and before them a group of

Druids was gathered, five or six of them, hands tucked into white sleeves, listening intently and smilingly to one of their kind. He was tall and brawny. The sleeves of his tunic were folded back, revealing brown, hard-muscled arms crossed on his broad chest. His beard was a vibrant, luxurious brown, and the spasmodic sunlight flickered on a dozen bronze rings tied into brown hair that fell tousled and healthy to the middle of his white-clad straight back. As they watched him, he unfolded his arms, pointed to his head, and laughed, and his companions laughed with him. Then he saw the silent band and swung toward them, arm outstretched, teeth bared in a wide, warm smile, and Caradoc stiffened in surprise while Caelte breathed a sigh of shock and behind them both, Eurgain started. The man's eyes were blue. Not the deep, rich flower blue of Eurgain's own, or the green blue of the ocean, but the palest, most delicate shade, almost no shade at all, almost milky in their opalescence. They did not glitter, nor did they reflect the plays of light and shade around them, and the pupils were pale also, the gray of an overcast dawn. If Caradoc had not seen them pass quickly over the group he would have believed that this Druid was blind. Bran took three steps and bowed.

"Master," he said, "I bring you Caradoc, his wife, and his train."

"Yes, yes, I know," the rich voice answered. "I dreamed of you last night, Caradoc, and the night before. I saw you sitting with your back to a rock, and it was night. I have been expecting you." The arm tinkling with silver clasped Caradoc's own, warm and strong, and seeing Caradoc's shock, the full mouth parted again in mirth. "You did not expect me, though, did you, my friend? You imagined the master of Druithin to be an old graybeard like Bran, bowed with the weight of wisdom? Well, I am sorry to disappoint you!"

Caradoc looked into the young face with its old eyes, and suddenly Bran did indeed seem to him to be a wizened, palsied dotard. He wanted to bow but could not, and then the master was beckoning behind him.

"Eurgain, come here." She walked forward, and he took her hand, stroking her cheek, her hair, then he kissed her softly. "I saw you also," he said, "with your feet sunk in the earth and your fingers straining for the stars. I saw you at your window, suffering for the mysteries of both. You should have been a Druid, Eurgain, for then your feet would never have touched the earth and you would not be torn. Ah well." He smiled. "Fingers are all very well, but they cannot carry the heart where it wants to go. And you." He turned to Cinnamus and a moment of pain clouded his features, but his eyes did not change expression. They seemed to be a mirror looking only upon his inner world and reflecting back to him his visions. "The precious seed

285

is strewn upon the ground," he murmured, "and trodden underfoot. Yet how else shall the new crop spring up? I salute you, Ironhand. An arrow is not good enough for you." And to everyone's amazement he knelt before a bewildered Cinnamus and kissed his sword, but before the moment could become an embarrassment he sprang up and enfolded Caelte, laughing as he did so. "Caelte, Caelte!" he exclaimed. "Your soul is like the crystal flow of the purest forest spring! A gift to you would be like a stone flung at a mountain, for you have the greatest gift of all, and do not think that I speak of your beautiful voice!" He let Caelte go, tightened his girdle with one swift tug, then turned away. "Come into the Council hut," he ordered. "We will eat and laugh and talk of nothing at all, for this is holy Mona, and here you may rest."

The hut was spacious, clean, and warm after the chillness of the wind. Even at that hour of the morning it was full. Men stood around the fire over which a cauldron sent gusts of fragrant steam to the ceiling. Women squatted or sat cross-legged on the skins that were scattered everywhere, clutching children or bundles of possessions and looking anxiously to the Druids who moved among them. No one even glanced at Caradoc and his train as they shed their cloaks and took the bowls handed to them by Bran.

"We must serve ourselves here," Bran said. "Every servant who could be spared is threshing the grain, and as you can see, there are new refugees from Gaul. My brethren are busy." They drew bowlfuls of hot soup and found space by the door in which to sit, and they sipped it slowly, savoring it, while one by one the newly arrived families went out with a Druid, the men swinging their children onto their shoulders, the women gathering up their few treasures and hooding themselves against the cold. Soon the crowd thinned to a few chiefs who had just returned from hunting and small groups of Druids who sat or stood and ate silently, their eyes on the master who at last came to sit with the Catuvellauni.

"You had some difficulty with Emrys, Caradoc," he remarked, stirring his porridge with a polished stick which he then licked clean and stowed away in the folds of his tunic. "I am not surprised. He and his kin have been tucked away in the mountains for many ages and the events of the outside world have not touched them at all. They never come to the Samain court, for they never have cases to settle with other tribes, and it is a pity. They have become too proud, too sure of their own invincibility, which causes them to be vulnerable to the glib tricks of a clever speaker."

Caradoc stopped eating and glanced at him sharply, and he smiled.

"Your words to them were true, of course, but I do not think that you yourself believed them, did you?"

"I don't know."

"Well, it does not matter. You have stirred them up, and I think that I must go and stir them still further. I would like to see my cousin again."

"Your cousin, Master?" Eurgain queried, and he nodded, his mouth full.

"Emrys is my cousin. I came to Mona when I was seven to have my dreams read, and I am still here, as you can see!" He laughed and Caradoc turned his face down to his own bowl, suddenly disappointed in this virile, muscle-bound man who laughed too much and seemed bereft of the dignity that surely ought to belong to the master of the Druithin. His feeling of depression and isolation increased and he wished that he had never crossed to Mona. He preferred his daydreams at his back, the thoughts of a powerful and mysterious figure of magic and secrecy who could weave spells against Rome while he himself wove military strategy. Now here was the master, grinning at Eurgain and scouring his porridge bowl with a piece of bread in his nimble fingers, while his bronze-ringed hair fell about his arms. Caradoc felt cheated, used somehow, and the old niggling seed of regret and longing for the past began to grow in him once more. Camulodunon, he thought sadly. My home. Why did I not surrender to Claudius and live there in peace and contentment? The master handed his bowl to a young attendant and rose. "I would like to show you the island," he said to them. "Are you warm now? Is your hunger appeased? Good! Then let us go. Bran, you need not tire your limbs with us. Stay here."

They walked many miles that day, through country that was more populous than any they had yet seen, more so even than the thick-scattered people of their own tribe. Everywhere huts were going up, round the edges of the fields and in under the oak groves' rims. The landless fugitives from Rome's peace had brought their dishonored gods with them so that each clearing guarded an altar or a stone deity, and many held the pits or pools into which the offerings were thrown. Apart from the armed chiefs who had guarded the Council hut they had seen no weapons, and Cinnamus asked why.

"The people come from every tribe," the master told him, "and here on Mona we wish only peace. Their weapons are given to their gods as a thanksgiving for this refuge, and I put them to work instead of to fighting. We have been able to clear many new fields since our population has grown, and grain is produced most plentifully. The gods are

287

pleased with their new home, and bless the soil, and the Ordovices grow fat!" He chuckled, then turned in under the shelter of a wind-break woven from young oak saplings and squatted, and the company went down with him. The whistle of the steady wind dropped to a low humming, and they loosened their cloaks and dropped their hoods with relief, looking with surprise at the distance they had come. Behind them the land had been steadily rising, and before them the ocean sparkled blue and lacy-white where a wide, calm bay had been carved. Fishing boats lay on their sides in the sand and their owners sat and gossiped around the fire they had kindled, but the company was so high that neither the crackling of the burning wood nor the voices of the men could be heard.

"Master, where are the halls of learning?" Eurgain asked him tentatively. "I had thought . . . I had hoped . . . Where are the secret places?"

He sat back on his heels, his hands clasped loosely on the ground. "The halls of learning are all around you, Eurgain," he replied. "Did you not notice the groups of young men and Druids, pacing here and there? The long, slow absorption of knowledge takes place wherever the teacher wants to teach, be it sitting in a field, walking by the river, or standing in the shrines, and his pupils move with him. The whole island is alive with the flow of thought, and after twenty years of study there is no tiny rock, no wrinkle in the rivers, no sacred tree that remains undiscovered and that does not have the power to recall some lesson to the mind of its observer. This is one reason why Mona itself is called holy. The very mud cries out to the initiate of all that he has learned. And those children who come for five years, or ten, take back to their tribes a fierce love of this, their true cradle."

"But what of the places of divination? The places where the stars are read? Where do the soothsayers practice their art?"

"You have a greed, Eurgain," he rebuked her quietly. "Beware. Yet for the love of your soul I will cause you to be shown a place where the evening star gives up her secrets. Caelte, there is a young man here who is engaged in making harps. Would you like to talk with him?" He chatted comfortably to Caelte, to Eurgain, to Cinnamus. Caradoc was silent, gazing out over the peaceful scene below him, aware that though the master had not addressed him once since the moment of greeting his whole inner attention was fixed on Caradoc alone.

Caradoc felt the probing concentration of him as a disquiet, a disturbance of his thoughts that had been growing ever since their boat touched the sandy shore. Memories long dead, long stripped of their

288

power, misted through his mind, trailing anger or remorse. Aricia was there, sitting on the floor of his hut at Camulodunon and giggling, and though he believed that he had conquered the pain of her, yet now he felt nothing but a full-blown desire and he knew that he had not healed himself. Togodumnus passed by, his eager, adoring chiefs trotting in his wake, and the wave of jealousy that shook him was so violent that his hand stiffened on the hilt of his sword. Jealous? Was I jealous of Tog? Ah no! he shouted in his mind. That was not true! He was my brother. I loved him! But after Tog came Eurgain, long, fringed blue tunic sweeping the ground, gold on the gold on her hair and silver on the whiteness of her arms, and the twinge of jealousy widened to a throbbing. Another lie! he called to the memory. I love her, love her, I have no reason to wish her harm, I do not keep her from her rightful place, it is not ture, I do not care how much of herself she hides from me!

He grunted aloud, and there was a sudden lull in the conversation. They all looked at him, and he met the nightmare eyes of the master with a new emotion. This man was a force more potent than the graybeards of his imagination, more dangerous than the strongest spell his shadowy, cloistered vision of a master had ever conjured in the cause of victory. Caradoc was afraid.

"I think we should return to the town and feed our bodies once more," the master said lightly, and they rose. As they did so a new and final memory blossomed in Caradoc's mind, as clear and sweet and fresh as the moment itself had been. Gladys came to him, walking along the clifftop to where the combined host had gathered in their fruitless wait for Plautius. Her face was tanned, solemn. Her eyes held sanity and steady warmth. The sea breeze floated out her long, dark hair behind her and wrapped the tunic tight about her legs, and as she approached he smelled the salt on her, and the seaweed, and the rock herbs of the cliff. His heart opened like the petals of a bruised flower under her cleanliness, her honesty. "Have you considered telling the omens?" she asked him. "I can do it, Caradoc." The master was watching him with a tiny grin. Caradoc turned and followed the others down the scrub-choked slope.

They returned to the town and ate a late afternoon meal, and by the time they had finished it the swift autumn dusk was beginning. The wind abated with its coming, and the scraped sky stayed clear. The master beckoned them all outside where a Druid waited for them, and Eurgain was introduced to him.

"He will show you the evening star," the master said, "but you must hurry. The sun is already setting." Without a word Eurgain turned away, following the glimmer of gray cloak, and the master pointed. "Caelte, follow the path that veers to the left. At the end of it is the hut of the bard-craftsman. Make merry music!"

"Cin, will you come?" Caelte asked, but Cinnamus yawned and shook his head.

"No. I will go back into the Council hut and talk some more with the warriors of Gaul. We have many stories to share. Then I will sleep. Caradoc, do you need me?"

Caradoc looked at the master. "No, Cin, I do not think I shall need you tonight. Sleep well."

"You also, Lord. A good night." He plunged back toward the door-skins, and Caradoc and the master were alone under the pink, paling sky.

The man gestured and moved away and Caradoc went after him, his body weary from the walking he had done that day but his mind wide awake. They glided swiftly along the track by the river, now placid with the last shreds of the sunset, then the master abruptly plunged in under the oaks to their right and was lost in shadows. Caradoc trudged after him, feeling the ground rising sluggishly beneath his feet. For half an hour they paced the silent forest, then all at once Caradoc found himself out on the crown of a hill. It was bare, and he could tell that at one time the trees had gathered right to the summit, for tiny saplings brushed his legs where the forest struggled vainly to regain lost ground. Now, three huge rings of stones marched peremptorily around the naked space, one inside the other, and in the center stood a low stone altar. There were no stakes, no heads, no god. Only the clean severity of weathered stone and long, frost-gripped grasses.

The master walked straight to the altar. He did not glance back to see if Caradoc was following, and with a wave of resentment it seemed to Caradoc that the man had forgotten he was there. He strode through the circles and came up to the altar to see the master remove a small leather pouch from his belt and tip a pile of powdery, grayish grains into the hollow that had been scooped out of the stone. Then he spoke. "See how dark it has become," he said. "I can hardly see you, and you cannot see me," and suddenly Caradoc noticed that full darkness had indeed fallen, and between the Druid and himself was a wall of blackness that his eyes could hardly pierce. "Now we wait," the master said, turning to face the east, and Caradoc also turned, wondering what marvel he would see. But the night was calm. A few stars pricked out, their light still muted, and as yet the moon had not appeared. In the trees a nightjar rasped his ugly song. The two men stood motionless while the stars swung higher, then all at once it was there, the moon, three quarters to the full and very clear, its blue-shadowed surface aloof. The master sighed. "Watch very carefully, Caradoc," he murmured. "Keep your eyes on the stones beneath the moon's face," and Caradoc strained to see.

After a few minutes, a ray of moonlight touched the base of one of the stones in the farthest circle. Slowly, almost imperceptibly, it traveled upward, until for a moment it crowned the blunt, plain shaft with a drop of dry water, then Caradoc lost it only to find it again, halfway up the stone that stood in the second circle, directly behind the first. Once more the light slid up, tipped the stone, then fell to begin another ascent of the inmost circle. Caradoc glanced up. The moon was higher, though he had not been aware of the passage of time. He looked back. The ray of light was inching toward him now, seeming not to move, yet growing nearer, then it was crawling up the side of the altar. The Druid turned, flint at the ready. The pale light came on, and just as it found the incense cup he struck a bright spark. Immediately the powder began to smoulder, and a cloying but sweet-smelling odor filled the cold, tasteless night air.

"Look behind you," the master ordered, and Caradoc swung round. "Do you see the star that perches glittering on the top of the farthest stone? That is your star. I saw it first in that position when Bran returned from his first visit to you, when you were a very young man. Now it sits there again, full of the knowledge of your years between. Stand on the other side of the altar and breathe on the incense." Caradoc did as he was told, leaning over to be enveloped for a second in warm smoke. "Now stand very still and keep your eyes on it. Do not look at me."

Caradoc felt the man withdraw into himself, and he suddenly felt lonely. His body cooled and he began to shiver, and his thoughts slipped past the plume of incense, past the tall, gray-folded figure opposite him and the old, spell-hugging circles, to his son, and Emrys, and Madoc. What were they doing, back in the country where solid flesh met warm, solid flesh, and all one needed to understand was that swords can kill? Were they limply asleep around a warm Council fire? He pictured Llyn's curling hair spread upon his pallet, the room dim, the shadows red, the fire falling into embers. He saw him breathing softly, deeply, lost in his dreams. Dreams. He glanced across at the master, and felt horror race for a moment across his skin. The man was staring at him, eyes wide and fixed, and the moonlight had sucked all pigment from them so that now they seemed white. The rest of him was dim, dark gray tunic, a cloud of darkness that was his hair and his swarthy face, but those two grotesque, inhuman orbs wreathed in incense were full of a pale, sickly glow. Horror turned to fear, and then to panic.

For the first time in his life, Caradoc wanted to run away, run, swim, scramble sobbing through the mountains, anything to escape the coldness seeping to him from the man who no longer seemed like a man. He looked wildly at the sky. The moon was setting. Incredibly, the hours had gone by. The sight of the stars calmed him and he dropped his gaze once more to the thinning plume of smoke, and then he saw a hand reach out, cover the incense cup, and the glow abruptly died.

"You make me tired, Caradoc, with your terrors," the master said dully. "I am nothing more than a man, and nothing less." There was no timbre to his voice now, no tones of virility, no laughter. It came quietly out of the darkness like the voice of the stones themselves, heavy, ageless, without inflection. "I am a seer, the greatest seer the Druithin have ever known, but the burden is great, and what use are visions if they cannot be interpreted? Come. Let us sit under the trees and talk."

He led the way, walking slowly like a cripple, back hunched, and they both sank onto the grass beneath an oak. "I am tired," he went on after a moment. "I would like to sleep for one night, just one, without dreams." Then he seemed to recover. His hands found the interior of his sleeves and he shrugged his tunic over his knees. "I had few words for you today, Caradoc, because visions for an arviragus are not for public ears. Yet the day was not wasted. You have been seeing yourself. The magic conjured here can do that to a man, for all the unknown secrets he brings with him become clear to him, and he goes away with no hiding place anymore."

"You made the magic," Caradoc snapped, his terror gone, his voice sounding harsh and loud in his ears. "You gave me memories, Druithin, but they were false."

"Were they? All of them? I can bring truths to the surface of men's souls, Caradoc, but I cannot take away the lies. And I tell you that the memory which seeemed to you the purest was in fact the most untruthful of all. I see you look at me, and there is bitterness. Why am I chosen? you ask me in your heart. Has my life never been my own, after all? What is an arviragus, then, but a stupid gaming piece of the Druithin? You are beginning to see, aren't you, Caradoc? And did you know that beneath the memories is hidden a lingering affection for the men of Rome? Truly the child still holds a ghostly knife to the throat of the man."

"No! No! You are wrong!" The master's words flayed him as though

292

he were a dead white bull, a sacred offering being stripped of its skin. The blood of his slaughter gushed from his throat, his body was rigid with pain. "I have given all for you, I have followed Bran into suffering, I have denied myself a peaceful home and the company of my children! I am empty. Empty! Do you hear me? Even an honorable death was taken from me!"

"You are lying to yourself."

"No," Caradoc snarled. "No, not I. You wander in your visions, master, but who can say which ones are true and which are the dancing images of madness? If you knew the secret twistings of my mind you would not push me as you do!"

"I do know them," the master said gently. "And I also know that without them you would be simply Caradoc, Catuvellaunian warrior. The Druithin do not hold you a witless prisoner, Caradoc. You, and only you, have the power to say yes or no to us, as you have done before. Indeed it is you who hold us in your hands, every one of us, and all the tribes besides. An arviragus is lord over the Druithin, as well as his followers, for strong reasons, and above all men, he must be master of himself. This is why I show you the darkest places of your heart. This is why you are tormented by your own visions and dreams. An arviragus is unique."

"But I am not an arviragus yet."

"No, you are not, but you will be. So I must give you not only your past, but such of your future as I have been able to divine. I am not infallible, Caradoc. I see not one future but many, path upon path, and those paths branching into other paths, all leading only to the possible. I cannot often disentangle truth from shadow. I am not permitted to tell you what I have seen, but I can advise. Will you listen?"

"Yes."

"Very well. The omens and visions are very mixed for you, perhaps because you and Albion are intertwined, and your fates are bound together. I can tell you little. I have seen you victorious, I have seen you ambushed and killed in a lonely valley, I have seen you in a great battle. Once, many years ago, I saw you at Camulodunon, living at peace with the Romans as your overlords, but that avenue of vision is now closed. I can tell you what you will do tomorrow with certainty, and the day after that with probability, but then the visions multiply, split, become unsound because of all the decisions, your own and others, crowding into the moments of each day. All I know with certainty is that you are the chosen one, you will be arviragus for good or ill, and that the universe is indestructible!"

"What use are your dreams then, Master, if you cannot tell me whether I shall succeed or fail?" The man beside him leaned back. The colorless eyes were hooded as he bent his head.

"I did not say that I was powerless before the dreams, Caradoc. I have been dreaming now for nearly thirty years and I have learned to catch the fleet heel of truth as it goes rushing by me. Also, I read the stars, and meld what I learn from them to the message of my visions. If there is no agreement between the two, then there is no truth."

"Well, tell me then! Do not leave me to the daily agony of seeing my people die and never knowing whether their deaths will be in vain!"

"The stars tell me that you will fail, and that your failure will be turned to good, but my visions tell me that you will succeed. Therefore I see it thus. You will come to a point in time, Caradoc, a place, a moment of great destiny, and so fine will be the line dividing failure from success that even the stars waver and dare not fearlessly predict the outcome. Neither must I. I cannot make conjecture. You have flaws, arviragus, but whether those flaws will destroy the tribes is entirely up to you, and I know also that there is no finer, more cunning warrior in Albion. So the only advice I can give you is this. Trust only your own judgment in all things, and then test that judgment in your heart. But when you are in grave doubt, listen to Bran. He is not a seer but his intuitions are perhaps more valuable to you than my visions."

Caradoc was stiff with the cold of the approaching dawn. He was stiff with anger also, yet, though he wanted to call the master an impostor out of his own disappointment, he did not dare. He sat with knees hunched to chin, his heart chilled, his mind in a ferment, and the master chuckled. "You hate me, Caradoc, and you wish to believe either that I am keeping truth from you or that I am a false seer, but you know that truth is many-faced and subtle, and that not only am I a seer but I can see into your thoughts when you let me. You can shut yourself off from me, Caradoc, if you are strong enough!"

Caradoc knew that the master was joking with him at his expense and in spite of his irritation, he smiled. "Forgive me," he said. "I wanted a great blast on the carnyx of truth, Master. I wanted all my doubts laid to rest."

"Even if I could have done this, I would have refused. The Druithin are bound by ancient laws, Caradoc, and we break them at our peril. One of those laws states that no man may be told his future, for then the power of choice is removed from him and he loses his soul. This means that my brethren and I must learn to circumvent the will of the people, to move from Council to Council with words that are not always welcome, and to clothe our advice in riddles."

"Will you at least perform the last test?"

"The Bull Dream?" The master shivered a little, then scrambled to his feet. In the east a thin band of gray light was growing, and now Caradoc could see the night's lines grooved into the handsome face of the Druid, and the toll his dreams took of him. I should go mad under such a load, Caradoc knew suddenly. This man must be as strong as a mountain. They began to walk back down the drowsy path together.

"Yes, I will, but know that I pay a high price for doing it. What will you give me?"

A single bird began to trill, high in the oak branches, and the morning breeze began to lift the hair from the master's bent shoulders. Hope came to Caradoc. He felt as though he had lived a thousand ages this night, fought a thousand battles with himself, yet he could not remember a single coherent thought. He flung back his head, and smiled. "I will give you back the whole of Albion," he said. "Is that enough?"

"Oh I think so," the master retorted, then burst out laughing, and before long the still-silent huts of the town came into view, clustered by the dark, cool waters of the river.

They all ate together two hours after the dawn, then the master embraced them and bade them farewell. "Remember, Caradoc, speak ill to no man or woman, friend or foe, for from now on you will not be able to discern either," he admonished. "Love the gods, but love your honor more. Now go." They bowed to him and he strode away whistling, then they made their way back to the beach and the waiting boat, and the gray, forested line of the mainland.

"Tell me, Eurgain," Caradoc said as the little craft skimmed over an ocean that was as calm and limpid as the sky. "What did the Druid show you?"

She was silent for a moment, trailing her fingers in the dark water, then she said, "He showed me many marvels in the sky, and told me many wonders." She tried to speak again, struggled with the words, then burst into tears.

For three days they lingered in the village that gave onto the narrows and the island, then a snow took them by surprise, sweeping on the wings of a wind that shifted suddenly to the north, and Caradoc was galvanized into action. "We must go," he told his hosts urgently. "We must not be cut off from your ricon." He was afraid for Llyn if they had to winter here, afraid of Emrys's dark, unfathomable warrior's mind, afraid of the mountains, afraid of the time passing. There was so much to fear, he thought in despair, so much, and I am only a man. "Do not return the way you came," he was told. "Go south along the coast until you reach the Demetae border, then turn east. There is a track, good in summer, and the ricon uses it to send the refugees to us."

But it is almost winter now, Caradoc thought grimly, looking out at the swirling whiteness that obscured the island. Yet we must go. They farewelled the villagers and thanked them for their kindness, then checked their swords, picked up their packs, and disappeared.

The snow did not lie for long. It was too early in the season. It melted and the sun shone bleakly though the wind knifed through the travelers with a cutting edge that could only grow keener. Almost at once they entered Gangani territory, but the chiefs of the village had told them not to worry. The Ordovices had a temporary treaty with the men of the peninsula and they would not be molested. They could have cut the peninsula off but Caradoc, after consideration, decided to keep to the coast. He had no wish to be caught in more unfamiliar country with winter on its way, so they slogged forward, bent against the wind, exposed above an uninviting, forlornly vacant coastline. Caradoc's thoughts went to his sister as he walked, the thunder of the cold surf in his ears and his face stung by spray. Where was she? Had Rome executed her or was she a slave now, chained to some officer's household? Gladys would not live long in chains, he knew. If she did not kill herself then the loss of the freedom she prized so vehemently would drive her mad. But he could not feel, he could only think. He had no emotions left.

In two weeks they turned inland. They had no difficulty in spotting the track, for it was wide and well worn, but within three days of their leaving the coast the first real snow of winter fell, and it did not go away. The track narrowed. Bran led them, having walked it many times with the refugees he had escorted to Mona. His gray cloak was hard to see against the whiteness of the still, cold world around them, and they plodded doggedly after him, their faces and hands blue with cold, and their feet wet and frozen. The track began to rise, feeling for the drier heights where the traveler could have some view of where he was going. They had to follow it at the risk of becoming lost, though the gorges had offered shelter. There was none on the crests of the increasingly sharper hills and they ate and slept without warmth, buffeted continually. At night they huddled close together, arms around each other, trying with the heat of their bodies to comfort each other, locked in the silence of exhaustion. The wild animals had gone to ground and Cinnamus often came back to them empty-handed. Caradoc found his sanity stretching out, the thread of reason thinning daily, and with an effort of will that took all his energy he hung onto it, leaving his body to obey the other bodies that pressed against it, shivering in the nights. If he gave in all battles were lost, all visions gone for naught. He no longer slept. He dozed between fiery waves of dizziness when the wind shrieked at him with a fell voice, and he dreamed that Eurgain came to him, soft and beautiful as she had been in their first youth together, whispering of the peace of abdication and the blessed rest of defeat. He wanted to rip out his brains and fling them away. He wanted to take out his sword and skewer his eyes in an effort to reach the seat of his anguish, but he clenched his teeth, closed his eyes, and night after night he held on, while Eurgain and Caelte crushed against him, and Bran watched him with black, expressionless gaze.

It took them three more weeks to reach the Ordovician town. Weeks of hunger, privation, and wet, chilled misery, but gradually the land smoothed out until they were striding the backs of the rolling, dark-forested foothills. Snow turned to sleet, became rain. Cinnamus speared a deer, dazed with cold and hunger, and Eurgain found dry wood under the protecting branches of the oaks. The worst of their journeying was over.

Two days after Samain they were greeted at the bridge by Llyn, Emrys, and Sine. They came to a halt and stood before the chieftain, their packs falling to the wet ground, and Llyn ran forward and embraced them all. Still they did not speak and Emrys, looking from one to the other, nodded. They were scarecrows, the tattered remnants of their once-gay tunics and cloaks flapping against bodies from which all softness had been eaten away. The skin of their thin faces and hands was burned dark brown and it peeled in places to the tender flesh beneath, and their eyes were cups full of mountain magic, an essence compounded of suffering, loneliness, and fear and pounded in the pestle of their souls by the proud, jealous peaks themselves. The Ordovices blooded their sons by sending them into the mountains and they all, the ones that returned, came back with those eyes, and the mystery never left them. Emrys nodded again and Sine removed her bronze mask, meeting Eurgain's gaze with the same plumbless detachment. Caradoc took one step.

"We have conquered," he said hoarsely. "Now call your great Council. I am going back to the Silures."

"You have indeed," Emrys answered. "If you had not your eyes would show it, but you have Ordovician eyes now, you soft lowland chiefs, and wherever you go you will carry the mark of the mountains on you. Caradoc, I can call no Council until the spring. I beg you to winter here."

But Caradoc shook his head. "There will be messages for me from my spies," he said, his voice hardly above a croaking whisper, "and I want to know how Madoc has fared. Give me meat and bread, Emrys, and let me go."

Suddenly Emrys glided forward and took Caradoc in his arms. "I did not believe that you would return," he said, "though a slave was drowned for you in the cauldron. I salute your tenacity, my friend."

Caradoc did not respond. He picked up his pack wearily and followed Emrys into the Council hut.

They rested for another week with Emrys and his silent chiefs, eating and sleeping, sitting for hours by the big fire while the rain drummed down outside, then they packed and left. Bran did not go with them. "I will stay," he told Caradoc, "and wait for Emrys's decision. I think I will also take a little trip to the Demetae. Their minds should be made up before the spring." He smiled warmly at Caradoc. "Do not despair!"

"What is despair?" Caradoc countered dully. "What is happiness? These words have become meaningless to me, Bran."

The Druid touched the long fingers laying limp on the knee beside him. "It will not always be so, and you know it. The stars promised great things for you, warrior, many years ago while you were yet heedless and carefree, and the stars do not lie. Look up! The end is in sight."

"I don't care. I care about nothing anymore but slaying Romans. I know that the stars do not lie but neither do they always tell the undistorted truth. What comes is often in a very different guise from what was seen, and destiny may be fulfilled as dust and ashes in the mouth."

"Ah," Bran whispered, almost to himself. "But what is truth? Can you tell me that? It is the thing that has evaded my brethren through countless years, though we pursue it to death and beyond."

"It is the backside of a lie," Caradoc replied. "It is what you see when you turn the coin over. It is nothing, a word."

"Perhaps. But somewhere there is a truth that will not become a lie tomorrow."

"I do not wish to discuss it," Caradoc said harshly. "You are well named, you Druithin. You fight with words and spells, but give me a sword and an enemy I can see."

"You have both," Bran reminded him calmly. "And it is impossible to insult a Druid, Caradoc. You have work to do, and so have I. I did not spend twenty years on Mona for nothing. I learned much wisdom and many mysteries but I did not waste my time in the weaving of spells, I have told you that before."

"Well, what did you do?"

Bran chuckled. "I learned to roll the dice of destiny."

298

The Catuvellauni made their way back slowly to the place Eurgain thought of more and more as home. They arrived on a day of inter-mittent rain squalls and a fresh, blustering wind when the sun flashes in and out like a spark that would not ignite wet wood. Madoc and Jodocus strode to meet them, and Madoc, laughing and roaring, flung his short, mighty arms around each of them in turn. "Rest and peace!" he shouted. "So the mountains let you go, Caradoc! How did you fare? What did you think of our noble cousins? Come and eat!"

The black beard wagged frenetically, the black eyes warmed them, and Caradoc was suddenly glad to call this big fighting man his friend. After the cool, silent danger of the Ordovices he seemed like a torrent of welcome hot water. Llyn disappeared in search of his friends. Eurgain left them immediately to find Annis and the girls, and Caradoc, Cinnamus, and Caelte walked to the Council hut where the fire leaped high and there was a dry place to sit. The smoky, shriveled heads seemed to grin in welcome as they pushed through the doorskins, and the Silurian chiefs ran to greet them. But there was no Fearachar waiting to serve his lord with meat and beer while pouring out a steady stream of woes, real or imagined, and with a sudden pang Caradoc missed him. He crossed his legs and sank to the skins, the fire's heat warm on his face, and a Silurian slave was there with a platter, boar's meat, flat bread, apples, and beer. Eurgain returned and his girls ran to be hugged with cries of delight. He held them briefly, astonished that the baby softness had turned in the months he had been absent to lanky bones and the clumsiness of two leggy colts. Eurgain was eleven now and Gladys ten, and as they left him to ply their mother with excited questions he thought how they had grown without him and now were almost unknown to him, two little sword-women that he had fathered in a time he could not re-member by a Catuvellaunian girl who had changed, like him, so much as to make her, too, almost unrecognizable. Or is it only I who've changed? he wondered dismally. Eurgain settled onto the skins with the girls, Tallia prepared to serve her, and Caradoc's eyes met hers without expression. He turned to Madoc.

"How did the summer raids go?"

Madoc frowned and his monumental shoulders lifted. "Not well. It is time to change our tactics, Caradoc. The road is patrolled now by soldiers on the watch for us, and every dispatch rider and wain is strongly guarded. We have lost too many men, and the Romans too few. We must strike elsewhere. The spies wait to speak with you. There have been rumors that Plautius is to be recalled to Rome and a new governor appointed, but we do not yet know who it will be. It is too bad. Plautius has been reluctant to push farther than his border across the lowlands and it would have been much easier to mount a campaign away from the mountains."

Caradoc digested the news, then shook his head. "No, my friend, it would not. Let the Romans lose their heads and try to fight us here. This is country we know, and they do not. The odds would be even. Now we can only wait for the other tribes to make their decisions." Madoc looked curiously into the thin, gaunt face. The Catuvellaunian chieftain had changed. Well, it was to be expected. No man spent months wandering in the mountains and remained as he was. Madoc was conscious of a fleeting sadness, but he grunted, forthrightly shoving it away. "Patience. Yes, I know. But let them not take too long or the Silures will have to take the battle paths on their own. Where is Bran?"

"He stayed behind to bring the decisions to us in the spring. It will not be long now. And I need the time of quiet left to us to order my scouts."

"So the time of testing approaches, eh Caradoc? Soon we shall say farewell not only to Plautius but to every cloddish soldier on the island. That reminds me. There is a strange Druid waiting to speak with you."

"Oh?" Caradoc went on eating.

"He has been here for two months and he says his message is a personal one, not for the Council. He will give it only to you."

Caradoc sighed. He wanted sleep, his mind needed forgetfulness for a while, but a Druid should not be kept waiting and this one had been waiting for a long time. Perhaps the message was important. "Find him then," he said. "I will hear his news."

"Jodocus!" Madoc roared. "Fetch the Druid!"

Caradoc finished his meal and sat still, gazing into the fire, mesmerized by the glowing heart of it. The hut was quiet. Rain rustled in the roof's thatching and then abruptly ceased. The little girls and Tallia had gone but Eurgain sat on, cup in hand, watching her husband's face through the steady flames. She knew there was nothing that she could do for him, and that she had lost the power to reach him. Her glance strayed to Cinnamus sitting silently beside his Vida, and her mood lightened. Cinnamus. He too had been changed by his trials in the mountains but he did not carry Caradoc's load. He was still warm, human. She looked away, shocked at her thoughts. I should go, she told herself. What more can I do? It is too late.

Jodocus swaggered in, followed by a tall, white-swathed figure. The Druid was young, his beard as black as night, his bronze-ringed hair curling below his ears. Joducus pointed and then sat down and the Druid came and stood before Caradoc who rose, wrenching his mind from the reveries that always waited for him in moments of inaction.

"Greetings, Caradoc ap Cunobelin," the man said smoothly. "I have waited long to deliver my message, but I was told to seek you and give it to none other, and that I have done. I have news. Will you hear it?" He tucked his hands into the sleeves of his long tunic as Caradoc nodded. "I bring words from your sister."

Eurgain sprang up and came closer and Caradoc felt himself tense. Gladys! He quickly stilled the whirl of conjecture and excitement that churned within him. She had escaped, she sent vital news of the legions, of course, of course, and he began to tremble as the clean, well-remembered face swam before his mind's eye. Brown braid hanging over one shoulder, black cloak fastened with pearls, self-sufficient, sea-filled eyes meeting his own. His heart turned over. Gladys! He wanted to shake the Druid in his impatience but did not dare, for the man had closed his eyes and Caradoc knew that the words he would hear had come from Gladys's own mouth. In a sing-song, phraseless monotone, the Druid began.

"To my dear brother Caradoc, greetings. That you still live is a joy to me, and it is also joy to hear your name whispered with hope among the enslaved tribes who look to the west for deliverance. I, too, am enslaved, but not with chains of iron. Listen to me, my brother, and forgive if you can, remembering that it was I who stayed to face Rome alone, I who fought beside you at the Medway, and I who slew Adminius, traitor and coward." The listening Catuvellauni sucked in their breath, looking at one another dumbfounded, but they dared not cry out for fear of breaking the Druid's concentration. Only Caradoc did not move. He stood with heavy stiff limbs like lumps of stone and the Druid went on. "My chains are forged of love and my freedom gone to my beloved. Forgive me, Caradoc. This was the final battle and I have lost it. I have been lonely for too long. You understand. All my life I have prized my freedom and fought for it in pride and with honor, but I can do no more. My sword hangs on my beloved's wall and I will never take it up again. I am to marry." Oh do not say it, Eurgain pleaded with the Druid silently. Not now, not here, it will kill him, and Caradoc, his head suddenly exploding in fire, heard the words shouted at him. Plautius! Plautius! The Druid seemed unaware of the dumb outbursts around him. He went on quietly. "You see why I must beg forgiveness, Caradoc, for my husband is to be Aulus Plautius, a man of honor who offers me his hand. You are his enemy, yet even enemies can command respect, and this man, Caradoc, is worthy of your respect. He is recalled to Rome and I go with him. Do not think hard of me. Sacrifice for me to Camulos, dear brother, for it will be a bitter thing to see the shores of my land for the last time with no member of my kin to bid me go in peace, and I will never cease to mourn for the days of our youth together. May you and your destiny drive the legions into the sea, and may you rule our own Council once more. Greet Eurgain for me. I swear to you that I will do all in my power to lighten the load of the tuaths. Farewell."

The Druid stopped speaking and opened his eyes. "Here the message ends," he said. "I am permitted no comment of my own, Lord, but I will say this. She is well, she is happy."

He stalked out of the hut, leaving a stunned silence. The color had drained from Eurgain's face and she leaned against the wall, feeling faint. Gladys and a Roman. It was not possible! What is happening to the world? The possibility of a trick flashed through her mind and was instantly dismissed. No Druid would carry a message that was a lie, and Druids had a way of knowing whether the truth was spoken to them. Caradoc stood with lowered head and she could see his hands slowly curl and clench, then all at once he threw back his head and began to shout.

"Slave! Slave and Roman whore! I disown her!" He pulled out his sword, grasped it by hilt and tip, and the blood sprang from his fingers as he tried to smash it in two against the lintel of the door.

"Caradoc, no!" Eurgain screamed, running to him, but he pushed her away roughly and cast the sword at his feet, stamping on it, his eyes wide, and his mouth contorted and flecked with foam.

"The tuath disowns her! The kin disowns her! Henceforth she is Catuvellauni no more, but outcast and slave. Let her be cursed of Camulos! Let her be hunted! Queen of Panic take her mind! Raven of Battle tear her in pieces! May she sleep, eat, walk, and fight in peace no more!"

"No!" Eurgain shouted. "No, no!" But he shouted back. "Her honor-price is forfeit to the people. I, Caradoc, ricon, declare her cast out from the tuath. I forbid her name to be spoken." He was shuddering all over now, gripped by spasms of madness as he repeated the terrible words of banishment. "Sword-woman no more. Honorable no more. Sister no more. And may this curse follow her into the world to come." Cinnamus was frozen. Caelte had hidden his face against the wall. Then Caradoc turned and swept out the door, and his going unleashed an excited babble as the Silurian chiefs gathered about Madoc. It had been the right thing to do and they said so loudly and gleefully, while the Catuvellauni present stood horrified under the holding spell. Eurgain was the first to recover and she sped after her husband into the rain.

Caradoc ran. He neither knew nor cared where he was going. He simply fled, his own words echoing in his flaming brain with the thud of his feet. Whore! Whore! Whore! Trees closed about him suddenly but he did not pause. Branches lashed his face, brambles tore at his cloak, but rage and shame drove him on and he could not escape. He opened his hands and it was good to feel the shreds of his reason dissolve into the boiling cauldron of his suffering. He felt as though his head would burst with the bursting of his straining lungs. Roman whore. Faithless slave. He stumbled, flung out his arms, and they closed about a huge oak. He embraced the tree, panting, his eyes closed, his forehead pressed against the wet, woody-smelling bark, and pain like the twisting of a sword tearing at his entrails and head. He sank to the ground and sat with his back against the tree, his arms around himself, rocking to and fro in his extremity while rain pattered gently through the stark branches above him and fell cold on his already soaking breeches and his shoulders. There was no sound but his own ragged breath, the thumping of his own burdened heart, and the confused shouting in his own brain. Whore. He opened his eyes. The clearing was dim, full of a suffused gray light, choked with dead leaves that lay sodden and thick under emaciated dead trees. Dead, dead, everything dead and rotten and old. I, too, am old and dead, all life and laughter gone, all love and honor burned away. Better for me to fall on my sword and let the Romans come. They will find nothing but shadows to haunt their fine new forts, and ghosts to watch them under the forest's blanket. I did not choose this fate, it was thrust upon me. I am only a man, one man. I have done all that is humanly possible, I can do no more. He felt for his sword but it was not there. Then his attention was caught by a flick or color on the opposite edge of the clearing, like a red leaf settling to the earth, and he stiffened.

A fox padded into sight. It stopped, looked at him enquiringly, then sat, curling its furry russet brush neatly around its tiny feet. It yawned, showing pointed white teeth, and its pink tongue caressed its whiskers, then it fixed him steadily with its black, beaded eyes. He moved a hand but it did not stir. It sat there staring at him. Caradoc felt a peculiar giddiness. He scrambled to his hands and knees, and the fox yawned again. "So you do not fear me," he whispered. "Why? Do I bear no scent now but the scent of an animal?" The fox blinked, a warm splash of bright fuzzy color, and Caradoc felt the bubble of pain move from his stomach to his chest. The agony of it was unendurable. He gasped and struggled for breath, then it was in his throat and inching into his mouth. Oh let me die, he begged, doubled over, let me die, and then the bubble burst, and tears poured down his face. Bitter tears, scalding and hot, hurting him, and the pain of their flowing was as great as the crumbling of the dam that had held them captive for four long years. He flung himself on the ground and wept with his face buried in his arms, great racking sobs of torment and desolation, and he could not stop. The rain eased, the sun shone out, only to be hidden again, and still he cried. The days of heartbreak and failure, the lonely burdens thrust upon him, the losses and treachery and ceaseless strain all washed away into the soft cradle of the earth.

When he was spent he lay quietly, inhaling the thick, wet smell of the empty forest, his swollen eyes pressed shut, and his arms flung out to feel the solid strength and comfort of the soil he loved. Then he sat up slowly, wiped his face on a corner of his cloak, and looked about him. The fox had gone. He rose stiffly. His legs were tender and trembling, and his belly was empty and, blessedly, his mind was too, peacefully empty, then he turned and saw her standing by the path, one hand against an oak, her blue cloak falling to the ground. He walked toward her unsteadily, and a moment of pride flickered and was gone. She waited motionless, watching him come, only her eyes betraying the price she had paid in humbling herself and running after him, and he knew that she would not speak. The word must come from him. He stepped onto the path and halted, taking his fierce, uncompromising Catuvellauni spirit and bending it with the little strength he had left.

"Forgive me, Eurgain," he said huskily. "I have belittled you. If you wish I will give you what I have and you can leave, but I beg you to consider carefully before you do so. I need you."

She did not smile. She looked long into his face seeing the eyes clear and whole again, the mouth with no bitter twist, and she took his dirty, bloody hands, turning them palms upward, and kissed them. "Where would I go to escape from you?" she said, her voice quivering. "We are bound together, Caradoc, whether I go or stay."

He drew her to him and they clung to each other, full of words too charged with emotion to say, then holding hands they started back down the path. When they reached the edge of the forest he turned her gently and kissed her. "Can we go back?" he asked, and she smiled. "We can try," she said.

The Silures and the Catuvellauni spent the rest of the winter hunting and waiting. The weather was changeable that year, frost and sun, rain, a few brief snowstorms, and Caradoc's spies had no difficulty moving in and out of the territory. The rumors of Plautius's recall were confirmed, as Caradoc knew they would be. In the spring he was going back to Rome to claim the honors Claudius was preparing to heap upon him. It was even said that he was to receive an ovation and the emperor himself would walk beside him in his triumph, but Caradoc thought of his sister, stared at and whispered about by the fickle, gossipy-hungry mobs of Rome, facing a strange country and strange people. He had done right to cast her from the tuath, he knew that, even though he had broken the sword in a fit of madness. Cunobelin would have done it. Yet he pitied her. If Plautius was not the man she said he was her life would be dreary and miserable. Her name was never spoken again in his hearing, but she lingered in his and Eurgain's thoughts and sometimes, sitting late at night by the cheery comfort of their own little fire and listening to the wind, they would fall silent and Gladys would rise between them, dignified and cool, leaning on her enameled, pearl-studded ceremonial shield and smiling enigmatically. Her odd, abrupt defection symbolized for them the precariousness of their own life, and insecurity helped draw them closer together.

They rediscovered each other slowly and wonderingly that winter, knowing that to each the other was irreparably changed, a different person from the one who had pledged so long ago on the grass outside Camulodunon in the sunshine. But it was an adventure, an odyssey. New delights were born. Old habits died. Only sometimes, in the long, cold nights, did they privately mourn for the time that had gone and the couple that had been.

Spring came, with blossom and bird song, and the tuath flung back its doorskins and emerged blinking and cramped, to calving and Council. Bran returned. He came striding easily along the valley, his head thrown back to sip the scented air. Before he rested he went straight to Caradoc, who was watching his cattle being herded for the trek to their summer grazing, with Cinnamus and Caelte beside him. Caradoc saw Bran coming, a white dot toiling up the hill to the wooden shelter and the pens, and he left his freemen and his restless, lowing herd and ran to meet him, his train behind. Bran stopped and watched Caradoc come, hands that might betray him nudging into the cover of his cloak, and eyes swiftly searching the face. The sturdy lope was sure and confident, the face a little fuller. Eyes like dark wine smiled at him with no trace of obsession or anxiety and Bran nodded to himself. The crucible had been scoured and now lay clean ane empty, waiting for a new holocaust.

The two men embraced. "Bran! How well you look! Are the passes open already? Have you news?"

"I have news, and do not bother with formal greetings, Lord. I must be rude, for I cannot wait to tell you." He went down, and the three chiefs squatted with him. "The Demetae will oath to you. In three weeks their chieftain and his men will arrive to do it. The Deceangli will also, for they know that the easiest path for Rome to take in order to strike at Mona and the heart of the west is through their country."

Caradoc nodded gravely but Cinnamus burst out, "What of the Ordovices, Bran? By the Mother, if we have tramped through their precious mountains for nothing I will go back and twist that Emrys's neck for him."

Bran laughed. "It would take stronger wrists than yours to twist his neck, Ironhand, but you need not fear. Emrys and his men will oath to you, Caradoc, and they have already set out, but you should know that the Council was long and bitter and the issue only decided on the word of their invoker and a visit from the master Druid himself."

"It does not matter. They oath, and that is the important thing." Caradoc stood. He looked out over the greening, peaceful valley. His gaze traveled the blue-hazed hills beyond, the dimpled, fast-rushing water, the clouds puffed white and covering the distant peaks, and suddenly he wanted to leap and dance and sing, crow like a wild pheasant, shout until the world was filled with the sound of his triumph. He looked down at Bran. "Arviragus," he whispered.

Bran inclined his head. "Arviragus. A work well done, Lord, and a greater work beginning." He stood and reached into his tunic. "I have a gift for you, sent by my master on Mona." He withdrew a small pouch and drew from it a round object, wrapped in hide. He handed it reverently to Caradoc, and Cinnamus and Caelte rose and craned to see what it was. Caradoc gently loosened the covering. It was a pocked, gray and white cartilaginous object, the size of an apple. Cinnamus and Caelte sprang back but Caradoc fondled it with awed fingers, feeling the steady, strong spell of it mingle with his breath.

"A magic egg," he said.

"Yes. The master Druid performed the bull dream for you, Caradoc, and in the dream he saw a green snake form this egg with its own spittle and roll it behind a rock. When he woke he sent one of my brethren to find it, and here it is."

" 'Greater wisdom than any man, a stronger sword arm than any man, and power to make a kingdom.' " Caradoc gingerly wrapped it again and put it in the pouch, tying it to his belt. "Thank you, my friend. For years uncounted no chief has possessed such a gift."

"Not since Vercingetorix," Bran commented lightly, and Caradoc shot him a quick glance. Many of the Silurian chiefs had been saying quite openly that the soul of Vercingetorix had been waiting patiently to possess the body of Caradoc in order to rise as arviragus again and this time be victorious. For the first time, questing Bran's brown face, Caradoc wondered if it might not be true. The weight of his new responsibility to the people and the uniqueness of his position suddenly smote him and he felt a wave of depression, but the die was cast and his feet were on the path he had chosen. "Vercingetorix failed," he snapped, and Bran's smile grew broader.

"But you will not," he said.

They filed down out of the mountains, Emrys and his lithe Sine, the tall, noble Ordovician chiefs, the black, uncouth Demetae, the tribesmen of the Deceangli, spreading through the town like a glittering, many-hued river, filling huts and spilling over onto the tiny fields, camping out under the summer stars. There were no squabbles. Each tuath kept to itself, cooked its own food, sang its own songs. When the passes lay empty and the western paths were still, Caradoc called his Council in the open air around a great fire, sitting on a chair with gold on his brow and a carnyx across his knees. The artist had come to him when the news of the tribes' capitulation had sped through the town, standing before him and thrusting a new torc into his bewildered hands. "To replace the one you gave to your son," the taciturn young man said. "It is a gift. And you still owe me for two brooches and an anklet, Lord." Caradoc turned it over. It weighed heavy and he knew immediately that it was pure gold, worth more than anything he owned, and he did not know what to say. The curving thickness of it was covered in gay leaves that seemed to flutter on a warm wind, and the faces of goddesses with flowing hair smiled at him between flowers that opened trumpetlike under a gentle sun. There was no hint of blood, fear, or secrets, and Caradoc asked him why. He smiled briefly. "An arviragus is lord of death and often forgets that he is also protector of freedom and life. My gift will remind you." He bowed absently and wandered away and Caradoc set the torc about his neck with an incredulous, blithe lightness of heart. Lord of death, and protector of freedom. Arviragus. Now anything was possible.

In the late evening light, when the sun hung in the west, too drowsy to set, the chiefs walked proudly to Caradoc's chair and flung their swords at his feet. Eurgain leaned over his shoulder, taking a count, her blonde hair wisping about her face, and Llyn stood beside his father, his own sword under Caradoc's feet. Cinnamus and Caelte had also oathed afresh and now sat beside him, bathed in the red summer glow that preceded a long, warm twilight, their helms on their heads and their torcs and bronzes sparking gaily. When Emrys came he did not add his sword to the shining pile. He drew it forth slowly and deliberately, kissed it, and laid it on Caradoc's knee. "You are first among equals, Lord," he said softly, and Caradoc met the dark, veiled eyes and smiled.

"As it has always been, Emrys. Do not fear. The time will come when you and I can return to raids and feasting." Emrys did not bow. He merely inclined his head and went back to sit with his wife.

With the first faint pricking of the stars the weapon count was complete and Caradoc rose, stepping around the haphazard mound of swords and putting the carnyx to his lips. Taking a deep breath he blew it, and the harsh, haunting note rang in the hills and returned, bringing with it an echo as if a ghostly host waiting in far-off blackness had answered the call. "Does any man deny me my destiny?" he shouted, and the men rose in one seething mass and yelled back, "Arviragus! Arviragus! Caradoc for freedom!"

"Does any man deny the task?"

"Death to Rome! Albion for the tribes!"

He handed the carnyx to Cinnamus behind him, raised his arms, and the people settled to silence. "Then I give you my first orders. Return to your tuaths, and bring back all your freemen. Arm your freewomen as well. Leave the peasants to harvest the crops and care for the cattle, but bring what grain you can. Forget your huts, forget your hunting grounds and your friendly hearths and your jewels. Henceforth you live where I am, you hunt only men, and your riches will be in Roman heads. Make haste!" He dismissed them and beckoned to Bran. "Take a message to Mona," he said. "Tell your brethren that they must double the shipments of grain to the Ordovices, and I want three Druids to accompany every tribe that moves with me. I want no quarrels while I am arviragus." Bran nodded and he turned to Eurgain. "You, Vida, and Sine will see to the women and children, Eurgain." She began to protest angrily but he held up an impatient hand. "I want them turned into warriors and I want them drilled. No gossip, dear heart, no silly boasting on behalf of their men. Teach them to boast for themselves. Every male and female over the age of sixteen will fight."

Llyn thrust forward. "But father, that leaves me out! I am a chief! I bear a torc! I demand to fight!"

Caradoc laid a hand on his stiff shoulder. "For you I have other work, Llyn. I want fresh spies placed where my first spies have settled, so that the seasoned ones can be free to come and go, following every move of the legions and moving between myself and them. Take your Silurian friends and make beggars and urchins out of them. A few more in the new towns of the south will not be noticed, and I need young ears in the streets."

"Do you know what you will do to those children?" Cinnamus asked quietly, and Caradoc looked into the expressionless green eyes.

"Of course I know, and so will they. Some will die, but all will say that it is better to die free than live to row in Roman galleys or labor in Roman mines." He and Cinnamus held their glance for a moment longer. Then Cinnamus sighed, "Ah, Mother," and dropped his gaze. The change was completed. His lord, his friend, had become arviragus.

Spring, A.D. 50

CHAPTER TWENTY

*B*OUDICCA STOOD STILL while Hulda draped the heavy scarlet cloak around her shoulders, then she lifted her chin and the servant fastened the folds to her tunic with a small gold brooch. The room was big and gloomy, full of the damp drafts of a wet spring night, and though she could hear laughter and the desultory conversation of the freemen who came and went past the house, she felt isolated, cut off in this quiet, orderly room. She walked quickly to her table, picked up the gold circlet studded with warm, glowing amber, and set it on her brow. "Where are the girls?" she asked, and Hulda came to her, holding out her cup of wine.

"They went to the hall. Lovernius promised to teach them the new board game tonight, and to let them try his harp."

"Well, go and sit with them, Hulda, and make sure that Lovernius doesn't bring out his dice. Prasutagas doesn't want them gambling. You can go now. I don't need anything more."

The servant bowed, took up her own cloak, and Boudicca was alone with the soporific, slow-dancing shadows. Prasutagas was late. He was always late these days, for his arm pained him constantly when the weather turned wet and the fumes rose from the marshes, but he hid his discomfort well and never complained. I would complain, she thought. I would scream and rage and drink myself into a stupor rather than smile like a suffering Druid and wait to be asked how I felt. Ah, Andrasta, what's the use? She drained the cup and set it with a bang onto the table, then she folded her arms and paced slowly between the fire and the rich, thick hangings that concealed the door. Surely the accounting would be done by now. But I suppose he is talking with the procurator's assistant, exchanging polite snippets of news while the freemen ride empty-handed back to their farms and I wait here getting angrier and angrier. I did not want to go tonight, he knows that, and yet he keeps me pacing while he fritters away the time. Now Favonius will be able to make yet another condescending comment to his pristine, perfumed Priscilla. These barbarians are without manners, my dear, time means nothing to them, and Priscilla will cluck like one of her outlandish, weird birds called hens and send her slave running to the kitchen with orders to keep the food warm. Boudicca smiled at the image, reached for the cup, and finding it empty, flung herself into a chair. No, that is unjust. They are good people, Favonius and Priscilla, doing their best to civilize us wildmen. What a dreadful, thankless task! Oh Subidasto, fierce and true son of the Iceni, what do you think of us now? Are we not fine, with our soft Roman hangings and our couches and our beautiful, silver plate? She shot to her feet abruptly and began to pace again. Not tonight, I must not think tonight, I must be sweet and charming. Hunger is making me careless.

Outside she heard swift footsteps and the chief on the door saluted, then Prasutugas hurried in, peeling off his cloak, fumbling with his belt, and she ran to help him. "I am sorry, Boudicca, but I could not get away. The procurator's assistant was unable to balance the accounts and neither could I. Where is Hulda?"

"I sent her to watch the girls. Let me do that." She drew the flower-patterned tunic gently over his head, easing it past the stump, but in spite of her care he winced. "Are you in pain today?" she asked, going to the chest and taking out a fresh tunic, and he waved a hand.

"No more than usual in the spring. It has started to weep again."

"Favonius will call in his doctor, and then you will feel better." She pulled the tunic over his head, belted it, began to comb his hair, and he stood meekly, like a child. "We are going to be very late." She flung down the comb and hung his cloak around his shoulders. "I think we should ride."

He selected four silver bracelets and juggled them over his fingers and onto his wrist. "I can't, Boudicca, not tonight. The chariot is waiting." His voice was high, almost a whine, and she knew then that the pain was very bad. A Druid could have given him a drug, but no Druid lived in Iceni territory anymore. The doctor would put salve on it, and wine would do the rest. She touched his cheek.

"We don't have to go, Prasutugas. We could sit here by the fire, and eat mutton and drink good beer, and then go to bed." She spoke without hope, and even before she had finished he was shaking his head and moving to the door.

"It is too late to refuse the invitation now and, besides, I want to go. Favonius will have plenty of news to tell us." With a shrug she blew out the lamp that hung beside the door and followed him.

Rain gusted in their faces as they took the few steps to the chariot, and Boudicca raised her hood against the warm, wet wind. The moon swung low in the west, a rising crescent wan and gray above scudding clouds, and the trees surrounding the town dipped before the first of the spring gales. They mounted, Prasutugas balancing easily, Boudicca reaching for the reins, and clattered along the road that swept gently down to the gate and the truncated earthworks and the brown hump that had been the dyke. It was filled with earth now, and grass grew where once the water had lapped, and as the chariot bumped over it the Roman sentries straightened and saluted. Boudicca sang to the horses and they rolled into the shelter of the tree belt, already seeing the lights of the little garrison twinkling out through the fresh darkness. In a few moments they had arrived. More sentries raised lamps, opened the tall wooden gates wide, and they trotted into the compound and came to a halt, climbing down as the stable boy ran to take the reins.

An officer strode to meet them. "Greetings, sir," he said. "A wild night. Please follow me," and they returned his greeting, walking across the packed earth of the assembly ground, past headquarters, then turning left to where the officers' houses stood, a tidy row of wooden neatness. Favonius's door stood wide, candlelight and lamplight mingling with the rain and turning it to glimmering cold fire, and the three of them stepped up onto the veranda, their booted feet sounding hollow on the sturdy boards. Boudicca tossed back her hood and shook out her hair, and the officer bowed and left them as Favonius himself came out to greet them, his arms wide, his fleshy face wreathed in smiles, and his elegant white toga falling to big, sandaled feet.

"Greetings, Prasutugas, and to you also, Boudicca. We thought perhaps you were not coming. Enter, enter!" He ushered them in and the servant closed the door and turned to take their cloaks. Favonius, seeing the drawn, tight look on Prasutugas's face, clucked sympathetically. "You are not well tonight, my friend. Is it the arm? Longinus!" His servant bowed. "Run and find the doctor." He turned back to Prasutugas. "You should have sent word that you were unwell and could not come. Priscilla would have understood."

They moved into the room. Against one wall the fire roared up the

311

chimney, crackling merrily. To the right of it the flames glowed red on the household shrine where Jupiter Greatest and Best, Mercury for luck, Mars, and Mithras received the daily offerings. Favonius was devoted to Mithras and it was said that he had achieved the grade of Lion, though none but his fellow initiates and he himself knew the truth of the rumor. The Mithras men were honest. They lived by a strict, almost ascetic philosophy of personal discipline and forthright dealing, and Prasutagas had told Boudicca many times that the Iceni were fortunate to have their business in the hands of such a one as Favonius. But Boudicca, glancing with distaste at the god flanked by his stern torchbearers as she had so many times in this room, was unimpressed. Give me the clean winds of the groves of Andrasta, she thought as Priscilla, flushed and pretty in her yellow stola, came forward. Her black hair was piled high tonight, and yellow ribbons were twined in it. Flounces covered her tiny, soft feet, golden bracelets tinkled, and a cloud of strong perfume made Boudicca's nose twitch as the two women embraced, smiling in mutual dislike.

The Roman women were toys, Boudicca thought, decorative as the delicate curls of spun sugar that adorned their precious cakes, and about as useful. Priscilla was no exception, though her husband had brought her to the dark edge of the empire and faced her with every danger and inconvenience. As for Priscilla, she regarded Boudicca with well-concealed disdain, considering her a mannish, rude barbarian, typical of the uneducated mass of squalid natives who did not know the meaning of tact or gentleness and sought to resist her efforts to enlighten them with an unparalleled scorn. She pitied Prasutagas, who had the makings of a good Roman citizen if only he could shake himself free from his overbearing wife. In his weakness, Priscilla surmised, he allowed her to tramp all over him. No Roman would have stood for it. With the ritual of greetings now thankfully over, Favonius waved them to the couches and they reclined quickly, their stomachs growling. Priscilla nodded to the servant who waited, arms folded, by the door. "Gustatio," she ordered, then turned to her guests with a bright smile, while wine was poured into the blue glass goblets and the wind rattled the window.

"How is the grapevine?" Prasutagas asked Favonius. "Is there any sign of life in it yet?"

"It seems to be shooting afresh," Favonius answered, "but it is very slow. If the grapes this autumn turn out to be as sour as the ones last year I shall give it up and concentrate on the roses. They seem to thrive on the dampness."

"We are putting in a hypocaust this summer, ready for the winter," Priscilla interposed. "I nearly froze last winter, and Marcus was coughing from December to May." She chattered on and Boudicca sipped her wine and pushed it away. They had flavored it with honey again and she found it sickly sweet. Everything about them is sickly sweet, she thought cynically. Poor dear Marcus and his cough. But she liked the boy for his clear, frank eyes and his straight talking, and as the servants filed in, burdened with plates, she pulled the goblet to her and swallowed more wine, glad to see that there was a salad tonight, made of the fresh shoots from the detachment's garden, barely green. The servant bent, placing a dish before her on the dazzling white cloth, and she sighed inwardly. Oysters again. She did not understand the Roman greed for the shellfish of her coast and she watched, amused, as Priscilla licked her lips and picked up her spoon.

"How are the girls?" Favonius asked her, chewing hard. "I saw Ethelind dashing by on her horse yesterday. How she's growing!"

"She will make an excellent horsewoman," Prasutugas answered for his wife, seeing her abstracted mood. "She has a natural seat. But she is reckless."

"Marcus rides well, too," Priscilla said. "He can't wait until he's old enough to join the cavalry. Favonius has sent to Rome for a tutor for him but it's so expensive, getting an education out here. I can handle the grammar and history lessons, when the young demon will settle to listen, but he's old enough now for philosophy and rhetoric and that is beyond me."

Philosophy! Boudicca thought. Rhetoric! Andrasta most High One, that boy is worthy of a chieftain's training and she wants to give him philosophy.

The servants began to clear away the empty plates and the doctor entered, his bare head slicked with rain and his feet leaving little puddles on the tiled floor. Favonius greeted him affably. "Come and have a cup of wine. I'll have it heated for you. And look at Prasutugas's arm, will you, Julius? It's giving him trouble again."

The doctor greeted them all and went to sit beside Prasutugas, taking the stump gently and lifting the empty sleeve away from it. Priscilla looked away. It was raw again, seeping a yellowish fluid, and the doctor exclaimed in annoyance. "I may have to take some more of it off," he said brusquely. "The salve isn't doing it any good at all."

Prasutugas withdrew and shook down the sleeve with his healthy arm. "You have hacked at it before," he protested, "and it still will not heal. In the summer it will improve. Just give me more salve for now."

The doctor rose. "I'll send it along to you tonight. No wine, thank you, sir. I won't interrupt your dinner." He bowed out, and a silence fell around the table. The servants returned with the next course, steaming, fragrant mutton that filled the room with the odor of rosemary and thyme, and began to place servings on the glossy, coral-colored plates. Boudicca looked up. "Is there any news out of the west?" she asked, her grating, hoarse voice louder than she had intended, and Favonius raised his eyebrows at his wife and looked into Boudicca's brown, gold-flecked eyes. What a woman! he thought with admiration. She dominates this table like a predatory eagle, and her conversation is about as subtle as an eagle's croak. The ruddy skin around his eyes crinkled as he smiled and replied.

"No, there is nothing new. Rumor has it that the governor intends to put forward a great effort this season and encircle Caradoc and his tribesmen, and there has certainly been much activity at Colchester lately. The last of the active legionaries have all marched west and the veterans are busy taking their places. The natives don't like it, of course. The veterans are entitled to land and it has to come from the peasants. There will be trouble if Scapula is not careful."

"He has stopped being careful," Priscilla remarked, spearing mutton with her knife. "He is absolutely obsessed with Caradoc. He even dreams about him. Every day he has the auguries read, hoping that his luck will change, but that wild chief goes on scattering soldiers like leaves on a wind. The governor has even raised the price on his head to six thousand sesterces and offered Roman citizenship to the native who brings him in."

"More wine, Priscilla?" her husband said quickly, leaning over to pour it before the waiting servant did, and he whispered, "Say no more! You will embarrass them!" He straightened and smiled. "Are you hunting tomorrow, Prasutagas? If you are, I think I'll come too. I want to see how the dogs are working."

But Boudicca was not to be put off. "Six thousand! Were there eyebrows raised in Rome, I wonder?" She laughed, a gravelly, harsh bark almost masculine in its tone. "It will take more than the offer of money to persuade the chiefs to forget their oaths to him. It has been three years since Scapula arrived in Albion to find the Cornovii and the Dobunni in a shambles and the legions demoralized, and still the situation is only barely in hand. What a man! I met him once, did you know that, Prasutagas?"

Favonius was looking at his plate. Priscilla blushed painfully, cleared her throat, and prepared to divert her guests, but Boudicca had the bit between her teeth and with a sinking heart Prasutagas saw the evening disintegrating. He shook his head noncommittally as though he were not interested, looking at his wife with a desperate pleading, but she smiled knowingly at him, raised her goblet mockingly, and drank.

314

"I was six. My father took me to Camulodunon with him when he went to make some protest to Cunobelin. I do not remember what it was about, but I do remember taking Caradoc's hand, and riding his horse. He seemed as tall as a giant to me, and very handsome. He had thick brown hair and warm eyes, and he laughed at father and me when I told him that the Catuvellauni had the Roman disease." Prasutugas groaned audibly, Priscilla swallowed, her appetite gone, but Favonius leaned back on his couch and fixed Boudicca with an expression from which all geniality had fled. I know you, lady, he thought, seeing how the flames of the fire leaped behind her, turning the rich chestnut waves of her hair into vibrant red life, making the amber stones on her circlet glow deep honey golden. She was smiling at him, the pale, freckled face was alight with mischief, the light brown eyes sparkled, and the nails of her blunt, capable fingers tinkled against the glass of her goblet. I know why the Iceni elected Prasutugas as lord instead of you. Tease me all you like, I will not be roused, and if your hostility finds rest in this way, I applaud. Your hands are tied and you know it. Your chiefs want peace and prosperity, and you can rant all you want. I rule here. "How foolish of him to laugh," he commented drily. "You must admit, Boudicca, that under him the Catuvellauni have been destroyed as a tuath."

"As a tuath, yes, but not as a free people, those that are left. To you he is a crazy, ragged outcast with a price on his head, but to the men of the west he is arviragus, a savior."

"Savior from what? His followers die like flies from starvation, from the sword, when at one word from him they could lay down their arms, go back to their towns, and live in peace. I say he is a murderer."

"It would be the peace of the soul's death," she replied softly, her eyes losing their sparkle and turning hard. "Favonius, I apologize for my rudeness tonight, but you know me well enough by now to realize that I will not sit here and smile my principles away. Scapula has forgotten that he is here to govern. He has mobilized all the legions to one end and one end only. The capture of one lonely, hunted man. What has such madness to do with prosperity and peace for the province?"

Favonius signaled to the servants. "Bring the mensae secundae," he ordered curtly, then he looked back at her. "Boudicca, even you see the answer to that. When Caradoc is captured, all resistance can cease. And it will. He alone keeps the war going and when he has gone to Rome in chains, as of course he will eventually do, the people will settle down to a normal life once more."

She shook her head violently, the wine in her goblet splashing over her hands. "No, they will not. Oh, Favonius, this is what you cannot understand. The people do not want your peace and your prosperity. They want only their freedom."

"Bah!" he snapped peevishly. "Freedom is a word that children use. No man who ever lived was free. What kind of freedom do they want then? Rome can give them freedom from war, want, disease, and fear. What else could they possibly want? What?"

"They want to be left alone."

A dismal silence settled over the table, a pall of embarrassment and unease, and while the servants dished up the pastries and set cakes and sweets and bowls of apples on the table, the four of them studied the walls. Favonius decided to drive his lesson home. Prasutagas and Boudicca had been guests at his table many times and there had been arguments before, but this time he knew that Boudicca's customary acerbic tongue lashed him from fear. The campaigning season had begun. Scapula, in a mood of angry desperation, had changed his tactics and the ships of the Classis Britannica were landing soldiers on the Silurian coast while all available men gathered in Dobunni territory, ready to spread out through the mountains and encircle the rebels. This time there would be no mistakes. The governor's reputation depended on the capture of Caradoc, and he knew it. He was running out of time, his health was not good, and the expansion of the province had been at a standstill while he bent all his powers on this manhunt. Things were coming to a head and Boudicca knew it. He did not think that she would be stupid enough to throw caution to the winds and mount her own little uprising, not again. Her chiefs had tried it two years ago when Scapula had ordered the disarming of the tribes before he left his rear thinly guarded in order to make his first move against Caradoc, and though she had not moved so much as a finger herself, she had done a lot of secret encouraging. So had Caradoc. His spies were everywhere, and Favonius had no doubt that it had been their insidious influence that had precipitated this spontaneous outburst of tribal defiance. But it had been quelled, Prasutagas had apologized, and Rome had been merciful. The Iceni had learned their lesson and now went about their increasingly lucrative business peaceably. Only Boudicca smouldered like a fire that had not been properly quenched. Favonius admired her, but her fierce, wild beauty did not blind him to her unreliability. As long as she was outspoken and quarrelsome he knew that Rome had nothing to fear, so in spite of her taunts he treated her well. But he watched her carefully for signs that her flamboyant wit was turning into quieter, darker channels. He and Priscilla had suffered through her sallies at dinner many times, but tonight he had had enough.

316

"I caught a spy yesterday," he said offhandedly, slicing an apple deftly on his plate. "My officers spent all night questioning him, but he would say nothing. I had him executed this morning."

She sat quite still, only the rapid rise and fall of her scarlet tunic betraying any shock, and he did not look at her.

"How did you know that he was a spy?" Prasutugas asked casually, his pleasant face fighting not to register alarm, and Favonius crunched his apple, washing it down with more wine.

"He lied to me. He said he was a traveling artist, come to ply his trade among your tribe, but when I had him stripped his body was a mass of scars. Artists don't usually fight. A pity. He was a good-looking young man."

"Artists used to fight," Boudicca ground out, her voice like pebbles sliding down a shingled cliff, "before Rome taught them that for artists to fight is not gentlemanly." She pushed her plate away and swung her legs to the floor. "How many innocent men have you executed, Favonius?"

"Not as many as you would like to think, Boudicca," he said quietly, his round, ruddy face calm. "And certainly not this time. Before my soldiers skewered him he flung up his arms and shouted 'Freedom!' "

Priscilla rose with determination. "It was a lovely dinner, and I am tired of the two of you spoiling my evenings with your eternal wranglings. At heart you agree, you know that, and I wish we had had music tonight to drown your words. Now let us sit by the fire, and talk of nothing but the weather."

Boudicca caught Favonius's eye and smiled and for once he responded to her impudent sympathy. She rose also. "Forgive me, Priscilla," she said smoothly. "I love a quarrel, as you know only too well. Will you invite me again? Tell me, will you take Marcus to Rome this winter, or will your hypocaust be ready?" She folded onto the floor by the fire, a smile pasted carefully on her sharp features, and Priscilla rattled on brightly, a spate of relieved, happy gossip, while Prasutugas signaled for the servant to refill his goblet and turned his attention to hunting and the pride of his life, his dogs.

When the guests had gone, Priscilla sat back with a sigh. "What a terrible woman she is, Favonius! You would think that by now she would have learned some manners. And that voice! Sometimes when I look at her she seems as old as Tiber's hills, but she can't be more than twenty-three or four. Poor Prasutugas. No wonder he is so quiet." Her husband came and stood looking down on her reflectively. "She's twenty-three. She has fought in twelve raids and killed five men. Because of us she has lost a kingdom and a way of life dearer to her than anything else. Don't you think, my love, that there is something

317

pathetic about this warrior-queen reduced to sitting at your feet while you prattle on about your melons and your child?"

She glanced up at him, hurt. "I was only trying to do my duty. I live in constant fear that one of these nights you and she will come to blows yet I go on inviting her here, at your request."

Contrite, he bent and kissed her. "I'm sorry. But you know why I hold these dinners. It is important to stay close to the pair of them."

She turned away pettishly. "That's not the only reason. Admit that you like her."

He smiled at the stiff, angry head of black hair from which the girlish ribbons trailed. "Yes," he said. "I like her. Now come to bed."

Boudicca slipped off her cloak, flung the gold, amber-studded circlet onto the table, and stalked to her chair. She threw herself into it, smiling ruefully up at Prasutugas. "I am sorry," she said hoarsely. "Very sorry. I have done it again, haven't I? And I did promise to be polite." She yawned. "I should never have asked for news from the west and started all that. If Priscilla thought me rude before, she will have utterly despaired of me after tonight."

He walked to the fire a little unsteadily, too much wine and the constant, nagging pain making him light-headed. "It doesn't matter. Favonius is a tolerant man, and I think you amuse him with your fiery speeches."

"Like a chained, performing bear, I suppose!" she flashed. "Ah Prasutugas, to what shameful end have we come? If my father had lived, Rome would be battling two fronts instead of one, and Caradoc would know that he has friends among the Iceni. He despises us, and with good cause."

He closed his eyes wearily, his face slack and gray. "Not tonight, Boudicca, please. I am so tired." She got up and went to him, helping him off with his cloak, undressing him, and he stood there limply.

"Shall I get Hulda to come and bathe your arm?"

"No. I want to sleep. If it is sunny tomorrow I shall feel better."

"We may have to cauterize it again."

He pulled back the covers on the bed and got onto it, lying down with a deep sigh of relief. "I don't want it cauterized anymore. It only helps for a month or two, and then the wound opens and I am back at the beginning. Curse the Coritani! I know how you feel, Boudicca, but I for one am glad that the days of raiding are over. The Roman peace is precious to me. If it had come sooner I would not have lost my arm and become less than a man." She took off her clothes quickly, combed her hair, and slid in beside him, alarmed at the heat emanating from his body, and his pouched, pain-stamped face. Each time his wound opened and his health failed her fears woke to new life, but he had always recovered to go back to his dogs and his horses and this time would be no exception. The evening had left a sour taste of old dreams in her mouth and she could not resist laying a hand on his good shoulder.

"One of these days your wound will kill you, my husband, you know that, and then what will happen to the Iceni? Rome's policy toward its tame kingdoms is quite clear, yet you refuse to see it. When Boduocus died, did his son succeed him? No! In went the procurator and his staff of vultures and stripped the Dobunni of what little wealth they had left, and then they found themselves governed by a praetor. And still poor Boduocus's son had to pay the inheritance tax, though his inheritance was more taxes!"

He struggled to sit up, and gave her a resigned smile. "Favonius has assured me that the situation here is quite different. Boduocus had made a mess of ruling the Dobunni and many of his chiefs had become uncontrollable through Caradoc's influence. Rome had to step in. But here it will be different."

"How? By leaving me out of your will you play straight into the emperor's hands. If you die before the girls are old enough to rule, Rome can quite legitimately march in to rule for them and there will be nothing I can do. The Iceni will have ceased to be a people. Rome will take everything she has not taken already."

"She has taken nothing," he said patiently, knowing that he would get no sleep until she had once more given voice to her anxieties. "We are the richest tuath in the country. Even our freemen wear the softest wool and can afford to hire the artists to make precious things for them. For the first time ever, our energies go into growth. No raids, no wars. We have never been so fortunate."

"One day you will die," she insisted, her throaty voice deep, "and all the money you have borrowed from Seneca in order to turn yourself and the chiefs into Romans will have to be repaid. Can the girls repay it? Only I could soothe the bloodsucker's worry. By taking from me any power in the event of your death, you leave the tuath open to ruin. Favonius knows this. He laughs at us behind our backs, poor ignorant savages trying to ape our betters; poor blind, innocent barbarians!"

"You are unjust and suspicious. The times have changed, Boudicca, since your father mixed hatred of Rome with your meat and fed you pride with your bread. Favonius works hard for us. I like him."

"I like him too, but I sit in the hall, looking into the past, and what do I see? The Gauls are Roman, the Pannonians are Roman, the Mauretanians are Roman, the whole world is turning into one vast

Roman province, ground under by men who speak of cooperation and prosperity in the same breath as atrocitas and extermination. Yes, the times have changed. Honor is giving place to an amused reason. The chiefs no longer wear swords on their belts, when only five years ago to be abroad without a sword was a matter of grave consequence. I am afraid, Prasutagas, and I ache with longing for the times that have been. It will not take long before the Iceni are no more, and people who look like the tribesmen, but are really Romans, will hunt in the woods and paddle their coracles in the marshes. Sometimes I wish I were dead."

He wiped the sweat from his forehead and slid back beneath the covers, closing his eyes. "The tuath elected me as lord because I offered peace with Rome and protection against the Catuvellauni. I have given them what they wanted. You are alone, Boudicca. You see the tuath the way you want to see it, not the way it is. Now be quiet and let me sleep."

She turned and kissed the hot lips, her heart liquid with memories, and he sighed. She felt his body relax against hers, a body so well-known to her, an old, comfortable habit, and she turned on her side away from him, pillowing her face against the palm of her hand and gazing into the quiet, firelit dimness. They had been together for eight years now, through times of disillusionment and despair, great fear, and moments of fragile joy. First love had turned to deep affection. There had been a sweetness about him, a gentleness that had attracted the restless, domineering spirit in her, and though her father had strongly disapproved she had married him. She discovered very soon that under the quiet, mild exterior lay a stubborn will as strong as her own, and all her efforts to rule through him were useless. For the Council elected him ricon, not her, and in spite of her ravings he had quietly given them the security they had wanted. Sometimes she hated him for his refusal to be drawn into the arguments she continually threw at him, when he would answer her with soft words and noncommittal smile. But he had kept her respect because of it, though he was fast becoming a civilized, genteel figurehead, malleable under the Roman hands that manipulated the tuath behind his thick blond hair and wide, slow smiles. She goaded him frantically, picking away at his dauntless, invincible sureness, beating him with rude words and sometimes even threats, but he would not be roused or driven. He loved his people. He loved the new security that had come with Rome. And he loved her, amused, not offended, by her actions. She was a child to him, tantrum-throwing and spoiled, only daughter of an old madman, and he took her too lightly. The swift uprising of some of his chiefs had shaken him, but not for long. He blamed the rebel of the west, not his wife.

Boudicca felt sleep draw away from her, though she willed it peremptorily to come. She could not still her mind. She had lied at dinner tonight when she said that she had seen Caradoc once, for she had seen him again, three years ago, when Claudius's beautiful white marble temple had been finished and the client lords and chiefs had come from every corner of the province to take part in the dedication.

Some came unwillingly, like Boudicca herself, for though no pressure had been placed on the tribes it was very clear that their rulers were expected to attend. Some came happily, greedily, like that Brigantian whore Aricia, dragging her miserable husband behind her as she went from celebration to celebration in the streets and houses of Camulodunon. No, it was Colchester now, respectable, bustling Colchester, a town where Rome ruled sunnily and cheerily by day but the ghosts of the mighty hillfort came out by night and drifted in the empty streets, their swords pale under the moon, their mouths and hollow eyes wide with reproach and misery. Prasutagas and Boudicca had stood with the others in the temple, looking with awe at the golden statue of the emperor wreathed in suffocating incense. Plautius had been there, his ascetic face already closed with thoughts of his coming voyage home, his sturdy, arrogant staff ranked behind him.

The rites seemed foolish and unintelligible to the tribesmen, who whispered and shuffled as the hours crawled interminably by, and Boudicca filed out into brilliant sunlight with a tired relief. A curious crowd had gathered at the foot of the wide, dazzling steps—servants and beggars, artists, peddlers and traveling bards come to watch the solemnities and to fleece the visitors if they had the chance, and Boudicca, looking down at them, was filled with an angry shame. No member of any tuath had ever held honor so lightly before Rome came, but now men who could work preferred to beg, and the artists forgot that their calling was noble and became imitators instead of creators, charging exorbitant sums for the rubbish they churned out with one eye closed.

She held back her sun-fired hair with one hand and prepared to descend the steps, and then she saw him. She was instantly certain that it was he. He was dressed in a shabby brown tunic, belted and covered by an equally disreputable cloak. Its hood was up, half-covering his thin face, but she could not mistake the eyes, and with the shock of it her feet stumbled and she would have fallen if Prasutagas had not caught her with his healthy arm. She moved on down the steps, drawing nearer to him, and he did not move. The crowd began

321

to jostle and she was forced to pause. She lifted her eyes to meet him. A spark of fear glowed and died in his eyes as he saw that she had recognized him, then he pushed back the hood a little and smiled disdainfully, hatefully. She was rooted to the step by that emaciated face. She tried with all her will to put into her eyes a little comfort, to say you are not alone, but he saw only the beautiful, pampered wife of the Romanized Prasutagas and with unutterable contempt he spat deliberately on the ground. She recoiled, shocked, and behind her Prasutagas nudged her.

"Move on!" he said. "Plautius is coming." The governor emerged from the columned shadows at the top of the steps, his tall, black-clad Catuvellaunian lover beside him, and for the last time Boudicca looked into the face of Caradoc. He was no longer watching her. His glance flew to his sister, faltered, then abruptly he turned and was swallowed up by the shouting, pushing people.

The shame of that encounter still burned and Boudicca turned over. Prasutagas lifted his arm sleepily and she snuggled into his shoulder. You must have forgiven me by now, Arviragus, she thought. You know how many of your spies I have protected in secret, how many weapons I hid from the hunting centurions, how many sacrifices I perform alone, no one but Andrasta and I in the hidden grove. You must think better of me than you think of the black Brigantian witch.

Aricia had gloried in her few days at Colchester, secure in the favor of the governor, and Boudicca smiled to herself in satisfaction when she thought of Brigantia's troubles now. Venutius was a tormented man. Two years ago he had repudiated his wife, beaten her lover to a bloody pulp, and fled with his chiefs into the west. For three months he had fought beside Caradoc, but his resolve was short-lived. He was like a man dying of thirst in the desert and she the mirage of cool, endless waters flowing just out of reach. He went back to her and Caradoc had understood, but Venutius had retained enough of his pride not to go crawling. His chiefs had surrounded her hillfort, she had impudently sent her henchmen out to fight, and an irritated Scapula had had to send her two detachments of cavalry and a century of precious legionaries before Venutius gave in. He had sent them both stern warnings but his thoughts were tangled around the treacherous passes of the western mountains and the man who crouched there, weaving brilliant strategies and waiting for him. When a wary peace descended on Brigantia once more he had forgotten Aricia. She and Venutius had been reconciled and the maimed lover was dismissed. Passion had crackled into new life between them but they had nothing in common save the blind cravings of their

322

bodies, and soon the tuath had resounded once more to the curses and recriminations of a disorderly house.

Boudicca pitied Venutius. He was an honorable man, loving his rapacious and complex wife with the same single-mindedness he brought to his gods and his people. Although he snarled and hurt he could not cut himself free from the net she cast around him with such consummate skill. She needed him. The people still loved and respected him and she doled attention out to him in doses just large enough to keep him hanging to her cloak when her tribesmen grew restive under Rome's yoke. But as she rose higher in Rome's favor, holding as she did the vast tracts of country between the tuaths hostile to Rome and thus saving the expense of untold manpower in patrolling the well-nigh unpatrollable border, her native animal caution waned. Her infidelities were notorious, even remarked upon in the dispatches to the emperor. Her love of luxury ate at her. Yet Venutius stayed by her, conscious of a deep well of insecurity within her, turning aside her insults and sparse endearments on the shield of his love for her. As Scapula gradually mobilized the forces of the whole of the lowlands, his conscience gave him no rest. Caradoc needed him but he was powerless, a puppet without volition, and the cries of his beleaguered countrymen went unheeded.

Boudicca dozed. Outside, the rain stopped. The Roman sentries paced quietly, bored and tired. Under the marshes spring stirred, and the surf broke monotonously upon the empty Icenian beaches.

CHAPTER TWENTY-ONE

LYN HEARD THEM coming first and he dropped to the ground, pressing his ear flat against the grass and closing his eyes. Caradoc waved his men to silence and stood looking down on his son, his arms loose along the rim of his battered shield. They were all tired. The morning was fresh and clear, and the sun climbed slowly in a blue spring sky, but they had spent the night lying high above the narrow path that wound from the fords and bit deep into Madoc's northern reaches, waiting for the Twentieth Legion. It had come quietly, just after midnight, moonlight glinting from the iron helmets, and the horses' hoofs muffled on the soft earth. Caradoc and his band had sprung from the trees, leaping upon the advance patrol of auxiliaries and archers and killing swiftly before the main body of the legion came into view. The tussle was fierce though the archers had not had time to draw bow, and the grunts and soft cries soon faded as the warriors melted once more into the night-hung trees, leaving the path deserted except for the bodies that sprawled loosely, stripped of their sword and armor.

Caradoc had allowed himself a grin of satisfaction as he loped beside the river, his men speeding silently behind him. He could imagine Scapula's face when he was told of the annihilation of his advance guard—rage held tightly in check, the red flooding of the rugged face, the renewed, sour griping of a stomach that contracted in pain every time the rebel leader's name was mentioned.

The war band had settled for another ambush some miles upstream, where trees clung to the sides of broken scree and overhung the path. They wriggled deep into the brush and kept sleep at bay with difficulty. Caradoc had spent the time of waiting with a busy mind, thinking of Emrys, Gervase, and Sine now also lying in some lonely high place, waiting even as he waited, far to the north. For Scapula was beginning his last and greatest effort, and all the west watched, feeling the hunters come. Caradoc knew that slowly but surely the west was slipping through his fingers. Madoc and the Silures had been forced further inland, steadily but irrevocably, away from their coast and their river valleys, fighting night and day, winter and summer, but giving back month by month. An encampment of the Second now lay where Madoc's town had once been. He had long since withdrawn from it, running to the hills before the dogged swords of the coastal squadrons and the naves longae, which had landed troops at the mouth of his valley. Now his people, men, women, and children, moved back and forth over the mountains with Caradoc's armies.

The Silures had suffered. With the ordering of a pitiless atrocitas they were hunted like animals, and often soldiers who became frustrated in their efforts to come to grips with an elusive, ephemeral enemy slaughtered the stragglers instead. Many of the Silurian children lay unburied under the forest's spreading arms, and the mothers who had ringed them in defence left their bones beside them. Eurgain and Vida with their war band guarded the flanks of each exodus, and the young women under them hardened swiftly to callousness. The sacrifices of each year were no longer slaves or criminal freemen.

Eurgain and her sword-women provided Roman captives and stood coldly by while the Druids chanted and Madoc wielded the sacred knife. Blood was cheap. It flowed without cease and Eurgain, looking back to the first night of Samain she had spent among the Silures, laughed now at the unease she had felt then. They were inured to death, all of them. Death was no longer a matter of honor or sorrow. One body was like another. The only importance lay in how many and who. Even Llyn gave no more thought to the men he slew than he did to the freewomen he made love to, women who went willingly into the strong young arms of the arviragus's son. Survival was all that counted, and survival meant killing. Only Caelte seemed unchanged, holding to his sunny, gentle world of music and poetry, singing all the old songs to himself and the forest, for Caradoc no longer called for the lays of his youth, and the songs sung around the campfires were all of death, and the freedom to come.

Now Llyn got up. "Perhaps two hundred men, with the wains, a mile away," he said crisply. "They are very late. I wonder why?"

Caradoc hitched his cloak impatiently, his eyes on his son's face. At sixteen, the soul of Togodumnus looked out from the brown, darting eyes, and the swift-sweeping, clean bones and cleft chin were all his uncle's. But Llyn had his father's cool ability to command without Togodumnus's impulsiveness, and the thin mouth was Cunobelin's, cruel and cunning. Women were drawn to him as they had been to Togodumnus, and like Togodumnus, Llyn did not allow them to become an enervating preoccupation. Caradoc, remembering his agonizing over the dishonoring of himself with Aricia, marveled sadly at Llyn's callous disregard for his conquests. But the times had changed, and honor now meant only the number of Roman heads one swung from the trees. There were no longer any youths among the western tribes. There were only warriors, or children.

"It does not matter," he replied brusquely. "They play into our hands. Off the path!" he called back, and the war band scrambled up the slope and disappeared under the trees. Caradoc and Llyn followed, and Cinnamus came and worked himself down beside them, digging deep into the leaf mold. Long ago Caradoc had forbidden the wearing of bright colors, and now the brown and gray cloaks of his men and women blended with the forest's subtle shades.

"Eurgain?" he snapped, and Cinnamus turned cool green eyes upon him.

"She and Vida are hidden farther along, to finish off any that escape us." He lay quietly for a moment, then he said, "Lord, we must leave this country. This is our fourth ambush in a week and we have lost too many men. If we wait for the Twentieth to close with the Fourteenth we will be encircled."

"I know. But I hate to do it, Cin. If we go north we leave the

Silurian territory to Scapula, and we may never be able to get it back."

"Emrys is holding them well," Llyn interposed, "even though the Deceangli are well-nigh finished. We can afford another season here, Cin."

But Cinnamus objected vehemently. "If we are cut off we must die. Let us join forces with Emrys and fight in mountains that Scapula cannot penetrate. Mother! I have no liking for the Ordovices, but at least they still command their territory untouched and, besides, there are the passes there, out of the west and into Cornovii country and Brigantia beyond. If things go ill we can always demand immunity from Venutius."

"He is not reliable," Caradoc said. "If we wanted to fight from Brigantia we would have to kill Aricia first." A thrill went through him as he said the words, and Cinnamus snorted.

"A good idea, Arviragus! I wish you had ordered the spies to kill her a long time ago!"

"Peace!" Llyn hissed suddenly, head uplifted. "They are coming!"

All eyes swiveled to the road. The bulk of the legion had passed an hour before under the hostile eyes of the war band, winding like an articulated, metal serpent into the dawn. The cavalry and few advance legionaries were followed by metatores and their equipment, then the men who cleared the path of obstructions that were often a prelude to engagement, the general and his staff with their mounted escort, more cavalry, the mules dragging the siege machines, officers, and the aquila sparking in the early light and guarded by its men. Then came the monotonous passing of the soldiers six abreast flanked by the centurions, rank after rank pouring into the west. But the baggage train and the rear guard of auxiliaries and soldiers had not come, and Caradoc was seizing the opportunity to take the grain. Food was always short and now, with the new offensive, the Romans held many of the valleys where the crops had been. Caradoc had ordered the Silurian fields and their precious crops burned and his command had been obeyed without emotion, even though the peasants knew that when winter came they would starve. They had ignited their little fields and vanished into the hills, and Caradoc added the burden of their deaths to the already crushing weight of his responsibility.

"Swords out," he ordered now, and the word was passed. They lay still, watching the vacant bend fill with the uneasy, lumbering vanguard. The wains were overloaded and the oxen strained, the men guarding them whipping at them futilely, the cavalry escort ringing them. The eyes of the perspiring soldiers flicked back and forth between the steep, brush-choked banks. They were afraid, Caradoc could see it. So much the better. He tensed and the eyes of his men turned to him but still he did not give the word, and the first of the wains reached the farther edge of the bend just as the last of the legionaries marched into view. Only then, when he saw that there were no more to come, did he jump to his feet, swinging the sword above his head. "Freedom!" he shouted, his voice as full and sudden as a summer thunderbolt, and the men rose with him and threw themselves forward, taking up his cry. "Freedom!" they called. "Freedom!" and the soldiers below scrambled to form fighting ranks, their own terror hampering the officers from bringing a swift order.

"Wains, Llyn!" Caradoc shouted, then he, Madoc, and Cinnamus were swallowed up in the melee. No quarter was ever given on these occasions by the tribesmen, and the soldiers knew it. They swung their shields forward and closed quickly, their short, lethal swords stabbing. Long ago the officers had given up any idea of mercy and it no longer mattered to them whether they faced the fury of the ragged men or the shrieking, wild-haired women. If they hesitated they were dead men, and they battled stubbornly to come together in compact phalanxes while Caradoc and his men struggled to keep them apart. Romans could not fight well as individuals, and Caradoc had had many successes by surprising and scattering. But this force was large, nearly two hundred legionaries, and the chiefs paid dearly for the grain that Llyn and his followers were calmly unloading from the wains, tossing the sacks to eager hands above on the bank. Beside him, Caradoc could hear Cinnamus's oaths as he laid about him, and Madoc was grunting and squealing like an attacking boar. For many minutes the issue was undecided, each side swaying back and forth, then Caradoc began to tire. The wains were empty and by now the grain was on its way to their camp hidden deep and high in the forest. He spotted his son, shieldless, dancing about a cavalry trooper who leaned down in a vain effort to reach the flashing limbs. Llyn held a knife in each hand. As the Roman's arm went out Llyn leaped aside, yelling "Now!" and one of his friends jumped onto the horse's rump, jerked the man's head back, and drove his knife deep into the exposed throat. It was a ploy that Llyn had painstakingly taught to his young warriors, and it always worked.

"Llyn!" Caradoc screamed above the din. "The women!" Llyn put a knife in his teeth, pulled the corpse from the horse, and leaped upon it, thrashing it and galloping for the band. Then the Romans knew that they would never leave that narrow, bloodsoaked place, for Eurgain, Vida, and the other women swept around the bend, fresh and terrible, and seeing them come their men fought with renewed vigor.

A handful of officers escaped, running weaponless into the dense wood, but by the time the sun had risen far enough to shine undiluted onto the path, the tribesmen had tipped the wains on their sides and piled all the Roman bodies on top of them, blocking the way. Then Caradoc ordered a swift retreat. He knew that before long a detachment from the main body of the legion would be sent out to find the missing rear guard, and there must by then be many miles between the weary chiefs and the scene of the ambush.

"What about the horses?" Llyn asked him and he paused. There were many horses and each horse still bore the soldiers' packs and equipment, but the way to the camp was rocky and tortuous and they would be slowed if they took time to lead the beasts. "We need the meat," Llyn pressed, and Caradoc gave in.

"All right, Llyn, but you and your chiefs can see to them. Hurry up!" He turned away and saw his wife sitting beside the path, a hand to her thigh, her face pale. He strode to her, wiping his sword on his cloak and sheathing it swiftly. "Eurgain, you're hurt." He knelt and she glanced at him, biting her lip and nodding faintly. He lifted the tunic gently, took his knife and slit the leg of her breeches, and exposed a jagged wound from which the dark blood oozed. He probed it carefully and she winced, then he took his cloak, cutting strips from it and binding the cut tightly closed. "It is not serious," he said, "but this is your third wound in two months. You are getting careless." He spoke roughly, worry putting an edge to the impersonal words, and she answered him through clenched teeth as he tugged his bandages tighter.

"We are all tired, Caradoc. We need rest. If you keep up this pace you will lose more chiefs through sheer exhaustion than to the gladiae."

He let her tunic fall and sat back. "That should stop the bleeding until Bran can attend to it. Can you walk?"

"I can try." She stood and put her weight on her foot tentatively, and he saw the quick flare of pain in her eyes. He beckoned to one of Llyn's chiefs.

"Bring a horse for the lady." Then he faced Eurgain. "You can ride with Llyn. How many women lost today?"

"Five, perhaps more. Caradoc . . ."

"Not now, Eurgain!" He begged sharply. "I know it all, who knows it better than I? Every decision I make costs lives, every move I make means more sacrifice, more hardship for the people who trust me. If you love me, keep your counsel."

"Yes, I love you," she said softly, and the grim lines of his face relaxed into a smile. "Like all your men, I am ready to die for you."

"But not yet, please Camulos!" He helped her to the horse and she swung herself up with difficulty, her leg already stiffening, her breeches sticky with drying blood. He left her then and she gathered up the reins, waiting for her son to give the marching order to the chiefs who were to ride, watching her husband walk in under the new leaves of spring. His words to her were always harsh and she knew that his love for her was just one more insupportable burden that brought him constant anxiety. No man could speak against her. No chief was allowed to bring her anything but the most respectful homage on pain of the arviragus's displeasure, and no woman, in spite of his attraction, ever got closer to him than the Council fires. His possessiveness was a part of his torment. She and his children were all he had left to him, and he felt that if he lost them his soul would be gone. Only Cinnamus still teased and chaffered her, argued with her, hunted with her in the easy friendship they had always had, and Caradoc did not mind. Cinnamus, too, was precious to him, as was Caelte, and he trusted their judgment, giving them the last word over Madoc and Emrys.

Now Caradoc swung along beside Cinnamus, his thoughts on the coming Council and the new decision that awaited him, and the war band melted with him into the embracing forest, leaving yet another scene of carnage to feed the raging fires of Scapula's obsession.

When they reached their camp hidden in a tiny valley, little more than a tree-choked gully with stubbed rock behind and a wide view of all the approaches in front, Bran was waiting for them with Caelte and the girls, and before any man ate they went to the stream. Bran made the incantations and the Roman weapons and armor were cast into it, for its goddess. Then they gathered about the fire, feeding silently.

An hour later Llyn and the horses came. He sent one to the freemen to be slaughtered and the others were tethered in the forest, then he flung himself down with the other men. Eurgain went to her tent and Bran followed to attend to her wound. The valley was quiet, each warrior wrapped in his own thoughts. The days of loud laughter, boasting, and squabbling were long gone. The men of the west had taken on the atmosphere of the lonely places that were their only home, and they had acquired the wild beast's facility of sleeping with one eye open wherever they happened to cast themselves to rest. Even the children were like animals, swift to startle into flight, suspicious of everyone.

Caelte sat with his back against a tree, humming as he fingered a tune on his harp, and the girls took their wooden swords and poked at each other, while Caradoc lay with one elbow propping up his head as he watched them. Eurgain was fifteen and Gladys fourteen, two unkempt, undisciplined girls, Caradoc thought, more at home with blood and sudden death than with dogs and hunting, or with the suitors who should have been courting them. They were both old enough to be betrothed but showed no interest in the young men of Llyn's war band. Or so he believed. He did not know them very well. Soon it would be time for them to join Eurgain's group of sword-women and take their chances with the other women who fought and died, blooded like all the young chieftains without ritual and without pomp. He sat up and took out his sword. "Cin," he said. "Give Gladys your sword. Eurgain!" The girls came to him panting and flushed and he held his sword out to his daughter, who took it eagerly, her fair hair falling about her face, and her strong brown arms hefting it. Gladys took Cinnamus's heavy blade, adjusted her grip on the hilt, and soon the clang of iron on iron rang out and the chiefs clustered to watch. Caradoc sat still, thinking of his wife and his sister sparring happily before the Great Hall, but Cinnamus could not contain himself. He got up and circled the combatants.

"Feet farther apart, Gladys," he commanded. "Eurgain, don't watch the sword, watch the eyes or you are dead." The older girl had her aunt's cool, steady swing, but the younger one was quick. They fought well but as yet they were no match for professional soldiers, and the weight of the shields would slow them still further. Caradoc got up and went to the tent.

Eurgain was lying on their blankets, wrapped in her cloak. She smiled at him as he unbuckled his belt and dropped it, and cast his own cloak down beside her. "Is your leg easier?" he asked, lifting the covering to see it, and she nodded.

"Bran packed it with herbs and it's closing already, but it will be very stiff for a couple of days. No fighting for me tomorrow."

"No fighting for any of us tomorrow. I have decided to go north and let Scapula have this country."

"He is no longer interested in the country," she said. "All he wants is you."

He grinned at her, a lopsided grimace. "But as Emrys would say, I am the country. We can open a new front in the north, Eurgain, and have the advantages of the escape routes into Brigantia and the more rugged territory. Also, we will be closer to Mona and our grain supply." Caradoc was surprised that Scapula had not made a concerted effort to break through to Mona and destroy the lush, productive fields. He himself would have done it, in Scapula's position, but Scapula was losing his judgment, allowing his preoccupation with the rebels to warp his good sense.

"In the north we will face the Fourteenth and the Twentieth," Eurgain pointed out. "We have had little to do with them so far. But of course you are wise. If we stay here we will be trapped."

"Scapula will find the Ordovices and their mountains a very different proposition," he replied. "Emrys tells me that Roman patrols have been seen quite deep in the mountains, and Scapula is obviously exploring the paths and passes. It will do him no good. He is losing men to us every day. We have held the west free for nearly five years. Think of it Eurgain, five years, and if only we can hang on for a couple more, Rome will declare Plautius's frontier zone to be the official boundary of the province and we will be free."

She lay back. "I prefer to think of you," she said softly. "Ah Caradoc, I love you so well. When you take me in your arms I do not regret that we may die tomorrow."

He took her luxuriant fair hair and spread it wide on the blanket and she raised her arms. He slipped off his brown tunic and his breeches and enfolded her, feeling her warm hands glide down his back and over his buttocks. She's like the rain, he thought, seeking her mouth. The sweet, cold summer rain that patters gently over the parched fields of my soul. Eurgain! He parted the cloak and lifted his head to see the nakedness beneath, running his fingers over skin as puckered and scarred with old sword thrusts as his own, yet still infinitely precious to him, still full of dark, appealing secrets. With a peculiar constriction of her heart she watched the ravaged face above her blur into softness.

"Arviragus," she whispered, "I do not care if the whole world is consumed with the fire of war as long as there is some corner where you and I may lie together." He smiled slowly and brought his hands to cup her face, so small, the blue eyes sparkling with humor and desire, the full lips parted, but a shadow fell across the tent flap and Cinnamus called, "Lord, an Ordovician embassy has arrived. Emrys is hard pressed and wants us to pack and move tonight." Caradoc sighed. "Give them meat and beer, Cin, and tell them to wait. Tell them that I am attending to important business."

They heard Cinnamus laugh and stride away, then Eurgain pulled his head down roughly. "What business could be more important?" she murmured and he chuckled, one of his rare, throaty eruptions of humor.

"None, my love, none at all," he agreed.

The Ordovicians had brought grim news. The Fourteenth and Twentieth Legions were gathering for a concerted push up the Severn valley and Scapula was with them, determined not to waste one day of the summer campaigning. He had mustered fifteen thousand men, all that the active legions could spare from the forts of the frontier and the peaceable towns, and the lowland lay almost undefended while he pursued his fey, fleeting enemy with angry singleness of purpose. Caradoc sat listening, two thoughts in his mind. If the Brigantians, the Iceni, the Trinovantes, had had one spark of honor left then this would have been the time to strike and strike hard, while he and his chiefs kept Scapula entangled in the west. But he knew bitterly that there was no resistance left anywhere but around himself, and this opportunity would go by, perhaps never to return.

He also pondered the coming year. Fate was drawing his time as arviragus to a close, he knew that too. Scapula had never before gathered such an army and Caradoc, chin in hand, unseeing eyes fixed on the faces of the Ordovicians, felt his thoughts stretch out, probing across the mountains, reaching for the mind of the man whose gaze turned stonily west, seeking him. What would Scapula do? Would he continue to press them with patrols? Would he mass his host and wait for them in some valley somewhere? Would he come to his senses and march on Mona, then sit and rub his hands while they all starved to death? If it came to that, could they slip into Brigantia and find a welcome from Venutius?

He waved the Ordovician down and he rose, squinting into the late sun. There were too many questions he could not answer. He felt his destiny throb in his veins, pulsing with his hot blood, returning to plague him with a force that was driving him like a runaway horse. He clutched the reins but was unable to control it. He could only look ahead with sudden fear to the time when destiny would come to a sudden, unpredictable halt and he would lose his hold and go tumbling on, bereft of all guidance. His hand went to the magic egg that hung on a thong about his neck and his fingers closed around it. The steady spell it wove served to calm him and he spoke evenly. "We will come," he said. He turned away.

"Madoc, Cin, you too, Llyn, have the camp struck. Leave nothing but ashes."

They all moved to do his bidding and Eurgain limped to him. "It is time to call out the full force of the Demetae," she said, but he disagreed.

"I will call on them, yes," he replied. "But I want to leave some chiefs to handle the coastal patrols if they can. Scapula thinks he can get at me from the rear, but he is mistaken. The Demetae can swim better than fish, and fight in their boats like water gods. He has a surprise coming to him, that dour old Roman with the stomach ache! Now go, Eurgain. Get your women ready to leave." She hobbled away and he stood very quietly, listening to the subdued, efficient

bustle around him, saying goodbye to yet another sanctuary that had
become, even briefly, a home.

For all Scapula's slowly mounting hysterical impatience, he did not
take Caradoc that summer. The combined Silures, Ordovices, and
Demetae held him off, giving him tantalizing glimpses of themselves,
forcing him to long, wearing marches, leading him on before they
melted away into the thick-treed, sullen fastnesses of their country
like mist before the sun, only to reappear and strike impudently at his
rear. His belly gnawed at him for days on end during that season. He
could not sleep. He swallowed his food with difficulty, knowing that
it would turn to acid and pain. He watched his long-suffering men
scrambling through rocky passes, fording deep cataracts that washed
away baggage and pack animals, losing themselves in forest that
stretched endlessly, with a deceptive, beckoning coolness and peace.
Many of them were never seen again. At night there was the howling
of wolves and the hooting of owls and in the morning there would be
a sentry missing here, a careless officer found headless there, horses
with throats slit. He captured no peasants, either, to assuage his burning thirst for knowledge. The land seemed empty under a hot,
thunder-heavy sky. In the south his coastal patrols were faring badly
and he reiterated his order to slay any human being unfortunate
enough to be taken in Silurian territory. When he had defeated them,
he decided maliciously, he would order them all killed, every last
dirty, treacherous one of them. But the summer was not entirely
wasted. He was getting to know the countryside. His surveyors and
cartographers were charting the tracks and marking the places most
suited for the building of forts, and they worked objectively and
thoroughly under his meticulous eye.

Romans and chiefs were relieved when the long, hot days began to
shorten and grow cooler. Scapula began to give thought to the placement of his winter quarters, but Caradoc, Emrys, and Madoc spent
long hours sitting with their faces to the fire, thrashing out a strategy
that would extend into the following spring. If Scapula withdrew for
the winter they would be powerless to harry him and would have to
cope instead with freemen who would have to stand to arms yet
remain idle, and the prospect was worrisome. As the air slowly dried
and the humid odors of summer were sucked out of the soil to blow
away on the keen, tasteless winds of frost-sharp nights, Scapula spent
sleepless hours growing more and more reluctant to disengage. If he
put the legions into winter quarters the rebels could spend the blind
months reestablishing their supremacy in the southwest and consoli-
dating along their weakened frontier. If he did not, he faced the slow

decimation of his exploratory patrols who would fight three enemies—
the weather, the terrain, and the elusive chiefs. He was not so sure
that the weather and the terrain were not sentient, either. Often the
mountains seemed to conspire gleefully against him, picking his men
off their shoulders and flinging them away, leading them astray along
fair, guileless paths that ended in cunningly hidden chasms, and the
weather had always changed when he did not want it to, pouring rain
to fill the gullies where the soldiers toiled and beaming with sun when
they had marched all day with no sign of a stream.

The mysterious, foreign magic shrouded him wherever he went, an
uncomfortably felt yet unseen cloud of malevolence that slowed the
reflexes of his legionaries and dulled their officers' judgments. The
dispatches from Rome were becoming increasingly critical. Too much
money was being fed into the new province, too many replacements
were needed in the ranks, and the returns were too few. Just why,
Claudius asked him in increasingly strident communiques, were the
tribes of the west not yet subdued? Scapula felt himself aging daily.

The legions did not go into winter quarters, and Caradoc began the
task of winter campaigning with his dying hope suddenly renewed.
Winter was a dangerous season for all, but more dangerous for the
freezing soldiers who struggled through snow on paths that were
unfamiliar, to a destination that had to remain unspecified. The
tribesmen took a heavy toll of them, though they themselves were
weakened by hunger and the necessity to keep moving without
proper shelter. There were babies born in tents to women who lay on
damp blankets between one day's march and the next, and many of
them died. Children who were not robust enough to survive long days
on their feet and nights of cold sickened also. But the strong among
them hardened to a swift toughness, to stand motionless in freezing
water while the Romans passed by, to hang from cliffs while their feet
scrabbled to feel solid rock beneath them, and to scratch under the
snow to find roots and iced berries to eat. The scouts and spies moved
back and forth. They were Caradoc's eyes and ears, his indispensable
link to Scapula's movements, and thanks to their information he and
his men were able time and again to lie above some bleak, snow-
choked crack in the mountain's armor and greet the already exhausted
soldiers with the final blessing of a savage, clean death. Samain came
and went, celebrated with a hungry ferocity by the assembled chiefs,
and the demoralized soldiers neared the point of mutiny when they
began to stumble across clearings full of wooden stakes crowned with
the ice-hung, tortured faces of their compatriots.

Scapula called a halt. The soldiers retreated gratefully into winter quarters on familiar ground and the chiefs rested their battered, emaciated bodies, their thoughts turning to their snug farmsteads, their sheep and cattle, the long-forgotten satisfactions of beer and meat beside a hot, friendly fire. They had oathed to their arviragus and they obeyed him willingly, but it had been four years since many of them had left their huts to take the war tracks, and it seemed to them that nothing was being accomplished.

Caradoc knew their doubts but there was nothing he could say. He had done more with them already than he had ever dreamed, brutally taking from them their pride in noisy, open combat and turning their rigid conception of what was honorable into an acceptance of the shame of battle without warnings and without triumphs. Supplies were running very low as winter deepened, and the freemen nursed their homesickness when there was no activity to drive it from their minds. Huddling around their small fires, chewing gloomily on salted meat and flavorless wheat porridge, it seemed to them that they were trapped in a slow wash of pointless, spasmodic little frays that settled nothing. They could look back on days bright with promises, sunny with the certainty of swift battle and easy victory. But when they peered cautiously forward they could see only more years of privation in exchange for the tiny handfuls of Romans who were slain each season.

The spring rains began and night after night they gathered morosely, sitting in water, drenched and miserable, thinking of the honor-prices they had relinquished into the dubious hands of their peasants, wondering how the spring calving would go and whether their little fields would be sown once more.

A rumor began to circulate, and try as he might, Caradoc could not discover who had started it. The freemen were whispering that they were surrounded, that their farms had been burnt to the ground months ago, and their cattle were gone. Scapula had not gone into winter quarters. A traitor had led him through the hidden valleys and even now he waited for the rains to cease before falling on them.

An insidious rumble of discontent grew. There had been outbreaks of incipient revolt before, but this time the grievances were dangerously focused on Caradoc himself. The arviragus had lost his vision. The gods no longer spoke to him. He was as lost and aimless as they. His magic egg had lost its power and he was deceiving them. He was a truth-sayer no more. It was not the Silures who complained. They understood Caradoc's patient, subtle policy of attrition. He had come to them first. They had sworn to him first, fought beside him before Emrys and his proud people, and they answered the rumors with scorn. But the Ordovices had listened reluctantly, acquiesced grudgingly, and now they wanted to go home for a season, just to set their affairs to rights. Madoc sought out Caradoc one wet, steamy evening.

"Call a Council, Lord," he said peremptorily.

Caradoc did not even bother to look at him. He went on braiding his hair. "No."

Madoc squatted before him, his gross flesh folding into his black beard, and his bushy black eyebrows jutting over eyes that held a stubborn concern. "Call them together and let them shout their doubts and longings aloud. Then they will be satisfied, and the rumors will cease."

"No!" Caradoc tossed back his plaits and put the comb away. "I am arviragus. They have all oathed to me. I order and they must obey, and I have the authority as arviragus that overrides any Council. Even the Druids must do my bidding. If I call a Council I will be admitting an uncertainty and my authority will be shaken. I cannot take the chance."

"They do not deny your right to order them, for they have oathed to you and their honor demands that they fulfill the terms of that oathing. They only wish to feel that they have a say in the ordering of their fate."

"But they have no such say and you know it, Madoc. As arviragus I am lord of their life and their death until such time as my mission is accomplished."

Madoc tugged unconsciously at his beard with one worried, beringed hand. "They love you, Catuvellaunian, but they are simple, ignorant chiefs who have suffered much in the cause of freedom. Let them speak, I beg you."

Caradoc looked swiftly at his friend. The bluster and raucous dogmatism were absent and the deep lines of crude mirth and lusty living that crisscrossed the chunky face now made him look like a sad, tragicomical old bard. Caradoc felt a groundless guilt prick him. "It does not suit you to beg, Madoc," he snapped, and color flooded the older man's face.

"We have all become beggars and outcasts, Arviragus, yet I am not ashamed. Cast a few crumbs of your vast pride before the people and let them give voice to their fears. What are you afraid of?" He rose, saluted, and strode away, and Caradoc glowered at the hazed, dim greenness that ringed him. I am afraid that the sound of their voices will give strength to their discontent and they will defy me and go home, and all the years of sacrifice will be worthless. Did you battle these things, Vercingetorix, as well as Julius Caesar's implacable juggernaut? After a moment he called Cinnamus to him.

"I am calling a great Council," he said. "Gather in the chiefs and freemen, Cin. We might as well while away the evening in fruitless bickering as sit idly by the fires."

Cinnamus pondered briefly, his green eyes thoughtful. Then he nodded. "I think it is wise, Lord. Let them berate us, and thus their sting will be drawn."

"I do not need you to tell me my thoughts!" Caradoc snarled at him. "Get about your business."

Cinnamus whirled smartly and strode away. "Mother!" he muttered under his breath. "I pity the poor freemen!"

They came eagerly to the fire that night and Caradoc, sitting cross-legged on his blanket, carnyx under his tense fingers and gold circlet on his brow, watched the hopeful, shameful gleam of a thousand eyes catch the flames' slow licking. They were still divided, even in Council. The Silurian chiefs sat closest to him, secure in his favor, but even they were careful not to step over the invisible line of power that surrounded him. The Ordovices glided silently and sank to the ground in a solid, well-ordered block, and the Demetae shoved and growled their way to the rear, heedless of crushed fingers or bruised toes. Madoc sat beside Caradoc, fidgeting and grumbling, and Emrys came, swinging smoothly over the turf to fold easily on his left. "You do not order your tuath properly," Caradoc snapped at him, and he turned slowly to fix his arviragus with a cool, quenching gaze.

"I am chief among chiefs," he replied, unruffled, "as you are greatest among greatest, Arviragus. I guide and judge but I do not order. The Ordovices are a free people."

"The Ordovices are a stubborn, stiff-necked people," Caradoc replied furiously, and Emrys wisely did not respond.

Llyn came and settled behind Madoc, and Cinnamus and Caelte, bearing harp and the arviragus's shield, stood arrogantly behind Caradoc. Eurgain and Vida sat with the sword-women. The chatter died away slowly until the only sounds in the clearing were the soughing of the restive spring wind and the incomprehensible speech of the deep forest. Caradoc handed the carnyx to Cinnamus and rose, his quick, jerky movements betraying to the gathering the foulness of his mood.

"I call for Council!" he shouted. "Slaves depart." Then he plunged straight on without bothering to unbuckle his sword, and no one dared to remind him of his omission. "You wanted a Council," he said briskly, "so I have called one, though what you hope to accomplish is beyond me. I will caution you to remember that you oathed to me, and any decisions made here must have my approval." He sat down

337

and Sine rose and walked to the front, a slim, brown-clad figure hung with bronze and topped incongruously by the glaring savagery of her wolf mask.

She spoke directly to Caradoc. "Remember, Arviragus, that I speak for the tuath and not for myself."

"I will remember," he said tonelessly. "Take off the mask, Sine."

She removed it and turned to the company. "Warriors! Freemen and women! For four long years we have lived together, sharing food and fighting, putting aside all our differences for the sake of the defence of the west. We have all lost brothers and sons, sisters and daughters, we have all suffered hunger and danger, but we have not complained, knowing that only in our hands lies the hope of Albion. Our arviragus's name has become a magic talisman, a spell of hope to the enslaved peoples of the lowland, yet the time goes by, the chiefs die and the children grow to stand in their places and die in their turn, and still we are not victorious. We wish to know how much longer we must be separated from our homes before the arviragus cries, Enough! We will not slide on our bellies like snakes through the forests anymore! We will stand and fight like men! Tell us, Arviragus, when we may don our pretty cloaks again." She stepped over the lines of people and resumed her place beside Eurgain and immediately a chief of the Demetae sprang up, the antlers on his massive helm bristling.

"The Demetae do not care about going home," he sneered loudly. "For us, home is wherever our swords wish to bite. But we care about killing Romans. Our swords are hungry. They are forced to nibble daintily at little morsels when they long to swallow whole legions. Give us battle, Arviragus, not ambushes and sneaking, shameful raids!" He had barely sat down when an Ordovician woman rose far back. "Strike at them now, Arviragus," she pleaded, "while they are tired and discouraged."

"How can they be tired when they have been lying in winter quarters for two months?" Caradoc yelled back furiously, and Cinnamus put a hand on his shoulder.

"Do not interrupt the Council, Lord," he warned softly. "They are in no mood to see the customs flouted."

Caradoc repressed an urge to strike his friend's hand away, and the woman went on in a high, nervous voice. "Never before have so many soldiers been gathered together in one place, within our reach. It is too good a chance to see go by." She sank into the throng.

Then Madoc sighed heavily, dipped his shaggy black head, and heaved himself to his feet. "I speak for myself, and for the Silures," he boomed. "We were warned by the arviragus to trust his judgment

338

even if it seemed strange to us, and we have done well to listen. Under him, the west is still free. Give him your obedience for a little while longer. I am a man who cannot talk with lovely words. I and my tuath honor our oaths and we will stay under his guidance as long as it is necessary." He sat down puffing from his effort and a moment of silence reigned. Then suddenly several people jumped up and began to shout.

"He has lost the Dagda's guidance!"

"He has lost the power to decide rightly!"

"He does not know what to do!"

The company rose to its feet in one angry, seething mass. The Silures reached for their swords but blades had already appeared in the hands of the Ordovices, and the children scattered. The clearing erupted into violence as the chiefs howled at one another, and a torrent of frustration was unleashed. Emrys sprang up and leaped into his tuath, laying about him with the flat of his sword, Aneirin and Gervase beside him. Madoc ran to his Silures' aid. Then Caradoc rose, put the carnyx to his mouth, and blew, and the seductive, plaintive note went echoing through the trees. Startled, the chiefs lowered their blades and looked at him, and he stamped his foot.

"The Romans pray to their gods for a madness such as this to overtake us!" he roared, his face chalk white, his hands trembling with rage. "Be seated, all of you!" Shamefacedly, without a word, they sank to the ground, their wary eyes on the tall, lean man who stood with stiff arms raised, his body black against the background of the hot, orange flames that ignited his torc and his circlet so that he seemed crowned and necklaced in fire. He stamped again, dropping his arms and putting his hands on his hips. Peasants! he thought, raking them with his fierce gaze. Stupid cattle! More dear to me than my life. "I have told you many times," he said deliberately, his voice shaking with suppressed anger, "that no tribe has ever met the legions in pitched battle and won. I will tell you again. If we gamble all the slow, painful progress of the last four years on one moment of stupid and reckless bravery then we will have lost everything. Everything! Your kin will have been butchered in vain. Your children will have starved in vain. We must continue as we began, striking unexpectedly and running away, playing on the soldiers' fears, luring them to death one by one. Then in two years, or three, Rome will give in, and we can all go home."

Gervase stood up. "Lord," he said quietly. "We have learned many hard lessons since we began this work together. Now we are tired. We cannot go on much longer. Listen to us, and let this battle be the last. We are ready. If we win there will be a song to sing that will never be forgotten as long as Albion exists. If we lose then we will have done our best and there will be no songs to remember down the long years of captivity. We are your beasts, Arviragus, and like beasts we have been hunted until our hearts have burst and there is no life left in us. The dogs of Rome are tireless, and ten years from now we could still be crawling through the forests. I beg you, let us fight, then set us free."

You are wrong, wrong, all of you, Caradoc thought in dismay, feeling the walls of the people's will close in around him. Claudius will tire of the money and men we are draining from him. He will have Scapula replaced. He will fix the boundaries outside the west. Oh why can't you see it, you fools?

"A vote," someone called softly, and the cry was taken up. "A vote! Let us vote, Arviragus!"

"You elected an arviragus," he reminded them arrogantly, "and where there is an arviragus there is no voting."

A hush fell. Their eyes were glued to him and he slowly scanned the honed, animal-thin faces before him, reading hope, fear, uncertainty, bewilderment, hostility, and underlying it all a love, and the final weight of a humbling trust. He met Eurgain's eye. Let them vote, he heard her cool voice say. Make an end, Caradoc. The time is here. He looked away. Bran's dark eyes also spoke to him, and the invoker's face was hidden under his white hood, but he sensed the futility of calling on the Druids. Well, why not bring all things to an end? Gervase may be right. The tribes may be ready. But something whispered bitterly within him that it was not the case, they were not ready for open battle and never would be, and Scapula would carry the aquilae with a vicious, gloating triumph into the west. He squared his shoulders. My destiny is accomplished, he said to himself. I can do no more.

"Vote, then," he barked contemptuously at them, and they quickened to life. "Those who will continue as I have begun, stand." Madoc and the Silures got up, and a few of the Demetae, and with surprise Caradoc felt Emrys stir and rise beside him.

"I cannot force my people," he said. "This is my personal vote." Sine remained on the ground.

"And what of the rest of you?" Caradoc pressed. "Do you want to be freed from your oaths?" The eyes slid away from him, but heads were shaken and a low chorus of No, Lord, Never, reached him. "I know what you want, you foolish people," he said gently. "Retain your oaths, and I will lead you to battle as you wish. If we are victorious you will never again question my judgment, and if we lose may you each be dishonored until the last Roman has left these shores. Do you agree?"

They did not want to agree but they were caught in the net of their own casting. Now that they had vented their spleen in open Council, many of them were thinking again, but it was too late to retract proud words without blood being spilt. They did not want to go into death dishonored, for the dead without honor could not rest and could not return to life until that honor had been avenged. The debt was eternal. But their fear drove them. Fear of more hardships and bereavements, fear of the gradual transformation of their tuaths into landless, witless peasants, little better than the animals they slew for meat. At last, with obvious reluctance, they agreed.

Caradoc dismissed them. The night was quiet and deep, and there were many hours to the dawn. He immediately called Madoc, Emrys, and the chiefs of the Demetae to him and they sat by the deserted fire discussing their last test, mustering all the lessons learned during the years of courageous and despairing recklessness that had brought them to the verge of doom. It had to come to this, Caradoc thought fatalistically. I have kept them together longer than any arviragus before me, but loyalty to the kin always comes first and they have given me more of that loyalty than I deserved. Now they take it back, and I cannot blame them. It is so much easier for me. I no longer have a tuath, no kin to goad me to jealousy. But, oh Camulos, I wish that they had chosen another time! The seed had been sown, and the shoot sprouted in such hope. Yet it is still so fragile, so new, and we are harvesting it before the appointed time.

"Let Scapula come to us," Emrys was saying. "We must choose the battle site and then wait for him to find us. And it must be done quickly, before the legions can separate us."

Caradoc nodded absently. He felt curiously empty, as though he had somehow lost the reason for his existence and had forgotten why he was there, and his drive and purpose had flowed away. He knew that in the morning he would have adjusted to new circumstances and could look ahead as he had always done, but now he sat with hands loosely hanging from his coarse-clad knees and his eyes on the ground.

By the time he awoke in the morning to drizzle and a warm wind, he had recovered command of himself and the people. He called his spies. "Go east," he ordered them. "Find the legions. Get drunk or fight. Do a little careless talking, but make sure that Scapula knows what we plan." He sent them away and turned to Cinnamus. "How many warriors will march?"

"Counting the women?"

"Of course. Have you been quarreling with Vida again?"

Cinnamus smiled wryly. "Lord, I have fought with Vida all my life. Did you know that when I went to her father to request the cup of marriage she turned her wine jug over my head and vowed that she would never wed such a ragged pauper as I? Mother, what a woman, I thought as I left her. I knew then that I had to have her. But she made me fight for her, the vixen, and I have been fighting for, with, and against her ever since . . ."

Caradoc smiled. "The head count, my friend."

"Ah yes. If you wish to count the women, then you command ten thousand warriors, Lord."

"And Scapula five thousand more. An even match, do you think?"

Cinnamus fixed him with that inimitably level, green stare. "It has never been even, Lord, yet we are still standing here in the rain and the west is still free. I think that answers your question."

CHAPTER TWENTY-TWO

WITHIN TWO WEEKS, an astounded Ostorious Scapula heard that the rebel had tired of his policy of slow attrition and was ready for a stand. At first he did not believe, preferring to think the news just another artful deceit to open the campaigning season with an explosion, but his scouts confirmed the rumor and for the first time in untold months he was able to sleep without the nightmares brought on by his churning stomach. At last, at last, Caradoc had played into his hands with the most incredibly naïve blindness. He stood with his tribunes under the shelter of his dripping headquarters and watched the soldiers hurriedly pack their mess kits, wanting to run in the rain and wade joyously in the puddles like a little boy. He had been right to hold on, to keep picking away at the west. The barbarian, in his simple animality, had caved in first, as Scapula had always known he would. Now, Divine Claudius, he thought happily, now we will see. The savage horde was moving north, still well within the cover of their mountains, and the scouts were pacing them, well-hidden in the dense, spring-hung bush beside the tracks. No attempt had been made to interfere with them, and by this Scapula knew that Caradoc was serious in his intent. He wanted Rome to find him. Scapula favored his second-in-command with a rare, beaming smile.

"I do not think the season will be overlong, Gavius. What a stroke of good fortune! Caradoc and his army, both together in one place and actually waiting for me! You would have thought that after all this time the stupid barbarian had learned some sense. He must know that we have no equal in pitched battle."

"I have heard that it was not a matter of good sense, sir," his tribune answered carefully, admitting to himself a certain disappointment.

The officers shared an admiring regard for the dogged, crafty enemy they had never seen, and their letters home were full of a speculation about him that the whole city of Rome had come to share. What manner of man was it who could resist not one but two legions, for over four years? Was he human, or a demon conjured out of the rivers where the tribes worshipped? Mothers disciplined their unruly children with the mention of his name. Young women dreamed of being captured by him, young men of fighting him and winning, and the bored, jaded members of Claudius's entourage enlivened the long winter days with titillating gossip about him. He was disfigured, a monster. He was the bastard son of a Roman trader who had seduced and abandoned his mother, and he had sworn revenge. He was Mars himself, come to jolt his lax worshippers into a new reverence. The permutations were endless. Even Claudius's new wife Agrippina played the game when she was not devising others that were less innocuous. But Claudius, remembering the hostile, disdainful eyes of the barbarian princess who had defied him all those years ago, did not join in the fun. He had forgiven Plautius for marrying her, indeed he could have done little else, for Plautius had arrived home on a tide of hysterical public acclaim and Claudius had presented the pair with another estate and a team of chariot horses for the arena. But he did not encourage them to come to court and they had retired thankfully to the Silvanus's ancestral halls. Claudius knew who the people's arviragus was. He was a man. Brilliant, charismatic, but still only a man, who ate and slept, fought and loved, and as such he would be defeated one day and come before him here, at the heart of the world. Claudius could wait.

"Caradoc did not choose an open confrontation freely," the tribune went on. "His chiefs have tired of harassing tactics and want the issue decided once and for all."

Scapula gave him a sharp look. "So you have set him up as some kind of people's hero, too?" He looked back at the gray landscape. "You will change your mind when you see him. He is nothing but a filthy, skinny, uncouth madman." The commander's voice rose a notch and his face began to flush.

"Yes, sir," the tribune said hastily.

Emrys walked over to Caradoc and laid an urgent hand on his arm as he stood pondering, his brow furrowed under the winged helm. "Arviragus, you must decide, and decide soon," he said. "For four days we have marched beside the river and passed many valleys, and we must stop. The legions are only two days away."

"I know," Caradoc answered automatically, "I know. Give me a moment, Emrys."

They had come down out of the hills for the first time in months, to the feet of the steep, rock-strewn foothills and the big river that rose near Emrys's town, and then they had turned north to seek a good place to give battle. Caradoc had known that the trees above them were full of Roman scouts, but he forbade Madoc to flush them out. Let them watch and count, let them run to Scapula, let him come swiftly, swiftly, and then, oh please the Mother, then a little peace, a little rest. Now he shook his head decisively and waved the leaders on. "This place will not do!" he shouted. Resignedly they began to straggle on, the late afternoon sun bathing them, and Caradoc, watching them go, seemed to see them all wading through a fine, blood-soaked mist. He swung after them. He was not sure what he was looking for, but no valley he had yet seen had smote him with the immediate certainty that this was the place, and something inside him kept his eyes ahead, to the next clean swoop of tree-clad land, the next high-running, gray-rocked declivity.

"We will camp around the next bend," he said to his train. "Madoc, it is the Silures turn to mount a guard. See to it." Behind him he heard the singing begin. The army had sung each evening since they clambered down out of the mountains' grasp and had plunged their sticky, wiry bodies into the water. Now the song swelled out suddenly, picked up by ten thousand throats as the sun became a fiery ball entangled in the trees. Tonight it was a raiding song, rich with words of victory, and he listened to it impassively, unmoved by the full, rolling tones flung up against the hills and cascading back to the river floor. His advance force had already vanished and he himself was nearing the foot of the spur of land that swept to the river. The sun dropped lower. He reached the spur and rounded it slowly, thinking of nothing but fire and food, then all at once he stopped.

He was looking into a valley that opened out on his left. Its mouth ended a mile further on, the new spur dim in the rapid shrouding of evening. The valley itself ran back, at first a flat grade strewn with

344

needle-sharp gray rocks that had tumbled from the plateau above, then rising swiftly and steeply to a haphazard, boulder-pitted slope dotted with stunted trees and hung with the girdle of some ancient fortification. The sun had almost gone and the whole silent, empty place was lit by cheerless and forbidding shafts of light that faded before the dismal shades of night even as he stood rooted to the spot.

Cinnamus came to a halt beside him and whistled. "This is the place, Lord, beyond any doubt. We can repair the defences halfway up the slope and not even Scapula will be able to fight up that hill!"

"I think you are right, Cin. Emrys, pass the word that I do not want the people camping down here. Send them up onto the plateau above the valley and they can light their fires in under the trees."

"Then you have chosen this place?" Emrys pressed him. "We will fight here?"

Caradoc shrugged. "I am not sure. I will tell you in the morning."

Emrys stood up. "By then it may be too late," he remarked, but he went away, and Cinnamus went with him.

Caradoc raised his head to watch the long, snaking tuaths scramble up the steep slope. It was almost full dark and somewhere on the other side of the river, lost in a murky, damp early summer twilight, fifteen thousand men waited to smash his people's pride. He felt lonely and friendless, and full of foreboding. He lowered himself onto a rock in deep shadow and sat for a long time while the night breeze sprang up, bringing to him the sweet, rich odors of the newborn leaves, running sap, and the wild, delicate tang of the thorny gorse.

I smelled that smell on my wedding day, he thought, Eurgain and I, young and innocent and full of brash hopes. I wish that men were not dumb, stupid gaming pieces of the Fates. I wish that I could take destiny and bend it to my will. Cin was right. No place but this could serve us so well, and that is a good omen. It would be foolish to march on and perhaps be caught by Scapula in a place where we cannot turn to fight. He put his head down onto his knees, lacing his fingers and placing them behind his neck. I will stay here. I will run no more. He felt his fate tighten its hold but he fought it off. I will be the master, he thought obstinately. I will make my soul mine to command. Yet he sat on, unmoving while the stars came out, and all the valley shone with the cold silver light of the rising moon.

In the morning his spies brought him word that the Romans had been delayed by the dispatches. Scapula was making very sure that his rear was safe before the final encounter. He felt that he could take his time, and the soldiers made their last-minute preparations while the speculatores returned to him with word that the lowland was quiet.

Caradoc ordered every man and woman to work, and they spent the day gathering rocks to repair the curving wall behind which they could shelter themselves and the freemen could use their slings. He, Emrys, and Madoc stood high on the lip of the plateau, looking out over a land bright with summer sunshine.

"I do not want the chiefs to fight to the death," he told them. "If the battle goes against us, tell them to run so that we may fight another day. Impress on them, my friends, that though it is honorable to die in battle, yet it is better to swallow honor and live to go on fighting."

"You doubt," Emrys commented, and Caradoc turned to him, annoyed.

"Of course I doubt! If we win tomorrow it will be the first time any gathering of tribes has done so. We have every chance of winning if only the tribes will obey commands, but you know as well as I that they insist on fighting on their own, and even I cannot keep them together in the heat of a battle. It will be up to you, both of you, to control your people."

For a moment they watched the activity below. The valley crawled with brown and gray-clad figures, sleeves rolled up, brawny muscles straining, and already the wall looked less untidy. The people labored in a mood of gaiety, laughing and singing as though they were preparing the spring sacrifices, and their light-heartedness irritated Caradoc. Children, he thought. All of them, children. He turned from them abruptly.

"Emrys, you and your tuath can take the middle of the valley. Madoc, the Silures must stand to the right where there is less cover for us. I will put the Demetae on the left," he pointed, "where the trees crowd onto the valley floor and the cavalry will be unable to get through. Gather your people right against the river so that we may assault the men with rocks and stones while they are trying to ford it. Then we can fall back behind the wall." They nodded in agreement. "And one thing more," Caradoc finished. "Tonight the people can cast their rags on the fires. We will skulk in the colors of animals no longer."

By sundown the wall was whole, sweeping the bouldered mile from side to side of the valley almost shoulder high, and the people retired to the height above to polish weapons and make their incantations. Their gods had traveled with them, and Caradoc, moving from campfire to campfire, listened to the rise and fall of soft voices grouped about the stone and wooden figures who squatted or sat cross-legged before their worshippers, three-faced or three-headed, grotesquely misshapen into swollen bellies, or thin as hazel sticks. He and the chiefs had stood by the river and watched as Bran dipped oak leaves

346

in the water, muttering his spells, and they had cast into the muddy, silted depths the last of the captured gladiae and pila. The goddess did not respond but a dead fish had risen suddenly, floating on the surface like a rainbowed sliver of winter sun or snow, and it was a good omen.

Night had come, an angry sunset of black thunderclouds with burning, orange underbellies, and the spies had come too. Scapula had arrived. Caradoc strode with them to the lip of the gorge and looked out, seeing the twinkle of a thousand cooking fires across the river, and even as he tried to count them he heard the trumpet sound the tuba for the evening ceremonies to Jupiter. He dismissed the spies and walked to his tent, glad that things were coming to a head. He raised the flap and walked in.

Eurgain was setting out his dress for the morning, yellow breeches fringed in gold thread, the blue tunic patterned boldly with black and yellow squares, and the long, soft scarlet cloak, tasseled with gold. She had opened the box that held their jewels and he went to it, lifting the silver bracelets, the coral-studded brooches, the circlets set with pink pearls.

"Cin brought your shield," she said. "Are you going to use it?" He looked to where his ceremonial shield had been laid beside the battered wooden one that had taken so many cuts, then he shook his head.

"The enameling would get scratched" was all he could say, a lump coming to his throat as he watched her brown fingers move among the treasured playthings of another time. "Eurgain," he said, "I want to hold the women in reserve. I do not entirely trust the Demetae. They fight well but they are all like Tog. If the first charge does not win the day they swiftly become confused, and I may need to send you and Vida to strengthen the left flank."

"And what of Llyn and his chiefs?"

He sank to the floor, pouring himself beer. "Llyn will fight beside me. He will protest, but this time I need him near me."

"And the girls?"

"They do not fight. They can stay in the rear, with the children and the old." He drank without pleasure, and Eurgain closed the jewel box and came to sit beside him.

"Caradoc, if we do not carry the day, what then?"

He put down his beer and pulled her closer, taking a braid in his hands and undoing it slowly. "Then we will run. Back to the west or into Brigantia. And we will start all over again." He shook the waving hair free and began to undo the other one.

"Sometimes I think that we will grow old and die in these moun-

347

tains," she said, "and never again know a home that is not a leaking tent, or a cloak that is not threadbare, or a moment when we can laugh together without fear and walk under the moon without danger."

He made no comment but gathered the golden, white-streaked cascade into his hands, and looked into the tanned face.

"Eurgain," he said. "I love you. How long has it been since I told you that?"

Her eyes widened in surprise and gladness. "I do not think that you have ever told me," she replied, her voice catching on the emotion that swelled her throat, and he kissed her longingly, knowing that time would not stand still for them and cruelly and inevitably the evening would give way to night, and the night to dawn, and perhaps he would never again hold her in his arms, the woman who was his other self. The coming battle lent a slow poignancy to their passion, bringing to their tired bodies the dark freshness of habits played out for the last time, joys to be savored with careful, subtle selection, and when there was nothing left to say they slept deeply, slumped against each other.

In the dawn's pale, somnolent light they woke and dressed quickly, strapping on their swords over the bright, flaunting tunics and lifting their shields. Then they said goodbye, speaking carefully as though the noon would find them together again at meat around the Great Hall's fire. They parted with a studied indifference, she to the women who were gathering under the motionless trees and he down to the valley floor, where Cinnamus and Caelte waited for him.

The morning was close and oppressive. Clouds were banked in one solid mass from horizon to horizon and in the east the tongues of lightning flashed soundlessly. The air was so thick that Caradoc felt his legs push through it, and it seemed laden with menace. Men's heads swam with the need for more sleep, and thoughts came sluggishly.

The three of them walked to the water and stood looking on the busy omnipotence of Rome. Far to the rear the cavalry cantered back and forth, the horsehair plumes of the mounted men hardly moving in the stifling atmosphere, and in the odd clarity of light that precedes a storm Caradoc could make out a knot of officers being briefed. He could even see their features. Was Scapula one of them? The army was milling about on a thin strip of flat land beside the river, thousands of helmeted, iron-clad insects, all dismally identical to the eyes of the chiefs. Right by the water a plume of incense rose straight into the air.

"What are they doing?" Caradoc asked curiously.

"Telling the omens," Caelte answered. "It is the second time this morning. The weather is upsetting the soldiers and I think they have demanded a clearer reading of the auguries before they will fight."

"Then their priests will have to lie to them," Cinnamus said promptly. "For we will win, and no one will dare to tell them so."

"Are all the chieftains ready?" Caradoc enquired.

Cinnamus nodded, and they turned to look back. The tribesmen were strung out over the whole mile-long front, a warm, vibrant splash of many colors, brilliant in the dull light. The chiefs proudly sported bronze, lazy-patterned shields and thick helms, and their spears were upright and bristling, and their cloaks were flung back, brushing the ground. In front of them the freemen ranged, some dressed in simple tunics, some naked, the dull blue of their intricate tattooing blending well with the gray of the rocks around them. All held their leather shields, and pouches full of stones and slivers of hard rock swung from their shoulders.

Caradoc turned to his men, taking them by the wrists and then embracing them. "Safety and peace," he said quietly. "You have served me well, both of you, my dearest ones. May you live again!"

They replied quickly, stumbling over the words, gripped suddenly in the same vise of presentiment that had brought unlooked-for tears to Caradoc's eyes. Then the three of them ran back through the ranks of freemen and up to where Llyn and his young chiefs strode restlessly back and forth, a light in their eyes.

Caradoc picked up his spear, unclasped his cloak, and let it fall. He turned. It all seemed so sickeningly familiar, and for a moment, with a horrible, unhealthy warping of the mind, he believed that he was lying in his bed at Camulodunon beside Eurgain and dreaming it all, but then the dizziness passed. The atmosphere was threatening, the cloud cover was low and black, and the valley held a sudden, expectant silence as both armies waited, all preparations made, for the shock of engagement. Terror stalked on the perimeter of Caradoc's consciousness, but he took a deep breath and fought it down. Suddenly the incursus rang out, clear and startling from across the water, and the first Roman ranks slid into the river. Caradoc raised the carnyx to his lips and blew with all his might, and the high, wild note struck the trees to either side and rebounded a hundredfold. Drawing his sword he jumped onto a boulder and swung it over his head. "A death morning!" he shouted. "A battle morning! Camulos for the Catuvellauni!" With a roar, the tribes sprang forward, beating on their shields, crying and screaming, and in the forefront the freemen twirled their slings. Legionaries were already dropping in the water, eyeless from the slingers' stones, but more poured in after them, and then all at once they were across and fighting, their fellows scrambling out of the water after them like waves of black beetles. Caradoc leaped down and ran, Cinnamus and Caelte behind him, Llyn and his band circling them with swords high, and they fell upon the soldiers with a grim, cold burning in their eyes and arms that dealt a pitiless revenge.

For three hours the tuaths fought like demented men, and under Caradoc they had learned their lessons well. Rome could not form ranks to drive a wedge through the whistling, slashing swords, and the soldiers found themselves isolated, forced to battle with no friendly arm beside them and further slowed by their fear of the gathering storm.

Scapula watched. He was not worried, and when he saw that his first shock wave of infantry could make no headway he ordered the release of the rest. They obediently forded the river, followed on the flanks by auxiliaries who fought with the tribesmen's own weapons, for they were recruits from Gaul and Iberia.

Suddenly Caradoc heard a great wailing go up. The Demetae had tired and the officers, seeing the tribesmen falter and break, had the trumpets sounded. Soldiers ran from the bank, dripping, and hurriedly formed ranks, driving into the disorganized Demetae who cursed, broke, and fled up the slope and into the trees beyond. Then Caradoc saw the women emerge from the wood, high above the chaotic clamor, with their swords raised. He thought he glimpsed Sine's copper-colored, stiff mask. They swept down the sides of the valley to where Rome was already driving purposefully toward Emrys and the Ordovices, and they fell upon the soldiers' unsuspecting rear like avenging goddesses. Then Caradoc could see no more, for the battle eddied toward him and he turned to fight.

The tribes slowly gave back. The rout of the Demetae had given the legionaries a chance to come together and now they faced the leaping, shrieking chiefs in well-nigh impregnable blocks of linked shields from which the little stabbing swords danced like snakes' fangs.

Scapula's spirits rose. Noon had come and he was hungry, really hungry, for the first time in nearly five years as he saw the chiefs backed against their wall of defence, watched them jump it, saw the land before it turned from variegated colors to a uniform gray. "Testudo," he ordered happily and the order was passed, and the trumpets blared. The massed legionaries melded into one metaled front against the rockwall. The shields were raised above helmeted heads, and the chiefs who leaned over to hack at Roman heads found their blades turned on an unyielding floor. Now the Romans scented victory. With hope revived they tore at the rockwall, while the tribes-men hurled missiles at them and reached to pierce that chinkless armor.

Caradoc, looking along the top of the wall, saw the impasse and shouted, "Back! All of you! To the top!"

He searched for Llyn but could not see him, and as he turned to flee to the plateau with the other torn, bloody warriors he heard a new howling. Arrows began to fall among the defenders as the auxiliaries found their range, and the scrambling men and women fell, pierced in the back. Caradoc ran. Cinnamus and Caelte joined the rout, and they stretched out, reaching for the lip of the valley with every nerve, yet not seeming to make ground, as though they were locked in a never-ending nightmare while the arrows sang around them. Cinnamus shouted, "All is not lost, Lord! We can turn and best them, and it will be their turn to struggle uphill!"

"Save your breath!" Caradoc snapped, and then he heard the high hiss of an arrow coming close, and he flung himself to the earth.

"Ah Lord!" Caelte cried out, and Caradoc heard another sound, a faint, abrupt hiccup. He whipped around. Cinnamus lay beside him, hands pressed flat to the ground, struggling to rise. Shock filled the round, sea-green eyes, and a gout of bright blood erupted from the wide mouth.

"Mother!" he coughed. "I am struck!" He slumped, and one blue-clad arm twisted behind him, scraping uselessly at the black-shafted arrow that jutted from his back, then the hand slid to his side, the eyes glazed over, and he was dead.

For one frozen moment the noise of battle ceased. Time stood still. The running chiefs slowed their steps and barely moved. Caradoc threw himself on the body of his friend, his cheek rammed against the blood-smeared blond braids, his arms spread out to embrace the tight-muscled back, still fleetingly warm beneath him. "Not you, Cin!" he whispered in amazement. "Mother, not you!" Tears gushed in a pain-ful flood of rage and loss and he raised himself to look into the placid, empty face, oblivious of the soldiers toiling toward him. Cinnamus gazed at him with a sad nobility. Caradoc sprang up and reached to him. He put a foot on the wiry back and with both hands wrenched the arrow free, then he broke it across his knee and flung it away, bending again to gently lift the body. But Cinnamus, for all his lithe grace, had been a solidly built man, and Caradoc could not raise him. Sobbing with frustration he squatted, and Caelte shook him by the shoulder, his own tears sprinkling the ground.

"Lord, it is fate. You can do nothing but mourn for him, and he would not have wanted you to die for him. We must fight on."

Caradoc nodded and rose, heedless of the fresh crop of arrows clattering in the stones about him. Swiftly, he unbuckled Cinnamus's sword belt, and his tears flowed afresh as he gently pried the blade loose from the strong-boned fingers. Then he leaned down once more, kissed the high forehead, and fled with Caelte to the cover of the trees. As they tensed for the final spurt, a sheet of white fire lit the heavens, there was a deafening, heart-stopping crack of thunder directly overhead, and the burdened clouds opened. A blinding wall of warm water poured down, soaking both of them before they ran in under the shadow of the forest, but they hardly noticed it. Caradoc ran and leaned Cinnamus's sword against a tree, then joined the others, for the Romans came on like soulless beasts and the chiefs, at last, turned at bay.

Their will had not been broken. For another hour they hewed the legions, the bitter memories of the long years behind them leading a brutal, superhuman strength to arms that had ceased to register weariness, but inexorably the battle turned against them. Rain streamed down steadily, turning the steep slopes into treacherous, muddy rivulets, and men fought and died ankle-deep in the loose, sloppy soil. Under the trees it was drier and here the fighting was fierce, but one by one the chiefs fell, and the afternoon wore drearily on. Finally Caradoc sought Madoc.

"Pass these words," he said. "It is time to run. Scatter into the forests, go west and north. No more must die if we want to fight on." Madoc lumbered wearily away and Caradoc began to hunt for Llyn, and for his wife, and Vida. Oh Mother, Vida, he thought in a panic close to hysteria. What shall I say to her? Around him he saw his army begin to vanish, speeding low into the gloom in twos and threes. But Scapula, across the river now and standing with his Second in the downpour, ground his teeth as he saw what was happening.

"They are getting away!" he said. "Order the cavalry after them! If Caradoc goes free again I will crucify every one of my officers!" His stomach lurched and began to churn and he wanted to double over at the swiftness of the attack, but he forced his shoulders back. The valley was strewn with sodden lumps that were the bodies of the slain. Please, Mithras, he begged, let one of them be Caradoc.

Off to his right Caradoc heard the whinnying of horses but he did not pause, running on as silently as his aching legs would allow. Cavalry were of no use in this densely wooded, gorge-ridden country, slit savagely with roaring streams that pounded down precipitous slopes to the river, and he was not afraid that he would be cut off. He did not know where he was going, he just ran, and the sounds of the seeking soldiers faded. Caelte sped with him. Presently they slowed,

352

and all at once a white-robed figure stepped out from behind a thick oak trunk. Caradoc reached for his sword, but Caelte whispered, "Bran!"

The Druid came swiftly to them, and he wasted no words. "Listen to me, Caradoc. Do not go around in circles. I will stay and find Eurgain and Llyn, and the girls, I swear it, and send them to you. Your life is more precious than theirs to the tribes, and you know it. Where is Cinnamus?"

"Dead," Caradoc said softly, feeling the cold simplicity of the word like an arrow in his own back, and Bran was silent for a moment, at a loss for words.

"That is a cruel blow," he said then. "The Ironhand was one of the greatest warriors ever to be born to the Catuvellauni. But do not mourn him, my friend. He died heaped with honor, and he will live again." He stepped forward. "Now. Do not go back into the west. Scapula will seek you without sleeping and without sanity, and for many months the men of the west will be hunted like animals. Before Madoc and Emrys can reunite them many of them will have died. You must on no account be taken. Go into Brigantia. Find Venutius. If he does nothing else, he will give you shelter and hide you." He embraced Caradoc and then pushed him away. "Run. Run! Even now Scapula is searching among the bodies for you. Keep the sun on your left shoulder." Without another word he turned from them, blending with the gray pall that hung about the trees and disappearing, and Caradoc stood listening to the silence.

The death throes of his people were far away. Eurgain, he thought, my heart, must I leave you? And my son, and my little girls? He heard the mournful drip, drip of water in the leaves. He smelled the secret, lonely smell of the forest. Slowly and reverently he ran his fingers down the length of Cinnamus's blood-encrusted sword, feeling an end, a gaping ravine in the smooth continuity of time which he would somehow have to leap, and then stagger on. "Well, Caelte," he said. "It is you and I. Let us run."

Within two days the west was crawling with patrols. With an intuition born of five long years, Scapula knew that Caradoc would not retreat into Ordovician territory. Not this time. His army was scattered, his painstaking labor destroyed, and he would need time to recover. Therefore the commander ordered auxiliaries into the hills that sheltered the gap between the west and Brigantia, and they rushed to cut him off before he slipped from their hands. Scapula knew his chances, and they were slim. The tribesmen had melted back into the impregnable, secret holds of the mountains and the soldiers moved with no fear of being molested, but it was like searching for one shadow in a land of shadows, and Scapula's only hope lay in reaching the gap and filling it with his men before the rebel got there. He paced angrily back and forth by the river, rain drumming on his breastplate and beating on his head, watching the bodies of the slain being slung onto the heaps for burning. His belly was on fire. Only some four hundred tribesmen had fallen in the battle. So few, and the rest had gone. Scapula was not so naïve as to imagine that the west was won. The tribes would quietly lick their wounds for a while and then Caradoc would return to them, probably with reinforcements lured by the honey of his words. Then Claudius would lose all patience and recall him to Rome, not to a triumph but to disgrace.

Sweat sprang out on his brow and mingled with the warm deluge. His reputation rested on two fine, ephemeral chances—capturing Caradoc and discovering the strongholds of the men of the west. Neither seemed remotely likely, but he had done all he could, and if he pitied himself, he pitied his successor more. Albion was a squalid, magic-ridden trap.

He turned to his second. "Gavius, I want the cohorts to move south and west. I want Siluria combed. The rebel has his most loyal support from there, and if we can destroy it then perhaps the other western tribes will give up." He looked to where plumes of black, stinking smoke were curling lazily into the curtain of the storm. "I want the Silures exterminated, all of them. Every man, woman, and child. Burn the fields. Fire the villages. There will be no resistance for some time to come." He did not wait for an acknowledgment. He swung away, striding to his boat and then the inviting solitude of his tent, aware that he was cold, wet, and unutterably miserable.

Caradoc and Caelte lay on the lip of the gorge, concealed by the thick, shiny greenness of the holly bushes that clung obstinately to the crest of the frozen wave of land. For three days they had run, pausing only to snatch brief hours of sleep when they were so exhausted that they could run no more, stopping to snare rabbits when hunger drove them, yet often not daring to light a fire, always aware of the unseen presence of the soldiers all around them. But running was balm, running was anesthetic, a blessed, mindless therapy of automatic motion when thoughts died and instincts were strained to interpret the sounds around them.

On the evening of the first day they had crossed a stream. They had stripped, taking their bright clothes and tearing off the tassels and braid, stamping their cloaks, tunics, and breeches into the brown mud, and for the first time Caradoc had regretted his dun rags. Then

354

they had sped on, clad without color like leaf mold and darkness, and even the moon had not marked their swift passing.

Now at last the gap lay below them, bottomed by the river that flowed turgid and deep, already full of the shadows of the evening, though the sun still filtered golden through the dark holly leaves, and between the watchers and the innocent, tree-lined banks the soldiers waited.

Caradoc looked down. Scapula had beaten them.

"We must go back," Caelte whispered. "We can cross farther south," but Caradoc did not reply.

Farther south there was a fort, and the valley leading out of the west was broad and full of villages. Besides, there was no going back. The forests were full of patrols. He lay very still, eyes closed, thinking. The men below were not regular soldiers. They were auxiliaries, men from Thrace or Gaul, skilled in tracking, able to flit through the woods like silent deer. They were his blood cousins, Caradoc knew, but he knew also that they could not be bribed. Although they looked out at the world through eyes as blue as Eurgain's, they were Roman to the heart, taken from their tuaths as children, and they hunted him relentlessly, as an enemy. He tore his thoughts from his wife, opened his eyes, and looked at Caelte.

"It must be this way," he said, "and it must be tonight. If we wait another day we will be caught. The patrols are already too close behind us. The moon is waning and there are clouds in the east so perhaps the night will be dark enough for us to get across the river without being seen."

"We do not know the fords," Caelte objected, "and of course we would not be seen. But we might be heard. We need Bran here, to put a holding spell on the soldiers."

Caradoc pointed. "We can work our way along the gorge and cross there, where the trees are thickest. There will be a sentry or two, but we will be just two more shadows. Now we must sleep. You first, Caelte."

His bard did not argue. He curled himself into a ball like a fox and was almost instantly asleep, but even in his unconsciousness there was a quality of watchfulness. Caradoc lay beside him, eyes on the kindly face and grieving at the empty grasses on his right hand, where Cinnamus's warm body should have been pressed. Resolutely, he warded off any thought of his family. Each one of us is alone now, he told himself. Living or dead, we can do no more for each other. The golden light faded to pale rose and in the dimness Caradoc lay with his shield-bearer's sword against him, and mourned.

Just after the moon was up they rose, bundled their cloaks under their belts, and set off. The valley floor was quiet as they slipped like wraiths back under the night-hung trees and slunk west to where the descent was more precipitous and the rocks would give them shelter. In an hour they found the edge again and cautiously lowered themselves over, feeling immediately exposed to the sentries who paced slowly beneath them, their boots crunching audibly on the loose stones. They inched from rock to shadowed rock, holding their breath, testing each foothold for fear they might send gravel rattling to the floor, not glancing down for fear the moon might glitter in their eyes.

At last they crouched together at the foot, peering along to where the little tents squatted. All was quiet. Only the sentries stalked, three moving up and down before the camp, six covering the river. The clump of trees directly ahead of the two men stood still and calm, a haven of shadows, but both knew that concealed in the depths more sentries waited, hands to their gladiae, eyes nervously straining.

Caradoc patted his chest and Caelte nodded. They lay on their bellies and began to slither over the rock-pitted ground, slumping into an inert stillness every now and then to press their ears to the earth. The trees drew nearer, became willows and vines, and Caradoc's sharp eyes picked a short, upright trunk that he was sure was not a tree. Caradoc rolled silently away, and Caelte followed.

The clouds had not floated in to cover the moon but clung stubbornly to the east, and moonlight brimmed the valley, spilling out aloof and peaceful to bathe the river. At last the fugitives felt moss and stiff ferns under their hands and the warm tree shadows danced on their backs.

There must be another sentry, Caradoc thought anxiously. Where is he? They were within hearing of the soldier who stood stolidly off to their left, and before they moved they carefully cleared the way of twigs and last year's still-crisp leaves, and while they worked, patiently and slowly, the moon reached its zenith and began to swing west. Caradoc saw a glint of light on water ahead of him. It was the river at last, but between himself and the water there was another shadow, tall, helmeted, and he knew that there was no longer time to find a way around. He cursed violently to himself, motioned for Caelte to lie still, and rose into a crouch, not knowing in the snug darkness whether the man was facing them or the river. He stepped forward, softly drew his knife, then sprang, one hand cupping hard against the sentry's chin to force it up into his shoulder, the other going for the exposed throat. The man had been looking across the water and it was a simple matter to drive the blade home behind his ear. He sagged in Caradoc's arms with scarcely a gurgle but the quick scuffle had been heard, and as Caelte glided past Caradoc and on into the river the other sentry called, "Did you hear something?"

Caradoc lowered the body to the ground, wiped his knife on the grass, and tucked it back in his belt.

"It was nothing," he answered, the Latin coming hard to his tongue after so many years. "A squirrel, that was all." The other man grunted, and Caradoc went after Caelte, dropping quietly into the cool, dark water. He was immediately out of his depth and before he had adjusted to his stroke, the current had carried him several yards downstream, but he took a full breath, sank beneath the murky surface, and battled grimly to the other side. As he dragged himself free of the weeds' slimy grip Caelte was waiting for him, and without pausing to wring out their clothes they fell to the earth once more, wriggling quickly into the covering darkness of the wooded slope beyond.

All night they pushed on through dense trees choked in old, half-rotten underbrush, and when dawn came and they could go no farther they fed on the tight-curled tendrils of young ferns and the rabbit meat they had saved. Then they slept together, pressed uncomfortably into the heart of a giant bramble. Their sense of urgency had diminished with the crossing of the river. They were out of Scapula's net now, and though the whole of Brigantia crawled with Romans, they were not actively seeking Caradoc, and he and Caelte had a good chance to pass themselves off as peasants when they came to the treeless, rolling country where Aricia's people herded their flocks. Caradoc thought briefly of her while sleep lapped at him, but he was too tired for the memories to do anything but fill him with a warmth of poignancy. He wondered where Venutius was. If he was with her, then they were running from danger into danger, but if, as his spies had told him, Venutius was once again in the far north with his chiefs, a new campaign could begin, perhaps next spring. The prospect was appalling. It filled him with despair. But he knew with a dull, tired stubbornness that it must come, that either he must die or Claudius must give in, for he was still arviragus, and could not lay aside his responsibility. He slept fitfully, uneasily, while the hot summer sun strode proudly across the sky, and far away Scapula waited for word from his auxiliaries camped by the river, looking for the wild boar that had already gored through the net and was gone.

In two days they came to a village and Caradoc decided reluctantly that here they must seek proper food and try to glean such information as they could. He took off his gold torc and the magic egg from around his neck, thrusting them deep inside his tunic, and he and Caelte walked slowly down into the circle of wattle huts. The village was quiet. Smoke rose from the roofs, dogs yawned and panted in the thin shade of the palisade, and one or two near-naked children played desultorily in the shallows of the stream that meandered tiredly out of the trees. In the center was the Council hut, a stone wall around it, and the travelers reached it before they were challenged. Then a tall, gold-bearded chief rose from the shadow of the gate and barred their way.

"Greetings," he said curiously. "Welcome to this village. There is meat and bread if you are hungry, but first you must tell me who you are."

"We are Cornovii," Caelte replied. "We are seeking a chief who will take us as his freemen, for the men of the west have burned our land and our lord is dead." The man's sharp eyes strayed to the swords hanging from their belts, and seeing his furtive glance Caradoc cursed himself. The swords should have been left in some safe, secret place, for most of the Cornovii and the Brigantians now went weaponless at Scapula's command, but all he had thought of was hot meat and perhaps a jug of frothing mead. He had not been so careless in a long time.

"Explain your swords," the chief said, an edge of suspicion to his tone, and Caelte hastened to assure him that they were booty, captured in the raid from which they had fled. But Caradoc could see that the man was not convinced and he wished now that they could turn and walk away, for he smelt fine mists of conjecture in the air that at any moment could condense to certainty.

"Remove them and leave them against the wall," the chief said curtly. "They will not be disturbed." He watched while they unbuckled their belts. Already several more chiefs were sauntering over, and as Caradoc followed the first man into the cool gloom of the hut he heard one of them say, "Look at this scabbard! Not western craftsmanship, I swear, and not Roman either. What do you think it is worth?" He hesitated, almost goaded into speech, but swung on his heel and turned to the chief who was waiting for him.

"Now I know where you are from," the chief said quietly. "I did not think that any man of the west could be so foolish. Sit and eat quickly now and then be on your way, for many of these people are in the pay of Rome and you are fortunate that I am not. Do not tell me your names. I do not want to know them." Caradoc and Caelte stretched out on the dirt floor, backs to the curving wall, and the man brought them hot, roasted mutton, apples, stale bread, and jugs of beer. He squatted before them, his level eyes searching their faces as they wolfed down the food. He seemed to be struggling with himself.

Several times he opened his mouth as if to speak then closed it again, but finally he sat, crossed his green-clad legs, and said softly, "If you seek Venutius then you must hurry. He is on his way from the north, back to the lady, and if you do not intercept him you might as well go back into the west. I cannot shelter you here, it is too dangerous for me and the freemen who are loyal to Venutius. Eat and go. Perhaps Brigantia the High One will give you luck."

Caradoc could not resist a question. "Is there any news of the legions?" he asked. The man looked at him for a long time before replying. Then he nodded. "The arviragus has disappeared," he said, his eyes lighting for a moment then dying, "and Scapula is taking his revenge on the Silures. He has ordered them wiped out, and already his soldiers range to and fro, killing the children and the old because they cannot find the warriors. Villages and crops are in flames."

I have done this, Caradoc thought, the meat turning to dust in his mouth. Perhaps the time has come to surrender myself even as Vercingetorix did, throwing myself on the mercy of Claudius in exchange for the safety of the people. But Madoc's face rose up before his eyes, and Bran's, and Emrys and Sine stood side by side to watch him with cold resolution. Freedom or death, arviragus. There is no compromise, and the mercy of Rome is like the adder's sting. He swallowed his mouthful with difficulty and picked up the beer. Where are you, Eurgain? Llyn?

"There was a report of prisoners taken," the chief went on. "But the news is very fresh and may not be truth. I pity the captives Scapula takes." Suddenly he leaned forward and spoke in an undertone. "Do me a courtesy, men of the west."

"We will," Caradoc replied, "if it is in our power."

"If you do not find Venutius, if you turn once more to fight in the west, if you should chance to meet the arviragus, will you tell him . . ." The lips shook, and the man looked down to hide his face. "Tell him that there are those in Brigantia who may be silent but who are not dishonored, and he is not alone."

"I think he knows that already," Caradoc said gently, "but if it should chance that he does not, then it will gladden his heart to be brought such words." He rose, Caelte beside him, thanked the chief, and left the hut. They picked up the swords and shouldered their way roughly through the gathering, walking swiftly to the edge of the village, taking care not to betray their urge to break and run from the hostile eyes fastened like leeches onto their backs.

They paced steadily for an hour, and once they were free of the village they relaxed. While the sun blazed overhead and the afternoon seemed to stretch interminably they traversed the last great forest before the long, gray-grassed horizons of Aricia's tuath, stopping often to drink from the cool, leaf-hung streams that splashed under the oaks. When the sun began to wester they rested, waiting for darkness to give them the cover the woods could not. They had just settled themselves beside a freshet and had taken off their soft leather sandals in order to soak their tired feet when Caradoc held up a warning hand and Caelte froze. Behind them, under the trees, came a soft rustling. They rose and drew their swords quietly, incredulous that here, at the last, they had been discovered, but it was not a Roman who pushed through the undergrowth with hands raised, it was a Brigantian chief.

"Peace, peace," he said hastily. "Put up your swords. I am unarmed."

Caradoc nodded at Caelte and the bard went to the man, removed his cloak, and quickly ran his hands over the short, chunky body. "His hair," Caradoc snapped, and Caelte felt among the tangled black tresses. Finally he was satisfied and stepped back, and Caradoc sheathed his sword. "So you have been tracking us," he said briskly. "Why?" He did not like the look of the man. There was something shifty in the face that reminded him of Sholto, and the black eyes would not meet his own.

"My lord set me to follow you," he explained. "He repented that he had not given you directions, and he asked me to guide you to Venutius."

Caradoc motioned him nearer. "We do not wish a guide," he said. "We prefer to travel alone. Go back and thank your lord for us."

"But without a guide you will not find Venutius before he returns to his lady in the town, and then you will not be able to see him, for the town is full of soldiers and traders.'"

"It is truth, Lord," Caelte said promptly. "We could wander over the trackless hills for days, and miss Venutius."

Caradoc beckoned him close and whispered, "I do not like the look of him, Caelte. I do not think he is a truth-sayer."

"Lord," Caelte hissed back, "we need a Druid to discover whether or not that is right and, besides, many of the people under the thumb of Rome have acquired the same look, for they are often forced into lies. The spies have it, yet they are loyal freemen."

"Yes, yes, I know, but there is a foul smell here. If I am wrong and yet refuse his aid, we are making a fruitless journey. If I am right and yet we go with him, he may lead us to a dark fate." He cast himself upon the ground, drew his cloak about him, and sat thinking.

The Brigantian watched him, impatience betrayed in the spasmodic clenching and unclenching of his hands, and Caelte watched the Brigantian with open mistrust.

Finally Caradoc stood. "I am loathe to put myself in your hands," he said heavily, "yet I must. It seems that time is running out for me, therefore I will go with you. May you guide us well!"

Caelte, his eyes on the man's round face, thought he saw a flash of satisfaction that was almost greed, then the chief nodded.

"I will guide you well, in exchange for your protection as long as I am with you. Will you share food and favor with me?"

"I will."

"And I."

"Then we will wait together for the night." He sat down in the grass and laced his naked fingers together, and Caradoc and Caelte put on their sandals. Their feet no longer ached as heavily as their hearts.

CHAPTER TWENTY-THREE

FOR ANOTHER THREE NIGHTS they journeyed, leaving the safe, dense woodland far behind. The two Catuvellauni hated the open country they now trudged across like wingless moths, exposed to the sweeping hot winds that flowed over the long grass and made it undulate like sea waves, and when they camped under the knots of stunted trees that sheltered in the valleys they were always reluctant to leave. Night after night the waxing moon hung fat and bloated above a vast, clean horizon, watching them complacently as they inched over the hills. The Brigantian urged them on. Hurry, he said, we will be too late, but they did not need his anxious whines to whip them on. With every step they were conscious that their fate lay waiting ahead of them. If they delayed it would contemptuously leave the meeting place and they would find only the impotent shreds of its capricious passing. They were oppressed by the landscape, by the long days of tension, by the silence that lay unfilled by any sound save the high calling of hawks. Sataida, Brigantia's Goddess of Grief, seemed to permeate the very earth beneath them, and Caradoc began to see the miles behind him as huge stones, jagged and cruel, over which his wife tried to clamber after him, calling him with parched tongue. Once or twice they lay prone in the grass while a cavalry patrol cantered past, but they were not spotted and finally, toward midnight on their fourth day from the forest, they crested a long, slow-rising spur of land and saw lights below them.

The chief pointed. "Venutius should be there."

"But that is a town!" Caradoc objected. "Venutius will be in an encampment."

The man clucked impatiently. "Why? When Brigantia is strewn with villages, why should he make a camp? I tell you he is there. We will go down."

Some sixth sense whispered a warning to Caradoc. Some old, long-forgotten memory stirred as he gazed down on the peaceful town. Was that the bulk of an earthwork in the center? The Brigantians did not erect earthwalls. But the man had already started down, Caelte after him, and Caradoc followed, his mind in confusion and his feet lagging. It was wrong, all wrong, it had been wrong ever since the accursed man had stepped out of the bush. He should have trusted his head, but it was too late. And really, he thought, I am almost too tired to care anymore.

Although the hour was late, the town bustled cheerfully. Traders carrying torches strolled to and fro, freemen sat before their doorskins and gambled or told tales, and here and there a soldier moved, bent on some business of their own. No one took any notice of the travelers as they passed through the gate sunk in the small defence wall, and there was no gateguard to challenge them. They began to climb the smooth, well-laid path that circled the town, rising in lazy spirals. To right and left of them the huts were built, well-spaced, neat, almost regimental in their placement, and Caradoc, rounding the bend that took them to the third circle, felt a wind that was laden with the pungent, rich tang of the sea. He stopped dead.

"We cannot have been moving north," he said. "The ocean must be very close, and Brigantia's coasts lie to the east." He took one stride and grasped the chief by the neck of his tunic, shaking him. "I closed the eye of my mind and trusted my safety to you, vermin!" he ground out. "Now tell me where we are or I will slice you in two." The man's eyes darted this way and that like a cornered rat and his teeth chattered under Caradoc's tossing.

"You swore me protection!" he bleated, and suddenly Caradoc let him go. He shrugged down his tunic, ran a hand around his neck, and looked at Caradoc reproachfully. "I have led you well," he sniffed, "and Venutius is here, as I said. Yes, we veered east, and we were almost too late, for the lady's town lies not far away, half a day's journey to the southeast, and tomorrow Venutius would have been with her again. Waste no time in foolishness, but follow me."

Caradoc and Caelte glanced at each other. Having once relinquished their instinct for direction to this man they had not carefully noted the way they had come. Now they were lost and they knew it. If they killed him and left the town they might never find Venutius. They were trapped.

Caradoc turned angrily. "Lead on then," he snarled, the tart, fresh sea-wind still buffeting him with doubt as they walked on together.

In the center of the first cycle, high above the town, they came at last to a house ringed by a high stone wall. Here the gate in the wall was guarded by a tall, black-visaged chieftain who was fully armed. His spear rested in his hand, his shield hung from one arm, and his sword hung from his belt. Beyond him, in the dimness of the court, more chiefs gathered silently, a bodyguard, and even before the three men had covered the last approach the gateguard had spoken a swift word and they came pouring to cover the gate. "Wait here," their guide whispered, and left them, going forward to speak with the chiefs.

Caelte leaned closer to Caradoc. "Now is the time to flee," he hissed. "I smell treachery, Lord, and I am sorry now that I swayed your judgment. Venutius is not here. He would never quarter in a place like this. The stench of Rome is overpowering."

Caradoc put an arm around his friend's shoulder. "All my decisions have gone amiss since I bowed my authority to the Council and thus angered Camulos and the Dagda," he replied wearily. "I am sorry, Caelte. I fear you are right, but it is too late to run anymore."

The man was beckoning them and the chiefs had drawn back, their black eyes full of a thinly veiled excitement. Caradoc and Caelte walked slowly through the group of men and on past the gate, which swung to behind them with a rude suddenness. The man made them wait once more and hurried away into the shadow, and Caradoc looked around him. Torches hung around the wall, casting a leaping, red light onto flagstones, fitfully revealing a large, wooden house built in the Roman style with four rooms all opening onto a raised covered porch. One of the doors stood open and candlelight gently warmed the gloom in a long yellow tongue. The feeling of treachery was claustrophobic, a suffocating pressure of deceit that filled the empty courtyard and turned the Catuvellaunians' blood to water. Caradoc looked behind him to the bolted gate and the chiefs clustered behind it. He looked to the walls, high, smooth, too high to leap, too smooth to scramble up. He looked to the open door, where even now the man was walking back to them, smiling. Fool! Fool! his mind shrieked at him. Trapped like an unblooded boy! His hand flew to the magic egg and clutched it tightly, but no calming emanation of Druithin spells warmed his fingers and he could only follow the Brigantian, who led them to the farther door, opened it, and bowed them through.

Caelte, brushing past him, noticed a new, bulging pouch hanging from his leather belt, but there was no time to wonder.

The man smirked. "A safe journey, Arviragus," he remarked sarcastically.

The door thudded shut behind him and they were alone.

They dismally surveyed their surroundings. A small fire crackled brightly in the hearth set into the wall. White sheepskins were scattered about, the walls were neatly plastered and painted in yellow and purple, and three wicker chairs were placed haphazardly. There were three niches set in one wall. One held a likeness of some goddess. Brigantia the High One, Caradoc guessed by the carved profusion of wild hair, the half-closed, glutted eyes, but the other two were strange to him. He turned to Caelte, but before he could speak the door opened again and the goddess herself glided to stand before him, flanked by four armed chiefs. He sensed Caelte move to stand to his left. He saw a Brigantian chief softly close the door and the others range in front of it, but the woman's face sucked all reality from the stuffy, foreign room and left only a whirl of shifting images, a fire-shadowed fantasy.

The black hair, now slashed with long tendrils of gray, still fell in an almost lewd profusion down her straight back, and the pale skin was even whiter than he had remembered, but it was tinged with an unhealthy hue that was somehow slack, as though the flesh beneath had been sucked inward. Some mysterious black stone ringed her high brow and her tall neck, and glinted sullenly from the belt that clasped her full, soft, red tunic to her, and imprisoned her naked arms. But it was her eyes that commanded the summoning of his will. They were still blacker than night but the impudent liveliness he had remembered with such a spasm of sick longing over the years, the hot imperiousness that had challenged him, had swelled to become the festering disease of devious selfishness. Caradoc stared with steady concentration, feeling the unslaked appetite of a deep self-hate come flowing to him from under lids that were swollen, folded at the edges into pouches of aging flesh, but he was oblivious to all save the thunderous crashing of the waves of memory and old desires washing within him. Aricia. Then, with a queer shifting of perspective that he felt almost to his bones, the room and the persons in it regained solidarity and she changed also. The fogs of that childhood obsession blew away and he found himself looking at a body that had once fascinated him, that had held a complex, tempestuous girl who had been left behind in the mirage of the past, and the well-remembered shell now held someone he did not know. The witch of his young lusts called once, a faint, dying echo, and he took a deep, free breath and spoke quietly. "Aricia."

"Caradoc." She smiled, a tiny twitch of pain and puzzlement, and then slid toward him, still with that easy, tempting swing. "But for the cleft in your chin and your way of holding your head I would never have recognized you. I left a brash, impulsive Catuvellaunian whelp to find a king wolf." She came closer and her hand trembled as she lightly touched his arm. "You do look like a wolf, you know. Lean and gray, lined and famished, burning with lost causes. It hurts me somehow, to see you like this. I have thought of you often over the years but my memories played me false, it seems."

He could not return her smile, and he took her fingers sadly. "Mine also, Aricia. I did not think that I had changed so much within myself until I saw you come into the room. It hurts me also, to have to bury my childhood at last."

"I buried mine long ago," she said, bitterness creeping into her voice. "On the day I left Camulodunon. You are lucky to have clung to yours for so long. I hated you, Caradoc, did you know that? For years I hated you. But now . . ." She shrugged. "Now I have no reason to hate any man. Love and hate belong to ignorant youth and grand dreams, and I have conquered both."

"Then you must truly be at peace," he said, wondering whether she knew that she was lying.

She shot him a dark glare and drew away a little. "I am content, which is more than you can say. I have followed your doomed path for years, Caradoc, ever since you deserted Gladys at Camulodunon. I have pitied you."

"Why?" He was still standing calmly but she had begun to fidget, the thin fingers pulling at each other.

All at once she turned from him and paced agitatedly by the fire. "Because the times have changed and left you behind," she replied in a high, hurried voice. "You and those deluded savages in the west. There must be change, Caradoc, men must change, or wither and die. The day of the tribes is over. Honor is a Roman word too, and it does not mean bloodshed." She suddenly stopped pacing and cried out to him, "Oh Caradoc! Why did you not accept, just accept, and be at peace?"

"Is that how you justify your own position?" he retorted, anger uncurling in him. "What has happened to you, Aricia?"

Her face hardened into a mask and the irrational rages that always simmered just below the surface of her control burst forth. "You dare to stand there in your stinking rags and ask what has happened to me? To me? What of yourself? All the blood in the west has not quenched the old dreams of conquest in you. Like your father and crazy Togodumnus you want to battle the world. You have used the poor, simple western chiefs without compunction, you have fed on their tender sheep's flesh, and they have gone down into death because you will not admit that you are wrong!" She almost ran to him, holding both quivering, outflung hands before his face. "You are only a man, only a man, you have faults and you fail and you hide shameful secrets, like everyone else! What gives you the right to destroy a people?"

He took her wrists in both his hands, feeling the anguished deluge of self-destruction pounding through her rigid body. "I cannot give you what you want of me," he ground out. "Do you want me to say that I am selfish, cruel, and unyielding? I know that I am those things. Did you offer money for my capture in order to hear me say that I wronged you all those years ago and that I admit it? I do admit it, Aricia, I treated you despicably, but do not lay the source of your torment at my door. Seek elsewhere." She wrenched herself free and he could see in her eyes the urge to strike him. "Nor will I say that I have donned the cloak of arviragus unworthily and led the tribes for my own ends. But you cannot deny this charge. You have ruined your people and your husband for no reason at all."

"Leave Venutius out of this," she snarled, walking to the fire, her red tunic swirling and her hair swinging with it. "You do not understand, Caradoc. You are an ignorant man." She turned from him and rested one limp arm along the mantel of the hearth and watched the embers glow.

All at once, in the moment of silence, he felt very weary. Fatigue scratched at his eyeballs and ached in his limbs and he wanted to sit down, but she looked suddenly across at him and smiled, and this time he saw her again, his fey, eager partner in the driving needs of youth.

"Ah Caradoc," she said. "It is a good thing that you no longer resemble that handsome son of Cunobelin or I might be tempted to keep you here with me. Tell me, is Eurgain well?"

"I do not know."

The black eyebrows shot up. "And your children?"

"I do not know."

"Where is Cinnamus Ironhand?"

"Dead."

366

Her lips parted in a sneer. "Brigantia, how ruthless you have become. The Druithin chose you well, didn't they? I do not think that even I pity you anymore." Her hands went to her temples and she massaged them briefly, then she nodded coolly in the direction of her chiefs. "Domnall, fetch the centurion." When he had gone, closing the door behind him, she walked to Caradoc. "The bloodshed ends here, Arviragus. Vercingetorix went to Rome in chains and so will you. Then perhaps there will be peace. I could have cut off your head, you know, and sent that to Scapula, but I decided that it would be better to send a living man to circle the forum. The tribesmen will not like to be shamed by an arviragus who has become a slave."

"It's not too late to find yourself again, Aricia," he said softly. "If Brigantia joined with the chiefs of the west then the Romans could not stand."

Astonishment wrung a sharp, choking laugh from her and she left the fire and came close to him, stroking his face, his neck, his hair with black-ringed fingers whose touch belied her words. "You poor, mangy old wolf! What ancient songs of victory still thunder in that muddled head of yours? I need the money you will bring to pay for the services of the architect I have engaged from Rome. You see, Caradoc, you are no longer worth any more to me than the price of my comfort." Her hands pressed down on his shoulders, and before he could draw back she had kissed him loosely on the mouth. "From one child to another," she whispered. She flung herself into a chair and crossed her legs, looking up at him soberly. "Forgive me, but if I do not hand you over, Scapula will think that I have changed my alliegance and he will march against me, whereas if I do my reputation as a loyal daughter of Rome will be enhanced a thousandfold. Do you at least understand this?"

"Yes," he replied patiently. "I understand."

"Oh you fool," she murmured. "Why did you allow yourself to be taken?"

There was nothing more to be said and they both waited in a resigned silence for the coming of the guards. Caelte had sunk to the floor where he squatted, head bowed, and the fire sparked joyfully on. Presently the door was flung open and six legionnaires rushed in, swords drawn, helmets and broad breastplates filling the room with a brisk efficiency. The centurion saluted Aricia and then turned curiously to the quiet, almost meek, bedraggled man who met his gaze with a steady scorn.

"This is their arviragus?"

"It is."

"You are sure, Cartimandua?"

"Of course." She was breathing quickly, lightly. "I have known him well."

Disappointment flooded the officer. He was such a common-looking chieftain. Where was the noble, cunning barbarian of his imagination? But then he scanned the face again, and he knew. "Optio," he snapped. "The chains."

Caradoc stood quite still as the heavy iron rings went round his wrists. He looked at Aricia as the soldier knelt to fasten them about his ankles. She was swinging her foot and gazing at the floor, and suddenly he shouted, "Look at me, Aricia! Or are you too cowardly? You wear them too, though you cannot see them!"

She did not respond, and as the optio hauled Caelte to his feet and chained him also, Caradoc struggled against panic. The man returned and unbuckled his sword belt, and Caradoc was a freeman no more. "Out," the officer ordered curtly, and the soldiers closed. Unthinking, Caradoc took a stride. The chains caught him and he stumbled, and then Aricia stood and laughed, a wild, undisciplined peal of glee. She spoke as he shuffled past her.

"One thing more, Caradoc," she said. "Your family is well. Scapula has them, at Camulodunon."

He turned slowly, seeing in her eyes the gloating eagerness to rip him apart, but he refused to bend under the weight of humiliation already setting upon him.

"You lie."

"Not this time."

"Bitch."

"A safe journey, a peaceful journey," she mocked, and then he was out under the soft night sky, warm wind in his face, and the door slammed shut behind him.

She slumped back into the chair and closed her eyes. Brigantia, I am tired, she thought. So tired, tired to my bones, and tomorrow Venutius will be here, with his hangdog, beseeching looks and his big, clumsy hands. Your hands were never clumsy, Caradoc, and you begged with honor, like a lord. What times we had, you and I, when our blood ran hot and the rain sang to us in the night! She reached into her tunic and drew out a small, wooden brooch, and absently her fingers traced the writhing snakes, smooth and warm to her touch. I have lived for this moment through all the long years of my exile, she told herself. Then why is it not sweet? Why this pain, this awful hurting? Her hand closed about the brooch, gripping it tightly, and desolation swept over her. Nothing satisfies me anymore, she thought with anguish, each triumph is a wasting and this, my greatest prize, is already spilling through my fingers. I cannot hold it. Suddenly she felt tears burn behind her closed eyelids and she opened her eyes. The walls blurred around her and the fire swelled to a rainbowed lake, but when she blinked the tears flowed faster. "Ah Sataida, Lady of Grief, leave me alone!" she whispered fiercely. "There was nothing else I could do!"

She spent the night in the wicker chair, drinking a little, feeding the fire in the small hours when her servants slept, seeing him in her mind's eye rocking and jolting in the cart toward Lindum, chained under the stars. Bitch, he had called her, his ravished face twisted into bitterness for a moment. She savored the epithet, turning it over slowly. Bitch. Well, so she was. She could not call Caradoc a liar. All the men she had met were lustful dogs sniffing around her—Caradoc, Togodumnus, Venutius, even Cunobelin in his way, all of them and the rest—so many tongues hanging out over the years, so many panting mouths! But, watching the night shadows move on her smooth yellow wall and feeling the firelight touch her cheeks, she knew that Caradoc had not meant this. Better, she thought, wincing from the sting, to stay away from all contemplation of what was his true insult. Honor in time of war was a luxury, in time of peace a safeguard. Nothing more. She should have told him so when she told him that men must change or die. She fell back in thought and explored the limits of her own change, realizing for the first time that it had not been deep enough. The young Brigantian ricon torn from the womb of Camulodunon still cowered, crouching in the recesses of mind and memory, bereft of honor, dependent on the frail support of a dead father, mourning in betrayal and hatred for her Catuvellaunian roots. Years ago she had taken a step away from that young girl, but it had not been wide enough. You poor, friendless little thing, Aricia thought as she emptied the wine jug. I thought I had killed you long ago.

Venutius arrived with the dawn. She must have been dozing, for she came to herself with a start to hear his deep voice raised in anger on her porch. "Out of my way, bastard whelp! Let me pass or I'll spit you like a suckling pig!"

She heard a scuffle and rose stiffly, her tongue furred and her head heavy from the wine. A yelp, an oath, and her door burst open, he lunging toward her, kicking the door closed behind him. He stopped inches from her and flung his sword onto the floor.

"Tell me it is not true!" he shouted. "Tell me before I throttle you with your own hair! Did you sell the arviragus to Rome?"

She faced him calmly, unimpressed by the rage she had seen so many times before, confident that in the end it would turn into fawning, pathetic apology.

"Yes, I did."

"Aaah!" He stood, fists clenched before him, long legs quivering, red hair falling over one shoulder. "I did not believe. I did not want to believe! You . . ." Words would not come.

"Bitch?" she finished softly for him. "Caradoc called me that too. I agree with him entirely."

"Why? Why? Every other indignity, Aricia, every other vileness. I have taken it all from you, but oh not this! A man of such miseries, such honor!"

That pernicious, meaningless word again. She shrugged. "I had to, Venutius. I couldn't turn him loose again. It would have been the end of Brigantia."

"You care nothing for Brigantia! You never did! Caradoc goes to his death so that you can at last warm your hands at the flames of revenge!"

"Think what you like. I did it, and I would do it again, and now get out. I've had no sleep tonight and I'm tired. Come and eat with me later—if you are in a better humor."

He did not respond as he usually did to the faint hint of waiting pleasure. Suddenly he half-stumbled, half-leaped upon her. Taking her by the shoulders he began to shake her viciously, snapping her head back and forth, and she could not find breath to cry out. Her necklace broke and jet showered them, catching in his hair, tinkling to the floor. He began to slap her face. At the first blow she fell backward into the chair, gasping, screams gathering behind her throat as he went on striking her and madness flickered in and out of his eyes.

"You will kill me, you will kill me. Stop, Venutius!" she shrieked.

At last, when she felt the skin of her cheek and temple split open and he saw the blood appear on his hand, he stood upright, breathing coarsely, loudly, and she slid to the floor, weeping and cradling her aching face in both hands, the jet stones hard and gritty beneath her knees. He was weeping also, the tears pouring down his cheeks.

"Even now I cannot make an end of you!" he sobbed. "Aricia, Aricia!" Reaching down he took her hair in one big fist, hauled her to her feet, and, dragging her to the door, opened it and pushed her out into the bright sunlight and warm wind.

Her bodyguard came racing across the courtyard, their swords drawn, but they found themselves cut off from her by their own kinsmen, Venutius's war band, who were planted stolidly in their way.

The men eyed one another in silence. Venutius brought her to the middle of the stone-ringed yard and let her go. Still weeping, he began to remove his jewelry—the black jet from his arms, his throat, his waist, the cloak's clasp from his shoulder—dropping the glinting pieces onto the ground. In one lithe movement he pulled his jet-embroidered tunic over his head and it collapsed gently onto her feet.

"I repudiate Brigantia," he whispered hoarsely, taking a little knife from his leather belt and quickly slicing across his broad chest. Blood leaped up to meet the blade from left collarbone to waist—slick, wet, and glittering in the sun, and slapping his palm against it he stepped closer to her and rubbed it into her face. "My blood!" he spat at her. He stooped and worked loose a clod of earth from the ground with the knife, breaking it in his strong fingers, then he slammed it against her cheeks. "The blood of Albion! You have slain us both. May I be cursed if I ever reach for you in love again."

She stood with head bowed before him, her hands trembling upward to hide her humiliation, and he turned on his heel and strode out the gate, blood spattering the ground around him. Aricia slumped onto the tunic, still warm from his body. She made no sound, but the men watching saw shudders jerk through her limbs. One by one Venutius's men sheathed their swords and followed until only her bard and her shield-bearer were left, squatting awkwardly in the dust, afraid to touch her.

The sun rose to stand at its zenith, and the sparrows, emboldened by the silence of the courtyard, fluttered down to scratch and squabble where Venutius's blood had already taken on the color of the earth itself.

Caradoc was taken to the fortress of the Ninth at Lindum, just inside Coritani territory, he and Caelte chained to an oxcart and surrounded by two centuries of soldiers. His arrest had been so swift and secret that none but a handful of Brigantians and the soldiers knew, and the green countryside lay peaceful and empty as they passed. The centurion was plainly nervous. Caradoc watched him striding up and down the tight lines of his men, the sting of fear goading them in his raucous voice, and his own eyes often strayed to the tree-shrouded hills that dipped to meet the road. But Madoc did not crouch with his chiefs above the gullies and no Emrys waited to sweep away his chains. In a day and half a night the gray, comfortably solid block of the fort loomed ahead. The centurion mopped his brow and sighed with relief but the prisoners, chafed and sore, knew as the vast gates thudded shut behind them that all faint hopes of rescue were vain and their days of freedom were gone.

The praefectus came out to meet them, and half the soldiers stumbled from their warm cots to crowd the cart, eager for a look at a legendary man, but Caradoc gave them no satisfaction. He did not growl and shake his chains like a captive bear. He did not stand and rain foreign curses upon their heads. He did not even carry a shrunken head on his belt, and many of them went back to bed, disgruntled. He stepped down calmly, swinging his legs together so that the chains would not trip him and make him fall before his captors, and he followed the centurion and the praefectus into his cell, with Caelte behind him.

The room was small and bare. There was no cot, no table, and no window, and dampness rose from the hard floor. The chains were removed but only so the two men could be stripped and searched, and Caradoc, standing naked and shivering under the praefectus's cool, cynical eye, saw the magic egg jerked from his neck and the pouch torn open. The soldier gingerly held up the egg, and the praefectus raised his eyebrows.

"What is it?"

"I don't know, sir. It looks like a lump of gristle from the guts of some poor beast." He poked it, tossed it up and caught it. "What savages these people are!"

The praefectus held out his hand, and the egg was passed to him. He turned it over, sniffed it, then threw it contemptuously at Caradoc.

"Here, you cannibal, catch!"

Caradoc's fingers closed around it. He held it fiercely, lovingly, his hand shielding it reverently from such ignorant blasphemy, and his face burned with shame on behalf of these unmannered men.

The torc was wrenched from his neck and Caelte's was taken also, but this time the praefectus held them respectfully, running his fingers along their delicate curves.

"These things are beautifully made," he said. "What odd fellows you are, you barbarians! I'll keep the bronze one, but I suppose the governor will want the gold."

Their clothes were slung at their feet and they were curtly ordered to dress, but they stood silently, incapable of movement, the nakedness of their necks finally bringing to them the full realization of despair. At another sharp word they slowly bent, picked up their breeches and tunics, and pulled them on, but Caradoc knew that clothes would no longer cover the bare, scoured bones of his soul, and the brand of his slavery flared out like an angry beacon in the night, invisible to Rome, but a roaring conflagration for every tribe to see. The chains were fastened again, and the centurion turned to his superior.

"Who gets the reward, sir? Does my detachment?"

The praefectus laughed shortly. "No such luck! Cartimandua gets it, of course, as she gets everything. The governor can hardly refuse her. It's so much easier to buy her loyalty, but all of us will breathe easier when she is dead and we can slap a praetor on Brigantia. She's too deceitful, that one. She'd sell her own children, if she had any, to whoever would give her gold." He was moving to the door as he spoke, and with his last words it was closed behind him and the prisoners found themselves in darkness.

Caradoc bent and felt about on the floor until his fingers touched the pouch. He picked it up, kissed the egg gently, and wrapped it away again, then sank down beside Caelte and closed his eyes. "More wisdom than any man . . ." What have I done to forfeit the protection of the gods? But he knew. He had not trusted his own judgment, that was all. So be it. He leaned against Caelte and they slept, their arms about each other.

Scapula motioned and the guards saluted and went out, then he rose from his desk and came around to the front, leaning back against it, his arms folded. His gaze slowly traveled the little group before him and they stared back rudely, the girls with a wide-open, frank fascination, the young man with hostility, and the woman with steady, courageous eyes. She was of average height, too thin, as were all the women of the west, the men too, for that matter. Her hair was thick and dark blonde, braided loosely in plaits that fell to her green, breech-clad knees, and wisps of escaping fronds curled on her wide forehead and about the brown cheeks. Her mouth was firmly closed, a warm, well-defined mouth, and her eyes, netted in fine laugh lines, were deep blue and composed. An intriguing woman, he thought. He barely glanced at the Druid who waited calmly, his white-sprinkled blond hair falling about his shoulders and his hands thrust into the deep sleeves of his grubby white tunic. He was a nonentity, a small fish caught by accident as the net drew tight about the giants, and Scapula unfolded his arms and hooked his thumbs into his belt. He had eaten well that morning, he was digesting his food with no pain, and the auguries had never read better.

"Now then," he said brightly. "We will not waste time on introductions. I know who you are. I have some questions I wish to ask you, and if you are wise you will answer me quickly." There were bloodstains on the woman's tunic. He had not noticed them before and he eyed her again, a rapid surge of disgust bringing pricks to his stomach. Animals! They lived like animals, they fought like animals, but thank the gods they did not reproduce like animals.

"Where is your husband?"

She smiled faintly. "I do not know."

"Of course you know! Where were you going when you were captured, if not to him? Now answer, Lady. Where is he? Did he go north or south when he slipped across the river? Hmmm!"

"Don't tell him anything, mother," Llyn interposed smoothly. "If he is so clever, let him find out for himself."

Scapula turned his head sharply and Llyn's dark brown, knowing eyes grinned impudently at him. A feeling of perplexity stole over him, as if often did. The longer he stayed in this magic-ridden, wet country the less he understood it, or its inhabitants. Just when his decisions were made, his policies clear, a mood of anxious confusion would take him like a sudden fog rising in his brain, and he knew that he could remain here forever and still be as ignorant as a child unrolling its first scroll. Here was a lad no more than seventeen yet a torc glowed about his neck, his sword was notched and well-used, and Scapula felt himself in the presence of a man with more experience of life than his own second. He despised them all, the blood-crazed chiefs, their unappetizing, uncouth women, people who did not spare even their children in their suicidal wars.

"If you interrupt me again," he said, "I will have you removed and whipped. No purpose is served by your rudeness." He looked back at Eurgain. "Did he go to Venutius? Or is he bound for the coast?"

"I told you, I do not know," she insisted. "He will go wherever there is sanctuary."

"There is no sanctuary left for him anywhere," he replied testily, "except in the west or with Venutius, but I have heard that Venutius and Cartimandua are reconciled again. So did he go back, with the other western chiefs?"

She said nothing this time. Her gaze dropped to the floor and he surveyed the bland, self-contained face with impatience.

"Lady, it can make very little difference whether you tell me now, or not. Before long he will know that I hold you and his children, and he will give himself up."

"No, he won't!" Llyn shouted. "Scapula, you are a fool! He is more than a man, he is arviragus, and he will let us all die, and he will fight on!"

Scapula signaled to his centurions. They moved to lay hands on Llyn but he whirled and marched from the room ahead of them, and as the door closed Scapula went behind the desk and sat, leaning back.

"If it makes no difference whether I tell you," Eurgain said mildly, "then why do you persist in asking me? Llyn speaks the truth. Caradoc will not come running to you like a trained dog just because you hold me. I am not innocent," she went on, her voice rising at last in anger. "I know very well that I face death, perhaps death with torture. Llyn knows it too, and the girls. But the girls really do not know where Caradoc is, and Llyn and I cannot be broken."

"Brave words," he remarked. "And probably true. So I will tell you where your husband is."

Her eyes flew to his and he held them steadily, watching carefully for a sign of betrayal as he continued. "He has fled to Venutius in Brigantia, and there I will seek him." It was a guess, intended to catch her off guard so that in her reaction he could read the truth, but her eyes did not falter or change expression and he was reminded of all the Druids he has seen die with the same blank faces. He wanted to smash that bottomless superiority, to feel bones crack under his knuckles, and to see the gentle mouth contort in agony, and as the color mounted in his neck he put his hands together and leaned over the desk.

"I will get him," he said deliberately, "and when I do you will all go to Rome, and after a time you will all be executed. If it had not been for your mad husband the whole of this country would now be at peace, the Silures would not now be hunted down, the Ordovices would still be wandering contentedly in their precious mountains with no cares. You are criminals, all of you, as blind to responsibility and morals as the rest of your kin, and your fate will be the fate of any common thief in the city." He swallowed hard, forcing down the gush of rage, thinking of all the months of doubt and sleepless nights behind him, all the good men lost forever, all the progress at a standstill, because of one man and this ragged, haughty family. The two girls were still gazing at him with dumb, wide eyes as though they were half-witted.

"Let me tell you something, Scapula," Eurgain said. "I do not care where he is. All I care is that he is free, and will remain free until he can gather yet another army and open yet another campaign. Whether I live or die is meaningless to me, and to him, if the west is to go on fighting. You have never understood what it is that you fight. It is not bodies, Roman, it is souls, and that is why Caradoc must stay free, and that is why you will not be victorious."

He opened his mouth to reply, color now blazing to the roots of his gray hair, but a knock came on the door and irritatedly he called, "Enter!"

His secretary came in, saluted, and held out a scroll. "A dispatch, sir, from Lindum." Scapula waved it away. "I am busy, Drusus. Put it with the others and I'll look at it after lunch."

"I am sorry, sir, but it's very urgent. The rider is waiting outside for your answer."

With an exasperated grunt Scapula snatched it. The sun had left the room and was standing high in the center of the sky, and though the shutters were open it was stuffy and hot. While Scapula broke the seals and scanned the scroll, Eurgain looked out the window.

So familiar, the blue-tinged haze of the wooded hill folding down to meet the river, the road, now paved, that left the gate and meandered through spacious oak groves and on to where the barges and coracles used to rock at anchor. Her mind's eye drifted to the estuary, a wide, reed-choked pool of ruffled water where the snipe and sandpipers picked their way on thin stick-legs, and then the sand, and the white cliffs, and the caves where Gladys would lie listening to the surf come rolling in. Nostalgia blew toward her on the flower-scented breeze and she looked determinedly back to the governor, now on his feet, his hands trembling as he clutched the stiff scroll. Suddenly he flung it onto the desk.

"Mithras!" he whispered. "It is not possible! At last, at last!" he almost ran from behind the desk and Bran took one quick step toward her as Scapula came to a halt, his face thrust close to hers, his eyes beaming.

"I have him!" he exulted, breathing heavily. "Lady, prepare to say farewell to Albion! He walked right to the door of Cartimandua's house, can you see it? He and his bard, and she wasted no time in turning him over to the praefectus at Lindum. His gods have deserted him, and my prayers have been answered. Caradoc! In . . . my . . . hands!" He emphasized his words gleefully, one clenched fist pounding on the tough palm of his other hand, then he straightened, went back to his desk, and sat down.

"Drusus, please ask the messenger to wait a moment and then show him in here. I want the rebel conveyed to Colchester as quickly as possible, before his chiefs wake to what has happened and try to rescue him." He rubbed his hands together meditatively, smiling. "Now for you, Druid. Drusus, bring in the guard."

The secretary went to the door, and Scapula continued. "Under the law you must die, but of course you knew that. The emperor has ordered the extermination of all of you, on grounds of sedition. If you have any message to this lady you had better give it."

Four soldiers entered and stood waiting impassively, their feet apart and their hands behind their backs.

Eurgain suddenly woke to the scene. She ran to the desk and fell across it. "No, you cannot do this! Not to this man! He is a good man, a gentle man, he has harmed no one in all his life! Be merciful,

Scapula, on this day of your triumph! Spare him as a thanksgiving to your gods!"

"How is it," he asked coldly, "that you beg for the Druid and yet not for your husband? What kind of a woman are you? Don't you know that Caradoc and his chiefs and indeed all the tuaths are only gaming pieces in the hands of the Druithin? You are a lost cause to him now, in any case, and if I set him free he would disappear back to his accursed island, deserting you in favor of a more hopeful throw of the dice. If it had not been for him and his brethren you and all your kin would still be here at Colchester, going peacefully and happily about your business, and you and I would have been friends."

"Never!" she began, a torrent of anguished invective about to pour forth, but Bran stepped to her, grasping her firmly by the shoulders and turning her about.

"Listen to me, Eurgain," he said quietly. "It is not important. There will always be stars to gaze at, in soft nights of wonder that steal away your breath, and crystals waiting for you in the rocks. Nothing else matters, do you understand?" She shook her head and laid it upon his breast like a tired, heartbroken child, and for a moment he enveloped her. Then he moved away. "Look into my eyes, little one." Slowly she raised her face, tears spilling down her cheeks, and he took her hands. "We will meet again, do not doubt it. Greet the arviragus for me." As she sought the brown eyes she felt the tears dry up, and a strange lightness touched her soul.

Scapula nodded curtly at the guard and the men moved forward. Bran turned to the door.

"A safe journey, master, a peaceful journey!" she called brokenly, and he replied steadily, "Peace to you and yours, Eurgain."

Then he was gone.

The door closed and there was a second of loud silence before Scapula rose.

"Back now to your cell. In a week your husband will be here. Is that not better than hearing that he is dead?"

She drew herself up to her full height. "No," she said.

Six days later, on an evening when the sun had just set and light lingered golden in the tops of the trees, the cohort from Lindum arrived at Colchester with its prisoners. Scapula had taken no chances. Five hundred men marched beside the wain, fully armed and standing battle watches on the journey, but no war cries had broken the warm night silences and the days had passed without incident.

Scapula personally took charge of his rebel at the gates and strode up the hill surrounded by bristling spears. He wasted no time by examining Caradoc. That could come later, but now he must be locked away, and guards set and changed every hour. He had sent off a jubilant dispatch to Rome, and soon the ship which would relieve him of an awesome responsibility would anchor, but until then he would live on nerves already stretched too thin. He knew his luck, it had never been good, and this sudden, unlooked-for concession by the fates would not last long.

The cavalcade wound its way up from the gate, past neat homes and gardens, trees, and busy shops, and Caelte looked about him in the failing light with astonishment. Nothing of their town remained. If they had not been driven through woods that had spoken to them mutely and sweetly of things they remembered with an increasing heartache, he would not have believed that this prosperous, self-consciously Roman community had been their playground. The whole mound had been leveled, and where once the climb to the Great Hall had been steep, now they paced up a gentle slope to a white temple, glowing softly pink in the late sunset.

Caradoc had seen it before and now he averted his eyes, thinking of the red-headed Boudicca standing with mouth agape on the pristine steps, Prasutagas behind her. He had been consumed with an acrid contempt then, he remembered, but Plautius and Gladys had emerged suddenly, and his rage had turned to shame.

Caelte gazed at it until they had shuffled past it and turned to where the governor's quarters, the headquarters, and the administrative buildings lay.

Suddenly Caradoc stopped and raised his head. Someone was calling his name, a high, urgent, tear-filled voice, and though he felt the butt of a spear strike his back he continued to listen. Eurgain. His eyes flew frantically from building to shadowed building and then he saw the white arm thrust between iron bars, and the blur of a face.

The escort straggled to a halt and Scapula shouldered through, nodding at his centurion. "Give them a moment," he said, and the soldiers parted.

Caradoc bent, picked up his chains, and half-ran, half-stumbled to the tiny window. Her fingers were on his cheeks, his lips, and he grasped the bars of her cage, the chains rattling against the wall.

"Eurgain! Aricia said that you had been taken but I thought she was lying. Has he treated you with courtesy? Where are the children?"

"In the next cell." She pressed her face against the cool iron and dropped her voice, ashamed of the question she was impelled to ask yet knowing that no peace would come to her until she unburdened herself. "Caradoc, why in the name of Camulos did you go to Aricia? You must have known that she would deliver you up."

He looked at her speculatively for a moment, then the harsh face split into a lingering, warm smile. "No, my love, I did not run to her because in my extremity I longed for her arms. I was seeking Venutius, and Caelte and I trusted ourselves to a guide who betrayed us. Is Bran here?"

She rested her forehead against his fingers. "They executed him. Ah Caradoc, so many gone! Sometimes I think that I cannot bear it!" Her voice began to tremble, but all he could do was stroke her face.

"Cinnamus fell beside me, Eurgain," he said gently, and she ground her head against his hand.

"I know, I know. Vida took her sword and vanished into the woods when Bran told us. They are at peace, all of them, yet still we go on suffering."

Llyn's arm reached out from the window beyond. "Father! Is that you?" Caradoc moved to touch him, but Scapula barred the way.

"That is enough," he said crisply. "Form ranks!"

"Freedom!" Llyn shouted after them. "Freedom, freedom!"

"Freedom," Caelte whispered as Caradoc returned to walk beside him, and they looked at each other with a wordless, gnawing hunger. Then the column began to move, and the timorous twilight edged quietly into the town.

CHAPTER TWENTY-FOUR

T HE LIBURNIAN FROM GESORIACUM docked in the estuary one week before the autumn storms were due to rake the channel. It was late, and Scapula hung about the crowded cells with griping belly and aching head, praying that the knifing, turbulent winds would be late that year and that he could get rid of his responsibility at last. Colchester was stiff with troops. They ringed the cellblock. They crowded the streets, they guarded three deep by the gate and fell over each other by the river, but Scapula was taking no chances. The dispatches from Rome had been excited and congratulatory and his messengers brought him word that the west was in confusion, his soldiers pushing unchecked through the forests. But night after night he stood by his window, looking out over the star-speckled countryside that dreamed quietly below him, anxiety keeping sleep at bay.

379

In spite of all the reports he did not believe that the men of the west would let their arviragus go, and he strode uneasily about the town at the thought that the weather might close in early and prevent the ship from leaving. He wanted to be rid of Caradoc and then hurry back to the west, for soon the snows would come, high in the mountains, and the legions would have to retreat to winter quarters, leaving the tribesmen unwatched. He had the dismal feeling that all was not over in that land of magic and madness. For five years his life had had only one purpose, to capture the spearhead of the people's desperate resistance and thus behead the insurrection. Now Caradoc lay in chains, but the undercurrent of hostility had seemed to intensify, the country seemed alive with whispers, and his hatred for it and its people flared up anew.

He had sent for the rebel the morning after his arrival at Colchester but in the end there had been nothing much to say. The two men had stood looking at each other while the hum of the town drifted cheerfully through the window, and, searching the dark, level eyes before him Scapula had felt his new confidence ebb away. He had captured a body, that was all. The spirit was still as free and light as a gliding bird, alien and frightening to him, and forever beyond his angry reach. He felt cloddish and heavy, a clumsy, ignorant soldier, and Caradoc had smiled at him slowly as though he divined the other man's muddy thoughts.

"It has been a good fight, governor," he said quietly. "But do not spend too much time in congratulating yourself. You think to send me to Rome, but I will not go. You are beginning to realize that, aren't you? Even now, in the west, a new arviragus will be rising, and my spirit stays here, with him."

"Rubbish!" Scapula blurted testily. "You fame has gone to your head, Caradoc. You are a talented man, wasted, I may say, among savages when you could have been a great general. With you gone the natives will lapse into confusion."

"I do not think so. Your predecessor understood us very well, and would not cross his frontier zone, but although you have been here for many years you have refused to learn."

"It was a matter of imperial policy!" Scapula knew he should not become angry but he could not help himself. "And you yourself forced that policy when you moved to unite the west!"

I can never explain it to him, Caradoc thought in despair. I will not even try. He let his glance stray to the patch of blue, milky sky, and after a moment Scapula shrugged.

"How foolish it is, Caradoc, to become incensed over what has already passed and cannot be changed. I will admit that you have broken my health, strained my relations with the emperor, and robbed me of the opportunity to continue the good and peaceful progress that Plautius began here. But all that is over. When you are gone the west will lie open to me, and in five years the people will be cursing your name for keeping Rome's prosperity from them for so long."

"Oh Scapula," Caradoc laughed. "How blissful is your certitude, how blind your confidence! The name of Vercingetorix is still breathed with love by the honorable chiefs left in Gaul, though for a hundred years the people have been enjoying the Roman prosperity! How true it is, that memory is more potent than the strongest wine!"

For a second they smiled at each other, acknowledging a respect that bordered on mutual admiration though if swords had been placed in their hands they would have battled to the death. Then Scapula dismissed him and Caradoc went back to his damp cell where Caelte sat with his eyes closed, already humming new songs, his indomitable optimism reasserted.

Scapula turned to his second. "Tell me, Gavius," he said. "Who was Vercingetorix?"

On a cold, misty morning, when the town stirred sluggishly under the grayness of autumn and the wet trees ranged motionless, their tips already crisped to red and yellow by an early frost, the cells were unlocked, and Caradoc, Caelte, Eurgain, Llyn, and the girls stepped over the threshold for the last time. Outside, their escort waited, dim shapes in the clinging whiteness, and in the moment when the final orders were given and Scapula mounted his horse and settled his cloak more tightly around his shoulders, Caradoc enfolded his wife, took his son's wiry wrist, kissed his daughters. "Have courage!" he whispered. The girls smiled at him tremulously, but Llyn shot him a mutinous glance.

"Do you think that the chiefs will rescue us today?" he hissed. "Surely my war band will not see me go into slavery without raising a hand!"

"There will be no rescue, Llyn," Caradoc answered emphatically. "The chiefs have not had enough time and, in any case, they are not so foolish as to attempt such a thing here, in the heart of the province. They will fight on, but my destiny is accomplished and the Druids will find a new arviragus."

A muffled command was given and the escort moved quietly down the road, past the temple, past the new, compact little forum, past the spacious houses still shuttered and dawn-drowsy. The hoofs of Scapula's horse rang flatly on the pavement and they filed out the gate to the waiting wain, the horses hung with dew, the breath steaming from their nostrils. The family and Caelte scrambled up and sat meekly while the chains were fastened to the sides of the cart. Another order rang out, and with a jolt they set off along the path that had seen chariot and war band, hunting party and reveller, lover and trader. Ghosts lined it, shades in gray cloaks, their pale, expressionless faces wreathed in streamers of thin mist even now dissolving under a benign sun.

Unmoved, Caradoc watched them glide by. Colchester was full of them, and beneath the bright bustle of a Roman town the deep, rich darkness that was Camulodunon would always flow, a river of pungent memories. He heard Scapula's strident, tension-strung voice shout "Close ranks! Hurry!" and with a start he realized that the silent shapes lining the route to the river were not ghosts but men and women from the surrounding territory who had gathered in mute, passive protest, and as the wain and the detachment passed they closed in behind, a weaponless army of sympathy.

At the river a barge waited, rocking gently in a cloud of river fog. The chains were unfastened, the prisoners embarked, the chains attached to the boat, and then they cast off, floating swiftly with the ebbing tide toward the estuary and the ocean. The river, too, was thick with tribesmen, hooded and cloaked, standing under the trees, and as Caradoc glided by them they raised white arms. Suddenly a voice rose, high and clear above the murmur of water, a woman's voice.

"A safe journey!" The words were like the first stone that rattles down to begin an avalanche. The holding spell broke. All at once they began to roar, a tumult of sound, an accolade, the final tribute of the people.

"A peaceful journey! A safe journey, Arviragus! We will remember! Freedom, Arviragus, freedom! Go in safety, Ricon, walk in peace!"

Eurgain's hand found his and gripped it with a fierce passion. His own closed around it and he sat with his chin high, a lump in his throat and tears in his eyes.

Scapula watched thin-lipped, his jaw tight with fury, but he dared not interfere. He did not want an eruption of mob violence, not now. The soldiers looked uneasily at one another and held their swords warily. One more bend and the ship would be in sight. At least the beach was heavily guarded.

The shouting turned into song. A few voices began it, the marching song of the Catuvellauni, and it raced along the riverbank from mouth to mouth, gained strength, and rose in one towering, raw-rhythmed crescendo of defiance and solidarity. The people clapped and stamped, flinging back their hoods and shaking down their hair, and as if at the sheer force of their singing the mists lifted. Sun sparkled fresh on the river and licked the flaming treetops, and soon the booming of the surf joined in the song, a joyful, vengeful torrent of liberty.

The barge nudged the landing stage and the soldiers jumped hurriedly to shore to ring the captives as they climbed onto the jetty and began the slow walk to the ramp of the tall-masted ship whose imperial flags hung limp. The captain stood at the foot of the ramp, his feet apart, his eyes darting from his passengers to the dense crowd that spread out over the sands. They had begun to gather before dawn, standing quietly just out of reach of the water, and for hours they had poured out of the woods, down the cliffs, rounding the headland, and he could do nothing but wait and watch. They had not been violent but had ignored him and his contingent of armed sailors with supreme indifference. His anxiety had mounted and he was more than glad that the governor had arrived on time. Two cohorts had been detailed to guard the last stage of this perilous undertaking and they were enough.

Caradoc and Eurgain, still holding hands, began to ascend the ramp, Llyn and the girls behind them. The sun was now fully risen and with it came a light, odorless breeze that flicked the crowds with a hint of the winter to come. It was a bright morning, a cheerful, gloriously brisk morning, a morning to set the blood racing and the eyes dancing.

Caradoc paused, let go of Eurgain's hand, and turned. Immediately, a hush descended, and the only sound was the slapping of waves against the ship's hull and the greedy mewing of the seagulls. He breathed deeply, his gaze traveling the expectant, multicolored host, seeing the eager, loving eyes meet his own in comfort. Blue eyes, brown eyes, clouded with age or clear with hope; black hair, blonde hair, a motley, haphazard multitude of peoples. With a growing ache in his heart he looked beyond them to the white cliffs, the rippling grasses, the thick-massed, dark trees already half-asleep, tossing fitfully in the wind.

Albion, Albion, he cried out in his soul. Turbulent and treacherous, wild and magical, you dreamed a dream with me. We dared to hazard a great thing together and I have emptied my soul but I have failed you. The ashes of my dearest dead lie cradled in your soil. Guard them well.

Slowly, he raised his arms, and brought his manacled wrists crashing together.

"Tell them I did not surrender and neither must they!" he shouted.

"The fight goes on! Tell them that!" He turned abruptly and walked forward, and when he reached the deck Scapula motioned him along the rail and the others ranged beside him.

"I am not an unreasonable man," the governor said. "You may remain on deck until the horizon is clean." The word was deliberate.

Caradoc flushed but did not reply, and Scapula received the salute of the captain and walked quickly back down the ramp. Sailors rushed to draw it up, and behind and below him Caradoc heard a shouted order and the regular boom, boom of the massive drum that beat to time the oarsmen.

How many of you down there in the galleys once galloped free across the meadows? he wondered as the ship began to move ponderously, with a weighty dignity.

Llyn clutched the rail and Eurgain stepped to her husband, but Caradoc's eyes were fastened on the crowded, still-silent shoreline.

For one moment all caution left him and he felt in his legs, in his arms, the frenzied desire to leap over the side and run the warm sand of his own beaches through his fingers once more. As a slave, as a miner, as a peasant laboring to build for Rome, I will suffer any indignity but ah, Mother, let me die in my own country!

As if in answer a call came floating. He could not catch the words but it seemed to embody all the loveliness, all the sweetest memories, all the hopes of his youth, and then the crowd surged into the water. He could see them dimly now, standing waist-deep in the heaving waves, casting brooches and bracelets, coins, beads, anything they had. Then they seemed to slide away from him and become a black line at the foot of the gleaming cliffs.

Eurgain was sobbing openly but he did not move to touch her and she did not invite his comfort. Llyn was leaning out over the side, light brown hair streaming behind him, the girls standing on either side of him with arms folded under their cloaks and faces stiff, like Sine's wolf mask. All at once Caelte began to hum, his eyes on the dwindling bay. The tune was familiar to Caradoc, vibrating a long-silent chord in him, and, as his bard began to add the words, he remembered a night of feasting long ago when he and Togodumnus had returned to Camulodunon to celebrate their first season of war against the neighboring tribes. All night the Catuvellauni had sung, drunk with power, drugged with heady dreams of an empire all their own, and he and Tog had flamed with the rash, reckless certainty of their own omnipotence.

> There was a ship, her sails were silken red,
> Peaceful she lay, upon a golden sea
> And all about, the graceful seagulls glided, crying . . .

384

He smiled in spite of himself, seeing Caelte's wry, sweat-streaked face as he rose to sing it in answer to the demands of the people. How good, how good it all was, in those days! And then, listening to the plaintive words, a new understanding came to him. The song had always had a strange power to touch the chiefs in a way that no other song could, and it was sung by every tribe. He had often wondered why, but now, with Albion sinking forever below the horizon, he thought he knew. A bard in some far-distant time had taken up his harp and conjured words of prophecy. None save perhaps the Druithin down all the long years since had understood them, but they had brought to their hearers the dim mystery of a truth, and that was why the song had never died. It was not the simple song of a warrior and his murdered love. Albion herself lay dying slowly under the trees and he himself was the warrior who died also, heart emptying while the ship took him away from her.

He turned to Caelte. "Why do you sing, my friend?" The haunting notes faltered, and Caelte met his question with a faint half-smile. "Why Lord, because I am alive," he said huskily.

Caradoc looked back. Sunlight glittered on a peaceful, emerald ocean and the horizon held nothing but a thin line of morning haze. Albion had gone.

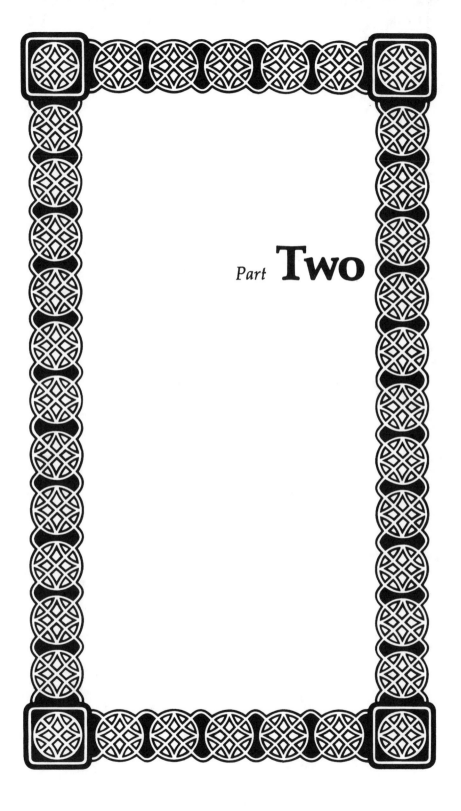

Part **Two**

CHAPTER TWENTY-FIVE

V ENUTIUS SPENT NO MORE than two hours in the town, and he left the same morning. Over the last two weeks, he had traveled far, bringing his kinsmen south, for Aricia had sent for him with words of regret and abasement and his heart had leaped at them. They had fought many times in the past. Many times he had ridden away from her to his holdings in the north, swearing bitterly that he would never again darken her door. Yet, as many times she had held out the carrot of reconciliation and he had run after it, always willing to forgive, always anxious to see her, touch her, hear her sarcastic, clever wit sharpened at his expense. He had learned to inure himself to her insults, and her stinging jokes no longer hurt him. He knew her need of him, deep under the coverings of her greed and hatred, of her returning fear of being alone. He had always come when she had sent for him. But this time was different.

He could hardly bear to bring to consciousness what she had done. Shame poured over him like a hot river of melted pride, shame for her, for himself, for Brigantia. The land was tainted with it, the people stank with it. His agitation was so deep, his grief and anger so strong, that he could not stand still, and as he curtly ordered his people to repack the goods they had just begun to strew over the field outside the town he strode from chief to chief, family to family, suffocating in his loss. They watched him warily, watched his flushed and contorted face, his clenched fists, his red-soaked breeches, his naked, mutilated chest where the blood was rapidly congealing. Long before he had reached them all, word of his wife's action and his own reaction flashed through the town and quickly spread over the territory.

Before Venutius was three days toward the west his group of kinsmen had begun to swell. The farmsteads emptied quietly. Families slipped away from their village huts. By the time he entered the vast forest that would take him south and then west again, he had a quarter of Brigantia strung out behind him.

Venutius had made no plans. Word of Caradoc's final, disastrous battle came to him disjointed, distorted, and he knew that the men he had to seek would be hard to find, buried far into the safety of their mountains. But he kept moving, the lash of his wife's great crime driving him unmercifully. He could not sleep. At night, when the fires of his followers twinkled out, he would leave his tent and walk in the darkness of the forests, for if he stopped, if he stood still, that tide of unbearable sorrow would reach out for him and he would drown. Aricia, he thought, threading through the stately, night-hung trees, but no other coherent words would come. Just her name. Aricia. His feet spoke it to the rustle of last year's dry leaves. His heart beat it through his blood, hot and sick and spellbinding. Aricia. Only when he was so exhausted in body and numbed in mind that he could no longer stand upright did he go to the small comfort of his tent and receive the blessing of unconsciousness for an hour or two before the dawn.

He took his people north of the half-finished fort at Deva, marching all one night beside the ocean to avoid detection. If he had been in his right mind he would never have done such a thing. A river connected the site of the fort with the coast and it was always busy with patrols, for the Deceangli continually harried the men of the Twentieth and the Romans there were all eyes and ears, but luck was with him. The marsh and the little estuary lay calm under a half moon. He did not know it but the Twentieth, emboldened by Caradoc's defeat and the scattering of the tribes, had emptied its fort and was scrambling to the south, where the feet of the Ordovician mountains rested. For four more days Venutius kept to the coast, and then turned inland. There were no paths. He had no destination, unless it was that of flight and healing. He moved through instinct, vaguely remembering the ways he should go, for he had spent three agonizing months with Caradoc in these mountains, half of him a rebel, the other half longing without pause for Aricia and the nakedness of Brigantia. He had deserted Caradoc, running home to his wife's arms like a repentant child, but he had not forgotten.

He knew that on his own he had no hope of finding Emrys and Madoc, if they still lived. They would have to find him, and they would be hidden within the cold heart of the mountains, bruised and wary. Day after day, he and his hundreds clambered to where forests grew perpendicular, rivers fell from sky to earth, and what valleys there were, so small, so secret, could be passed unknowingly. Occasionally they stumbled upon a farmstead, perched up against the slope of one of these valleys, always empty, the thatch rotting, the walls decayed, and the tiny field of the valley floor rank with weeds and tall new forest growth. Silence lay on the country like a watchful god, a silence that heard and saw them desecrate its jealously held domains. And though they sacrificed as best they could, and surrounded themselves with spells of immunity, the sheer weight of that ever present consciousness began to tell on them.

Then, one hot, still noon when they had stopped by a stream to drink and douse their tired feet, they rose from the grass to find themselves surrounded. There had been no sound, no warning stir of twig or wind, yet when Venutius got to his feet it was to find a sword resting against his neck and a dozen bright eyes fixed on him with hostility. His chiefs stood foolishly while thin knifes prodded them.

"Who are you and what are you doing here?" said the chief who was eyeing Venutius with such cold efficiency.

There were no words of greeting or hospitality, but Venutius had not really expected them. Relief made him close and open his eyes. "I am Venutius, chieftain of Brigantia, and these are my kin and my people," he replied. "I seek Madoc, or the Ordovician chief Emrys."

"Why?"

"I prefer to tell either one of them myself." He had thought of warning the rebels that his following was large and they should not decide on violence too hastily, but he realized that if these men were overpowered and perhaps killed he might as well turn around and go home. He smiled wryly to himself. He no longer had a home. Besides, if he harmed the rebels he would have no chance of leaving the mountains unscathed.

"I have heard of this chief," one of the men said. "He fought beside the arviragus for a while, but did not stay. One of his hands is joined to Rome."

"Not so!" Venutius flashed, but it was so, it had been so up until now, and how were these killers to know how his soul had been maimed?

The leader made up his mind quickly. "Bring them," he said quietly and was gone, swallowed up in the motionless noonday shadow. His companions gestured. Venutius picked up his gear, told his shield-bearer to pass the word, and went after the first man into the green gloom.

After only two hours of walking they came abruptly upon a camp, its brown tents clustered by the same stream Venutius had drunk from. Two people squatted on its bank, talking softly, and Venutius happily recognized Sine's bronze wolf-mask, her long, curved green back, the gray fringes on her green breeches. The man was a stranger to him. Without a word, Venutius's guide left him, and the two by the water stood. The Brigantians flowed around the camp and then squatted in silent twos and threes on the earth, their eyes on their lord. He waited, his spirit damp with an edge of fear, and then Sine was before him, the dark, hard eyes looking him up and down, the thin right hand resting lightly on the hilt of her sword.

"I know you," she said. "Venutius. Brigantian chief. We fought side by side for a while, did we not? And then you grew weary and hungry and you left us." Her voice was as curt as her eyes, as hard as the battered bronze of her mask. "You are not wanted here. We do not trust you."

He did not want to explain, not then. "Where is Emrys?" he said.

"He travels, gathering in the chiefs who were put to flight by Scapula."

"Madoc?"

"He has gone into Siluria to collect his people before they are all destroyed. The Second has gone mad. Its soldiers are setting fire to the forests there and killing every man or beast they meet." A sudden thought struck her. Venutius could see it bloom in her eyes and the fire of it made him step back. "There are rumors that the arviragus roams in the mountains, seeking us," she said, "but the strongest rumor is that he escaped into Brigantia, to you. Have you brought him back to us, Venutius?"

The wild hope in those black eyes brought the hot shame into his throat once more and he lowered his head. "No, Sine, Caradoc is not with me," he replied. She sensed that more was to come and nodded, the fire going out behind her eyes as quickly as it had been kindled. Venutius found that he could not go on. He swallowed. Sweat trickled down his temples. Pain swelled his tongue and beat in his thoughts, unrelenting. All at once he pressed both fists to his forehead. "Sine!"

392

he gasped, the words so raw, so jagged that they tore his mouth. "The arviragus will come no more. He sought me, but did not find me. My wife captured him and sold him to Rome. By now he will be in the fort at Lindum, perhaps, or on his way to Camulodunon."

A breathless and instant hush fell. Venutius could not look at Sine. She, too, was struggling to breathe. All around them a wailing began, a swiftly spreading tide of shock and loss that rippled out from Venutius and was soon lost under the trees. Sine put a trembling hand to her hidden face, but that was the only sign she gave that the news had devastated her. When she spoke again her voice was as cold and steady as ever, rising above the grief and rage exploding around them.

"Did she send you to us with this message?"

He had recovered a little. His fists unclenched and fell to his belt. "No. I have left her, and Brigantia, for good. I will not go back."

Suddenly she foamed with rage, snarling at him with her grinning wolf's mouth. "We do not want you here! We want no Brigantians here! You are a filthy, lying tuath full of dishonorable people who no longer merit being called freemen! Go away! Go away!" He could not tell if she was weeping. Probably not. He remembered her as being without softness, without pity or compromise. He stepped to her.

"Sine, I cannot go away. There is nowhere for me to go. I have brought men and women to you, fighting people, and more will follow as word of the arviragus's fall spreads. Let me stay. Let me prove to you that I am no longer the chief who deserted Caradoc out of weakness."

She stopped shouting and scanned his face, reading there more than his words could say. "What of Eurgain? Llyn? Where is his family?" she pressed.

He shook his head in misery. "I do not know. They were not with him when . . . when . . ." After a moment she folded her arms.

"Very well. You may stay. But I make you no promises until my husband and Madoc return. They may still decide to slay you."

"'I understand. You may wish to guard me, Sine, but I will not sneak away. My fate lies here now.'"

She watched him walk away, tangled red hair brushing his back, his long, thick legs swinging easily from the narrow hips.

"You will not stay long, Brigantian," she muttered. "You cannot stand the pace."

One of his chiefs had overheard her and came up. "You are wrong, Lady," he said. "He has sworn an oath, and his lady carries the weight of his blood. He will stay."

She rounded on him. "That is a serious ceremony," she snapped, "but it would have been more honorable for him if he had slain her. What does she care for the weight of his blood?" The chief bowed and left and she stood listening to the keening around her, her fingers still on her sword. Hurry back, Emrys, she thought. Hurry! Or I will kill him.

Emrys returned three weeks later together with the majority of his tuath. By that time the news of Caradoc's incarceration at Camulodunon had been confirmed by the spies, who paused only to add their news of Eurgain's capture and Bran's execution before moving on to tell the master Druid on Mona. Emrys heard it all in a resigned silence. He called Venutius to him, greeted him politely, then questioned him closely. Venutius had little to add to the tragedy but his own invisible wounding, and Emrys, after a night of fruitless argument with his wife, decided to let Venutius stay. He had, after all, brought fresh blood into the west, and after him had straggled many groups of angry and humiliated lowlanders to swell the rebel ranks. Day by day those ranks grew as the battered survivors of the battle wandered in, but there was no cohesion, no force of purpose in them. There was no Caradoc to bully and coax them into new life. Emrys was glad when a wounded but indomitable Madoc swaggered into the camp with three thousand of his people. Southern Siluria was no more. It was a blackened waste, and where the fires had not eaten, the soldiers had. But Madoc was not dismayed. There could still be a front there in the north of his tuath, a place of engagement—if only the arviragus could be found. When Emrys gave him the news, he reacted predictably, roaring like a wounded bull. He drew his sword and ran about, slashing at trees, then collapsed by the fire and sobbed. "What now, Emrys?" he asked when he had finished. "Without an arviragus, can we keep going?"

"We cannot surrender, therefore we have no choice," Emrys said firmly as Madoc wiped his face and sheathed his sword. "I think that we have all learned a hard lesson since my people's pride forced Caradoc into pitched battle. We will not be so foolish again. You and I, Madoc, must blunder on."

"The Demetae. The Deceangli. Will they listen to us?"

"I think so. But if they will not, it does not matter. They fight their own battles now, the Demetae along their coasts and the Deceangli against the Twentieth. The Deceangli must rely on us, for only we can provide the help they need."

"Ah, Mother, what a tragic mess!" Madoc breathed. "And all because your high and mighty freemen would not bend their necks to the arviragus's yoke!"

"I will not quarrel with you, old friend," Emrys said forcefully. "If you are wise you will not pour recriminations on our heads, for they are now bowed as low as any could wish. We must look ahead."

"I prefer not to," Madoc grumbled, "but you are right. Now what of the Brigantian? Sine does not like him."

"My Sine hates and loves what and whom she chooses," Emrys replied, his eyes turning to watch her briefly as she sparred desultorily with her shield-bearer. "But her emotions do not interfere with her good sense. Venutius must yet prove himself. We will watch him closely, but I think this time he is here to stay."

"Pah! A man who allows such a woman as the Brigantian bitch to order his thoughts is weak and not worth the effort of saving," Madoc rumbled. "But he is a very great warrior." Emrys did not reply. His chin had sunk onto his hand and his eyes turned back to Sine as she lunged and parried by the water. Madoc heaved himself to his feet and went away to sleep.

That evening, Emrys, Madoc, Venutius, and a few of the other chiefs met together. It was not a Council, for the calling of a Council would have meant a wait of days while freemen scoured the mountains for the stragglers still wending their way to the camp. The men had eaten and drunk, and now sat cross-legged in the warm darkness, just out of reach of the little fire. Around them the ever growing camp settled to rest. The scouts had been posted. Mothers hunted their children, and soft voices called on the night air. Somewhere a bard was singing a gentle summer song, and farther away the clang of iron on iron belied the peace enveloping the men. Emrys slipped his cloak from his shoulders and looked at them carefully, one by one.

"I wish to talk about Caradoc," he said. "Is there any chance of a rescue? Tell me what you think."

For a moment they considered, eyes downcast, then Madoc's gruff voice boomed. "Scapula has been trying to take him for years, and now he has succeeded. He will not sleep until Caradoc is on his way to Rome, and until that time Camulodunon will be so stiff with soldiers that they will be standing elbow to elbow, earthwall to gate. To attempt rescue would be suicide."

"If we had hope for the arviragus's return, even if it meant the death of every man in the war band, we would attempt it," another chief chimed in. "But there is no hope. The only chance we had was while he was on his way to Camulodunon, and since we did not know of his capture until after he arrived there we could do nothing. Now it is too late."

"I agree." Venutius spoke up hesitantly, aware that he was subtly separated from these men by their own choice, and would remain so until somehow he could prove to them the strength of his resolution to stay with them. "A rescue by force of arms could have been attempted on his journey south, but we have been too disorganized to plan such an ambush. A small group of men might be able to slip south as far as Camulodunon, but I doubt it. No tribesman is going to be allowed within miles of the arviragus's cell. We have lost the chance." He immediately felt their hostility. You lost us the chance, the silence around them said to him. You are to blame. Emrys loosely folded his sun-bronzed arms.

"Caradoc would not want us to come after him unless there were a good chance," he said. "He would say that we need every warrior we have left for the days ahead."

"What about women?" Venutius cut in suddenly, and they all turned to stare at him.

"Speak, Brigantian," Madoc growled, his eyes lighting shrewdly.

"Men could not get to Camulodunon, but women might, sword-women disguised as peasants. Not too many. Five or six, perhaps." They continued to gaze at him, then Emrys called to his shield-bearer.

"Bring me the scout from Camulodunon!"

They waited for him, an edge of excitement to their breath, their stance, then he came and squatted before them. "Tell us the deployment of troops around the town," Emrys requested.

The scout answered promptly, balancing on his bare feet. "Within Camulodunon, around the forum and the administration buildings where the arviragus and his family are held, are two hundred soldiers. No tribesmen are allowed there, none at all. Only Romans may pass to the temple and the offices of the governor and the mayor. Between there and the wall and gate are five hundred, stationed in every street. Between town and river, and scattered through the forest, are more than a thousand."

"Are you sure?" The numbers seemed ridiculous, nearly two thousand men to guard one family.

"Quite sure. I sometimes clean harness in the stables, with a centurion's servant. He likes to talk. Unless a man can fly, the arviragus will go to Rome, and soon. In one month."

Emrys thanked the man and sent him away, and the excitement went out of the disappointed men. "I do not think we will attempt any rescue," Emrys finally said. "Your idea was a good one, Venutius, but by now the Romans know that the hands that grip our swords are without gender. Caradoc would understand."

They all sat there without speaking, one wild scheme succeeding another in their minds, knowing that all schemes were fruitless. Between them and Camulodunon stretched many miles, and at Camulodunon itself there was only death. Yet none was willing to be the first to leave the fire and admit failure, so they all sat on until silence reigned in the camp and the soft summer night sky became laden with stars.

Venutius knew that he was being closely watched. Only his hours of sleep were his own, though his kin and his tuath mingled freely and with an increasing comfort among the other tribesmen. Each morning Madoc or Emrys would send for him, very politely, very gently, and he would spend the days going from camp to camp. Sometimes Emrys or Madoc would travel, for a new network of communication was being woven throughout the mountains between camps of a dozen, a hundred, even five hundred warriors. Venutius was able to begin a map in his head and slowly fill in its outlines with supply tracks, scout tracks, war tracks between one rebel group and another. He saw the genius of the arviragus for the first time as Emrys and Madoc painstakingly rebuilt what had been blown apart by Rome. An invisible carpet of thin threads held the west together, and along those threads, like quiet, busy spiders, flowed grain from Mona, men, and news. Orders were passed, strategies queried and confirmed. Emrys and Madoc patiently began to repair those threads that had snapped, and in Venutius's mind the west suddenly acquired a wholeness as north to south, east to west, it came together. The west was an army, its units scattered over miles of rugged terrain, too far-flung for a Roman general to control. But it was not too separated for a gifted warrior if his compatriots were versatile and able to interpret a change of order swiftly—if they could be cut off from the source of power, yet maneuver still as part of the whole. The units changed position, changed shape, grew or were diminished, and those vital threads shifted with them, ever fluid, ever static.

Only a man of exceptional ability could have created and maintained this living cobweb, and Venutius came to understand that his wife had destroyed something, someone, irreplaceable. As he strode the passes with Ordovician or Silurian, sadness and anger for Caradoc grew within him. The Druithin had made no move to replace the arviragus. An arviragus was first made, then chosen. It was too soon. But it might never happen.

He began to note the camps of strength, and weakness. He noted how grain from Mona followed one route for miles until it was deep into the hills, and he decided that this was a dangerous practice. He sat alone at night, moving the units about in his mind like gaming pieces, not trusting too much to their honor, as Emrys did, or countering his orders out of doubt, as Madoc often did, and within his head the west acquired a new shape. He said nothing to his still-mistrustful guardians, for his advice would have been suspect. He watched,

learned, and waited. Sine sometimes came to him in the evenings, still
hostile but very polite, and they spoke of inconsequential things. He
sensed that she was feeling for something deeper than the words, but
he did not know what it was. The core of him, perhaps, the soul. It
finally occurred to him that Emrys sent her but he did not care. The
long, carelessly folded legs, the wind-blown, unkempt black hair, the
air of clean, savage honor emphasized by the wolf's frozen leer, comforted him. She was so unlike Aricia. No maze of complex, half-
digested needs and cold, cloaked machinations disturbed their conversation, and peace began to settle its blessed veils around him. He
began to heal.

One month later, when autumn was a change in the smell of the
wind, one of the spies from Camulodunon found Emrys and Venutius
together, eating a noonday meal of venison and berries. He squatted
swiftly, sharing the food with them before he gave his news.

"The arviragus has gone," he said finally. "I was there. Many tribesmen had gathered to sing him to his fate. He looked very tired, but
otherwise well."

"Did he speak?" Emrys had been expecting this message but even
so there was shock, and the ever present, dormant hurt whipped into
life.

"He did, but not many words. 'Tell them I did not surrender, and
neither must they,' he said. I do not think that he could have managed
more, knowing that he was looking his last on Albion."

Emrys sighed gently. "My thanks, freeman. Return to Camulodunon. I need to know now what Scapula is planning for the winter
but you must not bring word yourself. Send it along the chain." His
next order cost him much. His voice was husky. "When word comes of
the arviragus's execution, I want to know as soon as possible."

"I understand, Lord." The man rose and went away, and Venutius
and Emrys could not look at each other. An unexpected loneliness
descended upon them. While Caradoc had been in Albion his presence had somehow continued to brood over the west, but now the
two men felt spiritless and empty, without direction. The force and
warmth of a mighty man had been withdrawn, and it left them lost
and empty.

Venutius was the first to rise. He tossed back his flaming hair, got to
his feet, and stood looking down on Emrys. "You heard his last order
to us," he said harshly. "We will not surrender. Never. As long as
there is one warrior to call the west his place of freedom we will fight
on. We will not dwell on the past, and I will no longer feel shame for
something I would have given my soul to prevent if I could. Nor will
I skulk here, dependent on your forgiveness. I will walk the camps

freely, with my spine straight. Up, Emrys! We must not fail him now."

Startled, Emrys glanced up at him, the look in the rugged face bringing him to his feet. For a time they stood eye to eye, exchanging a charge of determination, an agreement to fight or fall together. But it was not friendship. They understood one another, that was all.

CHAPTER TWENTY-SIX

THE VOYAGE WAS SHORT AND UNEVENTFUL, but after disembarking at Gaul's port of Gesioracum, Caelte, Caradoc, and his family were taken to the steps of the temple and chained together, while all day, in the dust and growing heat, the people of Gesioracum, coarsened by many more years of subjugation than the people of Albion, came to mock and to spit, to pile insults upon the bewildered, defenceless Catuvellauni. The Roman guards stood by and watched idly, bored with a spectacle they had witnessed many times, and as the hours went by the marketplace filled with the curious, the bitter, the scandal-seekers, all come to see with their own eyes the man who had become infamous throughout the Roman world. In all the years of his isolated struggle for survival, Caradoc had given no thought to his growing legend. Cut off in the silent fastness of the west, his days and nights revolving around campaigns and mere sustenance, he had been oblivious of the furor of speculation that had raged from Gaul to Thrace. But now, drowning in the ocean of angry, gleeful faces, he understood, and was devastated. He was booty. He was a prize, a toppled god to be ground into the mud by unforgiving, disillusioned worshippers.

"Sons of dogs!" Llyn exploded in his ear. "Cowards! Their hands have not held swords for years uncounted and they know it! That is why they jeer at the greatest warrior in the world!" He blustered on, but Caradoc felt the trembling of his body through the thin rags and watched the girls in tears, their heads bent, their hair hanging over wet faces, their hands unable to wipe shame away.

"Look at you!" someone bawled out. "Lice-ridden peasant—what kind of an arviragus are you? If you are the best Albion has to offer, no wonder the Romans disdain you."

Caradoc felt Eurgain stiffen beside him. "I love you, Caradoc, I love you," she whispered over and over again, while the small stones grazed their bare arms and clattered down the dazzling white steps. As the afternoon grew hot the offal of slaughterhouse and kitchen began to stink around them, but Caradoc stood seemingly unperturbed, his eyes on the far side of the square, dirty, matted brown hair falling about his broad shoulders. Something in his face drove the mob to a fury and his proud, aging features still imprinted with nobility brought a raw, frightening animosity surging around the little group.

Did you endure this also, Vercingetorix? Caradoc wondered. And was it the least of your trials?

The afternoon inched away with a ponderous, spiteful slowness, a sick dizziness overcoming them as the stench of packed, unwashed bodies rose under the sun. The girls moaned softly under their breath. Llyn and Caelte leaned together, supporting each other's aching legs. But Caradoc and Eurgain stood straight and aloof, a reproach, a living resurrection of hurtful memories to the people of Germania.

It took them a month to reach Rome, and in every town and village along the way the same exhibition took place. The same jeering peasant crowds gathered, the same worn insults were hurled, the same stifling, slow-moving hours were endured. While autumn was advancing swiftly in the clean, wet woods of Albion, here, as they journeyed slowly southeast, it was still late summer.

It seemed to Caradoc that the same contorted faces were following him and by some cruel trick of time he was really chained to the same temple in the same dusty marketplace, but he knew by the cringing of his soul and the deepening shame that they were not. It became harder and harder for him to keep his head high, to ignore the stupid, spiteful words. There were days when he wanted to grovel on the warm pavement, to crawl before the people in subservience, to beg forgiveness for something, anything, so that their harshness might be turned to a soothing pity.

The girth and might of the Roman Empire was greater than he in his arrogant naïveté had ever imagined, and in the dark, blessedly silent nights, sitting cross-legged in his cell, he marveled at his own temerity in having had the bravado to challenge it. He had been nothing but an irritating flea after all, nipping uselessly at the almost insensible hide of a giant. For a while the giant had scratched at him in vain, but then it had found him and brushed him off. He was nothing—a nuisance, a petty, piping annoyance—and Albion was nothing also, a tiny crumb beside the open maw of an empire. Cunobelin's empire had been a tawdry, cheap thing, less even than an imitation, and he and Tog, Cin, Caelte, all of them, had sported and boasted like innocent babes in . . . what was it that Bran had called it? . . . a fool's dream world. The Druithin knew. No wonder the silly little raids, the empty squabbles, the vain strutting of the tribes had driven them to desperation. I am nothing, nothing, he thought, the darkness of his despair more blinding than the close blackness of his cell. The Catuvellauni are nothing, Camulodunon was nothing. Ah Mother, nothing! His thoughts returned to his family, to love and laughter, and, though painfully, he was able to say—yet I am myself. I live. I have a rightful place, just as does the Emperor of Imperial Rome. I will not say that my life has been wasted, for I have been true to those things I know are right.

They were small comforts. He saw the splendor of the cities of Gallia Narbonensis with the dreary eyes of awakened disillusionment. He walked beneath Julius Caesar's triumphal arch at Arausio and felt his barbarism. And when at last he stood with his captors and looked out over the vast sprawl of the city of Rome itself, the death of his innocence was complete. He was looking at an everlasting power, and he knew it. He heard its constant rumble, he smelled its pungent mixture of spices and dung. He felt the inexorable ocean of its brute force against which no people could stand. He bowed his head and followed his guard along the road.

But he had grossly underestimated his importance, as Claudius had known he would. The emperor had ordered his exposure in the towns in the hope that he might arrive in Rome thoroughly cowed, for he did not want a swaggering, bumptious chieftain turning his triumph into a circus. He knew the tenor of the citizens over this, his greatest prize. For years the city had waited to see the infamous, impudent rebel in the flesh, and now Claudius, whose public image had suffered because of the excesses of his favorite freemen Greeks and his family, had the chance to swing that fickle opinion back to himself, and he grasped the opportunity in both greedy hands. He was giving the people a delicious nightmare in the flesh. At last he had brought the chieftain under subjection and there would be a military review, and a special session of the senate, and, of course, a parade.

On that last night, Caradoc and the others were housed in barracks just inside the city walls. Caradoc and Eurgain knew what faced them on the morrow, and they spent the hours of darkness in silence, holding each other tightly, their hearts full of pity for their unsuspecting children. Over the last month, the girls had lapsed into sullen, bewildered brooding, and Llyn had stopped cursing the gods and his luck and had begun to realize that his life was almost over. He was stunned. Death was something that one brought to others, and at the thought that it was now stalking him he was engulfed in panic. He sat in a corner, his face in his hands, grappling with his terror.

In the morning, they were brought water and clean clothes, and a soldier stood by while they washed and quietly dressed themselves. Then they were led outside. Sun beat down on the white dust of the wide, tree-lined Via Sacra and the wind was stale and somehow draining. They were given no food. They could hear the dull roar of the huge crowd that had already gathered, and before them the chariots rolled back and forth, and the officers, in red cloaks and sparkling bronze helmets crowned with gay plumes, waited impatiently for the order to begin.

Caradoc took advantage of the moment of confusion and he embraced and kissed the girls. "Walk slowly, with your heads up," he advised them gently. "Look straight ahead. Remember, all of you, who you are. You have nothing to be ashamed of, nothing to regret. If we are to die today then let us die proudly, not disgracing our tuath."

They turned huge, terrified eyes upon him and Gladys clutched at him with strong, panic-stricken fingers. "I cannot do it, father, I cannot!" she whispered hysterically. "I am faint, my legs will not hold me! I am afraid to die!"

An officer walked toward them, chains over his arm. "It is time," he said. "The young women are to go first, then the bard, your wife, your son, and then you."

"Father!" Gladys began to scream and the officer nodded at his escort. Two burly soldiers tore her from Caradoc's grasp and dragged her away, her sister following numbly, already in a daze.

"She will recover," Llyn said. "She has seen death too many times to be prostrate for long." His words were casual but his voice shook, and Caradoc hugged him briefly.

"Farewell, my son. Today we will cheat them of a spectacle." Llyn inclined his head and kissed his mother, and then Caelte bowed to Caradoc while the officer returned.

"I thank you, Lord, for a good life," he said. "You have been just to me, and I will not forget."

Caradoc took his wrist. "Farewell, Caelte. I thank you for your music. What songs you will sing for me yet, when we sit together around a Council fire again!" Caelte smiled and was gone. Caradoc turned to his wife. "Eurgain," he said, the tears undried on his face. "Do you weep also? You, who have always been my pool of sweet, calm water?" She tried to smile but her lips were quivering uncontrollably. Then they were in each other's arms, eyes closed against the pitiless bright sunlight. "Sword-woman," he whispered.

402

"Arviragus."

They broke apart slowly. "A safe journey," he said quietly.

"A peaceful journey, Caradoc."

They stepped together to the waiting chariots. Caradoc stood obediently with wrists together, and looked ahead while the chains went around them and the soldiers swiftly hammered them to the rear of the chariot. The street was thick with generals, commanders, tribunes, senators, each mounted or riding behind a charioteer. It seemed that all the aristocracy of Rome wished to be a part of this triumph. Llyn, chained to the chariot in front, turned and smiled at him and he smiled back, his eyes straining to where, far ahead, he caught a glitter of sun on purple and gold. The emperor. His soldiers stepped away, satisfied. Somewhere up ahead a trumpet was sounded, and the parade was under way.

What shall I consider now? Caradoc thought as the chariot began to roll with a jerk that nearly dislocated his shoulders. Shall I think of you, Vercingetorix, and your lonely torment? Shall I think of you, Cunobelin, and how your wiles were only the simple deceits of a wayward child after all? Shall it be you, Madoc, you black old reprobate, or you, Emrys, so proud?

The dull roar of the thousands that lined the route drew nearer, and the stiff, ironclad legionaries of the city cohorts that lined the street stood closer together, only their eyes betraying their excitement. The trees had abruptly given way to buildings and Caradoc walked on, his ears deliberately stopped to the wild clamor around him.

I shall think of you, Cinnamus, of your green eyes and bright sword. I shall remember your dry wit, your understanding smiles, your fearlessness and loyalty. You were devoted to Camulos and the Great Mother, but what are they beside Jupiter and the invincible gods of Rome? No, no, do not think of that. Think of what he would say if he were here, think of his scorn.

The sunlight was dazzling, an undiluted outpouring, blinding to his unaccustomed eyes, and the hard stone of the paving hurt his feet. The road had become a broad, straight avenue cutting through tall towers, lofty temples, row upon row of shops, a never-ending, harsh river of solid stone where no soft green thing grew, and it seemed to Caradoc that even the stones shouted at him, Barbarian! Barbarian! If his eyes strayed from the dancing plume of the general behind whose chariot he was chained, he was immediately smitten by the complexity of this mighty city and he could not begin to assimilate the impressions that rained upon him.

Cinnamus. Cinnamus Ironhand.

The faceless, screaming masses pressed and strained against the restraining arms of the cohorts, delirious with excitement, an ocean of waving white and brown snakes, a sea of blurred, open-mouthed faces.

Cinnamus.

The trumpets blared. The sun flayed him.

He heard a man yell, "Well done, barbarian!" and he came to himself and stumbled. All at once reality deluged him.

"A good fight, barbarian!"

"We salute you, barbarian!"

"Caradoc, Caradoc, well fought, well done!"

They were not vilifying him. They were not calling in a white rage for his execution. It was not garbage that struck him, it was flowers—pink, yellow, soft crimson, delicate blue. They were hurling flowers at him, their faces generous and inquisitive, their smiles broad, their shouts encouragement.

"Laurels for the barbarian! Freedom for Caradoc! Mercy for him, Claudius, mercy!"

He scanned them incredulously. It was true. His final humiliation had become the parade of a victor. Up ahead he saw Llyn pick up his stride and shake back his hair. Caelte was ambling along as though his lord had just called for a new song in honor of spring. And suddenly his own spirits took wing and soared high to meet his destiny once again. It seemed that he had conquered Rome after all.

The procession slowly wound to the Forum and halted, and the mobs poured into the plaza behind it. Claudius dismounted and walked slowly up the wide marble steps of the Curia, his purple cloak floating out behind him. When he reached the splash of sunlight at the feet of the soaring columns he turned, and raised a gold-braceleted arm, and his wife stepped from the shade to stand beside him. The mob exploded, screaming their appreciation. For a moment he stood thus, imposing, raised high above his thundering citizens, then he stepped back and lowered himself onto a shaded, purple-draped chair. The trumpets brayed raucously once more and the procession began the slow, solemn circuit of the Forum, at the forefront the praetorians in full regalia.

In all his wildest dreams Caradoc had never imagined such splendor as this. The sun filled his eyes with a blinding dazzle, glowing white and pink and honey golden on the pure, swift-running pillars of Julius Caesar's temple, flowing under the severe arch of Augustus. It wove mutely in and out the myriad arches of the Basilica Julia, battled silently with the proud shadows of the temple of Castor and Pollux, and Caradoc forgot his chains and craned this way and that in awe. He was in a frozen forest of giant white trees, stone trunks, jealously

404

and arrogantly sheltering the soul of the world as the oak groves of Mona guarded the heart of his people. Living trees grew old and died, even as the men who tended them, but this immobile forest would stand forever, as the soul of the Roman Empire. He trudged past the arch of Tiberius and Germanicus, glanced up at the temple of Saturn where thousands seethed on the steps and clung high on the pillars, and then his chariot swung to the left and past the temple of Concord beyond which, high on the hill, the temple of Jove reared proudly, flanked by the Tabularium.

Such grandeur. Such magnificent, opulent splendor! And I have fought all this, he marveled to himself. I must have been mad. He thought of Aricia's pride in her little wooden imitation of a Roman house. He thought of the tiny forums in which he and the others had stood, sweating and dirty under the stares of the crowds, then stared up at the emperor, a little man dwarfed by eternal stone, sizzling in sunlight. Suddenly he wanted to laugh.

His chariot finally came to a halt, and while a tribune and a soldier strode to unfasten him, he searched for Eurgain but could not see her. Claudius beckoned, the trumpets spoke again, and Caradoc and the tribune mounted the steps together, the chains clinking against each marble rise.

Claudius watched him come and his wife leaned toward him and whispered, "How tall he is!" her voice thick with titillation. Claudius nodded, his eyes on the lowered head, the arms outstretched with chains between them, guarding for a fall. He knew the fate of this man, and it gave him no satisfaction. The years ahead would kill what the executioner's spear could not. He had attended the special session of the senate the day before, and sat listening while the senators rose and came down onto the cool, tessellated pavement of the Curia to speak of Syphax and Scipio Africanus, of the clemency of Aemilius Paulus toward the great Perseus, their suave hints dropping like tinkling fountain-water into his ears. This barbarian king had been an enemy to respect, an antagonist worthy of the might of Rome. Besides, the populace held him in favor and Claudius needed that favor also. Attentively, the emperor heard them play on his reverence for the Roman past, his pupilage of the great Livy, and though he smiled a trifle cynically to himself, he was flattered. The people demanded a gesture of magnanimity from their noble, well-educated ruler, a proof of disinterested superiority and humanity, and the senate subtly demanded it, too. So be it. Rome would be merciful. The times had changed since Julius Caesar had had Vercingetorix strangled, and Rome would show that she was not threatened by her most ungrateful province's response to occupation.

Agrippina fidgeted with excitement as Caradoc breasted the last few steps and came to a halt before the emperor. Claudius motioned him in under the shadow of the columns.

"So we meet at last," Claudius said, bending his mild gaze upon the other's face while the uproar beyond them continued unabated. "It was a gallant fight, barbarian, but hopeless from the start, as I am sure you realize. You have the right to speak before I sentence you, if you wish."

Caradoc looked into the sad, worldly face, reading weariness there in the droop of the stern mouth and the tiny furrows between the wide eyebrows. Try as he might, Claudius could not still the minute, uncontrollable wobbling of his head, and already his nose had begun to run with the stress of the occasion. Caradoc was filled with pity. This man may be at the pinnacle of the empire, he thought, but he is not as free as I, though he is swathed in soft purple and I stand before him in peasant's garb and chains.

He did not look at Agrippina but noticed the empress's hands gripping the sides of her gilt chair, her black eyes consuming him from a white, carefully powdered face that hid the encroaching signs of age. Her perfume filled his nostrils with its musky, heady scent and the jewels that studded her piled hair and clustered in her coronet winked at him invitingly. With his sharp, animal divination he smelled the odor of rapacious corruption under the graceful, rich folds of the stola, and he knew that she was to be feared more than her husband.

He kept his eyes on Claudius, and wondered what to say. He was not speaking to a ragged tuath, he was addressing an empire, and for a moment shyness seized him, but then he recovered. I am arviragus. I love my people. For their sakes I will not bow my head, nor will I bring disgrace to those who have died for me. He began to speak slowly, feeling his way.

"Had my high birth and rank been accompanied by moderation in the hour of success I should have entered this city as a friend and not as a prisoner. You would not have hesitated to accept as an ally a man of splendid ancestry, bearing rule over many tribes. My present position is degrading to me, but glorious to you. I had horses, warriors, and gold. If I was unwilling to lose them, what wonder in that?" His voice strengthened. Power slipped to his tongue like golden mead and unconsciously he raised his manacled arms and flung one foot before the other, a gesture of pride. "Does it follow that because you desire universal empire, all must accept universal slavery? Were I now dragged here as one who had surrendered without fighting, no fame would have attached to my fall, or to your victory. If you punish me they will both be forgotten." For you, Eurgain, I say this, he thought

406

deliberately, and for you, my Llyn, and the girls, but I will not beg. He threw his head back defiantly, and the eyes that met Claudius's were haughty and cool. "Spare me, then, as an eternal example of your mercy!" The words rang out, echoing through the dim, regally clustered pillars of the Curia, and Agrippina began to smile.

Claudius watched the heaving chest, the feet planted sturdily apart, the flashing, unapologetic eyes. You ask me to spare you as though you were challenging me to a battle, he thought with an amused respect. Now I can understand poor Scapula's desperation. You are formidable, you wild chieftain. With a graceful gesture he rose.

"Listen to the people, Caradoc," he said. "They honor you, they shout for your deliverance. Never let it be said that Rome does not reward valor, whether it be in her own beloved citizens or in her noble enemies. You are deserving of our reward for your fearless resistance. Therefore, in the name of Jupiter and the gods of Rome, I pardon you. Strike the chains!"

Members of his bodyguard moved smoothly, and in an unbelieving daze Caradoc felt his wrists and ankles suddenly lighten and heard the chains clatter to the marble. Free? Just like that? So quickly, so easily hope returns to bear me once more on its wings?

Claudius stepped to him and, laying an arm across his shoulders, turned him to the populace, and together they went into the sunlight. Claudius slowly raised his other arm, the purple cloak slid back, a great howl of delight and approval went up as the people saw their emperor and their enemy side by side.

Caradoc did not heed them. The holding spell of his amazement still gripped him and his eyes searched among the throng below for his family. He caught a glimpse of Eurgain's shining blonde head but could not read her face. For a moment he and Claudius stood pressed against each other, and then the emperor drew him back into the welcome coolness.

"There are conditions, of course," Claudius said. "You must swear on whatever gods you worship that you will never again bear arms against Rome."

Now, hope, your silvery wings falter, Caradoc thought, and again my feet must brush despair. To swear this thing is to hold out my hands once more for the chains of slavery, yet what difference will it make in the end? Living or dead, Albion must fight on without me.

"I will swear," he answered unsteadily. "I swear by Camulos, by the Dagda, by the Great Mother, that . . . that . . ." His courage almost failed him but he rallied. "That I will never again raise sword against the people of Rome."

Claudius nodded. "Good. That was hard for you, I know, but necessary, Caradoc. You must also understand that you are exiled from your country. You may have your freedom within this city and under certain circumstances within five miles of it, but any transgression of this edict will bring immediate death."

Caradoc met the gray, shrewd eyes and saw his own thought mirrored there. You must be strong to die the slow death, Claudius was saying to him even as he said it to himself. Immediate death would be kinder but mercy has nothing to do with kindness.

"The senate has voted you a house and you will be supported at public expense. You have already cost us a great deal of money," he went on with humor, "but I suppose we can spare a little more."

I feel it already, tightening around me like a hunting net, Caradoc thought in fear. How long can I cling to what I am? How long will the children speak to me in the accents of their home, and share with me the memories of times past? This too you know, you cruel, implacable Roman. Then know that I resist, and I will go on resisting until the day my body dies. He made no comment, and finally the empress got out of her chair and came forward, reaching for his hand.

"Grieve if you must for your damp little island," she said, "but do not grieve too long, barbarian. You will come to be happy here, for Rome is a city of endless fascination." And so am I, her impudent, cool glance told him. "I congratulate you on a fight well fought." He withdrew his hand and did not reply, but she was not offended. She merely smiled knowingly and went back to her chair.

"I have arranged a small surprise for you," Claudius said, and with a spasm of shrinking Caradoc suddenly knew what was coming. He turned to run, but there was nowhere to go.

"Plautius, my friend, come out!"

Caradoc swung to the dimness behind him, his heart galloping. Two figures were emerging from the shadows, tall, quiet-moving, and the bodyguard parted to let them through. The man was straight, gray-haired, with a thin, commanding face and sea-gray eyes. He was smiling as he came forward with his sure, soldier's gait but after one quick stare, Caradoc looked past him, emotion strangling in his throat, blood pounding in his ears and throbbing in his limbs. She had not changed much, his sister. She was plumper, the once-angular, taut lines having become curves of contentment. The smooth black hair, now heavily streaked with gray, was bound up on top of her head. But the eyes, though nested in myriads of fine lines and filled with tears, were still steady and full of mysteries and there was the same self-contained beauty in her regally black-swathed figure. They stared at one another for a long time, his face gradually becoming whiter and whiter, until he abruptly closed his eyes and wrenched away. "I cannot," he said. "I cast her from the tuath, I cannot speak to her. I swore an oath!"

"Caradoc," she said huskily, slowly. "By Camulos, how changed you are. I recognize an arviragus, the stamp is on you, but where is my brother? What have they done to him, those lost years?" She spoke to him in his own tongue, lyrical and full of melody, threaded with a precise Latin accent. "I heard that you broke a sword in wrath against me. I heard you spoke the curses and swore an oath. Then I wept, Caradoc, having no tuath and no kin. I felt myself abandoned by all, even as you felt yourself to be. Yet I have been happy. My choice, if it were choice, was a good one." She walked to him then but did not touch him, though her arms ached to hold her own flesh once more. "Caradoc, I know that you will not forget your roots. What Catuvellaunian could ever forget the soil that bred him and the forests that blooded him? I have been in Rome for almost ten years and no day has gone by that has not been a day of longing for the smell of wet oaks and the touch of a bright sword in my hand. I am without tuath or kin, by your command. And now you stand here, also without tuath or kin, by command of the emperor. Dissolve your oaths, my brother! Let us support one another and share together the load that we must carry. I fought beside you, risking my life for the tribe whose ricon cast me out. Now I beg him to recognize a debt, out of his own extremity."

Caradoc listened to the soft voice, his face still turned away to where the crowd seethed in the swelter of the noon sun. "I cannot unsay the words of banishment, and you know it," he said flatly. "When I left the Great Hall that night, fire all around me and guilt in my heart, you were leaning against the wall all alone. I never dreamed I would see you again, and it was with such pain that I fled into the west. Ah, Gladys, where has all the time gone? What does it all mean?"

"Caradoc, please." She could see the muscles of his neck drawn tight, his shoulders hunched as though warding off a blow. Claudius, Plautius, and the soldiers stood watching quietly, caught up in the ebb and flow of a private misery voiced in a language full of sweet, wistful cadences, carrying the breath of a way of life beyond their comprehension. But Agrippina sat drumming her long fingers against the arm of her chair, suddenly bored and hungry for food.

Caradoc turned slowly, almost unwillingly, as though invisible hands pulled at him from each direction and he could not direct his limbs. "Sometimes it is necessary for a man to put aside the right and wrong he has been taught, and shed one truth to find another." He said it with difficulty. "So say the Druids. I do not think that the

Druithin had such a shedding as this in mind, Gladys. Nevertheless, I will attempt it." He took a step and then another. His arms rose, and all at once she ran across the polished pavement and flung herself upon him.

Claudius smiled like a beneficent uncle. Plautius felt a vast relief that did not betray itself on his face, for he had spoken in the senate urging clemency for this, his relative by marriage, knowing the amusement his speech had brought to his fellow senators. His wife had asked nothing from him, but for the last month she had been unable to sleep, pacing his tiled halls in the dead watches of the night, her arms folded on her breasts and her head down. There had been no word of his that could comfort her. Agrippina yawned under her ringed hand.

Claudius inclined his head and the bodyguard came to attention. "Now we will eat together," he said. "I trust, barbarian, that you will have no scruples about tasting my wine as your foolish sister did, so many years ago!"

"Elephants and emperors never forget," Plautius whispered to Gladys as she left Caradoc's embrace and went to link arms with her husband. "It seems that I shall have to wait yet again for that private dinner I desired with your brother when I saw him striding the ramparts of Camulodunon!"

The ramparts of Camulodunon. Gladys let the quick spurt of longing catch in her breath, and then held out a hand to Caradoc.

Agrippina rose. She and Claudius proceeded slowly out into the blazing sun, the others following to where Eurgain, Llyn, and the girls sat at the foot of the steps, a tiny pool of sane familiarity amid a desert of dark, foreign faces.

End of Winter, A.D. 52

CHAPTER TWENTY-SEVEN

THE SPY WORKED for one of the governor's secretaries. He kept order in the offices of the administration block at Camulodunon. He ran errands. He was a very willing, very eager servant and the secretary called on him a great deal, knowing that his demands would be carried out faithfully and promptly. But the spy, the servant, was ill, and the secretary, though irritated, accepted a replacement for a while. But he had come to rely on the man's quiet efficiency and he was annoyed.

The spy left Camulodunon, trekking like a shadow. He cut west through the Catuvellaun forest until he reached Verulamium, but he did not enter the town. He struck north, following the road that ran straight to the Roman garrison at Viroconium and the pass into the western mountains beyond. He grinned to himself as he loped under the brittle, sleeping trees, keeping the road on his right but not leaving the forest to tread its smooth surface, even though he often had to detour impenetrable undergrowth. He was almost disposed to bless Rome for this obliging guide. The weather was bitterly cold. Spring was still three months away, and Albion lay quiescent under winter's stiff white hand. In the south, rain mixed with sleet had driven the spy to keep moving, deep within the forest where there were still dry places to rest, but the cold had not allowed him more than a few hours of troubled sleep at a time. As he crossed the border of the Coritani the rain dribbled away and there was only sleet, ice-cold and stinging, and he dared not light a fire to dry his clothes or cook hot food. He sat hunched under the dubious shelter of the thorny bramble bushes, his eyes on the thin slice of road visible through the trees, shivering yet not daring to leave the concealment of the forest to travel more quickly. He had been tempted, but every twenty miles or so along this road there was a posting station, fortified like a miniature garrison, and the speculatores and patrols often clattered past him as he forced one sodden, frozen foot after the other. He reflected, with grim humor, that his life in Camulodunon had softened him, but he was not yet soft enough to lie down and die. He slipped like a forest wight past the posting stations and came to last to Viroconium, one link in Scapula's chain that stretched from Glevum in the south to Deva in the north, the governor's western frontier.

Snow had begun to fall, but there was no wind. He circled the garrison with infinite care, walking in the places where the snow had not penetrated so that he would leave no footprints behind. He stood facing the pass that would have taken him south into Silurian country, sniffing the cold, wet air. Then he turned and plunged north, swimming across the river in the middle of the night, holding his damp cloak over his head. He reached the other side and looked up. Forest beckoned him, and he could sense an infinitude of rock far beyond the snow's gray blindness. He began to run. He knew where he was.

He staggered into Emrys's camp six days later. The snow had stopped and a weak sun shone in the watery blue sky. The little tents were half buried, but fires blazed, and the dazed man gulped great whiffs of stewing pig. Emrys dropped his joint and ran to greet him.

"I am pleased to meet you at last, Lord," the spy croaked. "I have worked for the cause of freedom for many years, yet only the last link in my little chain has ever seen you face to face." He smiled, and Emrys's heart turned over. So this was Caradoc's chief spy in Camulodunon, a man who earned his bread from Roman hands, a man who had never left the town, yet who was more vital to the west's struggle than Emrys himself. The news must be very big.

"Come into my tent," he said gently. "Do not share until you have eaten."

"Hot food," the man said. "And dry clothes. I have enoyed neither since I left the south." Emry sent for Venutius and Madoc, and a freeman for food. He sat in his tent on his skins, saying nothing, watching the stranger peel off his sodden garments and pull on a pair of Emrys's own breeches and a tunic before he sank down to make his meal. It was a large one, but Emrys did not hurry him. Madoc and Venutius shouldered their way into the tent, bringing with them the strong, sour smell of wet wool. Then the spy gulped his beer, wiped his mouth, and at a nod from Emrys, gave his news.

"Two things, Lords," he said. "First, the arviragus has been pardoned. The dispatch came two weeks ago but I waited for confirmation before passing it along. It seems that Claudius has taken a liking to his enemy, or rather, the city of Rome has. The people demanded his release."

"That would not have been enough!" Venutius said sharply. "The senate must have voted for it as well. Could it be that Claudius pardoned Caradoc out of necessity, or . . ."

Madoc voiced the doubt in all their minds. "Or has Caradoc struck some dishonorable bargain with the emperor in exchange for his life?" They looked at each other, confused, but the spy spoke up.

"No," he said forcefully. "No. Never. I know him better than that. Claudius has become very unpopular lately. His family is a breed of degenerate animals and his Greek freemen shock even the Roman populace with their dissipation. He hopes that by pardoning the arviragus he will rise once more in the people's favor."

For a while the men digested his words, reviewed their own memories, and were satisfied. We are more like animals, perhaps, than Claudius's pathetic family, Emrys thought. I know no degenerate beasts of the forest—only men may be degenerate—yet we have grown to suspect ourselves and all those around us. His eyes brushed those of Venutius. "What are the terms?" he asked brusquely.

The spy shook his head. "I do not know for certain, but they will be common. Exile from the home of his birth, and death if he leaves the city of Rome."

To be exiled from Albion is death enough, Emrys thought again. There are many places in Gaul where a man might fool himself into believing he is home, but to have to live in that city forever, without forest or mountain, without clean streams and the silence of the golden meadows in a summer noon . . . Mother, Mother, I would die! He wanted to weep. "What of Eurgain? Llyn? His daughters?"

"None of them will suffer execution. They have all become heroes and curiosities in Rome."

The irony of it all came into Venutius's mouth, acrid and hot. "What other news have you?" he asked shortly.

The man smiled again, this time a grin of malice. "The governor is dead. Caradoc has finally killed him."

Only Madoc exclaimed. The others tensed in surprise, and the spy, seeing the reaction his words had evoked, went on. "The news of Caradoc's pardon was too much for him. After all, he had hunted the man for years, his health, his peace of mind, everything had been sacrificed to his desire to capture Caradoc. When he had finally done it he felt that he had fulfilled his destiny, but in one moment the emperor took all meaning from his triumph. He fell apart, Lords." The man's hands rubbed against each other. "His stomach burst, and something burst in his head also, for he died screaming. His agony could be heard all over the forum. So it seems," he finished, turning his head to look at Venutius, "that your wife did us a courtesy after all."

Us, yes, Venutius thought, but not Caradoc. He did not reply, and the man's brown eyes left him.

"Well," Madoc grunted. "What happens now? Can you tell us that, freeman?"

"I am a chieftain," the man responded pointedly. "But I suppose it does not matter. I cannot tell you with any certainty what will happen, but I have worked beside the Romans for long enough to make a judgment. The news of Scapula's death will not have reached Rome yet. The weather is not good. It will take the emperor by surprise, and he will be unable to select a new governor for some time. Again, the turbulence of the spring tides will prevent any man from coming to Albion until late spring, at the earliest."

And there must be a governor. Venutius's mind began to work fast. Without a governor the fools are rudderless, a boat without control or direction, a headless, useless corpse. It is time to tread the war tracks again. He hardly heard the man rise and address Emrys.

"That is all my news, Lord," he said. "I must ask food of you, and a

413

spare cloak, and I must leave immediately. I am supposed to be in my own house, ill, but there is so much confusion at Camulodunon now that I do not think anyone will seek news of my health until I am fully recovered." He bowed curtly and stepped to the tent flap, but Emrys asked, "Chieftain, who are you? What is your name?"

The man surveyed them all carefully. The knowledge they wanted could mean his death if one of them was caught and tortured, for Rome was feverish in its search for the eyes and ears of the rebels, yet he knew also that it was far more likely to be he himself who faced the torturer first. He inclined his head. "I am a Catuvellaun warrior. I used to be Caradoc's hunting companion, when he and I and Togodumnus were youths together, but lately I have been awarded Roman citizenship for my service in the governor's offices. Who knows? Perhaps one day I may be mayor of Camulodunon." He smiled to himself at his little joke. "I am surprised that you, Madoc, did not recognize me. My name is Vocorio." Madoc stared at him, breathing heavily, then he said, "You have changed, Catuvellaunian."

"I have grown older, even as you have, Silurian bear. You too have changed. Only one thing changes a man more than the passage of time." He shrugged and went out, the flap whispering closed behind him.

"What might that be?" Madoc muttered. Emrys laughed. "Why the constant reliving of bitter memories," he answered. "So say the Druids."

Over the next two months, news continued to trickle in. Claudius had indeed been taken aback by the sudden death of his governor. He could not provide a replacement before the early summer; he had no one to send before then and perhaps not even shortly after. Juggling the men best qualified for the job was an expensive and tricky business, and while he dickered the chiefs of the west met to plan their summer engagements. The winter had not been wasted. Once more the tribesmen were fully armed, the lines of communication reforged. The west was ready for combat, and with hopeful eyes the leaders watched the spread of confusion that had begun at Camulodunon with the death of Scapula. The legions received no orders, and their legates dreaded the coming of the campaigning season without directives from Camulodunon. Scapula's second-in-command did not know what moves to make, either. He could have taken over the task of the summer fighting, but Scapula, secure in the belief that with Caradoc out of the way, the west would surrender meekly, had not formulated any moves. The second, like his emperor, dithered. On Mona the refugees and servants of the Druids prepared once more to sow the crops that would fuel the rebels, and in the Ordovician mountains Emrys sent out a request to the Demetae and Deceangli chieftains to come to council. They sent no reply but came at once, with the returning messengers.

Council was assembled on a soft overcast day, full of the drip of melting snow. Five hundred chieftains, the leaders of their people, sat with Emrys, Madoc, and Venutius at the foot of a well-guarded cliff, rock at their back and a small lake edged in forest before them. After the opening ceremonies were concluded, Emrys rose, took off his sword, and briefly told them all the state of the province.

"This is a good time to strike the first blow of the season," he said. "Now, early, before the men in Camulodunon decide that they must make some kind of a move against us, governor or no governor. But we must discuss where our blow will fall. You are free to speak."

One of the Demetae sprang up. "We no longer have an arviragus!" he shouted. "Therefore we must rule ourselves. I ask the Council for more aid in the south. We Demetae have battled the coastal patrols from our boats. At great loss to ourselves we have kept the soldiers from creeping into the west and falling upon your backs. But now the south of Siluria is lost to you, and we cannot battle the Classis Britannica from Silurian shores. We are not mountain fighters, but we will be forced to be, this summer, now that Rome holds most of Siluria. Come farther south, you Ordovicians! Help us, as we have helped you."

He sat down and Sine stood, removing her mask and sword. "Your words are true," she replied. "But if we leave this country and move farther south the Twentieth Legion will devour the north. Then the Deceangli will be cut off from the rest of the west and destroyed, and it will be a simple matter for the Twentieth and the Second to push us front and back. Let the Demetae understand that they, like the Silurians before them, must hold their coast until they can do so no longer and then fall back to join with us. We can do nothing. There are not enough of us. Holding the Deceangli border against the Twentieth must be our first priority."

The Demetae scowled blackly and muttered to one another, and Sine sat down pricked by many angry eyes. However, what she had said was true, and none could gainsay her. A Deceangli warrior got up then, a quiet chief, who reminded them all that the Deceangli faced not only the Twentieth but also those of Aricia's Brigantian chiefs who were not patrolling the middle lands for Rome. The Deceangli had suffered more than any other tribe with the exception of the Silures. Any new push by Rome seemed to be aimed at them as Rome probed for the west's suspected weak spots. Also, as Sine said, if they had retreated at all Rome would have sped after them and another piece of the west would have been lost. He spoke unemotionally, not gesturing, not begging, and Venutius watched and listened, his mind busy. After the Deceangli chief had fallen silent the Demetae rose once more, and the wrangling began. For an hour the jugs of beer were passed, and the heated arguments flew back and forth. Emrys watched also, his heart sinking. Oh Caradoc, he thought. I can do nothing. I have no authority to order any but my own tuath. Madoc was twitching and cursing in his beard but he, too, was impotent. There was no help for the Demetae, and precious little for the Deceangli. The Ordovicians and Silures must face east.

Venutius touched Emrys's arm. "May I speak?" he asked in a low voice, and Emrys, seeing a glow of something strange in the dark eyes, nodded. Venutius stood, flung his sword to the ground, and bellowed. "Silence! All of you! I would speak!"

The haggling swiftly subsided, but a voice yelled back, "Sit down, traitor's plaything! What right have you to speak?"

Venutius's face whitened. His lips compressed briefly, but he did not yield. "I speak by right of Council!" he roared back. "If you will not listen, then go away!"

Something in his voice, the glare of his furious eyes, quelled all objection. He waited for a moment but, seeing no one leave, he hooked his thumbs into his belt and pitched his voice lower. It carried strong and clear, and no chief missed a word. "I brought one quarter of all the free people of Brigantia into the west with me last summer," he said. "Since then, more Brigantians have found their way here. No chief who loves freedom is left under my wife's dominion. I do not know how many Brigantians I now command. Five thousand, perhaps, or more. I will send them into your territory, Demetae chieftains, to fight with you, on one condition." Now he had the attention of all. They watched him out of immobile faces, their eyes following his every gesture, and Venutius saw Sine clap the mask to her face to hide her surprise. He went on calmly. "I want the Demetae massed together at the place where the north of Siluria borders on the Dobunni's land, just above the Second's fort at Glevum. I want them there for no more than one moon's cycle this spring. And you Deceangli." They turned bewildered eyes on him. "Do you want to see the threat of the Twentieth removed? If you will put your trust in me and in the honor of the Ordovician people, the Twentieth will fall before the summer. Ask among yourselves, both of you."

"What are you doing, you crazy Brigantian?" Madoc hissed up at him.

Venutius turned and smiled down at the old Silurian. "Have patience, Madoc. I will unfold my plan to you and the others presently."

He shouted again to the company, "I know a way to destroy not only the Twentieth but every garrison and posting station along Scapula's frontier, but it will not work unless you obey me. Think about it, and come to me before sundown." He went back to his place and Emrys spoke to him angrily.

"What are you trying to do, Venutius? Do you wish to control us all? Is that what you have been considering all these months?"

"No, Emrys," Venutius replied emphatically. "I do not want to be arviragus unlawfully."

"Then why have you not discussed this plan of yours with Madoc and me? Why must we sit here open-mouthed and shamed like the others?"

Venutius gripped him firmly by the arm, his eyes blazing with excitement from within his sharp animal face. "Because I did not want it revealed until the tribes had had their say, all of them, and were satisfied with the quarreling and the beer. Their talk is all of small things, a garrison here, a detachment there, more defence than attack. But this is the time for attack, Emrys, along the whole of the border! Let us take the initiative, while Albion has no governor!"

Emrys did not withdraw his arm though Venutius's fingers bruised it in his agitation. "If you council pitched battle I will forbid the Ordovicians to have anything to do with you," he said. "What other way is there to defeat a whole legion?"

Venutius shook his head impatiently. "No, no. I am not such a fool. There is another way, Emrys, but it depends upon the willingness of the tribes to take their orders from one man, just for a little while. They must thoroughly understand what I am trying to do and they must not feel threatened by me. I want power over them, but only for a little while."

"Very well." Emrys sought his wife's face and found it, far back. The eyes shone with a shrewd knowing delight from behind the wolf's grimace. She has listened to Venutius and she already understands, he thought. She is happy. "I suppose I can wait for sundown to hear your idea, Venutius." Venutius released his arm, not realizing he had been clutching it.

"I would have told you, Emrys," he said more gently, "but I wanted to be sure the Demetae would come to Council, and the Deceangli. Without them it cannot work, and I would have raised your hopes only to have them dashed in the end."

Emrys laughed. "Truly you have not been in the west for long," he chuckled. "Else you would know that for us there is no such thing as hope or despair. We walk the middle way, Venutius, and so keep our sanity. And our lives."

That evening twenty chiefs came to sit before Venutius, ten from the Demetae, ten from the Deceangli. Their bards and shield-bearers hovered in the background. "We will hear your words," they said sullenly, doubtfully, driven more by their curiosity than by the belief that the Brigantian had anything new to offer them, but Venutius smiled at them, unoffended. He took the knife from his belt and swiftly sketched a map of the west on the ground—no coastline, no rivers, no roads—only Deva, and Glevum, the string of garrisons in between, and the west's own lines of communication.

"Good," he said, as they craned to see. "Now listen. You Demetae will leave your territory, every one of you, and move east, to here." His knife scratched with sureness. "You will find Madoc and the Silures waiting for you. You will divide your forces into as many units as there are garrisons, from Viroconium to Glevum, but you will leave the fort alone. No whisper of what is taking place must come to the ears of the legate there." Something clicked in Emrys's mind and he glanced into Venutius's face with a dawning wonder, but Venutius was speaking again. "To the north, the Ordovices will divide in two, one-half of the tribe under Emrys's command, the other under Sine. And you Deceangli," he said, pausing to smile at them, "you will mass together here, on your border, and march on the fort at Deva." Loud cries of denial broke from them, but Emrys was silent, marveling at this man who had silently paced beside him from camp to camp, absorbed all the spread of the mountains and the units hidden within them, and then made this ambitious, this impossible, yet not so impossible, plan. Venutius held up a hand. "Let me finish. The legion will be waiting for you. Rumors will have gone out a little time before and the gates of the fort will open long before you reach it, but you must give battle here, well away from the forest. For in the forest, half of the Ordovician force will be waiting. Now. The fort will empty. You will engage the enemy. You will, of course, stand no chance against them. You will begin to retreat toward the forest. Then, when the soldiers are well away from the safety of the fort, pursuing you with great joy," here his mouth quirked, "either Emrys or Sine, preferably Emrys, will leave the forest and fall upon the legion's right flank. If the surprise is complete enough the legate should be well confused. When his confusion begins to turn to a hastily laid plan of retaliation, then the rest of the Ordovices will come upon his rear. Having occupied the empty fort and set fire to it, they will have cut off all chance of a Roman retreat. The legion will be surrounded, but not all at once. Shock must follow shock, so that the legate can put no firm battle plan into operation.

418

"He will send south along the frontier for reinforcements," one of the chiefs said hesitantly.

Venutius shook his head slowly. "He will send, but in vain. The Silures and the Demetae will have destroyed every garrison along the frontier. They will attack while the Deceangli are approaching the fort. Then, when victory is ours, the Deceangli can go home to rest and the Ordovices will march south to join with the Demetae and the Silurians and attack the Second at Glevum. When the Second falls the Demetae can likewise go home, and the rest of us can choose any point in the south as our next target."

"The Second will not fall as easily as that," Madoc remarked.

Venutius nodded again, scuffing out his map with his hand and sitting back on his heels. "I know. But we can try it, Madoc. If we have no luck we can leave it alone. What can it do but follow us south, and once we have gained the lowlands other tribes will join us. We will march the Second all over the south."

"The Fourteenth?" Emrys could not still the incredulous excitement rising in him. It shone from his eyes.

"We cannot look that far ahead. If we kill off the Twentieth and the garrisons we will have done enough. Then we can plan again. Well?" he urged the Demetae and the Deceangli. "What do you say?"

They rose. "We will talk together," one of them said. "And we will give you our answer with the first light of tomorrow."

After they had gone Madoc grumbled, "I do not want to fight with the Demetae. They are an uncouth tribe."

"But mighty warriors," Emrys pointed out, and Venutius, watching him, knew that he had won.

"You must go south and meet them, Madoc. That country is yours. Besides, it would be good to mingle Silurians with the Demetae when you divide into groups and face each garrison. Then the Demetae cannot change their minds at the last moment and go home," Venutius continued.

"Caradoc could control them," Madoc still protested. "I am no Caradoc."

But perhaps *you* are, Brigantian lord, Emrys thought, looking at Venutius's withdrawn face with new respect. Perhaps it is not such a foolish idea, that the west may yet win this vicious, eternal war. What would you say, Caradoc, my old friend, if you could hear this wild, wounded sheepherder? Is there a flaw in his reasoning? What will the Druids say? "Venutius," he sighed. "It is a good plan. Reckless perhaps, but when have we been less than gamblers here? I am with you."

"And I," Madoc wheezed. "I will do my best to be polite to the Demetae chiefs."

"Then we must wait for the dawn," Venutius said, and his eyes were dark with his seething thoughts. "I am hungry now. Shall we go to the fire, and eat?" He rose confidently, a new consciousness of dignity on him. Emrys and Madoc saw it and followed without another word.

Venutius's strategy worked with almost ludicrous ease. The Demetae chiefs went back to their territory and returned, bringing their warriors with them. They and the Silures quietly strung themselves out at the edge of the forest, two miles from Scapula's frontier garrisons, but their scouts lay hidden in the brush where they could watch the Romans. Any bold patrol foraging in the woods could have found them, but the garrison commanders were waiting for word from Camulodunon and did nothing. This was Venutius's gamble. If Rome was better organized than he had counted on, he would fail. The Ordovices flowed into the north, divided, and Sine led her host south again and east, single file into Cornovii country, working her way back north to come up behind the fort at Deva. Hers was the greater gamble. The northern Cornovii were sympathetic to the rebel cause but belonged to the province, and spring had arrived. The snow had gone and the trees had budded and opened, their shiny, crumpled, pale green leaves like wet, new butterfly's wings. The Cornovii peasants and freemen were sowing their little fields, and though Sine did her best to avoid detection by Cornovii tribesmen, there were peasants who saw the silent Ordovicians gliding past and did not live to tell what they had seen. Venutius watched the Deceangli assemble on their border. He knew they were unhappy that they had to trust him and the Ordovicians in order to save themselves from being cut to pieces. But the years with Caradoc had taught them that, at the last, no one tribe could exist alone. They were dependent upon one another and, even more, they could not have continued their fight for one day if they had not been buttressed by Emrys and his people. Venutius went among them, explaining over and over again what they must do, and they understood. In the evenings he briefed his scouts, men and women he had chosen carefully to run between himself, Sine, and the Deceangli. When they had gone he lay in his tent, on his back, his hands behind his head, and thought of Aricia and the cage she had made for him, and the west and its own cage. Somehow the two were tangled in his mind, as though if he could break out of the west he would also break free from his wife's invisible prison, in which, he knew despairingly, he was still trapped.

When the time came, and he was sure that he had overlooked no contingency, he gave his final orders. "Hold them for three hours," he told the Deceangli. "Then begin your retreat to the forest. Do not allow them to push you to either side. You must have your backs to Emrys."

Word came from Sine, lying behind the huge, unfinished fort that was rising beside the Twentieth's temporary quarters, and finally Venutius divided Emrys's force in two and set them beside each other. He himself commanded one half. "You bolster the Deceangli directly from the rear," he said. "I will bring the others onto the Roman flank. Sine will send men into the empty fort and then fall on their other flank. Thus they will be completely surrounded."

At dawn the Deceangli emerged from the forest, feeling naked and pitifully alone, and Manlius Valens, legate of the Twentieth, ran to his wall and stood in the cover of his lookout tower, watching them approach. Swiftly gauging their number he ordered out his auxiliaries and the gates of the fort swung open. They remained so. After an hour of battle he saw that auxiliaries were not enough. He sent another one thousand infantry. Then, resignedly, he ordered out the rest of the infantry, cohorts, and his cavalry. He climbed down from his vantage place and rode onto the field himself, the aquila glittering beside him in the strong spring sun. Another hour of furious engagement took place, but the Deceangli were no match for the legionaries. Valens had the battle well in hand by the time the natives broke and began to speed for the forest, leaving the grass piled with their dead, and Valens calmly ordered pursuit. The cavalry leaped to obey. The infantry opened ranks and ran, and the comforting bulk of the fort dwindled to a small gray box behind them.

Then a carnyx sounded. Valens heard it, faint but clear, a mocking, defiant note, and he knew. Screaming for a speculator he reined in, gave a hurried message to the man who answered his summons, and watched him gallop safely away south to where there were garrisons and men and salvation. He shouted to the trumpeter. "Get the first cohort back here. The aquila must stay with me, we must on no account see it fall." The call rang out, and now Valens could see them, rushing out from the trees, wave upon wave of grim tribesmen in brown and gray and dark green tunics, their shields outflung, their great swords held high. Orders fell from Valens's mouth, a tumble of concern, but as yet he was not afraid. He sat with his tribunes and his staff mounted beside him, answering each challenge as his unit commanders sent for orders, seeing the Deceangli turn back on the tide of this fresh onslaught, seeing his soldiers quell the impulse to turn and flee. Then someone close to him cried out. Heads turned. With a thud Valens's heart sank cold and painful, for off on his right flank another

421

dull-colored cloud was rolling from the forest, and even as he watched, it formed a crescent. He opened his mouth to shout warnings, useless words, for orders would not come. Fear choked him, but it was not yet terror. He kicked his horse and sped away with his staff bunched tight around him and the aquila shining in the hands of the aquilifer. As he flew the orders at last took shape in his mind and he gave them voice. His wavering flank rallied at his coming but he heard, he sensed, the break-up of his legion's confident unity. He could not fight here. Nothing at his back, and the tribesmen on three sides. "Close them up!" he shouted. "Retreat to the fort!" The trumpet broadcast the order, but when Valens glanced behind him the fort was not there. It was hidden by another cloud, low and menacing, advancing upon him. Terror wrapped its hot arms around him and his thoughts ceased to make sense. They have learned, he thought over and over again.They have learned, Jupiter save us, they have learned. He did not realize he had been screaming the words until his senatorial tribune gripped him by the arm.

"What orders, sir, what orders?" the man begged, his voice high with panic, but no orders could save his men, who were falling like wheat before a reaper's scythe. Valens did not answer but wrenched on the reins and pounded to where his cavalry escort milled in confusion. He tugged the aquila from the fingers of the aquilifer. "Save yourselves!" he shouted. "The legion is finished!" Then he was gone, and after one horrified glance at the wet, stinking carnage around them his escort surged after him. They did not notice the horizon, where the clear, fresh morning had been without mist. Now the far distance was fogged with a haze of gray. Scapula's frontier had collapsed.

Late Spring, A.D. 52

CHAPTER TWENTY-EIGHT

FAVONIUS ABSENT-MINDEDLY ACKNOWLEDGED the salute of his sentry, and he and Priscilla walked out the gate of the little wooden garrison and down the path toward the copse. It was a sweet, scent-heavy, late spring day in Icenia, full of mild sunlight and fitful, gentle wind, but Favonius had no eyes for the weather. He moved slowly, with his head down and a frown on his face, and his wife's gay stream of chatter was no more to him than the equally strident musical piping of the birds that nested in the thick, cool trees he now plunged under, still in a mood of brooding detachment. Priscilla chirped on, her pretty face raised to his, sun and shade dappling both of them, but as Favonius graced her with no more than a grunt or two she took his arm and tugged him to a halt.

"Honorious, what's the matter? I asked you whether I could take Marcus to Colchester for a few days. Is your response meant to signify yes or no?"

"Yes!" he snapped, the frown still set like a sour, irregular furrow on his forehead. "I mean, no! Oh Priscilla, your requests grow more ridiculous as time goes by. First it was a hypocaust, as though we were building a house in Rome instead of inhabiting a rough wooden house on the edge of the empire. Then it was silverware for the officers' table, as though we entertained the governor. No, Marcus does not need a few days at Colchester. Perhaps next year."

He moved on and she slid her arm through his once again. "What a nasty mood you are in today! Leave the garrison to run itself for once, my dear. The dispatches never reveal anything exciting anyway. How safe and peaceful it is here! As you have forced me to attend this display of barbaric prowess and coarse merrymaking you might at least do your best to help me pretend to enjoy it."

Testily, impatiently, he quickened his stride then sighed and turned to her, smiling in apology. They were nearing the edge of the little stand of oaks and could hear the roar of the crowd that was gathered outside Prasutugas's town. It was the day for the annual horse and chariot races that had gradually replaced the rites of Beltine, and a hubbub of shouts, whistles and laughter wove into the tuneless clatter of harness bronzes and the intermittent neighs and whickers of the ponies.

"You might consider the dispatch I received this morning to be exciting," he replied. "There has been a battle, Priscilla, and the Twentieth has been defeated."

Her mouth fell open. "Honorious, but how sudden. Is it just a rumor? It must be. No legion in Albion would allow itself to be defeated!"

Favonius wearily looked down at the girlish, pert red mouth and the blinking, vacuous eyes, and considered for the thousandth time whether he had been wrong to petition for her presence here with him. It was not usual for garrison commanders to enjoy the company of their families while on active service. Fort commanders, legates, and their officers, often did, but then a fort was not usually erected until an area was relatively safe. He had arrived in Icenia eight years ago with his men, built the garrison, and by the time Ostorious Scapula had landed in Albion he already was the envy of every other garrison commander on the island. Icenia was one of the safest places to be and, after Camulodunon, the most congenial. Its tribesmen were rich and relatively friendly. Its ruling house was not only willing but eager to foster the Roman cause. Favonius had requested the presence of his wife and infant son and the request had been granted without any deliberation on Scapula's part. Indeed, a cozy Roman family in the garrison was thought by the governor to help lessen the impression of military occupation presented by the soldiers in Icenia. But Priscilla was no hardy plebeian pioneer and had no intention of becoming one. She lived for the day when her husband would be transferred. She could not imagine any posting as arduous as Icenia and said so, often and volubly. Favonius answered her brusquely.

"Don't be a fool, Priscilla. You ought to think before you speak. If it's only a rumor the dispatch would have said so. Manlius Valens escaped with his cavalry escort. The rebels tried to fire the fort but apparently they were not successful."

"What does all this mean for us?" As always, her first fears were for herself and her son and she had lightly brushed off her husband's reproof.

"Nothing much. We couldn't be further from the arena of action unless we waded in the ocean. But we have been asked to stand an alert. There is also a rumor that the garrisons along the late governor's frontier are in trouble, but no solid news has come from them yet." He rubbed at the frown that still creased his forehead. "Five years ago the thought of a whole legion's destruction would have been ludicrous. Something new is rising in the west, Priscilla, something big. A fresh approach to their war, or even another arviragus rising. I don't like it."

She laughed and dismissed it all, her brief moment of panic gone with his assessment of Icenia's safety. "Now you are being silly. It is all so much nonsense. A new dispatch will arrive before long, Honorious, and we will be told that it was only Valens's cavalry escort that took a little beating and the messenger got it all wrong. Nothing ever comes out of the west but contradictions. Besides, the Twentieth is such a proud legion. It would rather die than acknowledge a defeat."

Favonius clamped his teeth together and sighed inwardly. "Perhaps you ought to be appointed the next governor," he said with heavy sarcasm, but as usual it was lost on her. She wrinkled her nose.

"Smell the horse dung, Honorious! They should scoop it all up and

424

put it on their fields, but I suppose it will lie and stink for days under this sun. Don't go off with Prasutugas today and leave me to Boudicca's sharp tongue. I shall hate you forever if you do."

He was sensible enough not to answer and together they broke through the trees. Immediately they found themselves thrusting their way through a choking, jostling press of excited freemen, all talking at the top of their voices. The meadow that encircled the town was thronged with them and their sweating ponies. The sun danced gaily on the bronze-traced wheels of the chariots and on the necklaces and arm bands of the freemen who struggled to yoke and harness the ponies in the press. A large fire burned by the gate, sending thick black smoke into the blue sky, and Favonius and Priscilla pushed their way to where Prasutugas and Boudicca sat. People came and went to the fire, nibbling on pieces of mutton and hunks of cheese, and by it the beer barrels stood behind a pile of wooden cups.

Marcus ran to Favonius and Priscilla as they approached, his face smeared with mutton grease, his scarlet tunic flying behind him. His legs and feet were bare, but though the day was warm he wore a long chieftain's cloak of green wool. In one hand he clutched a pair of breeches, purple with silver fringes, and in the other a mutton bone, which he waved under their noses. Before he could speak his mother pounced on him.

"Marcus, where did you get those clothes? And what is that . . . that thing around your neck?"

"It's a talisman of Epona, the Horse Goddess. Do you like it, mother? Prasutugas gave it to me. He gave me the clothes as well. They were his when he was my age." He threw his shoulders back and stalked before them. "Don't I look fine? Do you think I would pass for a chieftain?"

His father looked at the olive skin already darkening to a rich brown, though the summer had only just begun. Marcus's hair hung black and shining to his shoulders. A country child's clear, untroubled gaze met Favonius's own, and Favonius glanced to the hand holding the bone, the hand that already knew the tug of chariot harness and mount's rein, the feel of a knife's hilt and a tree's rough branches bending under the boy's questing weight, the slippery coldness of a jerking fish. But not a sword, Favonius thought. Not yet.

"No, I don't," he replied gravely. "You have no torc."

"Go and take those ridiculous things off!" Priscilla snapped. "Anyone would think this was Saturnalia!"

Marcus grinned at her. "This is more fun than Saturnalia," he answered her back, and he flung the bone away and stepped quickly into the breeches. "Father?"

Favonius could not refuse. "All right, Marcus. I don't really mind. Will you race today?"

"Yes, but I'll lose against the young freemen. Not a good thing for Roman honor. Ethelind wants to borrow my horse and Brigid has dared me to go in the chariot races."

"No!" Priscilla exclaimed.

This time Favonius agreed with her. "No chariot, son," he said firmly.

Marcus shrugged the cloak higher on his shoulders and smiled at them. "Well, I don't really care. Conac nearly broke his neck this morning, practicing the turn. I told him he should wait until he grew up to attempt the chariot and he knocked me down." He fingered the charm at his throat. "With Epona giving me her protection perhaps I shall win my race today." Then he was off, jogging through the people, calling to this one and that one, leaving Priscilla white with fury.

"Epona! Some savage blood-hungry native god! Really, Honorious, I find their religious taste extreme, and I won't have Marcus tangled in it."

"Oh hush!" he blurted. "What does it matter? What is a charm, Priscilla? The boy is healthy and happy. What more can you ask?" He spoke more harshly than he had intended, for uneasiness pricked him suddenly, but then Prasutugas saw them and rose to his feet, and Boudicca's freckled, volatile face was upturned to them.

"Welcome, welcome!" Prasutugas smiled. "We are honored that you came. Favonius, I want to show you the pair I have selected to race for me today." Favonius acknowledged the greeting, worry still nibbling at his mind, but he was not so preoccupied that he did not notice the flush of health on Prasutugas's face, and he was glad.

"My surgeon has been having some success with your wound?" he commented. "He has been longing to try the new salve he concocted."

"It is not your surgeon's stinging brew," Prasutugas responded cheerfully. "It is the warmth of the new sun. Three of my mares have foaled, Favonius. Come and see them, and tell me what you think." He and Favonius began to move away, and after one sharp protest Priscilla subsided, settling herself sulkily on the grass beside Boudicca and batting ineffectually at the hounds who came bounding to nudge her with cold noses. Somewhere nearby a carnyx blared and the people scattered.

"This is the third race," Boudicca said. "Soon the chariots will be put away and the horse races will begin. So far there has been only one broken arm and one splintered ankle. Is Marcus going to ride?"

Priscilla glanced at her, searching, as always, for the unspoken

426

taunt, the hidden sneer behind the gruff words, and as always she seemed to find malicious spite where there was only humor and a mild, polite dislike. You would be happy if Marcus broke an arm, she thought hotly. "Yes, he is, but I do not think he will hurt himself," she said aloud. "He rides too well for that."

Boudicca's head turned, and she quizzically surveyed the stiff, disapproving little face beside her. "I did not mean to imply that Marcus would finish the day with a broken limb," she growled. "Really, Priscilla, why must you always see insult where no insult is intended? That boy of yours has become very dear to my husband and to me, and I would not like to see him hurt. I asked you a simple question." There is something else on your mind, Roman lady, she thought. I wonder what it is?

They felt the turf begin to tremble beneath them. The crowds around them craned forward. Then six chariots came pounding into view, horses stretched out with heads down, charioteers straddling the wicker floors with whips held high, and cloaks and hair ripping behind them. The crowd began to scream and leap up and down and the contestants flew around the corner and were gone. "The first circuit," Boudicca observed easily. "Iain will win again. You know, Priscilla, Marcus could win his race this year if he would only put behind him his riding master's instructions and leave all to his instinct. He still sits on his mount as though he were not one with it."

"He has a good seat," Priscilla replied stiffly. "He only needs time."

How miserable she is, Boudicca thought. How uncomfortable, sitting here in the grass with me, doing her duty for Favonius's sake. I wonder if she ever stops to think that in all the world she has not one friend, and it is her own fault. "Are you hungry?" she asked kindly. "Thirsty? Would you like to walk about a little?"

"Not really," Priscilla said curtly. "I will eat when Honorious comes back. If you have duties, Boudicca, do not let me hinder you."

Boudicca sighed and rose as the chariots came thundering around the bend again, strung out this time, and the shouts of the charioteers rose hoarse and unintelligible over the screamed encouragements of the people. "I will return in a moment," she said, leaving Priscilla to watch her stride easily down to the meadow, a tall, sturdy woman in green fringed breeches and blue tunic, her fine, waving red hair undulating with her mannish gait.

Boudicca arrived at where the chariots were rolling to a halt, a tangle of cloaks, whips, harness, and foam-slicked horses. Marcus and Brigid ran to join her, and with a spurt of jealousy Priscilla saw how Marcus's brown face was raised to hers, how she reached down to cuff his black head in playful affection before leaning down to listen to her daughter and to fondle the white-gold tresses that hung down her back in three dazzling braids. The nine-year-old Ethelind sauntered over to the group, her own red-blonde curls dancing in the wind, and Priscilla suddenly felt lonely. She looked at her son, the talisman glinting at his throat, indistinguishable from every other chief's young child. The emotion did not reach to danger and was contained by her self-concern, but it came close, a loneliness mixed with homesickness, and she hunched up her knees and looked about vainly for the security of her husband's smile.

Boudicca spoke to Marcus and while he ran to the beer barrel and drew a cupful, Iain jumped from his chariot and ambled to her, grinning and panting.

"Another win!" Boudicca exclaimed, tossing him the pouch that had hung on her belt. Marcus came and lifted the cup to him and he drank quickly and noisily while the other contestants came to fling themselves on the cool grass and the chariots were led away.

"You ought to share this one with the other chiefs or they will become discouraged and refuse to race anymore!" Marcus said, grinning.

Iain stuffed the pouch into his tunic. "What I ought to do and what I am going to do are different things!" he shouted, careless with victory. "This money will buy cattle for me, and an offering for Andrasta!"

Immediately a hush fell. The people glanced furtively over their shoulders but the Roman soldiers were ambling about, oblivious to the little drama, and in an embarrassed quiet they melted away, leaving Iain with red face and awkward hands clasped about the cup. "I am sorry, Lady," he said. "I forgot myself."

She looked him straight in the eye. "On the contrary, Iain, you remembered yourself, and so did the people," she said gently. "No matter how long the time has been, you will never forget."

He turned away. "It is better to forget," he answered. "My tongue remembered, that is all."

No, Iain, that is not all, she thought. Andrasta sleeps in your heart too, and one day your heart will remember her as well as does your tongue. Ethelind tugged at her tunic.

"Mother, make Marcus lend me his horse for my race! Brigid rode mine this morning and he is blown. If I don't have a good mount and win I have to pay Rittia the birthday belt of amber that father gave me!"

"I told you, Ethelind, that you may not have him!" Marcus shouted back. "I want to win my own race this year and I don't care about your stupid wager!"

"If you don't lend me your horse then I won't let you use my snares anymore, and I won't teach you how to make your own!"

"I don't care! Lovernius will show me how to do it!"

"He won't! I'll order him not to!"

They had forgotten Boudicca and moved away, still quarreling until Brigid stuck out a foot and Marcus tumbled to the earth. "That will teach you to refuse a princess," she said in her high, childish treble. Ethelind burst out laughing and Marcus, pale with rage, took Brigid's braids in his hands and pulled viciously. Then they were off, the three of them running hooting over the grass, and Boudicca turned at the pressure of a hand on her arm. It was Lovernius, his harp slung over one shoulder.

"Smile at me, Lady," he said. "Smile and then laugh, so that those who are watching us may see a few jokes being shared."

She allowed her mouth to obey him, but her eyes measured his own with a sudden alertness. "What is it?"

"Great news. The Twentieth has been chewed to pieces and the garrisons along the frontier are on fire. Venutius and the rebels have left the mountains."

She blinked at him, her face tingling, the smile slowly growing broader as his words sunk into her brain. "Tell me again, Lovernius," she ordered. "I want to be sure that I heard you aright."

He unslung his harp and picked deliberately at the strings, his eyes on his fingers. "The Twentieth has suffered a crushing defeat at the hands of the Ordovices and Deceangli, and while the legion died, the Silures and the Demetae fell upon the garrisons. I have sent the spy away again, but I have no fears for his safety today." Ping, went his harp. Trrrring. "The men of this garrison are enjoying our little celebration."

She wanted to hug him. She wanted to reach her arms to the blue of the sky and shout. She threw back her head and laughed and he laughed also, his harp echoing the crescendo of their joy, and heads turned in their direction. "Who planned this thing?" she asked more soberly, the smile still flashing uncontrollably.

Priscilla, sitting just out of earshot, looked at her curiously. She had never seen the Icenian queen's masculine forthrightness dissolve into this girlish, uninhibited laughter before, and she wondered if the free, musical stream of humor was directed at her.

"The spy told me that the tactic was Venutius's," Lovernius continued.

"Indeed? So he is still with Emrys and Madoc. I did not think that he would last this long, in spite of all Aricia's treachery." She stepped closer to Lovernius. "Could this be the beginning of the end for

Rome, Lovernius? Have the tribes agreed to follow Venutius?"

"I do not know, Lady, but I doubt it. I think this strategy was so beautifully thought out that it took them by surprise and they agreed to submit themselves to him, but only for a while."

She clapped both hands to her cheeks. "I cannot think! Such gladness in me, Lovernius, such mad happiness! What now?"

"Talk to Prasutugas." He spoke the words softly, then bowed and walked away, whistling. Boudicca turned to see her husband and Favonius approaching Priscilla and ran to meet them. Prasutugas, looking at her glowing face, smiled inwardly, not without a twinge of anxiety. So she knew. Favonius had given him the news while they stood leaning against the corral that protected Prasutugas's foals, yet already Boudicca's brown eyes sparkled with the knowledge that had brought him a stab of fear. He knew she sheltered spies who took news of the daily doings of the Icenian tuath back into the west, but it disturbed him to think that the western chiefs regarded her so highly as to send their own to her. Looking at Favonius, he felt guilt. He had never been able to bring himself to tell the Roman that his tuath was riddled with spies and up until now it had not mattered. The chiefs and freemen did not care what the fools in the west were doing, but now the frontier was down. The province lacked a governor, and the summer stretched ahead, long, hot, and unknown. He looked at her and she at him, and in that moment he was glad of the sense of honor that bound her to him under the oath of fealty. That, and her love for him. Without her honor and her love he knew she would have wasted no time, but would already be coaxing and bullying the chiefs into some kind of action. She smiled at him smugly and he frowned back, but she was not reckless.

That night Favonius and Priscilla went back to the garrison in the comforting belief that only Prasutugas knew of the chaos that was spreading on the island. The day had been good. Marcus had not won his race but had come in a close second. Ethelind had not won either, and was sulking over the loss of her belt. When dusk fell and the Romans withdrew, the tuath settled to singing and drinking around the fire, and the meadow that had been scored with chariot wheels and horses' hoofs now lay warm and fragrant under the bare feet of the carousing people. Marcus, Ethelind, and Brigid wandered through the company for a while, then stole away into the copse to play hide and seek in the darkness and tell stories to one another. Prasutugas, tiring more easily now, went to his house, and Boudicca went with him.

"Favonius did not enjoy himself very much today," she remarked as he sank into his wicker chair and stretched his long legs out before him with a groan. "And Priscilla was very glum. I wonder why?"

He answered the roguish grin with a slight movement of his blond head, and smiled back unwillingly. "Do you want to play with me for a while before you pounce?" he murmured. "Very well, Boudicca. Favonius had certain matters on his mind, and I will wager that Priscilla had words with him over leaving her to your sweet and tender care. She is terrified of you."

"The poor, silly thing! I am terrified of her also, afraid that if I should happen to bump into her someday she will shatter. Do you think that Favonius is happy with her? Should we offer him some coarse, strong young freewoman for a second wife?"

He laughed. "Romans do not have more than one wife at a time," he said, "and besides, I think those two understand each other very well, though they seem as mismatched to us as we do to them."

She looked startled. "Are we mismatched, Prasutugas?"

"Of course. Your father and the Druids thought so. The whole tuath thinks so. Only you and I are not yet aware that we were not born for each other."

She softened, coming to him and kneeling at his feet. "How can you be so good to me, knowing what I am going to say to you?" she whispered. "For ten years I have fought you. You are like some once-gay shield now gored and split under the sword of my tongue. Yet still you stand and take my blows."

He did not move but just lay back in the chair, his eyes on the ceiling, his legs crossed loosely at the ankles, a faint smile of amusement hovering on his lips. "I stand and face the sword of your tongue," he replied. "I do not lie down under the weight of your feet. There is a difference. Say what you must, Boudicca. We both know why Favonius is worried."

She got up and went to look out the window, standing still and gazing to where the fire roared to the sky. He rolled his head to watch her, the red reflection drenching her face and neck and glittering in her eyes, the color of blood. The cheerful sounds of the maelstrom beyond came to him clearly, and for just a moment he missed the strong, distinctive odor of the bonefires of Beltine.

"They cannot win, my dear," he said, pulling his legs in under the chair and sitting straight. "They have destroyed one legion, but three more must be faced, and Venutius cannot take them by surprise with a subterfuge as he obviously did the Twentieth. The frontier is down. What does that mean? You know as well as I. A chain of garrisons, but the lowland is littered with garrisons. The most they can do is delude themselves into thinking they have made headway for a while by ranging to and fro unhindered. The governor will come, mobilize the legions, and it will all be over."

She swung from the window as though she had been waiting for the signal of his words. "It does not have to be that way! Prasutagas, have you ever seen such bravery, such tenacious love of freedom, such a capacity for suffering? Every time I think of them, my heart is pierced by shame. They forgive us our cowardice! They no longer plead with us for help!" She rushed to him and stood over him, her arms still folded tightly across her dusky blue tunic. "They are so pitifully alone, Prasutagas. Yes, yes, you are right—they will be driven back. But not if we do something. This is the moment, my husband. The time has come. Never again will such luck favor the cause of freedom. A legion gone, no governor, the officials undecided about what to do! Think!" Her arms left her body and spread wide. "We could fire our garrison in one night and sweep out of Icenia. Who would expect it of us? We could be at Camulodunon before the news of our actions had even reached the town . . ."

"No." The word came out sharp and final. His mouth was no longer soft but set into an obstinate line, and his eyes scanned her coldly.

"Yes! Yes! This time we will have a good chance of success. We have the people, we have the weapons, we . . ."

He was on his feet and in a flash she found her wrist imprisoned in a cold iron grip. "Boudicca, what have you done?" he whispered rapidly, harshly. "What weapons? We have no weapons. At least," he went on grimly, his grip tightening until she gasped, "*I* have no weapons. Where are they, Boudicca? Where have you hidden them?"

"I cannot tell you!" she shouted in pain. "If I do you will go running to Favonius."

"You know me better than that!"

"No, I do not! I cannot afford to!" For a long time they glared at one another, she on the verge of tears, caught in his one-armed grip, he with blue eyes blazing.

He let her go abruptly. "I have been more lenient with you, perhaps, than I ought," he said, as she rubbed at her wrist. "I have given you everything a ricon's wife could desire and more. I have been patient with your madness, I have kept your little secrets from Favonius, I have taken your public insults, because there is love between us. I thought there was trust also, Boudicca. It seems that I was wrong. Burying weapons is a treasonable offence, punishable by death, and you know it. Such folly could endanger the whole tuath. You force me to tell you now that if you make any moves to incite the chiefs into rebellion, if you conceive any plans that might endanger

432

the work Favonius and I are doing in Icenia, I will remove you from my bed and from my life."

She stared at him aghast, her eyes wide. "Prasutugas! You would do that to me?"

He nodded. "I would. I have done all I can, Boudicca, I have taken all I can. No more."

"Yes," she said bitterly. "You have indeed done all you can. To you I am nothing but a bad-tempered, seditious child. Yet, Prasutugas, you have not given me all you could. I do not have my freedom."

His face hardened. "You are free to leave me whenever you choose."

"That is not the kind of freedom I mean!" The cry tore into him but he did not flinch. Her arms encircled herself once more, an embrace of shock and deep fear, and she was bent before him, her magnificent hair tumbling to hide her face. "I feel my chains, Prasutugas; every day they bite into my soul like red-hot iron. You cannot know how I suffer, how my words to you are soft and pleasing compared to the words that scream from my soul. Perhaps I am mad, but if I am, then so is the whole of the west. I hate your sanity."

"And do you also hate me?" He spoke quietly but was as appalled as she at the swiftness of this chasm that had finally opened between them and was still widening with terrifying speed. He wanted to leap over it, to take her in his arms and hold her until the rift snapped shut again and they were whole once more, but its cold blackness beat him back.

"I do not know!" she sobbed. "Ah, help me, Prasutugas, I do not know! I only know that I have taken all I can as well as you, and I can think of nothing but those poor, bloodied people carrying the weight of freedom on their dying backs for all of us!" Her head came up and he saw her face, disfigured by tears. "How long has it been since you wept, Prasutugas? How long?"

He put out his hand but could not reply, and after a moment she straightened and stumbled out the door, her hands moving blindly, uncertainly, before her. Prasutugas could not move. He stood there in the dimness, surrounded by the flickering orange shadows, his heart leaping and falling erratically, the tears trickling slowly down his cheeks.

She waited in the shadow of the porch for a moment, leaning against the lintel and wiping her face on the hem of her tunic. She could not think. For ten years they had slashed and parried with each other, their loyalties deeply and irrevocably divided, and all the tuath knew it and wondered at such unity in diversity. She shouted, he yawned. She threatened, he smiled and did not shift one jot from the course that he, as ricon, had chosen. Their arguments had acquired a formula, a stately, invisible dance of words, and each of them had followed the steps because to break the pattern would have been hurtful. But this time he said new things, she thought, tears flowing fresh and hot once more. This time he broke the rules, he did not play fair, and what had become a game between them after so many quarrels was shown to be a matter of life or death after all. What did he say? Shock had driven the words from her mind. She remembered only his face, hard and strange, showing her a depth of resolve she had not believed possible in him. The door of the adjoining room opened and Hulda came out onto the porch.

"Where have you been?" she scolded loudly. "This is no night for you to be wandering about on your own. Your father would be angry if he knew. Come inside!" For a moment Boudicca thought the servant was addressing her, but then she saw Ethelind and Brigid wandering slowly up to the house. Boudicca shrank back into the shadow and the girls brushed by without seeing her.

"I would have pushed him out of the tree," Ethelind was saying stoutly. "Everyone knows that if father didn't want the Romans here he would send them away. But I feel sorry for him, having someone like Priscilla for a mother. She can't even ride." The two disheveled girls disappeared into their room, oblivious to Hulda's admonitory words. The door closed, and the lamplight was cut off.

Boudicca stood in the darkness a moment longer. The big fire was dying, its flames a gentle glow, and fewer freemen and chiefs ambled back and forth, silhouetted against it. Night had fallen, full and soft, but as yet the moon had not risen, nor had the stars become wholly visible. There was no sound from the room behind her where Prasutagus lay on the bed, stiff and unsleeping, and she did not consider going back to talk with him. As yet, there was nothing more to say. The night air was still chilled with the fading ghost of winter and she shivered, but her cloak lay inside that fast-shut door and not for anything would she have gone to pick it up. She stepped off the porch and walked alone through her town, flitting past huts full of chatter and laughter, feeling like a being from somewhere else, from a star perhaps—not human, not wanted, not of the earth but of the night and the wind. I did not know, she thought as the gray paths glided by under her bare feet. I did not know that more than half of me is Prasutagus and without that half I am a wraith, gibbering helplessly in the cold. Is any cause worth this terrible self-destruction? If there is a choice between my husband and freedom—if it has come to that—is one worth anything without the other? Has it come to that? She stopped outside her bard's doorskins and rapped softly on the lintel.

"Lovernius, are you there?" she called, and presently the skins were pushed back and he greeted her and ushered her in. His hut was bare of hangings or fripperies. He had only his bed, a table for his lamp, and his harp. Yet his home was warm and welcoming, as though its walls had absorbed something of the music that he made, sitting by himself in the evening, forming an invisible blanket of sweetness. He stepped with her into the room, his quick eyes on her tear-swollen face.

"Have you come to gamble, Lady?" he enquired. She sat on his cot and folded her arms yet again, groping for an assurance of substance. She felt fragile and empty.

"I have given up gambling with you, Lovernius. You either cheat or have become too expert for me, I don't know which," she said with an attempted humor. Her arms clutched tighter. "I have spoken with Prasutugas. He got the news from Favonius. As usual, he will do nothing."

"It is not usual for him to reduce you to tears, Lady," he answered forthrightly.

Her tears began again with his refusal to circle her distress. "He is afraid that I will incite rebellion here in Icenia," she said brokenly. "He will put me away from him if I do. He said so. He has never threatened me thus before, Lovernius. He does not say it, but he means that if he must choose between me and Rome then he will choose Rome."

Lovernius squatted before her, looking up into her face. "I do not think so. He is simply begging you not to force him to the point where that choice must be made. He must consider all of Icenia, Boudicca, not just his family. And in his eyes, Rome is good for Icenia. You must never force that choice upon him, for he will indeed choose Rome, and then die of a broken heart. If the choice between your husband and freedom for Albion was put before you, what would you do?"

"I do not know!"

"And neither does he. You must trust each other, for if you cease to trust then your marriage is finished."

Trust. She loosened her arms. Yes, that was the heart of the matter. Not Rome or freedom or love or hate, but trust. He did not trust her anymore. She should have told him about the weapons, she should have assured him that it meant little. But she had not told him because it did not mean little. It meant much, it meant everything, and she could not lie to him. Sometimes, living is worse than dying, she thought bitterly. To die is simple. To live is too hard. She rose abruptly. "Lovernius," she said. "I want to hunt tonight."

435

He nodded. "If you like. I don't know what game we can flush though, Lady. The wolves have gone away now that spring has come but we should be able to find a boar, even in the dark."

"I do not want a wolf," she went on quietly, "or a boar. I want to hunt the Annis."

He felt the blood leave his face. "What?"

She turned swiftly to him, and in her eyes he saw such anger, such pain, that for a moment he was afraid of her. Then he understood. Like her father before her, her wounds could only be healed under the balm of furious action. She was a creature of movement, not contemplation. I hurt, those big eyes told him. I have never hurt like this in all my life before, and I must hit back or die of my pain.

Nevertheless he tried to dissuade her. "An Annis has not been set loose since your father's time," he objected. "If we are caught, Favonius will have us executed immediately. Besides, there is no time for the ceremonies of choosing."

"There will be no choosing."

"The season is not right," he went on desperately. "Winter has gone and spring is well advanced."

"I do not want to kill winter," she shot back. "We will kill Rome. Rome is our eternal winter. Rome is our Annis. No choosing, Lovernius. Get me a Roman. Turn out the hounds."

"Lady," he pleaded, "think again. It is a terrible thing, to hunt the Annis. It will reawaken the demons."

"Yes it is a terrible thing," she agreed, "but the times are terrible also, Lovernius. I will direct the powers of the forest toward Rome."

"If they do not turn to rend us instead. I am afraid, Lady."

"Then I will hunt on my own. I don't care. Have there been any foxes snared lately?"

"Ethelind brought one in yesterday," he admitted reluctantly. "She cut off the brush for Marcus, but the carcass hangs outside the Council hut."

"Are there chiefs to hunt with us?"

"There are chiefs who are loyal to the cause of freedom, Lady, but none whom I would dare approach to hunt an Annis."

"Then it is you and me." She was still crying, but Lovernius saw that she was unaware of the tears that had already soaked the neck of her blue tunic. "There is always a soldier sent to the river from the garrison, to draw water for the morning. We will take him."

"He will be missed."

"Of course he will be missed!" she shouted. "But if he is found, Favonius will believe that the wolves got him."

"In the spring?"

436

"What other explanation will there be? A Roman Annis, Lovernius. It is right. It is just. Now go and leash the hounds. I will bring the fox and meet you by the river, where it flows closest to the garrison."

They left the hut and parted, Lovernius creeping unseen to the kennels and Boudicca to the Council hut, now quiet and empty but for the few chiefs who had been too drunk to find their own hearths and had curled up on the warm sheepskins on the floor. The night held the town under a wide, star-splattered sky, and the wind was drowsy and fitful. The huts no longer showed light under their door-skins or spilled the warmth of human commerce into her ears. They humped solid and black like tombs, the now-risen moon giving them streaming dark shadows through which she waded silently. The fox was not hard to find. Boudicca's questing fingers brushed its cold, soft pelt, and she drew her knife and cut the rope that held it to the eaves of the hut. She slung it over her shoulder and began to make her way to the low stone wall that surrounded the town, and then to the silver and soft blackness of the meadow beyond.

Lovernius was waiting for her, six hounds leashed and muzzled beside him, and as she ran in under the darkness of the trees they smelled the fox she carried and began to whine. She dropped the dead beast with a thud onto the grass and Lovernius hauled back the dogs.

"You wait here," she whispered. "There are four sentries standing watch tonight instead of two—I suppose because of the alert—and if they hear the dogs they will come and investigate. I will waylay the water carrier."

"No need," he whispered back. "I nearly ran into a sentry in the woods to the west of the town. Favonius must be taking his orders seriously and has placed men under the trees, but singly, not in twos. He is not very clever, our commander. Take one of them, Boudicca, and I will go deeper into the forest, north, away from the river." She thought for a moment, then nodded, and he picked up the fox, kicked at the dogs, and was gone.

With a steady, purposeful silence Boudicca worked her way through the trees until the garrison lay between her and the river and she had counted three soldiers standing uneasily just within the eaves of the forest, their backs to the garrison's squat security and their faces to the slow-shifting night shades of the trees. They were out of sight of each other and out of earshot, also, Boudicca thought, but she would take no chances. She chose the fourth man after watching him carefully for some time. He was nervous, changing his weight from one sandal-clad foot to the other, turning to face the garrison, peering to right and left, his hand never leaving the hilt of his gladius. She wriggled closer to him, blending with the ever fluid shadows, came around to his back, then stood and stepped to his side, clamping one strong hand over his mouth and hissing in his ear.

"Do not be alarmed, soldier. It is only I, Boudicca. Do not cry out."

His fingers clawed at her arm and his eyes rolled toward her. Before he could drag her hand from his face she whispered again. "The men of the west are coming. My bard and I have caught one of their scouts but we dare not march him to the garrison alone. Please come. Do not disturb your friends. They should stay where they are in the event that more scouts have broken through into Icenia."

He was bewildered, she could see his doubt. Taking a chance, she released him and tugged at the short sleeve of his tunic. "Follow me," she called softly, moving away from him. "Hurry!" She did not look back, but after a while she could hear him trotting after her, breathing heavily. Smiling, she quickened her pace until he began to pant. Annis, her feet rustled to her, blind Annis, black Annis, even if you wanted to turn back now you could not. Already the spells have begun to coil around you, already Andrasta has turned her gaze upon you. She led him north for two miles and then veered west, slowing so that he could catch up with her.

"What were you doing so far from the town?" he asked her, now into his second wind and jogging by her side.

She glanced across at him and grinned. "Hunting" was all she said, yet there was something in the way she said the word that caused him to look over his shoulder. He was not sure where he was. Each dusky tree resembled the one next to it and the one after that, an infinity of night-painted trees, and suddenly all the stories he had heard about Icenia's chameleon, blood-drinking goddess came back to him. He had laughed at this primitive deity who could transform herself into a raven and go flapping about in the forests. His commander had instilled in him a scorn for her, together with a distaste for the Druids who served her, but now, deep into the vast oak groves that even in daylight seemed to trap some dark essence of night, her presence sprang into life. The Icenian lady did not seem afraid. She half-ran, half-loped in the natives' awkward gait that nevertheless covered the ground without tiring the runner, her eyes ahead, her hair tangled on her shoulders, her limbs moving in a weird, complex rhythme. She did not look as she usually did. There was something foreign in her face. Her eyes were swollen, as though she had been weeping, and as she ran her lips moved. They had come farther than he had imagined they would and she showed no signs of stopping. He wanted to rest, to grasp her arm, drag her to a halt and demand from her a new

438

explanation, but the impulse seemed to die before it reached his body, and the sense of unreality grew around him. They hurried on.

Then all at once her pace faltered. She raised her head, and the man could have sworn that he saw her nostrils dilate like an animal taking a scent. Then she was off again. Minutes later he heard something, a snuffling and pattering. She spurted ahead, and before he could snap this new puzzle together she had shouted, "Lovernius, take him! I am tired," and he found himself face down in the earth, his arms wrenched up and back between his shoulder blades. Stunned, he lay there trying to get his breath, twigs and dead leaves scratching his cheek. His helmet was tugged from his head and he heard it go bumping into the undergrowth. His belt with the gladius and his knife followed. Then hands began to unlace his sandals and he struggled to turn and sit up, still in the grip of his unseen assailant. The hands loosened, but only so that other hands could unbuckle his breastplate. "What are you doing?" he demanded at last, and the lady tossed the breastplate into a bush.

"Turn him about and let him sit, Lovernius," she said, moving to untie his leather jerkin.

"Lady, have you lost your mind?" the soldier shouted, and those other hands hauled him around until he was sitting upright. Boudicca coolly took her knife and cut the linen tunic from him, and his iron-stripped apron came with it. Then he saw the dogs, leashed to a tree, saliva dripping from their huge muzzles, but even then he did not understand, though an icy mouth suddenly pressed itself over his heart. The Lady reached for his undergarments and though he exclaimed sharply and tried to pull away, the man behind him tightened his hold and forced him to his feet. The soldier found himself naked. The cold, night-darkened eyes of the lady did not change expression as they flicked over him. She walked away and bent, and when she came back to him she had a dead fox under her arm. A quiver ran through the watching dogs. She laid the carcass down and with one sure stroke of her knife opened it, then felt about inside it, pulling the flaccid intestines out to slither gray on the grass. Her slimed hand came up, the knife glinted, and she stood, the fox's bladder balanced on her palm. The soldier could smell it as she walked to him, a stench of old blood, an odor of putrefaction. The dogs began to whine, an excitement rising in them, and Boudicca lifted the obscene thing under his nose.

"Annis," she whispered to him soothingly. "You have not allowed yourself to be chosen, and for that I am sorry. Nor are you a criminal. For that I am sorry also. But I must put upon you every evil that your countrymen have done in Albion, Roman, and especially I put upon

439

you my husband's dishonor and my own suffering. Do you understand?" She spoke calmly and reasonably as though she were explaining something to a child. Puzzled, he looked from her face, to the thing she held in her hand, to the straining hounds, and then he felt the teeth behind that ice-lipped mouth fastened to his chest. Annis. A pack of hounds, a fox's bladder, the huntsmen, and Annis. The victim. The hunted. Now he understood. Now other memories came to him, other stories, of things so dark, so full of dread that even his fellows believed it brought bad luck to speak of them. He began to scream, eyes wide and staring, pale limbs thrashing in a mindless burst of terror, heedless of the cracking in his arms as Lovernius attempted to restrain him. Boudicca waited while the two men wrestled, detached and oddly calm, Prasutugas's face fading in and out before her. Then the Roman was on the ground, Lovernius's knee on his chest, his spasms of resistance dying feebly away.

"What have I ever done to you, Lady? What?" the soldier whispered, his voice a trembling whimper, but when she looked down on him she did not see him.

"That question is mine," she said, seeing a thousand dead lips ask it, lips parted in bewilderment, lips contorted in pain, lips long closed by Roman spears. "What have we ever done to you, Rome, that you should seek to destroy us?" Prasutugas had opened his lips. I will remove you from my bed and from my life, he had said, and her eyes closed against the remembering. Yes, those had been his words. "Hold him well, Lovernius," she ordered harshly, going down on one knee beside him. "You are our hunger," she said, and the knife carved a nick on his shoulder. "Carry it. You are our disease," and the knife sank into his other shoulder. "Carry it. You are our impoverishment. Carry it." She went on building the spell, Lovernius muttering it with her, and when it was completed and the naked chest was a mass of bloody cuts she added the final burden. "You are our winter, the winter of our sorrows, the winter of our oppression. You are Rome. Carry it." The knife trailed another bloody furrow and the man cried out. Lovernius then lifted him to his feet and turned him and Boudicca held the bladder over his head and pierced it with one savage movement. The contents dribbled over the Roman's head, a foul, pungent shower, and suddenly the dogs went mad. They threw themselves against their leashes, leaping into the air only to be snapped back by the strong leather, but they could not howl because of the muzzles' restraint. Their eyes ignited in the dimness, a fire of bloodlust. The young man seemed dazed. His glance dragged slowly from the dogs' crazed dance to Lovernius's grim visage to Boudicca's own impassive face. Beyond him the forest was sunk in blackness, a blackness with a listening, gloating presence, and only moments of accidental moonlight came to whiten his already ashen face. The blood trickling over his body was black also. "Carry it all, Annis," Boudicca said. "Carry it, die with it, take it from us. Awake!" He blinked. Slowly his eyes met hers and now there was consciousness in them, behind the drugging terror.

"Wh . . . wh . . . why?" he asked stupidly, but she ignored the question.

"I will help you," she went on. "Do not climb a tree. If you do, the dogs will simply sit at the foot until you fall out. Do not go in a straight line. Seek running water if you want to save your life. You have a certain amount of time before I release the dogs. Use it well. Now run." Lovernius let him go but he stood there staring at her helplessly. "Run, you fool. Run!" For a moment he continued to gaze at her, his mouth working, then he swayed, staggered, and began to run.

They watched him lurch away into the trees, a pale sliver of stumbling flesh. The dogs launched themselves after him but were jerked to a halt by their leashes. Lovernius and Boudicca stood motionless, blind to the still world around them, feeling only the long movement of second sliding into second, minute into minute. They did not need to seek the moon's face to tell them how the time was going by. Its flow mingled with the pumping of their blood, hot, tense, alive. For an age, for the life of a man, they stood there, then Lovernius said softly, "Dawn is three hours away."

"I know," she replied simply. "Unmuzzle and release the dogs."

The man careened through the trees, blundering wildly through thorns, vines, and bushes, not knowing or caring in which direction he pounded, sobbing as he went. The stink of the fox's bladder ran with him, catching in his throat, his nostrils. Run . . . water. Run . . . water, he whispered breathlessly to the broken rhythm of his feet. His side began to ache and then to pierce him with sharp stabs of pain but he ran until the pain sliced through him with every breath. He would have gone on until his heart had burst if his foot had not gone down into some small animal's hole, twisting his ankle. With a cry he measured his naked length on the ground and lay there, heaving and weeping. Run! his mind shouted, but now the first incredulous shock, the numbing fear, was giving way to reason, and he was able to think past the clamor of self-preservation. I cannot be more than five miles from the garrison, and beyond the garrison is the river. Flowing water. How did she bring me? From which direction did she come with me? I must not run away from them. Somehow I must angle back and around them, but how can I tell my direction with no moon to see by, no stars to guide me? The wind. Was there wind on my right cheek, and then on the back of my neck? Jupiter, my feet are raw already. I am a dead man . . . He scrambled upright and craned to listen, but behind him the forest was plunged in silence. So she had not released the dogs yet. He shuddered and began to whimper, but he tore a low branch from a brittle, dying tree, wrested the twigs from it, and knew that he could ram it down one slavering throat before the others pulled him down. He considered rolling in the soil but dismissed the idea and ran on, more steadily this time, trying to match his gait to his breath. Nothing but a hard scrubbing with sand and wood ash would relieve him of the miasma of death. That, and water. Water. Flowing, running salvation. He sped on, peering every so often above him to where the branches arched high and blotted out the night sky, but he did not see the moon. Nevertheless he strained to catch a breath of wind on his face. He ran with a fixed, frozen grimace on his mouth, oblivious to the throbbing of his chest where the knife wounds oozed blood, and still he did not hear the sound of his executioners. Annis. I am Annis. Four hours ago I was Dio Balbilla, soldier of a garrison, and now I am Annis. I wish I could reach the commander. I wish I could warn them all. I wish I could go on living, but I am Annis, and I must die. She smiled at me yesterday when I stood at the fire to receive meat from her hands, but now I am meat, and she did not recognize my face. He wrenched his mind back to the chase. What would an animal do? he wondered. I am a hunted animal, I am as the wolf, the boar. What should I do? Find water, or a burrow. A thicket is no good. The dogs may not get me but the hunters will. Do not climb a tree. No, no, the dogs would put their great paws against the trunk and howl for me, but the hunters . . . He was gasping now, the sweat pouring down his spine, his breath ragged, his throat dry. I must rest again, I cannot go on. How far have I come? Why is she holding them in? She is playing with me. She knows that no matter how far or how hard I run, I am dead. I should lie down here and close my eyes and wait. The image of himself prone on the grass in the darkness with the hounds coming closer brought another scream to his lips, and he forced his scratched, aching legs to obey him and move one before the other. Suddenly he halted. Above him he had caught a glimpse of the moon, and what he saw brought a surge of delirious hope. He had been describing a circle. No, more than a circle, an arc, a detour to safety. He muttered feverishly to himself, hands to his head, trying to remember where the moon should stand if he were standing guard at the gate of the garrison. Then he heard it, the sound he had heard a hundred times already, in his cowering imagination, the coarse baying of the hungry hounds. He slapped his elbows against his waist and sobbed aloud, falling forward once more to run, to stagger, to cover a little more ground, just a little. He forgot the moon. He forgot his true name. He forgot the contours of his face. I am Annis about to die, he cried. Annis to die, Annis . . . die. I carry . . . I carry . . . The broken, excited baying rose to one concerted howl as the dogs found the scent to be fresher and rushed on.

Like an exploding vision he saw it, a faint glimmer of light on water. Ah! he gibbered. Ah! His eyes widened, his legs found new strength, and there it was again, the moon's rays silvering his hope, his sanity, his life. He burst out of the trees and fell with a scream of passionate relief into the river. Before he had sufficiently returned to himself to be able to swim, the current had carried him around a bend and out of sight of the dogs that scampered up and down the bank, tongues hanging out, fangs snapping on nothing. The man struck out for the farther shore. He still did not know where he was. There was no town beyond the water, no garrison, only more black-enfolded forest, but he did not care. He had only to walk a little way in under the trees to be hidden from the farther bank, and then follow the river as it washed down to the ocean. Somewhere between himself and the sea was the garrison. Light, voices, swords, safety. He pulled himself up and did not pause to glance behind him but plunged straight in under the forest's eaves. Darkness embraced him, but this time he did not fear it. He began to walk, unsteadily but with light-headed gaiety. I am Dio Balbilla, he said to himself. That is my name. Ah, such bliss, such incredible happiness, that I should remember my name.

He heard a dry rustling in the leaves above his head and he stopped dead in his tracks, his fragile joy evaporating, leaving only horror. The rustling came again. Summoning his courage, he looked up. There, in the thick darkness of the leaves, he thought he could discern a thicker shadow, something black that gave back the light of the moon. His heart faltered and his knees gave way. As he slipped to the earth he thought he heard a whisper come echoing down to him, like dry leaves rubbing together, like the slow spreading of giant feathers. A-nnis. A-nnis, it fluttered. His heart gave a lurch, hot and agonizing in his chest.

"No!" he croaked. "I am . . . I am . . ." The pain in his heart raced to his loins, along his limbs, and blossomed like white fire inside his head. He did not have the time to speak his name again.

The hunters stood on the bank of the river and the dogs raced up and down, baying their loss. "He got away!" Boudicca said unbeliev-

443

ingly. "He found the water! How did he do that? Even I myself would have had difficulty in finding it without moon or stars. The spells failed, Lovernius. Why?"

Lovernius squatted in the mud, his hands passing slowly over the deep, blurred footprints where the Annis had launched himself to freedom. "Because Andrasta has ceased to listen," he answered. "Because Rome is here to stay forever and the spells have no more power. What will happen, Lady, when he tells his tale to Favonius?"

Boudicca stared at him. "Favonius will not believe him. Would you, if you were Roman? We must hurry back to the town and in the morning deny everything. Prasutagas will believe, but that does not matter anymore." Her deep voice cracked on the words, and such desolation swept over her that for a moment the cool promise of peace, the eternal forgetfulness that rose from the dark bosom of the river was almost too strong to deny. Just take one step, it crooned to her, and you will never need to feel pain again. Lovernius knew her mood as she leaned out over the gurgling water.

"Only cowards take their own life because they are afraid of hurting," he said quietly. "A freeman may destroy himself when he knows that for him all things are ended, but it is never an act of cowardice, Boudicca. Feel it, taste it, and then go on. There is always a tomorrow."

She unwillingly drew herself back from the edge. "You are right, of course," she said regretfully. "Andrasta has gone and I have lost my husband's trust, but my world has not yet ended. My time has not yet come. Leash the dogs, Lovernius. We will go home."

They went back to the town in silence. Somewhere the Annis still lived, and the winter of Rome's omnipotence would reign unchecked in Icenia. Despondency flowed from the couple to the dogs who slouched ahead of them, their tails dragging, and even the trees seemed formal with mourning. They circled the town, climbed noiselessly over the wall behind the kennels while the dogs scrabbled and leaped after them, and parted without a word. Lovernius caged the dogs, and Boudicca went wearily to Prasutagas's Roman house, opening the door quietly and slipping into the warm, fire-scented dimness. Outside, the cold conflagrations of the stars were diminishing and the night lay less heavily on the town. Inside the room the darkness was still full of sleep.

He was lying on his back on the bed, still fully clothed, his hand behind his head. She paused. He had not moved, but something told her that he was watching her.

"Are you awake?" she whispered.

The answer came back immediately, quietly. "Yes. I have not slept this night." He spoke without inflection but she knew then that his own hurts had kept him sleepless. All at once she could not bear it anymore, this aloneness, this stupid, murdering wall of words that had risen between them. She ran across the room and knelt beside the bed.

"Prasutagus, nothing in this world is worth a separation from you. I have thought about it, and I would prefer to die than to hear you say that because of our differences you do not love me anymore. Perhaps you disagree. Perhaps for you the welfare of Icenia under Rome is greater than what we have together. If that is so, do not tell me. I do not want to know. I only know that to try to live without you would make any cause meaningless, and if we cease to be one and become two, as we once were, then the world and everything in it is a lie. Do you still hold a love for me?"

He tried to speak and could not. He sat up slowly, swinging his legs over the edge of the bed, and his arm encircled her. He drew her up beside him, pulled her to him. "Boudicca," he said huskily. "I cannot withhold my love from you. It wells up like pure water and overflows me, and spills out into every corner of my life. Even the grief we bring each other is joy beside the grief that I would suffer if we parted. We have been drifting. If we had not, then how could you have asked me how long it has been since I really wept? You would know. Let us begin again now, tonight. Let us say that tonight, for the first time, I have wept. Let me tell you tonight, for the first time, that I love you. Can we do this?"

She held him tightly, her face buried in his chest, and tenderness, shame, and relief were strangling her. "I don't want anything to come between us ever again," she said. "But ah, Prasutagus, how easily, how subtly it happens! Words push us away from each other. Only your embrace tells me the truth. I will not lie to you again with the lie that is not spoken. Now I believe the Druithin when they say that of all the lies, that lie is the worst. Lovernius and I, and some of the other chiefs, buried enough weapons out in the forest to re-arm the whole of Icenia at the time when Ostorious Scapula ordered them taken from us. The hiding places are marked with signs that you would probably recognize, but no Roman would. I swear to you on my sword, by the power of my honor, that those weapons will stay where they are until you change your mind. If you do not change your mind, then they will rot where they are."

"You do not swear by Andrasta?" he teased her gently, and felt her tense.

"Andrasta has deserted me," she whispered in a sibilant flow of bitterness, and he began to stroke her face.

445

"Why do you say that?"

"The spells have no power anymore. They have become only words. I know this. My honor is worth more than the dead magic of the Queen of Victory."

He did not pursue the matter, nor did he ask her where she had been all night. "Dawn comes," he said, "and neither of us has slept." He pushed her onto the bed and lay down beside her, pulling a blanket up over both of them. "Close your eyes," he ordered. "Rest. Soon Brigid will be hammering on the door, wanting to go and meet Marcus at the garrison, and I must visit my farms today and talk to my freemen."

She obeyed him, sighing and turning to fit her body against his. "I am so tired," she murmured. "I could sleep all day." For a while they dozed, warmed by each other, exhausted and at peace.

Then Prasutugas said, "I heard a pack of hounds baying tonight, very far away. Were you out hunting, Boudicca?"

She did not stir. Her eyes remained closed. But watching her face, Prasutugas saw a shadow of sadness pass over it. After a long time she answered him.

"Yes," she said.

They slept late and had only just eaten their first meal of the day in the Council hut with Lovernius and Iain and a few of the other chiefs when Favonius rode up, dismounted hurriedly, and pushed his way through the idle throng at the door to the hut. Boudicca, seeing him come with worried face and brusque stride, felt her heart quicken its pace. She glanced at Lovernius and he at her. Then Favonius was before them. He did not say the words of greeting.

"Prasutugas," he said, "I want you to come with me and take a look at a puzzle. I cannot make head nor tail of it and it concerns me." Once again Boudicca caught her bard's eye, this time in wonderment and alarm, but Favonius was still talking. "I will say nothing more until you have taken a look."

Mystified, Prasutugas handed his cup to a servant. "Of course I will come. You are upset, my friend. If I can help, I will." He followed Favonius out the door and Boudicca stepped to Lovernius's side, but there was nothing to say to him. I want you to take a look, Favonius had said. Not—I want you to hear a tale. She longed to run after the two men, but good sense prevailed. She sank to the skins and began to wind a lock of her hair around one finger in a bemused, brooding impatience. Favonius had not even looked at her. What could have happened?

Prasutugas slid back over the horse's withers and Favonius swung himself down, flinging the reins to the aide who waited. Together the men walked the little parade ground, passed the administration building, Favonius's house, and then his officers' houses. They turned to the rear where the barracks and storehouses stood in neat, crisp lines. Favonius nodded to the soldier fronting one of the small grain-storage huts and the man opened the door. Favonius waved Prasutagas within and the door closed behind them.

The hut was dim and it stank. Prasutagas recognized the sickening odor. The sheeted form, which lay on a wooden plank slung between two sawhorses, seemed to glow in the shadow and he felt the hairs at the back of his neck prickle as Favonius beckoned him closer and pulled away the covering, his eyes on Prasutagas's face. Prasutagas went to the body and looked. At first what he saw made no sense to him, as it had made no sense to Favonius. The man was completely naked. His limbs were soiled with earth-mold and crisscrossed with scratches from briars, as though he had forced his way through the forest with no regard for the maiming of his flesh. His chest was crusted in places with rust-brown, dried blood, but in other places it was clean. Where the nakedness showed, white and startling between the patches of old blood, there were neat, shallow cuts whose lips gaped open and dry.

"Turn the head and look at his face," Favonius said.

Prasutagas obeyed, grasping the matted black hair and rolling the head toward him. Involuntarily, he stepped back. A terror as naked and tangible as the decomposing body itself was imprinted on the features. The eyes were open so wide that the whites rimmed the brown irises. The mouth, too, was wide, and stretched into a grimace of horror that had been frozen by death. The teeth glinted at Prasutagas as he raised his hand to his nose. The choking smell filled his nostrils, strong and unmistakable, mingling with a memory blown to him from his boyhood days when Subidasto ruled the Iceni and Andrasta was queen. His suspicions, become certainty, fell upon him like rocks. The nauseating contents of a fox's bladder. Hounds baying late at night, far away, yet disturbing as he lay on his bed unable to sleep. Were you out hunting, Boudicca? Yes. I should have asked you what you hunted, but never, never would I have suspected this. Annis. You poor young man.

"Take a look at this," Favonius said, beckoning Prasutagas, who woodenly went to stand with him. He lifted the feet, and Prasutagas saw that the soles were ripped and raw and the nails gouged. "The man was running from something, running hard with no thought of his feet," Favonius observed. "From what? What was he doing, miles from his post, stark naked, covered in knife slits which may have been painful but would not have killed him?"

Prasutugas found his voice. He knew that Favonius was watching him carefully and he strove to make the words even, natural. "What did kill him?"

"You tell me." Favonius dropped the feet and folded his arms. "He was brought in by the men I sent out early this morning to find him. He left his post sometime last night. The body was three miles up-river, lying on its back under a tree."

"Did he drown?" Prasutugas made the question come, knowing that it was expected of him, but the pain was back, deep inside him, a nagging, sick hopelessness as his thoughts revolved around his wife. Yet she had said that Andrasta's power was gone. Perhaps this was not her work after all.

"No. He was too far from the bank to have been washed up. He walked or ran to where he was found. The tracks are clear. And if he didn't drown, then what? He looks as though some great bird has clawed his chest. Whoever cut him made it look that way, but why? Why cut him up and not kill him?"

"Perhaps he went mad and cut himself. Perhaps his fear of the forest at night was too much for him."

"Perhaps." Favonius eyed him shrewdly. "What killed him, Prasutugas?"

Prasutugas swallowed and made his eyes meet the Roman's. "Look at his face, Favonius. He died of fright."

"What frightened him?"

"What frightens any man? Fear is a disease, like any other. It begins in the mind, not outside the body. And like any other disease, fear can kill."

"Certainly. But fear cannot cut man's chest to ribbons." Prasutugas made no reply and Favonius seemed undecided whether to say more. Then, when the stench in the hut became unbearable, he opened the door and both men went gratefully outside.

"I think you know more about this than you will say," Favonius remarked heavily. "I will conduct a few enquiries, but I am sure that they will bear no fruit. Do I have your word, Prasutugas, that no more soldiers will die of fright?"

Prasutugas faced him angrily. "I had nothing to do with the circumstances of this man's death," he snapped. "I can surmise, but so can you, and my surmises will be no more fruitful than yours. I rule many people, tribesmen who have been loyal to Rome and who have given you very little trouble, Favonius, and whatever happened to that man was incidental, a minor outburst of someone's frustration. I refuse to make you any promises. That would be ludicrous."

448

"I wonder whose frustration burns so deeply?" Favonius rapped back.

Prasutugas summoned a smile. "The annoyance was light and fleeting," he replied smoothly. "Use your good sense, Favonius. The man was tortured a little, a very little, and then freed. No living hand struck him down. He died of his own fright."

Favonius hissed sharply through his teeth and stamped away, and Prasutugas went out through the gate, down to the copse, and in under the trees. No living hand struck him down, he kept telling himself. That is true. But to have been murdered by his own terror he must have been pushed over the edge of sanity. Boudicca, the poor young man was a Roman. How could he have understood his part? Annis. I know you, my love, I know your daily burden, that I made suddenly too heavy to bear. I, too, am responsible for the soldier's death. When he reached the hut he called her sharply outside and she left the skins and came to him. He drew her away from the crowd that always stood about the hut, and when they were alone he said to her quietly, "You were hunting last night, Boudicca. What quarry did you flush?" If you lie to me now it will all be over between us, he thought so clearly that he was afraid he had spoken the words. I will put you away from me in body if not in soul. He was perfectly calm, everything within him poised and waiting for her answer, and she smiled sadly across at him, squinting a little against the bright sun, her red hair fluttering under her square chin in the warm breeze.

"You do not know for sure, do you, Prasutugas? And if I never tell you, you will be left with nothing but suspicions. Therefore I will tell you. Lovernius and I set loose the Annis."

Relief flooded him and he exhaled, then anger coursed through him, washing away the weakness. He did not need to ask her why she had done such a desperate thing but he mastered the rage and said, "Did the hounds bring him down?"

She looked at her feet. "No. He got away. Think of it, Prasutugas! An Annis has never outrun the hounds before! Oh, I know what you think of me, I know how mad my act must look to you, but don't you think it odd that an Annis escaped?" She looked up again, and now he saw that tears were not far away. "The gods have left Icenia. They went years ago, when the Druids went away, but I did not believe until now." Her lips shook. "Andrasta has gone. Only the Roman gods have power in Icenia now."

So she did not know. In spite of the warmth of the morning, a shiver went through him as he thought of that face disfigured by horror, and he grasped her shoulder and shook his head. "No,

Boudicca, Andrasta is still the Queen of Victory, though she may be forgotten by all but you and Lovernius. She heard the spells."

For a moment she frowned, bewildered; then convulsively, she clutched his wrist in both hands. "Prasutugas! What did Favonius have to show you? You know something!"

He stood quite still, and she did not miss the note of sadness in his words. "Favonius showed me the body of a young man with the marks of the Annis blooding on him and the odor of the Annis scent in his hair."

"But I do not understand! The dogs did not slay him, I swear it to you, Prasutugas! I am telling you the truth!"

"I know. He was not torn to pieces, Boudicca. He died of fright. I wish you could have seen his face."

Amazed, she let her arms fall limply to her sides and Prasutugas released her. "So Andrasta took him after all," she whispered. "I cannot believe it. She came to him in the forest . . ."

"He was killed by fear, and that is all we know," he broke in emphatically. "Boudicca, I must ask you to swear an oath to me that the Annis will never be hunted again in Icenia for as long as I am ricon."

"You ought to tell Favonius, oughtn't you?" she said softly. "Prasutugas, I am so sorry. Already it begins again between us, doesn't it?"

"No," he smiled at her. "This time it is different. This time there are no secrets in our little war."

"None. That I do promise. And I will swear the oath by Andrasta never to hunt the Annis again, if you will swear not to tell Favonius where the weapons are."

"I will swear, but if I discover them through another, Boudicca, then I am bound to report them."

"You never will!" She grinned impudently. "How good it is to swear by Andrasta once more!"

They parted, she to find Lovernius and he to order his farming freemen. I do not deny you, Andrasta, he thought as he made his way to the stables. I have never denied you. But I do not wish to live my life in fear of you. You must understand that your power was curtailed by me on behalf of the people. I do not begrudge you one Roman, but I will not see you spread your phantom wings over the whole of Icenia again. The forests are yours, and with that you must be content. He mounted and set off to ford the river, and thence through the woods to his fields. All the way his mind was full of Icenia's two queens, his magnificent, impulsive wife, and the black mystery of Andrasta. His thoughts strayed once to the news out of the west, but he, like Favonius, dismissed it as unimportant to Icenia. The west was a mirage, the west was another world. Here his crops were springing up fragile and green, and his new calves and lambs cavorted over his meadows to remind him that he was rich and secure. If his wound throbbed with his horse's stride, it only served to bring to mind a past that he had successfully obliterated and that he would never allow to come again to his people. Rome had put its strong, sheltering arms around the land, and Prasutugas was happy.

CHAPTER TWENTY-NINE

I T HAD BEEN A SUMMER OF VICTORY and of hope. The door of the west had swung open and the eager prisoners had poured through it. The Demetae did not want to go home; neither did the Deceangli. For a while the rebels strode exultantly up and down the frontier, revelling in their new security, while at Glevum the Second cowered behind its impregnable walls. Venutius decided to leave it alone, knowing that it could withstand a siege indefinitely, for the whole summer if need be, and he wasted no time on it. The mood of the tribes was one of madness, a gay, light-hearted insanity. Gradually the tribes separated to probe deeper into the east and the south, and Venutius, who knew that his power over them had come to an end, saw them go with no more than a twinge of misgiving. They wanted plunder now, their right as victors, and the Cornovii and the Coritani meekly gave up what they had to the bands of westerners who roamed the summer-heavy forests. Emrys, Madoc, and Venutius kept their tribes together, and as one they crept south, resting, riding slowly through the lush countryside, but always toward Camulodunon. There the officials scurried about like frightened rabbits. The procurator reluctantly assumed military control and ordered the Fourteenth to march to Camulodunon but later he countermanded it, and the legate of the Fourteenth, like the legate of the Second, ignored both orders and stayed where he was. But Venutius was conscious of them and of all the legions crouching in their forts and waiting for the new governor to arrive. The Ninth in Brigantia. The Second in Dobunni country, behind them now. The Fourteenth, also behind

451

them, smack in the middle of the Coritani. Three legions, and if the governor should arrive, if he was quick-witted, those legions could cut off any retreat into the mountains. He spoke of his fears to Emrys.

"We must tempt the legions to do battle, one at a time," he said. "We must defeat them all this summer if we are not to find ourselves back in the west this autumn."

"They will not be lured from their forts," Emrys responded bitterly. "They know that if they wait long enough the governor will come. I wonder what we have really gained, Venutius."

Venutius did also, but together they went against the smaller bastions of Rome, the garrisons, the posting stations, a few villages where much grain was stored in the winter for the soldiers. Sometimes they were successful, sometimes not.

Finally the Ninth braved the unsettled lowlands. It left its fort and began a march south. Its legate did not know where the rebels were, but he knew that the governor had landed at last and that he would be called upon. He was right. The news of the coming of Aulus Didius Gallus reached Venutius also, but too late and too stale, for the spy had not known where to find him and had followed only rumors.

"The new governor is here," the spy said. "He is an old man. I know nothing more about him. If you hurry you may take Camulodunon and kill him before he can plot your downfall."

Take Camulodunon? Venutius and Emrys looked at each other. No active legionaries were quartered at Camulodunon anymore, only veterans who lived on farmsteads taken from the Catuvellauni, or who amused themselves in the town while slaves worked their land. The spy left them, and Venutius wasted no time.

"Camulodunon," he said tersely. "We can reach it within two weeks if we ride hard."

They arrowed swiftly toward Catuvellauni territory, but four days later another spy intercepted them. "The orders have gone out," he said. "To the Second, Ninth, and Fourteenth."

"So soon?" Emrys was dumbfounded. This governor had moved fast for an old man who had seen nothing of Albion but his maps.

"We will keep going," Venutius snapped. "We can burn Camulodunon. Is it possible to kill the dispatch riders before they reach their destinations?"

The spy looked at him as though he had lost his mind. "No, Lord. We do not know how they have gone. With the countryside in such a state they have not set out on the roads."

"Of course." Venutius tried to shrug off the old, familiar ache of failure but it settled snugly around him as though it had never been lifted from him. Nothing had been accomplished after all. Nothing would be resolved. Albion was caught in some strange trap where time was suspended as it was each Samain Eve, and he and Emrys and Madoc, all the chiefs, would never die, the warfare would never stop, and eternity meant advance, kill, retreat, advance, kill, retreat forever, constant despair and fatigue an eternal background. He wanted to lie down on the grass, never to get up, just to close his eyes and surrender everything.

Emrys saw the broad shoulders droop. "Venutius?" he said. "Do we go on?"

"You are asking me, Emrys?" Venutius smiled wanly. "You?" He did not answer the question. He got to his feet and signaled to his host, and they surged on.

The next day other news came, this time from the north. The Ninth had reached the Fourteenth and together they were angling across the island to the south and west. The Second had shaken off its lethargy and was on the march also, south and east. Venutius knew what their directions boded. They would meet, an unbeatable front of three legions against which he and his people could not stand.

"There is still time to reach the governor," Emrys urged, but Venutius savagely disagreed.

"If we waste our time plundering Camulodunon we will be cut off," he said. "Our only hope is in immediate flight." He swore, then to Emrys's surprise he knelt and dug his hands into the sweet grass. "Ah freedom," he whispered. "When? When? How long must this soil be watered with the blood of your children? Well, once more we will run." He got up slowly and awkwardly as though his own blood had thickened within him. "If we hurry we can go straight through Glevum, for the fort is now empty."

There was no more talk. Emrys wondered what the Demetae and the Deceangli were doing. Word would have come to them sooner than it had come here, but were they scattered and running or were they planning to try to hold the land they had gained? With patient fatalism he saluted the horizon, then turned to follow Venutius, shouting to his chiefs as he went.

They sped north and west, hounded by the fear that their retreat had already been cut off. The summer had been a delightful fantasy, a dream, a respite, but once more they were the hunted, and like the hunted they moved swiftly, instinctively, fear blowing steadily behind them. Snatches of news shredded them as they went. The Demetae had disappeared back into the west. The Deceangli had attempted to engage the Ninth but had been repulsed and were also in flight. The waves of tribesmen rushed across Albion, straining for safety with all that they had, eyes, ears, hands, feet turned westward. They reached Glevum, the fort deserted and quiet, but they ran on, not stopping until the summer was a memory.

Autumn found them back in their camps, subdued and embittered, but though their bodies ran no longer, their hearts and minds still fled.

Early Summer, A.D. 53

CHAPTER THIRTY

*I*T WAS AN EARLY SUMMER DUSK, warm and redolent with a promise of heat to come, and the vast hall was crowded and noisy. The lamps flickered upon mighty brass stands, their perfumed smoke mingling with the heavy odor of food, and jugglers, naked but for white loincloths, tossed their bright balls high into the air while a fire-eater sat on the ground with his torches and fuel, waiting patiently to be called to perform. Caradoc, Caelte, Eurgain, and young Gladys paced beneath the echoing, painted dome and threaded their way through the tables and reclining diners, to approach the emperor. He lay on his couch, rumpled toga around him, one ringed hand fidgeting with the silver tableware. Claudius saw them coming and extended an arm, smiling broadly as Gladys ran over the tiles to kneel at his side. His Greeks were clustered nearby, gossiping desultorily, while beside him the empress, resplendent in pearls, gave one ear to their conversation and the other to her son.

Gladys kissed his cheek, bobbing to Agrippina before she did so. "Oh Emperor, you look so tired tonight!" she whispered. "Don't you ever sleep?"

"It is not sleep that I need," he answered, patting her face. "I am old, little warrior. Find me a cure for that. You look lovely tonight. Come and sit beside me for a moment." He made room for her and she snuggled onto the couch. He glanced up at Caradoc and the others. "Well, my noble barbarian," he went on. "Before you ask I can tell you that nothing of any note is happening in Britannia so you may eat in peace. The new governor has only just arrived."

454

Caradoc smiled, feeling the hostile eyes of the Greeks on him. "Thank you," he replied. "By that, you mean the situation has not changed."

"Do not grin at me! I see the pride all over your face."

"Sir, if you would like to see more action in Albion, then send me home. I promise you that I can stir up this Didius Gallus and make his dispatches to you very interesting."

Claudius grunted. "In all the years since I visited your primitive land you have only meant one thing to me, Caradoc, and that is money. I have no intention of spending more on you or Britannia than I do already. Now go to your couch. Eurgain, I greet you also."

They were dismissed. They bowed and went to the couches reserved for them, behind the royal tables, their servants trailing after them. The trumpets blared and the first course was borne into the hall. Agrippina nodded at the fire-eater, who got to his feet, and Gladys slipped from the emperor's side, pushed through the Greeks, and found her couch opposite Claudius and the empress. Now she could talk to him as she ate. Food was placed before her and she began her meal with gusto.

"You should not come to table with your hair down, child," Agrippina said to her smoothly. "You presume too much upon my husband's liking for you."

Gladys looked into the expressionless black eyes, knowing an enemy. You call me child, she thought, yet you do not know that according to the custom of my people I ceased to be one two years ago. I walk a precipice here in this luxurious death cell and I must walk it as a child if I am to stay alive. I love you, Claudius. You are a dear old man, and lonely. But you, Lady . . . my father knows that you sometimes let down your own dyed hair and then you are more dangerous than these fawning Greeks who hate me for taking the Emperor's favor from them. You sick animals. All of you with teeth invisibly bared, tearing at my poor old emperor.

"Lady, I must dress as my mother decrees," she answered seriously, "and my mother insists that my hair be loose or braided, according to custom."

Nero leaned forward, his own eyes hot as they ran lightly over her shining hair, the green silk tunic that clung to her body, the emeralds wound around her throat from ear lobe to collarbone, Claudius's gift to her.

"Oh leave her alone," he snapped rudely at his mother. "I like her with her tresses in the gravy. I have written another poem, Gladys. I shall read it to you later, and you must tell me what you think."

She smiled politely at him, quelling the fear and unease she always

455

felt in his presence. He got everything he wanted, that one. His mother doted on him, loaded him with money and precious things, surrounded him with every pomp, gratified his every whim. So far he had done nothing but follow her with his eyes, touch her occasionally in passing, and tease her with a vicious precision, but Gladys knew what he really wanted. So did Agrippina, and at Nero's words she smiled loftily and turned away. Gladys tried to answer him as lightly as she could, keeping her face averted from his ingratiating smile, the short, pudgy fingers that stroked and pulled at the straggling, soft beard he was trying to grow.

"I know nothing of poetry, Nero, therefore my praise or criticism is worthless to you, but read it to me if you like."

"Ignorant little barbarian," one of the Greeks muttered, just loud enough for her to hear. "Claudius is entering his dotage, to be captured by one such as she. I hate children."

Gladys picked up a peach, stuck a peacock feather in it, and flung it at him. It struck him on the cheek. "You have none, and will never produce any," she answered him rudely, "and you lie when you say you hate children. I have heard it said that you like little boys."

Nero began to clap. Agrippina smiled. The Greek turned his smooth, painted face to her with a look of loathing.

She answered it mutely, holding his gaze, then pointed her spoon at him. "The feather is to go through the ring in your nose," she said, and Claudius raised a hand.

"That is enough, all of you," he said. "Be still. Stop bickering. Gladys, you have not told me how you liked the glassware I sent to you."

She reached across the table and took his hand, contrite. "Oh Emperor, I forgot to thank you. I am so sorry. The glass is very beautiful, but so fragile that I am afraid to put it to any use. I have the pieces set out beside my bed so that I can admire them. I am preparing a special gift for you but do not ask me what it is. I want to surprise you." They smiled at each other and then Claudius went back to his dinner. Applause for the fire-eater broke out and he bowed and began to collect the coins that had been showered around him. Gladys met her father's eye and she suddenly wished she could climb on his knee and bury her head in his chest. She wanted to feel safe as she used to in the days when she was a baby. She remembered how much he used to laugh then, how full of vigor he had been. Now he smiled often, but laughed no more. She glanced away and found Nero's gaze fastened on her. Her fingers fumbled as she picked up her silver goblet.

Music began to float through the hall and the dancers came and bowed to the royal table. Caradoc felt a hand on his leg and looked to see Britannicus waiting for him to make room. With an apology Caradoc swung his legs to the floor and Britannicus perched beside him. "So you came," Britannicus said. "I didn't think you would. It has been a long time, Caradoc, since you deigned to attend my father. Have you been ill?"

Caradoc smiled at the boy who had been named in honor of his father's one and only military excursion. I suppose I should hate him, this living reminder of my agony at Camulodunon, Caradoc thought, but it was hard to hate Britannicus. He was eager, pert, cheeky, and charming. He and his stepbrother disliked and constantly intrigued against each other, Britannicus fighting for some of the limelight Agrippina arranged determinedly for Nero, and Nero himself using his rising popularity to bully Britannicus. But at twelve Britannicus, for all his unnatural sophistication, still had the engaging ways of a little boy.

"You know very well that I have not been ill," Caradoc answered him, offering him wine, "and you know also that I am not overfond of great feasts."

Britannicus laughed. "But you have spun me enough tales of the night-long feasts that used to go on at Camulodunon," he retorted, "and I have not yet grown weary of your stories. Never mind, Caradoc. I know why you do not come here more often. Did my father tell you how boring things are in my province at the moment? Are you happy or sad?"

"I try to be neither. What is the use? I am content, which is safer. Tell me, Britannicus, where is Nero's wife?"

Britannicus's face became shrewd. "How should I know? Do you think that Octavia's presence here tonight would make any difference to Nero's lascivious slobbering over Gladys? My brother fancies he is already a god and his mother entirely agrees with him. He is probably bored with little Octavia and she is sulking."

Caradoc sighed inwardly. They were a family of ferrets, all of them. Beside him Eurgain lay on her couch neither eating nor drinking, her eyes on the echoing upper story of the dome where the statues gazed at one another in the gloom, but she was listening intently to the ebb and flow of the various conversations around her. Britannicus put his elbows on the table.

"Perhaps it is not because of her husband that she sulks," he remarked. "I have heard a rumor that my father is about to acquire another daughter." He slyly looked at Caradoc out of the corner of his eye as Caradoc registered shock. "No, no," he went on. "The empress is not pregnant, and even if she were I doubt if it would be by Claudius. My father wants to adopt your Gladys."

Eurgain sat up slowly. Caradoc stared at the grinning face turned to him, the rich food beginning to sour in his stomach. "I have heard many rumors since I came to Rome," he said quietly, "and almost none of them, Britannicus, have had any basis on fact. This is just another rumor."

"Well, I hope for your sake and for Gladys that you are right. The empress would not like it at all because she would fear for the future of her precious Nero." He waved airily. "Oh I know what she wants for him and you see, Caradoc, if my father adopted Gladys I would immediately bend every effort to marry her and thus wriggle closer to the emperor and my rightful place." He patted Caradoc's knee. "You must not worry. I really like her a lot, even though she is four years older than I. Married to me she would be a good deal safer than she is now." He did not wait for a reply, but got up and walked away, his short tunic flowing against his thighs.

Caradoc and Eurgain exchanged glances. "I feel sick," Eurgain said finally. Caradoc said nothing. Suddenly his daughter's laughter soared and he saw Claudius bend to wipe his mouth with white linen. Agrippina was whispering to Nero, who still fingered his pathetic little beard, his eyes on Gladys. The Greeks were arguing violently over something. Britannicus was leaning against a pillar talking to his tutor, a small, secretive smile hovering on his lips. Music twanged and twittered, and then Caelte bent to his lord.

"She will survive," he said softly. "She survived the years in the mountains, and the dangers here are not very different. Trust her, Lord, and do not fear. As long as she has the emperor's protection she is safe from his wild ones."

"You are wrong, Caelte," Caradoc managed at last, seeing himself, Gladys, all of them with hands to the bars of this cage that had held them tightly for nearly two years, their feet balancing on the shifting morass of Claudius's good will. "If the emperor declined to honor Gladys with his attention we would all cease to be of any interest in the palace and could sleep without knives under our pillows. I ought to have forbidden her access to the imperium."

"One does not disobey the emperor," Caelte reminded him, "and it was Claudius who took a sudden fancy to Gladys, long before she grew to like him. Perhaps she is the daughter he wishes he had had."

"There is nothing wrong with Octavia. She is the most honorable of them all."

458

"True. But for some reason Claudius prefers Gladys. Perhaps Octavia reminds him of her mother."

"Perhaps. Ah, Caelte, how tired I am of every 'perhaps'!"

Caelte would have spoken again but a slave approached him deferentially, murmured to him, and he lifted his harp and rose. "The emperor wants me to sing. I hate to sing here, Lord. The Greeks laugh at me and my music."

"Then refuse him," Eurgain said suddenly, "and then let us take Gladys and go home. I will not come here anymore, Caradoc. I have never in my life inhaled such a stink of corruption and evil. I see no lips around me that are capable of uttering one truth." She spoke loudly, defiantly, but the rising of Caelte hid her words from all but her husband and her slave. Caelte walked to the emperor and bowed.

"You wish me to sing tonight, Lord, but I cannot. I have drunk too much wine. My throat is sore."

Claudius frowned in disappointment. "You hardly ever come when I ask you to," he grumbled. "Now you are here and you will not sing." His voice was querulous, his face flushed, and his stutter more pronounced than it had been all evening. Gladys, after one anxious glance at him, sat up.

"Oh please, Caelte, just one song. Is your throat so sore that you cannot sing one?" Claudius was wiping his nose and Gladys sat straighter, her fingers laced together under the cover of the tablecloth. The emperor was tired. He was about to become angry.

"Not even one," Caelte answered her quickly.

"For me?" Her eyes pleaded with him, and all at once he knew his danger. Resignedly he nodded.

"Very well. I will attempt one song for you, Lord, seeing you are kind enough to ask to hear me. What shall it be?"

"I do not care," Claudius quavered. "Anything. Cheer me, barbarian."

"I know no happy songs anymore, sir."

Gladys's shoulders slumped, then went slowly back. Her chin rose. "Caelte, I have a request," she said loudly. "I want you to sing 'The Ship' for me."

"No!" he barked, shocked, but she rose to her feet and stood gripping the edge of the table, her eyes suddenly blazing.

"For me, Caelte! I want, I need to hear it. Sing it to me now, in this place, for the good of my soul, I beg you!"

"Oh Gladys," he returned sadly, in their own tongue, "What are you doing here? Shall I bow to this old man and lay my honor at his feet?"

"No," she flashed back, her eyes still glittering and color coming and going in her cheeks. "Together, among these savages, we will lift it high. He is a good old man, Caelte."

"The ship has gone down."

"Not until there is no one left to sing its funeral songs."

"What are you prattling about?" Agrippina broke in suspiciously. "Gladys, is he going to sing or not?"

Caelte inclined his head to her. "I will sing." He unslung his harp, Gladys began the song. Caelte's voice had changed as he aged. It was deeper and had more volume. It no longer rose high and melodious to mingle with bird song and wind but forced itself against rock and pillars and the deaf, hard ears of the city. Until tonight the city had remained impervious to its music, but this song carried with it its own magic. Gladys stood and swayed, humming it softly with him. The empress crossed her legs and sat back, watching. Claudius craned to catch each tone, for though he could not understand the words, the subtle weaving of the tune fascinated him. Nero was plainly impressed. He watched Caelte's long fingers pluck the harp and he held his head to one side. The last note was high, plaintive, an unresolved question, a gentle plea, and Caelte closed his mouth, stiffening against the snickers he believed would come, but the Greeks looked at him blankly as Gladys went to him and kissed him.

"Thank you," she whispered. "I will not ask such a hard thing of you again." Agrippina applauded briefly, uncomfortably, moved for one fleeting moment. The emperor stopped blowing his nose.

"That was good," he commented without hesitation. "Come and sing it to me tomorrow." Caelte opened his mouth to refuse, but Gladys imperceptibly shook her head. By tomorrow the emperor would have forgotten the song. Nero sat up.

"I think I could sing it better," he announced. "Teach it to me. Show me the notes on my own harp. What manner of song is it?"

"It is a love song," Caelte replied. "A very magical and mysterious song. I do not think that it would be safe for you to sing it, young sir, even if you could learn the words. It belongs only to my people."

"Oh. Well, I want nothing to do with spells, and for a love song it sounds a bit gloomy. I prefer something more robust when I sing of love. You can go away now."

Gladys did not resume her seat but went to Claudius and put her arms about his neck.

"Emperor," she said in his ear. "I think my mother and father want to go home now, and I should go also. Have I leave?"

"I like dutiful women," he said, beginning to stutter again. "Of course you have leave. I may send for you tomorrow." She kissed his wrinkled cheek, bowed to Agrippina, and walked to where Caradoc

460

and Eurgain were already walking back under the dark height of the dome, Caelte and the slaves behind them. Moving in the air, she realized she was drenched in sweat.

They emerged onto the terrace that swept down, losing itself in the dusk. They stood for a moment looking over the city while a slave went to summon their litter-bearers. No one spoke. Gladys began to shiver although the night was warm, and Eurgain folded her arms and kept her eyes on the ground. People came and went around them, occasionally calling a greeting, but not even Caelte could summon a word. The litters arrived, but before they could be seated a messenger came hurrying from the torchlit caverns behind them.

"The empress wishes to see you in her own rooms," he told Caradoc. "Follow me, please."

"Father, be careful," Gladys began, but he kissed her and settled her on her litter.

"Go straight home," he said evenly to Eurgain. "I will not be long."

"It is about Gladys this time," she replied quietly. "There is nothing that terrible woman does not know. Are you armed?"

"I have my knife. Don't worry. If she wanted to harm me she would not have sent a message."

Eurgain spoke curtly to the slaves and Caradoc watched them sway out of sight, Caelte striding beside Eurgain's litter. He turned and paced after the messenger, who led him back inside, through a garden and the huge, still pool in the pillared atrium, up wide marble stairs lined with stiff troops and the garish flicker of torches, and they plunged into a maze of gleaming passages. Caradoc knew vaguely where he was. They climbed more stairs, silent now, far from the uproar in the dining hall, then abruptly came upon a broad, moon-splashed balcony with a high door to its right. The messenger knocked, bowed, and vanished.

She opened to him herself, beckoning him impatiently within and closing the door quickly behind her. He went and stood in the middle of the bright room, no longer awed, as he had once been, by the tall, painted ceiling, the red-and-white mosaic floor, the rich hangings, so heavy that it took two men to carry one of them. Windows framed a black night sky full of stars and funneled to him a breath of wind, clean-smelling up here above the smoke and odors of the city. His eye rapidly scanned the corners, seeking the places where a man might stand hidden, and she laughed gently.

"Now what would be the advantage in that?" she asked him. "None in particular for me. I would be rather sorry if it became necessary to murder you, Caradoc. I like to look at you. You are the only honest man in Rome and it shows in your walk and your face. You still flounder around in the palace and city like a gasping fish on dry land, saying and doing things that would have meant the silencing of a more cunning man long ago, but I suppose that honesty and forthrightness provide their own protection." She began to take the jewels from her arms, then from her hair. "You may relax, barbarian. I no longer plot against your life. You made me very angry once, you know that, don't you?"

He loosened and smiled at her. "Yes, Lady, I know."

"I am surrounded by old men, eunuchs, and perverts," she went on matter-of-factly. "When you refused to submit to me I was grieved and astonished, for no man refuses me if he values his life, but I must admit now that if you had done so you would have disappointed me. Your beautiful image would have been tarnished. Perhaps you would have disappointed me in other ways also, for surely an honorable barbarian must lack the requisite imagination." She smiled wryly, her fingers busy with the pins in her hair, and he grinned suddenly, wondering whether she had guessed his true reasons for declining her invitation to share her bed.

He had constantly been afraid during his first few months in Rome, afraid of the city, of the emperor, of the undercurrent of directionless power that blanketed those he met, giving them a strange, warped view of themselves and of the world. It had bewildered him. She had hinted that for his own good and the health of his family he ought to comply with her whim, but he simply could not. He had been incapable of doing so. She was too foreign, too unknown. Then, as he had begun to recover from the emotional strains of his capture and journey, he resisted her for other reasons, knowing instinctively that to submit would mean his eventual death. She would quickly have wearied of him and discarded him, and he knew that many of her lovers lay mouldering in their mausoleums.

He watched as she released the tight ringlets bunched on her head, letting them bounce against her neck, ghoulishly framing the tiny, pursed mouth, the flesh of her cheeks, once firm and round but now sagging inward toward her broad, curiously undelineated nose. Her eyes are old too, he thought, old and tired and full of the knowledge of man's degradation. Yet she is one year younger than I.

"It is perfectly true that hardship and poverty can deprive a man of this, ah, imagination," he agreed with humor. "You would not have liked me at all, Lady."

"You are probably right." She flung a cushion into a chair and sat leaning back, her fingers still busily pulling at the coils of hair. "But I did not summon you to discuss the past. You blunder about, Caradoc, doing no harm, in fact you are well liked by certain senators and other influential people, I suppose because you can be trusted. But this time your family is blundering into a situation that you do not understand. I will speak frankly with you, because if I do not, you will fail to appreciate the point."

In a flash he understood very well what she was going to say and could see all the ramifications making secret and invisible paths in the palace and in his own home. He went to the floor out of long habit, squatting before her, his fingers laced lightly together, balancing on the balls of his feet. She continued. "I have tolerated your daughter in the palace because she has provided diversion for the emperor and has asked nothing for herself. In short, she is as unambitious as the rest of you. But I want her here no more. Claudius is talking of adopting her, changing her name to Claudia, bringing her to live in the palace. My son moons after her like a lovesick cow. If she would settle for a nice, quiet affair with him, then all would be well and he would soon get over this odd passion of his, but knowing you all, she would not agree. Nero lets nothing go until he is ready or until he has glutted himself and," she said, smiling cynically, "you can see how our family concord would be destroyed. Britannicus would use her to recover the good graces of his father and further his own ambition. He is only twelve but that means nothing here, Caradoc. My son might even make an effort to divorce Octavia, or worse. With two daughters Claudius would be torn, and you yourself would suddenly acquire a new and dangerous position."

Dangerous indeed, Caradoc thought. Dangerous to you. With Gladys in the palace there would be a sudden focusing of everyone's slow machinations, and you cannot take the chance of losing control.

"She is a very sweet young girl," Agrippina went on. "But I know what sudden favor and power can do to sweet youth. If Gladys lost her head she could cause untold trouble. If Claudius approaches you with adoption plans you must refuse. And you must not let Gladys come to him so often. I am becoming tired of spying on her."

Caradoc rose. "I understand perfectly," he said. "But I wonder if you do, Lady. You are afraid of me and my family, aren't you? You think that a whiff of power would be sufficient for us to scrabble after more. But all we really want is to live in peace and anonymity with our hurts and our memories. Has it never occurred to you that Gladys really loves the emperor? We will bargain."

She shook her head. "Oh no, barbarian. I make bargains with no one."

"This time you must, Empress. I will refuse the adoption and ease Gladys away from Claudius, but only if you for your part keep your son as far from her as possible. She wants nothing to do with him."

She thought for a moment and then rose also. "Agreed. I shall find another playmate for Nero. But you had better keep your part, Caradoc. Do not forget the Greeks."

He looked at her, eyes narrowing against the threat, and she drove it viciously home. "Claudius is very fond of his freemen. They wield more influence over him than anyone else. They despise Gladys and are jealous of her. A few words of this matter would be enough to ensure that you lose a daughter rather suddenly."

"May I go?" he enquired stiffly, shoving away his anger.

With a snap of the wrist she dismissed him. "You may. Take your family to Aulus Plautius's summer residence this year. The country air might do you all good."

He closed the door softly and traversed the cool, dark passage, the slave who had led him there running after him. He knew that he ought to be grateful to Agrippina for the chance of extricating himself and Gladys, but all he could think of was his own knife in her back. He followed the slave blindly. How hard it was in this, the most civilized city in the world, just to stay alive. He came out onto the terrace and immediately turned to the steps that zigzagged down through the imperial gardens and would carry him part of the way to his own home across the Clivus Victoriae on the brow of the Palatine hill. Darkness obscured the view over the Forum and the river with its graceful bridges, but he did not care. He hated it all.

Llyn and his sister Eurgain left the house with Chloe, Eurgain's Greek slave, and slipped softly along the street, mingling easily with the evening crowds. The sun had set but darkness had not yet fallen, and as they reached the foot of the Palatine and began to cross the concrete and marble maze of the Forum, angling south and west toward the river, they had to battle the loiterers who gathered to gossip before going home to supper. They walked in single file, not talking, Eurgain in the lead, Chloe trailing behind, but when the Forum was behind them and the streets became narrower, the shops and apartment houses closer together, Llyn led and Eurgain fell back, watchful of every passer-by. The light failed but they did not pause to fire their torches, and they moved steadily and unerringly on through the shadows. The men and women who still passed them were shoptenders and tradesmen, intent only on finding their own tables and the comfort of their families, and the young trio was not challenged or accosted. The night was too young. At last Llyn halted. They were on a corner. To the left the street snaked back into the choked quarter where the poorer citizens lived and worked, but to the right it narrowed and dived suddenly into darkness and the murmur of river and tavern.

Eurgain pushed back her hood as she came up to Llyn. "Well," she said. "I will see you tomorrow, Llyn, unless they dredge your body out of the Tiber. Don't lose too much money."

"Why should I care?" he answered lightly. "It isn't my money and anyway there's plenty more where it comes from. You keep my secret, Eurgain, and I'll keep yours."

"Will you come with me?"

"No, thank you. There may be something left to live for, who knows, and I am not ready yet to be tied to a cross or ripped to pieces by goaded lions. Tell me, is it true that those people roll babies in flour and then kill them and eat them?"

She smiled briefly. "No, Llyn, it is not true. They would never kill anyone."

"In any case, they ought to know better than to plot against the emperor. You are a fool to associate yourself with them."

"They don't do that either. Their God has told them that they must obey those in authority over them."

"How very dull. They won't hold your interest for long, Eurgain."

"I can't say, Llyn." She kissed him. "I think that they have discovered the unchangeable truth the Druithin have sought for ages beyond ages, and, if they have, then nothing else in the world is so important to me."

"You look like mother," he grumbled good-naturedly. "Take care of her, Chloe." He waved and turned, leaving them to go their way.

"I can take care of myself!" Eurgain called, her echo following him into the dimness.

Llyn ran down the crooked street, plunged into an alley, and emerged at a place where the heavy, stagnant smell of rotting debris came to his nostrils, mixed with the wet earthiness of the river. For a moment he considered making his way to the warehouses and the docks, to stand on the bridge and gaze at the quiet flow of the Tiber, but he soon discarded the idea in favor of the well-lit tavern and his gambling friends. The merchants employed watchmen who patrolled the riverbank and the warehouses with their piled cargoes. He had once escaped arrest only because he had lain in a doorway, pretending to be in a drunken sleep. He did not need that danger now. He jogged along quickly, thinking of his father and mother and Gladys, reclining at the emperor's table. Gladys must surely be baiting the Greeks. Llyn slowed. Not me, he thought. And what's more, to have to avoid Nero's eye. Gladys is braver than I. Ahead, the lights of the tavern streamed yellow from the open door and the hoarse, painful laughter of his friend Valog, the Gaulish gladiator, drifted out into the warm, cloudy sky. Llyn unslung his cloak, cast a last look into the night, and went inside.

A dozen voices greeted him as he pushed his way past the long wooden tables to the rear of the tiny room. A group of men sat around another table, beer before them, and they made room for him. He bundled up his cloak and unhooked the purse from his belt.

"Linus, you are very late," Valog complained. "We thought you had done so well last night that you would not be back for at least a week."

"What are you doing here, Valog?" Llyn retorted cheerily. "I thought you were fighting tomorrow. I'll tell Plautius why he goes through so many gladiators. He should lock you all up."

"He canceled my fight," Valog said sulkily. "He has to visit his farm."

"Well, if he knew you as well as I do he'd never give you the freedom of the city. One day he'll find his merchandise damaged." .

"By you?" Valog grinned. "You cheeky young rabbit."

"Careful, Valog. I might make him an offer for you. Would you like to fight for me?"

"Are we going to play or not?" the man at Llyn's elbow complained. Llyn turned to him. "Not on duty tonight, Publius?"

"No. Double duty tomorrow. A soldier's life is not an easy one, Linus!" He shoved beer across the table to Llyn, who drank, emptied his purse, and looked around expectantly. Dice appeared and the men settled to gamble, oblivious of the noise around them. "Will you come to Sabella's with me later on?" Publius asked Llyn, but Llyn curtly shook his head.

"I'm not going there again. Sabella has sold Acte, I don't know who to, and the rest of the girls are diseased."

"It's not true."

"I didn't mean in their scrawny bodies," Llyn snapped, sweeping up the dice, and Publius rolled his eyes to Valog and laid his coins on the table.

The evening lengthened and passed into cool night. The coins passed from hand to hand. Llyn's luck was with him and several of his friends got up and drifted away, but he, Valog, and Publius played on desultorily until Llyn got out his purse and began to put his winnings away.

"You go on," he told them. "I'll sit here and watch." The dice rattled in the leather cup, but Llyn called for more beer and sat with his chin in his hand, silent. He was drinking too much, and he knew it. Al-

466

bion's beer was dark and thick, and it glided into the brain with mellow slowness, but Roman beer was light and cunning. It strikes all at once like a snake, like a Roman assassin, he thought, like a Roman emperor. But at least it obliterates thought unlike any Catuvellaun brew. He gulped at it. Valog looked distracted, and shifted in his seat, while Publius smiled at him greedily. They had forgotten about him, and Publius scooped up the last of Valog's money, but they sat on, swapping stories, for another hour. Llyn drank steadily, purposefully, until he saw the room floating in a soft, blurred glow. The patrons seemed to shrink, and the voices of the gladiator and legionary sang with intermittent melancholy, seeming to be about him, senseless, insulting him. Their laughter echoed in his head and their movements became perpetual and slow as the sun's crawl. He drank to take off the edge. One more try, he thought absently to himself. Just one more. Yet even in sleep I cannot escape.

"I don't really like you, Publius," he said with labored precision. He carefully put both arms on the table and his tongue worked hard at the words. "I've killed too many of your kind to ever like you. I don't like you at all."

Publius glanced at him casually and then grinned at Valog. "He's drunk again. Is it your turn or mine?"

"Yours," Valog said sourly. "I'm not going up on the hill again."

"Well, at least he walked for you. Tonight I won't be so lucky. Perhaps we should leave him here."

"And have his purse stolen and his head split open? No."

"It will happen eventually."

Valog watched, fascinated, as Llyn's head slid to rest between his elbows. "You don't understand us barbarians, Publius. One day he will stop swilling beer and feeling sorry for himself. The next we'll see him sitting in the Coria with the senators. One day when it pleases me I'll stop fighting for Plautius and take to singing. It doesn't matter, you see. It's all the same."

"It may be all the same to you, but I have to haul the young fool through the Forum. I might be arrested for manhandling him."

"There are no fools," Llyn muttered, and his eyes opened. "There are only those who do not understand."

"Linus, can you walk?" Valog asked him loudly.

Llyn lifted his head from the table and blinked slowly. "Those who cannot walk must crawl, and those who cannot crawl must die so that they may run," he answered.

Publius made an exclamation of annoyance and stood up, hauling Llyn with him. "He always talks such rubbish when he's drunk," he complained. "Yet he's likeable. Help me, Valog."

"Have you paid for the beer?"

"What with? You took it all."

Valog reached gently into Llyn's purse and took out three coins. "He won't mind, Publius. He can win it back next time." They left the money on the table and together eased Llyn out the door and onto the street. Publius cursed. A light rain was falling, but Llyn leaned against the stone wall of the tavern and smiled vacantly into the night. "I'll walk with you as far as the street of spicesellers," Valog said. "Come, Linus. And keep your mouth shut. I want no more Druithin maxims tonight." They put their arms around him and started up the street, now lit only by such pale light as came from the windows of those who were not yet in bed.

The rain was cool and refreshing, and Llyn rolled his face to it, letting his feet go where they were led, that tiny, untouched part of him still whispering of oak woods and hot firelight. "The crooked path seems straight to those who walk it," Bran's voice droned on. Llyn's head whirled. Death is an illusion. Truth is an illusion. Reality . . . reality is anything you want it to be. And freedom . . . He began to laugh, quietly at first, but then growing louder, unable to stop.

When they reached the corner where he had left Eurgain and Chloe, Valog bid them both a good night and strode quickly away. Publius took Llyn's arm and swung it around his own neck. "I don't know why I do this for you," he said, knowing the answer to his own question.

Llyn staggered beside Publius, humming under his breath. "If you sing I shall drop you and run!" Publius hissed, but Llyn did not sing. He went on humming, one or two citizens passing them with anxious glances. They came out onto the edge of the Forum and after skirting it safely Publius departed without a word, leaving Llyn standing, swaying, still humming softly. Above him, the slopes of the Palatine boasted the sumptuous sprawl of patrician homes, their frail lights glinting out and in as the wind stirred the trees that filled their gardens. He began the long, slow climb to his father's house, following the curving line of the stone wall and alley. But halfway up he knew that he could not go on, and he lay down with his face to the sky. The rain had quickened. It pattered over him enquiringly and he listened to it strike the leaves of some hidden tree. How many times, he thought, have I lain under the oaks straining past these notes for the sound of foreign soldiers? How many times have I seen blood dilute Albion's rain, dying her ferns and flowers scarlet? Albion. He said the word slowly to himself. You exist somewhere, in a place of greenness and silence, but I find it hard to believe that the world is not made of unrelenting stone, of ceaseless noise. Perhaps Albion is only a pretty story. He spread out his arms, feeling his tunic weigh heavy with water. The fabric stuck to his skin, but it was a good feeling, clean. Gladys is forgetting, he thought. Fear brought him clumsily to his knees and he scrabbled to his feet and went on, groping in the darkness, until he came at last to his father's gate and the porter's lodge. He did not have the strength to climb the wall but the porter heard him slip against the iron gate and came out, greeting him and opening for him without raising an eyebrow. He reeled through, hearing the gate click to behind him, and then under his feet there was grass and over him the branches of trees. His father's graceful portico loomed majestically ahead, gray pillars like the trunks of dead willows, and he sensed rather than saw the soldiers who did duty under their shadows. He bowed to the house profoundly, saluted with a mocking wave, and wended his way around it, still cupped in trees, until he came to the wide terrace and the lawn dotted with rose beds, alive with the monotonous music of the fountains. He crossed the lawn and came to the chest-high wall where on a bright day one could lean and look down and out over the whole of the city. You reward us with the insult of your pardon, he thought. You answer our desperate cries with the soothing poison of riches and hold us down while we eat it. Emrys, Madoc, have you forgiven us yet for living on? I took my first head when I was only a little boy. How strange that I should remember that. I carried it to the well and watched it sink. Madoc was amused. Something in me died that day, and Madoc was amused. Madoc. Emrys. He began to say their names aloud like some spell, gripping the wet stone with eyes closed. All the names he could remember, those he had fought beside, those who had died, those who had given all so that he could stand in a Roman garden with a house of unimaginable magnificence behind him, and be painfully drunk on Roman beer. He raised his voice and the names flowed faster, then he scrambled up onto the wall and began to shout.

Caradoc woke suddenly, thinking that he heard Togodumnus calling to him. He had returned from the palace too uneasy in mind to go to bed and he had been dozing in a chair beside the pool of his wide atrium, lulled by the spatter of raindrops on the water. Now he sat upright, still half in a dream, and there it was again, the high voice of his brother, shouting for him over the noise of rain running down his gutters and swishing over the paving of his terrace. He groaned and stood up, turning to seek his bed, then the voice came again—Tog's defiant, imperious voice, but the name he heard was Cinnamus's. For a long second, dread tingled in his fingers and pricked cold on his scalp. Tog was dead. Tog had been dead a long time, and none knew what body his soul now inhabited. He woke fully and half-ran across his yellow tiles, through the colonnade, out into the rain-washed garden of the peristyle, and under the cloistered walk. He ran down the terrace steps, slippery and black with water, across the lawn that squelched under his feet, and then he halted. Tog was standing on top of the wall, a lithe, dark shadow against the darker sky, his hair streaming out behind him, his arms flung wide, names pouring from his mouth. It was Mocuxsoma now, the dead calling to the dead, a summons to this alien garden, a judgment. Caradoc stared wildly, his heart drumming against his ribs, then the figure teetered, regained its balance, and Caradoc let out a sigh. Fear piled on fear tonight, he thought, walking forward. Agrippina and now Llyn. Anger started within him. He reached the wall.

"Llyn. Get down. And stop shouting."

Llyn peered at him. "You are not dead," he slurred, then he turned to face the city. "Rome!" he screamed. "Murderers!"

Caradoc reached up, grasped a flailing arm, and jerked his son roughly from the wall. Llyn came down in a tumble of naked wet legs and sopping, flapping tunic. Caradoc bent, and shaking him viciously, set him on his feet.

"You are drunk again," he said vehemently. "I feel a sickness when I look at you, Llyn. Where is your honor? Your pride?"

"Where is yours, Ricon?" Llyn sneered, rocking to and fro, his face pale and twisted. "You should have slain us all and then yourself when you first saw this marble and damask prison. They are dead! Dead! They believed in you and now they are dead so that you can live here and grow fat on Claudius's largesse. You had a price. The tribes didn't know that, did they? Did Cin know? Rome paid it. Rome has seduced you."

Behind him, Caradoc heard a flurry of movement as his servants came hurrying, some with knives, and his wife sped toward them barefooted, her white and blonde hair loose and her robe clutched tightly to her breast. He did not turn. He stood looking at the rain-darkened, stringing hair, the half-glazed brown eyes, the slack, sullen mouth, then he bunched his fist and drove it into Llyn's jaw. Eurgain cried out as those watching heard the crack of his knuckles connect with his son's face, and Llyn thudded backward onto the lawn. Caradoc reached down, grabbed him by his tunic, hauled him up, and dragged him toward the nearest fountain. Then with one swift movement he kicked Llyn's feet from under him, pushed him hard, and Llyn toppled into the cold, clear water. He came up spluttering, his hands groping for the green and white stone rim, and when he had found it Caradoc squatted before him, taking a handful of slick hair and winding it until Llyn exclaimed in sudden pain.

"They did not fight for *me*," Caradoc whispered, his voice shaking with rage. "They did not die for *me*." He flung out an arm, pointing over the wall to where the invisible city lay waiting for dawn, his extended finger rigid, and he jerked Llyn's head around. "It is there!" he shouted. "It will not go away, no matter how much beer you swill! It has broken better men than you or I, and it will go on breaking them long after you and I have gone! It gloats to see you destroying yourself." The stiff arm began to tremble with an intensity of rage. "If you wish to kill yourself, then do it as a warrior, with a sword, not as a craven peasant, with a flagon. Grow up, Llyn!" All at once a memory smote him. Cunobelin stood over Togodumnus, rubbing his knuckles as Tog lay stunned from the blow, but before he could hear his father's words, Caradoc stood up and forcibly sent the remembrance back into the past.

"Take him out of there and put him to bed," he ordered the servants, then he walked quickly back into the house, Eurgain striding beside him. When he stood under the shelter of the colonnade he slumped and turned to her sadly. "Llyn is right," he said. "I should have killed us all as my ancestors would have done, and awakened the conscience of this city."

"Rome has no conscience," Eurgain replied. "Rome would have been astonished, and then laughed, and would not have understood. Do not reproach yourself for Llyn's unhappiness. We have all had to learn to survive."

"Only Gladys has learned," he said bitterly, "and I sometimes wonder when I listen to her how deep she has allowed the lesson to go. I have never heard her express such passion as she did last night when she asked Caelte to sing. We all play games, Eurgain, like everyone else in the city. Should I blame Llyn for being himself?"

"Are you going to talk to Gladys in the morning?"

"I don't know. I can't think. Go to bed, Eurgain."

She left without a word and he sat suddenly on the floor, his back against a pillar, listening to his servants coax a sick and angry Llyn toward the stairs. I refuse to feel sorry for him, or for myself, Caradoc thought firmly. He must determine not to lie down under the blows of fate. He must learn to fight.

In the morning he told Eurgain and his daughters what had passed between himself and the empress. They were reclining at table in the triclinium, eating bread and fruit while the early sun blinked lukewarm on Eurgain's silver dishes and a damp breeze, full of newness and vigor, stirred the hangings beside the windows. Llyn's couch was empty. He seldom rose to share the first meal of the day with them. They could hear their morning guards outside dismiss the night sentries, and the gardener trundled by, his cart full of spring seedlings. They finished the simple meal in silence, then Caradoc sent out the servants and sat upright. In a few words he told them what Agrippina had said. "Gladys," he asked his daughter, whose face had begun to flush pink with anger, "did you know what the emperor is planning for you?"

"No. At least, I had heard rumors, but he has said nothing to me about it. Oh the poor old man! Agrippina sits there like a crouching cat, waiting for him to die so that she can spring into his place with Nero in her jaws, and those damn Greeks fawn upon him and suck him dry! Well, I will not cease to visit him. He needs me."

"He is not a poor old man," her mother put in gently. "He would not be emperor of Rome if he were, Gladys. I think you must be careful to see him as he is, not as you wish to see him. He is aging, certainly, and plagued with infirmity, but he has a mind as subtle and deep as Agrippina's. You feel sorry for him, but you should fear him also."

"I have tried to, but I can't. He is good to me, and kindly, and we say many things to one another. I comfort him."

Caradoc and Eurgain exchanged glances. Then Caradoc said, "Gladys, he could not protect you against the empress whether he knows it or not. He might try. He might surround you with soldiers, appoint tasters for your food and women to sleep with you by night and companion you by day, but sooner or later Agrippina would kill you. It is as simple as that. I think she is right when she says that we are blunderers. We have no business being in the palace at all. We are like sheep to be led astray and slaughtered."

The younger Eurgain looked sharply across at her father, but Gladys had begun to answer him and her gaze dropped back to her plate. "I will refuse an adoption if he asks it," Gladys said. "I love him, but I have only one father. But how can I refuse to go to him when he sends for me? He will be hurt. His fondness will turn to anger."

"Not if he really loves you in return," her mother pointed out. "Tell him that you need more time for your studies. Tell him that your tutor is becoming tired of filling his time in gossip with the steward." None of them considered telling Claudius the truth. All believed that he was probably well aware of the ambitions nurtured secretly within the hearts of the members of his family, and it did no good to speak them aloud to him.

"He will miss you," the younger Eurgain said softly. "He looked for Aunt Gladys's honesty in you, and he found it. Octavia is honest, but timid. She will not give him much affection, out of fear of the empress. Agrippina wants no one close enough to Claudius to turn his affections from Nero."

"And then there are the Greeks." The voice was Llyn's. They turned to greet him and he came into the room, pale and grinning wryly. "I have been listening to you all, standing outside the door to keep the servants ears away. Really, you are all too careless."

"You are a fine one to talk!" Gladys retorted. "I know what happened last night. The whole city was subjected to your insults."

He flopped down on his couch. Caradoc pushed bread to him but he shook his head. "I think you should all insist that Gladys be adopted by Claudius," he announced. "She would move into the palace and before long be betrothed to sweet little Britannicus, that paragon of all Roman virtues. I will court Octavia, and together we will do away with Nero. Sooner or later, probably sooner, Claudius will die. Now where does that leave us?"

The younger Eurgain smiled. "It leaves us in control of the Roman Empire."

"Exactly." Llyn picked up a bunch of grapes, sniffed them, and put them back. "Without Nero, Agrippina would be a broken branch. What a delirious thought! The House Catuvellaun, ricons of Rome!"

"What would you do?" Caradoc asked him, amused, and slowly the blithe, teasing light went out of his eyes.

"I would withdraw the legions from Albion and Gaul, set fire to this city, and go home."

Silence reigned. Then Eurgain spoke. "Llyn is right about the Greeks," she said evenly. "You see them only as feasters and parasites, Gladys, but most of them are powerful and capable men, doing more than their share of governing. Claudius relies on them, and often with good reason. They hate you already, for they are continually probing the future. They see what Llyn sees. Even if Agrippina softened toward you, they would not."

Gladys flung down her napkin and rose. "You are right," she said loudly. "And I am sometimes deathly afraid of that city within a city on top of the hill. I will try to explain to Claudius why I can come to him no more."

"Explain to him today, Gladys," Caradoc warned, and she nodded, thin-lipped, and left them.

Llyn yawned. "I suppose you want me to tell you today that I have mended my ways," he said to his father. "But I can only say that perhaps I will think about the words you hammered home with your fist. Do you realize that you were just my age, Ricon, when I was born to you?"

"Yes, Llyn," Caradoc answered him gently. "I know. But that was my life. You must live your own."

"Platitudes!" he snorted. The two women rose.

"You will have a chance to think about it very deeply, Llyn," his mother said. "We are going to spend this summer on the Silvanus estate."

"Oh," said Llyn. "With or without the emperor's permission?" He got up and shouldered past them, and they listened to the echo of his angry feet rebound on the pillars of the atrium.

Claudius stood still and watched her come swinging to him under the trees, the long, healthy stride of a country girl undisguised by the graceful folds of her red tunic. She had changed since the day when she faced him for the first time, he reflected, but she would change no more. He knew that also. The heart of her was as solid and innocent today as it had been then, though it had been overlaid by fear and awe. It was that heart which drew him, called forth in him the young boy who fifty years before had been shy and innocent, a lover of books, a dreamer. He had thought that youth was dead but then she had come, with her fearless smiles, and something in him had reached out to her. They had told him that the barbarian women were all killers, that she had blood on her hands, but for once he had not believed it. Of the mother certainly, and the elder sister probably, but not of Gladys. She had been trained, in their savage way, to kill, but somehow he knew that her sword had remained clean. He had blood on his own hands, plenty of it, and it distressed him no more than the thought that his wife's fingers were also red. But the young, insecure, unloved child who had grown to be the most powerful man in the world held out to this fresh girl a hand as eager and pure as her own.

She met his welcoming smile with a broad grin of her own, and coming up to him she kissed him. "Emperor," she said. "I am wearing the emeralds again, isn't that foolish? But I like them so much. How good the gardens smell this morning, after the rain! I cannot bear the heat of summer." She took his arm and they strolled along the path, his court behind and before. "I have only an hour, little one," he said, "But you will stay and eat with me tonight? Gladys, I want you to come to Capri with me this year when Rome gets too hot to bear. Bring your family if you like." She did not let go of him, but he felt her grip tighten. "I can't," she replied, and in her voice he detected regret mixed with something else. Fear? "My uncle has invited us to his summer home. I expect father will soon request permission from you to go."

"Well, I will refuse. You can all come to Capri this year. The sea air will do you good." His stutter had become more pronounced and he stopped walking in order to wipe his mouth. Gladys let go his arm. He was upset today, and she knew that she should attempt to calm him before incipient irritability turned to anger, but there were things to say that could only annoy him further. She swallowed, her throat dry.

"Please don't do that, Emperor. If you refuse us permission to go to Plautius's house we will stay in the city, but I cannot come with you." The regret was still there but that something else had sharpened her words and seeped over her face. It was fear, he knew it now. They had drawn level with a stone seat facing down an avenue of white, naked statues flanked by fruit trees and he sat, motioning her to a place beside him.

"Why not?" he half-shouted, showering her with spittle. She whitened, but the hands lying in her red lap did not stir.

"Because I am falling behind in my studies and my tutor is not pleased," she answered equably. "My father wishes me to spend more time attending to my duties."

"You have no husband, therefore few duties!" he said loudly, "and as for your studies, bring your tutor with you. You will not defy me, Gladys."

She looked at him for a long time, excuses flitting quickly through her mind, plausible lies, then she dismissed them all. "It is very hard to have two fathers," she said with a smile. "It seems that I cannot please both at once, but I have an idea. Come with us to the Silvanus estate, Emperor, just you alone, and thus I need defy no one. We will have a wonderful summer. I can read to you, and we can walk together in the hills, and Caelte will teach you my tongue and sing for you."

Laughter exploded from Claudius's entourage but the emperor did not share in it. He stared at her, his gaze intensifying, and she stared back smiling, a knot of terror in her chest. Then he leaned back, squinted up at the sun, and a tiny quirk came and went on his mouth.

"Gladys," he said. "I have no doubt that certain rumors have come to your ears, and you and your family have discussed them with gravity, and your father has ordered you to tell me that you can no longer come to me. I want the truth from you. No evasions. In return I will give you my thoughts."

The knot pulled tighter and Gladys could not breathe. Claudius saw her distress but made no move to help her. The listeners whispered among themselves. Then Gladys called up her Catuvellaun pride and took his hand.

"It is a matter of survival, dear Emperor," she said. "If you take me for your daughter, I will not live long. You must know this. Are you so selfish? Let there be no obligations between us, let us owe nothing to one another, so that I may go on living."

There was a breathless hush. His hand curled around hers as warmly as ever, but he no longer looked at her. His eyes were fixed on the pergola at the end of the avenue, a glimmer of white stone. Then suddenly he sneezed, withdrew his hand, and stood up. Astounded, she heard him change the subject, and the pain in her chest grew so acute that she wanted to go away and lie face down in the grass.

"I have a mind to tear up these gardens," he remarked, "and sink piles into the hill and extend the whole out over the lip. The view would be improved, don't you think?" Slowly they all straggled after him. He ignored Gladys until they had paced the full length of the avenue, then he turned to her, drawing her away from the others.

"Go home," he said to her shortly. "But I expect to see you back here tonight. And I have not yet made up my mind about the summer."

"Emperor," she replied, close to tears. "If you did not want the truth you should not have asked for it. You did not need to ask, for you knew it already. You are omnipotent, but not omnipresent."

"Men have died for less. You know that, don't you?"

"I am sorry. Give me leave to go, Claudius."

"Go."

She walked away from him blindly, came out from the shade of the trees into sunlight that beat up from the flagstones of the terrace in a jubilant dazzle, and her litter-bearers strolled toward her. But before she reached them Britannicus ran out from the gloom of the entrance hall, his dogs dancing with him.

"Gladys! Are you going home so soon? I am going to the market to watch the slave auctions. Come with me. We can go to the arena later."

"No." She did not look at him. She got onto her litter, twitching the curtains closed, but they were parted again immediately and she found his pert face thrust close to her own.

"Well, at least give me a kiss."

She regarded him coldly. "Someone should give you a whipping, Britannicus."

He flushed. "Upstart!" he shouted, and she pushed him away, lying back with her eyes squeezed shut as her slaves lifted her and set off down the steps. Save me, she thought, panic-stricken. I am in deep waters, over my head, and they will hold me under until I drown. The

476

litter was stuffy and hot but she did not open the curtains. When she was set down gently outside her own home she could hardly summon the strength to alight and walk between the pillars, a tunnel of drafty chillness, and into the sunny peristyle beyond.

Llyn was lying on his back, fingers laced behind his head and eyes on the puffy clouds sailing slowly high above. He heard her come and sat up, greeting her cheerfully, but when she walked past him without speaking he scrambled to his feet and strode after her, catching her by the shoulder and turning her around. "Did you stamp too hard on the royal toe?" he enquired with a smile, and then he saw her face. His arms went around her, and she suddenly clung to him sobbing. "So the poor old man is an emperor today," he commented dryly. "Come inside and drink some wine with me, Gladys. Father received some news after you left this morning that will make you feel better."

"I cannot take it anymore!" she choked. "It is like walking on fields of broken glass. Llyn, what shall I do? He will not allow me to go, I know it."

"You are a warrior," he soothed her, putting an arm around her and pushing her toward the house. "You will go on fighting."

Together they crossed the atrium, while the fish in the glittering pool darted away at the sound of their approach. They entered the reception room, which blazed with midmorning sunlight. Llyn put a goblet into her hand, and filled it full, then lifted his own high before her. "I offer a toast," he said. "To freedom."

Tears still trickled down her face. "Are you mocking me, Llyn?" she asked him, and he put a finger to his lips. "Claudius sent a copy of a dispatch he has just received from Gallus in Albion. The governor arrived and was met with complete confusion. The Twentieth has been smashed. Scapula's frontier is down. The west is wide open."

She stared at him, wide-eyed and tense. "Llyn! Ah! What has happened?"

"Someone in the mountains is busy pulling the tribes together again. I wonder who it is? Emrys, perhaps. Will you toast with me?"

She lifted her cup in both hands, her fears forgotten. "I will. To freedom, Llyn, and to hope." They drank and then stood smiling at each other, and the excitement seemed to leap and sparkle around them. Then Gladys put down her goblet. "Perhaps that is why the emperor was so abrupt," she said. "Where is father?"

"Out leaning on the wall, where he always goes when there is news. You go. I will stay here and finish the wine."

She ran out of the room, flew along the cloister, took the terrace steps three at a time. "Father!" she shouted and he turned, watching

477

her come speeding over the lawn, the emeralds at her throat glittering. He opened his arms and she flung herself upon him. "Is this the time?" she shouted breathlessly. "Is Rome finished in Albion?"

"I don't know, Gladys. Everything depends on what kind of a man Didius Gallus is. But this will be the summer of hope."

"Call Caelte! There must be a new song!"

He released her, threw back his head, and laughed, the grim face breaking into youthfulness. "Indeed!" he answered her. "I think we must sing. And drink, and dance. Let the emperor and his minions feast on each other. We will dine on freedom!"

Claudius soon recovered his temper, and Caradoc's slaves prepared to empty the big house as the weather rapidly heated toward summer. But the emperor remained silent with regard to the situation in Albion. Gladys tried to draw him out but he would not be prodded, and the family left Rome carrying their anxious ignorance with them. The country estate of Aulus Plautius lay two days to the north of Rome, a sprawling stone mansion originally built by Plautius's great-grandfather and added to cheerfully and haphazardly by the succeeding generations of the Silvanus family, so that now it resembled an airy warren, casual and comfortable yet with an unplanned beauty. A day further north lay Plautius's farm, and after a week of sleeping in the sun and kicking the dust Llyn took a horse and a slave and went there, reappearing every once in a while, bronzed and acid-tongued as ever, only to vanish again to ride Plautius's fields, argue with his stewards, and dream of the honor-price he had never seen. Occasionally he accompanied Gladys back to the city, for the emperor insisted on her presence out of some perverse fit of pique, and Gladys made the journey to Rome four times before the season ended. But Llyn always returned to the farm, much to Caradoc's surprise. They all waited impatiently for news from Albion, but the thick, cloudless days followed one another and it was as if the province of Britannia no longer existed. They ceased to speak of it to one another but it lay there heavy and sad between them, the wondering, the hours in which hope and certainty would alternately become the knowledge that freedom could never return either to them or Albion. Then Plautius came, and Caradoc pressed him for something, some word, some rumor, but Aulus knew nothing other than that Gallus had mobilized the legions.

"I no longer have the military contacts I once had," he told Caradoc as they sat under the shade of the cloister one broiling afternoon. "And my friends are like myself, growing old and drifting far from the heart of active service. If I knew anything, I would tell you."

"I want to know how the Twentieth was defeated," Caradoc said, "and how the frontier went down so easily. Someone is there in the west, someone with a new authority, and I cannot sleep for wondering who it is."

"Do you think the Druids have chosen another arviragus?"

"It is possible. But he could not be a western chief, Aulus. The Druithin would fear internal jealousies. I lie in bed, trying to imagine who has left the lowlands."

"What about Venutius? He and his wife have finally parted, or so Scapula's last dispatch would have us believe."

"He has left her before, only to go running back," Caradoc answered, his voice curiously flat. "And besides, he is not trusted in the west. Yet who else is there? Whoever it is, I am sure that he is not arviragus yet. The time is not right."

"Could it be a woman?"

Caradoc smiled across at his friend. "No. An arviragus is always male. The Druithin have never yet gambled on a woman, either in Albion or Gaul. No situation of that kind has ever arisen."

They drank their chilled wine in a companionable silence for a while, looking out from the breeze-stirred shadow to where the high sun beat white upon the garden, then Plautius took out a cloth and wiped his hot face. "Why do the Druids hate the Romans so much, Caradoc? Why do they keep the peoples' hostilities burning? We are not harsh masters. Indeed, we bring prosperity and stability to all our provinces. It seems to me that they are guilty of all the unnecessary blood that has been shed in Britannia."

Caradoc watched the listless air stir the topmost branches of the dusty plane trees and his fingers strayed to his throat where the magic egg still lay hidden under his tunic. Once, he thought, I would have vehemently denied that Rome offered anything but terror and death to its conquered nations, but now I must admit that what Plautius speaks is part of a truth. Have I changed? Has that slow death I saw in the emperor's eyes when I stood before him in the Curia begun to creep on me? I hate the city of Rome. I despise the soldiers, the land and money grabbers, the superior, high-handed officials, yet I have met men of honor, like Plautius himself, and in doing so I have found kin. Are the Druithin relics of an age that should not linger, manipulating simple and guileless people into a different subjection? What do the Druithin fear? What is so precious to them that it must be defended at all costs? But then his memories lifted him out of the sluggish Roman afternoon and he continued to gaze at the garden without seeing it. He remembered the master on Mona with his nightmare eyes, his dark magic. He saw Bran's face, bearded, alert, laying a certain choice before him in the wet dimness of his own forest, while behind him Camulodunon was consumed by Roman fire. There had always been choice. Freedom meant choice. Rome removed the choices. Freedom could not exist without honor, and honor went hand in hand with freedom. I have not changed, he thought. I have mellowed, I have allowed myself to become a chameleon, but my heart still asks why there is no peace for me here.

Plautius was waiting for his reply, and Caradoc blinked and answered curtly. "With or without the Druithin, the hostilities will never die. The decisions of a Council have always overridden the directives of a Druid, Aulus, and it would be a lie to say that the tribes are under the thumb of the wise men. Rome was not invited into Albion. Rome came like a thief and a murderer, willing to kill in order to snatch land, people, and treasure that was never hers. How would you feel if this country lay under the rule of the tribes who had taken everything, including your values, from you, and then told you that you ought to be grateful? You would like to believe that the Druithin keep the people from peaceful submission, but it is not true. Vercingetorix . . ." He stopped suddenly, his throat swelling. Vercingetorix. How could I forget you? They encircled you. They starved and flogged you. You flung your sword before Julius Caesar and knelt before him when you could no longer bear to see the people suffer. And for loving the soil that nourished you they put you in a hole without sunlight. I sit here discussing freedom as though it were some abstract idea brought out to pass the time of day, when you felt the longing for it like fire in your sinews and your blood. Seven years you squatted in that darkness, before Caesar remembered you and sent someone to strangle you.

"Yes?" Plautius prompted, and Caradoc turned to him, tasting suddenly the bittersweet blossoming of compromise on his tongue.

"Forgive me, but I do not want to talk about it anymore."

Plautius nodded equably, seeing the hurt and quietly saluting the pride that buried it almost instantaneously. "I should not have brought up the subject. But it would have pleased me, Caradoc, to see your religion become fashionable in Rome as it might have but for the Druids implacability. The emperor had no choice but to proscribe it as treasonous. The Jews could also have worshipped in peace but for their constant intriguing. Now the followers of The Way must die as well. Religion should never be mixed with politics."

"Religion is politics. Religion is life. It will survive after the empire has collapsed into chaos. I would rather see every Druid wiped from the face of the earth than see the empress with oak leaves and bronze rings in her hair, or the Greek freemen sniggering as they try to fathom a spell or enliven their boredom bandying truths about. Speak of something else!"

"Very well. I am expecting a guest this evening. I think you will like him. He is anxious to meet you, but the last time he saw you the earthwalls of Camulodunon stood between you."

"Who is it?"

"Allow me to surprise you, Caradoc. Are you expecting Gladys?"

Caradoc glanced at him uneasily. "Yes, and Llyn will be with her. Claudius knows full well how he is putting her in danger, yet he has not gone to his summer residence and Gladys has been back and forth to Rome three times."

"Have you spoken to him?"

"No. Gladys wants to accomplish this thing on her own."

"She is no longer a budding warrior, Caradoc, though perhaps she thinks she is. She has softened, as your other daughter has softened, since you settled on the Palatine. She should not be too confident of repulsing any attack."

"She may have softened in body, but not in heart," Caradoc retorted. "And it is for her heart that I fear. Britannicus is an old man with the charming face of a child, and Nero . . ."

Eurgain and Gladys appeared, still out of earshot, striding side by side and deep in conversation, and Caradoc watched them come with a lightening gladness. He did not know his children as well as he knew wife and sister. Llyn, Gladys, and the younger Eurgain brought to him only the loneliness of change, but the two older women made him remember who he was. Plautius also saw them, but made no move to rise.

"Nero has the seeds of both greatness and corruption in him," he said. "When he was born his father Gnaeus commented in public that the son could not help but grow to be a monster considering the depravity of both his parents. Did you know that?" Caradoc shook his head. "But he is still in the hands of his tutors, Seneca and Bhurrus, both struggling to counteract his mother's pernicious influence. So far they have done well. Nero did a good job as praetor while Claudius was away last year. There is ability in him."

"It will not last long," Caradoc snapped back. "One day he will tire of his tutors, and then Rome will get the kind of emperor she deserves."

"Britannicus will rule."

Caradoc looked around and had to smile at Plautius's cynical face, though his thoughts were dark. "You know he will not live long enough to wear a toga, let alone govern the empire."

The women were pacing the cloister now, their sandals patting the cool paving. Both were dressed in short, sleeveless tunics, their hair bound high, their brown arms clicking with bracelets, and they came up to the men and sank onto their heels.

"Give me your wine, Caradoc, it is so hot," Eurgain said, and he passed it to her. She drank thirstily.

"Gladys is back," the girl's aunt said, sitting down and leaning against her husband's legs. "I saw Llyn going down through the vineyard." As she spoke the words the young Gladys herself appeared, coming slowly down the long pillared walk with her slave behind her, black hair loose, and Caradoc thought how it could have been his sister nearly ten years ago, fighting to hold to the love that had been more to her than kin or honor, alone here with her Roman husband in this lovely foreign house. He looked at her. Plautius had a hand on her shoulder, with a touch of protective concern, a reminder to whom she belonged, and as his daughter bent to kiss him Caradoc stilled the moment of annoyance. In some subtle, quiet way, Gladys did not belong to the House Catuvellaun anymore. There was often a faint strain about her as she sought to be Roman wife and barbarian's sister, and this more than anything else convinced Caradoc that he was old. His years were not many, thirty-eight, and Eurgain still had the face that had meant sanity to him in the mountains, but he knew that he was as used up and useless as Cunobelin had been in his last years. The younger Gladys looked drawn, and she murmured a few words of greeting to them and went into the house. She did not reappear until the evening meal.

In the coolness of evening Plautius's guest arrived. The steward ushered him into the reception room where the family was gathered, sitting clustered by an open window that gave out onto the scent of roses and a velvet darkness, and Plautius rose to embrace him. "Rufus! How pleased I am that you could come. I have been playing a game tonight, for you did not know that our noble enemy is here and he did not know who was coming." Gladys rose also and kissed him with affection, then left him to Plautius, who led him further into the room to face the enquiring eyes of the others. "Caradoc, this is Rufus Pudens, who was my second-in-command in Albion. Rufus, here is the man who escaped us."

Pudens looked startled, then a smile crept over his face, broadened, and his hand went out. "Caradoc! Many times I have wanted to meet you. I knew you were in Rome but I have been in the east with my legion and then on business at my estates. Welcome to Rome!"

Caradoc took his wrist, searching the features. He was tall for a Roman, with straight shoulders under the white toga. His nose was straight also. His black eyebrows, the alignment of eyes and thin

482

cheeks, the fringe of black hair, were all straight and clear-cut, almost painfully so, and he carried with him the brisk air of the serving soldier. He took Caradoc's wrist in the native fashion, still smiling, and Caradoc could find nothing to say. He was conscious all at once of the irony of the situation, and he quickly turned to Eurgain.

"I thank you for your greeting. This is my wife Eurgain, my daughter, also Eurgain, and my son Llyn."

"Well, sir," Llyn said as Pudens turned to him. "Tell us what you thought of Albion, if you remember. You must have seen many another defeated people since then and perhaps we all look the same after a while."

Pudens's dark eyes became watchful, and he answered bluntly, taking the goblet offered to him by Plautius's steward. "Albion is unique, Llyn."

"Linus," Llyn snapped, and Pudens's eyebrows rose.

"I understand. Linus. Your aunt also refused to allow us to call her by name, but now she does not mind when I twist my tongue around it. Albion will always be a mystery. I have never seen such squalid living conditions coupled with such delicate and marvelous works of art, such noble and proud people. I could never decide whether they were very innocent or very clever."

Admiration crept into Llyn's eyes. "I think I will like you," he said gruffly. "I might even tell you one day whether we are indeed very stupid or more highly civilized than Romans will ever be." He sat down abruptly and went back to the wine, and Plautius's steward came to announce that it was time to dine. Gladys had still not come down.

Pudens was placed on a couch opposite Caradoc, and though he talked gravely and with a friendly attention his eyes kept straying to the lined, still face framed in gray-and-black waving hair, and finally Caradoc leaned forward.

"You may stare at me if you like, Pudens, I don't mind at all. Look well, and then tell me what you see."

Pudens was not embarrassed. "Thank you, I will," he replied. "I have long wanted to study your face." He propped himself higher on his couch and Caradoc lay motionless, his eyes smiling faintly. Then Pudens gave a nod that was half-gratitude, half-confirmation.

"My sister used to tell her children that if they did not go to sleep the monster of Albion would get them," he said. "She meant you, Lord." They all laughed, and in that moment Pudens thought, I see a strength that was once power, grooves of agonies that still make scars. I see eyes that grieve quietly and are still full of visions, eyes that hide far more than they reveal. No wonder the empress was tormented for a while. Aloud he said, "I see one of the greatest men of our age. Forgive me, Lord. I do not mean to discomfit you, but I have heard many men speak of you in this way and I must now confess that I agree." He shrugged helplessly. "You are arviragus. You will know far better than I what that really means, but I was in Albion long enough to begin to understand. Now may I impose another indignity upon you?"

Caradoc smiled, then gave one of his rare laughs. "I should have known that any friend of Aulus's would be thoroughly honest. Attack my dignity if you will!"

Pudens sat up, his food forgotten. "Tell me how Ostorious Scapula came to defeat you. Only four hundred of your warriors were killed. Why was it not possible to rally the rest and make a victory?"

Caradoc gazed at him, the smile slowly dying. There was a valley, he thought. Ah Camulos, yes, I remember. The moment the master spoke of, the moment when the path of destiny forked, and I sat on a rock, not knowing which way to go. And you died, Cin. They shot an arrow into your back. He sat up deliberately, and taking a napkin he made it into a crescent and laid it on the table, his eyes meeting Eurgain's for a fleeting second and reading his own pain and bereavement mirrored there. "I will answer you," he said steadily, and his hands moved swiftly, scooping up pieces of bread and utensils to make two armies. "The napkin is the place of engagement. There was a valley . . ."

Plautius drew his couch nearer and the slaves stood patiently, waiting to lay another course on the table, but the three men were soon engrossed in Caradoc's little tableau. When Gladys heard her husband say, "Why put the Demetae on the flank if they were unreliable?" and saw Llyn edge closer to his father, prepared to argue also, she signaled to the standing servants.

"Put it all down here. We can serve ourselves tonight." She smiled across at Eurgain. "Why *did* he put the Demetae there? It seems to me that if they had been in the center, and then broken, their places could have been quickly filled by others."

"Rome would have filled it first and, besides, he put them on the flank so that Sine and I could buttress them with the women. He thought that it was better to be pressed on the flank than have the tribes divided down the middle and the two halves isolated."

They ate and talked, stopping every once in a while to listen to Caradoc's even voice interspersed with Llyn's abrupt, impatient comments. "Caradoc is happy," Gladys said softly, "but you are so quiet tonight, Eurgain. Is something wrong?"

The girl lifted her blonde-haloed face to her aunt and smiled. "No, nothing. I was out looking at the grapes today, before it got too hot. They are still green but filling nicely. I think Aulus will have a good crop this year." Her mother glanced at her out of the corner of her eye. She was a mystery, this girl. Thoroughly self-contained, with a quiet assurance, she seemed to fear nothing, or if she did she kept it to herself. Eurgain had wanted to talk to her about her wanderings in the city but somehow had not dared, and it was certain that she did not drink and gamble night after night as Llyn did. She had conquered her sword with quiet stubbornness, fought beside the other women without complaint, and been blooded, yet she did not yearn after Albion as Gladys and the others did. She seemed to accept her exile calmly, realistically, and her mother, watching her from day to day, knew that in Albion, this child would have eventually left Camulodunon and vanished into the magic-drenched fogs of Mona. No one crossed the younger Eurgain. There was an authority about her, exercised only rarely, a cool self-possession that brooked no resistance, yet was not Llyn's bullying rudeness. Her mother did not know it, but she was the distillation of Eurgain's own essence, stronger, deeper, more powerful. The invisible stamp of Druithin calling was on her. Her mother met the formidable challenge of her blue eyes, and smiled.

"The crop will be heavy if the local children can be kept away from it. I wonder if I should send someone to see to Gladys?"

Her daughter shook her head. "She will come down before long. She and Caelte are in her rooms, singing. I heard their voices as I passed the door."

The men talked on, hunched over the table, and then there was a flurry of movement outside the archway and Gladys and Caelte swept in. Caelte hugged his harp to his breast. When Gladys saw a stranger at table she paused. "Oh Aulus, I'm sorry," she said. "If I had known that you had a guest I would not have stayed in my room." Pudens had risen to his feet. The other daughter, he thought. Of course. Like a man awakened by shafts of sunlight lying across his face, he stared at her, the emperor's favorite, Nero's infatuation. She was dressed in native fashion. A long, midnight-blue tunic fell from her shoulders to brush the floor, belted tightly by a thin, intricately tooled leather belt. Her hair was loose and falling straight and shining to her waist, and it was prisoned to her head by a circlet of silver surmounted by one large, milky green stone that dully reflected the candlelight and sat in the middle of her forehead. Around her wrists and on her fingers the same stone caused the light to slide softly over her skin, and as she stepped to her uncle he saw another band of silver around one ankle. Plautius introduced them and she took his wrist firmly. "Forgive my bad manners," she smiled. "You must put it down to my barbarian temperament."

"You look very much like your aunt," he observed, and the smile widened.

"Then I must be beautiful, for my aunt is," she mocked him gently, her eyes sparkling into his own, but then he saw the shadows under them, the faint marks of nervous strain, and in her gaiety there was an undercurrent of tautness. He felt all at once desperately sorry for her, why he did not know. She reminded him of someone, and as she found her couch and the others began to eat again he tried to remember who it was. Then he knew, and it was all he could do to stop himself from exlaiming aloud. She was like the Icenian lady, Boudicca. Not in the way she looked but in the angry misery inside. You hate us, don't you? he had said to her, and she had replied affirmatively with brutal frankness. There had been something beneath the honesty, a vast lake of sorrow, and it had touched him. He could not tear his gaze away from Gladys as she ate, and he wondered how old she was. Not more than seventeen, he was sure. He quickly reminded himself that he was well into his thirties, and at last turned to Caradoc, who had made some remark to him, but he could not free himself of the consciousness of her presence.

Later they drifted out onto the lawn and sat or lay in the dry grass, wrapped in whispering darkness. As the stars flared silver and the moon glowed white and small, Caelte sang for them, one soft song blending into another, his head bent over the strings of his little harp. Plautius and Pudens listened contentedly, enjoying the alien flavor of the music, but the Catuvellaunians hung onto it with an intensity that Pudens could feel, and it gave him pleasure. The bard was folding back memories for them, showing them years gone by. So strong was his ability that Pudens found himself gradually drawn into half-glimpsed dreams of places he had never seen, in times he had never known, as though the language, which he had once learned hastily and had as hastily forgotten, was once more insinuating itself behind his mouth and under his skin. Caelte glanced at him and smiled, and Pudens wondered for the first time since he and Plautius had left Albion whether magic was more than a matter of the imagination.

After an hour of wandering melodies Caelte suddenly sat straighter and changed key, and the Catuvellauns' eyes swiveled to him, glittering. He began another song, plaintive, wild, one that Pudens could not remember having heard before, and it brought a shiver of delight and fear to his spine. One by one they joined in, and in the dimness

486

Pudens saw their hands reach out unobtrusively and clasp. Immediately he felt shut out, and the gentle thread of communion in his mind snapped, yet the song held him. There were tears in the voices, even in Linus's warm tenor, but the white faces swaying in the night were all dry. When it was over Llyn yawned. "I am sober," he remarked. "Do I get a laurel wreath? I am also tired." He got up and walked into the house, the shadows opening to swallow him, and the others rose also, politely bidding Pudens a good night.

Starlight was sunk deep into the stone on Gladys's forehead as she came to him, and he searched her black, veiled eyes, wanting idiotically to put his hands over them, to feel the lashes flutter against his palms. "Will you come again?" she asked him, and when he had nodded and she had turned away he remembered what the gems she wore were called. They were moonstones.

"Stay the night, Rufus," Plautius said to him. "It is very late. You can go on to Rome in the morning."

Moonstones. He made an effort and turned his attention to his host. "Thank you, Aulus, I think I might. I am not expected until the day after tomorrow."

"Good. We can talk. I want to know how the Pannonian legions have survived without me!"

"You left an enormous gulf to fill, Aulus, and you know it! Goodnight!"

"Goodnight. Gladys will show you to the guest room."

For a moment Pudens's heart gave a jolt, then he laughed at himself as he left the garden. Stupid fool. In the morning you will see her as she really is, without her jewels, without her beautiful soft gown, and the sun will not play the tricks on you that moonlight and candlelight do. She is a child.

The next morning Pudens talked of military matters with Caradoc and Plautius, and in the afternoon they all went riding over the windy hills surrounding the estate. He had been prepared to dismiss his reaction to Gladys as a momentary fascination but when she and Llyn came running down to the stable where he and the others waited for the horses to be led out, he found himself fighting a new entanglement. She was clad in native breeches and short tunic, and her feet were bare. Her hair hung in four tight braids, her arms were free of ornament. She greeted him gaily over the clatter of hoofs on the courtyard, and with one bound she leaped onto her mount's back, holding her seat easily as the startled horse shied and chaffered Llyn. He and the rest of the family mounted also and trotted out the gate and along the road that ran through the grove of trees Plautius's father had planted. Pudens kneed his horse until he was jogging beside her and she looked across at him and smiled. The signs of strain had gone.

"Where are your estates, sir?" she asked him, and Plautius called out behind her, "You are riding next to one of the richest men in the empire, Gladys. He owns half of Umbria."

"And I suppose you own the other half, my uncle!" she retorted, and Pudens laughed.

"No," he said. "The emperor owns the rest. I am on my way to Rome to hire a new steward."

"Rome is that way," she pointed, grinning. "Hire yourself a scout while you are about it. You have a terrible sense of direction."

True, he thought. Suddenly I do not know where I am going. I thought I did, but you sit there with your braids bouncing against your supple back, the sun in your eyes and your toes dusty, and you have hidden my chosen path from me. She dug her heels into her mount and streaked away, Llyn after her, and he watched her go, wishing that the afternoon would laze on forever.

He did not go to Rome the next day. Somehow plans were made that he wanted to share, and he spent another two nights in the quietness of Plautius's one remaining guest room, lying sleepless and restless, thinking of her lying somewhere under the same roof, deep in her dreams. He rose early on the third day, and leaving a message of thanks with one of Plautius's servants he slipped out of the house, picked up his horse and his slaves, and swung onto the road to the city while the sun shimmered red and new on his left. With a sense of depression and frustration, he knew that he was in love with this girl who was little more than a child. He did not want to be in love. He had made a good career that fulfilled him, and he had carefully planned its course. He had a mistress on his estates in Umbria and another in Ostia where he went when he could in order to see to his ships. His family often urged him to marry, but he could imagine the buzz of outrage there would be among his sisters if he were to wed a barbarian, and a half-child at that. Ridiculous, he thought to himself. She would never have me anyway. She is less than half my age. Yet he could not prevent his thoughts from diving around her like fleet swallows.

Caradoc and the others returned to Rome a month after Pudens had gone, and Claudius immediately called for Gladys. She had made the journey regularly from the estate to the palace in spite of Caradoc's anger, and though she tried to talk to the emperor he either behaved as though the words had never left her mouth or he refused the subject as soon as she broached it. She did not know what to do. She felt trapped. A measure of security came to her as the visits went on and nothing happened, but Caradoc grew more and more uneasy until at last he told her that she must either tell Claudius that she would come no more, or he himself would do it. She promised, flying into an uncharacteristic rage which betrayed her heightening nervousness, but she returned from the palace white-faced and exhausted.

"Did you tell him?" her father demanded, and she nodded.

"Yes, I did. I said no pretty words. But he just looked at me, and smiled, and patted my hand. He gave me no answer, he never answers me, and soon he will send for me again."

Caradoc looked at the tight shoulders and shaking fingers. "He will answer me," he said roughly. "I am tired of this game, Gladys. He is using you, taking his wife's attentions from himself and fixing them on you, and it is time to tell him that he may not trifle with your life as though it were a trinket. Agrippina will not warn me again, and her patience must be running out."

"I do not believe that he has no affection for me."

"Of course he loves you, but in his own selfish, old-man's way. The next time you are sent for, I will go."

"He will lose patience with you. He imagines slights and insults where there are none, and he has slain because of a glance his way."

"Then for once I will give him a real fear."

"Father!"

He rounded on her savagely. "Would you rather I cowered at home until your body is found floating on the Tiber? Honor demands . . ."

"Judgment," she choked, her mouth quivering. "And sacrifices, and retribution. I know. All useless, father! Sometimes I think that we are all marked for a violent death. Before long, someone will put a knife in Llyn when he is drunk, because he will not curb his tongue. Nero or Agrippina or even Claudius himself will shorten my years. Eurgain must eventually be arrested because of those mad followers of The Way, and she will die in some monstrous fashion. You believe that it was hard to be ricon of Camulodunon, and harder still to put on the yoke of arviragus, but, oh Camulos! It is a daily torment for us to be your children here in Rome!" She made as if to run from the room but his arm shot out and pulled her back. He thrust his ravaged face close to her own, restraining her gently but firmly.

"Tell me this, Gladys, and tell me in truth," he whispered. "Has the time to choose death already come? Shall I take a knife to you all and then to myself? Would that be enough to retrieve your honor, and mine, Llyn's and Eurgain's and your mother's?"

"No!" she spat back at him. "That moment passed forever when Claudius pardoned you! Now there is a new battle. We fight to live, we fight with everything we have for as long as we can, for this city is still the enemy, and we are still the warriors of the mountains." She tore away from him and walked quickly away, calling for Caelte, and he stood shaken, unable any longer to recognize himself, or her.

Rufus Pudens called the next afternoon. He was shown into Caradoc's reception room, and together they sat facing the atrium, watching sunlight glint on the water of the pool and lie somnolent upon the red tiling. They talked easily, but Pudens sensed that behind Caradoc's polite comments the mind was far away, pursuing some other train of thought. The house was quiet. The slaves could be heard upstairs, their soft voices echoing faintly down the central hall, and birds perched on the guttering above the pool and fluttered and chirped, watching the fish below, but the pillared rooms sat silent and empty. Conversation began to lapse, and then Pudens said bluntly, "Lord, I am not certain of the customs of your people and so I may offend you. If I do so, forgive me. I would like to address myself to your daughter Gladys."

Caradoc dragged his gaze away from the water and looked at him blankly. "I do not understand. You are quite free to address yourself to any of us when it pleases you."

"I did not mean like that." Pudens searched the other's face, feeling as he did so the weight of dignity and alien experience that separated them. The man sitting loosely beside him, dark hair resting on scarlet shoulders, an elbow on the arm of his chair and fingers curling around the cleft chin, was no more than four years older than he was himself, yet Pudens knew he could never approach Caradoc as an equal. He was rich, influential, well-educated, but could not match the agelessness of the eyes that suddenly became alert and probed him. Caradoc smiled.

"Ah. I think I understand you now. Do you have a wife, Pudens?"

"No."

"Then the matter is none of my business. I ask only that you treat with her in honesty, and that you do not forget a young girl's freshness and innocence may seem charming to an older man, but only for a while."

"I believe that your women fought and died before they reached Gladys's age," Pudens rejoined gently. "How old is she?"

"You must discover that for yourself." Caradoc stirred. The fingers moved to run over his face in a gesture of weariness. "Sometimes I think she is older than I."

"May I visit her often?"

"As often as you like, but I ought to warn you that before long you may not want to be seen in this house." The smile came and went but it was not warm. It held only grimness, and Pudens raised his eyebrows. "I think I am about to make the emperor very angry," Caradoc explained. "If you are concerned with the imperial favor, leave us alone. Gladys will have finished her studies by now. Go and look for her in the garden."

The man bowed and left, and Caradoc watched him cross the altrium, a tall, black-haired soldier with an easy stride, his toga billowing white from his straight back. When he was out of sight Caradoc rose and went to the foot of the stairs, raising his eyes to the landing, squinting in the sun. "Eurgain," he called. "Come down." Presently she appeared and glided to him, and he beckoned and led her around the pool and through the cloister. Before them the terrace opened out, and then the steps and the long green sweep of the lawns. Together they stood watching as Pudens went in under the shade of a tree whose branches overhung the wall and sheltered Gladys. They saw him greet her where she sat, with her embroidery frame before her. Eurgain looked at Caradoc enquiringly.

"I am not sure," he said slowly, "but I think that you are looking at the man who will deliver Gladys from the empress's spite."

She understood at once and he studied her face as she scanned the bright garden, then she turned to him abruptly. "Only if she loved him, and it is too much to hope that her affections may go to a man over twice her age."

"Then you would hope for this?"

"She will never see Albion again," Eurgain answered bitterly. "None of us will. There are no young chiefs to court her. I can only hope that he will love her as Aulus has loved your sister."

"Do you still love me, Eurgain?"

She stepped back startled. "That question comes from you as though we were already looking back upon a lifetime gone," she said, wondering why his self-sufficiency was suddenly shaken. "Why do you need my reassurances? Have I not always been beside you when you needed me?"

"I feel old!" he burst out angrily. "There is not a man in Rome who could best me, my body is strong and healthy, but I feel as though I should squat in a corner on a pile of blankets and relinquish my life as my father did. I should have died beside Cin, in the mud, with an arrow between my shoulder blades."

"Perhaps you did," she said softly, and the purposeless rage in him brimmed over.

"Did *you*?" he snarled, then his arms went around her and he kissed her. "Forgive me," he said huskily. "I have wasted your life, Eurgain."

"No. There is only waste when love dies, and I love you."

Gladys heard him approach and looked up from her work. "So it is you," she said. "If you are looking for my father, he is somewhere in the house."

Pudens greeted her. "I have already spoken to him," he replied, and she glanced at him quickly before dropping her gaze. "I did not know that Albion's warrior women were interested in embroidery. What are you making?"

She sighed. "It is supposed to be a hanging for my emperor, but I don't know now whether he will want it. I have been learning to embroider but I must confess that I find it very difficult and I think that when I have finished this I will not attempt it again." She waved at the frame, tucking her needle into the cloth and rising, and he came closer, bending over it, acutely aware of her brown face frowning inches from his own.

"You have almost completed it." As he looked at it his interest was aroused. There was an ocean of peacock blue, flanked on one side by a scarlet eagle, beak open and talons hooked, and on the other by a bird without plumage, black as night. The eagle's claws were tipped in red but the black bird stood on silver—graceful, aloof, somehow above the eagle's blatant predatory stance. He was about to stand straight when something else caught his attention and he peered again, hearing her laugh quietly beside him. The black bird's eye was not an eye. There was a woman's face, contorted into anguish, and her hair flowed out of the socket to mingle with the bird's shining feathers. "I understand the eagle," he said at last, "but what is this bird?"

"She is the Raven of Nightmares." With a slap of her hand, Gladys spun the frame so that the picture was hidden. "She cannot be the Raven of Battle, for all battles are over, nor is she the Raven of Panic, for those days are also gone. Only the nightmares remain."

He did not know what to say. He went and sat on the wall, looking away from her and out over the haze of the river and the city, and after a moment she folded her arms and spoke calmly. "Britannicus wants to climb onto my back and ride into his father's affections," she said, "and Nero wants me on my back for other reasons. What do you want of me, patrician?"

His head came round, and he found himself looking into eyes as full of dark experience and inexplicable knowledge as her father's. Nothing, he should have said. I want to pass the time of day, that is all.

492

But instead he said quietly, "I think I am in love with you, Gladys. I want nothing from you that might hurt you."

She expressed no surprise, nor did she simper or laugh. "You can say this after having met me such a short time ago?" she asked him, and he left the wall.

"I am no longer a boy, falling in and out of love for fun, nor do I want to grab at love for the pleasure I can wring from it," he replied. "I am thirty-four years old, I am set in my habits, and I have a family that will be horror-stricken when I tell them I want to marry a young barbarian. But I can handle these things if you will tell me that I may again sit with you in your garden and make a fool of myself."

She studied the face, seeing there the pleasant arrogance of his blood, the marks made upon it by his soldiering life—the face of a man used to having his orders obeyed, who knew his own direction. "Roman men marry money, property, a vehicle to carry their children," she said softly. "I must be more than those things to the man I marry, Rufus. I have been reared very differently from your sisters."

"I know. You forget that I have had a taste of Albion's gently reared sword-women! How old are you, Gladys?"

She answered him with a straight face, but humor lurked in her eyes. "I am thirty-four." He began to smile and she came up to him, "And you are sixteen. Am I right?"

"I think you are indeed."

"Then let us walk by the fountains, and you can tell me about this snobbish family of yours."

For an hour they strolled Caradoc's paved paths and lush, carefully groomed lawns, standing to watch the fountains spew rainbow-colored water that arched and glittered in the late summer sunlight; then Pudens took his leave. "I was actually on my way to the baths," he said. "Martial will be wondering where I am, for I promised to meet him there."

"Martial? The poet Martial? He is your friend?"

Pudens smiled at her obvious delight. "Yes. Would you like to meet him?"

"Very much, and I am sure Caelte would as well. Bring him to dinner soon. I will ask father for a time. Do you live far from here?"

He drew her back to the wall and pointed down and to the south. "I rent three rooms in a house on the Clivus Victoriae," he said. "You cannot see it for the trees, but it is almost directly below here. I am seldom in Rome, and when I am it is usually for business, so three rooms are sufficient."

"The gray stone house that fronts the street directly? I know it. Tell me, Rufus, do you have many friends at court?"

He was pierced by the hint of pathos in her tone. "I have a few," he said simply, and took her hand. "Now I must go. I am afraid I have become thirty-four again. Forgive my stupidity, Gladys, and let me come to see you again."

"Tomorrow!" she shouted as he walked toward the gate, and he turned and waved before disappearing among the trees.

He spent three hours at the baths, but it was only when he and Martial lay side by side on the boards in order to be oiled that he unburdened himself. Martial grinned across at him. "Your dear mother will die of shock," he said. "And truthfully, Rufus, I myself think you are touched. You will end up blowing her nose for her when she cries, and singing to her when she has nightmares."

"She wants to meet you. Her bard will enjoy you as well."

The black, heavy eyebrows went up. "Oh. Then she must be reasonably civilized if she appreciates my work. But I don't know about the bard. All love and flowers, I suppose."

Pudens saw himself back in the garden on Plautius's estate, in the night, and Caelte's head was bent over his magic. "Not exactly. Why don't you reserve judgment until you meet them?"

Martial groaned as the slave's hands dug into his spine. "Don't rub so hard! Well, what do we do? Sit cross-legged in a circle and tear at beef with our hands?"

"They will end up tearing at you with their hands if you behave like this and believe me, Martial, I would sooner face a lion's claws than the anger of that family. When were you last at court?"

"Three weeks ago, when the emperor returned. He did not approve of my verses and told me so, which of course ensures that they will be repeated all over the city. I had commented on the empress's crow's-feet."

"Then I am surprised that you did not see my Gladys. She is the emperor's darling."

Martial whistled and sat up, waving the slave away. "So it is *that* barbarian! And already she is 'my Gladys.' It looks as though I am going to be the only eligible bachelor left in Rome. Whatever will Lucia say?"

"It is none of her business."

"True. Pass her on to me, Rufus, if under your indulgent hand she has not become too unruly."

"Perfume, sir?" the slave enquired, and Martial spread his arms wide.

"Of course. Let me know when I am to appear on the hill, Rufus. I really am delighted to be of such interest to foreigners."

494

Pudens smiled at him. "I will see you in a day or two, Martial, and I will ask Lucia whether she wants to join your household."

The poet cocked an eye at him. "You'd better wait a while. Your little barbarian might disappoint you."

"Never." Pudens picked up his towel and went out.

For two days he visited Gladys, walking with her in the garden, sitting with her in the shelter of the cloister while a swift squall of rain combed the roses free of their wilting petals. On the second night, Martial came to dinner and charmed them all with his scathing wit. "I am a satirist," he told Caelte after hearing him sing. "You are the true poet," but Caelte disagreed.

"We are brothers and besides, sir, I am more musician than poet. Melody comes to me more easily than words."

The third day was cold, for summer was almost over, and Pudens had to spend it sitting in the senate chamber. Gladys wandered through the house touching this and that, looking out at the windy garden, caught in the seemingly timeless lull between the seasons. The slaves had stoked the hypocaust, and warm air followed her in and out of the halls, up and down the stairs. Eurgain kept to her room and talked quietly with Chloe, her body servant. Llyn had disappeared soon after daylight, and Caradoc and his wife sat on in the triclinium with Caelte. As Gladys drifted past the archway she heard her mother say, "But there must be news. Someone is keeping it from us, that is all," and Gladys's steps slowed until she halted, reaching out to lean against a pillar with her eyes closed. News. Day follows day. We eat, sleep, and laugh, we dress and go about the city, while in Albion's forests children die, and the struggle for survival goes on. Beneath the masks that we prepare for each passing hour are gargoyle faces of longing and despair, and my emperor knows this and holds all news close to himself, to punish us. Shall I take you at your word, Rufus Pudens, and marry you, and cast another warm cloak around my own small unhappiness? What agonies of love and regret must have torn you, my aunt, as you fought to decide whether to give your freedom for Plautius or sink it deep back into Albion's soil. I do not believe I could make that decision. She walked on, melancholy and slow-thinking, out under the windy sky.

The evening meal was eaten in near silence, and Llyn had still not appeared when the family finally left the triclinium to the slaves and scattered. Gladys, passing through the deep shadows that always lurked in the corners of the atrium, on her way to her rooms, caught the movement of a darker shade beyond the lamps' glow, and paused, stiffening. The shade moved again and a hand came out of the gloom, beckoning to her. With her fingers on her little knife she turned toward it. A man waited in the covering shadow behind the pillars—short, bulky, dressed in a ragged tunic. His feet were shod in dirty sandals, and his face was covered by a black, greasy beard. As she approached him he reached out and pulled her deeper into the dimness. "Who are you?" she said loudly. "How did you get into the house?"

He put a finger to his lips. "Quiet, Lady. I come from Linus. He is in trouble. He is gambling tonight with strangers. He has lost all his money, and the men he is with will not take a promise of payment tomorrow. They are holding him until you bring it."

She peered at him warily. "Then go to my father."

"Linus does not want your father to know. He said that your father's anger would be great if he knew."

Gladys stared at him, suspicious and alert. It was no use asking for a note from Llyn, some written confirmation of the man's gruff words. Llyn had never bothered to learn to write, though he now spoke Latin with great fluency, and she knew that she could not put money into these grimy hands and send the man away. She had never plunged into the maelstrom of humanity that lined the banks of the river as Eurgain had, and she thought of asking her to go, but then dismissed the idea. Eurgain would argue as the man waited, his glance probing the huge, deserted hall. "Very well," she said, uneasiness filling her. "Wait here. Can you guide me to him?" The man nodded and she left him, climbing the stairs, walking the landing, turning in at her own door with a feeling of danger churning around her.

She went to her box, lifted the lid, and her body servant came to her. "Do you want to play a game, Lady?" she enquired, as Gladys drew out her leather money purse and strapped it to her waist.

"No, not tonight, and if anyone seeks me, tell them I have retired early." Picking up her cloak she went out softly, and the girl closed the door behind her.

The man still hovered in the corner of the atrium, and when he saw her coming he slipped toward the cloister and out into the garden. Gladys ran down the terrace steps behind him, seeing him vault the wall and disappear into the trees below. Of course. No guards did duty there. Gladys determined that she would ask her father to request more sentries from Claudius, then in spite of herself she smiled grimly. She did not think the emperor would want to grant any more Catuvellaun requests. She scrambled over the wall, tumbled into the rough grass on the other side, and sped after the man. He moved surely ahead of her, glancing back now and then to make sure that she was following, and one behind the other they cut across the

496

smooth width of the Clivus Victoriae and on down the hill, skirting the walls of other estates, jogging down alleys, until the Palatine loomed behind them. The man did not cross the Forum directly. He zigzagged on the periphery and Gladys fought to keep him in sight. Then he angled down through the blocks of apartment houses half-hidden in trees to where there were shops and an occasional expensive drinking house. It seemed that he was being careful to stay in sight, yet he obviously did not want her to walk with him, and she padded after him, her breath coming short, realizing for the first time how soft she had become with her litters and her host of slaves to escort her about the city. Now there were no gardens, no trees, and the streets narrowed and began to twist. Taverns and brothels lined them, bringing to her a low murmur of a life she had never known, and as she flitted past, there seemed to be in the dark doorways the unmoving huddles of a dozen grubby secrets. Llyn, how could you? she thought. There is so much gay strength in you, so many alternatives. Why this? Is it a deliberate denial of your captivity, a calculated choice?

The man strode on in the odorous darkness, often cutting from one street to another through an alley, and she stumbled on, sweating in spite of the chill wind. She was about to call to him to go more slowly, to wait for her, when she ran around a corner and he was not there. She halted, leaning against the rough stone, straining into the gloom, but no footsteps rang out under the laughter and oaths that spilled from the tavern at the end of the tiny street. She cursed to herself and shouted, "Where are you? Wait! Wait for me!" But there was no answer. She stood there panting, and the moments went by. She was about to call again when out of the corner of her eye she saw a man emerge from a doorway on the opposite side of the street. It was too dark to see more than his silhouette, but she knew that he was looking at her. She glanced away and saw another shape detach itself from the shadows ahead of her and come pacing slowly toward her. There was still the length of the street between them—it was still beyond the light-limned door of the tavern, but it drew closer with a determination she could feel. It was then that she knew, and her heart stopped. I am in a trap, she thought incredulously, and I am going to die. Trapped like the witless, lazy Roman wench I have become, trapped here in the bowels of the city, and they will say that I was carousing with Llyn, they will say that the sailors killed me, or the thieves and drunkards who roam these streets. The man facing her came on unhurried, sure of an easy prey, and the one standing in the doorway stepped out onto the paving. I cannot live! she thought, panic stricken. I have forgotten much, I have forgotten it all, I am lost and there is no moon to shine between the trees and tell me which way to go. The intestines of this city twine about themselves forever, dark and corrupt. Father! Help me! Then sense returned. The tavern. Better to face the dangers of a room full of curious men than the certainty of imperial knives. There might even be a Praetorian or two, Llyn himself might be in there.

She took three awkward steps, and then the tavern door opened and another man came out, hitching up his belt. She drew breath to cry to him but before she could make a sound there was another sound, and she saw that he had drawn a knife. "Take her!" the one coming down the street shouted, and the other two sprang into life. Gladys screamed, spun on her heel, and fell forward into the labyrinth that waited, leaving all light and sanity behind. It was an alley. At the end of it, looming high, there was a wall, and with near hysteria she prepared to turn at bay, but she saw the tiny path that began at its foot and she stumbled up it, squeezing between wall and wall, hearing the heavy thud of their footsteps. Hurry, she sobbed, oh hurry, hurry, then she was out in another street. No friendly lamplight fell on this one, nothing but shadows and silence, and she had no time to try the doors. She sped along it, hearing another shout as the three men saw her go. She did not know where she was, and as she ran she tried to think, but the clean stateliness of the Palatine and the Forum could have been a thousand miles away, in another world. Something rushed by her head and fell with a clink and she screamed again, knowing it to be a knife well thrown. She came to the end of the street and turned, ripping off her cloak as she did so, tearing at the belt that held her stola to her body. She dropped cloak, belt, and overgarment to race on, freer, in her white, thigh-short tunic. White! she groaned. Ah, mother! Must I go naked to my death? The sandals, flimsy things with golden buckles, pinched her feet and she kicked them off, feeling as she did so the shedding of her ill-fitting Roman self, feeling the ability for coherent thought come seeping back to her. "Sword-woman, sword-woman," she heard the voice of Cinnamus whisper, as though she were once more his pupil, weapon in hand, eyes on his face as he admonished her. "Make them run, make them sweat," and she sobbed as she drove into yet another alley drowned in night, the assassins fleet behind her. Dear Cin, it is I who run, I who sweat, I whose muscles are flaccid from too much good food, too little care. I haven't a chance.

She could smell the river now, and in her imagination she tried to picture it flowing through the city under its lordly bridges, curving as she stood in the garden and looked down upon it. Then suddenly it was there, starlight reflected on its smooth surface, the shadows of the warehouses rippling dark. Watchmen, she thought. Watchmen, but she dared not shout for help. Upstream or down? Camulos, where am I? She ran into an alcove and tried to get her breath, one hand over her mouth to stifle the sound, her head hanging, her ears tensely straining. Then she heard them step out of the maze of dockside streets and knew that she must move or be cornered. She flung herself from her hiding place, but not before the glimmer of her tunic had betrayed her. A man lunged for her, with arm raised, shouting to the others, and the impetus of her start carried her against him, faster, harder than he had thought. She could not have drawn back if she had tried. He stumbled, and his arm was driven back against the stone wall of the warehouse. Before she realized what had happened, Gladys saw the knife fall. She pounced on it, fell to her knees, and drove it into the man's chest with both hands, as hard as she could. The other two were almost upon her. She got to her feet and ran. First blood, she sobbed to herself. The first blood of my life, and she turned downstream, not caring that she could be seen, for now the city had relented and voided her out of its stinking bowels like a tiny white worm. Ahead and to her left the Capitoline hill bulked, and beyond it, far, oh heartbreakingly far, the Palatine mocked her with its lights. I learned once how to run, she told herself. Now obey me, my body. Falling into the graceless, ground-eating gait of her people, she sprinted, as the river lapped beside her, and the pounding feet and labored breath came on behind.

One man. Where was the other? No time to wonder. The river began its wide inroad on the west side. The Capitoline became the whole horizon as she swung with the water, and now the temples of the Forum were visible. Suddenly she veered, her bare feet finding grass for a moment, the Capitoline in front of her now, and cast a glance over her shoulder. The river's shadows were empty. She stopped dead. The man had gone. Where? Why? Shuddering with exhaustion and fear she forced herself to study the tangle of buildings ahead, behind. He was not there. She closed her eyes and felt for his presence, but there was nothing. For a moment she sank to the ground, but she was not such a fool as to believe the jaws had opened so easily. Where? Where? I must cross the Forum directly, with such people as might be out tonight, but then what? The trees on the Palatine are dark, and I dare not seek a Praetorian, not now. How many of them are in her pay? She got up, straightened her tunic, now soiled and bloody, and made herself walk slowly across the plaza. No one gave her a glance, and she knew that no citizen would dare interfere with a disheveled girl covered in sweat and blood, for fear of those pursuing her.

It took her a long time to traverse the Forum, and she wanted to linger in the hope that she might see a face she knew, but the rise of the Palatine loomed, a mass of darkness between her and its crown of lights, a forest that held death. Then she saw him, standing on the edge of the road that branched into the rising Clivus Victoriae. He watched her come with impudent patience, and her heart began to palpitate wildly again. Sobs of disappointment ached in her throat but she stood still, gathered together every thread of energy left to her, then leaped away like a hunted doe, running for the foot of the Palatine, around the other side, plunging courageously into the darkness that could smother her or be her salvation. He saw her purpose and sprang after her, trying to cut her off, to keep her circling at the foot, but the insanity of her last effort for life had given her an edge and she found herself looking down on the road, the man pumping behind her. There was no time for stealth. With an awkward jump she landed on the road and began to half-run, half-stagger along it, upward, around the curve, following a wall that ended in a row of gray stone houses which fronted the street directly. She knew that she was spent and could not clamber up through the trees to her father's wall but must stay on the road. There was a sound behind her. The man had come out and was gaining. It was then that Gladys knew she would never reach her father's gate. She had given all she could. There was nothing left. She ground her teeth together and turned. "Come then, animal!" she shouted, "But you will have to strike me in the back," and, turning, she took four more stumbling steps.

Then, like the shock of a sudden summer rain, she heard his voice, Rufus Pudens, . . . I rent three rooms in a house on the Clivus Victoriae . . . it is almost directly below here . . . A chance, she thought, relief and terror flooding her, and even as she reached the first gray doorway she looked up. The other man, the missing man, stepped out from the depths of the last house, smiling, his knife raised. She saw his face as a pool of whiteness, the knife as silver. "Mother!" she screamed, and beat on the door with both fists. Let it be this one, let him be home. The man stopped, aimed coolly, insolently, and threw. She flung herself flat against the unyielding door but the knife found her, pricking like cold fire between her ribs, and she sank sobbing, unaware that the door was opening. The porter looked down on her, aghast. When he saw the blood spurting from her side and the men hovering in the shadows, he began to close it again. "No trouble here," he said firmly, and Gladys raised a streaming, crazed face to the dimly lit peristyle beyond. Taking a last, pain-fired breath, she opened her mouth. "Rufus!" she screamed. "Rufus Rufus!" and the men waiting for the door to click shut looked at one another and started to melt away into the night. The porter stood irresolute, and then there was a flurry of movement. Rufus Pudens came striding through the peristyle, Martial behind him, and when he saw her on her hands and knees on the doorstep, her tunic torn, mired, and bloody, blood already puddling the tiles of the entranceway, he ran, side-stepped her, and vanished. A moment later he was back, kneeling beside her. "Gone," he said. "Jupiter! How could Caradoc allow this to happen? Help me to get her upstairs, Martial, before the others in the house awaken."

"I will have to tell my master," the porter said, worried. "I hope that you are not interfering with imperial business."

Pudens gritted his teeth. "I will tell your master myself," he said, "Now get out of the way."

Together he and Martial carried her through the peristyle, across the atrium, and up the stairs to Pudens's rooms. "Get those cushions," he ordered, "and shut the door." They placed her gently on the carpeted floor and Martial closed the door and gathered up cushions, while Pudens eased off her tunic. "Find some water so that I can clean this," he said after a while. "It is not deep, only painful and unpleasant. Gladys! Gladys!" She lay there crying while he washed and bandaged her and found her a blanket. She sat up with difficulty, wincing at the stiffness already spreading over her ribs and down her side.

"There were three of them," she said shakily. "I killed one, Rufus. My first blood. A Roman in Rome. I killed."

He and Martial exchanged glances. "You killed a wild beast, that is all," he replied. "It was not combat, Gladys. They were hunting you like the animals they are, and you should not concern yourself about such a killing. Tell me how it happened."

She did so quickly, her hand stealing into his, and Martial watched her critically, and not without amusement. Whoever was behind it all had bitten off a great deal more than he could chew.

Pudens listened without betraying the confusions of anger and worry in his mind, then he stood up. "I must take you home at once," he said. "Martial, go and roust my servants. I want the litter, and three or four of them can walk with us."

"Shall I arm them?"

Pudens considered, then shook his head. "No. I think our numbers will be sufficient, and it is not far."

Not far, Gladys thought. A pleasant little walk. It could have stretched ahead forever. She shuddered as Martial left the room. "Help me up, Rufus," she said. "I want to stand."

He put his arms around her and lifted her, and for a moment she rested against him, her body a single protesting ache of abused muscle and bruised tissue, then she kissed him softly on the lips.

"Thank you, Rufus Pudens," she said. "There are people at court who will hate you for what you have done, and you know it, and you may have to find other rooms to rent."

"I may indeed," he said gravely. "What a pity. I have been comfortable here."

She met the smiling eyes and stepped out of his embrace. "I do not find it funny, and neither will you when my father declares a blood feud against Agrippina."

"Will he do that?"

She sighed. "I don't know. Perhaps not, if I can show him an honorable way out."

"Marry me. Then your problems and his will be solved." He knew that he was taking advantage of a sordid situation but he did not care, and she stood staring at him for a long time, those black, deep eyes full of self-confidence and independence once again. She still had not answered him when Martial came to tell them that the litter was below, and they left the house in a tense silence.

Pudens took no chances. He sent a runner on ahead, and by the time they turned in at Caradoc's gate the guards were clustered, waiting for them. Caradoc himself was raging up and down the street, and when he saw the litter with Pudens and Martial flanking it, he ran up, tearing back the curtains. He said nothing. He met his daughter's gaze steadily and she saw again, for the first time since he descended the steps of the Curia with Claudius and raised both free arms in exultation to his family, the fiery wheels of power and authority rolling behind his eyes. "Arviragus," she whispered. "Do not blame yourself. This was my fault alone."

"Lady, it will be a long time before I approach senility," he croaked. "I was a fool to believe that my life no longer had meaning." He dropped the curtain, dismissed the sentries, and they came to the house. Here Martial bid them all a quiet good night and went away, and the rest of them entered Caradoc's reception room, Gladys walking slowly but unaided. The family came to its feet, their faces pale. Only Llyn stayed in his chair, sprawled loosely, fighting to regain sobriety, and Gladys went and sat beside him. "I heard," he said to her with exaggerated care. "I heard you run past the tavern. I heard the men who ran after you. It is not wise to seek trouble down there, and I was winning a lot of money from a stranger. I did not know it was you, Gladys."

"Llyn . . ." she began, but he turned his head away, white and sick.

502

The two other women stayed on their feet. Caradoc took off his cloak, and going to Gladys he demanded on account of the night in their own tongue. She gave it quickly, her hands moving unconsciously in the way of chiefs who sat by a Council fire and recounted their raids, and the others watched. Pudens stood in the doorway. The line that divided him from them had appeared again, as real as though Caradoc had taken chalk and drawn it on the floor. He was not one of their kind. They had closed ranks, suddenly and uncompromisingly, leaving him outside, the Roman, the enemy. One by one they squatted, going to the floor as though it were grass under their vast forests. He turned to go, but then Gladys put both hands together and brought them slicing down, the tears sliding over her cheeks, and she looked across the room and saw him.

"Rufus," she said in Latin. "Please do not go. I am in your debt. That is not a light thing."

"There is no owing between friends," he retorted, but he stepped into the room. When Gladys had stopped speaking there was a brief silence. Llyn sat with his eyes closed, but he was not asleep. The two Eurgains squatted and looked at the floor. Caradoc had folded his arms and was studying the wall. Caelte fingered his harp, but made no sound. Then Caradoc spoke.

"Eurgain?"

His wife did not even look up. "Blood," she said.

"Llyn?"

"Blood."

"Eurgain?"

The girl hesitated, then her mouth thinned. "Blood."

"Gladys?"

"Not blood!" They all turned their heads to stare at her and she strove to keep the pleading out of her voice. "The blood has been spilled. I was pursued and wounded, but a man was slain by me, and blood is not demanded unless there is murder."

"I agree," Caelte said softly. "No blood."

"Blood was intended!" Caradoc shouted at her. "Murder was intended!" and she faced him with full-blown desperation now.

"A blood feud cannot be sanctioned for motive alone. There must be a death."

"Will Agrippina come before a Council, and swear the oaths to leave you alone?" He was still shouting.

"No!" she shouted back. "But Agrippina will leave me alone, and Nero will forget me. I am going to marry Rufus Pudens!"

There was a sudden hush. Pudens heard her yell his name and then all eyes turned to him, and Llyn blinked and sat up.

"She has just said that she will marry you, Pudens," he commented. "Forgive our rudeness. You are marrying into a family of uncouth savages."

Pudens went to her and she rose, her chin high. "I do not want a debt paid off in this way," he said to her angrily. "You owe me nothing."

"I owe you everything, and you know it," she replied. "But I do not offer payment. I offer you my love, not out of fear, but because tonight I was able to take your measure. Will you teach me to love you, Rufus?"

He found her eyes. It is a beginning, they said to him, and he smiled sadly.

"The terms are acceptable," he said.

"There will be no dowry," Caradoc's harsh voice broke in. "I have nothing of my own and I doubt if Claudius will want to settle any money on you, Gladys, once I have spoken to him. I am going now, tonight. Who will come?"

One by one they rose. "I will come also," Pudens said, but Caradoc brusquely refused him.

"This is a family matter," he said brutally. "Gladys, you may not come either. The rest of you, get your cloaks. Take no knives. If we do we will not be admitted." He walked to Gladys, the embers within him still smouldering. "We will not be long," he said, "for I have few words to say. Go to bed." He swung around and went out and Gladys heard them all cross the atrium and descend the terrace steps in a unity of outrage, a tiny, living core of Albion moving clean and fearless through the city.

When they had gone, Gladys nodded to the wine flask and the goblets. "Pour yourself some wine, Rufus. I will return in a moment." She left him, paced the shadowed atrium where such a short time ago a man had waited to lead her into death, and went painfully up the stairs.

Once inside her own rooms she took off the tunic, pulled on another, and instead of looking for a stola she put her feet into breeches. Her servant was asleep beside the bed, curled under a blanket, and Gladys was careful not to wake her. When she was dressed she took the knife that she had left lying on her bed and went to the embroidery frame. The room was warm, dim, and quiet. "I curse you," she whispered. "Poor old victim, I curse you and yours, all your seed. I love you, but not enough, Claudius. Not enough to give my life away." She held the hilt in both hands, seeing for one anguished moment the man who had fallen and would never rise again, then she brought it down, slashing viciously. The material parted, the frame sagged.

504

Freedom, she thought. But not for me. Never again for me. She tossed the knife onto the floor and went out, closing the door behind her.

The Praetorian hesitated, looking at the five grim faces before him. "Wait here," he snapped finally and went away. They waited, while the sounds of feasting wafted to them, then he came back, tall and insolent in his superiority. "Are you armed?" he asked, and for answer they opened their cloaks. "Very well," he finished grudgingly. "Go in."

It was a long walk. They had all taken it many times in the past, but tonight, with the evening faltering toward dawn, the imperial domain had an air of negligent decay. Caradoc felt as though he were the only straight-backed creature walking the thronged halls, an arrow flying free to its target in an army of twisted nooses. Claudius saw them coming, like five tall birds, gods out of a dark past, their cloaks floating out together behind them, their strange long hair framing calm, impassive faces. Britannicus came running, tugging at Caradoc's arm, but Caradoc ignored him. The empress propped herself higher on her couch, an anticipatory smile coming and going on her small mouth, and her son whispered to her, "What have you done, you hag? Where is Gladys?" The five came on abreast, and the loud conversations in the hall slowly died away. They stopped without bowing, and Agrippina found that she had been holding her breath. They waited for the emperor to speak and Claudius kept them waiting, his eyes traveling across them, but their patience was indifferent, whole, utterly composed. Claudius pettishly mopped his dribbling mouth and rested his quivering head on one hand, then he suddenly capitulated. Barbarians who could stand in frozen water all day without moving, and go for six days on the march without food, could play this game indefinitely. I covet their pride, he thought. They do not hold the empire cheap. They do not consider it worth holding at all.

"Well, my noble barbarian," he stuttered. "You deign to grace us with your presence, even though you are uninvited. Do you want a favor? Are you in need of more money?"

But Caradoc would not be insulted. He smiled at Claudius, feeling as though a great weight was slowly lifting from his shoulders, feeling absurdly young again, and free. "I need nothing, Claudius," he replied. "Absolutely nothing. Your generosity is a constant shower."

The emperor heard other words beneath the odd compliment, and so did Agrippina. "One of you is missing," she said brightly. "I would have thought that Gladys would miss no opportunity to reiterate her affection for my husband. Where is she?"

You foul thing, Caradoc thought. You demon in a woman's body.

When is it the emperor's turn? "I once knew a woman like you," he said to her with seeming irrelevance. "She was very beautiful."

Agrippina's thin plucked eyebrows rose. "Oh? Was? Is she dead then?"

"I do not know, but I think not. Women like her continue to survive."

The empress shrugged off what she felt to be a clumsy barb. "Where is Gladys?" she repeated, and Caradoc felt Llyn stir beside him. No, he thought. Hold on, Llyn. This is not the time for dying, and if you throw the accusation out into this hall we will all die.

"She is not well," he answered. "She went out walking and became lost. It was a very long way home. But she will recover."

Slowly, Agrippina slid upright and began to smile. The smile grew, spread, and her eyes laughed into Caradoc's, full of vitality. She held out both hands suddenly in a youthful, exuberant gesture. "Hold them, Caradoc," she commanded, and after a moment he obeyed. "You must go home and congratulate your daughter for me. I am impressed. She must indeed have walked far tonight." She dug her nails into him with a sudden sharp venom but he did not start. He withdrew gently. "Send her here tomorrow so that I can offer her guides. She ought not walk about the city without them."

"She will come to the palace no more," Caradoc said, and Claudius stiffened. "She is about to be betrothed. Her future husband is a man with a jealous nature, and I do not think that he will allow her to be put on public display. He is a good Roman. I came to tell you this."

Nero leaned over to his mother. "Checked for once!" he hissed triumphantly. "They are too much for you, Empress!" Claudius said nothing. His face had fallen into a bland repose, and Caradoc could read nothing on it, though he tried.

"And who is this good Roman?" Agrippina asked smoothly. "He must be a foolish Roman as well."

"The fool sees foolishness in everyone," Llyn stepped forward. "As you, Lady, ought to know. You are surrounded by them. Gladys will marry Rufus Pudens. Will you summon enough vigor to object? None of us is really worth it."

Rufus Pudens. Caradoc saw the man swiftly reviewed behind Claudius's eyes. Rich, influential, a patrician, a man who holds the respect of the senate. The empress had suddenly lost interest in it all. Her eyes were on Llyn, and he grinned back insolently.

Claudius sighed. "I have news for you out of Britannia, Caradoc," he said, fighting his stutter, a malicious intent to wound now licking his face. The Catuvellaunians immediately fell silent and turned their gaze to him, but Claudius made them wait. Their patience was a humble, desperate thing, and he saw their invisible hands strain toward him. He knew that they were at his feet for the last time, and he relished every passing second.

"The rebels enjoyed a little freedom this summer," he said, breaking the silence at last, "but as usual they could not sustain their attack. My new governor chased them all the way back into their mountains, and there they will stay."

"Losses?" Caradoc whispered hoarsely, and Claudius waved.

"To us? None since the spring."

"No, damn you!" Llyn snarled. "To us!"

Claudius did not react. "None," he replied. "You ran. You ran back into the west like frightened little rabbits." He could see them thinking. It was survival again, retreat in order to live. He could see that they knew that. Then all at once, as though some hidden signal had passed between them, they turned and strode back across the hall, under the dome, out of his sight, leaving a painful dislocation behind.

"Kill them all," Nero grumbled, not meaning it, but Claudius did not hear him. He would miss the girl who had brought an unlooked-for freshness into his life. He had betrayed her trust in him, and he was sorry.

Once outside, Llyn took his father's arm. "I could get close to the old woman," he said. "I could easily kill her."

Caradoc rounded on him. "If you or any of you sets foot in this place again it will be I who kills," he said, and he swept down the steps and into the thinning darkness.

Llyn entered the tavern, elbowed his way to the rear, and flung himself down on the wooden bench. A month had come and gone since Agrippina had run an admiring eye over his healthy young body. Gladys had kept her word to Pudens and their betrothal had taken place, but not a whisper of agreement or censure had come from the palace. It was as though the emperor had never loaded his little barbarian with presents or strolled with her arm tucked under his, and the Catuvellaunians lived in a new and cheerful lightness. Pudens was a daily visitor to the house on the Palatine, bringing friends who more often than not ended the day around Caradoc's table, their curiosity merging into admiration for the man who greeted them amicably and presided over his household with under-stated authority. Martial was the most regular diner. Pudens brought young senators. Martial brought other poets, musicians, and thinkers who responded to the atmosphere of free informality, and soon came to regard Caradoc's house as a meeting place. Llyn escaped when he could, running from a house full of togas. Tonight his purse was full and his belly empty. He slapped his palm on the table, called for beer, and greeted his companions gaily. "Where is Valog?" he asked.

"He fights tomorrow," the man next to him replied. "I suppose he's sleeping."

"Where's Publius then? Has his wife put a ring through his nose already?"

"He's on special duty tonight. His unit is flushing out a nest of Followers."

"What followers?" Llyn asked, his throat going suddenly dry.

The man turned to him impatiently. "The Followers of The Way. The Christus people. They've been meeting not two streets from here. That's where Publius has gone. Are you playing or not?"

The beer came but Llyn drank all of it without tasting, and his mouth was still dry when he finished, as dry as the sandy floor of the arenas where the Followers spilled their blood everyday. "No," he said, standing up unsteadily. "I'm not playing tonight." He walked out of the tavern and up the street, and when he could no longer hear the din he began to run. Eurgain, he thought. Let the others line up for the slaughter like cattle, but not you. You will go like a warrior. He swerved to cut off a corner, flung himself at the wall he knew was there, and then was over the top, landing lightly like a cat. He straightened and pelted on. Another street. One more corner. A little linen shop, she had said, with a fish carved over the door. He came to a halt, drew his knife, and peered around the corner. With luck I have cut her off, he thought. But there is no such thing as luck in this hole. At the other end of the street he saw the soldiers, loitering, with one eye on the unpretentious shopfront, and he knew that at the rear there would be more. Wait until they were all inside. Publius had said it often enough. Get the whole lot together, a clean sweep. He grimaced with tension. What shall I do if she is already inside? The moments oozed by. I hate this, he thought. I hate it all. Traps everywhere for all of us, a city waiting to turn us into gutter rats and then strangle us. She was not a Roman citizen. They would crucify her, and out of pride she would not admit to being only a friend to the friendless. It would not matter to her, he knew that, but she was kin, she was his sister, and somewhere, at some time, there would be a place for her. And for you? His thoughts came back to him with cynical clarity, and he gripped the knife more tightly and swore gently to himself.

Then he saw her come, with Chloe behind her carrying a basket. She was wearing her favorite blue breeches, and the braids that she had never cut swayed against her knees. "Eurgain!" he called softly. She heard, but did not turn her head. She raised the torch in her hand a little higher, slowed, and then began to angle across the street toward him. When she was within his reach he grabbed for her, tearing the torch from her hand and throwing it to the ground. "You have all been betrayed," he said rapidly, pulling her farther into shadow. "The soldiers are watching the doors, front and rear. Now go home, and quickly."

"Thank you, Llyn," she said. "Now you can let go my arm."

He released her immediately but jerked her toward him again as she turned back to the street. "What are you doing? Eurgain, don't you understand? They will arrest you, and father will not be able to do anything."

"I must warn the others. Many of them are children."

"Let them be! They are all in love with death anyway."

Anger flared in her eyes. He saw it glitter in the dimness. "Do not pronounce so glibly on something you do not understand," she said. "Take your hands off me, Llyn. Will you stand here and send the followers home, while I go around to the back of the building?"

"I have a better idea. You are wearing your knife. Creep to the rear and dispatch the soldiers there. I can easily handle the two on this street."

She thought quickly, and he knew that her fingers ached to strike at something, anything, to rip apart the net and run free, then she shook her head. "No. The reprisals would be immediate and unpleasant. Oh Llyn, they are like children, all of them. Simple, brave, and utterly without guile! You would think that just the sight of a sword would send them scurrying, but I have never seen people die as they die, not even in Albion. Please, just tell them to go home and they will go."

"Eurgain," he said with wonder and bewilderment. "You have been to the arenas?"

"Yes. Now will you help me or not?"

"I will, but on one condition."

"Hurry up!"

"I will give up gambling, and do my drinking at home, if you will give up all commerce with these people and do your thinking at home."

She smiled, and then began to laugh softly. Suddenly she put her arms around him. "You need a woman," she said.

"No, I do not. I have as many as I want."

"I did not mean that. You need a woman to love, so that in loving you may find your fever laid to rest. Very well. I agree."

"A bad bargain," he grumbled. "Now we will have to entertain each other at home." Then he was gone, diving back into the darkness to come out farther up the street.

"Stay here, Chloe," Eurgain ordered, then she too vanished.

Later that night, in the tavern, Publius downed his beer with irascibility. "Someone made a mistake when they sent us after a weaver, a potter, and two slaves," he grumbled. "It was a wasted night. Ah well, tomorrow night Valog will be back. Are you coming, Linus?"

Llyn leaned back against the wall and put his feet up on the table. "I do not think so," he said. "I have decided to run for senator. I have no money or power, but I have plenty of charm. The empress would be delighted to make sure that I got a seat in the Curia. What do you think?"

"You talk too much," Publius said sourly, but he remembered how Valog had remarked about the barbarian temperament, and he looked at Llyn with a new and guarded respect. One day he might need a friend in high places.

Aulus Plautius and his wife moved into their winter home, a spacious house surrounded by vineyards on the outskirts of the city, and Eurgain spent much time going to and fro with her mother, questioning both women closely about the old religion and how the Druithin fostered it. At one point she mystified them both by declaring, "The Druithin do not believe in the gods. In their search for truth they have left the gods far behind them and only use them because the tribes are not yet ready to understand. There are no gods."

"But they have magic, they make the spells," her aunt objected, and Eurgain smiled wistfully.

"I did not say they had no power, but they are waiting. Knowledge weighs on them. The universe presses them to the earth with its mysteries. They are wise, yet they carry knowledge on their shoulders instead of in their hands. The universe suffocates them when it should be wreathed lightly about them like a precious garment. I wish that I could talk to them."

She, Llyn, and Gladys often went about the city with Pudens, Martial, and several of Pudens's other friends. It was a most irregular courtship, Pudens reflected. No one seemed to care how long he and Gladys sat alone in the garden at night, how late she returned home after dining with him. If there was any chaperon it seemed to be Llyn. He watched his sister and Pudens with a gleam of mischief in his eyes, but he no longer goaded Pudens's friends into hot argument. He seemed to be mellowing, curbing his tongue with a deliberate effort, and his father watched him change and wondered what new creature Llyn was calling into being within himself. He began to struggle with Gladys's lessons, rushing to learn how to read and write

510

with the same impulsive impatience he brought to everything he did, and he cornered whomever he could—Pudens, Plautius, the young senators—pouring forth a stream of questions on everything from Roman history to the working of Rome's watering system. He drank less but his restlessness grew until he measured the bounds of his family's captivity a dozen times a day, walking tense and preoccupied, disturbing the still air of each room with the burden of metamorphosis he pulled behind him.

He went to the arenas alone, or with his father and Plautius, and sat for hours with elbow on knee and chin in hand, gazing down upon the parade of death with a brooding, closed face, while the thousands around him screamed and cheered. The Catuvellaunians had never developed the taste for organized slaughter that moved the Romans to spend hours watching breathlessly, while life after life was ended in the sand and sunshine of the arenas. But they often went to see the gladiatorial contests, seldom losing the money they wagered, so expert were the eyes they ran over the protagonists, and the chariot races brought to them complete forgetfulness of who or where they were for a time, so deep was their involvement.

"Valog is fighting today," his uncle said to him one bright morning. "Will you come? Rufus and Gladys will."

"I suppose so. You should give that man his freedom, Aulus. You can afford a dozen more like him."

"He will ask for it when he is ready and, besides, what would he do with it if he had it? He could go back to his tribe and die of boredom, or brawl here in Rome until he became a nuisance and had to be put out of the way."

"That would not matter."

"Even to him?"

"No. The only reason he has never lost a fight is that he refuses to die unfree. Take him off the wheel, Aulus. You have plenty more. It would not matter to you."

"He makes money for me."

"I will take his place. Free though, of course!"

Plautius laughed. "You may be a mighty warrior, Llyn, but I would place no bets on you!"

"Why not?"

"Because you would not last a week. You hold your honor higher than your will to live."

In the end the whole family walked through the early afternoon brilliance to the arena, passing under its high, cool arches, up the stone stairs, and out to where the stone seats ran in a sweeping circle to enclose smooth, glaring sand. The seats were packed tight, and as

Plautius made his way to his place heads were turned and fingers raised to point in his direction, for no gladiator had survived as long as Valog and the crowds flocked to see his reputation grow. One day he would go down, everyone knew it, and no one wanted to miss the hour when it happened. Until then, however, he was the object of hysterical acclaim. They settled themselves on the cushions the slaves had brought for them, and their canopy was unfolded. Gladys leaned out over the row of heads in front, craning to see if the emperor's box was occupied, and Pudens gently drew her back.

"He is there," he said. "It would be better if you did not remind him of his troubles. Llyn, did you know that Claudius offered to buy Valog from Aulus for a ridiculously high price? But Valog said that he would not fight for the emperor."

"Neither would I," Llyn retorted. "It would be thumbs down no matter what when Claudius got tired of his gladiator. I would like to go down and wish him good luck, but I suppose he will be waving his talisman about and muttering incantations. Who is he fighting today, Aulus?"

A strange look, half-embarrassment and half-challenge, passed over the older man's austere face. "New blood, Llyn. A tribesman from Albion, owned by one of the Greeks."

The Catuvellaun looked at him blankly, then Caradoc barked, "Which tribe?"

"I am not sure, but I think he is a Trinovantian. I have not seen him, but the Greeks have an eye for a promising fighter. He will be worth seeing."

No one made further comment. Formality dropped around the family like a hunting net and though they did not move, it seemed to draw them away from Plautius and Pudens. Gladys withdrew her hand from Pudens's arm and her aunt turned her head from her husband to study the restless crowd around the imperial family. Then the trumpets shouted their arrogant fanfare and the gladiators came pacing slowly, wrapped in a fleeting regality as they made their way to stand before the emperor and give him their salute. There was a silence. "We who are about to die, salute you," Caradoc thought. We who are about to die . . . Always the expectation, the darkness held at bay by pride and determination over the years of battle, and yet here those words have a potency stronger than the day-to-day terror that lurked in the western forests. How many times has Valog spoken those words aloud to the emperor? Do they bear for him, as they do for us, a meaning that hangs precariously with each moment spent in this city? Claudius nodded indifferently, and the gladiators suddenly broke into pairs and ran to their positions.

Pudens turned to Gladys. "They will fight one pair at a time today, I hope. Do you want something, Gladys?"

"No. I am not thirsty yet. Look! There is Valog! Oh Llyn, the Trinovantian! How big he is!"

Llyn grunted, his eyes, also, on the tall, swaggering chieftain with the midnight hair who was glancing about him with such disdain, holding his net and trident high for the approval of the people. Then Llyn stiffened and turned incredulously to his father. "The man is wearing a torc! Father, he is a slave, he belongs to a Greek, and yet he has the impudence to sport a torc! I will wager that his father and grandfather were slaves to Cunobelin, and now he is here in Rome, strutting as though he owned the whole of Albion!"

"It does not matter anymore," Caradoc replied. "We are all slaves of Rome, Llyn."

Pudens overheard the remark but said nothing. Below, combat had begun, but the crowd watched with only half its attention. No gladiator had yet clawed his way into the great glare of popularity that Valog had won, and the people waited, their boredom a steady undercurrent of laughter and conversation. Plautius and Pudens talked politics desultorily and the Catuvellaunians sat tightly and uncomfortably, their eyes on the two natives. Claudius also looked bored. He sprawled back in his chair, well under the cover of his canopy, and those watching him could see the sunlight flash from his rings as he drummed his fingers on the arm of his chair. Then the trumpets spoke again. Valog lifted his mighty shoulders, drew his sword, and strutted out from the shadows into the full light of the arena. The crowd rose. "Valog! Valog!" they screamed and Valog slowly made his circuit. Even from where he sat, Llyn could glimpse the grin under his brown beard. Then he shouted something to the Trinovantian, a taunting superiority in his voice, and the Trinovantian answered with a shake of his trident and a leap that brought him within the whistling circle of Valog's sword. The people sat down and began to shout.

"Valog will win again," Pudens said. "The other barbarian is too sure of himself and he has not yet learned to ignore the yells of the crowd. But how light on his feet he is! Will Valog kill him, I wonder?"

"It depends on the crowd," Llyn said. "Listen to them! They would let him kill the emperor himself in return for such a show."

"Ah!" Gladys hissed. "The Trinovantian is down!"

But he did not stay down. Before Valog could move in the Trinovantian had bounced away, flicking his net free of Valog's sword. A cup of sadness was suddenly thrust toward Caradoc's mouth by some invisible hand but he angrily refused it. The honor of Albion, he thought. The clean, mighty state of champion of the tribe, reduced to this. Two slaves battling each other for the adoration of an ignorant populace. But I will not grieve. There is no point in it.

Suddenly there was a hush, as though the people had drawn breath and then been unable to let it go, and in the shocked silence Gladys craned forward. "What is it? What has happened?" she whispered, and her aunt said tersely, "Valog is down. The net tripped him."

"The net did not trip him!" Caradoc said loudly. "The cowardly Trinovantian threw it but he stuck out his foot as well. Who else saw that, I wonder?"

"Get up, Valog, get up!" Llyn said fiercely under his breath, his whole body tensed on the edge of the seat, but Valog did not get up. He struggled, and the more he kicked the tighter the net pulled itself around him. Scattered shouts rang out. "Get up, get up! Valog!" Then the whole arena was on its feet, chanting. "Get . . . up! Get . . . up!" The Trinovantian made no move to help him, and then Llyn knew. Most of the people had not seen that cowardly foot go speeding with the net, and their shouts grew louder, uglier. They still called for Valog to rise but their voices were impatient, as though he had toppled to the ground on purpose and lay there begging their sympathy. The Trinovantian stalked to his victim, placed a foot on his flailing arm, and raised the trident, holding his other arm high to the crowd.

"Surely the people will not accept!" Gladys said, shaken. "What is the matter with Valog? Is he ill?"

Plautius looked about him grimly. "I would put nothing past the owner of that healthy Trinovantian animal. He has the makings of the next favorite, but the first five or six bouts are crucial, and many potential favorites have never lived to take laurels. I wonder."

"Ah, no," Gladys whispered. The shouting had stopped. The people stood still and their mood came gusting to the family, irritated, petulant, and capricious. Valog had not fought well today. Valog had failed them. Perhaps Valog was getting old. One by one, tier by tier, the hands came out, waved, and the thumbs turned down. The Trinovantian followed the decision, turning his head slowly to see his majority, then he looked at the emperor. Claudius rose and came to the edge of the box, his own gaze traveling the sullen crowd. Shrugging, he raised an arm.

"No," Llyn murmured. "He was downed by a trick. No. No!" He got to his feet. "No!" he shouted, and he jumped down onto the next tier, pushing the people out of the way. He leaped again, stumbling, regaining his balance, and before Caradoc knew what he was doing he had tumbled into the sand of the arena.

"Aulus, stop him!" the elder Gladys said sharply, and Pudens half

514

rose in amazement from his seat. Llyn had picked himself up and was striding along the front of the arena, his arms held high, berating the astounded crowds as he went.

"Up, up!" he shouted. "Savages! Barbarians! Lovers of the stink of blood! Raise your thumbs, you cannibals, you slaves! You will never see another like Valog. Do you think that this treacherous man will delight you with his filthy tricks? Valog is worth a hundred, a thousand, of him, and you. Carrion! Vultures!" He paraded before them, insulting them, taunting them, and all at once a ripple of laughter began and spread quickly. The thumbs wavered. Claudius dropped his arm and waited. "Up!" Llyn screamed. "Up for a brave man, up for a champion! Has he not pleased you many times?" The laughter grew. The crowd had loosened, loving suddenly and with a fickle reversal this insolent, foolhardy young barbarian in his outlandish breeches and garishly patterned tunic. A thumb went up, and then another and another as Llyn continued to shout at them, but they no longer cared what he said. They worshipped him, begging for more, and their thumbs rose high. Claudius beckoned, and Llyn ran to him and bowed.

"You are either very stupid, or the gods of Rome have decided to love you, Linus," Claudius called down to him. "You could just as easily have been torn apart by them."

"But I was not," Llyn shouted back, smiling. "I am indeed stupid, and your gods do indeed love me. Is it up or down, Emperor?"

It was impossible to despise Llyn. Claudius raised his arm again, and the thumb turned to the sky. The crowd roared hysterically, and Llyn bowed again and ran to Valog, pushing the Trinovantian out of the way and kneeling to untangle the net.

"Are you hurt, Valog?" he asked quickly.

Valog sat up, rubbing his ankle. "No. He tripped me. Me!" Rising to his feet he waved his thanks, then he turned to Llyn. "I do not like to be in your debt, Catuvellaun. My honor is diminished until I repay you."

"There is no honor here," Llyn returned with a sneer, "as you well know. It did not please me to see them waste your talent, that is all."

They glared at each other for a moment, then the big Gaul stepped to Llyn and embraced him.

Llyn did not return to his seat. He pushed his way out of the arena and walked slowly home. Caradoc had expected him to make for the taverns like an exhausted homing bird but was surprised to find him sitting in the reception room, with a scroll across his knees. He greeted his father with a smile, and Caradoc asked him what he was doing.

"At the moment I am reading," he replied. "And tomorrow I am going to bully Rufus into taking me into the senate house."

"Why? You will never be allowed inside the Curia."

"Oh yes I will. I want to see how this mighty empire is administered. I am going to be a senator one day."

Caradoc stared at him and Llyn went on smiling, but the warmth of the mouth had faded to a cool cynicism and the eyes held no expression.

Two weeks later, on a sweet, windy evening, Caelte and the younger Eurgain sought out Caradoc as he walked pensively in his garden. He watched them come to him together over the sunset-blooded grass with their heads lowered, and something in their manner warned him of what was to come. He greeted them quietly, then turned from them and leaned against the wall where the city lay pink and peaceful and the river was still. "You have ill news for me," he said. "I know it. Tell me."

Eurgain went to stand beside him, putting a hand on his arm. "I love you, my father," she said unexpectedly. "I loved you in the mountains, and every day I feared for your life, but I think I love you more now, when the days of danger are gone and all that remains is helplessness." He turned his head in puzzlement and she kissed him. He saw that her eyes were blurred with tears. "I have come to say good-bye to you. I want to go away."

So it had come, drifting like the melancholy autumn mists of Albion into his soul, another parting, another face that he would never see again. "From the beginning we have all been together," he said to her. "We left Camulodunon together, we fought among strange kin together, and together we have endured this exile. There is a unity within the family that goes deeper than the loyalty owed to blood kin, Eurgain. Will you break it now?"

"Yes, I will," she replied, the tears brimming over. "I must. I cannot live my life chained to this house, and I do not want a husband who will move me to just such another house, and make my life a daily round of little duties, little pleasures, until I die still imprisoned in this city. The emperor will not miss me, and when he does it will not matter. It is you and Llyn he must keep under his old eye."

"Where will you go?"

She brushed away the tears and stood tall, the last light turning her blonde braids to ropes of living gold and bringing a glow of bronze to her calm, wet face. "To Eriu. I must talk to the Druithin. I do not want to go to Mona. I need peace, father, long quiet days in which to

516

think, and Eriu will never feel the pain of a Roman foot upon her shores. I will take ship to Albion, walk north, and take another ship out past Mona."

He lifted both her hands in his, and kissed them. "Eurgain," he said, fighting to keep his voice level. "The time is long past when you need my leave to go where you choose. Yet I will wish you a safe journey, a peaceful journey. Kiss the soil of Albion on my behalf, and may your destiny be fulfilled on Eriu." For a moment he could speak no more. Loss and panic suddenly rose in a great tide, mingled with a sharp and painful yearning for his murmurous beaches, his quiet, rain-washed forests. Change, he thought. Men must change or die. Who said that to me? Then he remembered. I cannot change, he thought again, and I refuse to die. But, my daughter, I can feel hurt. Long ago he had learned to bury the thoughts that led to reverie and then to memory, and he swung to Caelte.

"And you? Will you take your music away from me, Caelte?"

"Lord," Caelte said, "My music is going of its own accord. Every day it has less power, less beauty. The fire is dying, and I am afraid. I have sung you through love and hatred, wars and victories and despair, but I cannot sing you through your exile. Even if I wanted them to, the songs would not slide to my tongue as they once did. What is a bard without music?"

"Like an arviragus without people. Is your mind made up, Caelte?"

He nodded, white-faced, his harp rammed against his chest. "Forgive me, Lord. I will take your life farthest into the west, to Eriu, and there I will sing it to the generations yet to come, so that it will not slowly die and be forgotten here, among the savages of Rome. Release me from my oaths, I beg you, for I am no longer of any use to you or to myself."

Caradoc embraced him quickly and stood back from him, glad that the shadows were deepening and the light failing. "I release you, Caelte. Go in peace. I only wish . . ." He flung back to the wall. Presently he felt Eurgain's arms go around him and her head rest against him for a moment, and then he heard them go quietly away. Eurgain was sobbing openly, but before long the sound had died away and there was only wind, and the rumble of the city.

You, me, and Cin, Caradoc thought. From the beginning, when we were children, it was always Caelte, Cinnamus, and Caradoc. And somewhere, in some locked chest where time keeps its ancient treasures, I sit by my fire at Camulodunon, a young, brash chieftain full of the zest of living, and my bard runs his hand over his harp while my shield-bearer squats at my feet, gazing into the orange heart of the fire and dreaming his own rich dreams. A safe journey . . . a peaceful journey . . . To you, Cin, to you, Caelte, to you, my fearless daughter. With a mounting rage he fought the tears. You fool, he told himself. Only the weak feel self-pity. He covered his face with his hands.

Winter, A.D. 53–54

CHAPTER THIRTY-ONE

*A*RICIA WOKE WITH A CRY and sat up. Her heart was thumping and her lungs shuddered with dry sobs. Through the cracks in the shutters the first hint of dawn showed her that Androcretus still lay before her, tall and white-faced, draped in black, only the toes of his had slid to the carpeted floor. The room itself was dim, quiet, and cold, and though she shivered she felt her skin slick with sweat, her face swollen, her eyes puffy with unshed tears. She stayed upright for a moment, her hands gripping the sheet beneath her, waiting for the swift rush of panic to subside and the racking heave of her chest to be still. It was the dream again. It was always the same. Venutius stood before her, tall and white-faced, draped in black, only the toes of his muddy boots visible beneath the heavy cloak that exuded the stench of a charnel house. "What have you done, what have you done?" he whispered. "You know how I have loved you!" and his voice was the voice of Caradoc, husky with lust, vibrant with youth. She knew it was her husband who spoke to her, and she watched as his brown eyes collapsed in self-immolating flames. Yet the lined, cruel face belonged to the arviragus and the voice to Cunobelin's son, whose memory lay long-buried under the rubble of Camulodunon.

"L . . . lean and famished . . . famished . . . oh my soul . . ." she stammered, and Venutius, who was also Caradoc, who was also the ghoulish voice that had once played so consummately on every nerve in her body, took two steps toward her, that sickly odor rising in clouds around him.

"What have you done to me?" he began to shout, and though his hand stayed invisible under the darkness of the cloak she felt the words strike her, on the face, on the breasts, in the stomach, in stripes of pain. She began to sob, but no tears would come. "What have you done to me, to me, to me? I have loved you!" and the blows lacerated and burned.

"Burning with lost causes, all lost," she whimpered, her eyes closed so that she need not look. "I do not know you. Who are you?"

Then the shouting would stop. She would open her eyes onto ball-less sockets, rotten flesh falling from stained bones, red hair that clung in grotesque tufts to a skinless skull, and as she began to scream it spoke for the last time. Its jaw creaked open. "I . . . am . . ." and then she would wake.

She got off the bed and went to sit, still shivering, in the chair by the embers of the night's fire. I can bear it no longer, she thought dully. Night after night this torment, I will die of it. Who are you, what are you, that comes to tear me apart? Is it blood you want? I no longer sacrifice to Brigantia. Is it my soul you desire? I no longer plead before Sataida either, for I think my soul is dead. Ah, Great Mother, I am so lonely, so alone.

Through the thin wooden wall came a stirring. Someone sighed and coughed. Domnall, her shield-bearer, was rising from his pallet on the floor of the room she would no longer enter, the room where Caradoc had held out his wrists for the chains and looked at her dumbly out of cavernous eyes, the room where Venutius . . . She reached down to stir the ashes, finding them cool, then stood and began to patter her fingers lightly along the mantel, back and forth, up and down, anything, anything rather than remember. I do not want you, I never wanted you, you clumsy bear, you great oaf of a man! You cried out in your innocence to be used by me, and I used you! What right did you have to leave me? I am your welcome torturer and you are my habitual victim, and how can you live without that daily potion of pain? Is your life not pale and insipid without it? Venutius! You did not come back. It has been years now, two Samains have come and gone, and where are you? You need me, you cannot live without my scorn, my hatred, my body.

Her fingers suddenly stilled. Her chest ached. And in spite of her fierce forbidding, the memories were there, they had always been there like the dream, night after night, until she knew that she was slowly going mad. Something else had come, too, when Venutius had smeared her with his blood, something she had never before felt in her life, a cringing deep within her whenever she stepped unwillingly onto the treadmill of that one insupportable memory. At last she was able to name it. It was called shame, and neither the embraces of Andocretus, her bard, nor the gold that finally arrived from Lindum, her reward, her blood money for Caradoc, could soothe the cold despair that always waited to overwhelm her.

Now she walked across the room and pushed the shutters open. The dawn chorus had begun, with a hundred strident voices raised in praise of an invisible sun, and soft, muted light met her, mingled with cold, damp air that promised sleet. It was a chill, bleak winter morning, still and misty.

"Andocretus," she called without turning around. "Get up." After a moment the bedcovers heaved and he sat up yawning. She continued to stand gazing over the town, down to where fog hung in clouds and mingled with smoke from the huts, up to where an invisible slope rose to an invisible, treeless summit. My town, she thought, my hill. All the hills of Brigantia are mine; I ask for nothing more. Then why should I suffer? Behind her Andocretus got out of bed, pulled on his clothes, reached for his harp. He had sung to her last night, perched cross-legged on her bed, and she had knelt behind him, plaiting their long hair together, black and blond, but when he had laid the harp aside and turned to her, and she had drawn him hungrily, peremptorily inside herself, she had known that it was no longer enough. The dream had still come. The memories were still there, haunting the perimeters of her mind. She turned to him, her fingers going absently to trace the thin, silver scar running down her face.

"Find something to eat," she said. "And then find me a Druid."

He stared at her through eyes bleared with sleep, his face swollen, then her words penetrated and his eyes cleared. He walked to the basin and broke the ice on the water. Splashing his face and neck, he shuddered, then he knelt before the fire, laying sticks on the ashes of the night.

"That is not possible, Lady," he replied. "The Druithin can no longer be found unless they choose to be, and no Druid in his right mind, even if I could find one, would consent to come here. If I travel into the west in search of one, I will be killed."

She thought for a while, slowly, watching his supple fingers coax a spark from his flint. "I want a Druid—here. I must speak to one."

"Then call Domnall. He will know where to look." Andocretus looked up at her and they exchanged glances, then she went and squatted beside him, holding out her hands to the crackling new blaze.

"If I let him go, will he come back to me?"

"He did not go with Venutius when he had the chance. He is bound to you by his oaths."

"Honor, honor," she muttered. "Tell me, Andocretus, do you love me?"

520

He smiled faintly into the fire. "Do you need my love, Ricon?"

"No. I have all of you that I need, your body and your music."

"Then I do not love you."

Suddenly she enfolded his fair head in both her arms, drawing him to her, and kissed him softly on the forehead. He drew away wonderingly, for she was many things but she was not gentle. "Go and send Domnall to me. He is up, I heard him leave the house."

He rose, stretched, and went out quietly, and she banged the shutters closed and began to dress herself, not waiting for her freewoman.

When her shield-bearer came she was standing with her back to the fire, in her thick green tunic, belted with jet and falling to the floor. A yellow cloak enfolded her, and jet nestled also in her long braids, the color of darkness, the color of her hair. She looked at him for a long time. His straggling black hair met a bushing beard. The dark eyes were cold, and the orange cloak that he always wore concealed wide, solid shoulders. Many times she would like to have taken him to her bed, but something about him forbade her invitation. He was too self-contained, too unapproachable. She held him only by his oaths, and she knew it.

"Domnall," she said quietly. "Chieftain of Brigantia. I need your help, and only yours. I would not ask you this if there were any other way."

He did not reply. He just stood there, waiting. His very stillness upset her and her hands came up, twined together. "I have a . . . a dream, that must be interpreted," she went on hurriedly. "If it is not taken from me I shall go mad! It is sucking the life from me, Domnall, and I cannot bear it anymore. Bring me a Druid!" She had not meant to tell him all those things. His eyes narrowed, but he made no other movement.

"And where, Lady, am I supposed to find you a Druid?" he said sharply. "Most have withdrawn to Mona, and the rest travel with Madoc and the others in the west. If you order me to do this on pain of oath-breaking I will go, but I am not ready to die just yet."

Her fingers writhed about one another. "If you will bring a Druid to me, I swear that I will release you from your oaths to me, and you will be free to go into the west, to Venutius, where your heart is. Ah Domnall, do this thing for me, this hard thing! I am desperate! I am tormented! I know you can find one. You know where to search. Talk to the spies that wander through Brigantia. I know they are there, and so do you. Please!"

Your promises, Lady, can last a thousand days or a thousand moments, according to your whim, he thought cynically, but looking into her face he saw something he had not seen there before, a defencelessness, a poignant, lost hopelessness, and his chest tightened with pity for her. He inclined his head. "I will go," he said, "but do not count the days, Lady. My search will be long and difficult. I must have your oath that when and if I return with a Druid you will not molest him or give him to Rome to be slaughtered, and you will let me go from Brigantia with honor."

The fingers were stilled. She smiled without warmth. "I swear by the High One, on the grave of my father. And I thank you, Domnall."

His eyes widened in surprise and he smiled back briefly, hesitantly. Then he was gone and she turned again to the fire. Venutius, she thought, I miss you. When will you come back to me? But even as she said the words a loathing rose up to choke her, and she saw him weaponless and chained, even as Caradoc had been, and the bewilderment in his eyes brought a taste like honey into her mouth.

Winter deepened, sat on the land like a stiff, bitter woman, upright and unmoving, and Aricia fought a lonely battle. The dream came to her, fresh in terror each night, and she took to spending the hours of darkness talking to Andocretus and snatching sleep sitting up in the Council hall during the day. It did no good. Sitting or lying, by day or night, the thing came to her, accusing, clouded in the stink that seemed now to assail her nostrils even in her waking moments as though it rose from her own body, or from the earth under her feet.

Another nightmare was added to the first, constant terror. No progress was being made in the west. Scapula's successor, Aulus Didius Gallus, had moved swiftly and recklessly during his first month as governor, and the mountain men had once more withdrawn to lick their familiar wounds beside the secret, snow-fed waterfalls. Gallus himself had seen better days. He was well on in years, looked back to a lifetime of dedicated service to the empire, and resented another active post. He had come to Albion with Claudius, bringing the Moesian Eighth Legion with him, and hated the new province on sight. Claudius had soon sent him back to Moesia and later he had become governor of that infinitely preferable country. He had looked forward to serving his time there and then retiring back in Rome. He had seen action against that mystical and wealthy Prince Mithridates, received his surrender, and then gone on to defeat the Moesian Prince Zorzines. He had done his duty, he expected reward. Albion was no reward. It was a sickly, strife-torn, magic-muddled, wet hole that seemed to devour governors like a hungry beast. He had been greeted with frantic relief by his new legates, and before he could wash the salt from his face he had been informed that one of his legions was well-nigh finished and the western tribes were gleefully riding wherever they chose. Wearily, he had called for his maps, pinpointed his strengths and awesome weaknesses on it, and in two months the Fourteenth, the Ninth, and the Second were mopping up the lowlands and the rebels had hurried back to their miserable mountains. There was no reason why the Twentieth should have been defeated, no good reason why the remaining thousands of men should have huddled in their forts like frightened children. No good reason for any of the mess that he resignedly set about to untangle. It was just Albion, a province with a curse on it, a province that had never paid its way and probably never would. He had restored order along his predecessor's western frontier and doubled the number of troops patrolling it. He had talked to the procurator and looked at his ledgers—red, always red—and had decided that if over the next year or two the situation did not improve and stabilize he would recommend a complete withdrawal from Albion. Failure, costly and futile, and the emperor would not like it, but, still, he looked gloomily at the maps, tracing with a fatalistic finger the thin, snaking lines of his borders. So much country was still in the hands of the natives, almost the whole of the west, and the far north had not yet even been explored. For ten years Rome had fought for Albion, and yet so far it had not even been necessary to produce new maps. He had flooded Siluria with men, cleaning out pockets of resistance with distaste and boredom as though he were sweeping a house that might always be filthy, but he himself had not left Camulodunon. He had spent his time in his office, brooding, counting off the days of his bondage like a school child waiting for his holiday.

Since then, like some unholy, demon-filled body that has been stabbed again and again and yet refuses to die, the western tribes had fought on. A garrison fell here, a posting station burned there, an unwary cohort was never seen again, and though Roman reprisals were swift, it seemed to Aricia that the soldiers themselves, like her, watched almost paralyzed as the shadow of freedom for the west loomed steadily larger. She had heard all this from Caesius Nasica, Legate of the Ninth. She ordered men to her borders and spent much time wondering what Madoc and Emrys, and Venutius also, would do with her if they fought their way to her door. Perhaps they would give her a choice. Burning, drowning, or the swift blessing of a clean sword to end every dream, every pricking symptom of insanity. She saw them, the people she had never seen, in her imagination, slithering toward her over her snowy white hills, their eyes fixed greedily on her.

Andocretus laughed at her fears, sitting opposite her by the fire, clad only in his breeches. "When have the tribes ever held an inch

523

they have gained?" he said cheerfully. "They feed on lost causes, dreaming, sucking strength from them. But Rome has no cause. Romans inhabit this world only, and so they will triumph."

Burning with lost causes . . . Ah Sataida. Will no one save me? Rescue me from this pit into which I have fallen? "You are wrong," she said harshly. "Nothing is so potent a force as a dying cause. If Rome wants peace in Albion she will have to execute every western man, woman, and child."

"In that case she will. What ails you, Lady?"

"I want to die."

He sat watching her shrewdly, then he reached down beside him and lifted his harp. "A new song came to me this morning," he said lightly. "Would you like to hear it? There will always be music, Aricia, and good mead, and white teeth gleaming in laughter, and black hair swinging under the sun. Let those without music or love fight the wars."

"You are a bard to your very bones," she said dully. "Help me, Andocretus."

He sang to her with his smiling eyes fixed on her, his rich tenor lilting with the lift and fall of the shadows, plucking the strings of his little harp with delicate fingers. But when he had finished she knelt before him, gripping his legs fiercely, her face buried in the red cloth of his breeches. "It is not enough anymore," she whispered, and he laid the harp aside and took her in his arms.

CHAPTER THIRTY-TWO

SPRING CAME TO ARICIA like a jaded old whore, draped in false beauty to hide rampant decay. Domnall came also, grim and tired, plodding through the blinding wall of cold rain. He squatted before her in her house, too weary to stand, and water ran from him like tears.

"I have brought the Druid," he said tersely. "She waits on the porch."

"She? You have brought me a woman?"

He smiled. "I have brought you a Druid. I have sought long, and faced many dangers, and I came upon this Druid with the Silurian women and children."

"Did you see . . . did you see . . . ?"

He rose at last. "No, I did not. Do you think I am mad, Lady? And now let me remind you of your oath. This Druid came because I gave her my word that she would not be harmed."

"I need no reminding! But I ask you, Domnall, to stay with me as my shield-bearer for a little while longer."

"I will for as long as the Druid stays. No longer."

Resignation, fatigue, a stubborn uncomplaining stoicism, all these things she heard in his words and read in his face. With a gesture she ordered him out, feeling as though she were trying to shout to him over a high wall. "Very well. If the Druid has eaten, send her in."

"She has eaten." He nodded and went out, leaving the door open. Rain gusted in, soaking her fine sheepskin rugs, and she became aware of it thrumming on her Roman roof like the hoofs of war, or the thunderous sweep of the Raven of Battle. Then a shadow darkened the doorway, divided the streaming water, came forward closing the door behind it, and turned. Quiet reigned once more.

Aricia held out her hand. "Welcome to Brigantia," she said. "Rest and peace."

Before her was a thin, brown face, round eyes like black pebbles, and brown, wet-slicked hair. The Druid's coarse-spun cloak, caked about the hem with black mud, seemed too full and heavy for such a slight, short body. The feet were bare.

"Not for me," she replied, refusing the hand, her voice high and light like a child's. "I serve the master and the Raven of Battle, in that order. Neither one offers me rest or peace." She took off her cloak and laid it on the bed. The white tunic beneath was spotless. Spindly wrists jutted from the voluminous sleeves, and with a horrified fascination Aricia saw the thick silver bracelet, the silver ring on the brown hand. Snakes writhed there, silver fangs and forked tongues, in the same twisting, convoluted patterns of the brooch Gladys had given her long ago. The beginning and the end, she thought, paralyzed, the beginning . . . the end. Let me out!

The woman went to the fire and sat in one of the wicker chairs, looking up at Aricia with a frank interest. "So you are the famous lady of Brigantia," she said. "Beautiful and treacherous. And troubled also. Beautiful you are, Ricon, as beautiful as a lush summer night, and I can smell the treachery on you, and the stench of dead dreams, or living nightmares. No," she continued, seeing the expression change on Aricia's face, "I do not fear you. You bring to me more than I bring to you, sick Lady." Aricia shrugged and sat in the other chair, then her eye was caught by the feet. They were blue, but not from the cold. She bent closer. More snakes curled in intricate whorls, an infinity of sharp-toothed open mouths and slit, hooded eyes, tattooed under the tight skin. The Druid laughed, shaking back her sleeves, and more snakes crawled up her arms, coils unwinding, heads hidden where they reached for her neck. Aricia sat back shocked, the woman shook down her sleeves, and the blue terror was hidden.

"You cannot look into my face. You are full of disgust and scorn," the Druid commented. "Am I a woman or a monster? For to you, Lady, a woman is nothing but your soft, ever hungry body and everyone else is a monster. Well. Tell me what you want of me."

Aricia swallowed and forced her voice out into the huge, unbridgeable void between them. "I wish you to take from me a dream," she said harshly. "That is all. When you have done this you may go. I will pay you anything you ask."

The black eyes suddenly softened. "If you are not careful you will pay for my services with your soul. Tell me your dream."

Aricia told her. At last the horror spilled from her, loathsome and alien, while the wind rose outside and the rain slowed. The Druid listened in silence, her eyes on the fire, reaching beyond the words to the agony. When the words ceased and only the agony remained she closed her eyes, folded her arms, and withdrew into silence. Aricia waited. The afternoon dragged sullenly to a close. On the porch, just outside her door, Andocretus sat and sang quietly to himself, a rain song, a flower song, and the Druid sat enclosed in her thought, thin and stern, brown and white. Then she sat up and pulled a clinking leather pouch out of the folds of her tunic. She opened it and drew forth a bronze ring and then another, and began to tie them into her now-dry hair. "Ask!" she commanded.

"Who is this . . . this thing that comes to me? Is it my husband's death that I see?"

"No. Venutius comes to you out of your faithlessness, and the arviragus comes to you out of your lack of honor, but it is Albion herself who stands before you in her deathrobe, she who was unsullied and fairer than any other land, whom you have betrayed into rape, disease, and death. I am, she says, I am, I am Albion. Your roots are plucked up, lady of Brigantia. There is no longer any friendly soil on which to plant your feet. You have cut yourself adrift, and this is your madness."

"Albion is earth, rocks, trees! The land cannot change its character, no matter what race puts its feet upon it!"

"It can. It has. Two men have gone into your ravenous belly, and it is not enough for you. You are sick with greed, yet even the greedy may remain whole. You are torn in two because you are also sick with hatred of yourself."

526

"Take the dream away! Heal me!"

The other shook her head. "I cannot take it away. It is not an omen or a warning. It is you yourself. Only you can drive it away."

"How? How!"

The Druid tied the last ring and put the pouch away. Then she looked Aricia full in the face, with sympathy. "Send for your husband. Beg his forgiveness. Then join with him against Rome. If you do I promise that you will never have this dream again. Deep inside you, Ricon, you know the truth of my words, and you did not need to have me dragged halfway across Albion to tell you so."

Slowly, painfully, like an old woman, Aricia got to her feet. Her face was slack and gray, as Caradoc had seen it, as Venutius had struck it. "You are all the same," she said with difficulty. "Liars, impostors, caring only for the power that will give you back the tribes and the land, to manipulate as you wish. I ask a simple thing of you and you cannot do it."

"Listen to me, Aricia, and listen well," the Druid retorted angrily. "I am going to break one of the ancient laws by which I live, for if I do not, nothing will save you. Sit!"

Aricia sank back wordlessly, as though an unseen hand had pressed down on her head. "The Romans are going to cast you out of Brigantia. They will take your kingship from you and make you a beggar, and no one, not even a peasant, will give you shelter. They will see you for what you are at last, and their trust will turn sour. When Julius Agricola becomes the governor, remember my words. Then you must prepare to wander, you and your dream and your madness. Today, right now, you can make a lie of my vision. Turn back to Venutius! Cut Rome out of your soul and let your husband fill the void with his love and his sanity!"

"I despise my husband!" Aricia shouted. "I have always despised him, and I do not want him back! Ignorant fool!" She put her head in her hands. "I don't know what I hoped for from you," she whispered. "I should have known better. When I came to Brigantia I heard one of your brethren try to turn my people against me, while speaking of the evil of Rome, but they did not listen, and neither will I. Romans are men, Druid, just men, bringing to Albion more than they can ever take from her. I have terrors, but you have them too. What do you fear? Why do you hate Rome? Name your price and then go."

The woman rose and picked up her cloak. "You will do nothing?"

"No."

"Then my price is your soul. I will ask you for it the night I leave Brigantia. Now I think I will go to the hall and drink some wine." She went out, swinging the cloak around her shoulders. For a while,

Aricia could not move. She wanted to call Andocretus to her, she wanted to lie on her bed and cry, but she stayed with her head resting on her knees, her scarred cheek rough under her palm, eating once more a dusty feast of despair.

For three days she did not leave the room, and neither ate nor drank. The wind continued to swoop and keen over the treeless moors of Brigantia, but the sun shone benignly and the children ran into the fields to gather the first spring flowers. Andocretus came to her door each evening but she sent him away without opening to him. The lamb was roasted in the Council hall, the flagons were passed, the jokes shared without her. Then, late in the evening of the third day, she sent for the Druid. The woman came swiftly and Aricia stood in the doorway and watched her stride from the gate, white tunic billowing like a swan, ringed hair sailing also, out on the gale. She saw Aricia and slowed her pace, and Aricia stepped onto the porch and spoke quickly, urgently.

"I have made up my mind. I want you to carry a message to my husband, wherever he is."

The Druid looked at Aricia curiously. There were dark circles under her eyes. She was hunched deep into her yellow cloak, and her hands were shaking. "Lady, are you ill?" she asked.

Aricia shook her head violently. "No. No! Will you carry my message?"

"That depends on its content. What shall I say?"

Aricia stood straighter, with her head turned away from the bite of the wind and her eyes questing, and though she leaned against the lintel of her door the trembling in her knees and hands did not cease. "Say that I am deeply wounded because of my actions with regard to Caradoc's betrayal. Say that I beg his forgiveness. Say that I have been mad, blinded, but now I wish to right my wrongs. Tell him that if he will come back to me I will put Brigantia and all her chiefs and warriors into his hands, for the defence of Albion." The effort had cost her dearly. She closed her eyes, and the Druid thought that she would faint. "Tell him . . . tell him I have great need of him." A pulse fluttered in her throat, a visible sign of pain, and the Druid took her by the shoulders and drew her away from the lintel.

"Open your eyes, Aricia, and look at me," she commanded. Slowly, Aricia did as she was bid, lowering her eyes to the other's, feeling the stony gaze probe her.

The woman sighed and released her. "No."

"Why not? In the name of Brigantia, why not?"

"Because I am forbidden to carry a message that is a lie."

The silence stretched, deepened, became charged with hostility,

528

then the woman smiled wryly. "I see the thoughts chasing one another across your face. You want him back, but not for his good or Albion's or yours. What would you do with him if he should come? Has any plan formed in that hot, devious mind of yours? Poor lady! I wish to leave Brigantia tomorrow. Come with me. We can find him together. Leave your Roman house and your pretty clothes and your jewels. Come into the west. Be reborn, Aricia!"

Aricia struggled for a long second, for an eternity, her face all anguish and lines of aging, like a livid scar. The Druid withdrew from her, leaving Aricia to fight the battle alone, but then the grimace ceased and the full lips formed an ugly line of determination. Aricia's eyes fastened on some point far away beyond the wall, and the Druid knew she had lost her.

"If you are going tomorrow you must be paid," Aricia said.

"I will take my price, never fear," the Druid said, nodding. "If I walk from this town tomorrow, I will charge you nothing. The price has already been named."

"It is a valueless price."

"Perhaps. A pleasant night, Ricon."

Aricia went unsteadily back into her house and closed the door, and as she did so she realized that she could not allow the Druid to leave Brigantia alive. The certainty came to her full-blown, as a clear, cold thought. Horrified, she stood still, with her hands to her mouth. Kill a Druid? It was forbidden. No tribesman in all the long history of her people had ever raised a hand to the Druithin, and the curses on such a one would be so terrible that even the Druids did not care to think them, let alone speak them. Kill a Druid. Murder a Druid. But it must be done, I must do it now, tonight. If I do not she will find Venutius and tell him . . . tell him . . . Did she read my thought? Does she know what I wish to do with him? I want you back, Venutius, oh how I want you back. You will pay for humiliating me and going away. I want you here before me, chained, kneeling on my floor, your red head bowed. If I could have Madoc and Emrys, too, I would, but you will be sufficient. No, I cannot do it, not this. Not a Druid. Perhaps I can cut out her tongue, or keep her here, a prisoner, or . . . Or kill her. No! Not that! Never!

The knife lay in the wooden chest, under all the pretty gold-tasseled tunics and bright cloaks. She drew it out and then sat with it in her lap, her fingers cold and limp upon it. Darkness came swiftly, blown into the town like scudding black clouds before the wind. Her servant came to feed the fire and light the lamps, and she sat on, one half-formed thought succeeding another in her mind, and beneath them all, a still-growing malignancy, the certainty that the Druid must die.

She must have Venutius back so that once more time would move soberly and purposefully, from day to night to day, instead of whirling around her in aimless confusion. If the Druid spoke to him he would never come. If I could see him just once, she thought, his resolution would crumble. He cannot have ceased to love me, he cannot! And then, when he is here, when I have heard the words of apology from his own lips . . . She stood suddenly and went to the door on trembling feet, the knife gripped tightly in numb fingers. Then I will sell him to Rome.

Night had fully fallen and the courtyard was in shadow. The chill wind flapped at the cloaks of her motionless bodyguard, making them look like giant black birds, and as she left her house and crept, shivering, to the gate, the moon's light was hidden by a swift-flowing cloud. Before her men could come to her, she called to them to stay where they were, and she passed out of her stone-walled compound. The town was busy, cheerful. Voices that were raised in laughter, the sweet yellow shafts of torchlight, the patter and scuffle of spring-quickened feet, all came to her like fragments of some world that existed far out of her reach and that came to her only in dreams. It was some other world filled with solid things, shapes that did not dissolve with the touch of a thought, people who retained a core of reality and did not melt into nightmare—firelight, sunlight, candle-light, light that did not come gray and diffused from the back of her own mind.

She slipped quietly along the deserted paths that ran behind the wooden houses of the chiefs, and passed at the back of the Council hall, carrying with her a moment full of Andocretus's voice, raised in song within. Under her feet the ground began to slope away to the earthwalls and the gloomed moor beyond, and then the river. The guest huts clustered under the wall, to the right of the tall, unguarded gates, sunk deep in shadow. No lights showed beneath the doorskins. Aricia walked cautiously to the doorway of the first and raised the skins, but it was empty. The second hut was also cold and dark. But when her hand gingerly pushed aside the soft leather of the third she saw the faint orange glow of a dying fire and a still, softly breathing form on the cot, an almost indiscernible length of body dimly silhouetted. She stepped soundlessly within, letting the skins rustle closed behind her. She stood for a while, struggling to breathe as fear choked her, and she saw in her imagination the spells of protection and warning hovering over that sleeping monstrosity. Then she slipped the knife from her belt and glided to the bed.

The Druid lay on her back, a blanket draped carelessly over her, one snake-gripped arm hanging loosely to the rugs. Aricia bent down. The eyes were closed, the mouth was gently parted. Now I must not think, Aricia told herself. Do it, and afterwards think. Of Venutius running home to Brigantia, to me. Of Venutius rocking in the cart on his way to Lindum. But she stayed frozen, both hands clutching the hilt of the knife, her eyes on the peaceful, small face, so human now, so defenceless, so . . . so ordinary. Under her long cloak her body's muscles tightened and loosened in spasms of terror, and cold struck through the rugs to cramp her feet and calves. But she could not move, she could neither strike nor withdraw. She began to cry quietly, un-aware that she did so, the tears coursing down her face. If he were here this would not be happening to me, she thought over and over. If he were here . . . holding me back from myself . . . if he were here . . . Then she saw the glitter of eyes open in the darkness and her heart turned over and began to pound. The Druid did not move.

"No," she said. "No, Aricia. I do not want your soul after all. You may keep it. It is worth nothing to me." She closed her eyes again and turned over, and the snakes moved sinuously, easily, with her. After a moment Aricia lowered her arm and crept out of the hut, wounded, a broken animal.

In the morning the Druid came to say goodbye. Domnall was with her, and they both stood before Aricia on the porch of her house, new sunlight dancing joyously around them. She met them coolly, her shoulders back, holding out her hand to Domnall. He leaned forward and took it, meeting her eyes with his own. The warmth she read there was not for her and she knew it.

"So, shield-bearer, you are really going," she said. "To hunger, con-stant weariness, and in the end a sword through your gut or an arrow in your chest. And all for nothing. Will you consider again?"

He took his hand from hers. "No, Lady."

"And you, poor Lady?" the Druid said, those pebble eyes black on Aricia. "Will you consider again?"

I hate you, Aricia thought suddenly. I hate your arrogant purity, I hate your ignorant honor, your blithe, stubborn self-righteousness. You were not worth killing after all.

"No," she snapped back.

She did not wish them a safe, peaceful journey, but went into her house and slammed the door. Leaning against it, her eyes closed, she felt a change within her. The heat of shame was gone, and her head was clear. She was left with only her hatred and her maniacal will, for every other emotion seemed to have died with her shame. Demanded

531

or not, her soul had left her to follow the snake woman into the west.

Spring and summer pursued their accustomed courses. Lambing came and went, crops sprang up green and healthy, cattle wandered slowly over the bare, rolling land, and traders from Rome thronged river and coast. Autumn passed, and during winter, Aricia spent much time riding between her town and the fort at Lindum to dine with Caesius Nasica. They discussed the year's levy of Brigantian freemen to be sent to Rome, and talked of the sudden death of Claudius, poisoned, it was said, by a dish of mushrooms that the Empress Agrippina had prepared. The new contender for the purple was seventeen-year-old Nero, a vicious fool, in love with a nonexistent histrionic ability that led him to bore the courtiers with a feeble, piping singing voice, who fancied himself the new Augustus. Of more immediate interest to Aricia and Nasica was the state of her southwestern border. Many of her own chiefs patrolled it with the Twentieth where it touched Deceangli territory, and so far she had held her other borders without Roman aid, a fact that every succeeding legate of the Ninth had carefully noted in his dealings with the Brigantian ricon. She was worth all the gold and goods poured into her country, but only just. If the westerners decided to force Brigantia into combat and edge into the lowlands, the headquarters of the Ninth would move to her town and take over her kingdom, but the west was not yet that desperate.

Winter, A.D. 54–55

CHAPTER THIRTY-THREE

*A*RICIA LAY ON THE DINING COUCH in Nasica's spartan house. A littered table was between them, and behind her a native servant stood to pour her wine. It was late. They had eaten and drunk and eaten some more, while outside the snow fell straight and silent. The lamps had burned low and their conversation had slowed to an occasional dutiful, social comment. Nasica lifted his cup from the table and leaned back, pillowing his head in his other palm.

"I heard a piece of news today that might interest you, Cartimandua," he said. "Actually it is only a rumor, but a strong one." It had been almost a year since Domnall and the Druid had left Brigantia with light steps and lighter hearts, and he eyed her thoughtfully, carefully, his gaze level and bright with anticipation. "Word is going around that the men of the west have elected a new arviragus." He waited for her reaction, but she settled herself more comfortably into the cushions and stifled a yawn.

"I find that hard to believe," she said. "They have been on the move all summer, and the legions have only just gone into winter quarters. They have not had time to Council all together."

"The news I hear is that the decision was handed down by the master Druid himself, subject to each chieftain's approval. There were no objections. Shall I tell you who was chosen?"

"If you like." She smiled at him briefly, noting sleepily how the wine had brought a dull flush to his heavy, pock-marked features and swelled the flesh around his bleak eyes.

"Oh I like. And so will you. I have been saving this information until the end of the evening. I thought it might put the crowning touch on a good dinner." He smiled back at her, his mouth conveying only his ever present cynicism, his eyes an unwavering stare of observation. "The choice has fallen on Venutius, your husband. It seems that he is their new arviragus."

Nasica's smile widened as he saw the pale face blanch. He watched clinically as she leaned forward to pick up her cup, an almost imperceptible shake in her fingers as she brought it to her mouth and emptied it quickly.

"No," she said with a little gasp. "They would never choose him. Never! He is not to be trusted, he cooperated with me and with Rome for too many years. He . . ."

"He is to be trusted now," Nasica replied. "In fact, the choice is a logical one since he comes into the west from the outside. By choosing him no one tribe can be incited to jealousy of another because its chieftain has gained eminence. He brings a backbreaking load of wrongs and personal grievances with him. Hatred for Rome because of what she has done to his beloved Brigantia, and hatred for the tame natives—you, in particular, Cartimandua. You must admit that you made his life a living torment. And he has had three years in which to prove himself. But all that is behind him now. He is arviragus. He won't come back to you, no matter how you thirst for him. Personally, I find the situation amusing. You, one of our staunchest allies, married to our greatest enemy."

She snapped her fingers impatiently and the servant moved quietly from the shadows to refill her cup. Once again she tipped it high, licking her lips, then she flung it onto the table, where it clashed and rattled amid the debris, coming to rest against Nasica's empty plate. "I fail to see the humor. What will the governor say now?"

"Nothing. Why should he? I have sent on the news, and he will remember who it was that gave Caradoc to the emperor. He will not trouble you, Cartimandua."

She turned onto her back and lay staring at the ceiling, one arm raised across her forehead and the other tapping the back of the couch. Venutius as arviragus. That fumbling, hot-tempered innocent chosen by the master himself to pick up Caradoc's mantle . . . Her lip curled contemptuously. Impossible! Caradoc had had a brilliant, devious mind, a mind that could outwit Scapula time and again, a mind that projected power to his followers, a mind that was rich, whole, unrelenting. Ah Sataida, Caradoc, Caradoc! Venutius was a simple, foolish child, unable to plan his way from the north of his country to the south, let alone plot and carry out military operations year after year. Or was he? Have I ever seen him as a man? she wondered. Perhaps I do not know him at all. Suddenly she was greedy for him, and on the wave of this terrible hunger came an idea. She sat up unsteadily.

"Nasica, order the servants out." With eyebrows raised he did as he was bid, and when the door had closed quietly he turned back to her. She was sitting upright on the edge of the couch, her hands pressed tightly together. "Now," she said. "What will you give me for another arviragus chained at your door?"

You bitch, he thought, looking at her with admiration, seeing her tongue flick out to moisten red lips, the gleam of excitement in her eyes. You fiendish little bitch. How long will it be before there is no one and nothing left to sell, and you begin to feed on yourself? "The price will be the same, I imagine. I will have to send to the governor for confirmation. What makes you think you can do it?"

"While I am living he will not come near me, but dying . . . I think, Nasica, that I must begin to die, very slowly, very painfully."

He lifted his cup in salute and for a moment their eyes met in perfect understanding. Then she said, "Tell me, legate, how do Roman men make love?"

He was not taken aback. He had seen it coming for a long time and had been waiting with amusement. Now she was frenetic, fired, and her movements were jerky and continual. Her hands flew over the table and about her hair, in a tension within her like a tightly coiled spring. The languid sleepy woman had gone, swept away on the tide of this tight, hot-eyed animal. He knew better than she herself what

534

had caused this sudden burst of energy and lust, and something within him answered her impudent invitation with a callous affirmative. "I have no idea," he responded easily, "seeing that I have never been driven to that extremity. But I know how native women make love. With reluctance."

She laughed, and leaving her couch she came and stood over him. "Does a commander stoop to rape?"

"Not usually. It is better for a commander to buy his women." The smile had left his face and he lay relaxed and waiting, his eyes echoing the sarcasm of his words, and she began to strip the jewelry from her arms.

Aricia shut herself up within her house, and Caesius Nasica remarked to his officers during a staff meeting that the Brigantian queen was very ill. Before long the troops were speculating on the nature of her sickness and whether she would die, leaving Brigantia in the far more capable hands of a praetor. The rumor filtered slowly through the forts and garrisons of the lowlands and from thence to the native populations of the towns. By the time a new spring came eagerly elbowing winter out of the way the story had grown. Cartimandua was dying of a wasting disease that shrunk the flesh from her bones and made her unable to stand. Some said it was her goddess's judgment upon her, and a fitting retribution for her betrayal of Caradoc. Some said that the Romans were poisoning her. Some said that now, nearing her end, she had repented of her dishonesties and lay on her bed weeping and tearing her clothes, calling for her husband. Only her most loyal chiefs, Nasica, and the governor knew the truth, and all waited with bated breath for the gossip to reach Venutius's ears.

Spring waxed hot and strong, and Brigantia celebrated Beltine with gaiety. But Aricia, pacing from window to door and back to window in the dim, stifling prison of her Roman house, saw neither the sun dancing on the hill outside nor the black, star-frosted sky. She waited to feel the moment, the right moment, when she could be sure that Venutius had word of her distress and she could send Andocretus to him to confirm the rumors that would surely, she told herself, twist his heart and darken his days. She settled the affairs of the tuath through Andocretus and went no more to the Council hall. She had not bothered to replace Domnall with a new shield-bearer, for her arms had forgotten how to hold sword or shield. Finally she sent for Andocretus.

"Tell me the mood of the tuath," she requested. He closed the door quietly and came to her across the soft sheepskin rugs, his legs bare and tanned with hot sun, his blond hair loose and already bleaching to a gleaming white-gold from days spent with his flocks.

He shrugged. "It has not changed. Your chiefs know that you are not ill, but as Venutius took with him all whose loyalties were suspect, it does not matter. The freemen are busy with sowing and birthing, and I have distributed seed as you ordered, making sure they know it came from Rome."

"Then if I send to Venutius now, and he comes, no Brigantian hand will be raised in his defence?"

He allowed his gaze to travel the sun-starved, pale skin, and the drooping shoulders. The air of lethargy and boredom that enveloped her reached to him also, making him feel suddenly tired. "None at all. No Brigantian rushed to save Caradoc either. There was only your husband, Lady, and now he and his men have gone. You have nothing to fear from Brigantia anymore."

She glanced at him sharply, but innocence shone on his brown face. "Very well. I want you to take a chief and horses and go into the west. Find Venutius. Tell him that I am dying and that I wish to see him and beg his forgiveness. Make up anything else you like, I don't care, but convince him that he must come."

"How am I to reach him before the western wildmen shove a sword through my gut?"

"Do you think the rumor of my illness has come to his ears yet?"

"Yes."

"Then you can be sure that no strange tribesman taken in western territory will be slain before he has had time to give his news. Venutius will be mad for news of me. His anxiety will be destroying him, I know, Andocretus. He will be grasping at every whisper that comes to him out of Brigantia. You will reach him in safety."

"What of Rome?"

She walked away from him and slumped onto her unmade bed. "The governor is sulking. He wants to go home. Now that Scapula's western frontier has been refortified and secured he will not push the rebels because he simply cannot be bothered. He allows the forts and garrisons to defend themselves but he will not let them mount any attack. He feels that he has done his duty now that he has cleaned out Siluria for good. Nasica told me so. You will be able to cross the battle lines without hindrance."

"Gallus wants the emperor to order a full withdrawal from Albion," Andocretus said softly.

"That is why he does nothing. But he is a fool. If he would take a tour of his western frontier himself, he would understand how completely he plays into Venutius's hands by giving the rebels this long respite. Time to eat and grow strong again, time to rest, time to plot. But he does not care. He is nothing but a time-server, and if he leaves

536

Albion before Venutius explodes out of the west once more he will be luckier than he deserves."

Aricia looked down at the hands that had begun to twine about each other of their own volition at the mention of Gallus's desire for the permanent abandonment of Albion. The thought of Rome going away forever was too terrible for her mind to contemplate, but the subsequent thought, the one that brought real, incapacitating fear, was the bloody, fire-rimmed picture of the chieftains of the west, riding out of the mountains at last, like violent gods hunting her down. It will not happen, she told herself vehemently. If I deliver Venutius to the governor it will not happen.

"Our governors have not been lucky men," she said as lightly as she was able, and Andocretus felt his mouth dry up. Roman luck was a weak, pale thing beside Albion's hatred, and he must go on an errand for Rome and face the hostile eyes of Albion's forests, walk the narrow tracks of her mountains, with only Roman luck to ward away her virulence.

"I hate war!" he said suddenly. "My father used to taunt me and call me a coward because I loved my songs and not my sword, but I am not a coward. I simply hate war."

"Poor Andocretus," she said gently. "You should have been a Druid," and he did not hear the contempt in her voice. She knew that he was gifted and handsome and weak, but not in the way Venutius was weak—not weak with too much honor or too much love. Andocretus was weak with too much self-seeking, a mediocrity in everything but his talent. In the days when bards had been Druids he would have failed at both. But he was good to the eye, young and tall and fresh, and she rose to kiss him longingly.

"Go now," she said. "Practice your lying. If your eyes falter when you face Venutius, he will know all, and here. Take him this." She strode to her table and flung a heavy gold necklace to him, encrusted with jet and seed pearls. "This will melt his big heart. It was his wedding gift to me." He caught it and stuffed it into the pouch at his belt. "If you are unlucky enough to tell him your tale with a Druid standing by, and you are accused of falsehood, point out to him that the Druithin have always hated and been suspicious of me. Bring him back, Andocretus, as you love me!"

"But I do not love you, Lady," he quipped as he went to the door and opened it. "Does Nasica?" Then he began to laugh and she laughed also, and he closed the door behind him and walked out the gate under the steady summer sun.

He struck out due west, taking with him another young chief, a member of Aricia's bodyguard, and they went unarmed. When

Scapula disarmed the tribes he had allowed certain ricons and their nobles to retain their weapons, but the majority of Brigantians went without defences and Andocretus had decided that it would be safer for him and his companion to be seen as helpless. They did not hurry. They ambled across the Brigantian hills, their tans deepening under the ceaseless blowing of the hot wind and the bright cascade of sunlight. Their eyes swept across the vast, rolling horizon, and they filled their nostrils full of the odors of bending grasses and hidden flowers. They sang gay songs, and Andocretus was glad to be free of his aging, darkly complex mistress for a while. He could understand her desire to capture an arviragus on Rome's behalf but her constant appetite for a husband she did not love, indeed, one she had fought with through all the years since her return to Brigantia, puzzled him. He put her behind him and did not look ahead, content to savor the lengthening hours of sweet summer daylight, the nights swathed in his cloak listening to the stars' faint music. He and his friend ate well, demanding hospitality from the village chiefs as they went or sharing onions and leeks with odd Roman patrols that moved freely across Brigantia. It was with reluctance that they came at last to the western coast and turned south, walking their horses hock-deep in the gray, swirling foam that sucked at their hanging feet.

"Where is Venutius?" his companion asked him, his brown hair whipping into his eyes as he flung stale crumbs to the seagulls that had followed them every day in a squawking cloud.

Andocretus raised one shoulder, his eyes narrowed against the spray. "I do not know. We will keep to the coast until we reach Deceangli country, then take the first path that strikes inland. We will stop at the fort at Deva, I think, and get news of the rebels."

"I hope they are not summering in the mountains. I hope they have come down to fight. I am afraid of mountains."

"And I, too, but with luck we will have good guides." His friend nodded, smiling, and they cantered on.

A week after they had turned south along the coast they met a Roman patrol out of Deva. There was no laughter and loose talk with these fully armed, flint-faced, grim men who spent their time scouting the foothills. They were men who had lived for so long with the hourly expectation of a savage death that there was no longer anything but a wary animality in their eyes. If Andocretus had not seen them and hailed them fluently in their own tongue they would have shot the two youths from afar. Their centurion wasted no time in conversation with them but yoked their horses together and took them to the fort, he and his men moving swiftly away from the ocean through the Deceangli's brooding forest. Even when the great walls of

538

the fort loomed up out of its little valley, the centurion and his men neither relaxed nor chattered among themselves.

Once arrived, the centurion ushered Andocretus and his friend into the presence of the legate, leaving them without a backward glance. The legate, Manlius Valens, looked them over quickly as they stood before him, his arms folded on his desk.

"Who are you, where are you from, and where are you going?" he snapped crisply.

"We are Brigantian chieftains, seeking contact with Venutius, leader in the west," Andocretus replied smoothly and politely. "We are to tell him that his wife is dying and wishes him to return to her."

"Brigantia," the legate muttered, unfolding his arms to thumb through the dispatches lying piled neatly under his hand. "Brigantia." Andocretus and his companion waited while the man found the message he was looking for. He skimmed it rapidly and then tossed it back onto the desk, favoring them with a cold smile. "What do you want me to tell you?"

Andocretus stepped forward. "We need to know where Venutius is, where his host is summering."

The legate barked once in laughter. "Three days ago he and his men attacked a posting station not twenty miles from here and took all the horses. They killed thirty of my men. He is very close, gathering horses and massing his men, but the governor will not have us attack him before he can fall on us. You will have no trouble finding him. He knows that my hands are tied. Do you want a guide?"

The two young men looked at each other, then Andocretus shook his head. "No, sir. We do not want to take the chance of being seen with a Roman, but we would like supplies."

Valens folded his arms again. "Very well. Good hunting."

They realized that they had been dismissed. Awkwardly, they left the office and wandered onto the parade ground, uncertain who to approach, staring at the motionless men who stood guarding the aquila, the sentries high on the wall, feeling unwanted, a nuisance in this place of constant danger among men who stood endlessly to arms. Andocretus wondered how long it had been since the men of Deva had laughed for sheer happiness. Now I think on it, he mused, I have never heard a Roman laugh for nothing at all, for simply the joy of being alive. What a heavy people they are! Then the legate's secretary emerged from his office and beckoned them, leading them around behind the administration building to the granaries.

"Fill your packs," he told them. "Your horses have been victualed and watered. If you wish, you may stay here today and tonight, but the legate advises you to leave at sundown and put a few miles between yourselves and the fort before you rest. If the tribesmen catch you too close to Deva they will be suspicious." He left them to stuff the grain into their packs. Andocretus had no wish to linger in that forbidding, death-scented place. He and his friend went to the stables, led out their horses, and breathed a sigh of relief when the tall gates slammed shut behind them with indecent haste.

It was noon. The sun was high in a blue, cloud-dotted sky. They hurried out of the valley and entered the forest once more, veering south and slightly west, riding slowly and in silence. The trees closed around them and were immediately suffocating to them both who had been reared under Brigantia's wide sky, and they soon began to sweat. The forest was oppressively still. Occasionally a bird chuckled or the undergrowth rustled, but in the main a brooding quiet weighed down upon them, laying fear on their shoulders and about their necks like soft veils. They did not stop to eat but in the late afternoon, when light shafted through the trees and a slight breeze rustled the dark leaves, Andocretus reined in. "I cannot bear this anymore," he half-whispered. "I am going to climb a tree and see where we are." He stood on his mount's broad back and sprang onto a branch, disappearing upward with scarcely a sound. Minutes went by while the young man on the ground held the horses' heads and peered anxiously above him and around into the evening's first shadows. Then Andocretus sprang down softly beside him. "Far to the south the forest begins to thin," he panted, "and rocks and cliffs appear. But I think we have another day's march before we reach the foot of the mountains. We will make camp here."

They led their horses deep in under the arms of the oaks, to a place where the sky was utterly blotted out by high-soaring branches, and there they ate a cold meal and unrolled their blankets. Andocretus ventured farther into the wood to find a stream, for they were very thirsty, but his companion would not stir from the friendly sounds of the snuffling horses. When Andocretus came back, the full skins slung over his shoulder, the other said in a half-whisper, "Who are the gods of these woods, Andocretus, do you know? Who do the Deceangli worship?" Andocretus handed him the water and wriggled under his blanket. "I do not know. But all the men of the west, and the Romans too, move freely here. I do not think the gods of the Deceangli will molest us. Samain is far away." Nevertheless, they lay side by side while the shadows thickened and the sun vanished, gazing up into the moving darkness above them, their ears straining. Neither of them slept, and when dawn came, colorless and heatless, they got up quickly and left that place.

All day they plodded through an unending green ocean of summer-lit leaves. Twice they crossed little streams that gurgled hypnotically, running clear and very cold to disappear under last year's damp russet carpet. Andocretus did not bother to make sure the horses made no mark in the wet spongy moss overhanging the banks of the water. He wanted this silent, tree-prisoned journey to end. When the light began to fail they again left the faint but unmistakable track they had been following and made another fireless camp, noting that the ground was no longer soft and yielding and the soil was thinner, barely covering the broken rock beneath. The trees had been thinning, too, and their girth and height was less. Fear lay like ugly burdens on them now and they kept close together, lying back to back under a tree with their eyes wide open and their hands aching for knife or sword. Stars winked fitfully at them as the night wind stirred the forest's roof, and apart from the scratching of leaf on leaf, the silence was absolute. Then Andocretus, staring with tired eyes into the gloom, thought he caught the glint of moon on metal. He sat up. It was there again, a flicker of dull light, and he rose to his feet, dragging his friend with him. With their hearts pounding they strove to see with their ears, hear with their eyes, and then they found themselves knocked to the earth with a speed and suddenness that stunned them. Andocretus, the dark forest spinning around him, saw a nightmare bending over him, the frozen snarl of an angry wolf whose black mane tumbled over his chest. He closed his eyes.

"Kill them quickly and let us be gone!" he heard the wolf say. "We are too close to Deva, and the night is fine. The patrols will be out."

"Wait," a deep voice answered it. "Wait." Hands touched the jet necklace at Andocretus's throat, and the bracelet on his arm, and he lay very still and would not open his eyes. Then rough hands lifted him as though he were a wisp of grass and set him on his feet. "Open your eyes, Andocretus," the same voice commanded, and he obeyed.

The wolf was standing looking at him, its face a metal horror, but Andocretus, with a rush of gladness, fixed his eyes on the black-bearded chief whose hands still gripped him by his hair. "Domnall! Brigantia has given me luck! My lady is in such trouble but I was afraid that I would never find the arviragus! Will you take us to him?" Behind Domnall and the wolf, seven or eight chiefs stood in the gloom, unmoving, as quiescent and dark as the forest itself. Domnall released Andocretus slowly and the wolf turned its stiff face to him.

"Then the rumors are true!" it whispered. "Aricia . . ."

"Hold your tongue, Sine!" Domnall said, then he stepped up to Andocretus until his breath warmed the other's cheek. "I must now decide, my one-time brother, whether to kill you here or take you

541

with us. Your facility for lying is well known to me, Andocretus. Indeed, you lie better than you sing, and that is well enough. How come you here?"

Marshaling his scattered forces, Andocretus lifted his eyes to meet Domnall's. "I do not come willingly," he said in a low, hurried voice. "I am afraid of these forests, afraid of the mountains. But my lady is dying, Domnall. Day after day she lies on her bed, and her flesh has shriveled to her bones. The Roman physician can do nothing for her. She longs only to see her husband, to beg from him forgiveness for the wasted years. She sent me to find him, out of her desperation." Blue eyes locked with brown ones, but Domnall was no Druid. His gaze fell first and he frowned at the ground.

" 'Happy is he who dies slowly,' " he quoted, " 'for he may recover his soul.' So say the Druids. And yet . . . yet . . ."

"Kill them now and let us go!" Sine urged him. "That woman has never told a truth in all her life! Domnall, he lies to you!"

Domnall's wide shoulders hunched. "Be still, Sine. This is a matter of kin, a private matter, and you may not interfere."

"But your lord is now arviragus! His loyalty no longer goes to the kin!"

Domnall ignored her and Andocretus looked at her curiously. This was no wolf. Only a slender, weapon-girt woman, whose black hair fell over the bronze mask that hid her face. But out of that mask two moon-glittering eyes poured suspicion over him. Finally Domnall straightened. "I do not think that he lies," he said, "but even if he does, this matter is too weighty for me. My lord must hear. Tie them onto their horses!" he called to the men behind him. "Blindfold them!" Firm hands took Andocretus and the young chief back to the path, and Sine caught Domnall by the arm.

"You know what this could do to him," she said. "Even if the young man lies, the doubt will tear him in two. Domnall, I beg you, kill the messengers, kill the rumors. If it is true then no matter. Let her die as she deserves. If not you will have done him a great service."

"Sine, I cannot," he replied, the frown still furrowing his face. "He has ordered all strangers brought to him and, besides, if he knew that I had hidden such news he would slay me. There are Druids in the camp. We . . ." But she had swung away from him and was disappearing into the darkness.

For the rest of the night and far into the morning they glided through the forest, and Andocretus, sightless on his horse, his wrists tied together behind his back, marveled at how he seemed to be alone. No sound of human footfall came to his ears, no whiff of human presence, yet he knew that ten people accompanied him. They

542

gave Andocretus and his friend no food or water, nor did they stop to eat themselves. His horse plodded steadily onward, jolting him so that soon his muscles cried out, for they were climbing steadily, weaving back and forth. Wind began to play on his face. At last he began to hear something, or thought he did, a murmuring, a quiet sound of continual movement, and then a word was spoken. His horse came to a halt. Hands reached for him, pulling him down, and he stood shakily while a knife parted the rope around his arms and the blindfold was torn from his head. He looked around him, blinking in bright sunlight. Gray, tattered tents spread like clumsy gulls as far as he could see, half-buried in scrub and rocks. A few small fires burned without smoke, tended carefully by limber, squatting men, and men and women sprawled silently outside the tents or stood in quiet groups. His glance found the horizon, a long, tree-clad slope that ended in naked rock where sentries perched. Behind him the slope continued to a river and on to the eaves of the forest he had left, and more men and women stood like the trees themselves, unmoving, at intervals along the bank, their eyes turned to the cool green depths of the wood. His friend was beside him, pale and nursing sore wrists but unhurt, and they smiled tentatively at each other, acknowledging without words the bare discomfort of this forbidding place, the oppression in the muted sounds of a camp that should have been alive with laughter and shouts.

He and his companion were ordered to sit next to one of the fires, and they sank to the ground with relief. Food was brought to them— cold rabbit, bitter bread, an onion apiece, and hunks of white, strong-smelling cheese, all washed down with black beer that tasted of sour, rotting undergrowth. Then they sat in that animal quiet, their guard's eyes fixed on them, while the afternoon drowsed on. They finally dozed also, with two sleepless days and nights behind them, and they felt, in some odd way, completely safe.

Their guard woke them and they rose at once to dusk. Around them the fires were being extinguished and the last of the day's orange and pink light still lay gently on the lip of the little valley. The forest slumbered in its evening dimness, but long, thin shadows followed the three men who came striding up the slope toward Andocretus and his companion. With a beating heart Andocretus recognized Venutius, but he did not know the short, burly chief who swaggered beside him, or the graceful one who walked a step behind. He faced them, bowing to Venutius, and the familiar riot of red hair and beard, the wild, piercing eyes and swooping nose brought a sickness frothing inside him. Venutius knew that he was more than his lady's bard, but those alert eyes met his own without rancor. Only Venutius's mouth betrayed pain. It was slightly parted, ready to tremble into anger or contort with grief. Andocretus remembered that face twisted into agony, shamed under pitiless sunlight, and the blood that had fled down the shuddering chest. The sickness threatened to reach his mouth. He swallowed and faced his greatest test. "Greetings, Lord," he said. "I am glad to have found you at last."

Venutius did not hold out his hand, nor did he introduce his chieftains. He stood looking into Andocretus's face, afraid yet crying out to find there what he sought. In spite of himself Andocretus's own face drew into an expression of tense antagonism.

"You have eaten and drunk," Venutius said at last. "Now give me your news. No, wait. Emrys, have the Druid called to me." The chief went away sheltering a disturbing air of latent ferocity. When he returned Andocretus saw to his dismay that the same Druid who had come to see his lady in Brigantia was with him, striding like a man on naked feet, her small, bony shoulders swinging, and her thin face brittle with hostility. The young man beside him stirred and exclaimed quietly and Andocretus wanted to clap a hand over his mouth to him to keep silent.

"Well," she said as she came up. "It is the Lady Aricia's pretty singing boy." She halted beside Emrys, and Venutius made a swift, savage gesture, but she spoke again. "Now we will discover if the rumors are true."

Andocretus looked back at Venutius, whose face had turned ashen. "Speak!" he commanded, and Andocretus forced his eyes to hold Venutius's. It was hard, harder than anything he had ever done, more distasteful than he thought it would be, but he said the words.

"Lord, she is dying. She has so little flesh left that she is no longer like a woman. She begs you, she implores you to come to her so that she may tell you how she has wronged you before death claims her. She bade me give you this." He willed his fingers not to shake as he opened the pouch on his belt and drew out the necklace. "She does not ask that you remain with her, only that you give her a moment of forgiveness." He held out the jewels and Venutius slowly took them, turning them over in his fingers. Then his other hand came up to grip them also, and his head went down. "Druid," he whispered huskily. "Tell me again the words she used of me," and Andocretus saw Emrys and the stout, black-haired chief exchange glances. The Druid answered promptly.

" 'I despise my husband, I have always despised him, and I do not want him back.' "

Venutius's knuckles showed white. "You have called the rumors false," he said again to the Druid. "What do you say now? Look at this youth, and for the Mother's sake, give me truth!" His voice rose, a cry of despair, and the Druid looked coolly at Andocretus's beautiful, tanned face, the clear blue eyes, the blond hair that wafted shining to the slim shoulders. Andocretus kept his gaze fixed on her tiny mouth for fear his eyes would tell her everything.

After a time she sighed. "He is a liar," she said bluntly. "A magnificent, handsome young liar. Your wife is not dying, Arviragus. She is not even ill—that is, her body does not suffer. I give you truth."

"I told you!" the big chief grunted triumphantly, a smile weaving yet another furrow through his lined face. "Now slay this bird and think no more on the matter!"

Venutius looked up slowly, and in that moment Andocretus believed that he had won. No one would ever be able to tell the arviragus a truth about his wife. Though he himself had heard the words of hate and treachery from her own lips, though he had torn his body away from her, yet he still chose the mind's blindness, and in that blindness was a living, growing cloud of doubt that was anchored to his love, so that with her or away from her he no longer believed or disbelieved anything about her. Andocretus spoke again, gently, softly.

"Lord, you know the hatred the Druithin have for your lady, and so does she for them. That is why she sends you the only treasure left to her, your wedding gift, and begs you, as you once loved her, to listen only to her torment. She is dying. She needs you now."

"Ah Lord, how well she knows you!" the burly chief burst out. "Only this could bring you back to her, she knows it, so she is busy dying! This is a trap!"

"Peace, Madoc!" Venutius was controlling himself with difficulty. His glance slipped from the Silurian to the Druid, from Emrys's quiet pity to Andocretus, seeking one ray of certitude, one glitter of truth under the impenetrable cloaks of flesh around him. He passed a freckled hand over his face and groaned. "Emrys, come," he ordered and turned away, walking like a drunken man, swaying a little, one hand on his sword hilt and the other clutched tight over the necklace. Andocretus watched him go but did not dare to glance at his friend.

Out of sight of the camp, Venutius lowered himself to the earth, wrapping his arms about his legs and resting his head on his knees. Emrys sank cross-legged beside him, watching the night fall and feeling the wind come whispering to him, laden with the subtle scents of forest and water. It stirred the rich hair of the man sunk under the weight of misery beside him, it lightly and warmly fingered the bowed back. Emrys sat on, his thoughts passing slowly to the years of Caradoc, the desperate years, then past them to his own hearth, long cold, his own hut now tumbled into ruin. He surveyed the memories with wonder, he and Sine young and free together, so innocent then, so strong, but a war-battered stranger had come, with his son-child who was also a chief, and he and Sine had not known that he brought with him an ending. Caradoc. My brother, my lord, my fate. So many terrible partings in this life that is a constant death, so many heartbreaks. We did not believe that we could fight on without you, yet with the last breath you drew from Albion's air you ordered it to be, and lo, the master called forth a new arviragus. The red days stride on, giving us no rest, no rest at all. We are damned, each one of us, and now . . . this. At last Venutius stirred in the darkness, lifted his head, and Emrys put away the sadness and looked at him.

"Tell me what I shall do, Emrys." The voice was tired, formed thickly from a black mud of hopelessness. "Tell me quickly. Who lies and who hates? Who dies and who goes toward death?"

"I think it does not matter who lies or hates," Emrys replied gravely. "What does matter is that you are arviragus. You are lord of our life and our death, not your wife's, and whether she lives or dies is no longer your concern. You have been her prisoner all your life, Venutius. Set yourself free! Send the youths away or kill them, and put Cartimandua behind you. Since you came to us you have had a measure of peace, and out of that peace has come strengths you did not know you possessed. The Druithin chose you well. The time of our deliverance is at hand, you know it, you can feel it just as the rest of us can. The new governor has played wondrously into our hands. Before another moon's swelling we will have gathered together the greatest force since Caradoc's last mustering, and Deva will fall to us. That is the beginning, only the beginning. Freedom is in sight after all the years of loss and shame and murder. How desperately we need you, Arviragus! The new campaign is yours—you have plotted it, you hold its execution in your hands. If you leave us now we must delay, and if we delay too long then all is lost. Stay with us. We will smash Scapula's frontier again like rotten wood, and then the emperor will take the legions away, even as the rumors say."

Venutius listened, the hand that held the necklace unconsciously pressing it to his chest, and when Emrys's pleading voice fell silent, he asked quietly, "What would you do, Emrys, if you were I and it was Sine who called to you?"

"I would go," Emrys admitted without pause, "But Lord, Sine loves me and gives me only truth. We do not lie to each other as your wife lies ceaselessly to you. Forgive me, but I do not believe she is ill, nor do I believe that she is worth one thought from you, let alone a lifetime of unreturned love and lost honor."

"Yet, Emrys, suppose she is really dying? Suppose she calls to me out of a heart burdened with remorse? Must I refuse her?"

"Yes, you must. You have nothing for which to reproach yourself."

Venutius struggled to his feet and Emrys rose with him. Full night had fallen now, and the darkness folded them within itself. To Venutius it seemed that his soul was like that blackness, sealed in on itself, jealously imprisoning the long disease of his love and his hurt so that no cure could reach him. "If the Druids thought to heal me of my sickness by placing the mantle of arviragus around my shoulders they were wrong," he said harshly. "I am broken, Emrys, every day I am broken anew, my strengths are Madoc's, Sine's, yours, not my own. I must go to her, even if she would destroy me."

"Venutius, the whole of the west is paused on the brink of victory, waiting on your word! This is madness! Men and women have died, died I tell you, so that this day would come! I will not let you go!"

"I have no choice!" Venutius cried to him. "Surely you see that! Think of your Sine, and help me, Emrys!"

"Then let me go," Emrys said gently. "Sine and I will carry your words to her, and if I am wrong, if she is indeed near death, I will return to face your sword. You cannot, you must not go." In the darkness he could sense the struggle played out, and he was very glad that the night hid his arviragus's face from him. Venutius turned and leaned his forehead against a tree, his eyes squeezed shut. After a long time he whispered, "You are wise, Emrys. Very well. I will not go, but neither must you. You are needed here. I will send others."

"Who?"

"Domnall."

"No, he has not been with us for long enough and, besides, you will not trust the word of one man. Let Sine go, and perhaps a member of your family kin."

"Yes. I will send my nephew Manaw, and Brennia, his wife." He left the tree. "Forgive me, Emrys. I was not thinking. I will not break thus again."

Emrys did not answer, and Venutius turned and walked back to where the camp hunched almost invisibly in its protecting valley.

When Venutius handed the necklace back to Andocretus and told him that he could not go with him there was a moment of dumbfounded silence, then Andocretus exclaimed, "But Lord, if you do not come she will cease to fight for life! My lady will turn her face to the wall and die!" Tears glimmered on the long, fair lashes. Andocretus was indeed overcome with emotion, but it was at the thought of

Aricia's face when he had to stand before her and tell her that her husband was no longer altogether her slave. Venutius could take no more.

"Emrys, tell him," he said brusquely, then he turned on his heel and walked off in the gloom.

"He has not said that he will not go," Emrys told Andocretus coolly. "But until he can know without doubt that your lady ails he does not dare to leave the west."

"But he offends my honor! He doubts my word! I . . ."

"Young man," Emrys cut in wearily. "The whole of Brigantia is tainted with your lady's dishonor and you know it. No Brigantian chief is taken at his word anymore. My wife will accompany you home, together with the arviragus's own blood kin, and ascertain as quickly as they may whether you have told the truth. When they return, and swear oaths that she is indeed near death, then he will go."

There was nothing Andocretus could do. He nodded curtly to Emrys, thinking with dismay of the miles he and his friend would have to cover in the company of rebels, and what would happen to them if the Romans caught them and did not give him time to explain his errand. Emrys went away, and he shook out his blanket behind a rock and composed himself for sleep. No music fluttered through his mind that night.

The five of them left camp with the dawn, striking east through the pathless trees. "We will veer south through Cornovii country and then back up into Brigantia to avoid Deva," Sine had told Andocretus firmly and he had not dared to argue with her, afraid as he was of her battered metal wolf's face and her long iron sword. He vaguely remembered Venutius's nephew and his wife, two young, silent free-people with whom he had never shared a word in the days of growing, before his lady had called him to her bed. He was no more interested in them now than he had been then. They were the arviragus's blood kin, but they came from his brother's farm far to the north, where Venutius himself had been reared and where most of his loyal chiefs had grown up. Although Venutius loved his kin fiercely and had spent much time in the north with them after his marriage, they had not come to the town.

Andocretus mounted his horse in the stale, used air that waited to be blown away by the dawn's rush, feeling sick with apprehension as he saw Emrys and the wolf mask draw away from the company together into the morning mist and realized that Sine held him and his friend in the palm of her hand. He did not know Cornovii country or the routes into Brigantia from the little-used paths of the central south, and if the woman chose to leave them suddenly they were as good as dead.

Emrys lifted the grotesque mask from his wife's face and took her in his arms. "Do not trust the pretty boy for one instant," he said. "Do not let him leave your side to hunt or draw water, or for any other reason, and give him no chance to talk to his friend in private. If Aricia is whole, as I believe her to be, and one of those youths brings her word of your coming, she will kill you. Your only chance of return if she is well is to see her and run before she has time to collect her wits. If you feel yourself to be in the slightest danger on the journey, kill the Brigantians and come back. The arviragus's peace of mind is not worth your life." Be careful, he wanted to say to her. Be cowardly, be craven, be as the Brigantians are, but come back to me! He gently kissed the firm, cruel mouth that softened only at his word, smiled into hard eyes that only he could turn into wells of brief laughter or passion, and for a moment she rested her head against the warmth of his shoulder.

"This journey is so useless, so senseless," she whispered. "Why should he care anymore whether she lives or dies? Why should I risk my life for the sake of his stupid, doomed obsession?"

"For the sake of our own stupid, doomed obsession," he replied, his words lost in the blackness of her hair. "He must be free, the end is in sight, his mind must be wholly on war. He could be as brilliant a leader, in his own way, as Caradoc was, if only he could shake himself free of this woman." They stood straight and he handed her the mask. "Walk in safety," he said at last. "I love you, Sine."

"And I you, Lord. Go in peace." She raised an arm. Once more the wolf snarled a hungry warning at him, and she turned away and left him.

They trekked for a week, moving steadily south and east, though as far as Andocretus and his companion were concerned they could have been riding in circles. Sine led them silently and unerringly, Andocretus and his chief behind her, and the two young Brigantian rebels brought up the rear. At night Venutius's nephew spent a few hours hunting while the others sat in some hidden dell or cave, or beside some shallow stream without speaking, Sine and the woman somehow managing to interpose themselves between Andocretus and his friend so that private words were impossible. Andocretus's thoughts scurried hither and thither, becoming wilder as Brigantia neared, plan following half-formed plan, and he despaired of getting any word to his lady. She would greet them dressed in all her finery, standing strongly on her own two feet, and the reward for her husband's capture would stay snugly locked in the coffers of the fort at Lindum. When it was time for sleep one of Venutius's kin or Sine herself kept guard, and even when Sine lay down to rest, Andocretus could feel her eyes on him, unblinking and contemptuously hostile behind the bronze mask. She was like some wild wolf cub that the Brigantian children sometimes carried to their huts to tame, grown now into an unstable animal adulthood, still with the ferocity of its free, blood-hungry roots staring out from behind its wily eyes. He was afraid of her.

Andocretus's chance came late one afternoon, two days' march away from the town. The heavy woodland of Brigantia's extreme south was behind them and they rode now over the first rolling, wind-raked moors. Sine and Venutius's kin were tiring, and their weariness was exacerbated by the nakedness they felt under the wide blue sky, stripped of protection and uncomfortably visible, just as Caradoc had once felt on his way to this same town with Caelte and the traitor. But Andocretus and his friend drew deep lungfuls of the scentless wind and hope came to them as they were able to lift their eyes and gaze for unimpeded miles over small villages dotted like islands, and streams gushing fast and almost unbanked. Here and there in the depressions where the hills swooped down only to rise again, were trees, trees one could count, trees that did not encircle and engulf.

They were camped under just such a stand of thin trees, sitting in the pale shade while the sun beat down around them, when Sine suddenly put a hand to the earth. "Horses!" she snapped. Immediately, she lay prone with her ear pressed against the dry grass, and Andocretus watched her, his heart in his mouth. "I think it is a cavalry patrol," she said after a while, and before the words had left her mouth her companions were leaping to their own mounts, drawing them deeper into the copse's frail cover. Then all five of them were flat to the ground, waiting tensely. Andocretus found himself next to his chief. Softly, slowly, he inched his face against the other's dark hair. "When the patrol has passed," he breathed, "run." The other made no movement, gave no sign of having heard, but Andocretus knew he had been understood. For almost half an hour they did not stir, while the patrol came on slowly, easily, and even when it passed so close to them that Andocretus could hear the voices of the officer and his men, none of the five so much as blinked, and the horses themselves, long trained among the silence of the west, made no whinnies of greeting. Sine kept her ear to the minute trembling in the soil beneath her until long after all sound had been swallowed up in the wind's sigh, then she sat up and opened her mouth to speak. Andocretus did not give her time. He rolled over and flung himself on top of her, and with a grunt his chief sprang to his feet and shot out of the copse, bent low, feet fleet and light, speeding in the direction of a village whose smoke smudged the air two miles away. With an oath Venutius's nephew leaped after him, while Sine fought against Andocretus's smothering weight. Then Andocretus felt himself jerked from her and an arm went around his throat. Sine cursed and shot out from under the trees and Andocretus felt the other woman's knife cold under his ear. "Do not move, beautiful boy," she said, the first words she had addressed to him in all the days behind them, and he closed his eyes and shivered.

Sine drew her knife as she ran. She could see Venutius's nephew ahead, his arms and legs pumping frantically, but far beyond him the Brigantian flowed like water over the ground, settling into the stride that had once brought admiration to Brigantian freepeople from those tribes where the territory did not offer unlimited open spaces over which to run. Venutius's nephew had been in the mountains too long, and though his muscles were hard and firm he had forgotten how to run. Sine sprinted desperately, knowing that she would soon tire, forcing herself to breathe deeply in time to her lope. A little closer, her legs prayed, a little closer, her arms shouted, then she saw the fugitive stumble and then recover, and she had gained a little ground. It was now, or she had lost him. The blade of her knife slid lightly into her palm. "Down, Manaw!" she shouted and he immediately fell to the earth. At the same moment her arm came up and she flung the knife, and raced after it, not breaking her stride as it flew upward, outward, turning over and over, flashing in the sun. Then the Brigantian screamed, staggered, and fell, and by the time she had jogged unsteadily up to him he was dead. Stooping, she wrenched her knife from between his shoulder blades, wiped it on his breeches, and returned it to her belt and Manaw walked to her, still panting. "Take an arm," she ordered hoarsely, and together they dragged him back to the concealment of the copse.

"You stupid young fool!" she spat at Andocretus. "The lady would have been warned and would have killed us, and later she would have sent another victim into the west to enquire of the arviragus where her bard and her necklace were and why he himself had not come to her on her deathbed. But you did not think past such cleverness, did you?" She squatted in the shade and removed her mask to wipe the sweat from her face, and Andocretus saw her face for the first time, a brown face without sweetness or gentleness, yet coldly, caustically beautiful with its sharp bones, its huge black eyes, its thin, spare mouth and pointed chin. It was not a youthful face but he did not know whether that was because it had never had the soft curves of cheek and temple which belong to youth, or whether those curves had been planed away by the harshness of her life. Around her eyes went lines of weathering and war, but it was a simple, clean face, pure in its harshness. She could have been Emrys's sister, not his wife, they were so alike in grace of feature and body, in the music of danger about them. He stared at her as she wiped the blood from her fingers.

"Now I am convinced that your lady is the queen of liars. You did not consider that, did you?" The knife still pressed into his neck and he did not dare to shake his head.

"Let us slay this one also," the woman said, "and go back into the west," but after a moment of swift thought, Sine disagreed.

"The arviragus would not be satisfied," she said bitterly. "At first he might believe, but then he would begin to wonder whether this idiot," she stirred the corpse with one foot, "simply fled in an excess of fear, or whether one of us had mistaken an innocent movement of his and had slain him out of our own weariness and fear. No. We must go on and play this stupid game to its end. We will see this bitch with our own eyes, and then the arviragus will be content. Release him." The woman sheathed her knife reluctantly, and Sine leaned forward, taking Andocretus by the chin in a grip of steel. "And you, my fine, gutless little bird. Make one rash move and I will forget my mission and carve you into a thousand red pieces." Her tone was not malicious but matter-of-fact, and they rose and untethered the horses without another word.

Two days later, at about the same hour, they dismounted at the foot of Aricia's tall earthwall and walked through the unmanned gate, mingling with the crowds that sauntered unhurriedly to and fro in the soft, failing sunlight. Andocretus's quick eye saw that there were more than the usual number of Roman soldiers, standing in twos and threes or pacing among the freemen. Sweat trickled under his armpits as he thought of his lady, with all her preparations complete, waiting impatiently for him in her house.

Sine gave him no chance to catch a legionary's eye. She came up to him, drawing her knife under cover of her cloak. "Now," she said in a low voice. "I will lean on you, thus." She draped her left arm over his right shoulder, "as though I am very tired, and you will put your arm around my waist." He did so unwillingly, feeling the warm muscles, tight as a man's, under the short tunic, and her right hand came up and pressed the knife under his ribs. "If you signal or cry out I will kill you," she went on. "Lead us to the lady's house. How many men does she have to guard her?"

Andocretus swallowed. "Six."

"Ah. And I suppose all these Romans have been gathered to escort the arviragus to Lindum."

So she too had noticed. Andocretus relapsed into despair. "There are always soldiers and traders here," he answered and she nodded once.

"Do you think I am stupid? When we reach the house you must call her with excitement in your voice—excitement, mind you. She will step forth, and my task will be over. Lead on, liar."

Slowly, they wended their way up through the town. Sine made Andocretus take the alleys but everyone was out breathing the limpid air and many curious glances followed the group as they passed—the lady's young bard, a weary freewoman in a wolf's mask, and two foreign tribespeople. Andocretus did not even try to attract the attention of those chiefs who knew him. The knife pressed viciously into his side and in any case, he told himself, what would be the use? Venutius is not with us. I might have considered giving my life if he had been, but I will not die for the capture of these three.

Before long they were facing Aricia's high stone wall and her iron gate. Sine glanced back, as a steady sea wind lifted the hair from her hot neck. She could see beyond the huts and houses of the town, beyond the lowering earthwall, to where land rolled away to become clothed in the blur of the comforting forest, and the falling sun's streamers lay like red pools in the hollows and ran down the hills like rivers. For one moment she almost turned and fled, seeing herself running free again toward Emrys and the west. With the yearning in her the knife trembled against the young man, but she gave him a push and turned her metal face to the shadow of the gate. "Speak!" she whispered.

"Open!" he croaked hoarsely. "It is I, Andocretus!"

The high gate swung open, and Sine's quick scrutiny showed her a compound, a large wooden house, and a cluster of armed chiefs, all clothed in the coming night, all encompassed by that smooth high wall. The men holding the gate stood waiting but she hesitated, knowing now that if she stepped within and the gate was closed there would be no escape. And of course the gate would be closed. There would be nothing but that unscalable wall. She should have guessed, she should have asked the bard, but it was too late. I do not deserve this, she thought bitterly. After all the years I have managed to stay alive, against all the odds, to be caught at the last and to fall, not in battle, but trapped by a woman I could kill blindfolded in combat. Andocretus gasped as the knife suddenly slid through his clothing and pierced his skin, and a warm wetness blossomed under his tunic. Sine gritted her teeth and jerked her head, and together they walked toward the waiting chiefs. The gate boomed shut behind them.

In the middle of the courtyard Sine stopped, and Manaw and his wife came to stand close to her. "I have changed my mind," she muttered to Andocretus. "Order one of her chiefs to go into the house and tell her that you are here, together with the one she expects."

Andocretus raised his voice with an effort. "Go and tell the ricon that I have returned," he called, "and that the one she expects is here. He waits in the Council hall for word of whether she is well enough to see him."

The chiefs looked with suspicion at Sine, draped over their lady's bard like a lover, but as she slowly stood straight one of them muttered something to his fellows and strode away. Sine's heart began to beat in slow, even strokes. If the lady was ill they were safe, but that swift spark of longing for self-preservation soon died. They all waited in a tension of fear, their eyes on the now-open door of the house, as the sun rimmed the horizon far away and began to gather its light into itself once more.

Then she appeared, a tall, red-tunicked form darkening the doorway, pulling the firelight with her as she sprang onto the porch. Venutius's cousin gave a little cry. Sine felt an ache for her arviragus begin deep inside her, for this woman was beautiful despite the gray-streaked hair and the loose, age-marred face, and a man might lose his way in those hooded black eyes and forget who he was. Aricia slipped toward them, then halted. Sine held her breath.

"Greetings, Andocretus," the sweet, rich voice fluted. "You have done well. Now who is the creature that presses against you with such passion, and where is Venutius?"

Andocretus could not trust himself to answer her, and while he struggled, Sine's clear tones rang out across the gathering gloom. "Greetings, Lady. I am your husband's oathed freewoman. He waits for news of you in your hall. I will bring him to you." She released Andocretus, and Manaw and his wife turned with her as she walked boldly to the gate.

"No, you will not," Aricia called sharply. "Andocretus, you fetch him. You know what to do." Sudden suspicion edged her voice, then certainty exploded as Sine and the other two began to run. Andocretus slumped to the ground where he squatted, a hand to his oozing wound and his head reeling, and the rebels flung themselves upon the gate, clawing frantically, with desperation in their fingers and their scrabbling feet.

"Take them!" Aricia shouted, and her men leaped forward. Rough hands tore Sine and the others away from the gate, and there was no time to draw sword, no time to fight. Aricia walked to them with rage bubbling in the jet-studded fingers, the stiff, jet-hung shoulders. With one savage movement she tore the wolf mask from Sine's face, and

Sine, imprisoned by strong arms, gazed back at her, panting a little. Her life was over and she knew it, yet the eyes that met Aricia's own were steady. To end like this, she thought. How wasteful, how needless. Yet the arviragus is safe and surely nothing else can matter.

"Disarm them," Aricia ordered again, and sword belts and knives were efficiently removed and flung to the ground. She peered more closely at Venutius's cousin, then she suddenly laughed. "So! It is little Manaw. You should have stuck to snaring rabbits, boy, and left the snaring of men to those with the stomach for it." She would have taunted him further, but something in his eyes, a fatalism, a mature and sorrowless acceptance of his fate, made her swing back to Sine. "Where is Venutius?" she spat, and behind her Andocretus finally swayed to his feet and came to her side.

"He will not come until he is assured that you are not deceiving him," he said with difficulty, his hands still against his side. "His kinsmen must bring him word that your message is truthful."

She rounded on him savagely. "Then you failed! I should have known better than to trust such a matter to a mere boy!"

Pretty boy, he thought dully, angrily, beautiful boy, little bird. Pain was spreading up under his arm and the blood still slipped warmly down his thigh. For once in his life he spoke recklessly. "You call me other names when I am between your sheets, Lady!" he snapped. "I did not fail. Your husband would have come but his chieftains talked him out of it. Think carefully of what you do with them, for that one," he curtly indicated Sine, "is the wife of one of the rebel leaders, a powerful man. I am going to get salve for my hurt." He stepped past her, rapped an order, and the gate opened to let him pass through. Aricia looked after him for a moment, with narrowed eyes, then she swung back to Sine. Color flamed like red poppies in her cheeks, and insolently, happily, Sine grinned at her. "He will not come," she said. "He has found a larger love, Brigantian whore." With the speed of a striking snake Aricia's jet-ringed hand flew up, and blood trickled down Sine's cheek where the sharp stones raked her.

"Put them under guard," Aricia said, her voice shaking, her body shaking, the mist of a mad urge to tear and trample before her eyes. "Chain them to the wall, neck, arms, and feet. Take their torcs away from them."

She whirled away, marching into her house, and the door slammed shut behind her. Standing in the dark, silent room where nothing moved but the flames of her fire and her own heaving chest, she found herself still clutching the wolf mask. She looked it over carefully. The front, though highly polished, was buckled and dented, and she allowed her fingers to wander over the rise and fall of old sword marks, hills and valleys of pride and honor, the smooth bronze shine of a lifetime of dreams pathed in danger, furrowed in courage. Some fierce western man missed this woman. Somewhere his thoughts turned to her in longing and anxiety. Aricia reversed the mask. The underside was blackened with breath and sweat. On an impulse she fitted it to her own face. Immediately, her room seemed to lengthen. Details sprang at her out of the gloom—the sharp ridges of her table, a painful glitter of firelight on jewels, the curve and coil of Brigantia's face and hair, the late evening light forming a gray square around the shutters of her window. Strong odors filled her nostrils, odors she had been unaware of before. The sweet scent of woodsmoke, a cloying stench of tanned sheephides, the warm, familiar drift of sleep and pleasure from her blankets, even a hot, sparkling whiff of crystal and gold from her treasures. Startled, she put a hand to her bronze forehead. Then another smell wafted to her, faint but growing stronger, the sickly clinging stink of freshly spilled blood, and with it was mingled another odor, the odor of decay, the odor of her dream, rising in invisible fogs around her. She coughed, then suddenly could not breathe. She fought frantically to draw air into her mouth but the mask seemed to be pinching her nostrils and lips closed, and all the time that other insidious presence, blood and rot, caught in her throat and choked her. With fingers of panic she picked off the mask and flung it from her, and it clattered to the floor and lay sneering at her. The room snapped back to its proper dimensions. Her gagging mouth drew in lungfuls of warm, unscented air and she ran to the door, wrenching it open and screaming for wine. When it was brought to her, and her lamps had been lit, she sat drinking, pondering her next move. She thought of the three who hung chained to her prison walls, of her husband, slipping away from her, and of the kind of love that had never been hers. Her eyes were on the mask by her feet, and she tried to wash away with wine the jealousy and hurt she had felt when she looked into Sine's calm face, but she could not. The mask mocked her. Her own longing for something unnamed mocked her. The devotion of some chief she had never seen for his foolhardy wife, now in her hands, mocked her. She was alone.

In the morning she had Manaw's wife brought before her. "You will go back into the west," she said clearly, carefully, "and you will tell Venutius that if he does not come to me I will kill his nephew and the woman. I will not give them to Rome, mark you. I will kill them with my own hands, on my earthwall, within sight of the whole of Brigantia." The girl paled. Such a milk-and-water chit, Aricia thought derisively. Such a timid nothing of a face, such hesitant eyes, such nauseating sweetness. She did not hide her contempt, and the girl saw it there, in the lovely black eyes. She ignored it.

"Then you may do it," she answered levelly, though the color continued to recede from the delicate cheeks. "My lord and Sine discussed just such a thing last night. They knew when your guard came for me what you would say to me. And I say this to you, Ricon. If you wish to kill them, do it now, for I will go into the west and deliver your message, but I will not come back, and neither will the arviragus. You mean less than nothing to him now, and what are two more dead tribesmen when weighed against the cause of freedom?" She raised two ragged shoulders. "Send me if you will, but I would prefer to die beside my husband."

Aricia looked at her, baffled, conscious once again of the wall that had separated her from Venutius himself, and Domnall, and Caradoc, the wall that represented a perspective of life that had always seemed foolish and destructive to her. She turned away, realizing suddenly why it was that this young woman irritated her almost beyond restraint. She reminded her of Eurgain. "Oh, begone!" she snapped. "I have no doubt that you do not need a guide. I give you your life, and if you are clever, the life of your husband also. Bring Venutius to me!" There was no reply. When Aricia turned again, the room was empty.

Two days later, Caesius Nasica faced her angrily across his dining table, his heavy face livid with choler. She had never seen him lose control of himself before and she sat back and watched, bemused, as he stabbed a blunt finger at her. "You have bungled your moves this time, Cartimandua!" he rasped. "I should have you arrested for harboring criminals! You should have handed them over to me so that my men could have twisted the location of their camps out of them. You presume too far on Rome's good graces!"

She smiled at his anger. "You ought to know by now that they never talk," she remarked. "They suffer and die without one word."

He exhaled gustily and sat back. "It is always worth one more try," he said. "In any case, you should have asked your bard if he could lead us back to their camp."

"I did. He said that he was blindfolded when led there, and when he left the mist was too dense for him to retain his sense of direction." She snuggled into her cushions. "You know also how swiftly they move across the mountains, how often they strike their camps and vanish. At least this way I have one more chance at Venutius."

"He won't come."

"We will see. I think that he will. He has refused once, and only I know what that refusal must have cost him. He will not be able to do it again."

Nasica swung his legs off the floor and settled to his meal. "You overestimate your charm, woman," he remarked dryly, and she laughed at him, her eyes gleaming.

"It is not my charm that will draw him," she said. "This time it will be a fervent desire for my death."

He hid his surprise. "It is hard for me to understand," he said, dipping his bread in the gravy, "how any man can allow a preoccupation with any woman to interfere with his life. Certainly no woman is worth actually risking one's life for."

"I agree." She grinned maliciously over at him. "And of course your preoccupation with me falls within the realm of business."

He reddened. "Of course!" he said shortly.

The girl left the town just as the sun was stuggling free of the white, wet mists of morning. She took Sine's and her husband's horses with her and set off due west across Brigantia, cantering easily over the long, dew-hung grass. All that day she pushed on, stopping only once to steal food from a farmstead whose freemen and women were all on their land. When night came she wriggled into the bracken of a copse, curled up in her cloak, and slept long and deeply like a little animal. For a week she traveled thus, moving quickly and lightly over the barren hills, thinking nothing, blending with country and sky, the horses strung out behind her. She entered the forest, glad for a moment of the shelter it afforded, then once more sank all relief under her quiet vigilance. She was all eyes and ears, and nothing existed for her but each present moment. The direction of the wind stirring faintly on her cheek or hand, the woodland scents rising under her horse's hoofs, the slight, constant veer her mount wished to make, the angle of the unseen sun, these things were her life, her guide.

When, one evening, the breeze brought to her briefly a lungful of tart ocean air she reined in, her nostrils wide and lifted, then without sound or pause she turned her mount due south. She did not reason her decision. She had done that days ago, before she turned her back on Aricia's town. Now was the time of instinct alone, and to mingle it with reason would have been to dilute its power. Like a hound following a scent she flitted from shadow to shadow, and day went after day. She slipped past Deva, a night's march to the west of her, and hunger now sharpened her faculties and kept her sleep light. Then once again she swung west, into the dense forest on the Ordovician border. Only when the land beneath her horse's hoofs began to rise and grow rocky did she allow herself to remember that she was human and not wholly a wild beast. Her thoughts became full of her

558

husband and Sine and the evil that hung about Brigantia's lady, and she wept silently as she rode.

She reached the camp two weeks out of Brigantia, but the site was empty. Only her trained eyes could have picked out the faint hollows of the firepits and the rocks that had been shifted back into their places after holding down the tents, and those eyes picked other signs, down by the stream. She began to track her people and three days later found them, camped nearer to the fort, among the trees. She was challenged and answered softly, then she got down from her horse and walked slowly to the fire where Venutius, Madoc, and Emrys squatted together, drawing something in the dry soil. Her legs shook with hunger and the weight of her news. They saw her coming and rose, and Emrys, with his usual perception, knew what was to come.

Venutius embraced her. "Brennia! Rest and peace! Will you eat and drink before you share?" She nodded. "Forgive me, Lord. If I do not eat I shall faint. They took my weapons and I had nothing to kill with. I stole a little, but it has long since gone." She sank to the ground, tucking her legs under her, and Emrys himself brought her cheese and meat and clear, cold water. She ate slowly, chewing carefully, and the men sat around her and waited. When color began to flush the smooth cheeks again and her hands had stopped trembling, she spoke.

"My news is bitter for you to hear, Arviragus. Your wife is not sick. She holds my husband and Sine in chains and she sends you this message. If you do not go to her she will kill them both."

A deep silence descended, and though outside the circle of the fire's warmth men walked and spoke, the three around it had become blind and deaf to all save the girl's pinched face. Madoc growled, then sent a stream of spittle flying into the bushes behind him. Emrys sat quite still, always in command of himself, but his eyes slowly closed and his brows drew together. Venutius's head went down. He seemed to be fighting for breath. The girl sat loosely, her hands in her green lap, and tears slid down her face. "Forgive me again, Lord, for my weakness," she choked. "I should have laid myself down in the forest so that this word would not come to you. Sine and my husband would have died, but your mind would still be at rest."

"At rest?" Venutius laughed without warmth. "My mind will be at rest when I am dead." Yet even as the deep voice rumbled out, he did indeed find a tiny core of peace in his soul, a steady little white flame of dignity and sanity. He lifted his head. With this news had come death, but it was a good death, the death of his doubt. He found that he could think of Aricia without a fog of hesitancy and contradictions, and of his friends without the suspicion that they were deceiving him about her. He saw her now quite clearly as a cancer, a weeping sore, a blight. Somewhere under that putridity was his wife, the woman he loved, and though the death of his love had not come—that was an ogre, a monster that could not be slain—never again would he excuse her to himself.

He leaned over and clumsily wiped the tears from the cheek of his kinswoman. "I am glad of this news," he said quietly, and she looked at him, astonished. "It is always better, Brennia, to know the truth, even though it may bring pain unto death." He rose lightly, surely. "Madoc, call in the chieftains. I have something to say to them. Brennia, go to your tent and rest, and then Domnall will find you a new sword."

When she had gone, Venutius drew Emrys aside. "I would not blame you if you swept my head from my body," he said. "Emrys, Emrys, for only the sake of my own madness, my selfishness, I have taken from you your life's treasure. I can say nothing."

"Lord, if Sine had not gone you would have gone yourself," Emrys said thickly, fighting to keep his voice level, "and even now you would be waiting for a ship to carry you to Rome. It was your life or hers."

"No!" Venutius stood straight and shouted. "No, Emrys! It will be Aricia's life for hers. I have had enough, I can take no more. Because of my weakness, the bitch has reached right into our strongholds and controlled me still, but no longer. I will kill her. I will change the battle plan. She has gone too far this time."

"No, Lord," Emrys replied, though no other words in all his life had cost him so dear. "Let Sine and your nephew die. Put their blood away from you and let us do the thing we have planned. If they could speak to you they would only curse you for endangering the cause of freedom for their sakes. They would say that the responsibility is too great for them."

But Venutius, tight-lipped and resolute, brushed aside his words. "It can be done, Emrys. Look at it strategically. With Aricia dead the Roman hold on the north will be weakened and the adjustments the governor will have to make will drain even more men from the legions in the south." He went to the earth, picking up a stick in order to trace his thoughts on the ground, and unwillingly Emrys squatted alongside, his terror for Sine now overlaid with another fear. He did not believe that Venutius was strong enough to slay Aricia, and he saw tragedy as the end of any new move. The change in the arviragus had been too sudden.

"Now," said Venutius, drawing rapidly with his twig. "Instead of falling on the Twentieth once more at Deva, and then marching south through the foothills to the Second at Glevum and so across to Camulodunon, we can move against Aricia, destroy the town, and attack the Ninth at Lindum. Then straight south and west. We deal with the Second, then Camulodunon. By then the Twentieth will surely be on the march south, and we can turn from Camulodunon and intercept it."

"It is too complex," Emrys objected. "We should fear the Ninth, Venutius. We are mountain fighters, as are the legionaries of the Twentieth, but the Ninth has been quartered in Brigantia's open country for years, and it will be too difficult for us to fight a legion that is not bottled in a valley but can wheel and maneuver freely on the moors. The original idea is best. Leave the Ninth until the low-lands become ours and we have gathered men from the tribes there—enough men to overwhelm Nasica with numbers alone. Besides, we must cover too much ground if we go your way."

Venutius's hand still traced out the battle paths. "The Twentieth is alert and waiting for us. That cannot be avoided. But if we slip past it to the Ninth, unexpected, we can take Nasica by surprise."

"Not if we tarry in Brigantia." Emrys's foot came out and gently scuffed the map away. "Do not do it, Arviragus. It will not work."

"It will. I will make it work. Aricia will die, and then everything will work."

"Nothing we can do will save Sine and Manaw, Venutius."

They fought silently, eye to eye, the big-shouldered, flame-headed chieftain and a lean, stubborn Emrys. Then Venutius snapped, "Look you, Ordovician. We have the horses, we have the manpower and the tactical advantage. We also have the will, and we have had the time to grow strong again, and cunning. It does not matter whether we cut the Twentieth to pieces first or the Ninth. We will win. The governor is an old, bad-tempered man with a grudge against everyone. Young Nero sits in Rome, pondering the complete withdrawal of all troops from Albion on the governor's advice, and the legionaries know it. The fight is going out of them. Why die now, they say, when in a few months these shores may be abandoned for good. I say to you that no matter whether we march east or south and east, we will have the victory."

"In that case we will have plenty of time to deal with Brigantia when the Romans have gone."

"No." Venutius's mouth grimaced in hate, or passion. "I want her dead now."

"You have no right to intrude private vengeance, Arviragus."

Venutius stabbed him with his fierce gaze. "Private, Emrys? Do you not want her dead as well?"

561

Emrys continued to look at him steadily, but he was nearing the end of his control. "Not at the expense of a sea of unnecessary bloodshed." Venutius spun on his heel and went away.

Emrys did not attend the Council. He took his cloak and a blanket and walked into the forest until the sounds of the thousands who gathered to hear Venutius's words were far behind, and still he paced, his thoughts succeeding one another as silently and regularly as his soft footfalls. I could kill him, but what good would that do? The Silures, the Demetae, and the remnants of the Deceangli would not follow me, and the Ordovices cannot march alone. We have all become too dependent on each other for that. I could speak against him in Council, but then the host would become divided, and precious time would be lost while we quarreled. This time your visions played you false master, my strange-eyed cousin. The Druithin have made a mistake at last, and what a mistake! Why this mistake, cousin, why have your dreams failed you now? Is it an omen for the future? Is your power waning at the end? Venutius is no Caradoc.

He is flawed, like a rock with a seam of sand running through it.

Emrys found a tiny waterfall, splashing through green ferns down a tumbled rock face that was hidden in treetops, and he cupped a hand and drank. He sat beside the tinkling, ice-cold curtain and drew his cloak about him, folding his hands beneath it and staring into the forest. Sine, my Sine. I cannot remember a time when I was without you, and now time stretches ahead of me, an infinity of meaningless, dead days, carrying me from nowhere into nothing, and fate laughs at your pathetic, pitiful ending. You and I together. You and I apart. Forever. And the last chance at freedom is going also, lost because of a woman, one cheap, dishonored woman. I sacrifice you, I lay down your life—for what? For the chance of a chance. Die well, beloved, as you have lived. Sine . . . Pain crushed him at last to the earth. He put his face in his hands and wept.

He stayed alone in the forest that night, and when he returned to the camp in the early morning he found the tents being struck and the chiefs readying themselves to move. He sought out Madoc, who greeted him tersely, his black beard bristling and his wrinkle-set eyes bright with annoyance.

"I am getting too old for this constant running," he complained. "I should fall on my sword and let my son champion the Silures. Would that I had died under Caradoc's command!" He grumbled a little more, quietly, then Emrys asked, "Is his mind set on this foolish thing?"

"It is. We march immediately. Yet it need not be so foolish, Emrys.

562

There will be more ground to cover, of course, and less room for mistakes, but we have a good chance of success."

Mistakes. A good chance. Emrys suddenly laughed. "Caradoc warned us that we should never attempt pitched battle, and we did not listen. That is, not until we were scattered and he was a prisoner. Then we were wise, Madoc, oh how wise! We smashed the Twentieth by making good plans, even as we should be doing now, instead of crossing Albion in full view of everyone and then standing against a legion that will be ranked and waiting. All our victories since the Twentieth have been because we finally learned sense. Now we are about to repeat every mistake we ever made, and we will be defeated, and you and I will die still crawling about in our own mountains."

Madoc looked at him critically, noting the marks of a night of grief on the fine, thin face. "I am sorry about Sine," he offered gruffly. "Yet, Emrys, she will live again."

Emrys's eyes seemed to gather all the hurt on his face into themselves. "I know," he whispered. "But not with me, Madoc."

In two weeks the west had emptied. Venutius led his forces south and east, cutting deep through Cornovii country and then swinging north along the Coritani border. Long before the dry summer paths would have led them to Lindum they veered again, flowing quietly just under the eaves of the great forest that straggled the edge of Brigantia's moors. No one saw them pass. The Cornovii peasants were busy in their fields, for the harvest time was approaching, and the legionaries, at Gallus's command, spent their time patrolling the foot of the mountains and did not know that the mountains were no longer their enemy. The weather was hot, the wind stilled. Autumn waited patiently for the sun to tire, and the rebels waited also, riding enervated and sweating under the thin, stuffy shade of the trees. The night they made their last camp before moving out under Brigantia's revealing sky, Venutius called Madoc and Emrys to him.

"I will take the Brigantian war band and march alone to the town," he said. "Two thousand warriors will surely be able to defeat my wife's forces. You are to stay here under cover of the forest. I will send word when it is safe to march against the Ninth. This way no Roman need know that our host is gathered together here and that I have not come out of the west on a private matter."

It was a good compromise, a sensible precaution, and Emrys's spine loosened in relief. With the main force held back, perhaps they might still take the fort at Lindum by surprise. Venutius and his chiefs slipped away that night, riding hard, muffled in dark cloaks, and

Emrys and Madoc settled themselves to wait. Idleness hung heavy on Emrys. He had nothing to do but pace the forest, back and forth, and think of Sine. Had she come this way, on her journey to death? He watched the last full moon of summer shimmer like a silver globe in the soft night sky, but its plump beauty could not stir him. His heart was cold.

Venutius and his men traveled by night and lay in the folds of the hills by day, but they did not go unnoticed. A young sheepherder, wandering after his flock in the late evening, saw the last of the chiefs and their horses disappear into a thick clump of willows by the stream where the sheep liked to drink. His clear eyes had picked out the flicker of setting sunlight on helms and swords and, his heart in his mouth, he left his beasts and ran to his father's farmstead, and well before dawn a message was speeding to Aricia. At noon the next day she heard it, sitting before the Council hall with Andocretus and her other chiefs, and she got to her feet, astounded.

"A rebel force here? In Brigantia? Impossible! They must be messengers. Venutius is sending me another dreary mouthful of misery."

The chief shook his head. "My son saw horses and weapons. He said that there were many men concealed in the trees—he could hear their voices."

She looked past him for a moment to the peaceful sky, the smoke towers rising tall and gray from the fires of her town, and that other fear rose up to choke her. The men of the west creeping toward her, their eyes alight with grim anticipation, and she herself rooted to the earth, unable to run. She pursed dry lips. Venutius was coming, but was he coming with only a few of his bodyguard, as a token of dignity, or was he coming to fight? Had the eyes and ears of the shepherd boy deceived him out of fear? "My thanks," she said to the shabby, bronzed man before her. "Eat and drink before you return to your farm. My bard will give you payment later for your news." He bowed and walked past her into the hall and she moved slowly down through the town until she reached the earthwall.

"Andocretus, have the gates closed and a guard set," she ordered, then she climbed the wall and stood high above her world. Her eyes strained in each direction, but the horizon flowed on, uninterrupted by movement of horse and rider, and blurred into haze where the land met the forests striding out of the west. Most of my armed chiefs are with the Roman patrols, on the Deceangli border, she thought. I cannot recall them, it is too far away. She was unable to plan. Her mind felt helpless, muddled. What shall I do? He is one day away, and Nasica is two. He will come first. I have many chiefs gathered here, waiting for his surrender, but not enough to do more than hold the

564

town for a little while. A wind blew from the ocean where she was standing on the rim of her wall, and it brought to her the salt scents of Gladys and the merry tumult of old Camulodunon, but she knew, as the memories wafted in her nostrils, that her town was not Camulodunon and she was no Caradoc, though it was not Rome but a small war band that marched against her. She was afraid.

Before another hour passed she had sent a rider to Lindum. "Tell the legate that a small rebel force is coming this way," she said. "I must have help. If he does not send me soldiers he may find my town in flames." She did not wait for an acknowledgment. She almost ran into her house, standing before Brigantia with clenching hands and a beating heart. But she had no offering and no prayers. She had forgotten them all.

Nasica listened to the chief's message with a mounting exasperation, and when the man had gone he sat back in his chair with an exclamation of ire. "Oh damn the stupid woman! Why can't she handle her internal affairs properly? She should have left well enough alone when her first attempt to get Venutius failed, but no, she had to go on probing around in his wound until he lost his temper. If I had my way he could hang her from the nearest tree. How am I supposed to do my job efficiently when every time she has nothing to do she stirs up trouble with her husband?"

His secretary listened, smiling. "Sir, we may yet capture the arviragus or, better still, kill him in battle," he said, and Nasica waved impatiently.

"I know, I know. I must send her a few men, there's no way around it, because if I don't and she loses this scrap we will have a much larger problem on our hands. I am only angry at her ineptitude. Her usefulness to Rome is rapidly coming to an end and I intend to tell the governor so." He rocked back on his chair and flung an arm over it, raising his ruthless pocked face to his aide. "Have two auxiliary infantry units called out right away. No, make that two cohorts. Put the primipilus in charge. Send him to me first. I am going to have something to say to Cartimandua when this is over. Stupid . . ." He turned back to his desk, muttering, and the secretary saluted and left the office.

The auxiliaries marched out of Lindum that afternoon, but they were only halfway to Aricia's town when Venutius drew rein and pointed. "There it is. We will not pause to talk with her. Straight on, surround the town!" He surged forward, his men strung out behind him, and on the wall Andocretus gave a cry and slithered down to where the lower circles were packed with armed chiefs. Aricia ran to meet him.

"They are coming!"

"How many?"

"It is hard to tell. Perhaps a thousand, helmed and weaponed. They do not come to talk, Lady."

She put her fingers to cold lips, trying to think, trying to decide what to do. Her messenger had still not returned from Lindum and she supposed that he intended to ride back with the soldiers. Without Domnall to advise her, a Roman centurion to do her thinking for her, she was confused. Finally she dropped her hands, looking around her to the massed, jostling chiefs. "Open the gate!" she called. "Meet them out in the field!"

"Lady!" Andocretus shrieked. "No! Order them to the walls with slings! If you do not they will be slaughtered!"

"Why? They are Roman-trained, they will hold together, and Venutius will not be able to so much as touch the gate."

"But Lady . . ."

"Be silent, Andocretus!" The tall gates were already inching open and her men were flooding the meadow beyond, shouting and screaming, and the massed roar of an answering host came faintly. "I send forth at least twice their number. Are you afraid? Come up onto the wall and watch."

Yes, I am afraid, he thought, but so are you, Lady. Your lips are white. He followed her obediently up, while behind them the gates thudded shut once more and the streets lay empty under a blue and white patchworked sky. Her bodyguard straggled behind them, and they squatted beside her where she sat, far out of the reach of stones or spears. Venutius, lifting his eyes above the running, screaming mob of his erstwhile kinsmen who had come spewing out of the gate, saw her there. She looked high and small, her black hair floating around her on the wind, red cloak billowing out, her face a tiny white spot. The surge of love and hate that began in his belly did not have time to burst into his chest. Her henchmen were upon him.

All that morning the little battle raged fiercely. Contrary to Andocretus's gloomy expectations, Aricia's warriors were not cut to pieces within the first hour. They were no longer the naïve, hot-blooded tribesmen who would rush howling into a fray and expect their first charge to win the day. They had rubbed shoulders with Roman discipline for too many years, and some of the caution and coolness of the legionaries had been communicated to them. They stood in loose ranks, fighting shoulder to shoulder and back to back, and Venutius's men were forced to abandon their horses and do battle on foot. But gradually the long-learned fluid ability of the rebels to change tactics, an instinct born in them under Caradoc's relentless

566

hammering and Venutius's own foresight, began to tell. Aricia, still sitting with her stolid bodyguard atop the wall, saw her army gradually lose its cohesive mass and become ragged splinters of men surrounded by an increasing number of dun tunics, and suddenly she realized that the drab tunics were increasing, not because more rebels had come but because her own force was rapidly diminishing.

"Where are the soldiers?" Andocretus said anxiously. "If they do not come soon we are finished."

"It does not matter," she replied, her voice quavering, though she tried to keep the fear out of it. "Even if Venutius is victorious he will not be able to breach the gates before our help does arrive."

"Lady, my brothers are down there!" one of her chiefs reproached her angrily, and the others began to murmur. She kept her gaze on the plain below her, the tumult of battle pounding against her like ocean waves, and watched and listened to the destruction of her war band. She felt nothing, nothing, as though she sat on the highest mountain in the whole of the world and the wind blew right through her and moaned in her empty cavities, and out of that nothingness came a last terrible idea, a sacrifice to herself, an obeisance to degradation. She turned to Andocretus.

"Bring me a carnyx," she said slowly, "and have the two prisoners brought up here." He saw the hungry yellow tongues of power flaming behind her eyes, and he rose without a word and scrambled to the first circle. She turned back to the carnage below her, but now her fingers moved in the folds of her cloak, pleating and clutching, and her mouth worked soundlessly.

The burning noon sun stood overhead and then began to roll west, and just as Venutius paused a moment to lean on his sword and wipe the sweat from his eyes, the high, haunting note of a carnyx tingled in the air around him. He glanced upward, startled, conscious as he did so that the pace of battle was slowing to a halt. One by one the combatants fell apart to stare around them, seeking the source of that wild melody, and then the sword fell from Venutius's hand. Aricia had risen. She stood above the wall, the carnyx in her outflung hand, and beside her swayed the two tattered figures, their ankles and wrists chained. Behind them the cloaked chieftains of Aricia's bodyguard were bunched, their swords drawn and glinting in the early afternoon brilliance. Venutius sensed Domnall racing to him and staggering to a halt, but he had eyes only for the hunched, scarecrow pathos of Sine and his young kinsman, and Aricia's gloating, wide-stretched arms. She tossed the carnyx over the wall and shouted, her rich voice carrying easily over the corpse-littered field.

"Venutius! Do you see what I have up here? Come forward!"

A breathless quiet had fallen over the whole arena of battle. All eyes were turned to the sun-limned figures on the wall. Domnall gasped Venutius's arm convulsively. "Lord, do not stir! She cannot see you yet. She . . ." But Venutius was already threading his way over the blood-soaked grass like a sleepwalker, his movements sluggish, his frozen face upturned. Domnall walked with him. She saw him coming and gave a cry of triumph like a hawk's hunting croak, harsh and full of anticipation, then she lowered her arms and bent forward. He came to a halt at the foot of the wall, and at last his eyes left her and found the others. Sine looked down at him calmly, her head somehow small and foreign without her wolf-mask. Manaw stood with a stillness on him that was not the apathy of despair but an acceptance of his fate. "My wife, Arviragus?" he called down, and then Venutius shook off the webs of past memories and present horror and squared his shoulders, nailing down with ruthless purpose the fact that the mad woman leering at him was his wife, and placing on the coffin every cruelty he had suffered at her hands. Emrys had been right. She was not even worth killing, and he had sacrificed two people in order to prove it to himself. He answered his kinsman in a level voice. "She is safe, Manaw." He turned toward Sine. "Lady, I am sorry. I can say nothing more."

"Then do not try, Arviragus," she called to him lightly. "You are lord of my death. Greet Emrys for me."

Aricia sensed that more than words had been passed between them all, that nothing she might do or say would impinge upon the decisions they had already taken. Once again the invisible wall loomed, threatening and impenetrable, and rage rose in her also.

"This is your last chance to prove your honor," she yelled at Venutius. "I offer these two lives in exchange for you. Leave your sword and shield with Domnall and come within the gate, and I will release my prisoners. If you refuse and continue the fight I will slay them, and before you can breach my gate the Ninth will be here."

"Do not listen to her, Lord!" Sine called again. "The price is too high to pay. Even Emrys would not pay it."

I know, he thought with anguish, I know, Sine, for he said as much to me, out of his grief. Yet I have placed you wantonly in her hands. I need take only ten steps, and my callous selfishness will be washed away. The sun slanted down hot on his back and before his face, so close that he could have touched it, the earthwall exuded an odor of dry soil and warm stone. Without realizing it he placed both palms against the hard-packed earth, as though at his weight it would crumble and bury all his trouble. Caradoc, what would you have done if

568

Eurgain and your son stood under the knife and one word from you would save them? The battered, cruel face of the last arviragus appeared before him for an instant and he groaned aloud. Caradoc would not have hesitated. "Lord," Sine's voice floated down to him. "The plans are made, the victory is at hand. You should not have come here. You are needed more than I, more than a thousand men. I fall in battle, that is all, as other women have done before me. Refuse at once, and let the bitch strike!"

But it is not the same, beloved wolf lady, ah not the same at all! Slowly, he came away from the wall and raised his eyes to his wife. She smiled contemptuously. You still cannot make up your mind, that smile said to him. All your life has been one vacillation after another. The afternoon was so still that he could hear the rough breaths of the men around him. Suddenly he swore, a shout of defiance, a fierce, bestial word that was dredged from the limit of his endurance, and drawing his sword he struck the wall.

"I will not surrender! Farewell, Sine, Manaw. A peaceful journey, a safe journey. Cartimandua, you can harm me no more!"

Aricia nodded to her men. "Hold them. Give me a knife." It was passed to her and she stroked it reflectively. She had never killed a human being before, but it would be nothing, it would be easy. "This is your last chance, fool!" she screamed down to Venutius, and he shouted back immediately, "No!"

Aricia's left hand wound itself deep into Sine's tumbling black hair. "Do you pray, Lady?" she whispered, forcing the chin up, and the graceful brown throat strained. Sine swallowed.

"I do."

"What for?" Aricia's arm flew out, then across. A new, deep mouth appeared in the fragile neck. Blood spurted, drenching Aricia to the elbow, and Sine's body collapsed backward. Aricia dragged it to the lip of the wall and kicked it over, and Venutius stepped back as it rolled loosely, coming to rest against his booted feet. He looked down. The eyes gazed calmly toward the sun. Tendrils of dark hair lay over the bloodied, open mouth. Pain buckled his knees and swelled his own throat and he sank to the ground beside her, then another weight came thudding down. The silence lengthened, deepened. Rebel and Brigantian chieftain alike stood motionless on the field like victims of a Druid's holding spell, but up on the windy earthwall Andocretus leaned to his mistress.

"Dust, Lady! To the south. Rome is coming."

Venutius's force on the perimeter of the engagement had seen it too, and the spell was abruptly broken. Men grasped their weapons

569

again, and Domnall hauled Venutius to his feet. "She has alerted the Ninth!" he hissed. "We cannot fight any more today, we are tired, we must run, Lord."

Venutius nodded. "Then let us withdraw, quickly. We can surely outrun them on the horses. Send a message to Emrys to leave the forest and meet us immediately." Domnall sped away, shouting as he went, and the rebels began to leave the field, racing after him. Venutius forced himself to look once more to the top of the wall, but it was empty. Aricia had gone. On an impulse he knelt again and kissed Emrys's lady and his young kinsman, then he sheathed his sword and broke into a lope, wondering why he did not weep. But the time for weeping had long since past.

Aricia stood in her house, with Andocretus beside her, holding out red-encrusted hands. "I stink," she said. "The rebels' blood has a foul odor. Can you smell it?" He shook his head as she moved to the basin, stripping the tunic from her and reaching for the water. She washed slowly and thoroughly, and carefully explored her inner self. There was no hurt, none at all. When she had finished and was clad in a clean tunic she sat in her chair and pointed to a corner of the room. "Pick up that thing, Andocretus, and try it on. I want to know what you see." He went and got the mask.

"So you kept it," he said, turning it over gingerly.

"Yes. Put it on." She watched him intently as he wrinkled up his nose but dutifully lifted it to his face. His fingers flitted over it uncertainly. "Well? What do you see?" she snapped.

"Nothing," he complained. "It is as dark as night in here. Perhaps I have not fitted it properly." His eyes blinked at her out of the wolf's slanted sockets, then he tore it from his face. "It has a strange smell," he said. "Wet, rotting blooms, soaked, slimed leaves. I do not know how she could bear to wear it."

"Take it to the metalworker's shop and have it melted away," Aricia said sharply. "And send a chief with Rome, to track the rebels. I want to know what is happening. Then come back quickly, Andocretus. I do not want to be alone."

He took the mask and went out, but he did not go to the metalworker's shop. Something about the mask fascinated him and he took it to his own hut and hid it under his bed. Many times in the months that followed he lifted it out of the box where he had placed it and spent hours looking at it, but he never again tried it on. The memory of that pressing blackness within it was too real.

Nasica's auxiliary cohorts caught up with Venutius at dawn the next day. Venutius and his men and horses had been fatigued. They had eventually stopped to eat and sleep halfway through the night. But the primipilus and his soldiers had not stopped, and they gave battle one hour after the sun had risen. The day promised to be cooler. The clouds had moved in to filter the sunlight and a southerly wind brought the damp promise of the first of the autumn rainstorms, but the rebels spared no more than a glance at the weather. Domnall's message had reached Emrys and the bulk of the rebel host was already pouring like brown smoke across Brigantia's hills toward the arviragus, but before they could arrive there were a thousand Romans to take care of.

Venutius gave the order to mount and then spoke to Domnall. "Keep the chiefs on the move and tell them not to fight on foot. Only their officers are mounted. Nasica has sent no cavalry. Encircle them, and we will pick away at their flanks. We are in no hurry, and Emrys will arrive before long to help us finish them off."

The two forces met in the sweet coolness of the morning, the Romans ranked in orderly squares, the chiefs wheeling freely around them in a loose circle that lazily became tighter and smaller. The primipilus, who had not seen action for some time and who had planned his massacre around an expected, mad frontal charge, was nonplussed. With cavalry his job would have been done in half a day, but without mounted soldiers he was vulnerable. He set his slingers and archers to the fore, ordered them to shoot at the horses, not the men, and waited.

By nightfall the issue was still undecided. The rebels had lost most of their mounts but were not much dismayed. They fought with a new steadiness, and the hard-pressed primipilus, watching the bitter, silent struggle, reflected in surprise that the wildmen seemed to be learning their lessons at last. The legate of the Twentieth had said so to his own commander, and he of all the fort commanders ought to know, but then the Ninth had never faced the west. When darkness fell both sides retired, staggering with weariness, and toward the end of the third watch a soldier came to the primipilus.

"With your permission, sir, I would like to show you something," he said. The primipilus immediately got up and followed him, and he led him to the outskirts of their camp and beyond, to the crest of a hill that by daylight would have given them a long view west. The sentry dropped to his stomach and wormed his way to the skyline, a moonless roof of blackness above them torn with the white blaze of the stars, and pointed. "If you fix your eyes over there and wait, you will see it."

The primipilus did as he was bid. At first he could make out nothing but the dark waves of empty land, but then he saw it, a tiny red flicker, then another some way from the first, and then another, all of them miles away and barely visible. He knew immediately what he was seeing, and his heartbeat quickened. Campfires. Dozens, hundreds of them. Campfires in the west, not in the south where the Brigantian lady's town lay, nor to the east where villages hugged the banks of the numerous rivers that rose in the higher, wooded country. He left the sentry at his post on the hill, strode back to his tent, and called for his subordinate.

"Take a legionary and ride at once to Lindum," he said. "Tell the legate that a much larger force than he had supposed is seeking engagement, and he must mobilize the rest of the men. Tell him that if he does not, he may face a siege." He did not need to spell out the rest of the message. A siege could mean the kind of tragedy that had destroyed the bulk of the now-refurbished Twentieth. The man slipped away south and the primipilus prepared for another day of fatigue and blood.

By noon the next day, a day of intermittent drizzle and gusting winds, the primipilus knew that he must retreat or lose every man he had left. Half the rebel force was dead or wounded but he himself had lost all but two hundred of his auxiliaries, and by nightfall the main bulk of the rebel host would have arrived. A retreat across this barren, open country with no forest to melt into, would be near suicide, but to stay would be certain suicide. He ordered his trumpeter to sound the retreat, and his little band closed ranks and prepared to march. He put the slingers in the rear. He had no archers left.

Nasica heard his centurion out with an ominous silence that he did not break until the man had saluted and withdrawn. Then he rose heavily. "I will make no judgment until I have all the facts," he said loudly to the tribune who had come at his secretary's call. "Either the primipilus is an idiot, which I know to be untrue, or that Brigantian fiend has once again bungled it and incited her husband to a full-scale attack on Brigantia." He snatched up his helmet, and at his bellow his servant came scurrying, breastplate in his arms. "Have the troops prepare to make a forced march, every one of them. Send a speculator to Camulodunon, to the governor. Turn out the cavalry. Get them on the move as an advance guard." Disgust and anger welled within him. "Ah Hades!" he snarled, and pushed his way out the door.

The cavalry came to the relief of the primipilus and his hundred remaining legionaries a day and a half later. By the time Nasica and the rest of the Ninth caught up to them he had time only to swiftly deploy, for Emrys, Madoc, and the western tribes had reached Venutius and his exhausted war band, and Roman and chief at last clashed in full strength. By accident, for there was no time for design,

572

Nasica had the advantage of a hill placement, and he surrounded his men with his fifteen hundred cavalry. Emrys, Madoc, and Venutius strung out their men and women in loose lines, feeling defenceless without rock beneath their feet and at their backs and a forest's arms under which to hide and regroup. Venutius did not wait for Nasica to order an attack. He ordered a charge on three fronts and his people responded gallantly. He had the satisfaction of seeing the tight Roman block divide in two, the legionaries turning to right and left as his chiefs speared a passage through their midst and flowed up it. But the cavalry had simply moved outward, keeping their positions, waiting for their order, and though Venutius and his host had divided and surrounded the infantry, they themselves were contained by the lances of the mounted soldiers.

Nasica sat on his horse and watched critically. I could knock these wildmen into the greatest fighting force in the world in a year, he thought. It has taken them a long time to grasp the basic elements of civilized warfare but, by Mithras, now they are on the brink of a military sophistication that would make old Aulus Plautius blink. No wonder the Twentieth went down! But the Twentieth has always been too independent for its own good. Valens is a showy fighter, too many fancy tricks up his sleeve. The Ninth cannot be surpassed for sustained courage and solid obedience.

His senatorial tribune cantered up to him and saluted. "The tenth cohort is hard pressed, sir, and the second and third have become separated from the first but they are holding."

"Very well. Order one cohort of cavalry to the tenth. Swing the fourth cohort lower down the slope." The man rode away, the trumpets blared, and the battle swirled to new formation. Nasica hunched deeper into his cloak as a thin rain began to fall. It was going to be a long day.

Two days later Aricia stood in the doorway of the Council hall, snuggled deep into her blue cloak, looking out over a gray landscape. The rain had begun to fall in earnest the day before and now it sheeted down, turning the paths of the town into sticky yellow quagmires, and dancing off the dripping thatch of the huts. Sullen water filled all the potholes and dribbled past doorskins. Now the wind was rising, making the streams of rain quiver and undulate and blow wet against her. She hardly felt the new, chilling cold that spoke to her of the approaching autumn. She was anxious. The messenger she had sent to march with the troops that pursued Venutius had not returned. Her eyes vainly quested the northern trackway and encountered only the misted shadow of the gate and beyond it the wreaths of greasy smoke where her dead chieftains were becoming sodden black ashes. They are coming for me, she thought. They have defeated Rome and now they will rise out of the fog like gods. I will see them creeping slowly out of this pall of water, and they will stand me on the wall and cut my throat.

The town was quiet. Freemen squatted by their fires, women mourned dead kinsmen, and out on the hills the shepherds sheltered in the hollows with their dripping sheep, but though a fire crackled brightly in the dry coziness of her Roman house, and Andocretus and his songs were as close as a word from her lips, she had stood hour upon hour with the gloom of the Council hall behind her and her terror gathering ahead.

Andocretus left the shadows and spoke to her. "Come and get warm, Lady," he said, shivering as the wind sought the undefended door and found him. "Nothing is moving out there, and you will get no news until the rain stops and the ground dries up a little."

"He is coming for me," she said dully, her eyes still on the gray day. He laughed shortly, wishing that she would leave the hall and go to her house so that he could run to his own hearth and drink wine and sleep.

"It is simply not possible that the Romans have been defeated and you know it. You are allowing your foolish fancies to make you ill, Aricia."

She slumped, and her gaze fell to her mud-caked boots. "I suppose you are right. I will go to the house. But bring me men, Andocretus, for I want to be guarded." She raised her hood and left the frail shelter of the door. He snatched up his cloak and followed her, and together they picked their way toward her private gate and the wet-slicked stone wall. She had almost reached it when a shout spun her on her heel, and she saw a chief toiling to her. Andocretus cursed under his breath, his cloak already heavy with water, as the man came up to them.

"The legate of the Ninth is behind me," he panted. "He shouted until we opened the gates to him."

"Well, why are you telling me this?" Aricia yelled at him, relief dissolving the fear. "Of course you let him in! Why did you make him wait?"

"Because you told us not to open for anyone and because he is in a rage."

She thanked him brusquely and sent him away, and was turning to her gate once more when Andocretus took her arm. "Lady, I think I will wait for you in your house," he whispered. "Nasica is coming." He was through the gate before she could answer and she turned and stood still, watching the tall, thick-set commander splash bare-legged through the mud. His short cloak was plastered to his body, and his helmet and breastplate were shining with moisture. His face was grim. He did not look at her as he came up, nor did he greet her, and the fear was back. His men had been defeated, as the Twentieth had been defeated, he was alone, he sought help from her, he . . .

Then he was facing her, breathing heavily, the round pocks on his face standing out livid against the angry red of his skin. His eyes were cold, as cold as the icy rain that trickled down her throat and soaked the neck of her tunic, and she stepped back, felt the wall behind her, and could go no farther.

"I have lost a thousand men," he said quietly, and his low tone was more menacing than if he had screamed at her. "A thousand good fighting men dead, do you hear me, Cartimandua? And half that number are wounded. I had to drag out the whole damn legion and march it halfway across your accursed territory and fight every madman out of the west, because of you."

"I . . . I do not understand," she whispered, seeing his lips curve in a brutal smile and the spittle gather in the corners of his mouth. "Surely you did not take the whole legion after Venutius and his war band, you . . ."

He came closer to her, water coursing down his blunt face, his jaw thrust forward. "I sent you help as you requested, seeing that you could not handle your own petty quarrels, but you did not know that the whole of the west was coming for you, did you? I will fight no more of your wars!" he roared, and she shrank back, the hood falling from her black braids, the rain sticking the hair in tendrils against her scarred cheek, her chin. So it was true. All of them after her, all of them bent on destroying her. Nasica would desert her, it was not her fault.

"Please, Nasica," she whimpered. "How could I know? Everything went wrong."

"Everything always goes wrong around you, you greedy, grasping whore!" he spat. "The governor will not be happy when he hears about this, and I shall make sure he hears it all! It is time a praetor was appointed to set things to rights here. Brigantia is too strategically important to leave in your inept hands."

"My people would not obey a praetor!" she snapped back, rallying out of her desperate shock. "How many men can Rome spare to patrol where my chiefs patrol? You are dreaming, commander."

"No, you are the dreamer," he growled between clenched teeth. "Rome is the master of Albion, and every day of your rule is a day of sufferance from the governor. Even your life belongs to Rome. You forget this, Cartimandua. Rome lifted you up. Rome will cast you down. You have drained blood and manpower from the Ninth just once too often in your foolish persecution of your husband. From now on you are on your own." He turned away, and though she felt as though she would collapse with the humiliation, she called after him.

"Nasica! Venutius . . . the rebels . . ."

He stopped and shouted over his shoulder, "They were beaten, but just barely. I left their dead to be picked over by the wolves. Venutius lives. Try your aging charms on Valens next time, Cartimandua. He has been quartered far from female company for a long time and may not be too particular by now. He might even send you soldiers next time you are in trouble, if the price is right. You make me sick!" He vanished into the murk but Aricia could not move. She was trembling with cold and drenched to the bone. Nasica's scornful words hammered her like the cold needles of the storm, but she could not think of his threats, not yet, nor of how close she had come to annihilation at the hands of the men of the west. She knew the dream would come to her that night.

Emrys, Madoc, and Venutius pulled back into the forest. Without surprise their battle with the Ninth had cost them dear. It had been on ground that was not of their own choosing, and even if the autumn rains had not begun, they knew that the chance for a major thrust against the Twentieth and so into the lowlands had gone by. They knew that they would go back to their old, wearisome tactics that winter—carving up patrols, attacking baggage trains, resisting the attempts of the Twentieth to wrest just a little more of the border lands from their hands, and fighting to regain the Silurian territory and to keep the area too troublesome for the erection of a permanent fort. Emrys had gone to Domnall when they were at last safe around a welcoming fire. The Druids were going from chief to wounded chief in the thin rain that pattered through leaves which had begun to acquire the dry, yellow tinges of autumn, and shield-bearers and freemen sat oblivious of the wetness, cleaning and polishing weapons dulled and mired by death. He did not approach Venutius. He did not trust himself that far. Domnall was sharpening the arviragus's great sword. It lay across his knees, and the whetstone ground along its edge with a sound that gritted Emrys's teeth as he greeted the Brigantian and squatted before him.

"No man will tell me of my wife," Emrys said gently. "I am spoken to with a cloying pity, as though I were a child to be shielded from evil. Domnall, you give me the words."

Domnall's hand came away from the whetstone and the grinding ceased. He wiped his fingers on his cloak and turned the sword over. "Your wife is dead, Emrys."

"I know that. I have reason to believe that you saw her die."

Domnall glanced up, then back to his lap. The whetstone once more wove its rough circles. "Who gives you reason?"

"No one. Only rumors."

"Leave it alone, Ordovician chieftain. She died well, and that is all you must remember."

Emrys rested his elbows on his knees and linked his fingers together carefully. "How well did she die, Brigantian warrior?"

Domnall laid the whetstone aside abruptly and put both palms flat on his master's sword, but he did not look at Emrys again. "The Lady of Brigantia stood Sine and the young chief on the wall and offered their lives in exchange for the arviragus. He was ready to give himself to her, but Sine forbade him. She said that she would not have the responsibility. The lady cut her throat and threw her over the wall."

For a long time both men were still. Then Emrys said, "Where is her wolf mask?"

"I do not know. She was not wearing it when I saw her last."

Emrys rose. "Thank you, Domnall," he concluded softly and walked away, but Domnall sat on, his task forgotten, his eyes blind to the stained sword under his hands.

The rains did not let up. Autumn came in sodden and sulky, and the leaves dropped still half-green from the trees to mix with the mud at their feet. Rain turned to sleet and then to snow, heavy and thick, and in the mountains nothing stirred. It was impossible campaigning weather even for the rebels, who kept to their little tents and slept. In the forts the soldiers gambled and gossiped, bored and quarrelsome. Madoc nursed his stiffening joints, drank as much sour beer as he could get apportioned to him, and spent hours telling stories to his sons. Venutius sat in his tent, listening critically to the few spies who brought stale news to him and sharing with Domnall, in an unspoken empathy, his self-reproach and the bitterness of his failures. If it had not been for his mad hunger to see his wife, to kill her, to make her suffer at the expense of all else, they might now be knocking at the governor's door in Camulodunon. He had served his people ill, he had betrayed them cruelly, and that knowledge etched new lines of harshness into his face. Only Emrys ranged abroad, roaming the silent, winter-shrouded hills, seeking, in the tumbled rise and fall of the cliffs and the ragged grayness of the forests, a way to be whole again. But the soaring of the glistening peaks belonged to Sine, and the blinding sparkle of new sun on ice was hers also. The deep tracks of deer and wolf, the cold chatter of water over stones, even the air itself, chill and unflavored, told him only that she and he together had formed memories in these mountains that would stay on his tongue, in his nostrils, before his eyes, for as long as he was forced to wander among them. He wept with the streams, he called her name with the knifing winter wind. At night the wolves howled for her, the moon sought her, but though she spoke to him from the depths of each precipitous valley he walked, she did not come to him. The days were days of the most devastating aloneness. The nights were hours out of a past long gone. When the sun began to warm again he stopped his ramblings. He had come to terms once more with his arviragus, discovering, in his own agony, a tolerance for Venutius's pain, and the two men were together again when a spy squatted before them in the mud, his breath steaming and his legs caked with rotting snow and old leaves, from ankle to thigh.

"The passes are open, Lords," he said, "and there is news."

"Say on," Venutius urged him.

"The governor is to return to Rome before another winter. The emperor has made up his mind. There will be no withdrawal from Albion. Gallus knows that he will be recalled because he is no longer vigorous enough for active campaigning, and his replacement will be a younger military man." The spy grinned. "Word is that the emperor wants us dealt with once and for all."

Venutius stared at him. So there were to be no more chances. He had been given the greatest promise of success the west had had, his luck had blazed more brightly even than Caradoc's, but he had thrown it away and it would never come again. The west was no longer an incidental nuisance. The west had become the focus of the emperor's attention, and the emperor would not look away until there was nothing left in the west to see. Emrys did not help him. He sat beside him, saying nothing, but Venutius felt his accusation, his insulting, insupportable pity. So Nero, in a fit of pettish adolescent obstinacy, had made a bid for independence, dismissed his advisors, and . . . No withdrawal. No more hope. The metal fingers would squeeze tighter, feeling nothing, until the iron fist had curled in on itself and Albion was crushed.

"Is there anything more?" Venutius croaked.

"One scrap of interesting speculation. There is talk that Caesius Nasica will go with Gallus, and give the command of the Ninth to another man. He, too, has had enough of Albion."

Venutius's red head went down. New men, new enemies, untried, unknown, fresh, eager dogs snarling at his people's blistered, stumbling heels. He got up, went into his tent, and wept.

CHAPTER THIRTY-FOUR

T HE DAY WAS CRISP and sunny as Boudicca, Prasutugas, and their train of brightly-cloaked chieftains crossed the border that separated Icenia from the northern reaches of what had been Catuvellaun territory to find a military escort waiting for them. Camulodunon and the new governor lay three days away, two if they rode in haste, but they were in no hurry. The governor had invited them to meet him, dine with him, and see the town. The invitation, brought to them by special messenger, had been most polite, but when Boudicca stood in the Council hut and listened to it, she knew that their attendance was not a matter of choice, and that this Suetonius Paulinus, who had been in Albion scarcely a month, wanted to look them over.

"I wonder if he will be dead before we get there," she had said maliciously that evening to her husband, and Prasutugas had smiled at her in spite of himself.

"Why should he be? Do you think that Venutius's spies have become so expert that they can murder a governor in his own town? Since the execution of that man who had been a trusted servant of the administration for years, the one who heard the secrets of every secretary employed in Camulodunon, the Romans have tightened their security. What a blow to the rebels his death must have been!"

"A blow to Rome as well. How shaken they were to discover sedition even within the sacred precincts of the praetorium! But I was not thinking of murder, Prasutugas." She sat on the bed and picked up her comb. "Look what happened to Nepos. The emperor selects him with the greatest care and he promises Nero complete success in Albion within three years. He is young, able, the darling of the Roman populace, full of ambition, and he comes bouncing ashore at Londinium to replace Gallus with all the confidence in the world." She began to tug the comb through her obstinate, curling tresses. "Then Albion takes him. A year later he is as dead as mutton. Such frantic scurryings at Camulodunon! Such tuttings in Rome! With any luck the new governor will take a fever also."

"But not before we have had the pleasure of being observed by him."

She shook back her hair, put down the comb, and grinned at his tone of voice. "Prasutugas! Don't tell me you want to stay home!"

To her surprise, he nodded. "Yes, I do," and at his calm admission a shadow fell between them, bringing up the familiar anxiety to erase Boudicca's smile.

"It's your wound, isn't it?"

"Sometimes I think that I cannot bear the pain," he said. "It used to trouble me only in cold or wet weather but now it seems to ache all the time, like a rotten tooth. I can't remember the days when I was able to hunt or run with the dogs. Boudicca, I must face it. I think that I will die of this wound."

I faced it long ago, she thought as she sat with downcast eyes, not knowing what to say to him. There was a time when I used that knowledge to berate you, but no longer. Only someone without pity would be so cruel, for I see death stalking you every day. "Shall I go alone, and carry your apologies to this Paulinus?" she said aloud to him.

"Thank you," he replied softly. "Thank you, my dearest. How impossible it is for you to disguise your feelings! You would hate nothing more than to go to Camulodunon on your own, yet I know you would do it, for me. No, Boudicca, I must make the journey. I do not want the governor to be able to say that my allegiance to Rome sits lightly on my shoulders." She had said nothing more, but now, looking across at him, pale and stooped on his horse, his eyes on the approaching Roman escort, she cursed herself for not insisting that he stay in the sunny comfort of his town. He already looked close to collapse but she knew better than to interfere until he asked for her aid.

The officer and cavalry cantered up and saluted. "I am Julius Agricola, the governor's second-in-command," he said cheerily. "The governor extends his greeting to you and so do I." He allowed his eyes to hold theirs for a moment but he knew better than to stare as he would have liked to do. He had stood by Paulinus as Catus Decianus, the procurator, had shown the governor the figures that told of Icenia's security and wealth. No other tuath paid such monstrous taxes each year, but then no other tuath could boast that its freemen lived like chieftains and that even its peasants could afford the pleasures of imported wine and pottery. He had read the reports on Icenia's ruling house. A ricon who was wise, gentle, and totally committed to peace, and his wife who was impetuous, rude, and openly hostile to everything from Roman wine to Roman coin. Yet the marriage had worked for sixteen years, and Agricola found his interest aroused. He had welcomed his commander's suggestion that it would do no harm to have the pair come to Colchester, and he wondered whether Paulinus had also been titillated by the odd match, but then he rejected the notion. Speculation, unless it took the form of productive military musing, was not one of the governor's pastimes.

The Brigantian ricon, Cartimandua, had already been the governor's guest, and Agricola, fresh from Aricia's double-talk and endless innuendoes, was looking forward to what wàs reputed to be the Icenian lady's abrasive and mannish wit. His glance brought him disappointment, and her response to his greeting a deeper disappointment. She did not look like a man in woman's dress. She was tall, certainly, and well-built, but the turn of her wrists was graceful and the waving curls of red hair escaping from her four braids stirred against a face that was neither cragged nor harsh. The brown eyes, fanned at the corners by age, regarded him politely but indifferently and the large mouth smiled cordially as she thanked him for his words. Her husband seemed ill. His handsome, tranquil features were gray and the lines around his mouth had been placed there by pain. He looked much older than she, though Agricola knew that he was not, and the loose blond hair was too heavy with silver for a man only just approaching middle age. You have had a hard life, Agricola thought in surprise. The years have brought more sorrow to you than to your wife. How strange.

They rode on together for several hours, stopped and ate under the trees, then pressed forward again, talking of inconsequential things. Agricola's initial disappointment in Boudicca began to fade. Holding a conversation with her was like cautiously testing cooking water— one never knew whether one's fingers would be burnt. She answered every question decisively and frankly, her deep voice purring or scraping, and she spoke her mind with no attempt at evasion or feminine subterfuge. He began to see why she was always described as mannish. So she was, but not unpleasantly so. He was not charmed, and she was not the kind of woman to charm a man. But he was vividly impressed. He noticed that she rode close to her husband, and both her eyes and the eyes of their silent chiefs were on him constantly. Prasutugas himself said little. Words seemed to cost him an effort, and once, when his horse tripped and jolted him, he gasped.

Agricola decided to stop for the night, and he ordered out the tents. Autumn was soon to become winter, and though the days were warm at noon, the mornings and evenings turned breath to steam and reddened noses and knuckles. A big fire was kindled. Servants prepared hot food and heated the wine, but though Prasutugas drank it gratefully, his eyes closed, Boudicca brusquely refused it and sat with breech-clad legs crossed on the naked earth, quaffing cold mead with an evident relish that bordered on impudence. When darkness fell and the company went to their tents, Agricola stayed by the fire, his orderly beside him, watching the sliver of light from the Icenian couple's lamp steal out under the tent's flap.

At midmorning they came upon a work detail. The road had dwindled at the foot of a heavily wooded hill, but now half-naked Trinovantian slaves with iron collars around their necks groaned under the weight of great slabs of rock, while their overseer stood by them, whip in hand.

"The original track went over the hill," Agricola told them, "and our road ceased at the foot and continued on the other side. But as you can see, we have decided to link the road by scouting the foot. The trees have been felled and cleared away, the embankment raised, and the ditches dug. We must detour, I am afraid, but not far."

He turned his horse in under the trees that had lined the road and Prasutagas followed him, but Boudicca and Lovernius sat on, unable to move, watching the perspiring brown backs bend under loads no freeman would touch. The slaves staggered up the embankment, two by two, the dusty slabs dragged, pushed, and carried between them, the muscles of the naked legs bulging under the strain, and the sinews of the broad shoulders standing out like living cords. Black matted hair hid each face. The Trinovantian heads were as bowed as their lacerated backs, and Boudicca, looking over them slowly, saw three or four Catuvellaunians among them, their blond and brown hair tied back clumsily, their skin honey golden. Pity and anger budded in her stomach, and she could not have ridden on even if she had wanted to. At last the two silent, mounted watchers were noticed. One of the slaves lifted his head to wipe his face and saw them. He stood still immediately, and his companion looked up also. Soon, five or six of them were looking steadily at the green-clad lady and her bard, with eyes that held such hatred, such hot contempt, that Boudicca was paralyzed. The centurion was on them in a moment and the whip whistled and fell, but the men still stood there, and dumb, smouldering bitterness reached out from them to sting the Iceni. Boudicca finally found her voice.

"Tell me, centurion," she called. "Did these men dig the ditches and raise the embankment?"

"They did," he growled unwillingly.

"And what are they doing with the rocks?"

He glowered at her and answered her as though she were dim-witted. "They are laying the bed for the road."

"What happens next?"

The man sighed but decided to reply. "The bed is covered over with more rock, which is pounded very small, and with flint and slag from the Catuvellauni's old mines."

"I see. Will these men pound the rock and spread the gravel on the road?"

"Of course!" the soldier snapped. "Move on, Lady!"

"I see," she said again, conscious all the time of the devouring eyes, the listening ears. "Would you please tell me who will use the road?"

He roared at her in exasperation. "The speculatores, the beneficiarii, the legionaries, the . . ."

"Ah yes, yes," she cut in, her voice clear and unmistakable. "I understand. Thank you." The centurion waved her on and she turned her horse into the trees, but not before a ripple of mirth fluttered from mouth to mouth through the chained Trinovantes. The whip sliced the air. The centurion cursed, and the men bent reluctantly to their labor. But many of them were smiling, already treasuring the joke to spread among their fellows when they returned to the compound for their soup that night. Boudicca cantered to catch up to Prasutugas and Agricola. She was noticeably silent for the rest of the day.

Toward evening on the third day they drew rein and sat looking at Camulodunon. Boudicca tried to fit the memory of her last visit to the town, on the occasion of the dedication of Claudius's temple, with the peaceful scene below her, but somehow the two would not come together.

"It looks different," she said almost to herself. "The town has grown, of course, and yet . . ."

"Perhaps you saw it when the forest stood nearer to it," Agricola offered. "We have cleared much land, or rather, the natives have cleared much land, and there are more acres under cultivation."

"Yes," she said slowly, her eyes still on the sunlight that slanted long and mellow over the stubbled meadows. "There is more space around the town. But the fields are so big!"

"Our plows are larger and heavier than yours," he answered politely. "Consequently the fields must be longer. They can handle clay soil, too, which yours cannot."

She turned her head and smiled at him, with mischief sparkling in her eyes. "Of course the fields must be longer," she said. "Of course the land must be cleared. More land under cultivation means heavier yields, more grain for Rome and the legions, more money in the purse of the procurator."

"Very true, Lady," he retorted, as quick as light. "But what is good for Rome is inevitably good for her native subjects. More grain to fill everyone's bellies."

"More grain certainly ensures a limitless supply of healthy natives to be chained for work on the roads," she snapped back, and for the first time he felt anger. He stopped smiling.

"Let us go," he said shortly. "The governor expects us to dine just after sundown." He spurred his horse and clattered ahead of her over the road. Prasutugas threw her a half-amused, half-cautionary look, and she wrinkled her nose, tossed her head, and trotted after him toward the guarded gate.

They were quartered in a spacious house behind the forum, and an exasperated Agricola had to stand by and watch the chiefs pitch their tents in the neat, tree-filled garden. He had offered them lodging elsewhere but they refused to leave their ricon. As he took his leave of the lord and his lady they were already strewing their belongings on the dry dead grass and trampling the carefully nurtured rose beds.

"An aide will come to escort you to dinner in one hour," he said. "Meanwhile, the servants will see to your comfort." He cast a rueful glance in the direction of the bruised garden and went away, and Prasutugas walked from the door, across the red and white tiled floor, to where Boudicca surveyed the tiny pool sunk into the floor, her hands on her hips.

"It is too big to cook in, too small to swim in, and it would never raise fish large enough to eat," she said. "Therefore it serves no purpose."

"It is to look at," her husband responded. "I rather like it, Boudicca. The necklaces you wear serve no purpose either, save that they are beautiful and delight the soul with the intricacy of their design. This pool does the same."

"I would rather sit beside living, running water, with the sun on it. My voice echoes here, Prasutugas, as though I were in some temple where I did not belong. I hate it. Whose house is this, do you think? This whole street has been built since we last came. And fountains! I glimpsed them through the archway as we passed the forum. Fountains in Camulodunon!"

"Colchester. It is Colchester now, Boudicca, and do not forget it. I think it has been made very lovely, and will be lovelier still as the years go by. One day our own town will look like this."

"Andrasta!" The next cutting remark rose to her tongue, but sensing his preoccupation she left the pool and drew him back under the little pillars to where a servant was lighting the lamps. "You are weary. I can see it. Now, what are you expected to sit on?" The room was dusky, virtually unfurnished, and hung with brocades and linens of designs that the dim light made indeterminate. A dark oak table stood in the middle. Several folding stools were scattered about, and one deep basket-weave chair piled in cushions, its rich woolen cover trailing the floor. She went to it and dragged it toward the lamplight, determined not to allow the huge room with its long, unchecked shadows to intimidate her, but as her husband sank into the chair she

584

was suddenly homesick for their own tiny wooden house and the coziness of its unpretentious welcome.

"Who owns this place?" she snapped at the servant.

"A merchant and shipbuilder," he answered. "He is in Rome at the moment, Lady, and gave the governor his permission to house guests here."

"How very magnanimous of him. And he lives here without kin? How greedy! Go and bring the chiefs. I want them to stay here until my husband and I return." The servant bowed, a little stiffly, a little contemptuously, and Prasutugas said, "Don't be foolish, Boudicca. No one is going to creep in here and hide while we dine."

She ignored him, and signaling to the other servant she strode away. "Help him dress," she ordered. "I will change my clothes, Prasutugas, and be back in a moment. My feet are hot, and the walls feel warm. How Priscilla would love such luxury!"

Their sleeping room was also lighted, the lamps on their wooden stands glowing softly, and on a table by the bed were small jars of a delicacy. Boudicca picked one up and lifted the stopper. A pungent, lingering perfume assailed her nostrils and she sneezed and replaced it, picking up another. This one was squat, fat, a green and white marble pot filled with some thick oil that also hung rich and cloying in the air. She smiled. The merchant may have no kin, she thought with humor, but he does not live alone. She stripped quickly, and then a young girl appeared, as though she had been summoned. "Do you wish to bathe, Lady?" she enquired, but Boudicca, tired and dispirited all at once, asked only for a basin of hot water.

I want to go home, she thought, and she did not mean to the sodden, bird-clouded marshes of Icenia. What does all this strange, foreign way of life have to do with my Albion? She heard the chiefs crossing the cloister, and their voices were loud and excited, their feet clumsy and heavy in the exquisitely polite atmosphere of the house. We are like wild ponies—shaggy, ugly, shy and proud, and naïve in our simplicity. We are groomed and trained and put in the stable of some wealthy king whose horses are gently bred and highly strung. We do not understand what is happening to us, not even Prasutugas, who is able to bend with any wind. The water was brought, steaming and mingled with some other foreign scent, and when the girl moved to wash her, Boudicca ordered her out. When she was clean of her travel stains she dressed quickly, listening to the roars of masculine laughter around Prasutugas and the muted ripple of Lovernius's harp, and as she picked up her jewels and left the room she admitted to herself that she was as close to shyness as she had ever come.

An hour later a young officer presented himself at the door with an escort of four centurions, and Prasutugas and Boudicca left the house and walked with him through the windy night. Leaves tore from the trees that lined the street, and sailed around them, dry and curled, and Boudicca glanced up as she hugged her cloak more tightly around her. The moon hung bloated in the blackness as though its weight might bring it tumbling down, and racing clouds swept over its face, but she knew that it would not rain. The air smelled as dry as the leaves that caught in her hair. At the end of the street the group swung left, followed the stone wall that surrounded the forum, and passed under the arch that invited them to a paved plaza, fronted on three sides by buildings of solid stone and wood. The fountain in the center splashed dark water into its little basin, and the shower of autumn leaves swooped over the walls to scrape and rustle over the courtyard and pile up on the steps of the temple, whose silvered marble columns ran high and true. Boudicca's eyes followed their rise to the angled roof, then she shivered. The moon was above the roof, but between the moon and the roof's clumped shadow the clouds fled by, making the roof seem to be leaning toward her. It tilted, falling and yet not falling, and she stumbled under the thrall of its lowering domination. The officer's hand immediately shot out, and she thanked him absently. The sentries fronting the temple did not move.

"We could light no torches for you in the forum because of the wind," he apologized, "but you will see it better tomorrow, in daylight. There," he pointed, "is the office of the mayor. He is a tribesman, a Catuvellaun, but now a Roman citizen, of course, and he holds his office well. In the same building are the offices of civil administration. Beside it," and his arm swung to the left, "are the courts of justice where civil suits are tried. The legions have their own system of justice. The governor and the procurator share the next building, the praetorium. The temple needs no explanation. The building there, under construction, is being erected by the merchants who need a place in which to gather."

"Where was Caradoc held?" Boudicca almost had to shout over the keening of the wind, and he peered at her with hesitation.

"I . . ."

"The arviragus. Caradoc," she pressed impatiently, and she heard Prasutugas sigh beside her.

"That block of cells has been razed," the officer answered coolly. "The prison is just within the wall of the town now, but for important prisoners there are three cells in the courts of justice."

"Where are the public baths?" Prasutugas interposed hurriedly.

"They are still under construction, outside the walls and closer to the river. An arena is planned, but as yet no ground has been broken."

Not enough native slaves? Boudicca was going to enquire, but thought better of it, and they passed the temple steps, scuffing through the crisp leaves, and turned in behind the praetorium. Here there were more houses, still sheltered by the wall of the forum, where the governor, the procurator, and the higher-ranking military and civilian staff lived. It was a place of quiet by night but by day must be enveloped in clamor, Boudicca thought. Then they were standing before a massive oak door flanked by guards who opened for them, and they stepped into warmth and lamplight. Servants, silent and unobtrusive as the blue-gray tiles under their feet, took their cloaks, the young officer murmured a good night and vanished, and Agricola came toward them, his arms bare, his fingers ringed, his toga swishing about his sandals.

"I did not intend for you to be blown here by the wind!" he greeted them gaily. "What a welcome! But come. The governor awaits you."

Boudicca picked the skeleton of a leaf from her hair, and in the moment when Agricola turned she whispered to Prasutagas, "When shall I begin to snarl and curse? Shall I wait until we are all half-silly with wine? I do not want to disappoint our new governor."

For answer he kissed her swiftly. "No one could possibly be disappointed in you, no matter what you do," he whispered back. She took his arm and together they paced after Agricola.

The house was no palace but, like the merchant's dwelling, it was designed so that to shut the door was to shut out the hardships and dangers of a far, foreign province. The floors were tiled in blue, gray, yellow, and buff and from them rose well-spaced little wooden pillars. Folding chairs stood here and there, draped with warm red cloth that glowed against a background of green draperies. Sculpted heads sat discreetly in the small alcoves that they passed, and Boudicca did not know if they were gods or the governor's ancestors. Against the walls sat smooth wooden chests, and the feet of unnameable animals held up low, heavy tables. Everywhere there were cushions and hangings to make an otherwise sparsely furnished, rather austere house gay and comfortable. Servants glided in and out of the shadows, bringing with them whiffs of hot food and perfumed lamp oil. Boudicca's eyes scanned the walls, where Paulinus had already stamped his personality upon the house. Souvenirs of his governorship in Mauretania were hung about, strange curved swords in golden, filigreed scabbards, armor that had been made from the hide of horses, knives whose hilts glittered at Boudicca with blood-red gems that she had never seen before. Her fingers itched. They approached the atrium, its pool lying placidly in darkness, and the wind reached out for them from its shadow before they passed it and came to a halt at last in a brightly lit room full of servants. The table was laid, and silver sparked. The couches were drawn up to it, damask and more brocade, soft cushions in blue and scarlet, but she had time to do no more than pause, for a man was coming toward them, his gold-gripped arm outstretched, his purple-rimmed toga flowing with his thick, powerful body, the sandals on his big feet slap-slapping over the tiles. His smile came and went, a frugal nod to the proprieties, but as Boudicca took his wrist she knew that the small concession to good manners was not a deliberate affront. He was not a social animal, this Roman. His work was not done in the wine- and perfume-drenched rooms where ambitions were subtly advanced, and though he might be the perfect host, though the blue blood of Roman aristocracy flowed in his veins, he was a career soldier.

"Welcome, welcome," he said, and before he turned from Boudicca to Prasutagas a flicker of humor in his eyes warned her that there was nothing much about her he did not know. "I have been looking forward to this opportunity to talk with you, and it is a relief for me to put aside duty and indulge myself a little. I hope you find your temporary home comfortable?"

Prasutagas answered him calmly, asked him for his impressions of Albion, and Boudicca found a cup placed gently in her hands. Agricola ushered her farther into the room.

"You shivered," he remarked. "Are you cold, Boudicca? Come and stand against the wall."

"No, no," she said, smiling absently at him. "I am not cold at all, in fact I find your heating oppressive. Perhaps I am just tired after my long journey, and hungry also."

"We will eat soon. I believe that Icenian mutton is going to be offered, and the governor is very proud of the fact that he managed to procure a small barrel of mead, just for you."

"What a thorough man!" she exclaimed. "It is unfortunate that he cannot satisfy my other tastes."

"I am sure that he would be distressed if you lacked anything while you are here, Lady, but I believe you are talking about tastes that even a governor cannot satisfy, are you not?" Astounded, she looked full into his face. He was young, he was handsome, but for the first time she realized that he was also wise and had drawn her sting long before she had prepared to strike. These two are a team, she thought, perfectly matched even as Aulus Plautius and his second, Rufus Pudens, were. Fear stabbed her and she was bewildered, though she did not know why. She heard Prasutagas laugh, not a polite chuckle, but a full, healthy shout, and Agricola smiled into her eyes and sipped his wine. They have beaten me, they have beaten us already. Could these be the men who will defeat the west? she thought, and she answered him finally with a grudging respect.

"You know I am, and I have no doubt that every odd yearning I entertain is well known to the governor. Very well, I will not spoil the evening."

"Oh Lady," he protested, his eyes lighting even further. "Are you never tempted to live up to your fearsome reputation?"

"One day perhaps I will," she said lightly, "but until then I am content to provide you Romans with your best joke in Albion. Tell me what the governor has been doing since he arrived, apart from nursing a bad cold, of course."

"What makes you think he has had a cold?"

"Because so many of our governors have been unable to adapt to Albion's unique climate."

He grinned, then laughed aloud, acknowledging Paulinus's nod and ushering her to the table. "The Lady has been enquiring after your health, sir," he explained as Boudicca folded back her green sleeves and reclined and he sought his own couch. Paulinus did· not need to have the words spelled out for him. His economical, quick smile flashed out at her again before he snapped his fingers to the servants, who sprang to life.

"My health is excellent," he said to her. "It has never been better. I have lived for the last fifteen years in heat and dryness, it is true, but the mountains of Mauretania can be cold, wet, and uncomfortable, and I have had my share of all three."

"Were you sorry to be transferred to Albion?" Prasutugas asked him. He was not reclining. With only one arm it would have been impossible for him, and he sat upright in a chair that had been provided. Boudicca, watching him anxiously lest he should be unable to cut his food and thus make a fool of himself, saw that the portion being placed on his plate by the bending servant was already in small pieces. She looked down at her own plate and could not believe her eyes. Oysters. Oh surely not here, not at the governor's table, she thought in mild despair. What is it about oysters that turns Romans into greedy hogs? But the governor was talking and she gave him all her attention, picking up her spoon and swallowing the shellfish with distaste.

"No, not really. My first years in Mauretania were spent campaigning, but lately there was no fighting to be done and I must confess that the routine pursuits of administration bored me. It will be good to see action once more."

"You will get plenty of it here," Boudicca commented, washing down the last grayish lump of oyster with strong honey mead. "The emperor must be getting desperate, sir, to send the second most popular general in the empire to a rough, savage hole like Albion. Oh yes," she went on, smiling at the momentary surprise on his face. "We like to know as much about the men the emperor sets over us as we can. And I thank you for the mead. I appreciate your kindness."

He brushed aside her thanks, not deceived by the diversionary words. "Second-hand information can never take the place of a personal assessment, though, can it Lady? I have learned a great deal about Albion from the most surprising sources in Rome."

She almost choked. She put down her spoon and gave up all pretence to good manners. "You have spoken to Caradoc," she said flatly. "Would it be too much to ask how he fares?"

Paulinus raised his eyebrows. "You jump very swiftly to the wrong conclusions," he answered. "Do you think that I would seek to embarrass a man whose loyalties would forbid him to give me any pertinent information? I did speak with him. He told me more with his silences than he did with his words, and both were full of love for his country and longing to be home. That is all. I spent many hours with Plautius and his wife."

"And what did they tell you?" Boudicca glanced away from Paulinus's cragged face. The voice was her husband's.

"They told me that Albion will probably never fully submit. I listened, but I believe them to be wrong. She will submit to me."

"Ah well," Agricola remarked lightly. "If any man can clean out the west it will be you, Suetonius, but let us not do it tonight. I prefer to clean off my plate."

"No, please," Boudicca protested. "We are not discomfited. You both know my husband's allegiance to the Roman cause, and my own reluctance, but you must also know that I have promised him my support. If we must spend the evening wasting breath on social nonsense then our journey will have been for nothing. We wish to know you, and you wish to measure us. What is wrong with that? I hate the game of words."

"So do I," the governor admitted, "but I hardly think it right to swap animosities over the dinner table. You asked me a question, Boudicca, and I will answer you. Caradoc is well, though he looks older than he is. He and his wife have become good friends with my own friend, Aulus Plautius. His children are well, also. Gladys is married to Plautius's former second-in-command, Rufus Pudens, and has become a Roman citizen. Eurgain ran away, and if she was not drowned, lives on Hibernia, the island you call Eriu. And Llyn . . ." He paused. "Llyn does not like Rome very much."

"How much you do not say!" Boudicca rasped. "Well, I must thank you for what you give me." She met her husband's eye. It was all a long time ago, he seemed to be saying, it belongs to a different age. The Caradoc you knew lives only in your memories and dreams. I wish that I too could be at peace, she thought vehemently. I wish that I had been born like Prasutugas, or even Aricia, able to compromise, to wear a different face for every day, a different soul for every passing year.

"Here comes the Icenian mutton," Agricola said. "Tell me, Lord, are there any domesticated hogs in your land or do you prefer the flavor of wild boar you have speared yourself?"

"I am no longer able to hunt, unfortunately," Prasutugas answered mildly, "but I do prefer wild boar. My chiefs hunt every day, and I still train my dogs."

"The Mauretanian tribesmen hunt lions on horseback, with spears," Paulinus offered. "It makes great sport. Do you hunt, Lady? What game do you prefer?"

Boudicca felt Prasutugas's blue eyes on her again. She answered steadily, her mind suddenly full of the dark forest, a stink of dead fox, and a man's mutilated chest. "Yes, sir, I hunt. In the days when I was young I hunted men and cattle. Then when Rome came I took to netting the boar. Now I think I prefer the deer. They require more skill to bring down than either men or boar." She smiled at him and he took a moment to consider her, the sentences on the Icenian report passing slowly through his mind. The regular dispatches from the commander of the Icenian garrison had been well-thumbed by Agricola and himself and he knew that she was not lying, nor was she boasting. She had indeed hunted men. The dispatches said other things, too. She was all fury, all noise, but her danger was perfectly contained by her love for her husband. The garrison commander dismissed that danger. She was a woman who liked to talk, to stir up the dust, and that was all. Paulinus was unmoved by her flamboyant beauty. The long, soft green tunic fringed in silver which set off her curling bronze hair and golden brown eyes, the six or seven silver bracelets clinking loosely on each scarred arm, the profusion of necklaces, the coronet studded with polished amber, spoke to him only of the wealth that Rome had brought to her. He did not like or dislike her. She and her lord were simply two more factors to be taken into account as he filled in his swiftly complicating picture of the island, and he had already placed them where they fitted.

"I agree with you," he said. "The deer follow their instinct, but men ought to temper instinct. They ought to reason as well, but unfortunately reasoning will often lead them astray. I was struck many times by this faulty reasoning during my campaigns in Mauretania."

"How so?" Prasutagas was interested.

"The land is mostly desert," Paulinus went on. "Impossible to map satisfactorily because the sand is continually shifting. The tribesmen could have maintained hostilities indefinitely if they had behaved with an animal's instinct, but they did not. Instead of varying the routes their baggage trains took to and from food source to food source, they were unable to overcome the habit of hundreds of years. Of course, the terrain decreed that their food could only be grown near water, in the oases that dot the desert, and therefore the people had to return time and again to the same places. They could not live off the land when they ranged. It was a simple matter to discover the oases, destroy the food source, and then sit back and wait."

Slowly, the words seeped into Boudicca's consciousness. The food source. Destroy the food source. Food . . . destroy. All at once the full import of what he had said exploded in her mind and she felt as though she had been taken apart and put together again by a clumsy, inexpert hand. Her stomach churned. Her arms were so weak that she had to use both hands to lay down her mead. The men were not looking at her. Prasutagas had made a comment, Agricola also, and Paulinus was busily extolling the virtues of Mauretanian horseflesh. The tactic had been explained and dismissed in favor of a more satisfying subject of conversation.

He will do it, too, she thought incoherently. I knew it, I knew it. The moment I saw you, Paulinus, I knew. She could not take her eyes off him. Everything about him was blunt, powerful, ruthless, from his square-tipped fingers to the uncomplicated, clean lines of his face. She had heard that he had a reputation for cruelty, but not the warped cruelty of the weak. He was a keen disciplinarian, his decisions were swift, just, and final. He was, by all accounts, incorruptible. All these things . . . She forced her cup to her lips. The others had failed, all of them, but he would succeed. There was an air of solid, tenacious permanence around him. He knew who he was and where he was going, and once he had made up his mind, nothing would stand in his way. Neither gods nor men would sway him. He was going . . . he was going to Mona. The food supply. The source of the west's strength. Grain for their bodies, magic for their souls. Mona. She struggled, panic-stricken, against the nausea, unable to swallow the mead filling her mouth. What can I do? What? She was unaware of the silence until Prasutagas said anxiously, "Boudicca what is it?"

Her eyes fled from one to the other, startled, wounded. With great

592

effort she cleared her mouth of the thick, bittersweet mead. They do not know, she thought in amazement. Perhaps Paulinus himself does not yet know. But I know. "A piece of meat stuck in my throat," she gasped.

"Is there something wrong with the mutton?" the governor rapped and she nodded.

"You Romans do not know how to cook it properly," she joked desperately. "It is still red."

Paulinus clicked his fingers impatiently. "Take it away and bring another piece," he ordered. "I am sorry, Lady. Do you want some water?"

She shook her head mutely, aware of the question in Prasutagas's eyes, the probing of his thought. A fresh dish of mutton was placed before her and she picked up her knife, tearing at the meat with blade and fingers, forcing it into her mouth. Someone asked her something, and she answered without thought. Mona. I must get away, I must run. Venutius, it is over, all of it. Caradoc, did he tell his story to you? What shall I do?

". . . a new census," Paulinus was saying. "It is a nuisance but I cannot delay it. And your taxes will be going up, Prasutagas. The procurator is determined to raise them."

Prasutagas shrugged and smiled, but his eyes stayed on Boudicca's slumped figure. "They have gone up every year, but so has our revenue," he answered. "When we cannot pay our taxes I will let you know, sir!" They laughed. The dessert was borne in, and more wine. Fruit was offered, with strong brown goat's cheese, but the increasing weariness and pain Prasutagas felt was eclipsed by a mounting concern for his wife. She had not said one word for the last hour or more. She sat there like some meek, dumb peasant, bland-faced and seemingly shy, and though Prasutagas searched his mind he could find no reason for her sudden withdrawal. He was glad when the meal ended and they left the triclinium to the yawning servants and drifted a little unsteadily back down the cloister, past the wind-ravaged atrium, to the snug warmth of the governor's reception room. For another hour they drank and talked. Boudicca rallied a little, but her digs at the emperor and the governor were ill-timed and lacked her usual wit. At last Prasutagas rose, thanked Paulinus for his hospitality, and he and Boudicca left the house, stepping out into the wind-swept night, their soldier escort before and behind them.

"Truly, I do not know where Boudicca's colorful reputation comes from," Paulinus remarked to Agricola as they stood together looking out the door onto the chill night. "I suppose that like all reputations built on rumor and gossip, it has been exaggerated. The woman is no threat to Rome or anyone else. She was as meek as one of Icenia's lambs."

"Something upset her tonight, sir," Agricola objected. "I have never met a more forceful woman and I really believed that tonight she would give us a run for our money. Either you or I have offended her."

"Well, it was not done purposely," Paulinus snapped irritably. "Take them around the town tomorrow, Julius. I wish I could, but I suppose I must sit in the office and endure another day of the procurator's interminable figures. I cannot stand the man. I have never met a more greedy, grasping bootlicker. If it was up to me I'd get rid of him."

"He has his job to do."

"Yes, and thank the gods it isn't mine. He can go on counting money, and when I have finished with his stupid reports perhaps I can get on with my job as well. We can't do much over the winter, but in the spring I think we can begin a campaign that will see the end of all the hopeless indecision in Albion. Now go to bed. Good-night."

"Goodnight, sir. It was a successful dinner, all the same."

"H'm." They parted, Paulinus to his bed and Agricola to his own small house.

On the threshold of the merchant's house the four soldiers saluted and left them, and Boudicca and Prasutagas left the cold, insistent wind, shutting the door behind them. They found their chiefs sound asleep, sprawled in their cloaks on the tiled floor around the wind-rippled pool, and they did not wake them. In the sleeping room the lamps still burned steadily, casting a somnolent yellow light, and Prasutagas flung his cloak onto the floor. Although his suppurating stump throbbed unmercifully, and his head swam with pain and fatigue, he went to his wife. "Tell me," he ordered quietly.

Boudicca stood in the middle of the floor, still clutching her cloak around her, a new ravishment corroding her face. "He is the one," she said tonelessly. "He has the answer. Destroy the food supply, he said. Prasutagas, do you know what that means? How could you have missed it? He will march on Mona in the spring. He will do what Scapula was too obsessed with Caradoc to do, what Gallus was too old to do, what Nepos did not have the time to do. He will burn the crops, salt the fields, and then it will all be over. It worked for him in the deserts he spoke of, and it will work here in Albion. Venutius cannot order the mountains to sprout grain! Ah Prasutagas! This man

594

carries the odor of military success with him like a west wind laden with rain! I am afraid! I hurt!"

He considered her words slowly, forcing his thought through the pain that swam in his brain. "You are right, Boudicca," he said at last. "I think that under this governor the west will see peace. I only wish that he had been appointed in the beginning instead of Aulus Plautius. How many lives would have been spared!"

She looked at him aghast. "Andrasta!" she whispered. "Peace is all you think of, Prasutugas, peace at any price, any price at all. Can't you understand that peace is a delusion unless it means honor for Albion? What shall I do? Oh what shall I do?"

He went to her but was too tired to do more than rest his arm around her neck. "You know what you must do," he said firmly. "Send to Venutius. Tell him what you suspect. It will make no difference whether he finds out from you now, or from his own spies in the spring, when the legions are on the move."

She began to cry. Wordlessly, she began to help him undress. She was still weeping when he had laid his blond head upon the pillow and she started to prepare herself for bed. She slid under the covers beside him, her tears hot on his hand as he tried to smooth back her hair.

"Boudicca, please," he begged softly, and she tore herself away from him violently.

"Even with you I am alone!" she sobbed. "Alone! I cannot go! I am tormented if I stay!"

"You once told me that nothing was as important as you and I," he said presently, "and I believe it to be true. Let time carry everything else away, Boudicca, and remember only that I have loved you."

She turned to him then, her arms reaching for him, her wet face pressed into his shoulder, struggling to quell the grief that shook her, but even when she fell, exhausted, into a heavy sleep, despair still stalked her.

Agricola called for them in the morning. The wind still blew but the sun shone brightly as they and the chiefs followed him past the archway to the forum, now crowded and noisy, and down to the stables, a row of neat, sweet-smelling boxes just outside the wall. He chatted breezily as they went, his attention focused unobtrusively on Boudicca, but she seemed to have recovered her aplomb. Whatever had upset her had not followed her through a night's sleep, though she looked a little haggard. Horses were led out, they all mounted, and Agricola showed them Colchester until it was time for the noon meal. Although the foreshortened wall still stood where Caradoc's earthwall had reared, it now boasted four gates, and the town had spilled out beyond the wall in a seamy clutter of shacks, huts, and tents where landless, lordless peasants tried their hand at thieving and deception.

"They are cleaned out periodically," Agricola said as they jogged past the teeming muddle. "Some of them are shipped to Gaul and Rome for the arenas or the legions, and some are put in the Twentieth's old barracks and fed in exchange for their labor, but before long others have drifted in from the countryside."

"Why don't you give them a bit of land? Make them farm? Most of them will have farmed all their lives," Prasutugas said, and Agricola shrugged.

"Land is very scarce here in the south. The veterans from the legions are entitled to a farm when they retire, and they get it. Many of them prefer to live in the town, though, and leave their farms to be worked by natives. Here is the Twentieth's pottery. The last governor reopened it and it is turning out good plain ware, though the quality is not yet as good as the coralware from Gaul. We encourage the natives to continue to produce their own linen and woolen garments, also. At the moment there is quite a demand for Albion's dyes and finished cloth and some of the natives are becoming quite wealthy from it. The legion's demand for boots and sandals is constant, so there is another opportunity for some enterprising people to make money."

Once through the gate they walked their horses slowly along the wide paths. Only the street that ran from the gate to the forum was paved, but it was autumn, a dry, cold autumn, and the paths were packed hard under the feet of freeman and soldier, cart and oxen, horse and trader.

"What concerns me," Boudicca said loudly, "is that all these people, every one of them, in the potteries, shops, tanneries, are now completely dependent on you Romans for their very life. Turn them loose and many would starve. In another generation they would all starve. What happens to them if you go away?"

"But Lady, we have no intention of going away," Agricola replied smoothly. "Why should we? Certainly the people depend on us, and they consider themselves lucky. If we went away, Albion would immediately be plunged into the greatest bloodbath she has ever seen."

"How so?" she snapped.

"The tribes who cooperate with us would be attacked by those who do not. The whole island would become involved and it would be the war to end all wars."

"You really see it like that? You really think that would happen?"

"Of course it would happen!"

"What a low opinion of us savages you have, for all your fine talk," she spat bitterly. "Fighting is all we know, killing is the only thing we like to do, as though we were a pack of wolves. It flatters your Roman pride to imagine that you are the civilizers of the world, doesn't it?"

"Yes," he replied easily. "It does indeed. And we are. Ask your husband and your tribesmen if you do not believe my assessment, Boudicca."

She was quiet for a long time, then she said faintly, "That was not fair. That was a cut below the belt."

"If you give it then you must learn to take it," he said shortly, and she sneered.

"From you?"

They rode slowly past a row of shops that sold everything from locally brewed beer to Roman confections. The chiefs dismounted and crowded into the tiny, dark rooms to finger and exclaim over the goods displayed inside. They came out laden with gifts for their families at home in Icenia, for they did not lack Roman coin, and their pleasure seemed only to emphasize Agricola's insistence that Rome had indeed brought only good. And so she has, Boudicca thought. Then what is it that I mourn for every day? Why do the western tribes prefer to die than to wander down a street in Colchester with their purses bulging with money? The reason is so deep, so far beneath sun, soil, air, and light. The dignity of choice. The freedom to say yes or no without fear. Rome brings us everything but that precious right to choose our own destiny. She had struggled, through the years since the legions came, to put this thought into words for Prasutagus but she had failed. Yet here it came, clear and sweet and sane, with the wholeness of a Druithin truth. We are above the gods, for even the gods can be bound by spells. We are more than tame animals who do not care how their bellies are filled. We are men, whose existence as men depends absolutely on the preservation within us of a dignity that is tied to freedom. I must remember that. I must tell him. But looking at him quietly astride his patient horse, the reins held loosely in his one hand, his arm resting against the horse's neck and his back bowed, she realized that the time had come when she could no longer tell him anything that would bring him hurt. He was dying. It was in his face. Now she must swallow all dissent and approach him with nothing but her strength. She must do him the honor of divesting herself of all defence even though it would mean that before he left her she would not have time to rebuild that half of herself that was him now, and later would have to be composed of something else.

The chiefs were mounting again, their purchases stowed in purses or stuffed into their tunics, and Agricola led them to the end of the street to an open place where huge vats bubbled over fires and the ground was littered with frames hung in freshly dyed cloth. Boudicca slid from her horse. "I want to buy something that Hulda can make up for the girls," she said, and the little cavalcade stopped. The dyer came toward her, his arms stained purple to the elbows, and his wife and son hovered behind him. Boudicca nodded. "Greetings, freeman."

He looked her over swiftly, then smiled. "Is it the Lady of Icenia?"

"It is. How did you know?"

"Colchester is still small enough to be rife with gossip and, besides, there is only one ruling house whose lady has red hair and whose lord is one-armed. Shall I show you my wares?" She nodded again and prepared to follow him into his tiny hut, but Agricola's voice brought them both to a halt.

"Bring out your work and spread it on the grass," he called. "Perhaps others in the company might also like to buy."

Boudicca understood and she graced the Roman with an insolent grin. The man shrugged and entered the hut. "Aren't you going a little too far, sir?" she called back. "I might become offended, and complain to the governor!" Unexpectedly, Prasutugas laughed, and then the man was back, his arms full of gay bolts of material which he proceeded to unroll at her feet. "Are you under suspicion?" she whispered to him as he bent. Then in a louder voice, "They are quite lovely. Tell me of your dyes."

"Yes," he whispered back, his mouth hidden by his lowered head. "They watch me all the time." Then he raised his tone to match hers. "This cloth was dyed in primroses. You can see how fresh they were when picked. The color came out so bright and fragile that I decided not to pattern it. This one was steeped in elderberries, a very rich and thick dye, and the purplish blue it makes is now enjoying popularity. I find it too heavy, and would have it embroidered in silver to lighten it."

She bent also, running the cloth through her fingers. "I have never seen a paler green!" she marveled. "And the red patterning on it is so even! How do you make such a green?"

"You would have to ask my son," he replied. "He makes the dyes—and wanders far to find the ingredients that he needs. My wife weaves the cloth, and I attend to the patterning."

Wanders far. Boudicca did not miss the almost imperceptible emphasis on those words. "Prasutugas," she called. "Do you think that Ethelind would like the primrose yellow?"

"She would look better in the green," he replied. "Buy the yellow for yourself, Boudicca, and the red one there for Brigid."

She moved through the rivers of color, feeling and exclaiming, taking the dyer farther away from the men on horseback. She made her selections, called for a chief to roll them up and lift them from the ground, then said in a loud voice, "How much do I owe you, freeman?"

"Ten denarii." Then he said quietly, "Did you enjoy your dinner last night with the governor? I hear he is very close-mouthed."

"Lovernius!" she shouted. "Bring money! Not close-mouthed enough," she whispered. "I can give you no definite message. Tell them only to guard the holy island." She reached for her coins and Lovernius put them into her hand. She tossed them to the dyer and bid him rest in safety, then walked back to her horse. "Really, sir," she expostulated to Agricola. "If I had wanted to talk to a spy I could have waited until I reached home. You made the poor little freeman look like a fool."

"All I did was to ask him to bring his wares outside," he objected. "Who said anything about spies, Lady? You have a suspicious turn of mind."

"Dyers are all mad in any case," she concluded as they clattered on. "It comes of leaning over hot colors all the day long. They see nothing in black and white."

If Agricola heard her he gave no sign, and they spent the rest of the morning admiring the smart new houses going up within the old first circle of Camulodunon.

That evening Agricola entertained them in his own house, together with certain merchants and prominent moneylenders of the town. The men brought their wives, and Boudicca had to sit for an agonizing four hours listening to the women gossiping among themselves and the men discussing the latest rumors out of Rome and their own flourishing businesses. She felt more than ever like a creature from another world, though she sensed that these people were provincials themselves. She sat in a corner, well away from the circles of the lamplight. Both hands clutched tight around her cup of mead, and she felt as though she had stepped outside the flow of time. The rough winds of Icenia, the clean crackle of the cooking fires, the multicolored swagger of her bearded chiefs, all seemed as much a part of an old, discarded dream as did this gathering of complacent, over-perfumed foreigners. I belong in the west, she thought suddenly, where time has no meaning, where Camulodunon is still earthworks and Cunobelin stands outside the huge Council hall with fists on his big hips while his chiefs hew at each other on the practice ground. Where, in Icenia, Prasutugas and I are young and deeply in love, and Subidasto, my father, bows with the Druids in the groves of Andrasta. The past is there, in the mountains. The future is here, all about me in this hot, dainty room, and I sit with my drink in my hands and know myself to be cast out from both.

Prasutugas was drinking too much, sitting cross-legged on the floor as he did at home when the pain attacked him, his carefully braided blond hair lying against his black and scarlet chest, and the gold circlet shining on his head. His eyes shone also, a feverish blue glint as he glanced at the company and talked with seeming ease, but Boudicca saw that he was gripping his knee tightly, and every once in a while he reached out unobtusively to touch his shield-bearer's elbow. Agricola must have noticed, for toward the end of the evening he came and sat beside Boudicca.

"I did not realize that he was so ill," he said. "If I had known I would have seen that this trip was postponed."

"Well, at least you can now make your plans for the future of my territory," she answered bitterly. "It must be gratifying to be given so much warning of a royal death."

"What care is he receiving? Is there a surgeon stationed with the garrison in Icenia?"

"There is, but Roman medicine is crude. Cut off a bit, burn it a bit more, slather it with salve. He needs the care of a Druid but he refuses to disobey your senseless law."

He sat thinking for a moment, his eyes on her flushed, sad face, then all at once he put his hands around hers as they clutched the cup. "If there is anything I myself can do," he said softly, "anything at all, I hope you will lay aside your prejudice and ask me for help."

She did not stir, and he withdrew the warmth of his clasp. "It is not wholly a matter of my prejudice, Agricola," she said. "I think he wants to die. There is enough of the chieftain left in him to feel shame of his disfigurement, and I know that it angers him to become more of a burden to me than a joy."

"Why won't his wound heal? It was a clean severing, was it not?"

She did not want to talk about it but there was comfort in the young man, a moment of human concern that eclipsed his significance as Roman to her, and she answered him without sarcasm, challenge, or strain under the rise and fall of the conversation around them. "I do not know. Perhaps there was a spell of pain laid on the sword. The Druithin would say that it does not heal because there is a deep sickness in his soul, deeper than thought, but . . . I do not know. I only know that over the years it has closed and opened, and now will close no more. He may live to see another Samain, but not beyond."

"I see. And has he secured his succession in Icenia?"

The moment of mutual sympathy had gone. "He is not dead yet!" she snapped in a fierce undertone. "Ask the procurator what you want to know!"

Agricola rose. "I simply wanted to make sure that he had taken every step to avoid confusion," he said stiffly and went away, and the two Icenians went on drinking, Prasutugas to dull the pain of his body and Boudicca to kill tomorrow.

In the morning they began the long ride home. Prasutugas had admitted that he did not have the strength to face another day of official visiting, and so Boudicca, Iain, and Lovernius had gone to Agricola and requested that they be allowed to go. The request was granted, and the governor rode with them for an hour before he and his escort left them to walk their horses slowly under the now-leafless Catuvellaun forests. Then they turned their faces toward their own border, six days away. But Prasutugas did not reach it sitting upright and alone on his horse. Three days out of Colchester he collapsed, and was carried home on a litter fashioned from the pretty cloth his wife had bought.

Autumn, A.D. 59

CHAPTER THIRTY-FIVE

*B*RIGID SWUNG HERSELF UP onto her horse's back and leaned down to grasp the reins. She smiled across at Marcus. "Are you ready?"

"Ready. Once around the tree, on to the lake, and finish where the river enters the forest."

"But Marcus, that's too far. Last time we finished at the lake."

"Yes, but last time you were only thirteen. Today you are fourteen and you can go further," he teased her.

She made a face at him. "You must let me win, since it is my birthday. You haven't given me a present yet, you know."

"I know. This year I have decided that you are not worth the money I would have to spend. I'm saving for my trip to Rome, after all!"

She closed her eyes and lifted her face to the wind. "Oh Marcus, what a beautiful morning. Isn't it good to be alive on such a morning? Come on! My turn to start us!"

They backed their horses into line, shortened their grip on the reins, and while Marcus was still clucking to his restive mount, she called, "Go!" and her horse leaped out across the flat.

"Brigid!" he shouted, "that's not fair!" He pounded after her with his knees hugged tight to the warm horseflesh, and his tall body bent level with the whipping mane as the wind sang in his ears.

It was indeed a beautiful morning. The flat, scrub-dotted Icenian marshland lay clean and sparkling under a cloudless blue sky, and the thin wind that fretted the long grasses nipped with a dry, invigorating promise. She was already halfway to the tree, a speeding blur of bright scarlet, and he hissed softly at his mount and thundered over the soft turf. He saw her sit upright for a moment as she shouted to her horse. The beast skidded onto its haunches and veered, and she flogged it around the tree and careened madly onto the dimpling reaches of the north end of the lake. He skittered around the tree and then gave Pompey his head and he slowly began to gain on her. The lake edge flashed by, and the white birds, which had begun to settle once more to their feeding after Brigid had pelted by, rose again in a screeching, impatient cloud. He was gaining, and excitement flared in him and began to throb with his quick pulse. He was soon abreast, and he grinned across at her. "I'm going to win again!"

"But Marcus! My birthday!"

For a moment they hung neck and neck, but slowly he began to pull away. He quickly reached the willows along the riverbank, where he stopped short and slid from Pompey's hot, wet back, pleased he had time to turn and watch her canter up.

She tumbled to the ground, flushed and panting. "You ought to give me a head start at least, Marcus. I only lose to you because you have the better mount."

"No. You lose because you ride like a woman."

"And how does a woman ride?"

"Daintily."

"That's not true and you know it. I ride far better than you."

"Would you have been happy if I had cheated, and let you win?"

She sighed, still annoyed. "No, I suppose not. But one of these days my mother will retire this old lady to pasture and provide me with a real horse."

"Such excuses! Shall we go into the woods and look for cuckoo spit?"

602

"No. Let's sit in the grass, in the sun." She flung the reins about a willow branch. "This weather won't last, and when it breaks, autumn will be here."

"Brigid," he said softly. "I was only teasing you before. I really do have a birthday gift for you."

"Of course you do, Marcus. Every year you give me something lovely. What is it? Can I have it tonight at the feast?"

"You can have it right now. In fact you've been looking at it all morning." He smiled broadly at her mystified expression. "Do you want to guess what it is?"

She ran her eyes over him, then shook her head. "I can't see anything that it might be. Tell me quickly!"

He bowed with a flourish and waved at the horse, which had begun to crop the lush, wet grass beside the water. "There it is."

Her eyes widened in shock. "Pompey? You are giving me Pompey? Oh no, Marcus, I couldn't accept—you love that horse. And he's a fine animal, worth a small fortune!"

Marcus looked down, embarrassed. "I didn't know what else to give to a lady who has everything. Besides, Brigid, I want you to have him." He looked up at her shyly, grinning. "We will race again tomorrow, and then you will win!"

She did not know what to say and went to the beast, stroking its tangled mane, reaching down to carress its gray muzzle. "Thank you, Marcus," she said soberly. "I don't deserve him, and I don't deserve a friend like you, either. I promise to give up teasing you, forever."

"Oh I hope not!" he responded lightly. "At least it makes a change from my mother's nagging! Come on. Let's find a place to sit."

They left the horses and wandered into the meadow, where they cast themselves down in the tall, sweet-smelling grasses. Marcus rolled over on his back with a sigh of pleasure, lacing his fingers behind his head and squinting up into the deep, sun-filled sky. "I shall miss all this," he remarked. "No doubt Rome is a very enthralling place, but I think I prefer Icenia to the city's heat and stink."

Brigid got up off her stomach and sat upright. "Then you are no true son of Rome. Didn't Aristotle say that the countryside existed only to serve the towns?"

"No, he didn't. He said man is an animal that lives in the city. I don't think my tutor would get very far with you."

She began to pick the wildflowers that nestled in the dry grass around her, tossing them into her red lap. "I'll miss you."

He looked up at her, but she was studiously bunching the flowers together into a tight, colored knot. "There's plenty of time yet, Brigid," he said softly.

"But everything is decided, and you'll leave us for good and never come back." She dropped the flowers onto her tunic and slowly began to bunch them again. "Are you happy to be joining the cavalry at last?"

"I shall only be a general's dogsbody, you know. It will be years before I can even start the training."

He was not happy to go, and he watched the play of sunlight on the silken sheen of her hair. Her older sister was blonde also, a deep, red gold, the color borrowed from both Prasutagas and Boudicca, but Brigid had the palest, white-blonde tresses he had ever seen among this tribe of blonde, blue-eyed people, and he could never look at her without wanting to touch her hair. He had been fascinated by it even as a small child, when they had played together in the shade of the earthwall.

He had known no other life than the peaceful, fun-filled days in this wealthy little kingdom. His mornings were usually spent with his tutor, his afternoons with Brigid and Ethelind, riding the fields, hunting in the woods, paddling the coracles on the river or among the pools and the flat, muddy shoals of the marshes. He had been to Rome with his mother four times, and did not particularly like it. The crowds, the odors, the sophisticated, painted socialites, had bored and frightened him. He was a provincial, no matter what his mother would like to think. Icenia was his home, Brigid and Ethelind like his own kin, but now his father was about to send him away to start at the very bottom of a military career in a country he was born to but did not love. The prospect was alternately thrilling and horrifying. Until today it had had no reality, but today was Brigid's birthday and all too soon it would be time to pack and say farewell to his home, all too soon he would make the long trip to Rome where he would find lodgings and meet his training officer. Suddenly his dreams of success seemed hollow and forbidding.

"Do you want to fight, Marcus? Are you afraid?"

"I don't know. I've never even seen a man killed. Father says that in battle you don't have time to be afraid. He says that all you do is follow orders and that a battle is no different from an exercise, but I doubt it. There's no blood spilled in exercises."

"Mother says that she was always afraid, but that one just learns to ignore the fear. Once I took down one of the ceremonial swords that used to hang in the hall when I was little. I took it out of its scabbard, but it was so heavy I could barely lift it. It's hard to believe that girls really used to fight each other with those things."

"A formidable woman, your mother." He sat up and reached onto her lap, lifting a tiny, fragile bloom. "Look at this one, Brigid. It matches your eyes. Purple, like old blood!" Her eyes, like wet violets, sparkled at him.

"Marcus, how could you say such a thing! I'm glad that you're going away. Then I shall find a suitor who will tell me my eyes are like stars and my hair like the sun, without you smirking at him behind his back and making fun of him! Do you remember Connor?"

He grinned happily, his fingers moving busily in the grass, tearing up daisies. "Of course. I pushed him into the river. He was too full of himself, Brigid. He needed a wetting." Marcus began to weave the sturdy stems in and out, then he knelt before her. "A crown, for a birthday princess."

"That's pretty. Put it on my head."

He set it on her brow then sat back on his heels, frowning. "It doesn't look right. A princess shouldn't wear a crown unless her hair is free. Undo your braids, Brigid."

"No. It takes too long to plait them again."

"I'll do them for you. Please."

"Mother wouldn't like it."

"She isn't here."

Reluctantly, she pulled her braids forward and began to unwind them. He watched, his heart suddenly in his mouth as the freed hair cascaded over her scarlet shoulders and arms, and brushed the ground behind her. She tossed her head. "There. Now do I look more like a princess? I really am one, you know."

Spun glass, he thought. Gossamer in sunlight, hot golden thread in which to dress a goddess. "That's much better," he said huskily. "Now all you need is a throne."

She smiled and began to bind her hair up again, but he caught her hand. "Let me do it for you," he said, coming closer. Now he could smell it, a warm, sun-drenched, living smell. He closed his eyes and plunged his hands into the golden tangle, while she sat, rigid. He brought his face down and rubbed his cheeks with it, pulling it over his mouth. She turned her head to look at him and his lips brushed hers. She drew back.

"Don't do that."

"Why not?"

"Because . . . because it felt nice." Color began to stain her neck, and her mouth trembled. "Because mother would not approve. Because you are going away. Oh Marcus, don't go away!"

The knelt looking at each other, his fingers still locked in her hair. She swayed and fell back into the grass, Marcus with her. "Brigid," he whispered with a new wonder, "Brigid." He kissed her again, and this time her mouth opened under his and a stab of pleasure ran through him. Dazed, he lifted his head. Her violet eyes met his own in bewilderment. "How beautiful you are!" he began, "I think . . ." But she rolled from under him and sat up.

"No, Marcus, don't say it! Not now, not today on my birthday, not when you are going to leave me."

He shook his head from side to side and his arms went around her again. "I think I love you. Amazing! Marvelous! I love you."

"Oh, why did you have to say it today?" she cried out miserably. "Why didn't you say it yesterday when Pompey trod on my foot, or last week when I lost my best gold bracelet in the woods?" The color flamed in her cheeks. She was embarrassed, and she tried to smooth back her hair with flustered hands. "You are only saying it because you're going safely away and it won't matter."

"Don't be foolish!" he said quickly. "You know me better than that! I mean it, Brigid, I love you. Will you let me speak to my father, and your father? Will you consent to be betrothed to me?"

"But it's so sudden!" she protested shyly.

"Is it?" he snorted. Their eyes held for a moment. "No, it isn't," she said, dropping her gaze.

"Do you consent?"

She did not look up, and her fingers went on twisting about each other. "Yes, Marcus," she said in a low voice.

"Good! Now I can kiss you again to seal the bargain!" She smiled faintly and closed her eyes and, gently, he drew her to him, but a gust of wind whipped a tress of her hair between their mouths and then somehow his nose got in the way, and they fell back onto the grass, laughing breathlessly.

"Shall it be a Roman wedding?" she asked.

"But of course! Your father will want a tribal one first, but there will have to be proper nuptials as well."

"What is a Roman wedding like?"

He frowned, stroking her hair. "I'm not exactly sure. But I do know that you will be dressed in a long white robe, like a vestal virgin, and on your head will be a saffron veil. You and your family will walk to my house in the evening, carrying torches. Oh Brigid, I can see you now, the light dancing on your snowy robe! And everyone will shout, 'Talassio!' as I carry you over the threshold!"

She sighed. "It sounds so lovely." They sat with their arms about each other in a deep, new contentment for a while, but suddenly she tore away from him and wagged an accusing finger under his aston-

606

ished nose. "Marcus Favonius, now I know why you want to marry me! Of course. Why didn't I think of it before! You're just another penniless hopeful who wants a big, fat dowry!"

His jaw dropped and she sprang up. "I'm going to ride my birthday present. You'll never catch me now, you shameless adventurer!" All at once she was off, streaking across the meadow and shrieking with laughter, her pale, wild hair flowing behind her like a bolt of flung silk.

Brigid stabled Pompey and gave minute instructions on his grooming to the stable slave. She walked slowly through the circles of the chieftains' neat houses, braiding her hair as she went and humming under her breath. She wanted to skip over the gravel and dance in and out of the throng of busy freemen who passed up and down the path. He loved her. He had said so. He wanted to marry her. Oh birthday of my life! she sang to herself. Oh Andrasta, Queen of Victory, a white bull for you, and a wedding for me!

She entered the Council hall and stood for a moment, waiting for her eyes to adjust to the dimness. The great, airy room was cold. She glanced about but there was no sign of Ethelind, and except for a knot of chiefs in the far corner, the hall was nearly empty. The hides and skins covering the floor were scrupulously clean and the shields on the walls glowed even in the gloom. Pale patches still showed where ten years ago the weapons had hung, before Scapula had ordered the disarming of the Iceni. The fire was out and the grate had been scrubbed. Brigid began to cross the floor, and as she drew nearer to the little group she heard an angry voice raised above the others. It was Lovernius, standing with his cloak flung over one arm, his other fist clenched.

"He wants interest, he says. What is this interest? I am not the least bit interested in him! He has taken all my cattle and half my flock, and he says the other half is interest. He cannot even speak properly!"

"Lady," another voice interposed. "He has threatened to take my son if I do not give him the money. He stands there with strange soldiers, not men from the garrison, and he makes demands. What is happening?"

Brigid quietly came closer. Her mother sat in her chair, with her chin buried in one blunt hand and her red hair brushing her face. Her chiefs clustered around her, white and anxious.

"He brought slave chains to me," a short, belligerent man shouted. "He took away my freemen! Now who will till my fields?"

"I offered to gamble with him, for my sheep," Lovernius said. "But he did not even answer me."

Boudicca rose wearily. "Very well," she said harshly. "I will go to Favonius. Lovernius, take your harp and go to Prasutagas. Sing to him, see if you can cheer him. But don't tell him where I've gone. Tell him I am hunting." She strode away from the men and caught sight of her daughter, hovering in the shadows. "Brigid! Did you win today? Whatever have you been doing? Your hair is full of grass."

"No, I didn't win. . . . Mother, I want to talk to you."

Boudicca looked more closely at Brigid's flushed face and guilty eyes, and a hint of what was to come made her heart sink, but it was just one more trouble in an ocean of nightmares. "I can't stop now, Brigid. I'm sorry, but this is very important. Come to me tonight."

"What is happening? What's wrong?"

Her mother smiled grimly. "Your father is failing." She swept past Brigid, her tunic swirling about her ankles and her necklaces tinkling. Once outside she did not pause but went straight to the stable. "Bring my horse!" she shouted, and she fidgeted impatiently while the slave scurried to do her bidding.

A net was closing about the Iceni. She knew it. Slowly, invisibly, her tuath was falling apart. Yesterday and the day before she had gone to Favonius, begging to know why, but he had been embarrassed and evasive. I know why, she thought dully. Prasutagas. I told him again and again. I beat at him with my words but he would not listen, and now it is too late. The horse was led out, its harness glittering in the strong, raw sunlight, and she hitched up her tunic, tossed a leg over its back, and clattered to the open gate and the trees beyond.

For the last nine years she and the Roman surgeon had battled to prolong Prasutagas's life, but his time was running out and with it the last vestiges of self-government, just as she had foreseen. The path swerved in under the almost leafless trees and she slowed her mount to a walk. Anger and grief filled her and she knew that this time it would not go away. This time Prasutagas would die, this time there would be no reprieve. Boudicca struggled to swallow the uncharacteristic panic that curdled in her throat, acrid and painful. I must not look forward, she told herself. I must face each day, each hour, as it comes. Today I must beg help from Favonius on behalf of the chiefs. Tomorrow . . . She broke through the trees but did not pick up speed, and the horse picked its way disconsolately down the even slope to where the garrison lay quiet in the sun.

Caradoc, your life was wasted. Perhaps if you still led the west I might even now be riding over clean earth, my sword bright once more on my belt. But your sacrifices were for nothing, and I too must say that my own life has been one senseless, useless battle of words. If

I had capitulated this moment would still have come, but at least I would be able to look back to years of wholeness, of peace. I would have an inner strength to carry me through the dark days ahead, the terror of loneliness. She dismounted under the shadow of the palisade, threw the reins to the guard, and paced across the small parade ground. I remember you so well, Caius Suetonius Paulinus, she thought. I met you only once, sharing food with you in your beautiful house, and yet my thoughts have circled you continuously over the past year as though you were an absent lover. You are our nemesis. You will conquer. Venutius is not a worthy adversary for you. You have not left Colchester, and yet your garrisons have risen inside Siluria. No governor before you was able to accomplish that. Madoc may still be lord of the north of his country, but he will never again see his own village.

Shrugging off her doleful reverie, Boudicca marched briskly along under the wooden porch and thumped on the door. She could not worry about Paulinus, not now. She had her own troubles to fight. Favonius was busy at his desk, with papers piled around him. His secretary was standing beside him, reading over his shoulder. A soldier opened the door, nodded her in, and closed it quietly behind her when she had entered. She came to a halt in front of the untidy desk and Favonius glanced up in annoyance but then rose.

"Boudicca!"

Her face was parchment pale under the tan freckles, and her mouth was rammed tightly shut. She stared at him.

"Is it Prasutugas?" he asked her.

"You know what it is, Favonius. I came to you yesterday, but today there are fresh grievances. What are you going to do? Why do you allow these thieves to scurry here and there over my country, ripping homes apart like rats seeking offal? Whose order brought them here?"

He lowered himself slowly into the chair and waved his secretary away. "I told you yesterday," he said wearily. "Some of them come from the procurator's office, from Colchester. Some come from Rome. I have no authority over them. They are not my concern."

"You have not answered me. You don't dare. They come because Prasutugas is dying, don't they? Don't they?" she said, raising her voice as she placed her hands on the edge of the desk and leaned over him. "Poor impoverished Seneca is worried. He is afraid that when my lord dies his money will end up in other hands. Whose hands, Favonius?" She was shouting at him now. "Why is Seneca worried? Why are the procurator's agents here?"

He was silent while she spoke, his arms resting loosely on the desk before him, his eyes calmly meeting hers. "Seneca must know the terms of Prasutugas's will. When he dies his estates go to the emperor and to his daughters. But the debts will be honored. In all the years since Prasutugas borrowed from him, we have not missed one payment.

"No," she murmured, standing straight. "No. Another fear eats away at that avaricious old heart of his, and in the whole of the empire there is only one man who could take Seneca's money with impunity. And that explains Decianus's men." Her voice dropped a tone. "Tell me the truth, Favonius. What will happen to the Iceni when our lord dies?"

He raised one leather-clad shoulder. "I don't know. The governor may allow your daughters to take over the chieftainship, as Prasutugas wishes." His eyes slid away from hers and she jumped forward.

"Or the Iceni will be absorbed and a praetor will come! I am no fool, Favonius, and neither are you. Isn't it a policy, when the ruler of a client kingdom dies, to govern directly from Rome? Ah gullible Prasutugas! All the lies you told him, you glib, familiar son of a dog! All the fine dinners and lovely presents, all the reassurances! The Iceni are different, you said. The Iceni are our friends, our allies. Absorption? Never!" Her coarse masculine tones grated him, peeling away at the tender flesh of his honesty. "You lied, Favonius. Oh, Andrasta most High, how you lied! Decianus's men are here like wolves around a still-living carcass, and when my lord goes they will tear Icenia to pieces for Nero!"

"You exaggerate as always, Boudicca," he objected quietly. "Of course the men from the procuratorial office are here. When Prasutugas dies you must pay death taxes, and your daughters must pay inheritance taxes. The officials gather to see that the emperor is not cheated. As for Seneca's employees, you can understand their concern, can't you? But don't worry—it will all be sorted out."

"By whom? Prasutugas has tied my hands by his will. By his command the girls have been brought up to be pretty, useless decorations, like Priscilla." He did not flinch, but the almost bored, slightly amused light went out of his eyes and was replaced by a coldness. "Help us, Favonius. Seneca's wild dogs are already looting the people of their cattle, and freemen are being taken for slaves. They come to me, but I can do nothing without your support."

"It is not my job to interfere in dealings that were private agreements between the chiefs and Seneca," he said briskly. "If the chiefs did not understand the terms of those agreements, that is no concern of mine. I administer a garrison. That is all."

She drew back, astounded, marshaling all her forces of self-control,

610

fighting to speak reasonably. "That is *not* all. You are our link with the governor. You can petition him on our behalf. Go to Paulinus for us, Favonius."

"Impossible! You have not been listening to me, Boudicca. The procuratorial office is not responsible to the governor and never has been. Decianus is under the emperor only. And even if I did want to petition for you, I couldn't. Paulinus has left Colchester. He marches on the Deceangli, and then to Mona. His final campaign in the west has begun."

She gazed at him for a moment, dumbfounded, and then gave a little exclamation of pain and fell into the chair that faced him. "So soon," she whispered, half to herself. "Ah, how troubles pile up, one on top of the other, and as always I am helpless." She looked into the red, hard face. "I want a meeting with the procurator. Arrange for me to see him, Favonius. This lawless behavior must be stopped."

He got up impatiently. "It is not lawless, Boudicca. Roman law is fair and just. If the money was not owed, the men would not be here in Icenia."

She looked at him for a long time and her lips gradually settled into a thin, hard line. "Either honesty and goodness have blinded you, Favonius, which I most strongly doubt, or you have never been our friend, and over all the years of comradeship with Prasutagas you have been laughing at him behind his back. He is the one who has been blinded by honesty and goodness. He is worth a thousand of you! Will you do nothing?"

He spread out his hands. "I can do nothing. When and if Prasutagas dies, the situation will be put in hand and you will see that your fears are unjustified." He came around the desk and she rose. "I would ask you to share a cup of wine with Priscilla and me, but she is resting and as you can see I am hard at work." He made as if to touch her and she drew back. "I am sorry, Boudicca. I wish that Prasutagas could go on living, I wish that you and I could have been friends as he and I were."

She stalked to the door and the soldier opened it. "I, too, am sorry," she said hoarsely. "I wish that Caradoc were still arviragus in the west. I wish that Albion would strike down Paulinus. I wish I had never set eyes on you. I will not come to you again."

Once outside she ran across the courtyard to her tethered horse, mounted quickly, and whipped the beast into a gallop, disappearing into the woods.

The legionary closed the door and Favonius and the secretary looked at each other.

"Decianus is pushing too hard," the secretary said matter-of-factly.

611

"When Prasutugas dies the estates will come under the imperial seal as a matter of course. Why is he in such a hurry?"

"He is making his own profit first, as usual," Favonius replied heavily. "If I protest I will lose my post, but I may have to send some kind of objection if any chiefs are killed." He shuffled through the papers before him. "I like both Prasutugas and Boudicca, you know, and it angers me when I see our relationship with the barbarians put in jeopardy by the greed of one man. If Decianus knew Boudicca as I know her, he would think twice about such high-handed dealings." The secretary maintained a polite silence, and Favonius put away his uneasiness. "Well?" he grunted. "What's next?"

Boudicca left her horse at the stable and strode to the hall. Lovernius stood waiting, his gambling dice clicking in his restless hands, his harp slung over one shoulder. As she came up to him he ran forward. "What did he say, Lady?"

"Nothing!" she snapped. "He said nothing, he will do nothing. And we are as defenceless before Decianus as pheasants in a tree. How is Prasutugas?"

"He is very weak. I sang for him, and Brigid came and told him stories, but he fell asleep." The scored, homely face turned to her in worry. "What can we do?"

She was stiff with bitterness. "Nothing, nothing, nothing! It is too late. The chances have passed us by, Lovernius, and we must suffer the fate we chose all those years ago. Prasutugas spoke the words of welcome to Rome, and Rome said thank you, we will take it all, but do not worry, because for your generosity you may share our peace."

Boudicca turned and walked to her little hut. Someone had to order the tuath, and while he lived it had to be her. Some months ago she had moved from the house, leaving it to her husband. She could no longer bear his agony, the odor of rotting flesh that surrounded him, and the broken nights and anxious days. Nor could she bear to see him hour after hour, lying tormented in the bed they had shared so joyfully together. Sometimes, when he felt a little stronger, his chiefs would carry him carefully outside to sit in the sun and she would come to him and sit at his feet, her head against his thin knees. But the burden of his dying and the increasingly agonizing problems of the tuath often drove her to her own hut where she paced in silence, struggling to keep one step ahead of death and chaos. She no longer berated him. No hint of the tuath's distress was allowed to disturb him. Favonius visited him occasionally to talk of hunting. The girls told him jokes. Lovernius played and sang for him. But Boudicca herself came to him with silence, and he was not deceived. Words of

612

apology struggled within him but were suffocated under the weight of his ever present pain, and he could do no more than speak with difficulty of the weather, the feasts, the state of his vast herds. Before the Romans came he would have been killed and a new lord elected, but the Icenian chiefs were no longer devotees of the old ways. They worshipped other gods, the gods of riches and peace, and only Boudicca and a few of her own train still stood regularly in the groves of Andrasta, holding out empty hands to the savage, war-hungry Queen of Victory.

She pushed past the doorskins, ripped off her cloak and tossed it on her bed. She glanced at the dead fire and then sank into her chair and put her head in her hands. Quiet and darkness lapped at her and she exhaled in a long exhausted sigh. Now what do I do? The question had no answer. There was nothing to be done, and the days of hope in revolt were over. The island lay in Roman hands, and soon the long, stubborn resistance of the west would be a thing of memory.

Brigid found her an hour later still slumped in her chair, her long legs flung out before her and her head pillowed on one shoulder. The girl touched her gently.

"Mother, are you asleep?"

Boudicca opened her eyes and smiled faintly. "No, not asleep, just thinking. You wanted to talk to me, didn't you?" She sat up. "I am sorry, Brigid. This is not the best birthday for you."

"Oh, but it is! That's why I must talk to you." The young voice faltered. "It's about . . . about Marcus."

Now Boudicca was fully aware. "Tell me," she said, but Brigid found it hard to begin. She stammered, avoided her mother's eye, blushed, and twisted her fingers together—and Boudicca saw all there was to see in the changing expressions that flitted across the fresh, eager face. At last Brigid found her courage.

"He told me that he loves me. He told me today, on my birthday. He wants us to be wed before he leaves. I know that it is his place to speak to father on the matter and not mine, but father is so ill, and anyway . . ." Her voice trailed off. Anyway, father no longer rules the Council, she had been about to say, and Boudicca was suddenly overwhelmed by a feeling of despair. She sat watching the clear, untroubled eyes, the soft hands that had gripped neither sword nor spear, the sweet breathless innocence of the childlike mouth. She thought of herself at that age, already a formidable sword-woman, ready to be blooded like a man. I have betrayed you, Brigid, she thought. Your father insisted on this dangerous sheltering for you and Ethelind, but I could have done something. I could have taught you the lore of your people, betrothed you quickly to a young chieftain,

613

taken you into the woods and shown you the weapons buried deep, against a day that may never come. But I did not trust you, and perhaps what I did was not wrong. You and Ethelind and Marcus.

"Brigid, I want to tell you something." She spoke evenly, without emotion. "Marcus is very young. He is just beginning a long and arduous career that could take him all over the empire. A wife will only hold him back, and I'm sure Favonius will point that out to him. He has no money. He is not ready to marry yet, not for many years. You have grown up together, and perhaps your father was wrong in allowing you so much freedom. Marcus is a good young man, but he is not for you."

The violet eyes filled with tears. "Then you are refusing us? Just like that? He loves me, mother, and I love him more than anyone else!"

"Brigid," she said deliberately, "he is a Roman."

A moment of resentful silence hung between them, then Brigid went and sat on the edge of the bed. "I don't care what he is. Roman, Brigantian, Silurian, why should I care? I love him, and nothing else matters!"

"The survival of this tuath matters," Boudicca snapped back. "The honor of the people matters. Right now the Romans are stealing our flocks and herds, they are chaining our freemen and taking them away, and while you play in the fields with the son, the father sits in his comfortable office and will not help us. Right now, Brigid, right now while we talk! Can't you hear the wailing of the people? Rome brought this! And Marcus! They are the conquerors!"

"No," Brigid faltered. "Marcus is not like that. He would help if he could, I know he would. He loves this tuath. He doesn't want to go to Rome—Icenia is his home."

"But he will go to Rome, and there he will remember that he belongs to an empire. He will forget us, Brigid, and his memories of you will be of a simple, pretty little barbarian who amused him when he was too young to know any better."

"No!" The tears poured down her face but she did not move. "You don't understand! He has always been a brother to me! We learned to ride together, we snared our first rabbits together, I have never lived without him and oh, mother, if I have to live without him now I will die!"

Boudicca got up, reached down, and, grasping Brigid's trembling arms she pulled the girl to her feet and thrust her face close. "Listen, Brigid. If you wed a Roman the tuath will cast you out. Do you know what that means?"

"But those days are gone! Father said so!"

"They are coming back. Every herd driven south, every child torn from his mother and chained to be shipped to Gaul, brings them closer. Your father is dying, Brigid, and when he is dead Favonius and Priscilla will go away. A praetor will come, and a Roman town will spring up here, where we stand. The Iceni will have ceased to be."

Brigid raised puzzled eyes to hers. "Well, what is wrong with that?"

A surge of terror and loss took the power from Boudicca's limbs and she released her daughter. She went unsteadily to the door. "I want to refuse you," she said, "but I cannot. It must rest with Favonius. It is too late to undo the harm that has been done, and my ears are full of a suffering far greater than yours, Brigid. You may wed Marcus, if his father agrees."

Brigid sat looking at her, uncertainty chasing the bewilderment from her face as her mother swept from the room and the doorskins fell closed behind her.

Favonius looked at the glowering, mutinous face of his son. "You are not being reasonable, Marcus. It is far too soon for you to take a wife. Why, she would be nothing but a millstone around your neck, and at a time when you will need every denarius you can scrape together and all your energies will be going into your work. Besides, she's a barbarian."

Marcus flushed hotly. "That has nothing to do with it! In all the years we've been friends together the thought has never crossed my mind, and I believed you to be above such prejudice as well. You know, father, the great Aulus Plautius married a barbarian."

"He was much older than you when he did so, and he knew his own mind. Can you face the displeasure of your superior? The sniggers of the friends you will make in Rome? Have you considered that it might ruin your career?"

Marcus glanced away and Favonius absently toyed with the stylus in his fingers, a frown on his face. "You are letting sentiment override good sense, Marcus. She's young and pretty, but Rome is full of young and pretty girls, most of them a good deal more civilized than Brigid. You will forget her as the months go by."

Marcus folded his arms, a glare of obstinacy in his eyes. "What I feel for her is not sentiment. I don't give a damn for Rome, not really, and I don't know what you mean by 'civilized.' If you mean well-educated and rich, then I'm not civilized either."

"That's not what I mean!"

But it was, Favonious reconsidered. Marcus had spent his childhood running wild over the marshes and forests of Icenia, and his father knew his arguments were so much rubbish to a youth who knew more about the habits of the deer than he did about rhetoric. Marcus didn't care a fig for philosophy. Favonius felt himself trapped. He himself was a loyal Roman through and through, but he realized with a strange pang of regret that the young man standing before him with his feet planted so sturdily apart was a hybrid, a new breed of frontiersman who was neither Roman nor barbarian, but a little of both. Well, he thought, it could not have been avoided—I did not have the money to send him to Rome for an education.

Favonius dropped the stylus to the desk and ran a bemused hand through his graying, wiry hair. "There's another consideration, Marcus. Prasutugas won't last much longer and then the Iceni will come under the direct control of the empire like any other client kingdom. I don't think Boudicca will stand for it. There will be trouble."

Marcus grinned insolently. "All the more reason, then, to marry Brigid and take her away. But I think you're wrong about Boudicca, father. She grumbles and spits and curses us but she's not capable of anything else. She'll settle under direct rule like the rest of the chiefs, and then perhaps one day Brigid and I can come back to Icenia to live."

"You don't remember the uprising ten years ago, do you?"

"Only vaguely."

"Well, if you did you would not dismiss Boudicca so lightly. Oh, Marcus, stop dreaming! They are a dying people and we are their conquerors. No good can come of a marriage such as this! How will you support her? What will you do with her when she's homesick? I beg you to think again."

"No." Marcus stuck out his jaw. "She's for me as no one else is. If you don't give your permission I'll go to the governor."

Favonius laughed. "Spoken like a true son of mine. Very well, Marcus, you have my permission, but on one condition."

"Oh?"

"No wedding until you get your first leave."

"But that might be years away!"

"If she loves you she'll wait."

Marcus came up to the desk. "And of course you hope that I will be so wrapped in my work and so entranced by the city that I'll never give her another thought. You're wrong, father. Absolutely wrong."

"Take it or leave it, Marcus. I won't change my mind."

Marcus shrugged ruefully. "Then I suppose we must take it. At least you did not say no."

Favonius went back to his dispatch. "I didn't need to," he said lightly. "You will say it yourself."

616

CHAPTER THIRTY-SIX

SUMMER BLEW AWAY suddenly on a stiff autumn gale, ruthlessly lifting the leaves from the trees, almost before they could wither into crisp, golden sky-boats, while burdened clouds moved slowly and majestically over the now-dreary, deserted marshlands. Suetonius had joined the Fourteenth Legion and begun the march that would take him north and ultimately west, skirting the still-battling Ordovices and on into Deceangli country and so to Mona. The refurbished Twentieth marched with him, ready to quarter at Deva on the coast and there to await his order to advance if it was necessary. Half the fighting force of the province swarmed into the west, twenty-five thousand men, but Paulinus was unconcerned. He had laid his plans well and thoroughly mapped the paths he was now taking. Farther south and west, at Glevum, the Second Augusta carried out lightning raids against the battered but unbowed Silures, and it harried the Ordovices from their vessels, also at Paulinus's command. A perfect pincer, he congratulated himself, which will nip Mona without once getting entangled in the mountains of the interior. Then a short wait while the rebels starve, and I will have conquered the west. How absurdly simple.

He had remained at Colchester for the last campaigning season and kept in touch with his generals through dispatches, while they oozed slowly up to the passes and along the ugly, rugged coastline. But now, in the second season, he had gone to command in person, calmly and efficiently. This season would see an end to the years of bloody, vicious waste and the beginning of a true and lasting peace. His predecessors, with the exception of Plautius, had allowed themselves to become either too emotionally involved with the game, like Ostorious Scapula, or too anxious of failure to be decisive, like old Gallus. They lacked objectivity. Paulinus had it in full measure. First and last he was a soldier—cool, brilliant, with the ability of a born general to completely disassociate himself from the human element in warfare and move his legions like pieces on a gaming board. He had no defeats behind him, and looked to none ahead. With an uncharacteristic flash of insight Nero had chosen the perfect man for the task, and confidently, almost impatiently, Paulinus clattered with his cavalry escort around him, and his thousands before and behind, toward the treacherous, mist-clogged northern passes. All his thoughts were bent on Mona. The lowland had lain quiet for ten years and would continue that way for another hundred, and he was about to put the crowning laurels on a long and successful career. He was happy.

Boudicca sensed the growing light around her and was instantly awake. The night was deep and cold. She sat up, drew the blankets around her shoulders, and pushed aside the curtain to see how her fire had sunk to red embers and the snow had silted in long white fingers under her doorskins. The light stopped outside her door, wavered, and a chief bent his head and entered, a lamp in his hand. "What is it?" she whispered, and he came and stood by the bed.

"My lord is sinking," he said tersely. "He will not live through the night."

She slid from the warm womb of the bed and reached for her cloak and boots. "Have you sent for the doctor? Does Favonius know?"

"Not yet, Lady. Prasutugas forbade me to bring the Roman doctor. He is tired of being mauled. He wants to die in peace."

"Then he is conscious." She pulled on the boots with swift, steady fingers. "Rouse Brigid and Ethelind. Quickly!"

The chief bowed briefly and went out, and she stood, wrapping the cloak tightly around her. A dozen thoughts clamored for her attention and a great shadow of fear reared up at her back, but she raised her hood, pushing the welter of thick hair beneath it, and stepped outside.

It was snowing, a gentle, quiet drift that settled softly on her up-turned face as she scanned the night sky, and there was no wind. The air was wet and dense but not cold, only full of a clean winter magic, and she drew in deep breaths of it as she turned and walked past the Council hall to the imposing entrance of Prasutugas's Roman house. His chiefs had already gathered, squatting in silence under the shelter of the porch, and they murmured a greeting to her as she slipped between them and opened the door to the room where Prasutugas had lain, now, for six unendurable months. Lovernius closed it behind her, his bulbous features haggard, and she went to the big bed and knelt beside it.

He was awake and he lay on his back. His broad jaw was rigid, and his teeth were clamped tightly together. The sweat trickled down his temples to soak his pillow. He was breathing slowly, with great wheezing rasps of air that sounded like the huge, tattered bellows of the ironsmith's forge, and his naked, wet-slicked chest rose and fell, rose and fell, strained and shuddering. His eyes were wide open, fixed on the ceiling but not seeing it, his gaze turned inward to the labyrinthine disintegraton of his body. But when she placed a firm hand on his good arm he slowly turned his head.

618

"Boudicca," he gasped. "I have not fought an enemy in years, and this one is strong. I face him alone, and I am so weak."

"Say nothing, dear one," she broke in. "Die in peace. You are not alone, for I am here with you, and beyond my father waits, and your chiefs who fell with honor. Go forward."

He licked his cracked lips with a dry, trembling tongue. "My sword. I need it."

She smoothed back the white-streaked, blond hair and looked up at Lovernius. "Bring a sword."

"But Lady," he hissed, glancing sideways to the bed. "It is forbidden."

"If I have to get it myself you will be sorry!" she said in an undertone. "Go quickly. You know where to look."

He bowed unhappily and went out, and she turned back to her husband, laying her cheek against the frail, heaving chest. "I love you, Prasutugas," she whispered. "I have always loved you." He could not answer. All his will was bent on keeping silence, and the echoes of another reality were already floating fitfully through the dark confusion of his mind, like harness bells tinkling far away on a scented summer evening. Boudicca sat back on her heels, her arms folded on the edge of the bed where the damp sheets trailed the floor, and all in the room listened, trapped, to that agonized breathing. The girls slipped in, their cloaks clutched under their chins in frightened hands, their sleeping tunics mired with mud and snow brushing the floor, and they came and stood behind her.

"He will recover again, won't he, mother?" Ethelind whispered, but she did not answer.

How pitifully old you have become, my husband, she thought, her eyes on the tense, quivering muscles of his face. And how old I feel also. I die with you tonight. My life is over, though I go on moving down the long years. Oh take me with you, Prasutugas, take me with you, don't leave me here in this terrible coldness! Lovernius approached and she rose, taking the sword from him and laying it carefully beside her husband. It was dull, the blade stained, the hilt encrusted with wet earth, but his hand stroked it and he smiled and closed his eyes.

"Druid," he muttered, "Druid," and she leaned over him.

"He will come, Prasutugas." He shifted then. His back arched suddenly, his eyes rolled, then he lapsed into a stupor. Such a death! she thought in desolation. Such a rude, unlovely passing, with no Druid to ease his going with spells of loosing, and only a blunt, useless sword by his side. And the tuath goes with him, sinking even as he has lain ailing, dying slowly and miserably, limbless and impotent. She sat in the big, comfortable chair where he had often rested with his good arm in his lap, watching her with an amused affection as she paced to and fro by the bed and shouted her frustrations. The girls huddled close together, not daring to speak. The chiefs, Lovernius, and Iain, his shield-bearer, squatted at the foot of the bed and looked at the floor. The lamps burned with an occasional spasmodic flicker, but the shadows, like people frozen into a timeless tableau, were still.

He spoke once more before he died. "Andrasta! Raven of Nightmares!" he called, his voice urgent, then his breathing faltered. Boudicca sprang up. He took another shuddering lungful of air and opened his eyes, fighting to keep it, but then he had to let it go and it sighed from him in a long, quiet wind. He did not breathe again. His chest lay motionless. The pain-marred face relaxed as though with an enormous relief, and a new silence rushed in to capture the little group in its aggressive embrace.

After a long moment, Boudicca turned to Iain. "Go immediately to Favonius," she said tonelessly. "He will want to send a message to the governor, and to Rome. Tell him that if he wishes to see Prasutugas he must come in the morning. Tell him . . ." The large, sweeping lines of her face suddenly seemed to crumple inward and she waved him out, striding clumsily back to the chair beside the bed. Prasutugas lay quietly, his head turned toward her, his hand flung out to touch her like the hesitant reaching of a shy child. The other chiefs came crowding behind her, murmuring together, and at last Brigid began to cry, but Boudicca put her chin in her palm and watched him.

He was lain on a bier in the Council hall and for three days the Icenian chieftains sat around it on the floor, speaking to one another of his virtues. Boudicca, seated on a chair at the far end of the room with Brigid and Ethelind silent at her feet, listened impassively to the soft, respectful murmur. No chief rose to proclaim Prasutugas's might in battle or his bravery in raids. No one acted out his fights in single combat with the champions of other tribes. She drank her golden mead slowly and reflectively, hugging such memories to herself. He had been a peacemaker, her gentle husband, and perhaps it was right that the chiefs should bring to mind his careful wooing of Rome, yet she felt ashamed that in all the long history of the Iceni, Prasutugas should be the only lord remembered for his agility of mind rather than of body. He lay quietly in their midst, braided hair on his green breast and a silver helm on his head, with his great blue-enameled ceremonial shield beside him. But no sword rested under his limp hand, and the soft songs Lovernius sang now and then were as plaintive and tender as the lays of love.

The snow continued to fall. Sometimes it thinned and slowed as if tired of its duty but no wind came up to move the burdened gray clouds, and Prasutagus was carried to his mound through a thick, white curtain that hurried to cover him like a Druid's pall. Inside the barrow it was dark and cold but somehow welcoming—a safe, secret room where he could sleep undisturbed, far from the turmoil of living —and his chiefs put him reverently on the ground and began the last solemn rites. The spokes of his chariot gleamed in the torchlight. His richly chased silver plate, his golden brooches and bracelets, stored up the full, hot light against the long darkness to come and glowed in the shadowed corners of the little room. His men delivered eulogies, but with an embarrassed reluctance, and the words were all of gratitude and amity. Boudicca did not speak. She wanted to praise him for his sweetness, his tolerance, the steady, comforting years of loving he had shared with her, not for his peace, but these things were private and she could find no public deeds to glorify. When the ceremony was over she left the mound and went to her hut. Ethelind drifted to the stable, led out her unwilling horse from its oats and warm straw, and vanished under the snow-laden branches of the forest. But Brigid saw Marcus hovering beyond the cluster of men and she ran to him. He wore Icenian breeches against the cold and his long native cloak made him look like a young chieftain, but his thin, almost pinched face was Roman and his black, short hair, sprinkled with snowflakes, curled around his ears.

"I'm sorry, Brigid," he said. "We all knew it was coming but that doesn't make it any easier to bear. I feel I've lost an uncle, or even a father. He was always so good to me."

"It's all right," she replied. "I think he is happier in death. It was strange, Marcus, watching him die. I was terrified when Lovernius came to fetch me but somehow his dying was so . . . so small, as if it really wasn't important at all. Do you understand me? I expected something shattering to happen—time to stop for a moment, or the lamps to go out, something to mark death, but nothing has changed."

"I suppose death is a going away, just as birth is a coming in," he said awkwardly. "It is only people who change, Brigid." She brushed the persistent, gathering humps of snow from her shoulders and pulled her cloak more tightly around her. "Are you cold?"

"No."

"Good. Then let's take a boat and go downriver. The countryside

621

will be deserted today and we can build a fire later on. Would you like that?"

Swift words of teasing mockery rose to her lips but for the first time in their long relationship she had no desire to utter them. He was smiling, his eyebrows raised, and without a trace of awkwardness she leaned forward and kissed him on his cheek.

"Thank you," she said. "I would like that very much."

They went to the river, picked their way through the upending fishing coracles cluttering the pier, and cast off in a small boat belonging to the garrison. Marcus took the paddle and expertly guided them to the center, where they drifted, the sleepy current bearing them toward the sea. It was warmer on the water, though in the shallows to either side of them the still, forgotten pools were rimmed with ice and the thick brown rushes and waterweeds stood clogged with silted snow. There was no sign of life in the shrouded marshland that stretched away from them on either hand, only an occasional water rat splashed into the murky darkness and then swam strongly and was lost in the choked white riverbank.

The snow was turning to flurries mixed with sleet, and Brigid lifted her face to the low sky. "The weather is warming," she said. "Soon it will rain." He did not reply and they floated on, swathed in silence and pale coldness. They sat for an hour, sunk in their own lazy thoughts, secure in a mute companionship, then Marcus took up the paddle and deftly steered them toward a dim, tree-hung backwash. They climbed out, pulling the little craft high, then set about collecting dead twigs and branches, their blood slowly heating to tingle in their toes and fingers as they worked. Before long they had kindled a fire and sat staring into it, their shoulders hunched over knees drawn up against the damp. The stately sobriety of the day hung with calm wings above them and they gazed into the flames for many contented minutes without speaking. Then Marcus stirred.

"Brigid," he said hesitantly, his voice falling dull and flat in the close stillness. "Would you consider coming to Rome with me when I go?"

Her head snapped around. "What do you mean?"

"I mean that instead of waiting years to marry we would do it right away, in secret, and take ship together."

"But we can't marry without permission, you know that. And even if we could, how would I get all the way to Colchester without being missed?" Excitement shook her voice, belying the doubt in her words.

"We could think of a way. Ethelind would help, I know she would. As for the wedding, we could manage it once we got to Rome." He flung another log on the fire and turned to her, speaking rapidly and with fear. "If we wait we'll never be married. I feel it, Brigid. Something tells me that if I go away without you I'll never see you again. Call it a fancy if you like, but I can't shake it off. There's a doom coming."

She had never heard him speak so seriously and she edged closer to him. He put an arm around her and pulled her against him. "I trust you, Marcus," she said in a small voice, "but it is an unforgivable thing, to run from my tuath and my kin. If I go, mother will not take me back."

"There will be no turning back for either of us," he spoke into her wet hair. "I've done all I can, and if we are to stay together it's the only way."

"I'm afraid."

"You'll be safe with me, I swear," he promised with more confidence than he felt. "And once father is over the shock he'll support us."

She extricated her hands from the folds of her cloak and rose, then drawing one of the bronze bracelets from her wrist she ran to the water's edge and hurled it far. It sank immediately and she folded her arms and began to shiver. "Why did you do that?" he called and she turned slowly, trying to smile at him over the dying flames of the fire, her eyes filling with hot tears.

"For Andrasta," she said. "The Queen of Victory must not become the Raven of Nightmares."

For a month the tuath hung in a strange limbo. Two days after Prasutugas's burial a Council was called and his will discussed, and though the chiefs were not happy at its directives they accepted it. Brigid and Ethelind now ruled the Iceni, but all knew it was in name only. Favonius had sat with the freemen during the proceedings. He had not spoken, but the people were aware of him and all that he represented, and they did not forget that half the wealth of Icenia now belonged to Nero, his master. The officials from the procuratorial office hung about the town with the traders and Seneca's employees. They seemed not to know what to do, or they were waiting for something, and as winter deepened and the nights drew in, no chief ran to Boudicca with tales of abuse. She herself was quiet and subdued, riding alone over the hard, wind-raked turf, sitting for long hours by the Council fire, drinking thoughtfully by herself in the hut she was reluctant to leave for the past-haunted house. The snow had become rain but when the skies had cleared once more the temperature had dropped and remained sullenly low, and icicles hung from the eaves of the huts and houses. She was despondent and tense, caught in a mood that was more than the slow grieving for her husband, but she blamed the weather. Winter was hard on man and beast, and this winter could prove to be the hardest of all. The dense forest was locked in cold, and the trees stood with a brittle stiffness and glittered with frost. The river began to ice over. Men and beasts huddled together in the same mood of irrational, glum expectancy, and even the heatless glisten of the noon sun on the crystal whiteness of the marshes failed to raise their spirits. They felt that spring would never come, and if it did it would come too late—for what, they could not say. They knew only that something irreplaceable had passed with the dying of Prasutugas and as yet there was nothing to fill the chasm, and perhaps there never would be. The tuath was like a boat without oars, rocking just out of reach of a busy current.

Priscilla was unaware of weather or mood, and moved fussily about her little house in the garrison, packing and unpacking, for Marcus was to leave soon for Colchester and Rome. But Favonius found himself straying to the high gate in the palisade wall and looking out beyond the copse, to where Boudicca's town lay. He was uneasy. He had never taken the peoples' muddled religion seriously before, but now his mind dwelt on the war goddess Andrasta and her fierce Druids, long gone, and he could not drag his thoughts away from the sense of malevolent, brooding magic spreading toward him from the vast forests. Winter was a time of slackness for soldier as well as chief.

Marcus and Brigid no longer raced together. They paced among the somnolent trees, putting the last touches on their plan for Brigid's escape, and the silent weight of suspense around them became so heavy that even they spoke unconsciously in whispers.

Then, on the day before Marcus was due to bid farewell to Icenia, doom fell. Boudicca had dressed and was cloaking herself for the walk to food in the Council hall when Lovernius pushed aside her doorskins and walked in unannounced, stuffing his dice into his belt pouch, his face suffused with wrath, and a half dozen chiefs tumbled behind him, breathless with panic. "Lady, Favonius is here with a guest, and several hundred other men, most of them soldiers," he shouted at her. "I think it is the procurator."

"Decianus?"

"The same. Favonius sent me to . . ." But he did not finish. The chiefs shouldered past him and pressed about her.

"I woke this morning to find them driving off all my breeding cattle!" Iain yelled. "All of them! My freeman herder is dead!"

"They dragged my daughter out of her bed, Lady. I cannot find her anywhere!"

624

"My granary has been broken into, and all my winter store is gone!"

She listened impassively though her heart had begun to beat erratically and her throat went dry. She picked up her amber-studded coronet and set it carefully on her brow, then raised both hands and the furor died abruptly.

"Peace, all of you! The procurator is here, and all misunderstandings will be righted. Go to the hall and wait for me. Lovernius, Iain, you come." She pushed past them and they made way for her as she bent her head, passing under her lintel and out into the winter morning. The sun was free of the horizon and its light had already gone from pink to golden. A keen wind lifted her hair and flung it back in her face and she clawed at it, her heart still thumping painfully under her ribs. She strode through the hut circles to the gate where Favonius had already started up the path, with a loose, portly man beside him and a stream of jostling, laughing legionaries behind. Favonius looked alarmed. And well he might, Boudicca thought in sudden fear. His escort looks half drunk. Surely they are not serving soldiers! No officer would allow such behavior. She stood and waited, turned into the wind so that cloak and hair blew out behind her, and Favonius came up and halted.

"Boudicca, this is the procurator, Catus Decianus. He brings an edict from the emperor."

She met his eyes swiftly, and they were veiled, troubled, then she moved to scan his companion. Thick, bushing eyebrows almost met over large, watery eyes. His nose was thin at the bridge but swelled to wide nostrils, giving him a deceptively fastidious look. His mouth was red and wet, held permanently in a smile of polite insincerity, and he was breathing loudly, his belly heaving with his chest. She felt the welcoming smile on her lips stiffen into disgust, and she quickly stilled her face.

"I am glad you are here, sir," she said, striving to keep the distaste out of her voice. "Perhaps now my tuath can procure justice. We have been sorely used by your servants for some months now, and I am sure you are unaware of our plight. The emperor must know how loyally we have paid our taxes."

He went on smiling. "Of course the emperor knows, Lady," he replied, in a voice that was a painful wheeze. "He has instructed me to claim and catalogue the inheritance your late husband so generously awarded him, and with your cooperation it should not take long. Some of my men have begun already. Never let it be said that the members of the procuratorial staff are dilatory in carrying out their duty!" He chuckled at Favonius, and Favonius laughed politely.

"But your men are stripping my chiefs of all they have!" she exclaimed. "Their personal possessions as well! They are even taking freemen away! Surely this has nothing to do with the inheritance!"

Suddenly his eyes went as hard as agates. For years he had watched the Icenian tribute pile up on the docks at Colchester, a profusion of wealth outstripping the contributions of the other tribes and hinting at a far greater hoard to be picked over. Now his appetite would be assuaged. The Iceni had been growing in riches, therefore the Iceni had been dishonest in their dealings with their masters. The arrears must be set to rights. He hated the poor natives, but he hated the rich natives more. They had too much pride, they were invariably contemptuous and high-handed, but he knew how to cut them down. Paulinus did it with swords. He did it with figures. Either way, Rome benefited. And himself, too, of course. That was understood. He answered this raw-boned, red-headed queen with a careful disdain.

"You have not been honest with us, and the time of reckoning is here." He snapped his fingers and a secretary hurried to his side and handed him a slate. "Fifteen years ago the Divine Claudius loaned the Iceni a certain sum of money. You have not made one payment, any of you, on the sum itself or on the interest."

"That money was a gift to us in exchange for our cooperation! Only the money from Seneca was a loan, and that is being repaid faithfully!"

"Not according to the records. The imperium is tired of waiting." He licked his lips. "By order of the emperor I am here to assess the whole kingdom. All horses, cattle, and herds to be impounded. All jewels, personal possessions, anything of value to be brought forth for evaluation and taxing. Two thousand slaves are to be levied. It was two thousand, wasn't it, Sulla?"

The secretary nodded. "It was, sir."

"Good. Henceforth, all this land is under the imperial seal, to be disposed of as the emperor, and I, see fit. Have you any mines?"

She was shaking all over, her arms clutched tight to her bosom, and her face drained of all color under the sprinkling of freckles. "Does the governor know about this, this monstrous lie?" she whispered, and he handed back the slate and wheezed at her sharply.

"He knows that I am here. Do you object?"

"Of course I object! I object most strongly! How dare you bring this rabble here and terrorize the people!"

"Remain calm, Lady, and do as you are told," he said. "Then no one will be hurt and my business can be promptly concluded."

He dismissed her from his mind. "To work!" he huffed at the men shuffling impatiently behind him, their eyes already on the huts of the

626

defenceless freemen. "Empty the buildings! Pile it all in front! If any of the natives try to interfere, chain them." He hitched up his belt and trundled on up the path, and Boudicca swung around on Favonius, grasping his sleeve.

"Who are these men?" she demanded.

He answered diffidently. "Some of them are regulars of the Ninth, from Lindum. Most are veterans that Decianus had brought with him from Colchester."

"Favonius, do something! Look at them! They are here for booty, not tax, and you know it! Call out the garrison and have them driven away!"

He firmly picked her fingers from around his arm. "I've told you before, I can do nothing. Decianus would have me removed from my post. Besides, I didn't know about the debt to Claudius. I must say it was stupid of Prasutagas to ignore such a large obligation."

"You pig!" she shouted. "He was your friend for years, and yet you can believe this of him."

"Control yourself," he snapped, and he turned on his heel and left her, following the procurator and his eager, greedy men.

She stood for a moment, struggling for breath and forcing down the waves of violent anger, her bard and shield-bearer silent beside her. Then she jerked her head and they went after the men. An alarmed hubbub had already broken out as the people found themselves herded roughly from their warm huts, and as Boudicca rounded the last bend she saw Brigid and Marcus come out of the hall together and stand bewildered before the door. "Brigid!" she called. "Come here! Stay close to me." The girl murmured something to Marcus and ran to her mother, and Marcus set off in search of his father.

"What is happening?" Brigid asked, and Boudicca answered impatiently.

"Not now. I will tell you later. Where is Ethelind?"

"I don't know. She ate in the hall, but I haven't seen her since."

Boudicca swung to her shield-bearer. "Iain, go and find her. Bring her to me." Iain sped away, and the other three moved slowly to Prasutagas's gay Roman house, beside the hall. They halted there and Lovernius squatted loosely on the frozen earth. Brigid leaned against the wall, her eyes wide. Boudicca stood stiffly, with her arms folded, listening to the irritated protests that had now turned to wails as the people stood helplessly by, watching their possessions flung out at their feet. From where she waited she could see only a part of the first circle. Bright cloaks and pearled belts, trinkets sparkling in the sunlight, bronze mirrors studded with coral, silver-rimmed bowls and cups, old pink- and blue-enameled shields lay in glaring confusion on the white frost. Children stood with their fingers in their round mouths, and the women sobbed, their hands moving lovingly among their tangled possessions. But the men cursed and muttered, following the soldiers in and out of the dim huts, and Boudicca could feel the tension around her mount like a great, seething thunderhead. Already, one or two legionaries were picking over the tumbled heaps, tucking this and that into their packs, and all at once there was a shout. One of her chiefs had leaped at a soldier, his hands going for the throat, and the two men were locked in a vicious struggle, but two other soldiers were running, and in a moment the chief lay stunned among his precious goods, his blood staining the green and yellow tunics. A group of procuratorial servants and centurions came swaggering up the gentle rise. They did not look at her. They made straight for the Council hall and went inside. An excited burst of chatter was heard from within. They had found the wine barrels. Lovernius rose slowly to his feet and glanced at Boudicca, and she at him, and together they saw with sinking hearts the barrels being rolled into the open and the lids torn off. The grassy lawn before hall and house was beginning to fill with freemen who wandered aimlessly, and dazed women who clutched bleeding, trampled children. Then Iain came striding up, Ethelind with him.

"Brigid, Ethelind, go into the house and do not stir," Boudicca ordered quickly. "Lovernius, Iain, bar the door and stand just inside it. If the soldiers break in let them take what they want and don't argue with them."

"Where are you going?" Brigid asked in panic, and Boudicca kissed her.

"To find Favonius and the procurator and make another attempt at a reasonable settlement."

She hunted for them, stumbling over the debris of the once-quiet town, half-running from the imploring hands that reached for her.

"Lady, my linens! My hangings!"

"Lady, my brother is hurt!"

"Lady, they have taken away the twins!"

"Help us, Lady."

Lady, lady, lady . . . crying, screaming, beseeching, catching at her cloak, her arms, her long hair—drowning, dying hands, clinging, tearing, they were ripping her apart, and she felt herself cry out with the despairing voices, keening and moaning. The desolation filled her and overflowed in tears, but she walked on. The crowds thickened, milling about each circle in a dense confusion. The sun was high now, and

628

streamed a pitiless, indifferently glaring light onto the choked pathways and the littered, frosty grass. She passed the gate where the wains stood, many already loaded with booty. Soldiers relaxed against the wheels, sitting, gambling, laughing, their breath a hot steam. She paused, tired and beaten. Beyond the wains the countryside moved out to a far horizon. The marshes lay shining peacefully, dotted here and there with scraggly clumps of bush, and off to her right the forest invited her to run in under its protecting arms. She wiped her face with one sleeve and started back for the hall, defeated. She could not find them in this crushing, panic-stricken mob.

As she made her way, the crowd suddenly fell silent and parted, and a group of chiefs stumbled past her, chained to one another at the neck, their hands tied together. She felt herself grow faint and she drew back, but they recognized her and began to clamor, shaking their chains. "Lady! See! Vengeance, Lady! Freedom!" All at once she was a leaf torn from a dying tree and whirled onto some great dark river. Swiftly and mercilessly it carried her away. Voices cried from the bank. Freedom! Freedom! The years flashed by her, full of those proud, deafening calls. Caradoc, Madoc, Emrys, Venutius, the name-less dead, and now the tide was rushing her past her own kinsmen, and though the years had lengthened, the cry was the same. Freedom. She ran a trembling hand across her face, and her vision cleared. The chiefs and their jailers were disappearing and the black water in her head sloshed and receded. She went on unsteadily, coming at last to the hall, where she found Favonius, the procurator, and Marcus. She staggered toward them. The procurator had a sheaf of papers in both hands and a frown on his face. He was oblivious of the men who came and went from the now almost empty wine barrels, but Favonius shifted unhappily from one foot to the other, hearing the laughter and loud jokes grow coarser and more violent. Marcus saw her com-ing and ran to her.

"Lady, is Brigid in the house? I knocked and tried the door, but I could not get in."

She pushed him aside roughly and went straight to Decianus, terror stiffening her tongue as she glimpsed a group of soldiers reeling from the barrel to the farthest door of the house. "Decianus, this must stop," she begged urgently. "Men are dying, children are being kicked and punched. Possessions are nothing, we will give you anything you ask, but have mercy on the people!" The soldiers shoved the door open and peered inside. Several remained to continue the plunder, but the others moved on.

He leered his grotesque, meaningless smile at her and shuffled his papers with annoyance. "I am within the law," he said, breathing hard. "I am taking goods and slaves. Nothing more. If the people are foolish enough to get in the way, then of course my men must defend themselves."

"Against virgins and babies?" She began to sweat. The group had already thinned. More men had broken away to sift through the contents of the third room, but four of them even now were thumping on the last door.

He bent toward her. "You proud people are learning a long overdue lesson in submission," he snarled at her, his flabby face convulsed with hatred. "You belong to Rome. For years Rome has treated you well. Too well, in my opinion. And like the savages you are, you have grown arrogant and domineering. Now you are being put in your place." He pointed to the ground. "There."

Shock smote her, knocking all but a horrified disbelief from her mind, and before she could recover she heard the last door of the house splinter and a shout go up from the sweating soldiers. She spun around. Decianus had gone back to his papers. Then she heard a high scream, from Brigid or Ethelind she could not tell, and even as she felt life surge back to her limbs a body came hurtling through the jagged timber. It was Iain, the hilt of a gladius protruding from his chest, and he rolled over twice and came to rest in the shadow of the hall, his face down on the iron earth. She began to run, and behind her Favonius grabbed his son by the arm.

"We are going home now, Marcus," he said firmly.

The young man protested, white to the lips. "But father, I must find Brigid!"

"You'd never find her in this muddle anyway. Hurry up!"

They left Decianus and began to move toward the first circle. Favonius kept a tight grip on his son's tunic. "This is a nightmare," Marcus said quietly. "I love these people, and the trust you've built here over the years is being destroyed in one day. Surely the procurator is exceeding his duties! Would Paulinus approve? Can't you do anything?"

"Jupiter!" Favonius snarled, guilt and fear driving him to lose his temper. "Do you want me to call out the garrison and give battle to Decianus? I'd be executed! Use your head, Marcus, and be quiet!"

They slipped unnoticed through the throng and past the gate, and they mounted quickly and set off for home. The noise of the dishonored town faded, and the wind soughed a high threnody in the branches around them. They did not speak. Fear prickled down Favonius's back, and Marcus slouched on his horse, hoping that Brigid would have the sense to lie low somewhere. I can't help her if I can't find her, he told himself angrily. Besides, she's quite safe. Decianus would never allow a princess to be manhandled, he's not that stupid. But he knew that he was lying to himself. He knew where Brigid had been. He knew Decianus's rapacity. And he knew himself for a coward, after all.

When they reached the garrison, Favonius went straight to his wife. "Are Marcus's things all packed and ready to go?" he demanded, and she looked at him curiously.

"Honorious, what's the matter?"

"Decianus is completely stripping the Iceni. Blood has already been spilt, and there's more trouble coming. I can almost smell it. I want you to go with Marcus, as well, Priscilla."

"But I can't just pick up my cloak and walk out!" she said, stepping to his side. "Is there danger for you? Oh surely not!"

He patted her shoulder absently, his ears still full of the shrieks and sobs of the townspeople. "I hope not," he said heavily, "but I know them, these spell-sick barbarians. They will put up with anything as long as their honor is not abused. I only wish Decianus knew it."

"Is Marcus with you?"

"I brought him back. I suppose I'm being too alarmist, my dear, but it affords me great relief to think of you and Marcus safely on the way to Colchester. You will just have to be packed by tomorrow."

"I hate this country!" she burst out suddenly. "I've always hated it. Sometimes I hate it so much I want to vomit. When we get to Rome in safety I may never come back!"

If you get to Rome, he thought gloomily, then he laughed at himself. "And what would I do then?" He kissed her angry cheek. "We will see what happens, Priscilla. First things first. You must leave long before the sun is up."

Boudicca reached the shattered door of the house and burst inside. At first she was blinded after the bright sunlight and she had to stand inert, the scuffles and terror-stricken cries coming to her out of a thick dimness, but gradually her eyes adjusted and what she saw drove the last vestiges of control from her. Lovernius lay almost at her feet, crumpled into a limp heap of rumpled cloak and splayed limbs. At first she thought he was dead, but as she glanced down at him he stirred and moaned softly. The room was a shambles of overturned chests, smashed lamps, and piled hangings. One of the soldiers stood beside the hearth, with her golden jewel box in his hands. He upended it on the floor even as she watched, and he crouched to sift through the cascade of brilliant stones, lacy necklaces, thin, delicate circlets. But these things did not matter, these things were fragments

631

of a meaningless, idiotically disjointed moment of time, for Ethelind stood pinned against the wall. Her tunic was torn from her shoulders and it was imprisoning her arms to her waist, and her head snapped from side to side as she tried to free her hands. She was whimpering like a wounded dog, and as Boudicca stared, the soldier crushing her into the corner slapped a big hand across her throat and fought to bare her thighs. Brigid lay spread-eagled beside the bed, gasping, her hands pushing and clawing at the man kneeling over her. She was naked, one braid unloosened to carpet the floor in silver. Blood trickled from a gash on her right breast and she was fighting back with the strength of sheer terror.

The room stank of stale wine, fear, and sweat. "Lie still, pretty bitch, lie still," the soldier cursed her and the waiting soldier snapped, "Hurry up!" The other slapped Brigid across the face, back and forth with all the weight of his wrist, and she began to scream, a high, continuous ululation. He drove his knee between her legs, and then Boudicca came to life. She leaped across the room, howling with anguish and rage, and knocked the man sideways, her teeth ripping at his cheek, her fingers digging into his throat. They rolled together, and his hands gripped her wrists, trying to force them to relinquish their hold, but a madness had seized her and all he did was to drag those long nails lower and deeper. She felt warm blood gush onto her hands. Her mouth found the lobe of his ear and she bit hard. He screamed, and the sound of his pain mingled with Brigid's agony. His hands loosened. She wrapped her long legs around him, flung an arm about his neck, and began to force him backward, feeling his spine stiffen and crack under her relentless clutch. A fierce release of emotion shook her, a feeling of exultation and power, then brutal fingers entwined in her hair and jerked back hard and she lost her balance and fell choking.

"Mother!" Ethelind was wailing, her voice as tremulous and thin as a newborn baby's. "Mother, mother!" She was hauled to her feet. The soldier with the severed earlobe staggered to her, and clenching his fist drove it toward her mouth, but as quick as light she turned her head and the blow fell on the side of her jaw. She cried out, and he punched her in the belly. Then he weaved back to Brigid, and Boudicca found herself dragged into the open.

Nothing had changed. Decianus still stood frowning over his growing pile of requisition papers. The tribesmen still milled about, rudderless and speechless. But now Ethelind's screams provided an insane harmony to her sister's abandoned melody. The soldier pushed

Boudicca to the procurator and he looked up angrily, but before he could speak she began to shout from between clenched teeth.

"You dirty, disgusting animals! One day I will plunge a sword into that fat paunch of yours, Decianus! I will slay every filthy Roman I can find! I spit on you! I spit on your witless emperor! I spit on your honor!"

He was still smiling, but the fixed, wet mouth showed only a freezing, devouring malice. He looked at the bloodstained teeth, the grimed, sweating face, the glint of madness in the huge eyes that were veiled by her tangled chestnut hair. Then he looked back at his figures.

"Take her to the gate and give her twenty lashes with the barb," he said coolly.

"You'll kill her, sir," the soldier responded doubtfully, and Decianus smiled again.

"Well, twenty without it then, but make each one count. I don't care whether we kill her, but perhaps it would not amuse the governor to find that we had whipped a queen to death. Learn your lesson well, barbarian," he finished laconically, and before Boudicca could make any reply the soldier shoved her from behind.

"Walk," he commanded, and she stumbled down the path.

The freeman saw her coming and made way for her, and the stunned silence of the now-ruined town gave place to an ominous, incredulous whispering. The crowd let her and her guard pass, but it closed in behind and followed, and when she reached the gate and the laden wains and the lines of chained men and women it pooled out into a lake of white, puzzled faces. "You!" the centurion barked at one of the resting legionaries. "Bring me a whip!" A sigh of disbelief went up from the assembled people but it was ignored. Boudicca found herself led to a tall wooden post used for the tethering of guests' horses. Her arms were raised and cradled around it and roped securely, and she felt the man's fingers at her neck. With a jerk and a tear her tunic parted, and shouts of indignation went up all around.

"No, you cannot!"

"Why do you do this?"

"She has done nothing!"

The man's vacant eye flicked over them. He took off his helmet and laid it on the grass, unstrapped his leather jerkin and let it fall, and the other soldier returned and handed him a long leather whip, barbed at one end. He fingered the barb longingly for a moment, considered, then deftly removed it and threw it onto his jerkin. If the barbarian died he would be demoted. He flexed his muscles, put his

633

legs apart, and the first stroke came whistling down to leave a deep welt in the naked back from waist to shoulder.

Pain burst like raw, new fire in her brain and her head snapped back, but before she could tense her body, the next stroke fell, the tip of the whip curling under her chin, and she cried out. Blood trickled slowly down her spine, under her armpits. The third stroke was lower, searing, biting deeper as the centurion found his rhythme, and she sagged against the post, taking her lower lip between her teeth and grinding it. I will count, she thought, already light-headed. Before her she saw the friendly gray stone of her wall, patched with moisture where the sun had warmed the frost to water. She saw the thin winter light flowing through the leafless little copse that hid the garrison. She saw her chiefs, their necks in iron rings, their dark, murderous eyes fixed on the sweating soldier. Four. The pain was unendurable. I must scream, I must cry for mercy, Andrasta, I am dying and I cannot take this pain, then all at once her people began to shout.

"Courage, Lady!"

"Stand, Boudicca!"

"Remember Subidasto!" and at the mention of her father's name a final shred of dignity came to her. Six. Count well, my soul, she thought. For every lash, a thousand men will die. Her head was spinning and her thoughts echoed nonsensically. She thought she heard Prasutugas dying, his breath rasping in and out, in and out, but she realized that it was her own labored lungs marking time as the trickle of blood swelled to a stream and spattered onto her feet. Nine. Her head lolled forward and she closed her eyes, slumping to her knees, feeling the tendons crackle in her straining wrists. My daughters. My sweet, innocent daughters. I have betrayed you. Why am I so hot when it is wintertime? Dizziness roared in her ears. Eleven. Her body went limp as unconsciousness overtook her.

At last Marcus made up his mind. Turning reluctantly from the tiny window that showed him only the cold hostility of a winter night he picked up his cloak from the cot and moved quietly to the door. His father had told him that Priscilla would be leaving with him in the morning and they would go earlier than planned, with as little fuss as possible, and reading the anxiety in Favonius's eyes, Marcus had understood. There would be trouble. Perhaps it would not come tomorrow, but Favonius was taking no chances and he sent his son to bed with an uncharacteristic sharpness that betrayed his unease. Marcus had gone to his room and doused his lamp but then he went to the window and stared moodily out at the deceptively peaceful courtyard, filled with moonlight. What of his plans with Brigid? She was to have met him in the forest just before dawn and would have traveled to Colchester lying in the wain that was to carry his belongings to the ship. Now, with an earlier start and his mother's company it was clearly impossible. Miserable, he considered the alternatives and came up empty. There was simply not enough time to hatch another plot. Besides, he had no idea what was going on in the town. Had Decianus withdrawn his men for the night? If that was so, he had not returned to the garrison to sleep. What were they doing, the outraged Iceni, his friends, his other kin? Fighting back? Or submitting with that sullen, secretive cloak of seeming patience that he knew so well, drawn around them? He felt wretched. Guilt made him squirm. He should have stayed to find Brigid, gone from chief to chief and offered what help he could, interceded on their behalf with the callous, gluttonous soldiers. But that would have landed his father in trouble and, indeed, he thought with exasperation, who would have listened to a sixteen-year-old?

A sentry crossed the courtyard, his footfalls echoing against the shadowed palisade, and Marcus rubbed his eyes and sighed. How to get a message to Brigid? Shall I write her a letter and leave it with one of the secretaries, to give to her in the morning? Dear Brigid, the plan will no longer work as father has changed . . . No. Dear Brigid, when you read this I will be gone, but I will send for you the moment I am established in Rome . . . He groaned, thinking of her face as she read such a cold, precise proof of his desertion. That was how she would see it. No, the only alternative was to go at once and look for her, as he should have done in the morning. He fastened the cloak securely on his shoulders, tiptoed to the door, and softly let himself out into the still, frosty night. The moon was a swollen blue chariot wheel rolling slowly to its zenith, and its colorless light saturated the courtyard, throwing the barracks, the administration building, the storehouses, into sharp relief. He crept along the wall, reached the gate, and slipped under it like a purposeful ghost.

The copse was drowned in deep darkness and he hurried through it, looking neither right nor left for fear of what strangeness he might see. With a vast relief he broke through it and left the road that ran to the main gate of the town. Now he could hear life, a low, constant murmuring interspersed with shouts, the high calls of a stricken woman, the drunken singing of a satiated legionary. There were ominous red glows here and there, little flushes of color that looked to him like three or four suns about to rise, but as he sped silently over the grass and gained the slight hill that brought him to the low stone wall, the tongues of flame danced on his upturned face. The fires were not serious or extensive. By accident or by the hands of the procurator's men, single huts had been torched, and for a few beleagured families the winter had become a scorching, unwelcome summer. But Marcus was suddenly taken with a gush of real fear. He crouched beside the wall, consumed with a desire to turn around and run back to his bed to dream a safer dream. This black night shot through with orange flares, this blue, overburdened moon, these frightening sounds of rapine and desolation belonged to an unreal world that he had never before visited, even in his nightmares. These things did not belong to the sunny days of his carefree youth. He swallowed, closed his eyes, then stood and vaulted the wall in one clean spring. His doubts for Brigid's safety suddenly became terror-stricken certainties.

He made his way to the house above the first circle, hugging the shadows, avoiding the reeling, whooping soldiers, the freemen who scurried down the paths, the huddles of weeping, destitute families who sat before the doorskins of their empty huts. He was not challenged. The soldiers' orgy of destruction had glutted itself and the men were seeking rest beyond the gates. In the morning they were to join their fellows who had been in Icenia for months, and finish the business they had started. The townspeople no longer cared who flitted past them. He reached the house and cautiously went from room to room, but it was empty and cold, like the huge, dark mausoleum his mother had taken him to see in Rome on one of their trips, a place redolent with dampness and finality. He crossed to the hall and peered inside. A fire burned in the big grate, but the shadows were untenanted. All the rich shields, the skins covering the floor, the bright hangings, were gone. He turned away and doggedly began a search of the first circle and here he became aware of the hopelessness of his task. Crowds wandered aimlessly here and there, loosing and forming, grouping and then scattering suddenly, as though lightning had struck in their midst, and looking for Brigid was like looking for one white hailstone in a summer shower. But he did not give up. For two hours he lifted doorskins, clambered over discarded rubbish to disturb frightened families squatting in darkness, walked up and down the littered paths, and at last, weary and frustrated, he had to admit defeat. She might be anywhere, with anyone. He had tried questioning the people once or twice but had received astonished, brutal laughter, curses, and terrified silence. He found himself by the wall. The moon had shrunk and now was floating almost overhead. It was time to go. What shall I do? he asked himself as he scrambled over the wall and plodded across the grass toward the hostile, thick dark-

636

ness of the copse. What shall I do? What will she think of me? This is the end and I must go without her. How lonely I feel, how cold. Brigid, where are you? Must I go without ever seeing you again? His distress was so great that he plunged in under the black, gaunt branches of the copse with no hesitation and his feet followed the winding, narrow path through the overhanging trees while his mind wept. He felt as though his whole world had been blown apart, as though he had somehow lost control of his own destiny and another massive force had rushed in to march him along a way he did not want to go and could not see—like a man blindfolded and pushed onto a bridge with no parapet. The water churned and crashed below him.

Then she stepped from behind a tree onto the path before him. He jerked to a stop, dumbfounded, his gaze trying to pierce the pressing dimness, and he ran forward crying, "Brigid! Brigid! I have been searching for you everywhere, I had given up all hope, I was so afraid for you, ah Brigid!" He stopped suddenly and looked at her, puzzled. She was clothed in a torn tunic and her feet were bare on the frosty ground. A braid hung decorously over one naked shoulder but the rest of her hair fell in a silver tangle over her face, giving her a half-wild, half-prim air like a native god, like Andrasta herself, caught in the slow moment of change from the Queen of Victory into something else. Brigid's hands were behind her back and she was nodding at him, a fixed, idiotic smile on her mouth, her head on one side. His blood slowed and began to chill. "Brigid?" he faltered, and she swayed toward him.

"Marcus!" she hissed. "I have seen her! She is here! Sitting on a branch in the moonlight, very big, very black! With the moonlight glossy on her smooth, dark feathers."

He stood rooted to the spot, transfixed by a dawning horror, and Brigid bent closer. "She told me things."

He wanted to turn and flee from her monstrous aspect. He wanted to scream for his father.

"What kind of things, Brigid?" he whispered, fear beating with frantic wings in his chest, and she licked her lips.

"She told me to kill everyone. She told me to kill you."

Then without warning she leaped, her face contorted. The blade arced upward and came slicing toward him and even though he felt it bury deep within him, the explosion of pain was not as great as the shock of her derangement.

"Wh . . . wh . . ." he choked, but he crumpled slowly forward at her feet and died, without ever knowing why.

CHAPTER THIRTY-SEVEN

S HE WAS SQUATTING in front of the fire in the Council hall, watching the flames roar to the ceiling, and outside a winter gale was howling, throwing rain against the sturdy walls like handfuls of arrows. Her father sat cross-legged on the skins to her left, his gray braids resting neatly on his green tunic, his sword across his knees. He was shaking his head sorrowfully at her. "I warned you not to wed that milk-cow chief of mine, Boudicca," he rumbled, "but you would have him, even though the omens were bad and the invoker spoke against it. You see what ruin it has brought you."

She wanted to answer him sharply, to tell him to mind his own business and leave her alone, but there was a reasonless, empty ache inside her and she could not speak. The fire was too hot. It clawed at her back with fiery nails and she wondered why that should be, when the flames lit her face and colored her naked breasts. "Father, why am I naked?" she whispered, and he giggled suddenly.

"Because you have no clothes on," he smirked. The wind soughed in the smoke vents. Rain, it sighed. Rain and dew, cool rivers tumbling over smooth stones, streams trickling beside the green, shaded ferns of summer, water, sweet, cold water. She opened her eyes.

"Water," she croaked.

Lovernius tossed his dice onto the table, poured from the jug, and carried the cup to her. She lifted her head and drank thirstily, then put her cheek back onto the cool pallet. She was lying face down on her own bed, in her own small hut. Outside a storm keened and lamented, and rain poured onto the roof and spilled down the walls. It was dark. Her fire twinkled red and comforting, her lamps shone with a steady glow, and the dice clicked again in her bard's fingers. She closed her eyes once more and explored her body. Her head ached with a sick, nauseating constancy. Her legs and arms felt heavy and numb, her neck was stiff, and her back . . . Her back throbbed as though a thousand freewomen sat around it and plunged their needles in and out of the tender, swollen flesh. She wanted to sleep again but rest would not come and in the end she raised a slow arm and pushed the hair from her bruised, pained jaw. "How long?" she whispered.

He pulled his chair closer and bent to her. "This is the fourth night, Lady. I thought you were going to die." The hand level with her eyes opened and closed, opened and closed, and the dice rattled cheerily.

Which door shall I enter first? she thought. Which death-filled black hole shall I crawl into? Lovernius was waiting for another question, his brown gaze fixed impassively on her, and she noticed the purple bruises on his temple, the swiftly closing gash under his eye, but she did not want to ask. She wanted to lie thus forever in the peaceful dimness of her room, quietly ignorant, calm and passive, and let time snuffle past her, smelling out someone else.

"Tell me," she begged softly.

He did not look at her. His glance strayed to the bare wall beyond her. "The soldiers tied me when my soul returned to me," he said. "I do not know why they did not kill me. Lady, I am ashamed. I could do nothing."

"I know. Reproaches are vain, Lovernius. Go on."

He sat up, and stilled his hands. "Your daughters are deflowered, Lady," he said harshly. "Many soldiers came and raped them and threw them out into the cold. Ethelind has not spoken since and will let no one near her. Brigid . . ." His fingers went to the ragged wound on his cheek and Boudicca saw that they shook. "Brigid's soul has left her, Lady, and will not come back."

A wave of sick pain started at her back and shivered over her, and when it reached her head she crawled forward and vomited onto the floor. Then, white and gasping, she slumped weakly back onto the mattress. "Where is she now?"

"With Hulda, in one of the huts. A chief found her wandering on the edge of the copse and brought her home, but her feet are badly frozen and the wound on her breast will not begin to heal."

Boudicca carefully put aside the succession of images coming clear and small into her mind like visions seen from far away. "Decianus?" she said.

"He and the soldiers have left the town. They go to the villages now, and the farmsteads. Doubtless the agents have already chosen the ripest fruit for the picking."

"What is left to us, Lovernius?"

He raised his thick eyebrows, grimaced, and his fingers began to juggle the dice again. "Our lives—most of us. Our wits." Suddenly he realized what he had said and his face flushed crimson, but she did not recoil. She knew that if the Iceni were to be salvaged as a free people she must learn to sink all catastrophe, all evil news no matter how brutal, beneath the new wall she would begin to build around her heart—a high wall, smooth and impregnable, more pain-resistant than her customary straightforward honesty. "Our huts, a little food, a few clothes, the chariots and ponies."

"That is all?"

"Yes."

She pondered for a long second, glad to have her thoughts centered on something other than the pain that was ending waves of faintness over her. Then Lovernius sighed, pulled his chair closer, and dropped his voice. The wind still skeetered around the hut like a wild stallion, and the rain gusted under the doorskins.

"Lady, a doom has befallen Favonius as well. Marcus is dead."

She was not prepared for this shock. "Young Marcus? But how?"

"No one knows. He was found in the copse, a knife in his chest. Favonius and his guard have been going among the chiefs, asking questions and making threats, but he is learning nothing. I do not think the people are hiding anything from him, they simply do not know."

"Oh Lovernius," she said, grief making her tones even more hoarse and deep. "He was such an upright young man. Poor Priscilla."

"Favonius has sent his wife to Colchester, and I believe he is going to apply for another garrison to command. He has been asking to see you."

"Yes, I suppose he has, but I have no wish to receive him lying in my bed."

"Lady," Lovernius responded urgently, "Let him come. Let him see. what his countrymen have done to you. Is his suffering more bitter than yours? Happy is Marcus, who lost his life rather than his soul! Let him come, I say!"

"You are right," she said slowly. "Why should I care for my dignity anymore? I am a broken branch. My life oozes away like sap dripping to the earth. My daughters are children with scarecrow's eyes." She broke off and turned her head away from him so that he would not see the tears come hurtfully from beneath eyelids squeezed shut against them. "My people. My valiant ones. You trusted me, and I failed you," she whispered, and Subidasto muttered in her ear, "I told you, I told you. Now you know why you are naked." For a long time she lay quietly listening to Lovernius's restless movements, the capricious bluster of the storm, the hot, rapid rhythme of her own feverish breath, then she rolled her head to look at him again. "Lovernius," she said. "Bring me a Druid."

He stood up, the dice disappeared, and he began to smile. "Do I understand you, Boudicca?"

"You understand very well, but no one else must understand. Send someone you can trust, and send him quickly. Tell the Druid that the holding spell of the Iceni has been broken."

"He will know that already. Shall I allow Favonius to come?"

"If you come with him. And tell Aillil that he is now my shield-bearer."

He went out, with a spring in his step, and she dozed, exhausted,

640

falling at last into another drugged, sick sleep in which her father sat in the corner of her room, his sword still shining on his knees, a look of patient exasperation on his face. When she awoke, giddy and with another raging thirst, he was still sitting there in the shadows until she blinked, and he went away. Favonius stood beside the bed, muffled in a long cloak that reeked of old, wet wool. Lovernius was behind him, the water running from his shoulders and dripping from his loose braids. Boudicca gave Favonius no time to speak.

"Show him, Lovernius," she croaked, and Lovernius came to her and hesitated.

"Lady, the sheet is stuck to the wounds."

"Rip it off."

He reached down and reluctantly did as he was bid, and she cried out as fresh blood sprang to trickle along her spine. "Look well, Favonius," she gasped. "Do you like what you see?" His red-rimmed eyes moved from her face to her back and he did not flinch though it was a pulped mess of gored flesh, and in one spot where the lips of a raised welt clove deeply, he fancied that he could glimpse bone. Blood from the new-opened furrows slid lazily toward the mattress, and suddenly she dropped her head. "Cover me, Lovernius."

"You must believe me," Favonius said flatly. "I did not think that he would go this far."

"Didn't you?" she snarled, her voice muffled in the pillow. "Isn't that why you treated me with such embarrassed circumvention, like a newborn liar clumsily practicing his art? You suspected this, Favonius, and now it has rebounded on your own head." He winced, then all at once he sank into the chair by the bed and leaned back with unutterable weariness and misery. His whole face sagged as though ten years had passed for him in one night, and his eyes were cloudy. "I have sent a protest to the governor," he said, the strong, virile voice now no more than a thin whisper, and she managed to laugh.

"As I implored you to do weeks ago! Did you know that the soldiers raped the soul from my Brigid? Took Ethelind's voice from her? What can the governor do about that?"

He put up a hand as if to ward her away. "I don't know."

"Can yet another imperial edict bring back your son?"

Now he stiffened and leaned forward. "I will find his murderer, Boudicca, if I have to tear down the rest of the town to do it. Some chief saw his chance and took it, and a young boy lies dead."

"Why do you so hurriedly accuse the chiefs? Marcus often wore tribal dress—breeches and a chieftain's long cloak. Far more likely that some drunken soldier took him for an Icenian and struck him down in the darkness."

"No. The knife was no gladius. It was a knife for slicing meat, taken from the Council hall."

"And not even half the soldiers were serving legionaries, Favonius. Many were veterans without regulation weapons. I think you must ask the procurator who killed Marcus. Oh most impartial Roman justice! A fair hearing for all!"

He got up as though his body were a thick stone weight encasing him. "Truly the sword of justice has two edges," he said. "I will enquire of Decianus, but I will go on questioning the chiefs."

"You waste your time." Her lips were quivering and her white nostrils were distended. "You might as well admit your failure to family and duty, Favonius, and fall on your sword like a good Roman."

He went to the door. "Not yet, Boudicca," he said as he went out. "Not yet."

For a month the procurator and his assistants ravaged the countryside, and when there was nothing left worth taking they went back to Colchester. Then the people began to pour into the town, wending their way to her hut, and she lay hour upon hour with her eyes closed, her body flayed by the agony of her flogging and her soul shredded by the tales of murder, rapine, and loss. The people were like helpless lambs, softened by years of easy living and a growing wealth, now shorn of all they possessed, riches and kin, and left to shiver and bleat in the cold wind of Rome's treachery. She could give them no comfort. Sow again, breed what stock you have left again, get sons and daughters again she could have said, but it would not have been enough. Grain and meat would not satisfy souls that were crying out for redress. New babies suckling from old breasts would not warm hearts full of the ice of revenge. She sent them away, longing to promise them blood but knowing with some sixth sense that the time had not yet come to full ripeness. They must regain some strength. Shock must give way to implacability, and a blow struck prematurely would mean a final, stunning reprisal from which none of them would rise again. By day her chiefs ringed her bed. By night Subidasto came to her, shouting, threatening, cajoling, shaking his big fists at her as she had shaken hers at Prasutagus, but she waited.

The Druid came. One warm sleeting morning he pushed past her doorskins, took off the long brown cloak that had disguised him and tossed it in a shower of water to Lovernius, lifting the sheet without a word. He poked at her gently, grunted, then sent Lovernius away to find a bowl. Astonished, she tried to speak, but he held up a warning finger. "Shh!" he ordered. "The body's hurts first. The soul's later." He reached into his tunic and withdrew four small leather pouches which he opened, pausing to sniff each one, and a large pot of yellow grease. Lovernius returned with the bowl and the Druid emptied the contents of the pouches into it and scraped out the pot. He began to pound his mixture with a wooden pestle, singing some high spell of healing over it, and a cool, fresh odor filled the room like the wind that mingles with the clean snows of the mountains. Boudicca inhaled it, feeling a peace and sanity steal over her, then he squatted beside her and began to spread it over her back. Coldness and balm slowly pooled out, burying the heat and pain, and she sighed and relaxed. "You are most fortunate," he remarked, wiping his hands on his tunic and rising to sit in the chair. "It is a nasty suppurating mess with a good deal of purple flesh there, beginning to die. Now I would like wine." She felt like laughing. The pain was ebbing away, and as it receded she wanted to sing.

"Bring wine for our guest," she grated at Lovernius. "And bread for us both." He nodded and went out, and she turned to the Druid. "Welcome to the tuath," she said. "Food, wine, and peace to you."

He inclined his head gravely, the firelight glinting on the bronze rings in his blond hair. "The three necessities for the body's health. But what of the soul, eh?" He folded his short legs and the twinkle in his eyes suddenly gave way to a somber, piercing stare. "So you have come to your senses at last, Boudicca. I am only sorry that it had to happen in this terrible fashion. What do you want of me?"

She lay with her head turned sideways on the pillow, looking up into the genial, intelligent face. "I want you to go into the west and beg arms and men for myself from Venutius and the others. I want messages sent to every tribe in the lowlands. I want your advice."

He cocked an eye at her. "Such small things you want! I have come out of the west, Boudicca, where Paulinus is nearing holy Mona. My brethren are preparing for their last great battle, knowing that they are forbidden to raise swords themselves, and Venutius, Emrys, and Madoc have sent many of their chiefs there. They cannot come to you."

She went white. "Andrasta! Must the Iceni fight alone, then? What hope have we?"

"More hope than there has ever been since the Catuvellauni met Plautius at the Medway," he said. "Listen well. Over half the troops in Albion are with Paulinus, two hundred and seventy miles from Colchester, and the lowland is virtually undefended. The Ninth is intact but it lies to the north of you, not to the south. The Second is at full strength also, but divided. Oh, there are posting stations, detachments, the odd garrison here and there, but other than that, the towns of the south lie open. Do you hear me?"

Lovernius returned with a jug of wine, cups, and a platter of mutton and flat bread. He served them silently, then went to the fire and sat cross-legged, and soon the clicking of his dice punctuated their conversation.

"The Iceni can do nothing alone," she went on. "If the men of the west cannot aid us, who can?"

He swallowed his wine and broke off a piece of the black bread. "Once," he said, "the western tribes fought alone, and even they might have succumbed to Rome if Caradoc had not risen as arviragus. The lowland people became like shadows beside their fiery reality, and like shadows they have been forgotten. But Boudicca, the Iceni are a lowland tribe, and will you say that your people still walk in shadows? I tell you that in this month, this long, pain-wracked month, the tribes of the south have been waking. The news of your dishonoring has gone among them like the cold wind that heralds the dawn. They are shocked for you, they are enraged at their own trials. They have borne their slavery for many long years, but your betrayal has caused their uneasy grumbling to have purpose once more. If you call them, they will come."

"Why are you so sure? Caradoc called them, he called us, but we refused to listen."

"In those days, Rome's domination was new, gloved in soft words of prosperity, oiled in money and promises. They have slowly learned what domination really means, and now they see its claws, the claws you have felt on your own body. Trust me, Boudicca. I know. Begin a march south, and they will run to join you as you go."

She lay for a while with eyes closed, then she reached for her cup and drank slowly. "I wish I could believe you, but I know how deep the thrall of Rome can go. It has more spells and faces than Andrasta herself."

He tutted impatiently. "Do not say that. Rome is only a city. Romans are only men. Andrasta is the Queen of Victory. Believe me, Boudicca. Do the Druithin lie?"

"No, but neither have they yet discovered a truth that is the same tomorrow as it was yesterday. Do you surmise from intuition only?"

"No. Rumors and tales filter into the west, and this last month has seen an added fire blown from mouth to mouth. You can ignite a great conflagration."

"If you are wrong then the Iceni must march and perish alone, for march we will. Dishonor demands judgment."

"I see that you remember the teachings." He wiped his mouth, rose, and yawned widely. "First, a healing for you, Boudicca. Sleep. I will stay in the town until you can walk, but then I must return to the west and to Mona. Your fate is in your own hands. Instruct your freemen to carry messages to the tribes when you have made your plans, and do not fear. This is the time of reckoning."

Then, with a curiously humble gesture, she put out a hand and pulled at his tunic. "Do me a service, if you will. My daughter . . ."

He sighed gently and sat again. "I know, I know. I cannot return her soul to her, but perhaps I can relieve her of some of her torment. Have her brought to me."

She nodded at Lovernius. "Bring Brigid," she said, and he went away. They waited in a cup of quiet, while outside the sleet hissed monotonously. Then he said, "I knew your father once, long ago."

Her head turned to him. "Subidasto? So many changes since then, my friend!"

"Yes," he answered simply. "I myself was an Icenian. Once."

Surprise and shame flooded her. "I am sorry," she said, and he raised one eloquent shoulder and laughed.

"The time for regret is over, Boudicca, and I think I shall soon be an Icenian Druid again."

Lovernius returned, holding back the doorskins, and Brigid entered. She was dressed in a warm red tunic that Boudicca remembered from days of horse racing and fishing in the snow, but now it seemed to hang on her slim frame like a graceless sack, and her hair fell unbound in a pale river over her thin neck and shoulders. One hand rested in Hulda's, the other patted and pulled at her mouth as though she was constantly trying to set it in place. Her eyes, like drowned flowers, wandered the room and came to rest on her mother, but no flicker of recognition lit them.

"She sits on the roof of my hut," she said. "The rain gleams on her feathers and she croaks blood, blood, all night long. Where is Pompey? I am so cold. Pompey will warm me with his soft breath, and tell me where to go." The hand left her swollen lips and fluttered to her throat with an artless loveliness. "Blood is black under the moon, and eyes are white. My mother should remember, but she has gone to be the Queen of Victory, and I must go to Rome." At the mention of the city her hand left Hulda's and began to trace a pattern of distress in the dimness. "All men are filled with blood, black blood under the moon!"

The Druid rose and went to her, taking the aimless fingers of both hands and imprisoning them in his own firm grip. "Brigid," he said kindly. "Blood is warm and sweet. Blood makes music, blood makes laughter. Trees have golden blood and rivers have silver blood, and the sun is full of hot, life-giving, glittering blood. Look at me." The drenched eyes slowly found his, and he smiled. "Tell her about the

645

rivers as she perches above you and calls you in the darkness. Tell her about the sun, and the trees." The working mouth became still, then Brigid swallowed twice. She frowned, tried to speak, but her hands remained limp in his and her eyes were enmeshed with him.

"Trees," she whispered. Then suddenly she began to laugh, a shrill peal of coarse mirth, and her hands wrenched free. "I killed him, poor Marcus," she snickered. "Oh Marcus, my dear, my love. I stabbed him, pretty Marcus, and the trees clapped their black hands, black, like his blood under the moon."

Boudicca stared aghast at her daughter. Her own blood seemed to rush back into her heart, leaving her head, her arms and feet, lying iced and dead while in her breast a monstrous hot ball throbbed unevenly. "Why are you shocked?" Subidasto whispered in her ear. "She is naked too." Lovernius cried out. Hulda swayed. Only the Druid was unmoved, his sad, level gaze fixed on Brigid. Then all at once he stepped forward and enfolded her in his wide embrace. "Child," he murmured. She stopped giggling and began to sob, moving from his arms to the comfort of Hulda's hand, and Boudicca said wearily, "Take her away, Hulda. And braid her hair. She looks so disheveled that way."

"She will not let me," Hulda answered. "I thought it best not to trouble her with it."

They left, Lovernius with them, and the Druid raised his eyebrows at Boudicca, and his face was grim. "Heal quickly, Lady," he said.

She felt an enormous fatigue leaden her body and she sank her head into the pillow. "Ah desolation," she murmured, a catch in her deep voice. "Even though I should slay every Roman in Albion, the times have changed and nothing will ever be the same again."

"The times are always changing," he replied, swinging his cloak around him and going to the door. "It is the changes within ourselves which bring despair or contentment, Boudicca. I will come in the evening and anoint your back again." He pushed past the doorskins, and in a while Lovernius returned.

"She is settling for sleep," he said. "I think she is calmer."

"What of Ethelind?"

"Ethelind walks the town, and eats and rests, but she will still speak to no one."

"I want to sit up, Lovernius. Help me." He went to her, lifting her carefully and turning her around, and though her head suddenly swam and her back screamed a protest, it was good to view the room from a sane angle. "Bring me my comb."

He handed her the carved, delicate comb and she began to draw it

646

through the dark, red-lighted tangle. Not until her hair lay submissive and shining around her did she give it back to him.

"Now. Take Aillil and go into the forest. Find a nice, private clearing and build huts, and a forge. Dig up all the weapons and have them cleaned and sharpened. Make swords and spears and knives. Make torcs. Ask Aillil himself to check all the chariots and take any that need repairs into the woods. Make slings and axes for the peasants. I want every Icenian—man, woman, and youth—re-armed within two months."

"The young girls also?"

"Yes. Their mothers were sword-women and it is time they learned what that means." She folded her arms, gripping herself fiercely. "Ah Lovernius, is it too late? Can the people remember old skills after all these years? Will a thirst for vengeance be enough to rekindle their spirit?"

"If they remember nothing else they will remember that an honorable death is better than the life of a slave. We have nothing else, Lady."

"I know." They smiled ruefully at each other before she went on. "Take my own chiefs. Send them out to all the tuath. Tell them to give the people sword practice in whatever secret places they can find. Use poles, kitchen knives, anything, until the swords are ready. But make sure that no man from the garrison is killed, Lovernius. If Favonius hears even the faintest rumor of what we plan, then all is lost. We must have spies out in the forests and on the farmsteads to warn of any straying soldier."

He nodded brusquely and went to the door. "And no gambling!" she called after him. "Tune up your harp instead!"

"A man must have some peace!" he shouted back, annoyed, and she answered sharply, her voice like whetstone on rusty iron. "When you are in your grave!"

So, like a wondrous, invisible metamorphosis within the cocoon of winter, the Iceni began to change. Outwardly the tuath settled to a sullen peace once more. The people struggled to pick up the pieces of their shattered lives, rebuild gutted homes, collect whatever flocks and herds had scattered into the forests, but under the slow reordering a new and terrible embryo of militancy moved toward birth. The tuath lived two lives. By day the towns and villages went about their business, but by night the surrounding forests hid the low cries of warring men and women, the white fire of the perspiring metalworkers, the murmurings and whisperings of a thousand dark transformations. Favonius sensed it. In his grief and loneliness he walked the garrison late at night, feeling the minute stirrings of something alien and new on the chill winds. Beyond the soft, white wall of the Icenian cocoon he saw the shadows shape themselves, turning from nothing into something so faint that he could not discern what it was. In the end he attributed his anxiety to the turmoil within his own mind. He had not found his son's murderer. There had been rumors aplenty. He had even heard it whispered that poor, witless Brigid herself had struck him down on that mercilessly cold, catastrophic night, but he had not believed it, nor could he prove such a thing, and now it seemed that Marcus must lie unavenged.

The governor had replied to his small bleat of protest at the procurator's avarice with a brusque, almost rude communique. Paulinus had his hands full, he could do nothing until his campaign was completed. When he returned to Colchester he would look into the matter but until then he expected his garrison commanders to keep the peace. After all, that was their job. As to transfer, it could not be considered at this time. Such details were irrelevant to the business in hand. Favonius paced in the wet, late winter nights, full of an irrational fear. He had often had dreams where some unimportant, everyday event, like a morning cup of wine with his secretary between requisitions and dispatches, became luminous with terror. The people chatted and laughed and the sun shone, while all the time, like an insane, unrealistic backdrop, the fear rose up and became more real than the prattling, the paper figures, and the feeble sun.

He felt this way now, in his waking hours. His duties were performed, the winter bored them all, he read the letters from Priscilla in Colchester, but all the while this other thing lived within him and turned his world to fantasy. He was not an imaginative man, nor was he clever. He was simply a common, down-to-earth soldier of the empire doing the task his superiors had set for him, and now, though all seemed normal, he felt that the task had outrun him and had torn itself from his hands. He was puzzled, and afraid.

When spring was no more than a hint of change in the smell of the wind, Boudicca had a visitor. She was up from her bed now, and the wounds on her back had closed to become red, furrowed scars that were rough and sore to the touch. The Druid had gone with no word of farewell, vanishing toward the west, and though he had seen Brigid every day there was no suggestion that the girl's wits would return. She seemed meeker, more docile, but at the mention of trees or other innocuous things she would become agitated, pouring out a stream of chilling nonsense and driving herself into a frenzy. Ethelind, too, bore scars, but they were less visible. She kept her distance from all and would not speak, though sometimes she was heard crooning to herself in the long nights.

Boudicca forced a world between herself and her broken children, and filled it with the plans of war. New weapons gleamed in the huts of her people, hidden in barrels, under grain, in the thatching of the roofs, beneath beds; and bodies that had stiffened under peace became fluid with the dark oils of war. The disused wicker weaving of the chariots was ripped out and replaced, the harness mended and hung once more with the fierce, long-idle bronzes of Andrasta. Chiefs sat by their fires at night and fondled new torcs and freshly polished helms glinting with hope, and though the tuath shouted silently with an uprushing intensity, until it seemed that even the marshes and the meadows trembled with the word War, Favonius did not suspect the true cause of his anxiety. The gates of Albion had slammed shut on him before he had ever set foot on her shores, and he did not know it.

She was sitting in the denuded hall, Lovernius and Aillil beside her, and a sheep was roasting over the fire, turned slowly by a slave. Chiefs and freemen wandered in and out and occasionally one came to her for a word of advice or an explanation of the day. Ethelind sat against the wall, dipping bread into a soup bowl and eating quietly, her dark golden head down and her legs folded under her red and blue striped tunic. Around her there was a hiatus of loneliness, a space respected now by all the tuath, and her servant squatted well away from her, under the shadows. Brigid was in her hut, watched carefully all the time. She walked every day around the inner circles of the town but only occasionally was she brought to the hall, to eat with the freemen. She had upset them with her babbles about the Raven of Battle, but now that battle flared in every heart they had ceased to be wary of her and many regarded her as the special messenger of Andrasta herself, hungry for fresh Roman blood after the years of neglect.

There was a sudden commotion by the door, a flutter of excited voices, and Lovernius broke off his whispered account of the night's progress and ran across the hall, with Aillil beside him. Boudicca watched and waited and when they came back, a stranger was between them. He was tall, well-made, and dark. His free-flowing hair blew softly back from a high, lined forehead, his eyes were firmly guarded but not wary, and his mouth, above a broad, clean-shaven chin, was straight and delicate. She rose as he came toward her, and she held out her hand. "Welcome! Food, wine, and peace to you." He took her wrist in a swift, businesslike swing, and dropped it again.

"Show me," he said.

She and her men exchanged glances, then she turned and slipped down her tunic, covering her breasts with her cloak. He grunted, and for a second she felt his fingers light against her welted back, then she shrugged her tunic on again and faced him.

"Romans?" he enquired crisply, and she shook her head.

"None in the town," she answered. "They stay within the garrison. You are quite safe this night." Some of the tension left him, and they lowered themselves to the uncovered floor. A crowd of inquisitive freemen had gathered, and Aillil and Lovernius firmly placed themselves so that words could not penetrate. "You have news?" she pressed him. "Will you share it now, or eat first?"

"I will share." He took the cup of wine held out to him by a servant and drank steadily, tossing the dregs onto the floor for the gods of the Iceni. Then he tucked his feet under him. "I am Domnall," he said. "Chieftain of Brigantia." Boudicca let the shock enter her and crumple against the wall of her inner defences. So Aricia knew what they were doing and was going to inform on them, and his chief had come to warn. But how had she known, with the Coritani between the two tribes? Domnall saw her expression and shrugged impatiently. "No," he went on. "When my ricon betrayed the arviragus, and Venutius left her to go into the west, she sent me south to live among the Trinovantes and direct his spies there. I have been working for Rome, building roads and digging ditches." He spoke offhandedly, but she knew the price he had paid in setting aside his pride to do such work. "The Trinovantes and the remnants of the Catuvellauni have suffered hardest under the conquerors. You must know this. You surrendered here without raising sword and were rewarded with prosperity, but the arviragus's people and their former slaves who resisted have been punished unceasingly since that time. Many of them were shipped to Rome as slaves to fight in the arenas or to train with the legions. They have labored in the soil, they have died on the roads, they have starved, they have built fine houses for Rome and left their bones beneath the foundations. Colchester is growing. Now, more and more of them have had their lands stolen from them and given to retiring soldiers, who chain them in their own storehouses and make them farm their own lands, reaping the crops for masters who do not care that their children cannot be fed. Their load is crushing, and now they have had news of your humiliation. They wish to know if you will fight."

"And if I will?"

"They will fight with you. My spies tell me that other tribes will join if you win through to Colchester. They are ashamed, Boudicca. First

650

the arviragus is defeated, not by might but by the treachery of one of the people. Then you are wronged for no reason. They are afraid, trusting neither friend nor foe. This is the time, while the governor hunts men on Mona."

"Will they be led by me?"

"I do not know, but it is certain that there is no man remaining in the lowlands who can command. Have you weapons?"

She was silent, studying his face. He could be a truth-sayer or he could be just another tool of Rome, come to discover if certain rumors were true. If he were a spy and she opened her mind to him, the Iceni would be destroyed. If not, and she sent him away empty, the chance would go by forever. She looked at her men. "Lovernius?" He nodded imperceptibly. "Aillil?"

"We need a Druid," he said with worry, "but I think he says a truth."

"So do I. Very well. We will fight, Domnall, and soon. Our weapons lie hidden and the people have once again the wit to use them. Tell the tribes that."

His eyes searched the blunt, freckled face, the waving riot of red hair. How different she was from his own ricon. The last scion of the House Brigantia was slender, delicately beautiful, with eloquent eyes and fingers, but this hoarse-voiced, big, quick-spoken woman had a driving force of rough attraction, like the tugging gales around the vortex of a storm. Yet she had married a peacemaker and loved him until the day he died, whereas his own lady had wed a warrior and destroyed him. Men made good ricons, he thought, but women were either brilliant or ruinous.

Those flecked brown eyes were fixed on him impatiently, and he replied. "How soon, Lady?"

"Before the old moon turns young again." Her voice dropped to a racing purr. "Due south of this town, Domnall, between the two roads that desecrate my country, there are wooded hills that fold deep within the old Catuvellaunian borders. Do you know the place?"

"I know it."

"Meet me there at the time I spoke of, with all who will come with you. Bring food if you can, and chariots, and any weapons you can steal. But come quietly, I beg you. I do not want Colchester suddenly refortified and held against me."

"I am no fool, Lady."

"And send word to the lords of the west. Let them know what I am doing." Would Caradoc hear? she wondered with a pang of sadness. Would he then forgive? The tribes knew only that he still lived, somewhere amid the teeming maze that was the city of Rome. The thought of Caradoc brought another thought to mind. "The temple to Claudius," she snapped. "Is it still standing?"

"Of course!" Domnall retorted with surprise.

"And Decianus?"

"The procurator?" He could not follow the darting of her mind. "He is at Colchester."

"Andrasta, Andrasta," she whispered, her eyes shining. "Sharpen your blade. Deliverance comes with the spring."

In that last month, cold ungraciously gave place to warm, wet winds and intermittent rain, which sank beneath the drab sleep of winter and coaxed the first faint green of the coming spring from the rich soil. Boudicca's preparations were completed and at last she issued orders for the wains to be loaded. The people packed up their few belongings in readiness and then waited in an anxious, tautening excitement. No crops were sown that year. Seed was scarce, for the procurator had taken most of it, and besides, there was to be no going back, no second chance at peace. They would win through to the grain-stuffed forts and freedom, or they would perish. No one was to stay behind. The whole countryside was to be emptied. The old songs of battle and victory began to be hummed under anticipant breath, the old war cries sprang to life on tongues that thought they had forgotten what to utter. Andrasta and the Iceni. Death or freedom. Heads for the House Icenia, heads for greedy Andrasta. The time dragged by in sprinkling rainfall, and the trees began to bud.

The moon waxed, sat at the full, and then slowly waned. Favonius watched it from the window of his office, unable to sleep though the nights were sweet and warm. Boudicca saw it as she circled the town again and again, exchanging words of encouragement and cheer with the freemen. She stood before the dark Council hall in the small hours of the morning, her cloak wrapped about her, gazing at it as it floated in its lake of blue mist, and Subidasto muttered in her ear, "Hurry, Boudicca, hurry! Paulinus is nearing Mona. Soon he will turn again, and it will be too late." "I know, I know," she answered him aloud, the night drifting by. She felt the need to gather in her own forces as her people gathered in their weapons and goods. She felt lonely and afraid there in the spring darkness, unwilling suddenly to say farewell to the town, to take her sword and ruthlessly sever the past from the future. She shivered with this aloneness, wishing that she could turn from the calmness around her and walk to her house where Prasutugas waited in light and warmth, his shoulder an inviting hollow of security and love, his lips gentle on the wounds of her pain and rage. She knew that an uncharacteristic cowardice held her also, an unwillingness to say the word that would begin a time of agony and death.

She remembered the hours spent with Priscilla and Favonius, dining on oysters and mutton at their spotless silver-strewn table, drinking watered wine and arguing with mingled suspicion and respect far into the night. Those days had fled like visions glimpsed at the bottom of some still, dark pond. She went to her bed and slept a brief, fragmented sleep.

Then it was time. The moon had shrunk to a thin curve of ivory light and in the woods and meadows the first brave, tentative flowers unfurled pale colors to a strengthening sun. She called the royal war band to her and they set off through a cool, dark night to the garrison, clad only in breeches and short tunics, their knives tucked safely into their belts. The town they left was quiet, dreaming a last illusion of peace, and they slipped down the long, grassed slope and were lost in the fuzzed shadows of the copse.

Once through the trees she motioned them down into the new grass and lay with them, looking out at the lights of the garrison. All seemed quiet. The sentries stood on either side of the high wooden gate, torchlight flickering dully on their armor, their naked legs planted stolidly apart. In the detachment's stables the horses rustled their straw, and from somewhere behind the warriors an owl screeched and dipped low to flap heavily away beyond the road. Nothing else was stirring. Satisfied, she rose and gestured, and the war band crouched and flowed over the remaining ground to mingle silently with the dense shadows of the wall. She nodded to Lovernius and Aillil, pushed her knife farther along her belt so that her sleeve hid its glint, then the three of them walked boldly up to the gate. One of the sentries loosened and came forward, but when he saw Boudicca his suspicious scowl gave place to a respectful smile. "Lady! I didn't recognize you without your horse. It's very late to be calling on the commander."

"I know," she answered levelly, "but there is an urgent matter that requires me to seek his advice." Out of the corner of her eye she saw the other sentry lean back against the wall and yawn, and behind him a deeper shadow moved. "Do you think he is still up?"

"A lamp is still burning in the office. I think he is working. Shall I call someone to escort you?"

Lovernius began to sidle around behind the man and Boudicca folded her arms casually against her waist, feeling the hilt of her knife. "That will not be necessary. I know my way." He pushed open the gate and stepped back. "You should by now. A good night to you, Lady."

"Farewell, Roman." She nodded sharply at Lovernius as the vague shape under the wall solidified to become a chief that sprang like a lean cat upon the second sentry. She drew her knife smoothly, quickly. For a moment it felt alien in her hand, like a clumsy appendage, then Lovernius spun on his heel, clapped a hand of iron around the man's mouth, and as his eyes widened to white rims her wrist seemed to tighten of its own accord and the knife slid into the pale throat. With no more sound than the troubling of wind in pliant grass they dragged the bodies under the concealing blackness of the wall, then Lovernius whistled, the broken piping of a curlew, and the other men came gliding out of the dimness.

"A stiff gamble, but the stakes are high," he whispered gleefully to her but she did not reply. The stakes were high indeed, and now the dice had been thrown. Even if she wanted to she could not reach out and pick them up, and they must go on rolling to the feet of Paulinus. On noiseless feet they entered the wide, faintly lit courtyard and immediately spread out, the men hugging the inner walls and vanishing toward barracks, officers' houses, and granaries. She paced steadily and openly toward the administrative building while Lovernius and Aillil began the circle that would bring them there also, up behind the sentry that strolled back and forth along the porch, his silhouette crossing and recrossing the blade of yellow light cutting under the office door. Just before she reached it, the sentry paused at one end of the covered way, turned, and then seemed to drop backward into the shadow behind him. She came to the step, mounted briskly, knocked on the door, and went in.

He was alone, sitting at his desk with his head in his hands, and he looked up slowly as she closed the door and came to him. His eyes were bleary, his gray-peppered hair tousled, and he showed no surprise at seeing her there. "Boudicca?" he rubbed his face with both hands and sat straight. "I must have fallen asleep over my work. It feels very late. What do you want?"

Her eyes shifted about the room and came back to him. His breastplate stood in a corner, his helmet beside it, but his knife hung from his belt. "It is late, Favonius, but I wanted to talk to you. Have you heard anything from the governor?"

"Yes, I have. I intended to come and tell you what he said but I did not particularly want your company, just as I'm sure you would have hated mine. He has promised to look into the matter when he returns to Colchester."

"If he returns," she growled, her lip curling. "Have you had letters from Priscilla?" Now the sleep-swollen eyes became puzzled, then wary. "What is it to you? It is no business of yours."

"True. But Priscilla always hated living here. I simply wondered if she was any happier at Camulodunon."

654

Uneasiness began to stroke him. She had never before called Colchester by its ancient tribal name, and it tumbled into the thick silence of the room, bringing with it a new, raw menace. Her eyes were slitted, grinning at him, she was leaning slightly forward, her shoulders tense, and suddenly he was aware that his sentry's measured tread no longer pounded outside the door. Prickling with a cold presentiment he rose and went to the window, flinging wide the shutters, but the courtyard dreamed its cold dreams under a forest of white stars, and he turned back to her, mystified and alarmed.

"What do you fear, Favonius?" she asked him, a catch of derision in her deep voice. "The Druids are a memory. Andrasta is a tale for children who will not go to sleep. What brings sweat to your brow? Are there spells in shadows? Does the forest mutter incantations with the wind?" She moved toward him. "You thought you understood this land, but now you know that you do not, and that is why you ache for the familiarity of things turned suddenly strange."

"I certainly do not understand you tonight!" he snapped. "Are you drunk? Boudicca, I can do nothing for you or your daughters. Where is that sentry?"

Words hovered on her tongue—biting, murdering words, words of hate and wounding. Brigid killed your son. Brigid stabbed him. Brigid skewered him like a poor, ignorant young fawn and his blood pooled black under the moon. "Say them, Boudicca!" Subidasto urged her, his rumbling whisper a gleeful rasp in her brain. "Take off his clothes and begin to cover your nakedness!" But though she felt the need curl in her mouth like hot wine fumes on a winter's day, she backed up slowly until she had placed the desk between them.

"Andrasta has him," she said evenly. "Lovernius! Aillil!"

Then he knew. He tugged at the knife in his belt and hurled himself from the window shouting "Guard, guard!" but the door opened, her men rushed at him, and she slid aside from his waving blade and laughed.

"They are all dead, Favonius," she said. "The garrison is a tomb, and so on the whole of Albion will be a tomb also, a Roman charnel house. We trusted you, and you failed us. You could have given us your support but you turned your back and closed your ears to the screaming of my children and the sounds of my humiliation."

He did not struggle in the chiefs' strong grip. He just stood there looking at her sadly. "It seems that I underestimated your degree of pride," he said. "But Boudicca, you cannot win. All the odds are against you."

"Not this time, Favonius. The governor is miles away, with half the occupation forces, and the rest of them are straining their eyes after him. I am not going west, I am going south. I will burn Camulodunon to the ground."

His ruddy features paled, and she could see the odds regroup in her favor behind his bloodshot eyes. "I am to die?"

"Yes."

"Now?"

"Yes. If you have spells to bind your gods you had better speak them. I thought of taking you into the grove of Andrasta, Favonius, and setting your head upon a stake, but for the friendship my dear husband held for you I will give you a clean death. I think it is more than you deserve." She did not give him time to speak again. "Strike, Aillil," she ordered calmly; then she turned her back, and when she heard his body slump onto the floor she left the room and walked toward the gate. "Coward!" her father snorted furiously in her ear but she ignored him, thinking of Prasutugas lying pale and noble under the earth mound, sleeping his long sleep.

Before they left the garrison the chiefs hitched the horses to the detachment's wains and loaded up all the grain and weapons they could find. Then they tore the flaming torches from the walls and ran from building to building, thrusting them into the corpse-inhabited rooms, and soon the crackling inferno dwarfed the stars which were fading slowly toward dawn.

The tribe moved swiftly. The first blow had been struck and Boudicca was consumed with haste, knowing that time had begun to quicken its pace and before long the speculatores from Lindum carrying routine messages from the fort to the garrison would discover its destruction and spread the alarm. The tuath left its territory that night—chariots, wains, and people filing quietly away from the dark, deserted towns and villages and the leaping orange pyre of the garrison. For three days and two nights they journeyed south, snatching sleep and food when they could, as the wooded land began to rise to gentle hills. Long before they reached the appointed meeting place the Trinovantian scouts met them, and they moved through trees alive with horses, warriors, cooking fires, and shrieking children. There was no longer any attempt at concealment. The host mingling together now was too great. Colchester was barely a day's march away and it was already full of rumor and confusion. The only advantage left to the people was in speed. Boudicca greeted Domnall at last, in a clearing beside a small stream, and they embraced.

"So you came," she smiled. "I did not believe, but it seems that the Druid was right. The host is enormous, Domnall. We have been passing through it for hours. Who are all the people?"

They squatted together by the fire that his servant had kindled, and

656

he poured beer for her before he replied. "They are Trinovantian, Catuvellaunian, Coritani, some Cornovii, some Dobunni. The Druids have been moving among them once more, and they came. Caradoc said that the spirit of freedom was dead in the south, but he was wrong. It only slept, Lady, and you have awakened it. You, and the cruelty of Rome. Will we Council?"

She nodded. "Tonight. I bring arms and food, but not enough for this gathering. Do the people have weapons?"

"Most of them, and those that do not will soon be bearing gladiae and pilum. Food is short, but if we take Colchester we can replenish the wains."

Colchester. Camulodunon. She drank her beer and did not answer.

Evening fell into a dark, soft spring night, and before her Council began Boudicca went to her daughters. Ethelind was sitting under a tree, her chin in hand, gazing intently into the little fire that her servant had made for her. Her blanket and cloak were folded neatly beside her, and Boudicca stepped up to her. "Are you well, Ethelind?" she asked brusquely, her offhand, rough manner disguising the ache she always felt when she looked at the frozen face of her elder daughter. "Is there anything you need?" Ethelind did not look up but her hand came out slowly, a warning, a signal of distress, and after a moment Boudicca stepped back and turned away. Andrasta, she thought in sudden fear. What can I do with them? Somehow I believed that when we left the town they would recover, why I do not know, but how can I march and think and fight with this dumb pain always beside me?

Brigid was walking to and fro by the stream, which was now a black mirror trapping stars and leaves in its smooth surface, and her long silvered hair was swaying about her knees. "Come down!" she was calling to the rustling branches. "There is no moon to show you how the river's blood is full of little flowers. Andrasta! Come!" Hulda sat with the young chief whom Boudicca had ordered to guard them, both of them silent and grim, and Pompey quietly cropped the grass.

"Has she eaten?" Boudicca asked harshly, and Hulda nodded.

"Only meat, and water from the stream. Lady, what will you do with her when the fighting begins?" Boudicca looked toward the slim, shadow-dappled figure.

"How am I to know?" she snarled. "I cannot think of it now, Hulda, there is too much hurt." She stalked back to the clearing where the chiefs and representatives from the tribes were settling themselves before the fire. Sinking onto a blanket beside Domnall, she looked them over critically, and a warm feeling of homecoming stole over her. The stricken, lost mood of hopelessness about the girls began to fade. This was how it had been when she was a child. A hot, welcoming Council fire glinting and glancing on a thousand torcs, necklets, brooches, and bracelets. Bronze helms shining like bright gold. Sparkling, expectant eyes and the excited, sibilant rise and fall of many voices. The flutter of cloaks—red, green, blue, scarlet, striped, patterned, flowered. The clang of sword in scabbard. And of course the wine passing gaily from hand to hand, the spontaneous lifting of a fair voice in song, the stories, the quarrels, and over it all, the close, fierce protectiveness of the kin.

She rose, held up her arms, and the talking died away. She stepped forward, unbuckled her sword and handed it to Aillil, then she shook back her fiery and flame-haloed hair and began to speak. "Chiefs and people of the tuaths! You see before you a woman who has lived all her life in obedience to Rome, in cooperation with Rome, a woman who believed and trusted in the justice of the emperor of Rome to bring peace and prosperity to her people. Yet you also see before you a woman who has been grievously and cruelly wronged. In exchange for my full trust and cooperation, people of Albion, my tuath was robbed, my people dragged into slavery, my daughters outraged, and my own body tied to a stake and whipped without mercy. Do my words fall on ears already ringing with the same sad tales? Is it not true that each one of you carries a similar burden of pain? You are here because you are afraid.

"The Iceni, through all the years since Claudius came, have been the model of a Roman-loving tuath—the richest, the softest, the most privileged companions of the conquerors. We, of all the people, should have been secure. But what do you see now?" Her hard, masculine voice rose, abrasive as the tongue of a cat, and its cracked tones splintered around them. "What has happened to the Iceni," she shouted, "can happen to you in spite of your craven submissions, it can come with no warning. The Iceni have learned a bitter lesson. Rome is faithless, greedy, and lying!" She dropped her arms and lowered her voice. "So I will tell you what I will do. I will avenge this terrible wrong. On behalf of my poor, despoiled children I will burn Camulodunon, I will burn Londinium, burn, burn them all, and then I will turn to meet Paulinus as he marches home, and I will burn him too. I speak as a woman and a mother. If you wish to come with me and avenge your own wrongs, then let us march and fight together. Is there any tribe that will not come?"

No one stirred. No one spoke. Her words were true, and every silent chief was pondering them with a frightened loneliness. If this could happen to the Iceni it could happen to all of them. She waited for the space of ten heartbeats while the fire roared and the night

658

wind shared a spell with the compliant treetops, then she set her hands on her hips. "Good. We march tomorrow." She swept up her sword and sank beside Domnall but the people sat on, immersed in the private tragedies that had so suddenly become the pitiless goads to freedom.

Before dawn the tribes were on the move, swarming out of the hills and onto the Roman road that ran from Icenia to Camulodunon. They no longer went unremarked, and in Colchester a panic broke out. It had become almost a city by now, and little remained of Caradoc's old capital. It was a busy, well-planned Roman merchant town, always in the forefront of progress, and the huge defences of the Catuvellauni, once reduced to a low earthwall, had never been rebuilt. There would have been no purpose to it. Colchester was the seat of the governor, Colchester was at the heart of the occupation, and for years the inhabitants, Roman and native, had gone smugly about their business, growing soft and prosperous, hearing the tumult of Caradoc's war from far away like the whisper of battles among gods who could never touch the world of reality. Now, suddenly and shockingly, something had gone wrong. With no warning at all the gods had become crazed, bloodthirsty chiefs within hours of the city, and long-forgotten fears woke to drive the citizens into the streets in the middle of the morning. What they saw reassured them. The sun shone and their neighbors scurried about their errands. Children squabbled and played in the wide, tree-lined avenues. And everywhere the soldiers, traders, secretaries, officers, both civilian and military, wove in and out of the citizens like a safe, unworried river of calm. After an hour or two of excited conjecture the people reluctantly went back to their daily round. It was all so much foolish talk and anyway, the Iceni would be the last natives on the island capable of revolt.

The mayor was not so sure. He stood at the window of his office in the administration building that was part of the bustling forum, looking out at the sun-filled square and frowning to himself. The reports coming in had all been strident in their insistence on danger and he had alerted the legionary veterans on farms beyond the city. Many of them had come within the walls with their families, but they were the least of his worries. Should he order an evacuation to Londinium? The thought was not a happy one. Evacuation would mean congested streets, panicking women, accidents, and the complete disruption of all business. Besides, there were few active soldiers in the city to make a defence. Perhaps it would be better to arm the civilian men and keep everyone here. He had never in his life faced such a situation and he heartily wished that he had never run for office. He was a

Catuvellaunian, a man awarded Roman citizenship for his services to the province, and though he did not believe for a moment that there was the danger of any permanent rupture in the life of the city, his worry came from some vestige of tribal memory. He turned to his secretary.

"Send a speculator to Londinium," he said. "The procurator is there at the moment. Tell him the rumor, and ask if he can send us a detachment. We probably won't need it and I will end up looking very foolish, but it's as well to be prepared." He went back to the window. The graceful, clean lines of the temple gleamed in the warm spring sunshine, and below the steps a girl was throwing crumbs to the pigeons who waddled and flapped around her in a gray cloud. His breakfast curdled in his stomach.

The lone scout drew rein and sat gaping incredulously at the sight before him. The sun was about to rise, and a cold light washed over the smoking, still-warm ashes of the ruined garrison, a light without definition, without heat. The air was perfectly still. In the trees the birds had concluded their dawn chorus and were silent, and in the eerie, long moment before the sun rimmed the eastern horizon the soldier kneed his horse closer, his hands slippery on the reins. Nothing moved in that charred wilderness, and, dazed, he picked his way through the black stumps of the barrack walls. Then, mustering great daring, he put his hand to his mouth and shouted, but the echoes of his own voice frightened him and he clattered out of the stunted gate and in under the sheltering trees of the copse. Here he dismounted, and leaving his horse tethered to an oak he crept up to the town. For a long time he lay looking at it, but it, too, was dead. There was no smoke from cooking fires spiraling from the thatched roofs. No dogs barked and chased brown children. He knew that he should enter it but he shrank from the ghosts and demons that lurked unseen in the still-untouched shadows of early morning, and in the end he wriggled back to his horse, mounted, and hurried back the way he had come. There was a posting station ten miles on, and beyond that another three or four, all with fresh horses, and he knew that he must reach Lindum and the Ninth as quickly as he could. He understood the wind of terror that swept him along. The Iceni had disappeared and they were not in the north. That could only mean that they had headed south. His commander had been right. The procurator's actions had begun a war.

Petilius Cerealis listened to his exhausted speculator, and even before he had heard all his suspicions confirmed, one by one, he was issuing the order to stand to arms. The Ninth had had an easy time of it over the last few years. The only action they had seen had been against Venutius, and when he had melted away into the west his wife had settled so firmly over her tribesmen that the Ninth had done nothing more in the north than patrol endlessly. Cerealis, like all the Romans in Albion that year, had had eyes for nothing but the governor's campaign, and the tiny, almost unnoticed hints of trouble had blown toward him like leaves in an autumn gale, to pile up unheeded in the shadows of his mind. Complacency and blindness, he accused himself angrily. Now we all pay. He quickly dictated a dispatch to Paulinus; then he left his office and strode out under a high, windy spring sky. He did not know the strength of the rebels but he knew the direction of their thrust, the defencelessness of the city, and indeed the whole of the lowlands, and the impossibility of any engagement for the Ninth before Colchester was wiped from the face of the earth. Boudicca, he thought, standing for a moment to watch the gay glitter of the sun on the aquila in the center of the square. Who would have imagined it? If she makes her plans carefully the whole island could be in her hands before the autumn. I wonder if she knows it? He shrugged and moved on. Of course she did not know it. She was a barbarian, and as such could not think beyond a few severed heads and a wain piled with booty. In a week or two the Ninth would be back patrolling for Aricia, and the rebels would have scattered. He smiled at his moment of irrationality and went to meet his second.

"There it is!" Domnall called to her, and she reined in her chariot and stood looking down the valley while her horses tossed their heads, and all around her, in under the trees, her chiefs straggled to a halt. The country they had passed through with its small, neat fields, its fat herds cropping in lush meadows, had brought to her no memories of the journey she had made with her father nearly thirty years before, but she remembered only too well the low, snaking wall encircling the city, the brawling noisy sprawl of traders' and laborers' huts leaning drunkenly over it, the slow, gentle rising to treed streets, spacious houses, and the orderly wood-and-stone grace of the little forum. She shifted her gaze, her eyes narrowed against the sun, and thought she caught the dazzle of light glancing off the tall pillars of Claudius's white temple. Prasutugas, my husband, she thought, allowing the memory to tug her with sadness. How pleased you were to stand with me in its cool depths and watch the incense rise. How flattered to receive an audience with Plautius and dine on white linen with Aricia and the other ricons who surrendered. Now I am about to destroy everything you worked so hard to achieve. She held out a hand to Aillil and he gave her the new bronze helm cast with the soaring wings of the Queen of Victory on either side, and she set it firmly on her head. Around her waist went her own iron-studded belt, and from it hung a great sword that had been her father's, and his before him. Turning to Domnall, she smiled briefly.

"Are you ready?"

"Yes. The city is surrounded, although the last of the people, and the wains and children, are still some miles back."

"Did the detachment march straight through the gates or is it quartering outside?"

"It went in, or so the scouts say. I do not think the Romans are aware how great a force has been mustered against them."

She laughed once, scornfully. "It would make no difference even if they did know. There is no army south of Lindum as large as ours, and luck is with us." She gathered up the reins. "No prisoners, Domnall. No mercy for any. Lovernius, where are the girls?" He glanced at her, his heavy horned helm glinting in the sun. "They rest far back, by the river. They will be quite safe."

"Then let us ride. Sound the carnyx, Aillil. Vengeance is mine today."

The shrill, haunting battle call floated far on the fresh morning, and out of the shade of the thick forest ten thousand chariots rolled, the sun sparking on their slender spokes, harness clinking as the little horses cantered over the green flat. Behind them the freemen came running, pouring from the dimness into the full glare of light like multicolored insects, and Colchester turned from its morning optimism to see a lake of death lapping at is feet. Shouts rang out, and the charioteers could see the crowded streets empty suddenly. Helmets bristled above the low wall. Boudicca drew her sword and waved it above her head. "The House Icenia forever!" she yelled. "Andrasta, Andrasta!" and she thundered for the gate, red hair streaming on the wind, the rumble of chariot wheels and the cries and curses of the chieftains tingling in her ears. The gate loomed. She reined sharply and leaped down, and while the women of the town still screamed and ran hither and thither, shepherding their terrified, bewildered children, the rebel host flowed over the wall, the first onslaught carried by the sheer press of the thousands behind, and the new-forged swords of Icenia began their work.

It was a massacre. Only the two hundred soldiers sent by Decianus were active, serving legionaries. The men of the town were civilians or retired legionaries who lived in Colchester while their Trinovantian and Catuvellauni slaves farmed their allotted land. Most were unarmed, all were unprepared, and they fled from the carnage of the lowest circles to the stone-ringed safety of the forum. The civilians milled about in terror, but the veterans soon recovered and began to ransack the administration buildings and the homes of the first circle for weapons. Many were found, and the ex-legionaries pushed through the wild-eyed, screaming mob and ran to give battle.

For those who sought to jump the wall and run, there was no escape. The tribesmen were still coming, line after line, and all the land from town to forest was thick with men who had not yet given battle. The outer rim was already on fire as freemen looted, flung their booty over the wall to their friends, and set more huts ablaze, moving up the slope and killing anyone in their path. The detachment hurriedly retreated, met the now-armed veterans coming to join them, and managed to block off many streets so that for some hours the chiefs could not get through and were content to range about, tearing women and children from their hiding places and spearing them, broaching the wine shipments that were kept in the warehouses by the gate, and running with flaming brands in their hands to hurl at any thatch that had not caught. The lower town slowly filled with more freemen and fresh swords, and at the last, when nothing lived below the prosperous houses of the rich, they turned to battle once more. The soldiers fought grimly, back to back, but a spirit of insanity had entered the once peaceful Iceni and their cowed allies. It became an inferno of hate that burned up all pity and all mercy, and unleashed an orgy of bloodlust. The years of degradation and misery were being washed away in one howling, exultant moment of long-due retribution, and the soldiers looked into the red eyes of animals as they were slowly beaten back, closer to the packed, crazed citizens in the square.

Noon passed in a stinking heat of fear. Bodies choked the streets, the open gutters began to trickle red streams, and the gasping, staggering legionaries at last broke and ran, diving into the mass of unprotected civilians to be lost for a while. Then the tribesmen paused, and the terrified people on the fringes of the forum could see them standing in every street, swords wet, mouths grinning, agape. "Mercy!" someone screamed in a voice high and thin with fear. "Mercy. Ah, mercy!" And at that the attackers surged to new life. They rushed into the square, screaming, howling, cursing, their swords slashing, and the people went down before them like a crop before hail.

Boudicca lurched toward the administrative building, the din of slaughter battering her hearing. She kicked open the first door and reeled inside, but it was empty. She leaned against the wall for a moment, panting, then walked down the corridor and flung open the second door. A woman crouched in the farthest corner, sobbing, and as the vision of horror staggered toward her and raised a sword she sprang up, crying, "No! No! Boudicca, I am your friend! Look at me!

Do not slay me, oh please let me live!" Boudicca slowly lowered her sword. It was Priscilla, pressed against the wall, her graying hair loose and disheveled, her stola filthy with blood and mire, and her face gray with fear and her eyes wide. For a long second they gazed at one another, not moving, then Boudicca closed her eyes and swallowed. Her throat was parched, and her breath was coming in quick, painful spurts.

She turned to the door. "Someone else can kill you," she croaked, and she staggered out to where the bodies lay heaped, covering the square, and she walked ankle deep in a river of blood.

By the time a red evening light diffused through the town there was not one citizen left alive, and the drunken, satiated chiefs had to climb over bodies that were heaped in every street. The sunset passed unnoticed, for the conflagration burning in the lower circles roared into the darkening sky and obscured its last, placid light. But in the temple the men of the detachment from Londinium had gathered in a tiny, hopeless gesture of resistance, and much to the chiefs' surprise they could not break the lines of stubborn men strung behind the smooth columns that fronted the steps. Boudicca and her men stood at the foot, looking up to where night's shadows were swiftly multiplying. "We cannot leave them to spread and bring the legions down on us before we are ready," Lovernius said, and Boudicca nodded wearily, her mind and body almost too dumb to think.

"I know," she managed. "Domnall, have the chiefs tried to force a way through the rear of the building?"

"The doors have been barricaded as well as locked, but some of the freemen are trying."

"Good." She shook a trembling fist at its pristine indifference. "Citadel of eternal domination," she said, her voice half-whisper, half-raven's caw. "I will not leave until I have defeated you!" Turning to the chiefs she ordered them to determine if any sober freemen could be found, and to organize forays against the soldiers throughout the night. Then she laboriously picked her way through the now dark, corpse-riddled streets and the feeding fire to the gate, and the sweet, tree-filled silence beyond.

Brigid was asleep, curled up in blankets beside the little cooking fire, her face relaxed and full of dead innocence as her mother bent wearily over her. Ethelind sat wreathed in her voluminous cloak, leaning against the bole of a tree and staring into the tangled depths of the forest. Hulda and the young chief nodded, their heads full of sleep, and without a word, Boudicca cast herself down in the clean, dry grass a little distance from the fire and closed her eyes. Such cool, sweet-smelling grass, she thought. Such stupendous quiet, such unknowing peace. Andrasta, did you see? Did you clap your black wings together and dip your cruel beak deep into the entrails of my revenge? "More blood," Subidasto grumbled in her. "You are only half-clad. You look wanton and unkempt without your honor. More blood, Boudicca, oh much, much more!"

"Leave me alone!" she hissed sharply at him. "Stay dead, old man, and trouble me no more!" But she tumbled into a deep, soaking sleep and dreamed that he squatted over her, his rugged face impatient, his gnarled, hot fingers tracing the crooked paths of the lash upon her naked back.

In the morning she ate a little stale bread, drank deeply from the stream, and left the clearing before her daughters were awake. The sun was just rising, tipping the trees in pink as she got down from her chariot and entered the town. The stench of decay smote her immediately, a fetid, thick miasma that reminded her of the cattle slaughtering of Samain, and she retched as she made her way to the obscene, unmoving gathering in the square. The lake of blood had run down the gutters to the wall, there to pool out and find channels through the grass beyond, but the stone beneath her feet was sticky as she trudged to Domnall and the others. He greeted her in a parched whisper.

"They are holding. How, I do not know. I must rest now, Lady, but half the freemen have slept and are ready to fight again."

She waved him toward the gate and drew her sword, struggling against the sick fumes of death and burnt houses. "Today we must kill them and be gone," she said. "Aillil, the carnyx." The strident, high bronze voice spoke, another wave of tribesmen assaulted the temple, and the soldiers formed their ragged ranks within its shelter and parried with no sound, and no hope.

Morning deepened into a cloudy afternoon, and the afternoon into windy evening, and at last the chiefs stood in the square and admitted defeat. Most of the forces had retired long ago to the forest, there to load the wains with booty and grain taken from the storehouses, but five hundred of them now squatted or stood loosely amid the already swelling corpses, looking up at the baffling imperiousness of the unsullied pillars. Boudicca cursed hoarsely, wiped her face on her sleeve, and sheathed her sword.

"There is no choice now," she said. "We must burn them out. I do not want to do it, they have fought well, but they cannot be left alive. Domnall, bring wood. There are plenty of houses left. Aillil, make more fire. The stone will not catch but the interior is full of things that will burn." They ran to do her bidding and soon a fire blazed up at the foot of the steps. Within the shadows there was a small flurry of

665

movement as the soldiers knew that now they must begin to count the moments left to them. But Boudicca cared only to finish and be gone. At her word the chiefs began to cast flaming brands between the pillars, a shower, a storm of flame and shooting sparks in the cool dim air, and the men trapped inside ran back. The fire continued to rain into the darkness, then all at once a long tongue of yellow flame billowed out, followed by another, and a black smoke began to roll outward. For a few more minutes the people in the square stood silent, watching the fire take hold. Then the entombed soldiers began to scream and Boudicca turned abruptly toward the gate. "Fire the rest," she ordered and she forced herself to pace away slowly, the death cries of the Romans loud in her ears.

In the clearing a scout was waiting for her and she, Domnall, her bard, and her shield-bearer went wearily to the earth, taking the beer offered to them by Hulda and drinking thirstily.

"The Ninth is on the march from Lindum," he said. "Cerealis has emptied the fort."

"How far?"

"He had just arrived at Durobrivae when I left, but I do not think he will stay there long. He will rest the men for a few hours and then press on toward Colchester."

She thought deeply, drank again, then drew up her knees and rested her arms across them. "Do we wait here for him or do we go out to meet him?" she asked herself aloud. "If we wait we will have time for preparation, but there are too many trees, it is too hard to fight a legion in the trees." Her head went down but she raised it slowly. "We will move north and west to where the land is more open," she decided. "A legion will not be hard to find, particularly if the scouts keep moving."

"Colchester was no gamble," Lovernius cut in. "It was like slaughtering sheep. But a legion will be a fitting test."

She scrambled to her feet. "For the rest of this night we will eat and sleep. I want to change my clothes and wash." They left her then and she began to strip off the crusted, foul tunic and breeches, not caring who passed in and out of the fire's light. Her limbs shook with fatigue and her back was burning and sore. Stepping to the stream she lowered herself under the chill, chattering water and when she was clean she put on fresh clothes, drew her cloak around her, and lay with her head on her shield. The remains of the town burned all night, casting a lurid, dappled glow through the trees, and around her she could hear the sighings and mutterings of the thousands of people, and she could not sleep. She was afraid.

666

CHAPTER THIRTY-EIGHT

PAULINUS REMOVED HIS HELMET and then lifted his arms so that his servant could unbuckle his breastplate. It was hot in the tent and the air was hazed with acrid blue smoke from burning wood and shriveling bodies. The sound of axes came to him clear and rhythmical and he heard the crisp shouted commands of his officers as they brought order into what had been a chaos of destruction. Yesterday Mona was an island seething with white-clad, raging priests and the screaming curses of incensed women brandishing swords and flaming torches. Today the sun poured over dismembered corpses, smashed altars, and the sweating work detail who were slinging the limp dead onto bonfires and chopping down the thick, vigorous oak groves. He moved his stiff shoulders under the soft leather jerkin, flung the plumed helmet onto his camp cot, and eased himself into his chair. The burn on his thigh tingled and he rubbed at it absently, his thoughts still entangled with the day before. It had been close. Not the battle, of course, if one could call chasing wildmen up the beach and slaughtering refugees under the trees a battle. There had been no element of surprise in his attack, not with his legions on the march for days through the embittered, hostile countryside, and every native for miles around knowing full well where he was bound. He had had his share of false alarms—wrong turnings under the blanket of the brooding mists, accidents with the baggage train on the narrow track between ocean and mountains, and then the swift burning of the village opposite the island that loomed dark from the beach, fogged with sea spume. A camp was built, boats and rafts were constructed, and the water was probed for shallows in order that the cavalry could cross. And all the time Mona sat there like a spell-hung monster of the depths, humping malignantly and filling the horizon. The officers had been worried, claiming that the soldiers felt the magic of the place and were afraid, though he himself could not catch so much as a whiff of this so-called spell. Indeed, when the time came for assault the men huddled in the rocking boats and on the rafts, cowed into immobility at the sight of a shore thronged with yelling, cursing Druids, and until he himself had leaped into the water and plunged for the beach they had been paralyzed with fear. He had led the charge, the men had responded, and no superstition had turned their lethal blades after all. Naturally. He grunted a thanks to his servant who had placed wine before him, and dismissed the past. Back to Colchester now, a message to the emperor, and peace for the province at last.

"Your second is here, sir," the servant said respectfully, and Paulinus took off his arm bands and sipped gratefully from his cup.

"Show him in, then, and find me some good hot water. I need a bath."

The tent flap was pushed aside and Agricola bent his head and came forward, saluting gravely. Paulinus smiled at him and indicated the little leather stool. "Sit down and have a drink, Julius. How goes it this morning?"

The younger man pulled the stool forward and sat, running a hand through his curly brown hair. "Very well, sir, but it will take quite a few days to fell all the oaks and burn them, and a detachment has gone after the natives who escaped us. There were not many and they will all be dealt with in a week. How hot it is today!"

"A welcome change after the mountains. Our losses?"

"A score or two, not enough to mention, and no officers. Some wounds, a few broken gladiae. What shall we do about the crops?"

"Crops?"

"Many of the fields had already been seeded. Shall we leave them?"

Paulinus drank, considered, and answered bluntly. "No, not this year. Have them turned under. Next spring we can have them tended, for the soil seems incredibly fertile here, but the men will have enough to do on the island without becoming farmers. I don't think the western tribes will attempt to take Mona again, but until they surrender I have no intention of inadvertently providing them with more food."

"I'm surprised we got through with so little opposition."

"So am I. Conditions must be very bad for them by now. Well, Julius, we can relax for a week or two in the sun before we wend our way back to civilization." He picked up his cup, the gray eyes smiling into Agricola's brown ones. "A toast. To the emperor, and our success."

"The emperor." They drank happily. Agricola rose to go, but before he could leave the tent, Paulinus's servant pushed past him.

"There is a scout here, sir, from Deva, very upset. He will not give his message to a legate, he insists on speaking to you in person."

"Let him come, then. Julius, you'd better stay. I hope that Brigantian woman isn't in trouble again." Agricola retired to the stool, the servant bowed and went out, and a moment later the scout came into the tent. He was splashed in mud from head to foot and limping but Paulinus did not at once notice these things. His eyes were on the man's face. A thinly masked terror was there, veiled only by a soldier's discipline, and the big jaw trembled as he tried not to vomit the

668

words that for the last twelve days had whipped him all the way from Lindum as he rode alone. He came clumsily to attention, saluted with one weary arm, and Paulinus nodded. "What message do you bring, centurion?"

"Sir," the man answered, his voice husky with fatigue, "the Iceni have risen. They have destroyed the garrison within their territory and they are headed for Colchester. Thousands of them. The whole of their country has emptied."

Agricola left the stool and went to stand beside Paulinus, but the governor did not move. "Is this only a rumor?"

"No, sir. The speculator from Lindum saw the remains of the garrison himself, and said that he rode through countless deserted villages. The legate of the Ninth has taken the legion and left Lindum, marching south. He asks me to tell you that he will not arrive in time to save the city but will endeavor to engage the rebels as soon as possible. There is a rumor that the Trinovantes have joined the Iceni, but that is just a rumor."

The governor's hand came crashing down on the table, and he rose heavily. "The Iceni? It is not possible! We have had no stauncher allies than Prasutagas and his chiefs." But then a memory stole into his mind, a dispatch from the command of the Icenian garrison, a dispatch from the procurator. He had glanced over them briefly and handed them to his secretary with a few absent-minded words of vague instruction, all his attention focused on Mona, but now snatches of them drifted back to him. ". . . the chieftain of these people having died, and his will having been made known, I intend to proceed at once to Icenia . . ." "I do not believe, sir, that rapine and murder can be considered to be a part of imperial policy or the procurator's duty, and I respectfully request to be transferred from Icenia . . ." Icenia. Boudicca. Ah yes, Boudicca. A colorful, big, hoarse-voiced woman, a joke to the occupying forces with her outdated ideas of loyalty and her rude but harmless insults against the emperor.

Dead silence had fallen inside the tent, but beyond it the axes rang cheerily and a shout of laughter rose as a group of officers passed by. Paulinus walked to the flap, lifted it, and stood looking out on the sparkling green of the ocean. The Iceni, and perhaps the Trinovantes. Say, certainly the Trinovantes. Better to err on the side of safety. How many people? Fifty thousand? More? Could the Ninth hold them off, let alone defeat them? Where would they go after they had sacked Colchester as they undoubtedly would, perhaps had already done so . . . Londinium, of course. A cold feeling of impotence began to steal over him. Londinium was defenceless. So was Verulamium, almost.

So, he thought in resignation, is the whole of the damned lowlands. Ripe fruit waiting meekly to be picked and eaten. What was the matter with me? How is it that I did not put the pieces together and see the picture forming? If other tribes follow her lead, Britannia is finished as a province. If? Of course they would. He swung back into the stifling noon heat of the tent.

"Sir, there's the Second at Glevum," Agricola said, and Paulinus stood looking down at the table.

"I know," he replied tersely. "Let me think, Julius. I have the Fourteenth here, on Mona. I have the Twentieth at Deva, sixty miles away. Two legions. It might as well be twenty for all the good they can do, stuck here over two hundred miles from Colchester. That leaves the Ninth, somewhere on the march, and the Second. The Second could reach Londinium in time, perhaps. Mithras! So many ifs and perhapses! I am responsible for this fearful mess. I should have read the dispatches with more care. I should have left at least half a legion in the south.

"Go and find something to eat," he ordered the scout, and when the man had saluted and gone Paulinus turned to Agricola. "Send a speculator to Glevum and order the Second to Londinium."

"The Second is divided, sir, and the legate is away. It will take the praefectus castra some time to mobilize the legion."

"It can't be helped, there is no closer assistance. I want you to get half the Fourteenth off the island, march it to Deva, and join with the Twentieth. Then bring them both to Londinium. How long will that take you?"

"Forced marching? Two weeks."

Paulinus rubbed at the black stubble on his chin and sighed. "Again, there is no quicker solution. With luck, the Second will meet up with the Ninth and keep the rebels contained until you arrive. Has it occurred to you, Julius, that in conquering the island of Mona I may well have lost the island of Albion?"

"Not even Julius Caesar himself could have foreseen the revolt of a tribe such as the Iceni, sir," the younger man protested. "The greatest strategist in the world cannot predict all eventualities. What are you yourself going to do?"

"Take the cavalry and head for Londinium. The road is not completed, I know, but once we strike it we can make good speed. By the time we reach the city the Second should be there and the panic will be over." He spoke confidently, but a depression settled over the two men, and his words sounded shrill and boastful. Agricola found himself thinking of Veranius, of Gallus, even of poor Scapula, and his doubts found voice.

670

"This land is cursed, Paulinus. I sometimes think that even the ground under our feet hates us."

"Nonsense!" Paulinus dismissed him testily. "This is no time to be vainly imagining nonexistent perils. The real ones are bad enough. Send for the tribunes and my legates. We can surely hope that through the years of peace the tribesmen have forgotten how to fight."

Agricola saluted and hurried out and the governor put his hands behind his back and gazed at the gently sloping walls of the tent. I must retrieve this situation or fall on my sword, he knew suddenly, with no doubts at all. I am fighting not only for my career, I am fighting for my life.

As he stepped out into the full glare of the noon sun, the primipilus of the Fourteenth hurried to him and saluted. Paulinus was so preoccupied that he brushed by the man without seeing him, but the primipilus matched his stride.

"Sir," he said. "Forgive me for troubling you, but there is a small problem."

Paulinus stopped. "What problem?" he snapped, dragging his mind from the memory of his own triclinium at Colchester where Boudicca had reclined opposite him, drinking the mead he had ordered especially for her, smiling at him with mingled familiarity and impudence. "What are you talking about?"

"There is a body in under the trees that no man will touch," the primipilus answered almost apologetically. "Will you come, sir?"

"Go to your legate," Paulinus said brusquely. "Don't bother me with such a nonsensical detail."

"I cannot find him, sir, and the men refuse to return to work until this body is dealt with."

I have no time to give you! Paulinus wanted to shout at his senior centurion, but he controlled himself. His officers would be gathering, but it would be some minutes before he could address them. Take one step at a time, he thought. To run will be to awaken panic, and then disaster.

"Very well," he grunted. "Show me this thing."

The primipilus led him back behind his tent, past the roaring fires piled with bodies, which gave off a suffocating black smoke, and into the wood. It was cooler under the trees, and as they received the salute of the men hewing the oaks, Paulinus became aware of the breeze that stirred the upper branches and made the green leaves quiver. The drowsy sound served to calm him a little. The path curved, and as he and the primipilus rounded it they came upon a group of legionaries clustered a respectful distance from a huddle on the ground under a tree. When they saw Paulinus they broke apart and saluted, but one man stayed sitting on the ground, his arms about his bare knees, rocking back and forth. Paulinus strode to him.

"Get up!" he shouted. "On your feet, you cowardly young bastard!"

He looked up at the governor. His face was gray, and sweat stood out along his upper lip, and as he struggled to his feet two of his fellows bent to help him. Shakily, he gave the salute but he seemed dazed.

"What ails you, man?" Paulinus pressed.

The soldier swallowed. "I killed him, sir," he croaked.

"In other words, you did your duty," Paulinus rapped tartly. "Are you ill?"

"I killed him," the soldier repeated, as Paulinus turned in disgust to the primipilus.

"What is going on here?"

"These men have been detailed to collect bodies for the fires," the centurion replied. "They had been working well all morning, but then this body was found." He indicated the quiet form. "The legionary you just spoke to took one look at its face and would not touch it, and the other men refused also."

"I killed him," the young man said again, beginning to recover his balance. "As soon as I saw the body, I remembered, and then when I bent to lift him, and looked into his eyes . . ."

"Well? What? Hurry up!"

"I saw myself."

"Of course you saw yourself! What else would you see reflected in the eyes?"

"No, sir, not like that. I saw myself lying dead, my breastplate gone and my chest an open wound."

Paulinus grunted, a sound of impatient exasperation. "You are a fanciful young idiot who will have to be disciplined for disobeying orders and spreading superstitious rubbish."

"I saw myself also," another man interposed. "I was running through a forest, lost and without weapons." A murmur of agreement rose, and Paulinus turned to the primipilus again.

"You?"

The man looked uncomfortable, and answered softly. "Yes, sir. I saw myself and my brother, drunk and fighting. My brother had drawn a knife against me."

Paulinus favored him with one astounded stare, then strode to the body and looked down. It lay with its face resting a little to one side, blood-spattered silver glinting about the throat. The spear that had gored it still protruded obscenely from the broad chest. It was a man just past the prime of life, Paulinus thought, his eye traveling the wealth of waving brown hair, the rude health apparent in the long, strong legs, the well-muscled arms. He could have been a gladiator, but he was only a Druid. The white, sleeveless summer robe still shone, though much of it was crusted red brown with old blood. On the limp, curved fingers of one hand, rings of curious design winked as the leaves above moved to let the sunlight through. He squatted to scan the face more closely, aware as he did so that the men behind him were watching intently. His eyes found the other's, wide open, immobile eyes, and then he had to bite back a startled exclamation. He was looking at eyes that were the milky white paleness of a winter dawn, tinted faintly with blue, the eyes of a blind man. Or seemingly blind. He bent closer. For a moment, all he could see was the shadow of his own face, but the shadow darkened, took on color and defini-tion, and he found himself looking at Boudicca's freckled skin. Red hair blew about her face from under a winged bronze helm. Her own eyes stared back at him with a chilling purpose and she was speaking, the large mouth forming words he could not hear, but their gist was carried to him by the grim face, the thinning, hard lips. He inad-vertently craned to hear, knowing somehow that she was not ad-dressing him, then he found himself so close to the corpse's face that its outlines slid out of focus and he drew back carefully, slowly, so that his men might not see his agitation. Pale, blue-tinged eyes once more gazed over his left shoulder. He got up, and in the moment before he turned around he had composed himself. He deliberately glanced up at the dipping, tossing leaves high above, then he walked to stand by the primipilus.

"There is nothing to see but one more dead Druid," he said firmly. "If the eyes seemed to show you visions it was simply because the leaves above the body are troubled by the wind and their shadows pass back and forth over the face. Now pick him up and carry him to a fire."

They loosened and began to move reluctantly, and the primipilus sprang to life. "That was an order!" he roared. "Move! Hurry up!" Paulinus nodded to him, took his salute, and walked out from under the trees. Shadows, he thought. Of course. What else? This accursed place is the heart of the native superstition and I ought not to wonder at the fears of the men, but I am surprised at my own. Boudicca fills my whole mind, and the leaves in the wind did the rest. He did not see the men gingerly raise the heavy body, and place it on the litter. The primipilus walked beside it as the soldiers carried it out quickly from under the gloom of the forest into the bright sunlight, and as

673

they passed from shade into blinding light, he glanced down. The face still mirrored a calmness, but the eyes were no longer pale. They had turned as black as a raven's wing. Shuddering, the primipilus reached out and drew the lids down over the spell-burdened darkness he saw there. He had no wish to see his commander-in-chief enraged by another mutiny.

Paulinus left Mona with twelve hundred cavalry, and struck out south and east. There was no time to gather provisions and, in any case, wains and pack animals would have slowed them down. Each man carried his needs in his pack. The weather was mild and sunny by day and cool and still by night, a perfect spring melting into a perfect summer, but Paulinus, rolled in his blanket under the trees, had no time for the weather. Every hour was a nightmare that stretched his nerves tighter as the miles lengthened between the safety of his legions in the west and the dark, unknown fate that waited. At any moment he expected a horde of western tribesmen to issue from the dense woodland and end all hope, and by the time he and his officers made camp for a few brief hours at night his spine ached from the tension of imaginary spears in his back. He did not dwell on his position. The decision had been made, his escort was the elite of the army, and there was no panic and no grumbling. If the gods ordained that he should be ambushed in spite of everything, and die in some forgotten, lonely spot, then so be it. Sporadic sleep was followed by hours in the saddle. There was no time to send scouts ahead, no time to cook proper meals or erect a proper camp each night, no time for anything but haste and more haste with the whispering trees clustered before and closing in behind and the incessant thrum thrum of hoofs on turf. They felt their vulnerability under the white stars, and when at last the town of Penocrutium suddenly appeared before them, nesting in its little valley, and they saw the road to Londinium begin beyond its clustered houses, their fears were eased. There was a small detachment and fresh horses here, though not enough for Paulinus's host. Here also was a message for him, from Poenius Postumus, the praefectus castra of the Second. Paulinus stood with the commander and listened, shock giving way to an astounded rage.

"The praefectus cannot come, sir," the speculator told him uncomfortably. "The Second is divided and a quarter of the legion is keeping the western tribesmen engaged as far from Mona as possible, as you ordered. The praefectus sends his apologies."

"The praefectus sends his . . . But it was an order! I sent him a direct command! Didn't he understand the gravity of the situation? Doesn't he know that the fate of the province hangs by a thread?"

"I am sorry, sir. I only carry the message."

Paulinus swung away and began to pace, his agitation visible in the down-thrust head, the clenching hands. "It was an order! I don't care for his reasons, he has disobeyed an order, and when this business has been concluded I will have him disciplined to the full extent of the law. Such a thing has never happened under my command before! If the legate had been on duty there would be no such weak excuses. Well." He stopped pacing and looked up into the sun. "I must manage with the means I have, but without the Second I can do little for Londinium."

"Be careful as you move father south, sir," the detachment's officer said. "The land is strangely empty, or so my scouts tell me, and there has been no word as to the whereabouts of the Ninth."

Paulinus closed eyes already itching with fatigue. "There is no time for caution. Are the provisions ready?"

"Yes."

"Then we will press on at once. As for Poenius Postumus . . ." He turned to the embarrassed, worried soldier. "Take this to your praefectus. He is under arrest as soon as the legate returns. His behavior is cowardly and incomprehensible, and you can tell him so." That man has fought his way up through the ranks, he thought as he strode toward the road and to the quiet men who waited for him. He is no playtime officer. What ails you, Postumus? What strange spell of sudden fear turned your blood to water? He mounted quickly, took up the reins, and cantered onto the straight, deserted road lying like an invitation to a lonely nowhere. All of them had been emasculated by it at one time or another, he thought, settling deeper into his horse's stride. This cloud of ephemeral, primitive magic that seemed to stultify the brain and mysteriously weaken the will. Scapula, Gallus, Veranius, even his good friend Plautius—all of them, he thought defiantly, but me. I have not, and will not, succumb. His men strung out behind him, their brilliant red cloaks floating in the sun.

They bypassed Verulamium, and six days after they had set out from Deva, the governor and his exhausted cavalry clattered into Londinium, dismounting and walking to the administration buildings, which were surrounded by a crowd of hysterically relieved citizens. Paulinus had come. He had not failed them. Now everything would be all right. They cheered him frantically, jostling to press cups of wine and morsels of food into the eager hands of his men, but he did not pause to speak to them and his cragged face was closed and grim under the shining helmet. He left his men to rest where they could, and went straight to the office of the mayor.

"Where is the Ninth?"

The man almost embraced him, babbling with relief. "Oh, sir, thank the gods you have come! I did not think . . . we did not know . . . Have you brought the legions?"

"How could I bring the legions in so short a time, you fool! Pull yourself together and answer me! Where is the Ninth?"

The mayor drew back, puzzled. "You don't know?"

Paulinus removed his helmet and put it very slowly on the big desk, striving to hold onto his temper. "I am hot, filthy, and tired. I have ridden for two hundred miles, almost without stopping. I am faced with a matter of the gravest peril. Now where is the Ninth?" He roared out the words, hammering his fist on the desk, and the mayor fell back, his face white. Then he collapsed into his chair.

"The Ninth has been defeated. Petilius Cerealis was lucky to get away with his cavalry and a few auxiliaries. The last news was that he has retreated to the fort at Lindum."

Paulinus stared at him. "Colchester?"

"Burned to the ground. No one escaped. Then the rebels doubled back to the northwest and met the Ninth on its way south. They are coming this way now."

Panic gripped the governor's head in a quick, merciless vise. No Second. No Ninth. The Ninth defeated. Mithras! Defeated! The ablest, most proficient legion in Albion! He forced himself to think calmly, rationally, and all at once his emotions disappeared, leaving nothing but a cold, fast-rolling core of pure reasoning power. A defence of the city with only twelve hundred cavalry was clearly impossible. Cavalry could not fight in the restriction of the streets anyway, and if he stayed it would be nothing but a futile, empty gesture. The Fourteenth and the Twentieth were all that stood between the rebels and overwhelming victory, and the two legions could not possibly arrive in time to save the city from Colchester's fate. Nor was he, Paulinus, expendable. Without him, the province would collapse within weeks. He felt the sword of fate trembling above him, hanging on a slender, frayed thread that threatened to snap at any moment, and remorselessly he made the decision on which his reputation and the future of the province hinged. It was unfortunate, but Londinium would have to be sacrificed.

"Very well," he said. "Have the storehouses opened. I want all the grain my men can carry on their horses, I need it. Then burn the rest. Boudicca must go hungry."

676

The mayor whitened. "What are you saying?" he whispered. "Surely you cannot mean to . . . to leave!"

"That's just what I mean. I'm sorry, but I cannot take the dubious chance of saving a town at the expense of losing the province. Any citizen who can keep up with the cavalry may ride with me, and I mean ride. On their own horses. No wains, no carts, no people on foot. I must move swiftly."

"But you will be condemning us to certain death! Governor, there are more than twenty-five thousand people here, defenceless, decent people, women, children, looking to you for protection!" His voice rose uncontrolled, a burst of hysterical fear. "Do you have any idea what happened at Colchester? Blood lay in great pools, sir, it ran down the gutters like water after a flash flood! They burned soldiers alive, they skewered children on wooden stakes! I don't want to die like that, I . . ."

Paulinus strode to him and gripped his shoulders. "Pull yourself together and listen to me! I must buy time. I have twelve hundred men with me, and the rebels number in the tens of thousands. I must leave. If I can meet the Fourteenth and the Twentieth there is a chance, a slim chance, that something can be salvaged, but nothing will be served if my men and I sit here and die!" He dropped his hands and the mayor slumped trembling, his face hidden in his palms.

"What shall I tell the people?"

"Nothing. There is no time to tell them anything, but if you must, tell them that two legions are on their way. Where is Decianus?"

"The procurator?" For a moment the mayor rallied. "He stripped the treasury and fled to Rutupiae when we heard that Boudicca was coming. I suppose he is safely in Gaul by now."

Anger flared in Paulinus, and then sank beneath an icy determination. "The criminal fool. If I had minded his business as well as my own, none of this tragedy would have happened. See if you can have hot food prepared for my men, and lay hold on every horse available. Pay for them if you have to. I want to leave before sunset."

The mayor nodded shakily. "Sir," he said, "if you survive, will you make sure that the emperor knows of this . . . this supreme sacrifice his city is making?"

For a moment Paulinus was swept by regret, and a terrible, insupportable pity. His harsh face softened. "If I survive, the whole empire will honor you."

"Nevertheless," the man concluded, "I would rather have life."

Paulinus had recovered his self-control and his face fell once more into its sharp, ruthless lines. "You have had more than many who will fall here," he retorted, and he went swiftly out of the room.

Somehow the news of the governor's intention to abandon them to their fate was spread among the people, and they reacted with an incredulous disbelief that preceded an insane burst of terror. Paulinus and the cavalry ate hot leek soup and wheaten bread in the safety of an empty warehouse, squatting silently and listening to the turbulent uproar of the townspeople, who milled about in the streets shouting and imploring, begging and promising, driven to a despairing fury as the black doorway that gave onto annihalation inched open behind them. When the men had finished the food they slipped from the building, walked quickly away from the river and the now-deserted wharves where cargo lay untended and the ships rocked at anchor on the rising tide, and mounted their horses under cover of a grove of trees. It was now late afternoon, the mellow summer light lay rich and golden, and the air was full of the hum of drowsy bees and the intoxicating odor of wild blossom. With a word of command Paulinus swung quickly onto the road over which they had ridden only hours before, and someone saw them go. A wail went up, a swiftly multiplying howl of betrayal and loss, and though Paulinus gritted his teeth and slashed at his horse, the desolation in that cry haunted him well into the twilight.

Feverishly, the people set about packing their goods, and many punched and kicked their way to the free, open peace of the meadows that lay, tree-lined and calm, around the town. But for most of them it was too late. Three hours after the governor took all hope away with him, just as the sun touched the horizon with fiery fingers, a woman dropped her bundle and pointed north, screaming. A dark, low mass that was not an evening mist filled all the fields, and the last of the light flickered on swords as they were drawn. Boudicca, and death, had come.

CHAPTER THIRTY-NINE

S HE STOOD IN THE DARKNESS of the oak grove, and this time the hands she held out to Andrasta, Queen of Victory, were not empty. Her chiefs stood with her, and all around them in the moon's pale washing the wooden stakes were crowned—a hundred tattered, blood-spattered heads, mouths slack in the half-light, eyes dull under sunken sockets, a hundred souls imprisoned forever in this secret place between sleep and waking. "More blood," Subidasto whispered to her as she gazed upon her triumphs. "More blood, blood, blood, blood," and she saw him clearly in her imagination. His face had become thinner, darker. The color of his eyes had deepened to the black of Brigantian beads, and his hair clung closely to his scalp and glinted with a sheen, like oiled, dark feathers. "No," she murmured, looking down on her own blood-soaked palms. "No more blood. Only the legions. I am avenged."

"Blood!" he squawked angrily at her, his hooked beak creaking open, and she squeezed her eyes shut and turned on her heel while the night wind stirred in her hair and cooled the sweat from her neck.

"We must Council," she said to Lovernius, as they left the soul-crowded, silent grove and swung down the path to the twinkle of cooking fires and the laughter and shouts of the tribesmen. "I have things to say." He did not ask what things. He took out his dice and fingered them reflectively.

The chiefs were waiting for her, drinking beer and talking. The little meadow between river and forest was crammed with them, but they fell silent as they saw her step into the big fire's glow and stand patiently for their attention. When she spoke she had to almost shout, for in the days since the burning of Colchester, new members of the tuaths had been trickling in steadily to swell the rebel host, bringing their chiefs. Some came from fear that if they did not join their farms would be fired and they themselves slain, but most saw an opportunity come to them from the gods, to regain at last their long-lost freedom, and they threw in their lot with the Iceni with a fierce willingness.

Boudicca flung her sword to Lovernius and spoke. "Freemen and freewomen! The time has come to strike a last blow against the domination of Rome! I know that you are tired and hungry, I know that food is scarce, but if you follow me for a little longer you will have food in abundance! Paulinus was not in Londinium, as I had hoped. Therefore we must pursue him immediately and destroy him before he can meet the legions that even now are marching from the ashes of Mona. Then we can slay the Fourteenth and the Twentieth as we slew the vaunted Ninth, and Rome's oppression will be a matter for song, not everlasting mourning."

She paused for breath, but a burly chief rose swiftly and forestalled her next words. "Why should we turn from such rich pickings just yet?" he yelled at her. "The booty from Colchester was good, and the silver and precious things from Londinium were very beautiful. Now

Verulamium waits to be explored." He grinned around at the company and sat down, but before Boudicca could reply another chief jumped up, stuck his fat thumbs in his belt, and boomed at her, "Let the legions wait. We have made carrion fodder of one and we can do the same to the others in our own good time. Meanwhile, let us sink our teeth into the delights of Verulamium. The summer is young, and much booty waits to be carried back to the villages. My wain, for one, is not yet full." He sat down amid a ground swell of approval, and Boudicca exchanged shocked and angered glances with her men and with Domnall.

"What stupid dreams do you wander in?" she shouted. "Have you forgotten so soon what we face? You have lived long enough under that crushing heel! You ought to know the strength and cunning of Paulinus and his legates! If he joins with his reinforcements, the balance moves back into his hands. We shall not move against Verulamium! No more pillaging! No more killing of townspeople! The legions and Paulinus only." She sat down panting, and an offended muttering broke out.

"You are not arviragus!" someone shouted at her. "Who elected you to lead us?"

"Andrasta," she snarled, struggling to her feet once more, and above the rumble of disagreements she screamed at the top of her voice, "I lead you because you are all too witless to lead yourselves! Raven of Nightmares, without me you would have stood before the Ninth and let them cut you down! Fools and slaves! If I had not left Icenia you would still be digging roadbeds and sowing crops with chains around your necks! Verulamium is full of Catuvellaunian tribesmen, not Romans. You Catuvellauni, what do you say? Will you kill your own kin?" But the Catuvellauni sat sullenly, looking at the ground, and the tumult grew. Subidasto began to laugh, a gleeful, high-pitched giggle of smug mirth, and she put a shaking hand across her eyes.

"Let them glut themselves," Domnall said beside her. "Then they will be ready to listen to you. They have been ground into the dirt for a long time, Lady. Give them more time."

"There is no time!" she rasped at him. "Look at them! It is all falling apart, all useless." She got to her feet and stumbled away, and Lovernius and Aillil ran after her but she snapped at them, "Leave me alone!" and they fell back while she went blindly on into the rustling trees. Brigid was laying outstretched on her blanket, her eyes closed, breathing deeply and peacefully in sleep, and Boudicca threw herself down and gathered the girl gently into her arms. Brigid sighed but did not wake, and Boudicca cuddled the thin, warm body of her daughter for a long time, the tears trickling slowly down her cheeks and falling like bitter acid onto the fresh, unlined young face.

Before it was full dark, Paulinus left the main road that ran from Londinium toward the west. He did not know exactly when Boudicca would attack Londinium or how long she would tarry there before casting about for news of his whereabouts, and he was taking no foolish chances. He and his stoical, unquestioning men swung in a wide arc, moving as quickly as they could through an uncharted and unpathed wilderness, slipping past Verulamium, once more unnoticed by any save the inquisitive animal inhabitants of the forests. Now and then they stumbled across villages but they were all empty of life, and the tiny fields hewed out of the encroaching trees were untended, the vivid green spears of the young crops a sudden, lush splash of color. He sent no warning to Verulamium. He believed without question that Boudicca would make him her next imperative target and he pushed forward, aware that if he slacked his pace she could overtake him. He wondered what the Fourteenth and Twentieth were doing, how far they had marched, whether the men of the west had recovered from the shock of Mona and belatedly attacked them, whether they were lost, whether, like Postumus, their legates had lost their nerve and would not come at all. He knew that stress and desperation were eating slowly at his rationality and he forced himself to remember Agricola and the legions.

Once past Verulamium and the next posting station he decided that it was safe to ride the road once more, and at the next garrison he rested, commandeered all the grain they had, and moved on. He debated now whether to send scouts to the countless little garrisons and posting stations dotted throughout the lowlands in order to draw more fighting men to him, then decided that there was no time. It was vitally important not to linger. At three more posting stations along the road he took grain and men, then he reached Venona, and there he stayed. He took command of the little fort that was planted like a stubbed, friendly fist set down in the middle of miles of rolling, densely wooded country. He sent men further north to scout for his legions and back south to locate the rebels, and hour after hour he stood with his legs apart and his hands behind his back, searching the two roads that crossed where the fort was built with eyes dazzled by the dance of hot sunlight, fuming inwardly at his inaction. He had done all he could, but he knew that without a stroke of the most incredible luck it would not be enough. Paulinus did not believe in luck. He believed in intelligence and ability, and he knew that Boudicca had both. But he also knew the simple-mindedness of the barbarian temperament. They could not sustain any prolonged campaign, no matter how persuasive or brilliant their leaders, and he hoped that the chiefs would quickly tire of blood and booty and go home. He did not count on it, however. It did not pay to count on anything, and he rocked back and forth on his heels, looked up and down the roads, and waited.

He had been in the fort at Venona for barely three days when one of the scouts came hurrying from the south with news that astounded and heartened him. The rebels had swamped Verulamium. Paulinus listened to the same dismal tale of an almost total slaughter of the peaceful native townspeople. Tribesmen had carried off more goods to pile on wains, which must already be loaded with the spoils of Colchester and Londinium, and now they were running amuck through the Catuvellaunian countryside, burning every farmstead they found and killing everyone they met. Paulinus felt his spirits rise. For a moment he thought of how the three most progressive experiments in Roman integration with the conquered had been wiped out in as many weeks, but he dismissed any regrets. Boudicca was losing the precarious hold she had on her vast, motley host, that was obvious, and now, with good planning, he could snatch back the reins of control. She would rally them, no doubt, once they had worn themselves out by dashing all over the countryside, but by then his legions would have arrived, and any battle would be fought on his terms, not hers. He even whistled through his teeth as he went past the gates with the scout, and he acknowledged the salutes of the guards with a jaunty smile. He was a long way from safety yet, but now he had a fighting chance.

Agricola and the legions arrived with the next dawn, and in the pale, misty morning the two men greeted one another while the soldiers began to make camp.

"I took it upon myself to leave three cohorts at Deva," Agricola said. "I didn't relish the idea of having rebels at our front and the western wildmen at our back. I also picked up all the soldiers from the stations along the way."

Paulinus drew him within the high wooden walls to where the rich smell of stewing game coiled about him. "You've made good time. Are the men tired? How many do we have?"

"Ten thousand infantry, and of course the auxiliaries and cavalry. The men are a bit footsore, but a few hours of rest will cure that. Tell me, sir, what are we facing?"

Paulinus steered him toward the headquarters building, lowering his voice as he spoke. "The mayor at Londinium gave me the figure of one hundred thousand, but in his fear he may have exaggerated. In any case, that would include the families of the chiefs. I have some reports from scouts, though, that tend to support his estimate, and of course Boudicca is gaining recruits all the time. Say eighty thousand, Julius."

They reached the commander's quarters and went inside. Agricola took off his short cloak and stood bunching it in his hands for a long time, then he said, "And what are our chances, Paulinus?"

The governor pulled the shutters to, against the morning's chill. "I think they are very good. Don't let their numbers awe you, Agricola, for that is all they have. We have discipline and superior training. We have officers who know their job. And we have the advantage of time."

"Sir?"

"I intend to move farther north, not far perhaps, and choose a sight where we can meet them in pitched battle. It's no good chasing after them and ending up ambushed in some tree-choked spot. I intend to make very sure that Boudicca knows where I am. Then we shall sit and wait."

Agricola sighed. "Morale is not good. The men are jumpy."

"All they have to do is obey orders and fight. If they do that, and of course they will, the victory will be ours."

With a rueful inward smile, Agricola envied his governor his supreme lack of imagination. "Of course, sir," he said.

Boudicca stood with her chiefs, breathing the thick blue smoke that was spreading like a stinging miasma over the road and into the forest, and swore aloud. "I needed that grain!" she said angrily. "He has fired his own fort. Can't you smell the grain burning, Domnall?"

"At least we know that we must keep following the road," he answered. "Sooner or later we will catch him. He cannot march his troops into the sea."

"If we had left Verulamium for later we would have caught him by now," she retorted, a barb of contempt in her gruff voice, then she walked to her chariot and clattered back onto the road. Slowly, ponderously, the unwieldy horde straggled in behind her. The same whines, the same complaints and accusations rose to flog her with reproach. We have traipsed a hundred miles, and where is the governor? We are tired, we want to go home now, we have missed the legions, the men of the west got the legions, we want to go home, go home, go home.

Andrasta take you all, you idiots, she thought furiously. But you are not going home until I have Paulinus's head on the tip of my spear, for if you do, you will not live to see another Samain. Angrily, silently, she cursed them, her mouth rammed shut and her hands tight on the reins, but her bluster could not cover the steady pulsing of uneasiness as yet another mile crawled by. The trail of the legions was easy to read. Almost too easy. Pots, dishes, broken harness, cast horseshoes—it was as if Paulinus had deliberately thrown down this litter to lead her on, like a calf to the slaughtering. He has, she thought in agony. Oh, he has! What is he planning? What will he do? I wish I knew him as Caradoc knew Ostorious Scapula. I wish there had been time to listen to the intuition of a dozen years of confrontation. If in another day I have not found him the tuaths will begin to desert me, but I am afraid to find him, afraid, for I know that though I seem to stalk him, yet he is hunting me. Now I understand the frustrations that nearly drove Caradoc mad. You stupid, stupid people! Behind her the rumble of her disgruntled army was like a continuous, low thunder, a swaggering, quarreling, beer-drinking, well-nigh uncontrollable storm that reached back thirty miles and more, and she listened to its menace with despair. There was no food. The posting stations they had searched on the way had been empty of men and grain, and the people had only what each family trundled with them in their wains. Most of it was already gone, and in order to get more they must do battle soon. Where are you, Suetonius Paulinus? she thought anxiously. In what secret place are you hiding?

At noon she stopped to eat, sitting on the grass verge of the road with Lovernius, Aillil, and Domnall, but before long she was forced to take her sword and go among the angry tribesmen. Fights had broken out between those who still had dried meat and grain and those who tried to take it from them, and she strode from wain to wain, laying about her with the cutting edge of her tongue and the flat of her sword and followed by a crowd of delighted children and hopeful dogs. She returned to her chariot hot and angry, but just as she was about to give the word to move on, a scout came pelting along the road from the north. He fell from his horse and raced toward her.

"They are there!" he shouted. "Camped in a valley, seven, eight miles ahead! And so few of them!"

Her heart lurched and she turned swiftly to her men. "Lovernius, Aillil, pass the news quickly. We will spend the night here, and meet them in the morning."

"Is that wise?" Domnall asked quietly. "A night without purpose brings risk."

"I know." She considered briefly, while all around her the news was being spread and excitement took the place of boredom. A night of more quarrels and pointless bloodletting, of too much beer and not enough sleep, and she acquiesced to him reluctantly. "Very well. We

684

will go on, and fight today." She glanced swiftly at the summer sun, now perched high above the treetops. "Perhaps it is a good thing. If we do not win we can rest for the night and continue fighting tomorrow."

They went on at a faster pace now, buoyed by the thought of Paulinus turned at bay and his sacks of precious grain, and only Boudicca and the Iceni remembered why it was they had been brought to this hour, what was at stake. The Icenians fell suddenly quiet, and the chiefs drove their chariots with unconscious skill, not shouting across to one another. The freemen strode after them grim-faced. As the last miles were covered, Boudicca's thoughts were on her daughters, each in her prison of loneliness, and for the last time she mourned for Prasutugas, and the wise, gentle strengths that were gone forever.

Then, suddenly, the land rose, and where for a short distance on her left the soil changed its character the trees had not rooted, and defiles gaped crookedly toward the road. On her right the forest still pressed close, leaning over the ditch and bank the Romans had built. It ran the length of the road to give clearance on either side, as though straining to regain the ground it had lost, but on her left cheek a wind blew steadily, hot and damp, and there they were, like gray pebbles shaken from the almost bare slopes behind them and still rattling against each other, soulless and dry on the bed of the valley, faceless and smooth, heavy and impassive.

Aillil gave a whoop and stamped his foot. "Look at them, Lady! Packed into the valley like dried fish in a barrel! How could Paulinus be such a fool?"

She did not answer. Her eyes roved slowly. Paulinus was many things but he was not a fool, and fear wet her palms and slithered cold down her back. Outwardly it appeared that he was beaten before the battle had even begun, for, as Aillil had said, the soldiers were crammed into the small place far back, where the valley began to narrow, and they had left the broad flat that bordered the road quite empty. It was not a sharp, high ravine. Its sides, thick with scrubby, stunted thorns, briars, and twigged elder bushes, sloped gradually to a naked plateau, and between her and the army, perhaps two miles, there was sand and gravel, a perfect arena for a chariot charge. Too perfect, she thought. This arrangement is much too perfect. Yet there are so few of them, a tiny handful that would be lost in the great ocean of the tuaths. Surely, no matter what is passing in the mind of Paulinus, we can swamp them with numbers alone. The constant undercurrent of sound around her was rising, breaking up into exultant yells, war cries, taunting shouts, and the deafening crash of sword

685

on shield, a mounting furor of glee and anticipation. Far back, underlying it all, she heard the rattle of the wains and the shrill, excited baying of the dogs. "Call the chiefs," she said.

The Romans were moving about quietly and methodically, ignoring the mad cacophony of noise on the road, and Paulinus addressed his unit commanders, looking out behind them to where the ranks were forming up. Legionaries in the center, elbow to elbow, six deep. Auxiliaries to either side, loose and wheeling freely, the mounted archers and slingers preparing to harass the rebels as they themselves formed up. Paulinus was fervently grateful that these auxiliaries—Thracians, Iberians, men from Germania—were predominantly and traditionally archers. The cavalry made the flanks, sitting easy and tall on their gleaming horses, their plumes waving proudly. The whole front was less than a thousand yards across, but it would suit his purposes.

"Impress my words on your men," he said. "You have already received your battle commands, but in this situation, orders are not enough. Pay no attention to the noise the savages make, and close your ears to their empty threats. There are more women than soldiers in their ranks. They have no understanding of proper warfare, and they are badly armed. When they experience the weapons and courage of troops who have often beaten them before, they will turn and run." His clipped, crisp words rose above the purposeful bustle around him, and the commanders listened gravely. "Tell the men this, also," Paulinus went on emphatically. "In an army of many legions, few win battle honors. Think what glory will be yours, then, a small band which fights for the honor of the whole army! Keep your ranks. Throw your javelins, strike with your shield bosses, and drive on. Above all, do not pause for booty. Win the battle, and you win all. Is that quite clear?" They murmured their assent and quickly dispersed, and he, his tribunes, and Agricola mounted their horses.

"If we can hold off their first charge we have them," Paulinus said. "Boudicca can't throw all her chariots at us at once because the mouth of the valley is too narrow. Julius, I do believe that the day will be ours."

Boudicca spoke rapidly to the impatient, jostling chiefs, her voice scarcely heard above the blowing of carnyx and the roar of the people. "This is my war," she shouted. "I am a woman fighting for justice and revenge, and my cause is right. I will not live like a slave, and I want the tribes to know that today there will be victory or death. The Iceni will charge in the center, the Trinovantes to the left, the others to the right."

686

"That is not fair!" a chief protested angrily. "The Iceni should not have precedence over the Catuvellauni!"

"Why not?" she snapped back. "The Iceni began this, the Iceni have brought you all to the brink of freedom. I say we fight in the place of honor."

Some of the chiefs cursed her with surly mouths but she turned from them in disgust. "Form up, all of you, and keep your men away from the beer barrels." They straggled away and she got into her chariot. The mouth of the defile was already choked with line upon line of chariots and the Roman auxiliaries swooped around them, loosing arrows and flying stones from the slings and then dashing back to their ranks, harassing the irate chiefs as they tried to hold to their positions. "They are playing with us," she said angrily. "Aillil, get some of the chariots moving on the flanks and answer them back." Then she whipped at her little horses and began a swift passage from tribe to tribe, admonishing, threatening, promising, joking. Far back, from his position above his own ranks, Paulinus saw her, a speeding flash of wide green cloak and floating red hair, tall in the afternoon sunlight, and he watched her until the praefectus cantered up and saluted.

"Ready to engage, sir."

Paulinus took a last deep breath of sweet, untainted air. "Very well. Sound the incursus."

In the few moments left to her she trotted back through the Icenian lines until there was nothing between her and the stolid, iron-clad ranks of Rome but glaring light on the smooth gravel of the valley floor. She unfastened her soft cloak, folded it, and laid it beside her feet. She tightened her belt and lifted the heavy, winged helm, setting it firmly on her head. She drew her sword and Lovernius stepped up behind her and took the reins. Then she paused. There was a flutter of astonishment in the chiefs around her, a flurry of consternation, and she turned to see Ethelind standing by the spokes of the big chariot wheel, her face immobile, the glossy, rich hair braided tightly around her small skull. Boudicca stepped down, shocked. A silence had fallen around them, a tiny oasis of tension in the desert of deafening madness, and Ethelind spoke.

"Give me a sword."

Boudicca stared at her, sucked into the poison wreathing from the venomous blue eyes, and when she did not respond, Ethelind struck the chariot with one stiff hand. "Boudicca, I demand a sword!"

A hundred objections sprang to Boudicca's tongue. You have not been taught how to use one, you could not even lift one, the soldiers will cut you down before you have made such a useless, wasteful gesture—but behind the dry wells of hating in Ethelind's cold gaze she saw a pathetic, soul-wrenching longing for death that eclipsed all memory and all claim to kinship between them. For Ethelind, as for Brigid, time had ceased to be when the soldiers pierced them with the hot flesh-swords of yesterday, and only another sword could bring a second, kinder death. Boudicca moved to embrace her but she held out both arms in a gesture of repudiation.

"No—no. Not that. Only a sword."

Boudicca sliced brutally through the net of caring and mounted her chariot again. We stand alone, she thought, each one of us, and you must fall alone, Ethelind. "Aillil," she barked. "Find her a sword." She nodded brusquely at her charioteer and they rolled away, the incursus blaring at last and the voices of a thousand carnyx shivering on the air. When she looked back, Ethelind had gone.

The chariots lurched forward, wheel to wheel, and began to pick up speed, thundering like a howling iron wind over the ground. The freemen poured after them, shrieking. The land began to lift gently but the thrust of the charge was not slowed and the auxiliaries came to meet it, plunging fearlessly into the clamor. For a furious moment the two sides clashed but the charge was still gaining impetus, swelling to a gale, and all at once the auxiliaries broke and fell back. The main body of the legions had not stirred. They stood motionless, rank upon silent rank, faces all alike under the helmets, and the tribes came on, with arms flung wide and shields high. Then an order rang out. The soldiers raised their javelins like mindless dolls and waited, and Boudicca, almost upon them, had time to marvel at their dumb, brave obedience. Then came another order. She could hear it, level and clear, and the next moment she was jerked from the chariot as one of her horses fell and the other was dragged to a halt. Screams rent the softening late afternoon and the charge abruptly slowed, but before she could scramble up from the ground, another shower of javelins came singing and clattering among the tightly bunched chiefs. The front line of soldiers stepped back smartly and the second stepped forward, and again the hail of iron-tipped death fell among the people. Lovernius helped her to her feet and she saw Aillil clambering to her over the bodies already hampering the thousands who trampled them.

"Why don't the idiots drive for the cavalry on the flanks?" she yelled. "I told them and told them! Aillil, get behind them and make them face the auxiliaries. We can do nothing but die bunched together in the front like this!" She swung her shield to cover herself as more javelins dove to transfix men and animals, and now the charge was disintegrating, for those chiefs who had not been killed were frantically tugging at soft, bucking javelin hafts that refused to slide easily from the wooden shields and rendered them useless.

In that moment, the trumpets rang out. The legionaries closed ranks swiftly, raised their long shields, and drew their swords, and now they were dolls no longer but crouched, shuffling beetles with stings in their hands. Boudicca's enraged shouts were swallowed up in the melee. The outlying tribes had not attacked the cavalry and auxiliaries on the fringes. If they had they might have broken through to surround the Romans, but while she swung her sword in readiness, and shook and cursed them all, they flowed into the already suffocatingly crowded center of conflict. The cavalry sat astride their horses unchallenged, and watched, and Boudicca, with Lovernius hewing steadily beside her, forgot all else but the need to destroy.

The implacable, emotionless wedges of the Roman forces pushed foot by congested foot into the seething mass of freemen, dividing and scattering, and the tribesmen found themselves fighting not one front but two as they were isolated in iron-walled groups and remorselessly cut down. Every now and then some cool voice would issue a curt command, and the engaging line would fall back to rest while fresh legionaries continued the desperate hand-to-hand fighting against swiftly tiring, blood-soaked men and women who had barely enough room to swing, let alone maneuver. The shield bosses crunched and thudded their way into defenceless ribs. The little sharp swords licked in and out like snakes' tongues, drawing blood from those who were trapped by their living comrades and by the soft but unyielding bodies that cluttered the ground and could not be kicked away. Boudicca found herself elbowed back roughly, and though she pushed and swore, the front line moved rapidly ahead. Swinging about she struggled for another area, and in the second of inactivity she looked about her. The soldiers had gained ground. A cold, drenching river of sweat bathed her as she saw the warriors in the forefront being inexorably pushed into the mass of freemen behind. The throng became thicker and more and more men died, standing hunched and impotent, crushed against their neighbors, while the Roman swords stabbed with no opposition and no check.

Andrasta, we are on the verge of a rout, she thought, horrified, and even as she jumped onto an overturned chariot and began to shout, the pace of the tuaths' grim onslaught faltered and their clamor died away. For a moment time seemed to hang suspended and even the earth seemed to hold its breath, and her voice rose hoarse and clear, filling the hiatus with a lonely cry of fearless defiance. "Remember your slavery! Remember your oppression and your endless mourning!"

But far back a trumpet blared forth, and her last words were drowned as the legions surged forward. The tide of battle had turned, and seeing its relentless sweep the tribes began to run, not knowing what had gone wrong, howling as panic engulfed them. Another trumpet spoke, and now the cavalry lowered their lances and charged into the struggling, bleeding mass. Lovernius pulled her from the chariot and dragged her away.

"The people will flee into the forest across the road," he panted. "We can regroup tomorrow and fight again. Run, Boudicca!" But she staggered suddenly as though a sword had found her back, and she fell to her knees. "Look, Lovernius," she whispered. "Oh look!"

There was nowhere to run. Across the narrow mouth of the valley the wains and carts were parked seven, eight, nine deep, a broad wall of heaped booty drawn up by the people in arrogant confidence so that the older women and the children could watch the victory. The valley was sealed, a tight, blocked tomb, and even as Boudicca rose horror-stricken, the leaping, careening chiefs saw it too, the wall without door or chink, the executioner. They flung themselves upon it hysterically, overturning wains so that silver cups, gay linens, bronze-plated chairs, all the gaudy knickknacks snatched from the tortured cities they had burned, went tumbling amid the dogs and screaming children. But it was too late. There was no retreat. The Romans saw it, too, and a great triumphant shout went up. The cavalry came pounding after them, the soldiers ran, and the chiefs died.

"Oh, no," she whispered. "Andrasta, no, no, no. Not like this." Then the thought of Brigid came sharply into her mind and the surge of groveling terror passed her by. Dropping into the mire of corpses and pink-sprayed gravel she began to crawl, Lovernius behind her, not toward the carnage of the wains but toward the side of the valley. It was not far. How well you chose, Paulinus, how well you chose, she thought, not looking to right or left where dead hands brushed her and dead faces leered at her with white reproach. But you will not take me. No chains for my ankles, no long humiliation in the dungeons of Rome. Then suddenly thorns were tearing at her tunic, and the dull green of an elder brush brushed her shoulders. "Now run, Lovernius," she called softly, but there was no reply. Getting to her feet she looked behind her, but she was alone.

Hulda and the young chief were standing close together, deep under the trees, and Brigid walked to and fro before them, her fingers entwined in her long hair and her eyes on the ground. Hulda ran forward when she saw who it was, then she halted. The blue tunic was smeared in blood. Earth and gravel clung to the fiery, disordered

690

hair, the helm was gone, and the face that wrung a cry from her was convulsed, scarcely human in its agony.

"Lady!"

Boudicca leaned against a tree. "The battle is lost," she forced out. "The tribes are laid to waste. Flee, both of you. Go north, go west, run, run!"

"But Lovernius, Aillil, where is Domnall, surely . . ."

"Dead, all dead. Now take your goods and run."

"But Lady, what of Brigid? Where can you go with her?"

"She is no longer your concern, Hulda, and if you want to save your own life you had better leave this place."

Hulda said no more. She went to the girl, kissed her gently on the forehead; then she gathered up her belongings and walked away, with tears slipping silently down her cheeks.

The chief unsheathed his sword and hesitated, his eyes on his lady, and she stood away from the tree and smiled painfully at him. "You also, my friend," she said quietly. "You cannot save us now."

He smelled it already, the sickly-sweet odor of death seeping slowly into the clearing, and he raised his sword in salute. "A safe journey, Lady," he said, "A peaceful journey."

"To you also," she responded, and he spun on his heel and vanished.

For a moment she stood listening to the violent, insane roar of the slaughter; then she laid down her sword, drew her knife, and went to Brigid. The girl stopped pacing and looked at her enquiringly, her hands leaving her hair to flutter over Boudicca's soaked tunic. "Blood?" she said. Boudicca pulled her gently forward and put her face into the warm, gleaming tresses. I don't want you to suffer any more, Brigid, she thought. If I leave you the soldiers will come and it will be as it was before, yet there is nowhere to take you, nowhere at all. We can never go home again. Her fingers found the ribs, so thin, so poignantly thin, and the blade slid between them. Brigid sighed, the pale, matchless beauty of the girl's head slumped against her mother's breast, and weeping, Boudicca lowered her onto the fragrant grasses. She lay quiescent, wildflowers between her fingers, her hair over her face and her tunic floating to settle around her, and Boudicca turned swiftly. Bending, she dug in the rich damp loam; then she tossed the knife away, swept up her sword, and rammed it hilt down in the hole she had made. She secured it with small stones, her hands fumbling, her eyes blinded by tears.

"Where are you going, Boudicca?" the voice of Subidasto the Raven croaked in her ear.

She straightened. "I do not know," she whispered aloud, "I do not know." Like a withering leaf lifted from the branch of a dying tree and whirled onto the surface of a river, she spread out her arms, and fell.

CHAPTER FORTY

T HE NIGHT WAS STIFLINGLY HOT but the shutters had been flung back and a fitful breeze stirred the hangings and made the dozens of candles and lamps gutter spasmodically like golden drunken butterflies. Gladys nodded, and the slaves moved silently and unobtrusively to clear the debris from the white-draped table and brought silver bowls laden with dusky grapes, fuzzed peaches, and shiny purple plums. Greedy hands reached out, and from behind the gilt couches the patient servants came with more wine, but Caradoc put his fingers lightly over his cup, smiling across at his wife, and Plautius refused also. Only Llyn held his cup to be refilled and drank quickly, his spare frame slumped deep into the inviting cushions, his eyes half closed.

"The wheel came right off," the younger Gladys said, "but the chariot went on rolling for a good sixty feet. You should have been there, Mother, the crowd went mad. We all yelled ourselves hoarse, but naturally it did no good. Poor old Aulus! That's the third race your team has lost, isn't it?"

"Did you bet?" Eurgain smiled at the black hair piled high in tight curls and hung with pearls, the swinging earrings, and the red, gold-bordered stola, and Gladys made a face and flung up her hands.

"Yes, I did, and Rufus lost a lot of money."

"Will you please let me finish my story?" her husband said with exasperation. "The servants have gone. Well, no one would have noticed if Vespasianus hadn't started to snore, but snore he did, like a bull, and the emperor stopped singing. 'Is someone ill?' he asked, and everyone froze and tried not to look at everyone else."

Eurgain spat a pip onto her plate. "Then what happened?"

Pudens shrugged. "Absolutely nothing, and don't forget that it was the second time Vespasianus has fallen asleep during one of Nero's recitals. The emperor ordered him out and then went on singing."

Plautius stirred. "It's not a good idea to spread such stories in these times, Rufus," he remarked softly, and the company fell silent, but Llyn struggled to a sitting position and yawned.

"Plautius's walls have no ears," he drawled. "If they did, we would have all been crucified or tossed into boiling oil for treason a long time ago."

"Ah hush, Llyn!" his mother urged hastily, but he only swilled more wine and closed his eyes again. Caradoc swung his feet to the warm tiled floor.

"Once again we have abused your hospitality, my friend," he said to Plautius, "and stayed too late." But before Plautius could reply his steward glided into the room. For a long time he whispered in his master's ear and the assembly watched anxiously as Plautius's face became grave and then bleak, and when the man had bowed himself out they began to fidget. Plautius seemed to be having trouble with his speech. He tried to form words, stumbled over them, spewed forth an uncharacteristic obscenity, then he rose slowly.

"There is news from Britannia," he said with difficulty. "The Iceni staged a revolt, and pulled most of the lowland tribes in with them. They almost succeeded in killing every Roman on the island, and three towns and a legion have been wiped out."

"The *lowland* tribes?" Caradoc stiffened incredulously, a long-forgotten wave of feverish gladness washing him. Llyn's eyes flew open. "Great Mother!" he whispered, but the elder Eurgain said sharply, "Almost succeeded, Aulus?"

Plautius cleared his throat and went on huskily. "It seems there was a pitched battle, and the rebels were overwhelmingly defeated. Boudicca took her own life."

"What else?" his wife demanded sharply.

Suddenly he sat down on his couch and rubbed wearily at his forehead. "I don't understand it. My good friend Paulinus is massacring the Iceni. Eighty thousand warriors fell in the battle and he is pursuing the survivors, hunting them down. Icenia is a wasteland."

No one moved. The wind sighed around them with a dry, dusty breath, and the darkness from beyond the window seemed to seep toward them, chilling their hearts even as the heat of the night brought sweat to their brows.

Then slowly, heavily, Caradoc got to his feet. "Your pardon, Plautius," he said evenly, and he left the room, walking quickly under the archway and into the shadowed atrium where a fat harvest moon was reflected on the motionless surface of the little pool and in the garden beyond smooth grass smelt of dew and roses. He went on across the deep, slanting shadows of the pillared courtyard, along the deserted cloister where his feet rang loudly on the pavement, and came at last to the little path, and then to the rustling plane trees and the wrought-iron gate. He leaned on it with his hands clasped together, looking out below him to where the myriad lights of the city twinkled in the velvet darkness. He heard its heart beating—a dull, never-ending roar, a ceaseless grind of industry, the heart of an empire whose blood was made of suffering, whose food was oppression, whose blind hands carried death. Little Boudicca with the red hair, he thought. What did they do to you, that caused you to deliberately spill your blood upon a soil already drowning under an ocean of such agonizing sacrifices? Why am I standing here, grown old and useless, while this same moon slants down through the wet, secret oak groves, and the hazel thickets are laden with ripening nuts, and the young deer run silent through the crystal-beaded grasses?

A warm hand descended lightly on his naked arm and Eurgain looked up at him, her face bathed in the pitiless moonlight that seemed to suck all color from it and make it drawn and lined. "The others are going home," she said. "All except Llyn. Gladys is putting him in the guest room." Caradoc unclasped his hands.

"It's no good, Eurgain," he said flatly. "They bow to me in the streets, the emperor calls me his noble barbarian, my daughter has made a good marriage, I am welcome in every senator's house as though I were some kind of god, yet I dream night after night that I am back at Camulodunon and the rain is falling, and Cin is calling to me." He sighed. "For ten years I have existed here, closing my eyes and ears to Albion's torment, then something like this happens and I know that I am nothing but a stranger mourning in a foreign land."

She rubbed her cheek against his shoulder. "I, too, want to go home," she whispered. "So does Llyn. Do you think that when the time comes they will let us be burned on some funeral pyre taken from the sweet Catuvellaunian forests?"

He put an arm around her and drew her close. "All we wanted was to be left alone," he said quietly. "Such a little word, freedom, such a small request, and yet the asking of it has consumed the soul of a people."

She rested against him and they stood together while the moon slowly shrank to a hard silver brilliance, its white beams flooding the shadowed vineyard, and below them the city hummed and pulsed.

Far away, in the swirling autumn mists of Albion, the light of freedom flickered and went out.

694